Absolutely brilliant!   —Bridget, Rea

a thoroughly engrossing time travel story that promises to continue as vividly as it started.   —Nan Hawthorne, *An Involuntary King*

a delightfully intricate tale of time travel, life lessons, challenges of faith, and redemption...moving, witty, and captivating...a page-turner...I highly recommend this novel.   —Jennifer, Rundpinne.com

Vosika spins a captivating tale.... The pacing flows from a measured cadence...and builds to a climatic crescendo reminiscent of Ravel's Bolero. I become invested in the characters. Both Shawn and Niall are fully fleshed and I could imagine having a conversation with each. Write faster, Laura. I want to read more.
—Joan Szechtman, *This Time*

fast-paced, well-written, witty...Captivating! —Stephanie Derhak, *White Pines*

Ms. Vosika wove these aspects...together in a very masterful way that...kept me spellbound. I could hardly put it down. —Thea Nillson, *A Shunned Man*

Original & intelligently written. I couldn't turn the pages fast enough.
—Dorsi Miller, reader

Ms. Vosika spins the web so well you are a part of all the action. If you love history, romance, music and the believable unbelievable...this book is for you. I couldn't put it down until I closed the cover on an ending I never expected.
—Kat Yares, *Journeys Into the Velvet Darkness*

...best time travel book I have ever read. Fantastic descriptive detail and a sweet love story are combined beautifully.   —Amazon reviewer

some of the best writing it has been my pleasure to read....
—JR Jackson, *Reilley's Sting, Reilley's War,* and *The Ancient Mariner Tells All.*

a very exciting tale....   —Ross Tarry, *Eye of the Serpent,* and other mysteries

Vosika is a master at creating engaging characters...a riveting plot, well-drawn cast, and the beautiful imagery of Scotland.
—Genny Zak Kieley, *Hot Pants and Green Stamps*

I love books on time travel, but this is so much more. The characters come to life in your heart and mind.   —Jeryl Struble, singer/songwriter, *Journey to Joy*

One of the most intriguing stories of Scottish history I have ever read...riveting.
—Pam Borum, Minneapolis, MN

I found myself still thinking about the characters long after finishing the book.
—Goodreads reviewer

To all the Shawns and Nialls
Who are often more like one another
Than they want to believe

Westering Home

Blue Bells Chronicles Four

By

Laura Vosika

G/H

Gabriel's Horn Publishing

Contact: editors@gabrielshornpress.com

Published in Minneapolis, Minnesota by Gabriel's Horn Publishing

Publisher's Note: This novel is a work of fiction. Names, characters, places, and incidents are either products of the author's imagination or used fictitiously. All characters are fictional, and any similarity to people living or dead is purely coincidental.

Cover photo by Laura Vosika
Author Photo Emmanuel's Light Photography, by Chris Powell

First printing December 2015
Printed in the United States of America

For sales, please visit www.bluebellstrilogy.com

ISBN-13: 978-1-938990-14-4
ISBN-10: 1-938990-14-5

Acknowledgments

No book is complete without acknowledging those who have done so much to make the book happen.

My thanks to Chris Powell, who has been a great source of encouragement for the *Blue Bells* story, and was almost solely responsible for getting me to Scotland for my most recent research trip, and who is working with me on several other books.

Thank you to the Night Writers—Ross, Judy, Lyn, Genny, Judd, Janet, Jack, Stephanie, Sue, Catherine, and Meredythe—for years of listening to Shawn's story, and your great input.

Thank you, Jack Stanton, for helping me think like a medieval madman and your expertise on harnesses. I couldn't have done it without you.

My thanks to Deb Shaw, my editor, who seems to be there at all hours of the day and night, answering questions, looking things up, giving feedback, and more.

My thanks and appreciation to Elaine White, who has welcomed me into her home in the beautiful Ochil Hills, on my most recent research trips, and helped me with Scottish idioms. I'm blessed to call you friend, Elaine.

Dear Readers:

Blue Bells of Scotland was originally a trilogy:

1. Shawn and Niall trying to get home
2. Shawn in Scotland
3. Shawn's adjustment to his own time

However, as the story and characters grew, they were better served by splitting the second and third parts into two books each. Hence, a five book 'trilogy,' as of this writing: *Blue Bells of Scotland, The Minstrel Boy, The Water is Wide, Westering Home,* and *The Battle is O'er.*

Westering Home is the first part of the original Book Three, which concludes with *The Battle is O'er,* now Book Five of the *Chronicles.*

Trasna na dTonnta

The Original Westering Home

Good-bye to loneliness and to the distant remoteness;
Bright is my heart and bright is the sun,
Happy to be returning [home]

I saw my fill of countries abroad,
Gold and silver, the wealth of the world,
My heart rises in me with the break of each day,
As I draw closer to the land of my people!

On my journey - oh! my heart rises!
The weather is beautiful and the waves are settled
Steering directly to land of my bosom
And I'll be [home] tomorrow!

PRELUDE

Once upon a time, not so long ago, there was a man named Shawn. "Shawn" means self, and "Kleiner" means centered, one of his—many—former girlfriends declared. Shawn wore her assessment as a badge of honor. His father had been good, very good—and it had gotten him killed. No, life was about having fun, living for himself!

Once upon a time, not so long ago, there was a woman named Amy who saw behind Shawn's public mask. He was self-centered, selfish, and self-important, that was true. But he was also diligent, generous, hard-working, and funny. He did good deeds in secret. He changed life for everyone when he joined her small orchestra.

Because none of us is all good and none of us is all bad.

But eventually the bad outweighed the good. She believed his public self was his true self. On the eve of the Feast of St. Columba, she left him in an ancient tower in the Highlands of Scotland as thick mist rose. He woke up in the wrong century, mistaken for Niall Campbell, and sent on a dangerous mission to raise troops for the battle of Bannockburn.

Once upon a time, very long ago, there was a medieval Highland warrior named Niall Campbell. He was everything Shawn was not: devout, responsible, a servant to his people. He could also be vain and over-confident.

Because none of us is all good and none of us is all bad.

On the eve of the Feast of St. Columba, his betrothed left him in their tower in the Highlands as thick mist rose. He woke in the wrong century, mistaken for Shawn, ordered to play an impossible concert as he learned Scotland's awful fate at the battle of Bannockburn, and sought a way back across time to save his people.

The story is told in three chronicles—Blue Bells of Scotland, The Minstrel Boy, *and* The Water is Wide, *of how Shawn and Niall turn the battle at Bannockburn, how two men who despised one another become brothers, and their attempts to return to their proper times; of how Amy, pregnant with Shawn's child, seeks Shawn across time, her heart now torn between Shawn and Angus, the*

Highland inspector who helps her.

Finally, racing across the country with Shawn's infant son, they find their chance on the eve of the Feast of St. Columba, at the tower where the original switch happened. Angus, working for the good of Amy and James, whom he has come to love, waits at the bottom of the tower as Amy races up through ghostly warriors to try to pull Shawn back through time, knowing she still loves Shawn.

In the heat of battle against their long-time enemies, the Thieving MacDougalls, at the top of the tower, Niall bids farewell, as Shawn, reunited with Amy and James, disappears in the mists of time.

This is a story of miracles.
This is a story of people who, like us, are good and bad.
This is a story of redemption.

FIRST MOVEMENT

CHAPTER ONE

Glenmirril Castle, Shores of Loch Ness

Helicopter rotors beat overhead, whipping hurricane drafts down on the ancient stone tower. Amy bent over her infant son's head, cringing into the rough homespun robe covering Shawn's chest, into the hard chain mail underneath. He held her tightly, his helmeted head bowed over her and James, sheltering them from the roar and the spotlight flashing down from dark skies.

"Come down from the tower!" A voice erupted over a loudspeaker. "Shawn Kleiner, come down from the tower."

James let out a high-pitched screech, squirming in the constraint of his parents' bodies pressed around him. Amy lifted her head cautiously into waves of sound pulsing through her ears, searching the small tower. Gray stones rose on all sides, sharp against the black night. Niall and the dying man had disappeared, the pressure of Niall's fingers on her wrist just a memory. "They're gone," she whispered.

Shawn's body remained tense, his arm tight around her.

"They're gone!" She lifted her voice above the pulsing rotors. The spotlight swished over them, slashing swaths of light across the dark.

"What?" he shouted back.

"Niall, the other man, they're gone. You're home!"

Shawn scanned the tower, poised for action, before relaxing. He looked down at her. A beard, more auburn than his long, dark hair, covered his jaw. The eyes that had been full of life still held flecks of gold; but now they were piercing and stern, wary and watchful, looking out from vertical eye slits in a medieval helmet. He looked once more around the tower, up at the hovering helicopter, and back down at her. Slowly, he smiled. "I'm home? You're real?"

"Shawn Kleiner!" boomed the voice from the loudspeaker overhead. "Come down from the tower!"

She nodded, biting her lip, then smiling, and laughing. Tears sprang to the her eyes. She nodded again, harder. "You're home! You really did it! You're back!"

He gripped her close and kissed her, the way he had the first time, under the dripping awning.

Glenmirril Castle, 1316

Backing into the wall where Amy had melted away just moments ago, Niall scanned the tower, bright with light pulsing from the night sky. Pain burned the length of his right arm. Ignoring it, he scowled down at Duncan MacDougall, huddling on the floor, and strained to listen, over the cacophony roaring over the castle, for men coming up the stairs. Hearing nothing, he prodded Duncan with his toe. His chain mail chinked as he squatted down. The light above swept away, leaving them in moonlight. He gripped the man's hair, yanking his face up.

Duncan's glazed eyes stared up in the moonlight. "Kill me, then," he rasped.

"Killing's too good for you," Niall said softly. "You can stay here and feel a wee bit of the pain you inflicted on Christina these years." He loosed the dark hank of hair. Duncan's head lolled back. "Call it mercy you've a chance to make your peace with God." Niall hesitated. His emotions railed against it. Duncan didn't deserve it. But Niall's nature was well-formed. He sketched the sign of the cross over him, praying for his fleeing soul.

Duncan spit at him. "Burn in hell!" he whispered.

Niall wiped the spittle from his beard. "Make your peace with God," he advised. Hefting Duncan's sword in his left hand, he edged into the stairwell, listening. From below came the harsh clang of metal on metal, but more scattered, less vicious than it had been when he stormed up the stairs after Shawn. From above, the horrible rhythmic thunder waned. It must be something from Shawn's age, though he couldn't imagine, even after all Shawn's stories, what.

Despite the silence in the tower, he edged cautiously into the inky blackness, his back against the curving stone wall, listening for the approach of enemies. He reached the bottom of the tower, as the last sounds of fighting died away. The unnerving beam of light sliced through the night clouds, illuminating the courtyard. It swept in great circles, glinting off the metal loops of the Laird's hauberk.

The Laird, despite his age, gripped MacDougall's arms behind his back. MacDougall leaned forward, his greasy black hair falling half over his face, grimacing. His men huddled together, guarded by Lachlan, Owen, Brother David, Taran, his sister's son, Gilbert, and the boy Red, with drawn swords and taut faces. Several glanced up nervously at the light. Allene stood among them, a knife in each hand, her red hair escaping its braid, and her fine blue kirtle smeared with dirt, waist to hem.

"Allene!" Niall snapped.

She spun, her face hard.

"You should have been with the women."

"Go, Allene," her father said. "Had I time to deal with you, you'd not have gotten away with that."

"Thank you would do fine." She pushed one knife into her belt. "Is he gone?"

Red turned to him, echoing, "He's gone, My Lord?"

"He's gone with Amy," Niall replied.

She peered into his face. "You're pale, Niall. Are you injured?"

"'Tis naught." Niall ignored the heat searing up his arm.

"Who's gone with Amy? Who's Amy?" MacDougall demanded.

"'Tis none of your concern!" The Laird jerked the man's arms, making him grunt and fall silent. "You'd no business in my castle threatening my people to begin with."

Allene glanced at the sky, and her eyes darted back to Niall. Her lips tightened. "He's really gone?"

Thunder pulsed over head, the light dimmed and glowed again, and a muffled voice echoed down from the clouds. *Shawn Kleiner come down from the tower!* All the men, friend and foe alike, looked to the sky. Several of MacDougall's men fell to their knees, staring upward with chalky faces, and making the sign of the cross.

Red turned fearfully to Niall, whispering, "Why is my Lord Shawn's name being called from the sky, my Lord?"

"Sh," Niall murmured back. Raising his voice to his men, he said, "Have no fear." With a glare at MacDougall, he jerked his head toward the tower stairs and said to the Laird, "He'll want to say his farewells."

"Duncan?" MacDougall's head shot up again, despite the pain creasing the corners of his eyes. "What've you done to Duncan?"

Red took half a step forward, raising his sword.

"Same as he was trying to do to me and mine," Niall snapped. "'Tis a risk we take when we invade other men's castles, aye?" Niall arched a single, grim eyebrow at the same time MacDonald released MacDougall. The man stumbled forward, gripping his injured arm. "You'd best hurry," Niall advised. MacDougall gave one last glare, and hastened past, clambering as fast as his battered body would allow, up the tower stairs.

The voice gave another faint echo above, the rolling thunder dimmed, and the light faded. "'Tis naught to fear," Niall assured his men. Allene gripped his arm, her eyebrows furrowed. "I believe 'tis summat from Shawn's time," Niall whispered to her. His eyes met MacDonald's across the courtyard. The light faded, leaving the courtyard lit only by torches flickering along the walls, and a scrap of moon glow eking through dark clouds. "He's gone," Niall said. His voice was flat with the finality of it. His life, too, had just lost the peculiar light it had had for two years.

Glenmirril, Present

Shawn lifted his head, staring into Amy's eyes, the deep blue he'd dreamed of for two years. He removed his helmet, cradling it in one arm as he touched her hair, braided long and thick to her waist, pushing escaped tendrils from her temple. "I'm home?" he whispered.

In Amy's arms, James howled, his face screwed up and red under thick black hair. Shawn's smile grew. He had never heard a more beautiful sound. He touched James's cheek, hardly daring believe he was real and solid this time, that he wouldn't fade away, back into a different century, as he had months ago in the monastery.

Amy nodded, touching his cheek. "You're really home."

He looked her up and down, from a hooded sweatshirt, to long black skirt and tennis shoes. "Are you in concert black?" he asked in disbelief.

"Shawn Kleiner, come down!" bellowed the voice from the helicopter.

"Later." Kissing James's head, Shawn pushed Amy behind himself. Despite her assurance, he replaced his helmet, and raised his sword as he inched down the stairs. Behind him, James cried in her arms. Shawn didn't blame him. After two years of medieval life, the pulsing rotors and halogen glare made his heart race, too, made every nerve dance, screaming to fight or flee, as he circled down the stone stairs.

"They're gone," Amy said, close behind his ear. "You don't need that."

"Being safe," he replied, and inched around the corner. He looked out the door at the bottom of the tower, into the courtyard flooded with the spotlight from above.

"Shawn Kleiner!" boomed the voice from the sky.

Lowering the giant sword, he stepped through the door. "I'm here!" he shouted, at the same time the voice echoed, "Come down from the tower!"

In the courtyard, a squad of police ringed the tower entrance, twenty feet back. Pools of mist wreathed their ankles. Shawn removed his helmet, leaving the chain coif covering his head, and stared at them, trying to work his mind around the modern clothing, the long, straight leggings and navy blues, starched and plastic-brimmed hats with white-checked bands, and clean-shaven faces—not a scarred cheek or puckered eye socket among them. They seemed young, fresh, plastic, unreal, with none of the scars that life brought. Behind him, James's wails settled to a few hiccups, and the courtyard fell silent but for the thump of rotors overhead.

It dawned slowly on Shawn that the police stared in equal confusion back at him. He wielded a claymore, covered in the blood of Duncan MacDougall, who had died in 1316. He wore a monk's robe over chain mail and held a medieval helmet. He lowered the weapon, point into the dirt, and pulled off the chain coif, shaking out the long golden hair that would be sweaty and dirty, nothing like the hair he'd taken such pride in, two years ago.

"I'm here," he said again.

The ghost who had appeared in Niall's room so many months ago stepped forward, parting the gloam. He was solid now, a tall, broad man with dark curls cut close, and cheeks ruddy in the cool night. "Shawn Kleiner?"

"It's him." Amy stepped from behind him, and the cop pulled her into his arms, hugging her and James, his head bent over her as Shawn's had, just minutes before.

"What's going on?" Shawn looked from her to the man. The cop and Amy exchanged glances, and he pushed her back, then held out his hand to Shawn. "Inspector Angus MacLean, Inverness Police. Welcome home." He gave a nod to the man beside him, who spoke into a radio. The helicopter above gave a start, and veered north, taking its spotlight away and leaving the courtyard lit only by floodlights along the base of the ancient walls.

Shawn shook the man's hand, disliking his touch. He turned to Amy. She didn't meet his eyes. "Amy." Shawn touched her arm, touched James's head. His stomach turned in a way it hadn't, even going into battle beside James Douglas. He'd spent two years, given up everything, to get back to her. "Amy, who the hell is this guy?"

♫

Shouts in the hallway jarred Simon awake. Angry voices. He rolled off his cot, dropping to one knee, tensed for action, before noting the moon spilling through the barred window and remembered: he was not in his own time. He relaxed. These people were weak and soft. There was no need to tense for action.

"Come along now," a voice rumbled.

"Get your hands off me! What law have I broken!" demanded a deep voice.

Simon started. The voice had a strong flavor of Simon's own time, the vowels like the Scottish lords he had known. Simon moved silently to the bars, pressing his face to them.

The group burst into the room, half a dozen men in blue, Angus among them. Simon drew back. But Angus passed, his eyes locked on the man in the center of the melee. He was tall and broad under a rough spun monk's robe. Golden chestnut hair escaped wildly from a leather thong trying to bind it back. Dirt streaked his face. He raised a hand to push at the men closing in on him, and Simon saw dried blood. From under his robe the distinct *chink chink chink* of chain mail. The group was gone as quickly as they'd come, their shouts fading down the hall.

"It's that musician," said the man in the adjoining cell. "Yer man who came back mad after a night in Glenmirril."

"And disappeared at Bannockburn," Simon said. "He turned up back at Glenmirril, did he?" So the old monk had told the truth—about that, at least. Shawn Kleiner was home. And he had missed his chance to cross back, to seize power.

Glenmirril, June 1316

MacDougall yanked viciously from his guards. But with his hands behind his back, rough rope biting into his wrists, he stumbled, barely righting himself against the stone walls, backing away from the cell. Duncan, his only son—dead! His army defeated! "You'll die!" He whirled on his captors. They were *boys*. It added insult, to have *boys* shoving him around like a common criminal. "You killed my *son!*"

The oldest lad inserted a large iron key in the door, ignoring him, but one of the younger ones grabbed his shirt, yanking him nose to nose. "You killed my *father!*" The boy's voice boiled with fury. He shoved MacDougall at the open cell.

"Dismiss the words of a fool, Taran," spoke the older guard. "Red." He tossed the keys to the youngest, whose vivid hair explained his name. "Lock the door."

MacDougall resisted, throwing his weight against the lad. The boy grasped his hair, dragging as Taran pushed, into the chamber. MacDougall landed gracelessly on the stone floor, jarring his bound wrists all the way to his shoulders. "I'll kill you!" he raged. "I'll disembowel every one of you, down to the smallest bairn!"

"I'll let my Laird know." The oldest set the tip of his sword to MacDougall's throat.

Taran's weapon flashed up. "Let me kill him, Gil."

Gil held up his hand. Taran's sword froze mid-air. "We follow our Laird's orders," Gil said. "Do not let anger drive you, Taran."

MacDougall glanced from Taran, his face contorted, his sword poised like a serpent overhead, to Gil, whose steady eyes never left his. MacDougall smiled slowly. His heart slowed. "Yes, Taran, do not let anger drive you," he mocked. He saw no wisdom in advising Taran that anger led to deadly mistakes. His own anger had not been wise.

Taran glared at him.

Gil gave a sharp nod of his head, and the boy lowered his weapon grudgingly. In the doorway, Red watched, his sword ready.

MacDougall remained still on the floor, his bound arms painfully propping him up, watching their every move. "What does MacDonald plan to do?" he demanded.

Not answering, Gil gave a jerk of his head, and Taran left the small space. Gil backed out, swinging the heavy door shut with a thud. Tumblers clicked into place.

Furious, MacDougall struggled to his feet, stumbling into the stone walls, and falling heavily against the iron cot. Outside, Taran hissed angrily.

"We follow orders," Gil said firmly.

MacDougall stood quietly, listening, but no more sound came from outside. He forced himself to think. Yes, they would report all he said and did to MacDonald. He could use that to his detriment or advantage. And nobody had ever called MacDougall a fool. Moreover, he reminded himself, a skilled military commander had more at his disposal than strength and steel. He had cunning and wits.

He peered through the grate. He could not see them, but MacDonald would not leave him unguarded. They were undoubtedly there. He turned to assess his prison in the gray light before dawn. It was long enough to squeeze a cot between two walls, and wide enough only for the space of floor on which he'd landed between the cot and a table pushed up against the other wall. A rickety chair pressed itself under the table. Its legs could be used as weapons, sharpened against the stone walls perhaps. The blanket on the narrow bed—strips could be torn from it to garrote or bind his captors.

Flexing his wrists, he strode to the barred window. Stars shone in the west, even as faintest dawn blushed in the east. He looked three stories down, into the shadowed southern bailey, with the vegetable gardens and dovecot in the center. From his vantage point, he could see across the stone wall into the northern courtyard where the battle had raged. His men were being ushered into a dark maw at the bottom of the northernmost wing of the castle, no doubt to the dungeons. He thought of Duncan in the tower, whispering, "Take vengeance!" before the glaze of pain in his eyes turned to the still glaze of death.

His thoughts turned to his wife, waiting at home for a son who would never return. She'd objected to the venture, forgoing her usual peaceful acceptance of his decisions, to plead, "Drop this hatred, Alexander! 'Twas not Niall Campbell in Duncan's dungeon, but a wandering minstrel!"

But MacDougall's hatred of Niall and desire for Christina burned side by side. He would have them both, the prisoner he'd justly sentenced to death, and the woman who had given him a promise. He had strapped his scabbard around his waist, striding for the door. He would have them! He would not be made a fool!

"Alexander!" She darted forward, her face a mask of anger. "Can we not finally live in peace! How many more must die?"

He pushed her aside, feeling only brief guilt when she stumbled against the bed, as he remembered Duncan throwing Christina across the room. But he hadn't thrown her. He hadn't hurt her. He'd business to attend, and she had spoken out of turn.

Now, her son was dead. He himself would not be returning to care for his lands soon—if ever. MacDougall's eyes narrowed, watching the shadowed courtyard as the last of his men disappeared into the depths. He twisted his wrists behind his back. He'd had every right to reclaim his prisoner. MacDonald should not have fought!

With his men gone to the dungeon to await their fate, he scanned the southern bailey. Across the way, smoke rose against the charcoal gray sky. Three men crossed the courtyard below, swinging swords, heading toward the plumes of smoke. They ducked inside, and soon a steady metallic clanging arose. The smithy. The armory was likely next to it. It was information worth knowing.

Two monks appeared, carrying baskets, to kneel in the vegetable garden. A boy led three ponies into the southern bailey. They pranced, heads tossing, nostrils filled with the lingering scent of battle, as he pulled them into the wing under MacDougall's own tower. The stables, MacDougall guessed.

He flexed his wrists, watching. His son was dead, victim to this hellish clan. *Take vengeance!* In the northern bailey, MacDonald emerged from the great hall, descended a short wooden staircase, and disappeared into the dark doorway that had swallowed MacDougall's army. Peace came over MacDougall. He knew one thing of MacDonald. He fancied himself a man of God. In truth, he but sought excuse for his weakness. With sudden certainty, MacDougall knew what the old laird would do.

He smiled. Yes, they would report anything he said or did. *Do not let anger drive you.* Anything they reported would, henceforth, be impeccable. It would be a slow game. But MacDonald would slip into trust. MacDougall had all the time in the world to plot the vengeance that would please Duncan the most.

Inverness Police Station, Present

Fluorescent lights glared down from a white ceiling. White walls doubled their effect, washing the whole room in blinding white. "I've died and gone to heaven," Shawn muttered. "Niall's going to be so disappointed to find me here." He lounged in a spindly chair designed for discomfort, his legs in filthy breeks stretched in front of him. He'd shed the robe and bloodied chain mail. They lay on the scarred, wooden table, under the huge claymore and two short, vicious *sgian dubhs*, between him and half the Inverness police force, several of whom threw the items curious glances at regular intervals, while striving to appear only professionally interested.

"Someone's called my mother?" Shawn asked for the second time. His lower leg burned. He suspected he'd been sliced with one of the MacDougalls' swords. "She's here in Scotland?"

"Aye, down in Bannockburn," said Inspector MacLean, with the short black curls and ruddy cheeks. In contrast to the other cops, he wore jeans and a rumpled navy blue sweatshirt. He stayed back from the table, against the wall. "Amy's on the phone with her now."

"Perhaps that should be Miss Nelson to you," Shawn said.

Inspector MacLean stared straight ahead, not answering. But his lips tightened. Shawn smiled.

"We must ask again," spoke the man who must be the chief, "where you've been for a year?" Beside him sat a middle-aged man Shawn had identified as Clive, with a well-padded paunch and thinning brown hair, reaching for a donut. But it was Inspector MacLean, standing calmly, avoiding his eyes, to whom Shawn's gaze strayed over and over. "Mr. Kleiner?"

Shawn forced himself to look at the chief. "I've spent about a quarter of the time at Glenmirril, and the rest at Stirling Castle, Cambuskenneth, Creagsmalan, Dundolam, and all over Jedburgh and Northumbria."

The chief banged his fist on the table. The coif slid off the hauberk to fall, clanking, against the sword. "You mean to say you've been going around Glenmirril, which is packed with tourists every day, dressed like that!" He indicated Shawn's trews and stained, torn gambeson, over a medieval *leine*. "With half of Scotland searching for you, and no one's noticed?"

Shawn shrugged. He looked again at the man who had hugged Amy and James. The Inspector gazed at the far wall, his cheeks high with color. Shawn looked back to the chief. "No one noticed because I was there from June 1314 until early this morning, June, 1316."

The chief bolted from his chair, pacing and glowering. "'Tis impossible, for starters, and your games are not appreciated. 'Tis a fortune has been spent, the Scottish police and your own people, looking for you, and you playing games! Besides which, you've only been gone a year."

Shawn shrugged again. A corner of his mouth quirked up. "I can't help but appreciate the irony that the one time in my life I tell the truth is the one time no one will ever believe me. You tell me, then. Where did I get medieval chain mail and a claymore?" He nodded at the things on the table. "Whose blood is all over them?"

"Aye, we'd like to know," Sergeant Chisolm said.

The chief stopped his pacing, staring at Shawn, waiting for an answer.

"Most likely Duncan MacDougall's," Shawn said. "I *hope* it's Duncan MacDougall's. Look him up in the history books and find out if he died June 9, 1316. I think you'll find he did. I *hope* he doesn't have a miracle recovery like

Lachlan." He closed his eyes, thinking of Lachlan...Owen...Red. He'd left them there, fighting for their lives.

"Lachlan who?" Sergeant Chisolm's voice came through the dark.

Shawn opened his eyes, disoriented to see a modern police officer in a white-washed room. The chief stared at him, jaw down. He sputtered, stumbled over a few words, and burst out, "You admit to *killing* a man?"

Fatigue washed suddenly over Shawn. "I sure tried to kill him," he snapped. "Duncan MacDougall. Son of Alexander MacDougall. Look him up. He was trying to kill me at the time, and he'd put his wife through enough hell, he deserved it." His jaw clenched, fighting the burning pain in his leg. "I think the statute of limitations is up well before seven hundred years, anyway, so I'm not too worried about it."

The chief spun on one of his men. "Look it up. Send men to search the tower!"

"We searched the whole complex," Sergeant Chisolm protested. "The tower is only ten by ten and empty. We'd not have missed a dead man!"

"You won't find him." Shawn sighed, and gazed at the ceiling. "Except in a history book." He closed his eyes in pain as the door slammed behind one of the men, rushing to order forces back to the tower and to look up Duncan MacDougall. Behind his lids, Shawn saw Niall's face, eyes bright and wistful, up in the tower. He smelled the blood of battle. He heard the clash of steel, saw Allene leaping on the back of one of MacDougall's men, fighting him off Niall. "I left them," he whispered. His chest ached with a pain beyond MacDougall's sword wound. He felt sick to his stomach.

"What's that?" asked Chisolm.

"Nothing." Shawn opened his eyes, drew his legs in abruptly, and sat up. "Look, I've got a nasty gash down one leg. As far as I know, it's not actually a crime to disappear. I'll pay back double what I gave that guy in counterfeit bills. Even though that wasn't really my fault. But I'd really like to have this leg looked at, and get home—wherever that is—to a hot bath and warm bed."

The remaining cops leaned close, whispering to one another. Shawn studied Inspector MacLean, standing apart against the white-washed wall. The man refused to look at him.

Chisolm rose from his seat, rounded the table, and squatted before Shawn. "I suspect he's done more for you than any of us will ever know," he said softly, giving a nod toward MacLean. "At great personal cost to himself. He's a good man."

Shawn's eyes remained on MacLean, not acknowledging Chisolm's presence in any way. As the cop returned to his seat, the door burst open. Chisolm spun. The policemen's heads snapped up.

The chief stood in the doorway, his face dark. "There's no body in the tower!"

"Told you so." Shawn said.

"For that, you're very lucky."

"Did you check on Duncan MacDougall?"

"What was his father's name?" The chief's eyes narrowed.

Shawn sighed. "Alexander."

"Age?"

"What is this, twenty questions?" Shawn glared. "My leg hurts. I've probably got an issue with blood loss, and as long as I'm here in the twenty-first century, I'd love a little twenty-first century medical care. Duncan, mid-twenties. Alexander, mid-forties. Letch." He spit out the last word, thinking of Christina.

"He died as you say on June 9, 1316," the chief replied.

"Thank God!" Shawn muttered, pressing a hand to his aching calf.

"I don't know what game you're playing," the chief said, "but 'tis not appreciated."

Shawn rose, glowering at the assembled force. His leg trembled. His head swam. It mattered not. He had been knighted by Robert the Bruce.

The officers drew back in their seats.

"Am I charged with a crime?" Shawn demanded. "If not, I'd like to leave. *Now.*"

Tension trembled in the white-washed room. The chief glared back, no happier with the filthy, bearded Shawn Kleiner standing before him in a medieval gambeson than he'd been with the arrogant mega star who'd invaded Inverness a year earlier with his orchestra. The men of the Inverness force looked to their chief.

"There's no crime," he snapped. "Inspector MacLean, escort him out."

♬

Simon lay awake as the sky faded to gray. One of the men in blue hurried through, calling to the man at the desk, "Duncan MacDougall. Chief says find out if he died in 1316."

The man at the desk swore. "Kleiner's nothing but trouble!"

The sky brightened to dusky pink in the small window, and the men bustled through again. Simon pressed himself against the wall, but Angus's eyes locked on the man—Shawn Kleiner—in medieval clothing. His robe and chain mail were gone, revealing a padded gambeson over a *leine* and breeks. The group passed through, followed by two men carrying his hauberk, monk's robe, coif, and sword. "Living in medieval Scotland," one of them said in disgust. "Feckin' star, thinks he can get away with anything."

They'd barely passed through when the door opened again, and the man at the desk approached Simon's cell. "Visitor," he said.

Simon rose warily.

It was the old monk. Brother Eamonn stood before the cell bars as if he'd materialized there, frail as a breath of wind, his few strands of white hair lying over his bald pate, his arm in a sling.

Venom rose in Simon's stomach, curling like a dragon, and crawled up his throat. But his loss of control, his attack on the old fool, had landed him here. The monk should have been gloating. But he didn't smile. He didn't speak.

"Why have you come?" Simon sneered, as if he were the one looking into a cell. "You know I'll be out again."

Eamonn's pale lips curved upward. "Aye, for I'm allowing it," he said, his voice as thin as old parchment.

Simon's hands curled around the bars, his nose inches from the monk's.

Eamonn did not draw back. "You still need to get home."

Simon's jaw tightened, unwilling to admit he needed anything from this villein.

Eamonn's voice dropped. "I can give you what you need. Perhaps."

A snarl, rose in Simon's chest. "You play a dangerous game, old man," he hissed.

"That we do." Eamonn smiled. "But the stakes are well worth it. Far higher than you know."

"You'll die," Simon whispered.

"Ah, threats, when I came to help you," Eamonn sighed.

Simon gripped the bars more tightly.

"Christmastide. Another door opens."

"Where is the crucifix?" Simon demanded. "Is it in Glenmirril?"

Eamonn frowned. "I think, now, on further thought, that the one in Glenmirril was a different crucifix. I do apologize for the mistake." He tapped his temple with his free hand. "Too old. You understand, I get mixed up. Brother Jimmy's brew and all." He began to shuffle away, but stopped suddenly, turning back. His eyes appeared watery and vague. "Wee James, now. Amy's outside with him. So close! What a fine braw laddie he'll grow up to be!"

Simon's knuckles turned white. "Where is it?" he hissed.

Eamonn chuckled. "'Twill do you no good before Christmastide."

"I'll be out," Simon snarled. "And then I'll kill you."

"That should be most unpleasant," Eamonn wheezed. "For you. For without my knowledge, you shall be trapped here." He stepped close to the bars, nose to nose with Simon, and Simon had the unpleasant sense the old monk had just grown taller and stronger. His words were firm. "As Christmas draws near, we'll speak again." He smiled, with thin, white lips, and sank back into a shaky, decrepit old man. His brown-robed back bent, he hobbled out of the jail.

Simon shook the bars, his lips tight in fury. He'd find the monk if he chose!

A pair of guards came through at that moment. "Fighting with the Bruce!" one of them said in disgust. "He expects anyone to believe that?"

Simon smiled. He didn't need the old man. He had Shawn.

CHAPTER TWO

Glenmirril, 1316

Niall stormed into his chambers. Blood spattered his tunic and mail. A ruby stain seeped through the white linen sleeve covering his upper right arm. "Niall, you must let me look," Allene insisted. Coral dawn streaked the opening of the arched stone window.

"What were you doing in that courtyard!" Anger turned his face dark beneath the auburn beard.

She stuck her chin out, the concern in her eyes turning to anger. "Helping. I believe you'd have had a knife in your back had I not. A few, perhaps."

"You are with child," he said. "Are you mad! You endangered our bairn!"

"Och, dry yer eyes," Allene snapped. "I'm fine, am I not?"

"Look at my arm," Niall insisted, showing her. The smell of blood grew pungent. "Have you no sense? This could have been you! It could have been our wee bairn!"

"My father needed me. You needed me." She lifted her nose. "It *wasn't* me, so all's well, aye?"

"Who was caring for the women?" Niall pressed. He glanced at the spreading stain, deciding it needed her attention, and began struggling with the hauberk, leaning over to let gravity drag it off. Dizziness rushed him; she leapt forward, heaving him upright as the chain slid to the floor in a chinking metallic puddle. She pushed him to the divan, fumbling to pull off his gambeson and torn, bloodied shirt, exclaiming in horror at the gash on his arm.

"Bessie!" she hollered at the open door.

"Who's protecting the women and children?" he asked again.

"Bessie, Christina, your mother." She glanced around the room. Bessie would be in the dungeons, far out of earshot. She took another quick look at the open gash, oozing heavy, thick blood, and ran for her needlework basket by the divan.

"Boiling water, the fire," Niall reminded her. "Shawn said we must."

"You're bleeding *now*," Allene protested.

"Clean it first. Shawn said."

She rummaged a minute before emerging from the basket triumphant. A sound caught their ears. They turned. Christina stood in the doorway of the chamber that had been Shawn's. "You need help," she said.

Allene straightened and became still, the needle in her hand. "You were meant to be with the women."

Christina lifted her chin a trifle. The look of calm Niall knew well, from his few days playing in her castle with her musicians, came over her face. Unease stirred in his gut. He'd learned it was a steel mask, holding in a great deal. Her hair was disarrayed, escaping its glossy braid. Her face was chalky white.

"Christina...?" He rose from the divan.

"Let us tend your arm." Christina spoke in the low melodic voice that had so entranced Shawn. She moved briskly to the hearth, stirring the fire, and pulling the large black kettle over the weak flames.

"Christina." Niall spoke sternly. "What has happened?"

Inverness, Present

"*He's* taking us?"

Amy, cradling a sleeping James on her shoulder, avoided Shawn's eyes. A police car had taken him to the hospital for stitches down eight inches of his left calf. "It'll match the other one," he'd said, and when she raised questioning eyebrows, lifted the hospital gown to show a rough red scar running the length of his other thigh. "Wolf," he explained, and smiled at the doctor who paused in his sewing. "I'm jesting," he'd said. "Kidding. I'm full of tall tales." But he made no further explanation.

"And what of the, uh, arrow wound?" the doctor asked. "The one I stitched last time I saw you. It's healed? Strange business, that."

"Like it never happened," Shawn answered. "Yep, strange indeed."

They brought in a psychiatrist, who concluded he was mocking them, but quite sane. But with police business over, clothed once more in filthy breeks, and bloody, torn shirt, he stared at the green mini waiting outside the hospital's glass doors.

"Who is this guy, Amy?" he asked. But he stared at Inspector MacLean.

"You're tired," Angus said. "You need a good meal, hot bath, and bed."

"We'll talk tomorrow." Amy pulled off her sweatshirt, revealing her concert black blouse with the bell sleeves, a match to the skirt. Opening the back door to nestle James in his car seat, she glanced up at Shawn. "Please, Shawn, get in. You can finally hold James and spend time with him." She looked from Angus, his face stiff, back to Shawn, who had clearly not missed the look.

To her relief, he climbed in the front passenger seat. She rounded the car to where Angus held the door for her. "It'll be aw' right, Amy," he whispered. "One day at a time, aye?"

She paused, one foot in the door. Her hand touched his, resting on the top of the door frame. Their eyes held one another. The memory of Shawn's kiss, up in the tower, tingled through her. She wondered if Angus could read the guilt and thrill in her face. *Shawn was back!* Fear and exhilaration trembled side by side, on the wings of that one thought.

"It'll be aw' right," he said again, and gently pushed her hand off the frame.

She sank into the car, her head dropping back against the headrest, and her hand resting on James's sleeping body.

Inverness, Scotland, Present

The sun climbed high as Clive finished the paperwork on Kleiner. The man was an eejit! Far worse than an eejit! Lying to the chief, making a joke of it all!

"Morning!" He looked up as Claire, the new secretary, came in with a donut and a mug of steaming coffee. "Angus is gone?" she asked. Her jet black hair bobbed in a pony tail. Freckles sprinkled her cheeks below cornflower blue eyes.

"Aye, they've sent him to take the eejit home," Clive said. "Wherever that may be at the moment."

"I'm sure you're needing coffee." She set the mug and the donut on the desk. "Where does he say he's been?"

Anger welled up in Clive. He glanced at the holding cell. The prisoner there, Seamus P. Martin by the identity card in his wallet, had gone barmy on an elderly monk last night. He'd been brought in raging like a mad man, with the strength of a bull, and paced his cell relentlessly for the whole hour before Angus had called, demanding they commandeer a ferry, and launching the whole department out to Glenmirril. Clive had a vague memory of Seamus Martin becoming still, holding the bars, watching with unblinking, snake-like eyes, as Kleiner was brought in, in the wee hours, and later, as he was herded out again. But the man lay now on his cot, paying no mind. "Kleiner thinks he can make a mockery of the entire force." Clive's irritation spewed out. "Kept insisting he spent two years fighting with the Bruce."

"They say he showed up in chain mail," Claire said.

"Aye, that he did."

"Where would he get such a thing?"

"Damned if I know."

"Are they taking him to a doctor, to see if he's a head injury?" Claire suggested.

"Aye, he's been. Though he didn't seem mad a 'tall, only as arrogant as ever, playing games with us." Clive sighed, reining in his anger, and took a deep sip of coffee. "The hell of it is, *Angus* didn't seem surprised or concerned he'd stick with this story. Everyone else is in an uproar." He looked down the hall. The prisoner gripped his bars, listening to every word. Clive bit into a donut, the chocolate thick on top, meeting the man's eyes. He'd been brought in only for disrupting the peace. But Clive swore there was something much uglier in the glittering black gaze.

Claire cleared her throat. "They asked me to tell you to release yer man."

Clive nodded. "Is Pete coming with his things?"

Pete entered before she could answer. Clive rose, the keys on his belt jingling, and headed down the short hall. "Time to go," he said. The hair on the back of his neck rose. Seamus Martin from Bannockburn, the man's ID said. Neither the name nor his fingerprints had turned up any record whatsoever. It seemed odd that a man with no previous run-ins with the law would attack an elderly monk.

But Seamus P. Martin had calmed down.   He was downright congenial, following quietly alongside Clive, cooperating as Clive processed his paperwork. Maybe it was a one-off, Clive thought, bad row with the wife, or a difficult client at work.   He handed him his things, and watched the stocky man head out to the street, as pleasant as the June sunshine.

♫

Angus guided the green mini through the afternoon streets of Inverness, with occasional quizzical glances between himself and Shawn in the passenger seat. The silence stretched in the car, taut as a bow, among the three.   Angus sifted through his mind for conversation. *How are things in 1314?* seemed flippant. *Are you going to take her from me,* far worse. He cleared his throat. "Straight home? A bit to eat at a pub?" He turned the car onto the last street before his own, row houses stretching down the block, each with fluttering lace curtains; but a pub was close enough.

Shawn stared at him, then turned to Amy. "Who the hell is this guy? What's 'home?' Are you living together? Are you sleeping with him or something?"

Angus slammed on the brakes and veered to the curb. Tires squealed.

Shawn lurched, hands slamming the dashboard.   "What the hell!" he demanded.

"Angus." Amy sounded nervous. "He didn't mean—it doesn't matter."

"It matters a great deal how you're treated."   Angus turned hard eyes on Shawn. "I've been with you all of two hours and I like you even less than I did before I met you. Apologize to her or get out."

"I've been up for about thirty-six hours now, spanning seven hundred years," Shawn shot back. "Maybe you could just loosen up and put this car back in drive. I think I have a right to know what's going on with the mother of my child."

"You've a duty to treat the mother of your child with respect, is what you've got."   Angus yanked the keys from the ignition. "I'm not your chauffeur."   He enunciated each syllable, before turning to Amy. "I'm going home. I'll carry James if you like, or you can stay with this eejit and hope his attitude improves. I'd not bet on it, even if I were a betting man."

Amy looked from one to the other. "He's just had a rough..."

"You were ever good at making his excuses." Angus climbed from the car, slamming the door, and walked away.

Amy jumped from the car, rounding it for James.

"Amy!" Shawn clambered from the car, pain shooting up his newly stitched calf. "That's my son!"

She wrestled with the straps on the car seat. James stirred, opening his eyes and squinting in the sun. "Look at me!"   She whirled on Shawn, her long braid swinging. "He's right. Two hours with you, and I'm right back to putting up with it and making excuses for you. What's wrong with me?"   She lifted James from the car seat. Half a block away, Angus turned, waiting.

Glenmirril, June 1316

"'Tis naught," Christina spoke briskly to Niall. "You've an arm to be seen to. Allene, I believe Shawn had a special needle made for such as this. 'Tis curved." She stirred up the flames in the hearth and pushed in twigs from a basket nearby.

"You were meant to be with the women." Allene searched the sewing basket.

"As were you." Christina took the curved needle Allene handed her, and, gripping it carefully in a pair of tongs, lowered it into the bubbling water. "Wash his arm. Niall, you'd best sit down."

He dropped onto the settee facing the window, exhaustion and pain washing over him. Allene exchanged a glance with him as she rinsed a cloth in the bucket of water on the hearth, and cleansed the sticky blood from his arm. He stiffened.

"What's been done with MacDougall and his men?" Christina asked.

"Duncan will bother you no more, Christina," Niall answered. "He's dead."

She turned from the fire, her face stiff, her eyes dull.

"As to MacDougall's men, they were being led to the dungeons when I left. Some of our people would like their heads on pikes."

"My father will not allow it." Allene studied the wound, running half the length of his upper arm, gaping with red, raw edges. "Whisky?" she asked, and promptly answered her own question. "Aye." She disappeared into the bed chamber and returned with a heavy flask, watching as he obediently downed half of it.

As his shoulders relaxed, she glanced at Christina, holding the tongs in the cauldron, one hand drawing her skirts back from snapping flames. She should have been in the dungeons, not in Shawn's chamber. It was not hard to guess why she'd go there, but her countenance suggested more than disappointment over his leaving.

Christina turned from the fire, clutching the tiny silver needle in the tongs. "You've thread?"

Allene nodded, unspooling fine white linen and biting it off. She took the needle and threaded it in one quick motion. "Have a wee bit more," she advised Niall.

He lifted the flask, gulping several times before his hand went suddenly limp. Christina caught the flask.

To keep his mind off the impending jabs, Allene asked, "What did my father say about MacDougall's men?"

Niall closed his eyes, gave a brief smile. "Good," he sighed.

Allene pushed the edges of the wound together, while Christina held it. "MacDougall's men?" she prodded as she pushed the needle in.

Niall stiffened, his muscle taut under the pull of thread and second jab of the needle. "He said Bruce believes mercy will heal our country."

"So it will," said Christina.

Allene knotted the thread tightly. In the arched window, shell pink lightened to pale blue.

"Bruce showed mercy even to Ross, after he betrayed his wife and daughter."

Niall sucked in a deep breath as the needle poked through again. "I believe your father is thinking deeply on that even now in the Bat Cave."

Allene nodded. "So he would." Her father spent a great deal of time in the large natural cave, far below the castle, at the far end of the dungeons. Shawn had dubbed it the Bat Cave, despite their insistence there were neither bats nor— especially!—robins in it.

"Why would he think there are birds there?" Niall mumbled, echoing her thoughts. "Why robins?" Allene was pleased to hear the slur in his words. He sagged against the settee, his head lolling, and didn't react when she pushed the needle in again, but to heave a sigh.

Allene sighed, too. At one end of the cave, far below them, hung a large crucifix, carved by MacDonald himself. She guessed her father would spend hours on the kneeler before it, skipping morning and noon meals, before deciding MacDougall's fate. "Ross has shown himself worthy of the mercy granted him," she mused, though whisky had clouded Niall's mind. "But will MacDougall? Or will we suffer still more at his hands? Has he not taken our cattle often enough, and tried three times to kill you, Niall? How many more times do we risk his evil? What else might he do?"

"'Tis impossible to comprehend the good and evil that live together in one man," Christina said. She let go of the wound suddenly, surprising Allene, and glided away, into Shawn's bedchamber, her long black braid bobbing against her green kirtle.

"Christina?" Allene looked from the wound, gaping once more, to Christina disappearing into Shawn's chambers. Niall's head lolled to one side, eyes half closed. She knotted the thread securely against his skin, and hurried to the door of Shawn's room to see Christina kneeling over a bucket, retching.

Inverness, Scotland, Present

"I'm sorry." Shawn stared at the ground, jaw tight.

"Are you sorry or do you just want a ride?" Amy asked. In her arms, James squirmed, stretching his fists.

Shawn's hands went to his hips. "Believe me, I'm quite capable of walking anywhere at this point." Christina flashed to his mind. *What kind of man are you?* He'd hated the disappointment heavy in her voice. She'd had such faith in him that he'd come back and do it right this time with Amy. She would be saddened to hear what he'd just said to her.

"Walk, then." Amy's skirt swirled as she turned to follow the cop.

"It's not about a ride," Shawn said quickly. "I *am* sorry, Amy. I had no right to say that." A few hours in his own world, and he was slipping right back to his old ways. He told himself it wasn't true. It was only that he had a right to know how things stood.

She turned back. "Especially after all your activities on the side."

The cop watched them. Shawn turned his eyes to Amy, wondering what she knew. He had a sinking feeling, seeing the calm certainty on her face, that this time she *knew*. His face colored. His eyes shifted to the row houses, all with brightly colored doors and lace curtain in the windows, and parked cars surrounding them. "I'm sorry," he said again. "Can we start over?"

The cop, Inspector MacLean, took two steps closer.

"But what's the deal with him?" Shawn glanced at the man, hoping he wouldn't come closer.

"We've been seeing each other," Amy said softly. "And I like him. A lot. More than that."

Shawn closed his eyes, breathing inward. He'd woken thirty-six hours ago, to a gray medieval dawn, to misty hills, to Hugh and MacDonald and Niall, Owen and Lachlan and the rest of the company stirring in their plaids, to porridge and bannocks hastily fixed over the fire, to an ambush against MacDougall's men, a hard ride back to Glenmirril, and another battle. He'd answered dozens of questions in the brightly lit interrogation room. His leg stung with the long, deep gash of a medieval sword, and a dozen or more stitches, as the anesthetic wore off. "I came back for you." The words came out softly. He felt his body sway, and opened his eyes.

Inspector MacLean stood beside her. "Has he apologized?" he asked.

Amy nodded.

"You may have had a rough night," he addressed Shawn. "But she and I have also been up for over thirty hours, chasing you through the night from Bannockburn to Iona to Glenmirril. We've covered a good quarter of the country ourselves trying to get you back. Get in."

♫

On the bustling street, between the station and the sparkling waters of the River Ness, a silver slash through the heart of Inverness, Simon drew a deep breath, tamping his fury. A child screeched in its carriage. A man bumped him. But losing control had cost him the chance to be at Glenmirril, and cross back to his own time.

It was tempting to seek the old monk. But there was time to deal with him before Christmastide. No, he would find the man, Shawn, just returned from Simon's own time. He couldn't have gone far.

Simon glanced back at the station. He didn't need them coming out asking why he was loitering. He looked up and down the street. There was no sign of Eamonn, or of Angus, Amy, or Shawn. Simon found a bridge crossing the Ness, and took it, flowing with throngs of hurried women, and bairns in cots on wheels, and men rushing with black cases swinging from their hands, to the other side. There, he leaned on a rail, looking across the water to the station, and considered his next move. Crowds swirled around him, talking, laughing, calling to one another. *Cars* let out shrill pierces. Huge *buses* lumbered by.

...going to lunch with her next week, a woman said behind him.

Simon tried to shut out the voices and think. The monk must have returned to the nursing home. Simon couldn't go there, but Eamonn had to leave its safety sometime. Until then, Simon had things to do. Talk to Shawn. Find the crucifix. Find Amy. Kill the child.

Put in the order to buy! Beside him, a man barked into one of the *foons.*

Simon glared at him. The man glared back, and strode away. Simon planted his arms on the rail, watching the jail to see if Angus came or went.

Two women stopped by the bridge with prams, sighing about the cost of *nappies*, whatever those were. Across the river, the girl who had spoken with Clive came out, chatting with another wench. The women with their howling offspring moved along. Two girls flounced up to the rail, taking their place. "Over there!" One of them pointed across the water.

Simon's lips tightened in annoyance.

"Do you think we'll see him?"

"Sure an' he's gone by now."

Simon gave them a hard stare. They didn't notice, in their fixation on whoever it was they sought across the water.

"Dave says he told the most outlandish story about being in medieval Scotland!" One of the girls giggled. "He said he's wearing medieval britches and shirt.

Simon became still, his irritation melting. God smiled on him.

"His orchestra's here," the first girl said. "Do you think he'll play with them?"

"Oh, aye, I'm sure of it," said the second. "He'll stay a wee bit. Dave says they've told him not to leave, in case they've questions for him."

He would bide in Inverness, too, Simon decided. All the players were here: Amy, Shawn, Angus, Eamonn, Glenmirril where the switch had happened and where, according to Brother Eamonn—though he was hardly trustworthy—the crucifix lay.

Simon left the girls, strolling south until he found another bridge down the river, and crossed back. He followed the streets winding behind the jail, strolling as if enjoying the sunshine, street after street, searching. Children ran in the road, tossing balls to one another, or playing with dogs. One cur stopped, a ball in its mouth, staring at him. Its eyes narrowed, and a low rumble came from its throat. Simon lifted a lip at the dog, meeting its eyes. It dropped its ball, turned, and ran.

Women swept steps, or bent over gardens full of summer blooms, weeding and nurturing. He watched every house, noting curtains fluttering in windows, and doors flying open as children tumbled out to play. He walked block after block, until he found what he sought. He glanced at it, strolled past, and returned in the late afternoon, to confirm. He smiled, and, noting the number on the door, and the name of the street, headed off to learn what more he could of Shawn before night fell.

Inverness, Present

Angus sits shoulder to shoulder with me, on the front stair of his house. We ate at a nearby pub, Shawn's eyes shifting from me to Angus, all of us short on conversation, and the other patrons casting nervous looks at his torn and bloodied medieval garb. One couple rose from the booth behind him, hands to noses, and slipped out. Angus stopped at a store on the way home to buy him clothes. Yes,

Angus bought them. Here in his own home, Angus showed Shawn the bathroom, laden with towels, and left him to it while he and I came outside.

James sleeps in my arms in the afternoon sun.

"I think we take a break now," Angus says softly.

My head shoots up, startled. "Just like that? He's back and you decide we're through?"

Angus sighs, staring at the row of houses locked together across the street, behind a barricade of parked cars. Lace flutters in every window. Each house sports a door in jovial green, blue, red, or yellow. A woman in a kerchief sweeps her steps. His hand drifts to the soft black down of James's head. "I'm deciding to give you space to deal with him and make your own decisions."

"You asked me to marry you, back at Monadhliath," I protest.

"Things changed."

"Because I reacted to the music he left? That's not fair."

"Because you're still in love with him."

I bow my head. I can't deny it. I can only say, "I love you, too." I knead a fold of my black skirt between two fingers. "I don't know what to say. I wish...."

"We both wish many things," Angus says. "I recall saying once 'life doesn't hand us neat packages to work with,' and you laughed and said 'that's the understatement of the year.' Little did I know."

I give a soft chuckle. "To think it could get even less neat than my boyfriend—ex-boyfriend—coming back from a night in a castle obsessed with Bannockburn, and disappearing in the middle of a re-enactment."

James stirs and stretches out a small fist. He smiles, his dark eyes boring into mine.

Angus leans forward to kiss the soft, pink knuckles. "You've given me a lot of surprises, these last months."

I laugh. Then my lip quivers; I squeeze my eyes against the tears. "I'm sorry."

His arm wraps around me. He kisses my temple. "Don't be sorry," he whispers. "'Tis I should be sorry I'm not a different kind of man."

"What does that mean?" I pull back, studying his face. "I told you I don't need Shawn's flash and glamour."

He smiles, but it's a sad smile. "I'm off to Clive's." He stands up.

"What do you mean?" I insist. "I like you the way you are!" I try to push myself up off the stoop, hindered by James cradled in my arm. Cement bites into my palm.

"I'll be back in the morning to drive you to Bannockburn. Carol is no doubt half mad to see him, aye?"

"Not even a last kiss?" I demand, as I struggle to my feet.

"I'll see you in the morning," he says, and walks away.

I stare after him, angry, hurt, and knowing there's no good answer. Shawn is back. It's what we wanted. And it's a problem.

♫

He'd been home eight hours, Shawn guessed, as he swirled sweet smelling bubbles into the filling tub—eight hours of police interrogation, psychiatric evaluation, and medical attention; a twenty-first century lunch in a modern pub, with a real latte. He put a foot in, sighing at the warmth, and sank down. He smiled as the water climbed to his chin, his injured leg propped over the edge out of the water, thinking of the sweet taste of the latte after twenty-four months of gamey meat, seafood, and porridge; of shopping in a modern department store, with people staring at his bushy red beard and battle-worn breeks and gambeson. They'd stared, too, at Amy's concert black, and Angus's jeans and rumpled sweatshirt. He'd cocked his arrogant grin back, and they'd turned away blushing.

He reached a foot to turn off the water, inhaling the scent, reminiscent of baths in medieval Glenmirril, with sweet-smelling herbs floating in the water; thinking of Niall, Red, MacDonald, Hugh, and Brother David. They would not have hot baths. There would be injuries to be seen to. He'd hoped fervently, prayed, even, that none of them had died at the MacDougalls' hands. They'd be setting the castle to rights, dealing with prisoners—there would be prisoners, right? It wouldn't end with MacDougall killing them? He squeezed his eyes tight, telling himself it *couldn't* end that way. What would become of Christina, of Allene, of Niall's son James, if MacDougall triumphed?

He forced his mind back to Amy as he stared at the ceiling of Angus's bathroom. Even now, she was downstairs, with the Interloper. But it couldn't really be anything serious. Still, his happiness cooled with the water. He rose from the tub, drying, shaving, and dressing in new clothes. The jeans were stiff and tight after two years in trews. He switched them for loose pajama pants, and descended the stairs, his mind a tangle of knots, his heart pumping hard at the sight of Amy at the bottom of the stairs, her hair escaping its braid, curling in soft tendrils around her face, her concert black emphasizing her porcelain skin and dark blue eyes. She held his son, their son, looking up at him. For two years he'd thought of her, imagined her, tried to reach her. He saw in her eyes, as she stood at the bottom of the stairs, the same flush of excitement at seeing him again, though she backed away.

CHAPTER THREE

Glenmirril, June 9, 1316

The rising sun turned the solar rosy in dawn's soft glow. With Niall passed out in his bed, his wound cleaned and sewn, Allene turned to Christina, once more boiling the needle in the cauldron. Her face had reverted from the cheerful young woman of recent months, to the stiff, polite mask with which she had crossed the drawbridge a year and a half ago.

"Tell me what happened, Christina," Allene said.

"We've men to see to," Christina said briskly. "The women will be up from the dungeons." She pushed the needle into a ball of thread, handing it to Allene. She smiled the mask of a smile, and swept from the room, calling back, "Come, your son will be needing you. And you need food and rest yourself, in your condition."

"I'll see to it," Allene said. She did indeed feel queasy. She followed Christina to the courtyard, where dawn turned the walls pink, and mist crawled along the ground. Men milled, talking, or drifted toward the great hall in hopes of food; only a few sat against the stone walls, in pain.

"Milady!" Red hailed her, as Christina headed for one of the men. "MacDougall is in his cell."

"Where?" she asked brusquely.

He nodded toward the tower in the southern bailey. Allene looked up. Three stories above, MacDougall glared down, his hands around the bars, his face a mask of rage. "He's well guarded?" she asked.

"Day and night," Red replied. "The Laird's orders."

"The women?"

"Hugh has fetched them. Your father has gone to the dungeons."

Allene nodded, as she scanned the courtyard, deciding where to start.

"Where has my Lord Shawn gone, Milady?" Red asked.

Her eyes cut back to him, and suddenly softened, remembering how young he was. Shawn and Niall had rescued him from an abandoned Roman fort. He had rescued them from the English at Carlisle, spiriting them away through the Greyfriars' sewer, while he stayed behind to cover their escape route and mislead the army. He would feel Shawn's loss as surely as he would an elder brother's. She touched his shoulder. "He has gone home," she said. "Be happy for him."

"In the tower?" he asked plaintively. "Why was his name being called from the skies? *Please*, Milady, tell me what happened here. Is it some witchcraft as MacDougall's men say?"

Allene smiled sadly. "'Tis no witchcraft, Red. Pay no heed to fools."

"Will he be back?"

Allene shook her head. "He will not."

"And you'll not say...."

"We must see to the men," she said crisply. "Help me."

He bowed his head, accepting the reprimand, and fell into step beside her as she went from one man to another, doing what she could. Owen, limping, fetched clean water and rags. She cleaned two men and stitched a wound on Lachlan's cheek while Red held his head still. The men had given him a healthy dose of ale, waiting for something more helpful.

"Lachlan," she chided, "you're testing the saints, now, aren't you? They've already given you one miracle, but you must help them a wee bit by staying clear of swords."

"Och, aye," he slurred, grimacing at the needle on tender skin. "I avoided the first two, sure 'twas the third I walked right into."

She tied off the fourth stitch, decided it was enough, and patted his head. "Margaret will think you the more dashing for that scar." She washed her hands, looked around to see her work was finished, and rose to her feet. Women and children streamed from the castle depths, flowing around Hugh, her father's giant of a brother. Bessie hurried toward her, clutching a peaceful bundle. "He's just after being fed, Milady," the girl said, handing the baby over.

Allene took him, glancing to the stairs that led to the dungeon and her father in the bat cave. He'd want to be alone. And she wanted to be with her son. She cradled him in the crook of one arm, smiling for the first time that long morning, as she looked into his small pink face, grateful. It could have ended so differently. His eyes fluttered open, and scanned her face, dark and intense as only an infant's eyes could be. Her free hand drifted to her stomach.

Perhaps Niall was right. She had risked leaving James motherless. She had endangered this new bairn. She shouldn't have. But then, would anyone else have seen the man coming up behind Niall? If Niall had been felled, who would have gotten Shawn to the tower and stopped Duncan? It was impossible to say what was right or wrong sometimes. She glanced at the tower, feeling sick. Someone would have to deal with Duncan's body.

It had been but hours since the battle in the courtyard; since she'd watched Shawn disappear into the tower. But the world had changed for them all.

Inverness, Scotland, Present

I carry James into the house, fighting anger at Angus, yet unable to blame him. Shawn is coming down the stairs, wearing pajama pants and a black t-shirt. I stare at him, at the face I spent two and a half years loving, at a chest and arms grown broad with hard living, at hair once more clean, and shining with copper highlights. *He's shaved the auburn beard, showing the smooth planes of his jaw.*

You take my breath away....

He left the song in a manuscript at Monadhliath. We arranged it together, side by side, through a long evening in his house, with the floor to ceiling stone fireplace in the great room. I close my eyes, feeling the ghost of the kiss in the tower, and hating myself for being so fickle. I want to walk away from him, turn and follow Angus down the street to Clive's; tell him not to be insane, not to walk away and leave me hanging. I take a step back, groping for the door handle.

"Amy..." His voice comes out low, husky.

I open my eyes, my arms around James. "I don't want to be alone with you," I say.

He takes another step down the stairs. "I meant it when I said I'm sorry. I meant the apology on the rock. You have no idea what I felt that night, thinking how much better you deserved."

"Angus deserves better from me." I turn away, my shoulder and head against the door, clutching James in his blankets.

"I came back for you." His voice rises in a question, pleading. I've heard him wheedle often enough, but never plead. "I came back to make it up to you and do it right this time."

I straighten, turning to him, studying his face. It's harder, stronger, more serious. He's lost weight and gained muscle. A hundred memories rush in: the first kiss under the awning in the rain, the first strange phone call from a woman. Watching him play A Train *at the jazz club, hang-ups when I was at his house. Weekends at his mother's new home in the country, driving him to the airport to fly out for another appearance.*

Angus has never given me a moment's unease. I glance around his narrow hall with the bisque cross, palm leaves sticking out behind it. I stood here talking to his father six months ago at Christmas. On my right is his front room, where Clive burst in, on my first visit to Angus. Down the hall in the kitchen, the table waited, set for two, while Angus blushed and told me it was in case his sister stopped by. I smile.

Shawn comes down the last step, reaching for me, touching the bell sleeve of my black blouse.

I edge away, the smile dropping. "It was the moment," I say. "The thrill of having you back. Don't kiss me again. It's not fair to Angus." James squirms in my arms. I hold him out. "Except for lunch, you haven't had a chance." I hesitate, unsure what to say. There's not exactly established protocol for 'ex boyfriend returns from medieval Scotland.'

Shawn takes James into his arms, his face lightening into a smile as he pulls the blanket back from his son's face. He nods toward the living room. "Come on. Can we sit down?"

My shoulders relax. "Yeah. That would be good." I meet his eyes once. They're bright, intense, burning with hope and memories. I see in a flash each and every intimate moment between us, and lower my eyes, flushing. "Uh, do you...?" I twist the ring on my finger, the large heavy garnet ring he threw to me nearly a year ago on the battlefield. I saw his face that day, determined, hard. He rescued a child. "Do you want, uh...?" At great personal expense, he saved a boy. "Tea? Coffee? Water?" My words fly out, tumbling over one another. I stare at the ring on my finger, at the umbrella stand, the crucifix on the wall, at anything but Shawn, who is making my heart turn over in my chest, like he always could.

Cradling James in one arm, he touches my shoulder. I stare at the floor. "Don't kiss me," I say. I wish Angus would come in, say something to settle my heart.

"I won't." He touches my hair and runs his hand down it, his fingers trailing down my back. "He has your hair." He speaks softly, his voice full of admiration. "It's beautiful and I never told you so."

"Coffee?" My heart flutters, at the sight of James in his arms. He's become all I wanted, those terrible, wonderful two and a half years we were together. I push past him, even as he says, "Sure," and hurry to the kitchen to run cold water into the coffee pot. My heart beats erratically. My hand trembles, making the pot clatter into place in the black coffee maker. The kitchen holds reminders of Angus. I push the filter, full of coffee grounds, into place, and lean back against the wall, arms locked across my chest, while the machine hums to life and begins a cheerful burbling.

It's beautiful and I never told you so.

I close my eyes, remembering the early days when he did tell me so, and later days when he suggested I do something different with it. Here in this kitchen, Angus ran his hands the length of my hair, telling me he loves it.

I open my eyes, studying his small kitchen. Everything in it is old: a battered washing machine and small refrigerator tucked under a counter that has seen better days, a wooden table with scratches from his nephew's pen knife under the frayed blue cloth. It would compare poorly with the large, gleaming kitchen in Shawn's small mansion—if I were the type to compare. But I was happy here, safe, loved. In Shawn's kitchen, in his home, I often felt unsure, off balance.

The coffee machine ups its tempo, spluttering and burbling at a frantic pace, and tweets. I give myself a shake. Shawn has changed. He sits in the other room, loving his son, our *son. My feelings rage with all the good I always saw in him, coming to life before my eyes. I fill two mugs, and take them, fighting the tremble in my hands, to the front room.*

Glenmirril, June 9, 1316

As the sun climbed halfway to its peak, with James nestled back in his cradle under Bessie's watchful eye, and Niall emitting drunken snores in the curtained bed in their chamber, Allene threaded her way through halls once more bustling with life, with the animated chatter of the castle folk comparing adventures or bursting in outrage at MacDougall's attack. Servants hurried to prepare the evening meal. From the courtyard came the keening of the new widow—Taran's mother.

Allene ducked into the entrance to the dungeons, took a torch from the wall, and followed the dank labyrinth, past the meeting room all the lords knew of, into an almost invisible side tunnel known to few, until last night. Another branch, so narrow her shoulders brushed the damp stone walls and so low she had to carry the torch before her, led to the Bat Cave.

Her father had found the cavern as a boy, exploring the tunnels when he'd been forbidden. As a youth, he'd built a door and added a lock to make it his own. As a man responsible for the safety and care of hundreds, it served as his refuge, a place to do the un-lairdly woodwork that gave him peace, a private chapel at the feet of the life-size Christ he had carved the year his wife had died and his son was executed by the English.

Allene rapped at the door softly. Moments later, her father opened it. He stood back wordlessly, ushering her in. She laid a hand on his arm as the door shut again, and studied his weathered face, bristling with the silver-streaked red beard. As long as she could remember, he'd had the scar running down one cheek. Dark circles edged his eyes.

"I'm no longer young." He gave a rueful smile. "'Tis a hard night, it's been." He nodded toward the crucifix. "We're after talking now."

Allene smiled. "And what does He say?"

"Mercy, Allene." He spoke heavily. "I don't much care for His answer."

"Nor do I."

"He's tried three times to kill Niall. For your sake alone, I'd not allow it again. But we've also the people of Glenmirril to think of. They need him." He turned and crossed the cave, to stand under the carving of Christ. A garden of candles in reds, blues, and greens, flickered under it, filling the cave with the scent of tallow wax. MacDonald dropped to his knees on the kneeler, looking up to the carving. "He's forever taking our cattle. How many of our men have been injured, retrieving them?"

Allene squeezed his arm. She, too, stared up at the carving. The multitude of flames sent flickering shadows up over the face, seeming to light the eyes. "Bruce believes mercy will bring our people together and save our country. I think often on what it took for him to accept the Earl of Ross back into his peace. Yet Ross serves Scotland faithfully."

"Time will tell," MacDonald sighed. "None would fault me for hanging him and all his men before sundown." After another minute staring up at the carved figure, he dropped his head onto his clasped hands. Allene stood silently by his side, her hand on his shoulder. Her own eyes closed, and a smile touched her lips. Only two days ago, she'd stood in this room, as she had so often in the last two years, side by side with Christina, listening to Shawn play her father's sackbut; listening to Niall play the harp while he and Shawn sang.

Now Shawn was gone. Though Niall would never say so, she knew a light had gone out of his life. First, his six brothers, executed by the English, dying of disease, and Alexander drowning; Iohn and William had filled that empty spot, only to betray him. Shawn, so unlike him, had become a brother, nonetheless. Now he, too, had gone. She squeezed her eyes shut, breathing in the tallow scent and sending up her own pleas for Niall. It was not only his arm that would need healing.

Her father shifted, and she realized she was squeezing his shoulder. "I'm sorry, Father," she murmured.

"There is only One who might fault me." MacDonald lifted his eyes to Christ. "Allene, I've been down here for *hours*, and I cannot seem to make Him see sense."

Allene bowed her head, disappointed and relieved. She had no wish to see rotting heads leering down from the castle walls. The stories of William Wallace turned her stomach. But still she feared for Niall's life.

"Those who wish to see their heads on pikes will be disappointed. What shall I tell them?" her father asked.

Allene sighed. "You tell them you are Laird and we will show mercy as God commands."

"And if he should kill you or Niall, or the children?" The weight of the responsibility dragged down his shoulders.

A chill shot down Allene's spine. She looked to the carving for a moment before meeting her father's eyes. "We will trust. You must do as you feel led."

"I am led to mercy." He pushed himself up off the kneeler. "But he'll not forgive the death of his son, though they themselves attacked. Pray God, Allene, that mercy will not kill us all."

Inverness, Present

Early evening sun danced through lace curtains, dappling the carpet. Shawn sank back in a large, soft armchair, his stocking feet up on a footrest. James, wrapped snugly in blankets, peered intently up at him with gleaming, dark blue eyes. Shawn smiled, liking the feel of his son, solid in the crook of his arm.

He held his finger up, letting James clutch it. His smile grew, as he whispered, *Thank you.* He'd expected a child well over a year. To find he'd missed only months of his son's life was a great gift. Maybe, he thought, he could move to civil speaking terms with God.

James's mouth opened wide in an answering smile, showing pink gums and dimpled cheeks. A gurgling laugh came from deep in his belly. Shawn leaned forward, kissing his jet black hair. He'd often held Niall's son, James, on his days of 'being' Niall. He sometimes walked on the small scrap of shore behind the castle with him, or took him to the stables to touch the rough manes and velvety noses of the Scots' tough hobins. He'd loved holding the child, though the people of Glenmirril found it odd for a man to carry an infant. Holding his own son was something different, yet. He couldn't get enough of the pink cheeks, rose-petal skin, and grunts and gurgles.

The pungent smell of coffee twisted under his nose. Amy stood in the doorway with two mugs curling out thin wisps of heat, looking nervous. The sleeves of her black blouse hung in graceful bells. The black skirt swirled to her ankles, and her hair curled around her face, pulling loose from her thick, waist-length braid. The sight of her brought back a dozen memories of walking with her by the stream on his property, holding her in his arms. His smile grew. "I don't bite, you know."

She bit her lip, swallowed. "I know."

It wasn't much to build a conversation on. James let out a cheerful squeal, drawing his eyes back. He smiled at the boy, who dimpled back at him. Amy set a mug on the table by his side. "Thank you," he said.

"You never used to say thank you." Amy crossed the room, as far as she could go from him, he noted.

It didn't matter. She was here. With him. She hadn't gone with the Interloper. Of course she hadn't. "I'm sorry. I should have."

She stirred the embers in the hearth, raising a small flame, before dropping into the chair. She looked fatigued.

"Do you want to go to bed?" Shawn asked.

Her eyes flew open.

"I meant sleep," he clarified. "I'll take care of him."

"You've been up all night, too," she said. "In rougher circumstances than me."

They regarded one another, punctuated by the soft crackle of flames and James's gurgling, before Amy asked, "You saw Niall?"

He studied her face. It remained passive. Niall had admitted to kissing her backstage after the concert.

"I thought it was you," she said.

He smiled ruefully. "Does my face give that much away?"

"No. But it's what your mind would go to. And after all the women..."

He stared at his stocking toes, resting on the blue and white striped ottoman. "I know. I have no right. You don't need to say it." He'd promised himself he'd apologize, tell her the truth. He lifted his coffee, sipping it, letting it zing his senses back to life. He'd missed coffee. Maybe that conversation could wait until he wasn't so tired, until after a good night's sleep. "I've spent the last two years with Niall. I spent half the time *being* Niall."

She cocked her head. "Tell me about it."

He told her, his eyes closed, leaning back in the chair, wrapped in the powdery smell of his infant son and the woodsmoke that might have been the Interloper's small fireplace or the great hearths at Glenmirril. Falling asleep while his pony followed Douglas instead of MacDonald...raiding churches...setting villages and fields ablaze...rescuing Niall from Creagsmalan's dungeon...MacDougall crashing Niall's wedding...finding Red starving in the Roman ruins...escaping Carlisle through the monks' sewer.

They'd all been alive, just yesterday. They remained alive in his mind, though the disturbing thought came to him that each and every one of them was now but bones beneath Scotland's soil, perhaps dead within minutes of his disappearance back into the twenty-first century.

His arms tightened around James, thinking of Niall's and Allene's son, willing that bright head of red-gold hair to live into old age. And the child on the way. He'd last seen Allene, despite early pregnancy, leaping on the back of a MacDougall as he went after Niall; she'd hacked at him with her knife, screaming like a banshee, her hair flying from its braid.

"What's Allene like?" Amy's voice broke into his fears.

He opened his eyes. A fresh cup of coffee waited at his elbow. Sunset glowed through the white lace.

She had released her hair from its braid and it hung in thick, black waves, though she still wore the rumpled black blouse and skirt. Faint circles smudged her eyes. She perched on the end of the couch, nearer him than she'd been. "You drifted off."

He looked at James, asleep again in his arms. "I might have dropped him."

"I've been watching. He was safe. What's Allene like?"

He smiled, drifting back to dozens of memories. "Red hair, freckles, temper. Thoughtful, courageous."

"Are they happy?"

"Aye." He chuckled softly. "You should hear Niall play *A Train* on recorder."

A corner of her mouth twitched up. "You taught him that?"

"Aye. And lots more. We'd spend half the night up on the parapets, talking about history and music and science. He wanted to know everything. He taught me Latin and French, and...a thousand other things." He settled into silence, his gaze drifting to the dancing flames, thinking of nights of geography, clan history, political discourse, sword fighting, and playing Niall's favorite pieces on harp over and over till he could do it for the castle people without raising eyebrows, on the nights he dined in Niall's stead. "I can ride a horse," he added.

"You can?" She breathed out, a soft whoosh of air. "You hate horses."

"Not anymore!" His eyes lit, remembering the thrill of racing Niall, the wind in his hair, and his pony nuzzling him, its velvety lips seeking an apple from his hand. "I'll buy you one. We'll go riding. We'll take James."

"Did you kill men?"

His smile slipped. He stared into the fire, remembering the feel of his sword thrusting through Duncan's intestines; of crashing to his knees after Skaithmuir with Douglas, vomiting at the bloodshed and gore and the beast that had possessed him, slaying dozens of men. "I think you know I did." He bit back a sardonic twenty-first century rejoinder: *How does that make you feel?* He wasn't sure he wanted to know.

She didn't answer.

"There was no choice sometimes." He turned to her abruptly. "I feel like I should have guilt about it, but I don't. We asked for peace, Edward refused. What were we to do?"

"I know the history well," she said.

"I stopped men raping! I stopped them desecrating the church! I did the best I could with what I was thrown into." He studied her, willing her understanding.

She leaned forward, touching his hand where it rested on the arm of the chair. Her hair slid forward, brushing his knee.

He eyed it, eyed her, waiting for her to pull back. Her hand tightened on his. He closed his eyes, relishing the tingles shooting up his arm.

"I believe you," she said. "I found your mark everywhere."

He opened his eyes, shocked at the intensity of her dark gaze probing his soul. He risked turning his hand over, twining his fingers in hers. She let him. "I must have carved thousands." In his arm, James gave a heavy sigh. Shawn smiled down at him. "I wondered if I was crazy."

"I thought it was Niall at first. I thought you were dead."

He gave a humorless snort. "I don't know how I avoided it. They say it was a miracle. There's a pretty ugly scar. I don't know how I'm going to explain it to doctors here. Or the one from the wolf. Or the one from last night. The police don't exactly believe my story."

"Angus does."

He gave another snort. "I don't think the Interloper is going to risk his neck backing me up on this one."

Amy yanked her hand back. "The Interloper?" Her voice had a hard edge. "He actually did risk everything to get me to that tower for your sake. I thought you were *dead* when I started seeing him, Shawn." She catapulted herself from the couch; James gave a squeak in his sleep and settled again; she paced the room twice and dropped back into the far chair. "He deserves far better than whatever he's feeling right now, camped out with a friend wondering what's going on between the two of us in his own home."

"So far, nothing," Shawn said. "I guess he can rest easy." He lifted the coffee mug again, drinking deeply.

"And being called names by you on top of it!" Across the room, her eyes blazed.

He set the mug down, surprised at her anger. "Don't tell me you love him or something?"

She stared into the flames. His nerves stretched, not hearing the immediate denial he'd expected. "Amy?"

"Yes," she said. "I love him. Or something."

Glenmirril, June 10, 1316

Niall woke in the night with the aftereffects of too much whisky pounding in his head, and infection burning the length of his arm. Flickering light from the wall torch outlined a pair of shadows swaying against the bed curtains. A bundle which must be a child passed between them, whispers reached him, the chamber door scraped against stone floor, and the bar dropped into place.

He sank into the heat in his forehead, disappearing into a snowy forest with Shawn, and coming through the trees into a castle with a massive black dais and shining harp of gold glittering in a pool of light. He touched it, stroked a chord that shimmered in the air, and enveloped his world in peace. No pain. No MacDougalls. No swords. No arms burning with pain. He looked up at curtains soaring high into the clouds, and the clouds shining down. *If you could take Allene and the Laird with you....* Shawn stood by the curtain, beckoning. *Bring them with you. There's no fighting here.*

Niall plucked a string; his fingers drifted over the melody of the sad tribute to Falkirk, where his father had died. A plaintive melody cried from one of their *oboes,* sending chills up his back. Shawn stood silently in the dark wings, watching. Allene appeared at his side, inching the curtains aside and letting in a cool draft. Torchlight and moonlight, shining through the arched window, played over the red strands of her hair, picking out one, now another, as she turned her head.

Cool dampness trailed across his burning arm. He dropped it off the harp, grimacing. Pain shot down the length of it once again. Shawn was talking, telling him something. He rolled his head, eyes squeezed tight, mumbling, trying to tell her.

"Sh, now," she said over and over. "You're speaking nonsense."

He opened his eyes. The stage was gone. The harp was gone.

Shawn was gone.

But he remembered. "Clean water." He pushed himself up, despite ale and infection raging through his body. "Shawn said."

She disappeared, letting the bed hangings drop to, and blocking off the cool draft. Her shadow swayed across the heavy curtains, waxing and waning. The heat of infection closed in on him. The oboe twisted into a terrible keening. His heart hammered. He struggled, pulling his legs from sheets and furs, pushing with his good arm at the bed hangings. His feet hit heavy skins covering the stone floor. They enveloped his feet in soft warmth.

And she was back beside him at the window, holding a pail of water and a cloth.

"Owen, Lachlan, Red?"

"They're well, as are Gilbert, your father, and Hugh."

"Praise God," he whispered.

"Ronan is injured." She touched the wet cloth to his arm.

"Badly?" His head hung, his arms bolstering him on the sill, trembling as the cloth traced the burning infection with a trail of ice that made him shiver.

"He'll live." She lowered her eyes. "Taran's father, however, lies in the kirk, awaiting burial."

Niall squeezed his eyes shut, hurting for the lad. He remembered the day of Taran's birth; his father's joy as he ran, heedless of dignity, through the castle, shouting that he had a son. "MacDougall?" he asked.

"He lives." She dropped the cloth in the pail with a soft splash, and set the bucket down.

"Why do the evil prosper and the good die?" Niall asked softly.

She laid her cheek against his arm, whispering, "Who can answer for the will of God?"

Niall stared out the window to the moon that would be shining down in seven hundred years, wondering how Shawn was spending his first night home. It wouldn't be at a wake.

"We are blessed," she said. "We lost only one man. Ronan will recover. We got Shawn home."

"Aye, that we did." Niall closed his eyes, giving silent thanks to God for granting what they'd sought, these two years since Shawn had appeared.

"My father stopped in," Allene said. "He bids you come to the courtyard early tomorrow morning. MacDougall's men will be gathered. You'll begin your duties as the next laird by telling them their fate."

"Which is?"

"Mercy, Niall. Pray it doesn't kill us."

In the moonlight, he studied her, touching a hand to the thick auburn curls. "Aye." He turned back to the moonlight glinting on the black loch, staring up to the stars twinkling above, and prayed a silent prayer. *My Lord and Savior, watch over Shawn and Amy, and please, watch over us. Please, can You grant that our mercy will bring peace with the MacDougall's? And can you grant me, maybe, just a little time home with Allene? I'd be grateful for even a week or two.*

Inverness, Present

I sit on Angus's old couch, watching Shawn in the firelight flickering in Angus's hearth. He's fallen asleep again, his arms wrapped around James, who snores gently on his chest. I study his face, the harder planes; his arms toughened by medieval living. I don't want to think about the scars carved on his body by wolves and weapons. I don't want to think about the people left behind to face those things every day, about Niall and Allene, and the people Shawn grew to love.

And still, I feel I've been whisked back into it. I'm trying to make a decision rather than be swept away. But it's hard to think clearly when waves of excitement and chaos and Things Happening are smashing and crashing all around me. It's hard to even stand up in the roaring, thunderous surf that is Shawn, never mind stop and think. Shawn was always good at sweeping me—or anyone—away. He swept the orchestra into his vortex. He swept me into the crashing surf that is his energy, his life, his passion for living. Watching James sleep, I step outside it all, asking, where am I? I was happy with Angus. I grieved Shawn, but I didn't miss my old life.

In my pocket, my phone buzzes. I pull it out. The voice mail icon blinks at me. Rising from the couch, I step into the hall to listen. It's Dana, my best friend since I joined the orchestra. "He's home!" her recorded voice gushes. "Amy I heard he's home! Is he really home?"

And the next: "His phone is out of service." She's emotional. Very emotional. "Tell him to call me!" A third: "Have you seen him? Where is he?" She sounds as she does when she's excited about Someone New. I know Dana well.

There are six more. Wanting to see him. Complaining that his phone isn't answering. Asking how he is, as I watch him smiling in his sleep, his hand protectively on our son's back. With each message, my certainty grows. I no longer doubt my senses. He's barely back, and it's hitting me harder than ever. My best friend. The old sickness returns. I delete the messages and block her number, watching Shawn.

He sighs in his sleep, his cheek against James's downy hair. This is not the Shawn who did those things with Dana. I know that with certainty. I check that James is secure, and go to the kitchen. Closing doors between me and Shawn, I call Rose, wondering where she is and what she's doing.

"Amy!" She answers promptly, breathless and happy. "It's wonderful!"

I smile, imagining her just finishing a concert, violin still in hand. I can remember her, from the time I was four, and she'd take me to her concerts, coming back into the green room, flushed with the joy of music, cheeks glowing, eyes shining. She'd sweep me into a hug, crying, "It was wonderful! Did you hear it?" And I always had, sitting there in a big chair in the green room, where no one minded a child, because they knew I'd sit and listen, entranced, often with my own eighth size violin in my hand, leaning forward in a chair too big for me, head cocked with an ear toward the speakers.

"He's back," I say. My voice is numb and flat. I haven't slept in two days.

"Yes, I heard," Rose enthuses. "It's impossible not to hear! It's been on the news twenty-four seven, shot after shot of Glenmirril, and that helicopter overhead, and Shawn coming out of the gatehouse in a monk's robe, and Shawn being led into the police station. You did it, Amy! You and Angus got him back! It's wonderful!"

I'm silent just long enough, and she speaks again, more soberly. "Oh, no, Amy, it isn't, is it? You're still in love with him."

"No, and yes," I say.

"There's Angus," Rose says.

I know her so well, I can see her backstage somewhere. Indeed, I hear the chatter of excited post-concert talk behind her, and a quick catch of a flute solo from Scheherazade. I know her so well, I know the violin has just sagged to her side, her shoulders fallen, her smile flitted away. "There's Angus," I agree. "He broke up with me. More or less. He told me to sort things out with Shawn."

"Well...." There's a brief pause; the sound of chatter fades in the background, as if someone has turned down a dial. And Rose speaks more softly. "Have you?"

"How?" My voice shoots up in agitation. "How am I supposed to sort anything out with Shawn when I don't even know who he's come back as? You won't hear it on the news, of course, but he was in Niall's time for two years."

"Two?" Rose asks. "He was only gone one year."

"Two years there," I confirm.

"That would change a man," she says. "What have you seen so far?"

"Same old arrogant Shawn," I say, and immediately, with no intention of doing so, I smile. "But different. Stronger, kinder, protective." I think about him pushing me behind him in the tower. Never before would he have thought to protect me, to shield me with his own body from danger. Indeed, it was he himself who harmed me. "Apologetic," I add. "He apologized to Angus for being rude."

There's a soft chuckle over the phone line. "Well, that's not the old Shawn!"

"But how long will it last?" I ask. "He was always capable of being wonderful for weeks, even months, at a time." I stare out Angus's kitchen window, into the small garden blooming with peonies and lilies. I think of him in the mountains, on the hike to Monadhliath, his head on my shoulder, telling me people like him need people like me.

I save lives, *he said,* but you save souls.

His beautiful garden bursts with life, color, and peace: a glimpse of his soul. I was at peace with him. "I got a dozen voice mails from Dana," I say. "She's awfully worried about Shawn."

There's a small intake of breath from the phone, and Rose says, "Oh." Her tone says it all. She knows what I'm saying. And she doesn't doubt my intuition.

"Even my best friend," I say, pain pinching my words.

She's silent for a moment before saying, "Remember one thing, Amy. He's not the same man who did those things."

"I know," I say. "But how do I know who he is now?"

You take the gift Angus has given you. Time to get to know him."

I sigh. "What about Angus?"

"It's his gift to you," she says. "And Amy...?"

"What?" I ask.

"Angus is one of the finest men I've ever met," she says.

I hear the But... *coming. And it does.*

"But I've known you since you were three. Shawn brought you to life."

I stiffen. "I'm nothing like Shawn. I don't need that life."

"You and Shawn fit like the parts of a fugue," she says. "You're nothing like him. But something in you needed him, the way something in him needed you. You'll be happy with Angus, but I wonder if you'll be as alive."

Anger rips through me. "I knew I was alive with Shawn, because I always hurt! I never hurt with Angus!"

"You didn't always hurt with Shawn," she counters. "Not at the beginning. And not for months at a time. And those parts of him that hurt you may be gone. Give it a chance," she says, softly.

Applause sounds over the phone, tinny as if over a speaker.

"Intermission is over," Rose says. "I have to go."

We say quick good-byes. I hang up without the resolution and direction Rose has always been so good at giving me. It's true I feel alive again, something woken up and called forth from me that I hadn't even realized was missing. My loyalty to Angus surges, here in his kitchen. I was happy with him! I love *him! I open the door softly and tread down the darkening hall to the front room. Dusk has fallen, finally, on this longest of days, leaving the room dim.*

I stand in the doorway, studying Shawn. My stomach clenches. It's all too easy to see him and Dana together. How could I have missed it? I feel sick. His mouth quirks upward. James sighs and nuzzles into the crook of his neck, smiling.

I sink onto the couch, watching them. I love Angus. I loved Shawn. I grieved for him. I watch his arms tighten around his son, and I think he's not merely the man I always thought was there...but someone even better. I want to know this new Shawn. And I miss Angus terribly.

Glenmirril, 1316

Late in the night, Christina sat on the bed that had been Shawn's, that was now hers, the gray robe of Brother Andrew folded across her lap. She ran her fingers over the rough material, thinking of the identical robe Shawn had worn on leaving Glenmirril just days before. Presumably, he'd been wearing it when the men returned and fought, when he climbed the tower stairs and disappeared back to his own time.

She bowed her head over the robe, missing him, remembering the times she'd seen them return, her heart fluttering with yearning as she tried not to watch the monk in gray, eager to see Shawn again. It was foolishness, clinging to a robe. Yet she was profoundly grateful to Allene for allowing her to take it. Without Shawn, Niall had no more need of it.

She rose, hanging it deep in her wardrobe. It was too early to know— yet she did. And she had to somehow face what was coming by herself, without him. But he needed to go back. He had things yet to learn, mistakes to repair. She had done right to tell him to go. Foolish though it might be, his robe would bring comfort as she faced what was to come.

CHAPTER FOUR

Bannockburn, Scotland, June 10, Present

"I told you where I was," Shawn snapped. His patience had long since worn thin. Rob swallowed, his Adam's apple bobbing, his knuckles white on the steering wheel. He stared straight ahead, at Amy's home in Bannockburn. It looked much like Angus's, two hours away in Inverness, one of a row of homes in red or pale bricks locked shoulder to shoulder, each with lace curtains, a brightly colored door, and a patch of garden, as they called their yards, in the front and another, walled or fenced, in the back.

"I can't see why you and Amy keep insisting on this crazy story," Rob said. "It's not like anyone's going to believe it."

In the back, Amy gathered James out of his car seat, cooing to him. He gurgled and gave belly laughs in return. Shawn leaned back against the head rest, eyes closed. "Because I'm too tired to think up a story. I mean, how do I *make up* a story to explain where I've been for two years?"

"You've only been gone a year," Rob said.

"Yeah, whatever." Shawn opened his eyes, studying the bright blue door that was Amy's, trying to fathom what her life had been this past year; wondering how often the Interloper had stood on that stoop and knocked; whether he'd kissed her in that doorway with the bright blue door framing them, or swooped her upstairs. "I'm surprised my mother isn't bursting out the door."

"She probably ran down to the shops," Amy said from the back. "She'll want to make you something nice for dinner, and we got down much earlier than I told her." They'd woken early to Rob banging on Angus's door, breathless. He'd heard Shawn was back—who hadn't?—and raced north to drive him home.

Angus had stood far back on the sidewalk, watching them on the front stoop. Shawn had paused, in loading his breeks and chain mail into Rob's car, watching with narrowed eyes as Amy, carrying James, had gone to the Interloper. They talked, heads close. Angus shook his head, as she laid a hand on his arm; he kissed James, turned, and walked away. Amy stood another minute, staring after him, before returning to Shawn and Rob.

"Everything okay?" Shawn asked.

"Are you ready to go?" was her curt reply, not looking at him.

The ride to Bannockburn had been long, with Rob pressing for answers and not liking those he got.

Shawn released his seat belt, and opened his door. "Come on in, Rob. I'll show you the scars." He opened Amy's door, taking her hand as she climbed out, juggling James in one arm.

"I'll get your things." Rob reached in back for the diaper bag and Shawn's duffel bag. Chain mail clinked inside. Rob frowned, and scratched his forehead.

Minutes later, in Amy's front room, with Amy already pushing his clothes into the washer and James in his bassinet, Shawn lifted his t-shirt. "Take a look, Rob."

Unwarned, Rob turned to the sight of the thick, red scar circling Shawn's waist. His face blanched. "Yeah, but..."

"There's another one from hip to knee on my right leg. From a wolf. And one on my left leg stitched up yesterday—from a fight in the castle in the wee hours, night before last."

"*Wee* hours?"

Shawn tugged his shirt down, wishing Rob would leave. "Sorry, I've gotten used to the word."

"None of it proves anything. Where did you really get them?"

Shawn sighed. "Thanks for the ride, Rob. Is there a room upstairs for me?"

Rob swallowed, blinked hard twice, and nodded. He turned and called down the hall, "Amy, where do you want his things?"

She slammed the washer and jabbed a button, before coming down the hall. "I'll take it." The weight of the chain mail jerked at her arm. Shawn took it, their hands grazing one another. She blinked, swallowed, and turned quickly. Shawn followed her up the stairs, watching her black hair swing at her waist. She turned at the top, heading down the hall, toward the front of the house, and used a key to unlock a door. It swung open on a small room with a desk, on which stood a laptop and piles of papers; walls covered with maps, charts, time lines, and dozens of highlighted notes and sticky sheets marking things.

Shawn stared. "What is this? A war room?"

"Our research, trying to track you down." She reached for a map.

"No, wait." Shawn stopped her from tearing it down, studying it. A yellow line trailed northwest from Stirling, around the top of Loch Ness, and down to Glenmirril.

"Angus figured that's the route you must have taken home."

The name of the Interloper grated. "How did he know I'd be going between the two at all?"

"Our research showed Niall—or possibly you—were at the parliament at Cambuskenneth in November."

"We both were." He smiled, remembering Brother David's shock when he stared at the two of them that day; and of the long, chilly ride home, the mysterious woman on the hill, with whom he'd left his cloak. "His hair hadn't grown out."

"His hair?"

"Bessie—that's—never mind. She shaved his head to get him out of Chez MacDougall. They were going to hang him."

Amy nodded. "We found records saying he'd been in MacDougall's dungeon and figured he wouldn't go around the bottom of Loch Ness, and we knew he wouldn't cross it, especially in winter. That left the northern route."

Shawn's finger traveled the yellow highlighter, seeing the snowy pine forests and hills along the way, the steep slope with the wise woman's cave nestled in it. She was long dead, like the rest of them. "You guessed well."

"*Angus* guessed well."

The name stabbed. Shawn gave his head a shake and glanced around the room.

Amy edged past him, into the hall, and led him to the third bedroom, empty but for a book shelf and bed. "It's your mom's room, but we can put your things here. I guess—I could sleep on the couch till we find you something. Or, um—have you thought ahead? You'll want to see Conrad while he's here, of course, but you know they've replaced you."

Shawn nodded numbly. She had mentioned it sometime in the last twenty-four hours, in the flood of catching up. He'd been replaced in her life, in the orchestra. Despite the evidence of her hunt for him, he wondered, for a fleeting second, why he'd come back. His world—the orchestra, Amy—had no need of him.

"I'll sleep on the couch," he said. "If I'm here longer, maybe I can find a bed."

"My lease is up in July. I have to find a new...."

Downstairs, the door burst in. Carol's voice erupted in a screech up the stairs. "Shawn!" Something fell heavily to the floor, before her feet pounded up the stairs.

By the time Shawn reached the stairs, Carol was there, hugging him, crying, pulling back to look him over and brush tears from her eyes, and crushing him again in another hug. "Where have you been?" she asked over and over, interspersed with, "You're home, thank God you're back safe!" She turned to Amy, gripping her hand. "Where was he, how did you find him? Where's Angus?" She paused, aware of the gaffe, and pulled Amy and Shawn both into a tight hug. "You're home, I have prayed more this year than ever in my life, thank God!"

At the bottom of the stairs, Rob gathered up spilled groceries.

Shawn held his mother tightly, breathing in the clean smell of shampoo. His eyes closed, he felt the dozens of times Niall's mother had kissed him on the cheek, thinking him Niall. She had smelled of sweet herbs and the castle's soaps. He pulled back, studying her. Niall's mother was long gone. His own mother stood before him, her hair a soft brown, in little fluffs around her face, her eyes smudged with tears. Hope rose like the sun in those eyes. It was no longer hope that he'd come back, he realized. It was hope that he'd changed.

He closed his eyes again, not wanting to see the pain behind the hope. He'd put that pain there, himself.

Glenmirril Castle, June 10, 1316

MacDougall's men, brought up from the dungeon, stood sullen and silent in Glenmirril's courtyard in the pale light of dawn. Mist twisted around their ankles. The younger ones stared at the strong, gray stone walls hemming them in with terrified, unseeing eyes.

Niall, his arm burning and aching, paced before them, his sword swinging at his side, a reminder of their possible fate. Having just left the kirk behind them, where Taran's father lay in state, awaiting burial, hearing Taran's footsteps, and the sniffing of his widowed mother, he desperately wanted to use the sword.

MacDonald stood behind him, a strong, silent figure with his thick auburn and silver beard; imposing and terrible with the scar running from eye to lip, and his men lined up by the dozens beside him, swords at hand. Lachlan and his archers stood with arrows nocked on the parapets. Taran and Red stood side by side, swords at the ready, their young faces stern.

Let them tremble in fear, MacDonald had admonished Niall. As if he needed admonishing. He admired Bruce. He respected Bruce's famed mercy. He felt his own neck half in MacDougall's noose already, by practicing that mercy himself. His claymore itched to end the threat to his life, to Allene's. But MacDonald's word was law. At the very least, each and every one of MacDougall's men must understand, must feel to the depth of his bones and soul, the power of MacDonald; must see their deaths hovering, must feel the rush of wind as the gates of eternity swung open, ready to accept their souls. Unless they felt that, they would not grasp the mercy extended by MacDonald in snatching them back from the very threshold of those gates.

Niall stopped before the youngest lad, a youth no more than fourteen, no older than Red, who rose only to his shoulder. The boy swallowed convulsively. Niall thought of Rob, Shawn's sycophant friend, swallowing nervously. Little did Rob know how little he truly had to fear. "Look at me," Niall commanded.

A sheen of sweat erupted across the boy's brow. His pale face went stark white. "Y-yes, my Lord." He tried, but failed, to raise his eyes.

Among the captives, a man fell suddenly to his knees, wailing, "My Lord, please my Lord, not my son! He's but a lad."

Niall stalked to the man, his ankles ripping through mist; hating the part he must play, hating the mercy, hating the thought of more killing, hating the risk in not killing, hating terrorizing a father who feared for his son. One day, it might be himself and James, facing an English commander.

Niall stopped, letting his leather toes step into the man's field of vision. His insides gave a taut, grim smile at the realization that this was a performance, as surely as his night on stage in Shawn's twenty-first century. He let the moment hang, as he would let a beautiful note hang on the air. He closed his eyes for less than a moment, wishing he had stayed in Shawn's world, playing music rather than threatening men with death; rather than threatening a man's son, a boy, with death.

"He's my only son," the man cried. "Please, my Lord. I give you my life."

Niall said nothing.

The man's dark-haired head inched up slowly. Niall could feel every eye in the courtyard on him, as every eye had rested on him on the stage in twenty-first century Inverness. He breathed in deeply. *God, I will do as You and my Lord MacDonald command. I am your servant. But I beg you, even as this man begs me, let the mercy You demand not be the death of my own son.* His first sight of James filled his mind, a pink-faced, red-haired bundle in tight swaddling clothes, screaming. *I beg you!*

"My Lord, I beg forgiveness for speaking out of turn." The man lifted his eyes, lifted roped hands in supplication. "Have you a son, my Lord? Take me as your slave, kill me, but spare the lad. He'd no choice."

"Aye," Niall said softly, too softly for any but the nearest to hear him. He wanted to raise the man to his feet, father to father. He wanted, too, to strike him down, an enemy who would have harmed Allene and James. Perhaps it was this man's sword that had slashed his own arm, even now throbbing with pain and red with infection that might yet kill him and leave James fatherless, and Allene a widow. "Aye, he'd no choice. Still, he'd have killed my wife or child, given the chance."

"Please, my Lord." The man's voice cracked. His head fell, and he dared clasp Niall's hands between his bound ones. "Please. He'll never harm you or yours, ever. Take my life, but spare him to swear it on my body."

Niall pulled his hands from the man's grip. He marched before the front rank of men again, meeting the eye of each who would look at him. Some faces showed fear, others defiance. "You, men of MacDougall!" He roared the words, snapping the heads up. "Your lives, each and every one, are forfeit this day for attacking without provocation, the castle, the men, the women, the children, of my Lord MacDonald. For injuring men who have done ye no harm!"

The wails of the father, still on his knees, rose as sharp and jagged as the keening of Taran's mother had throughout the night. Squelching his horror at the sound, at the grief he was inflicting on another father, Niall stopped before one quaking man, pushing his chin up with the hilt of his claymore. "My own arm is torn asunder by one of your swords." He glanced to the far wall, where Ronan stood, a bandage dark with blood wrapped around his head, and one arm strapped tightly to his body, supported by the widow Muirne and her oldest son. Niall turned back to the men of MacDougall. "My friends are injured by your unprovoked attack. A good man lies dead. D' ye look forward to swinging from a noose in our courtyard?"

"N-no, my Lord," the man stuttered.

Niall moved on to the next man, less cowed than the previous, though his bound hands left him helpless. His black eyes glittered back at Niall defiantly. "D' ye fancy your head on a pike?" he roared for all to hear. To his right, the father wept openly.

The man stared with hatred at Niall. "It matters little to me once I'm dead, aye?"

Niall's mouth curved into a tight smile. Maybe killing just one of them would be a good example. But he held his words, and instead circled the man slowly, breathing in his face, before leaning close and murmuring, "Tell me one thing I've done to you, me or my people, that you should come into our home and attack us."

"You steal our cattle."

Niall roared, "They are ours, but if 'tis truly the issue, then take the cursed cattle back, as we ourselves do when ye steal them from us." He raised his voice higher. "When have we attacked your home? When have we threatened your women and children?"

The man spit in his face.

A hush settled over the crowd in the courtyard.

Niall stared at him, wiped the spittle from his face, and turned his back slowly. His eyes met MacDonald's. MacDonald nodded almost imperceptibly. Niall whirled, heaved his claymore, and sliced through the man's neck, clean as wind through a glen. Blood shot, spraying hot and sticky over Niall's face and shirt. The head rolled to the ground. The body stood a moment, then swayed and toppled, hitting the ground with a thud.

Niall wiped the blood from his face. He felt the trembling of the men of MacDougall, palpable in the misty dawn. His own arm trembled. He suspected he'd ripped out several of Allene's stitches.

The boy blanched. His lip trembled.

Taran, his dead father even now laid out in the chapel, glared at the head, hatred etched on his face.

Red stared at it, his face a blank mask. He'd no doubt seen plenty of violence, Niall thought with regret. He lifted his eyes to the third story. In a window high above, Christina turned, her head buried in Allene's shoulder, a hand to her mouth.

Niall lowered his eyes. He stared around at the gathered MacDougalls. "Anyone else?" he asked.

Not one met his eyes. The severed head gazed up through tendrils of mist.

Niall waited a moment, as he'd once waited for his cue from Conrad, waited for the moment when his part would fit the music perfectly, waited till he heard a soft shudder from the boy, till he saw a strong man shake, before he took up pacing among them, letting them tremble, stopping now and again to ask, "Have you a wife? Bairns? Who's left to defend them if ye die today? The tailor?"

Behind him, the men of Glenmirril laughed dismissively.

"The baker? Will they protect your bairns with a needle and flour?" He assessed the growing concern on the faces of MacDougall's men. Many more sweated freely now, though dawn's mist kept the courtyard cool. More faces turned chalk-white. The boy trembled. Tears rolled down his cheeks, leaving pale streaks in the dirt of battle and his night in the dungeon.

Niall strolled to the front of the assembled men, past the headless body of their clansman, letting them sweat. "We desire peace. We desire safety of ourselves, our castle, our women, our bairns."

Several MacDougalls stared at the head on the ground.

Niall met another eye or two, before saying, "Each man who kneels to my Lord MacDonald and so swears on his honor never more to come within twenty miles of Glenmirril receives our mercy."

Grumbles arose among MacDonald's men. Niall spun on them, his eyes dark, and silence fell among them, too. He turned back to the enemy. "Your laird will bide with us to assure that his men develop peaceful habits."

One by one, the trembling stopped; faces regained color; the sniffles of the boy stopped. He looked to his father with brightened eyes. One by one, the men of MacDougall approached MacDonald, walking past the headless corpse to kneel and swear peace. And one by one, two by two, their bonds cut, the father and son clinging together, the men of MacDougall left Glenmirril, each with a bundle of bannocks for the journey home.

By midday, Niall stood before MacDonald, with the last of the MacDougalls filing over the bridge, prepared for the long walk home—MacDonald had kept their hobins as extra assurance against attack. MacDonald clapped him on the shoulder. "Well done, Lad."

"Some of our own men think not." Niall rubbed his throbbing arm.

"'Tis not their place to think aye or nay," said MacDonald heavily. "We bear the authority and must do as we see fit before God."

"Where is MacDougall to be kept?"

MacDonald smiled. "Perhaps we'll send him to the north tower and hope he disappears into Shawn's time, aye? Perchance he'll be struck down by a *plane*."

Niall grinned, pleased to see the old man still had his humor. "Not unless he's flying in the sky. It's *trains* that run on the ground. Where will he stay, my Lord?"

"The south tower, the highest room."

"Does Christina know?"

MacDonald's mouth tightened. "I'd not have kept him, for her sake. But I've little choice. He can do no harm, locked in the tower, aye?"

Inverness, June, Present

Shawn lounged at an oval mahogany table with the board of directors, at a hotel in Stirling. Conrad had aged in the two years—one year, Shawn reminded himself—he'd been gone. Loose skin sagged under his eyes. Heavy lines etched his mouth. Zach Taylor, the tall, young trumpet virtuoso who had taken Shawn's position, sat across the table. His friendly demeanor and open willingness to talk it out had already impressed Shawn. Bill, Dan, Peter, and Aaron completed the circle, none of them bothering to hide open stares of curiosity. "Medieval Scotland's beautiful this time of year," Shawn told Dan, catching him staring yet again. "Especially if you don't mind a little warfare."

Dan glowered. "It's hardly a laughing matter. Maybe you could try telling the truth for once in your life."

Shawn grinned.

The others looked away, finding interest in their nails, or the lilies in the vase on the table, or the paintings on the walls. Shawn glanced around the room, himself, at the plush blue carpeting and paneled walls of the hotel's conference room, much like the one they'd stayed in two years ago—a year ago. He'd already stumbled once, speaking of two years. They'd attributed the comment to whatever unknown trauma he'd suffered in his *year-long* disappearance.

"I'd like to see you play both trombone and harp," Conrad said. "They loved you playing harp last time. We've got two concerts left, and I'd like to make them celebrations co-starring you and Zach."

Shawn considered. He'd played harp often enough for the people of Glenmirril, on his nights being Niall. "I guess I could play harp," he said.

"You guess? You were *phenomenal* last time."

"Well, that wasn't me, that was Niall."

He paused, only barely, for Conrad to throw up his hands, muttering, "Niall, Niall! There was no Niall! Is this some joke you convinced Amy to take part in?"

Shawn ignored the question. "I can play harp if that's what you want. But we need to talk long term. Is there a place for me in the orchestra?" He wondered what Niall was doing.

Dan's face became stony. The others looked hesitantly between Shawn and Zach, lounging at the other end of the table, his hands locked behind short waves of blond hair. Shawn studied his replacement, from under lowered eyelids. The man was young, younger than Shawn's own twenty-six years. Twenty-five, he corrected himself. Zach had a quality of Niall to him, a forthrightness and confidence. Niall would like him.

Shawn let out a heavy sigh. Amy had been surprised early that morning when he'd asked where the nearest church was. He'd shrugged it off with, "Just something I got in the habit of. The Laird was a wee—rather particular about it." He lifted a finger, scratching his ear, thought of Niall's criticisms, and dropped it. His ear could itch for a bit. He quirked a smile at Amy.

"I don't get it, what's so funny?" she asked.

He couldn't explain, even to himself, why he found Niall's criticism of his ear-scratching in church funny. "Nothing." But he continued to smile. "Where's the church?" So they sat side by side, quiet but for James cooing in his arms. Thoughts of Niall, Allene, Christina, Red, all of them, crowded his heart as he stared at the crucifix. It had nothing on the Laird's. MacDonald's was a true work of art. Shawn hoped it had survived all these years. *I guess,* he thought, *I should thank You for bringing me home. You'll show Amy I'm the one for her, right?*

Mostly, he still had no idea what to say to God or do in church. Christina drifted to his mind. *Is it ridiculous to pray for someone who's here and now to me, when it all happened seven hundred years ago?* Of course it was ridiculous. Still, he offered a silent prayer for her protection, disturbed over not knowing her fate in the battle for Glenmirril. In the here and now, he had to get back to the States, see to his checking account, his house, re-establish himself.

"You don't want to be late to talk with Conrad and the board of directors." Amy touched the back of his hand. They'd left, shoulder to shoulder, if not hand in hand. He had wondered what she thought about, sitting in church—and how she knew where to find one.

"Is there a way to make it work?" Aaron asked. Shawn's attention snapped back to the conference room. Aaron pushed a heavy lock of black hair off his forehead. It promptly fell back. "Can Zach and Shawn switch off? Each of them work with smaller ensembles so we can have a couple performances at a time, record more?"

"I'm surprised to hear you of all people looking for a way to make it work," Dan replied dryly.

Shawn's mouth tightened. He and Aaron glanced at one another and away; the memory of Celine, soft-spoken and gullible, with flowing blond hair, hovered between them, as surely as if she were in the room.

"We'd best stick to professional issues," Conrad sighed. He pushed his fingers through unruly white hair. It stuck up like a dandelion.

"We've made our peace," Aaron said to Dan. "I believe he's a changed man, and I believe in second chances."

"I'm all for second chances," Dan shot back. "But sometimes, it just doesn't work. Two stars takes two orchestras. You can't just expect the musicians to double their playing time. The union wouldn't allow it, anyway. We're not asking Zach to walk, just because *he* decided to show up again."

"I'm not asking him to." Shawn reached for the coffee pot on the sideboard behind him, adding steaming brew to his mug—his black mug etched with the gold trombone he'd found in Amy's kitchen. Amy had said Niall used it frequently, during his time with the orchestra. An image of Niall, gripping his hand in the tower, burned on Shawn's retina. What had he gone back down to? Death? Injury? What about the Laird? Red?

"Shawn?"

"Sorry?" He jolted back to the present. Steam curled up from his mug.

"What *are* you asking?" Dan's tone left no question he'd already asked once.

"Nothing but ideas at this point," Shawn said. "I'd be happy to play second trombone like I originally auditioned for."

"*You*, settle for *second*?" Peter, the aging concert master, snorted.

"We moved Jim back to principal and hired the new guy for second," Bill said.

"So you mentioned. I'm just saying."

Just saying what? Allene had asked. *What I just said,* he'd replied. *You said we stole MacDougall's cattle. Those were our cattle.* He smiled, amused still by Allene's reactions to his idioms.

"I'm missing the amusement factor in any of this," snapped Dan.

"Sorry. Just thinking about something else."

"You know, it could only help if you'd give us a straight story about where you disappeared to for a year."

Shawn shrugged. "Events beyond my control. I've given the straight story to the police and they don't believe me. Neither do you." He pushed his hand through his hair, letting it fall to his shoulders. The novelty of having it clean and soft with conditioner again had not worn off.

Dan burst from his chair, hands planted on the table. "You're as arrogant as you've always been! You disappear, cause no end of grief, reappear with no explanation, and now you're...."

"Dan, can we...?" Conrad lifted a hand, begging for calm.

"...smiling at things that aren't funny and admiring your own hair!" Dan raged. "Yeah, I know, it's your signature. Get over yourself already!"

Zach leaned forward, drawing all eyes. His youth—*youth*, Shawn thought wryly, *he's barely younger than me, just hasn't fought as many medieval battles*—and short blond hair brought Rob to mind. But he had a straightforward manner Rob lacked. "The thing is," he said, in a voice that dispelled the illusion of youth, "Shawn has no more need of an orchestra than Trombone Shorty."

Nods went around the circle. Shawn leaned back in his chair, legs outstretched, interested to hear Zach's words. So far, he'd liked all he'd seen of the man. He'd watched at the concert the previous night, seeing how Zach handled the female admirers backstage, with nothing more than a friendly wave, and good-natured quips. He'd kept his wife and daughters close by, introducing them to one and all, pride shining on his face, and the women who had screamed his name while he played onstage became models of decorum.

"I think there's a win-win situation here," Zach said. "Shawn has the same talent and name that got him where he is. His albums—what, nearly a dozen of them?—are selling like hotcakes. He's all over Yahoo and MSN. He's on the most searched list on Google. In the last twenty-four hours we've taken a hundred calls from the States wanting him for talk shows and interviews." He looked to Shawn. "I think your manager, Ben, is already talking about a solo tour for you?"

Shawn nodded.

"He's in a perfect position to go solo, play with any choir, ensemble, or orchestra in the world. And we would be fools not to sign a contract with him right now to lock in three or four of those guest appearances each year. He's not going to have time to breathe, with the possibilities open to him."

Shawn breathed out on a smile. He liked this man. He took a deep swallow of his coffee, realizing he was still living in the fourteenth century, a man who didn't even fully exist; who, even when he existed as Niall, didn't want to be seen or found, as there were those who wanted to kill him. He was not yet thinking in twenty-first century possibilities. He'd forgotten, himself, just who he was.

He studied Zach, his appreciation of the man growing. He'd just kept his own job while offering Shawn something even better. Win-win, as he said. Shawn set the mug down. "Tell me what works for you," he said.

Peter frowned at Shawn. "Amy did say you came back a changed man."

Shawn laughed. "More than you'll ever know." Amy had smiled this morning, when he'd made her eggs. He treasured that, after all he'd done to her.

"Not changed enough to be honest and tell us where you were," Dan harrumphed.

Shawn spread his hands in apology. "You wouldn't believe me."

"You could at least try."

"I have," Shawn answered shortly. "Anything you want to know about James Douglas, just ask."

"I don't even know who that is." Dan scowled.

"That's a shame," Shawn said, and sorrow pierced his own heart. "He's a great man." He turned to Conrad, dismissing Dan. "What days work for the first guest appearance? I think Zach and I could come up with some crowd-pleasing duets. Maybe dueling antiphonal brass in opposite balconies?"

Zach's green eyes lit up. He leaned toward Shawn, the rest of them forgotten in finding his kindred spirit. "Amy could do a great medley mixing *Carnival of Venice* with *Blue Bells* with *Dueling Banjos.* Can you imagine that? Back and forth between trumpets and trombones?"

His excitement caught Shawn. "What about throwing in that lick from *Laughing Brass*?" he asked.

Quiet fell on the room. They all stared at him.

"What's *Laughing Brass*?" Zach asked.

Shawn cocked his head, looked around at the half dozen men, all of whom looked back, waiting. "It's all over the internet," he said. "Millions of views. The English boy who wrote it...he was fourteen, played all the parts himself on all the brass instruments, and morphed them together...." They stared at him blankly, but he couldn't stop the flood of words. "He was offered a job composing soundtracks when he was sixteen. You never heard of...?" He stopped, understanding. Everything had changed. If none of them had heard of Ethan Peters, it could only be because he'd never existed. He swallowed. A chill chased through him.

Shawn cleared his throat. Had they not changed history, Hugh, the Laird, and so many more he knew and loved would have died. He turned his mind firmly from the loss of the piece.

"I meant *The Devil Went Down to* Georgia." He laughed. "It still exists, doesn't it? They'd never expect that. Conrad, can you get permissions on that? Bill, do you have staff paper handy?" He turned back to Zach. "Start it in the violins and move it down the score order, till the tuba's doing it."

Zach took up the brainstorming. "Then back up to trumpet and trombone choirs in the opposite balconies for the grand finale."

"Unreal!" Dan tossed up his hands and headed for the door.

"Hey, Dan," Shawn called. "You have the numbers of those interviews? Is Lindsay still working for us? Can you ask her to start arranging those and maybe ask her if she'll do some work for me on the side?"

"Right on it, my Lord," Dan sneered.

"I'm not a lord," Shawn said. "Just a knight."

Glaring, Dan slammed out of the conference room.

Glenmirril, June 10, 1316

Christina lifted her head from Allene's shoulder, turning her eyes back to the courtyard three stories below, to the MacDougall clan filing past the headless body —their faces mostly averted from the grisly sight—through the gatehouse. Allene, cradling James in one arm, squeezed her shoulder. "He'd no choice," she said.

"Aye." Christina spoke calmly, though her face was white. Her black hair hung free to her waist, over a ruby red gown.

They stared down into the courtyard in silence. A cool breeze blew through the open arch, ruffling the cloaks of the men filing out. Taran kicked the severed head, sending it rolling through a tendril of gloam. Hugh put an arm around his shoulder.

"Poor lad," Christina said. "What will he do without his father?"

"He's his mother, still, which is more than some boys have." James squirmed in his blankets. Allene lifted him to her shoulder. "And there are men aplenty for him. Hugh, Niall, my father, Gil. Taran. He'll find solace in looking to Red, who has no kin at all." They watched as the last MacDougall left through the gatehouse, as the Laird issued orders, as the heavy creak of the drawbridge reached their ears. "Is it what you hoped for?" Allene asked.

Christina stared down into the bailey. "'Tis grateful I am not to have their heads on our walls. Especially the lad."

"Without the influence of Duncan and MacDougall himself, what are they?" Allene asked. "Perchance we'll find them to be men just like our own, who also wish to live in peace."

"'Tis still a risk, aye?" Christina replied.

Allene studied Christina as she stared down into the gory scene below. She seemed curiously remote. "Is it MacDougall?" She touched Christina's arm. "He can do us no harm," she assured her.

CHAPTER FIVE

West of Scotland, Present

In the car, Amy glared across the small road to the sandy beach and blue waters. "Why didn't you tell me this was where we were going?" She felt for her phone.

Thinking about calling the Interloper, Shawn guessed. The thrill of his victory with the board of directors wilted. He laid his hand on hers, stilling her phone. "Would you have come?" He studied her. Neither a year nor pregnancy had changed her. She had the fine, creamy skin he'd thought about so often; her thick, black hair hung free down her back, and her royal blue shirt set off her eyes. It was a color Christina often wore.

In the back, James let out a cheerful squeal. Amy's jaw tensed. "You don't think I had anything to say about it?" Tioram rose, a squat, solid bulk, on its spit of land.

He swallowed. "I didn't think of it like that."

"No, you wouldn't."

Silence hung heavily between them. In the back, James chortled and the sound of bells rang out, as he hit the toy hanging from his car seat. An answer dawned on Shawn. "We could leave if you want."

She turned to him, a dozen questions in her eyes. Finally, she nodded. "It took long enough for that to occur to you, but good answer."

"You want to leave, then?" He desperately hoped she didn't. He wanted to be here with her, where memories were strong and warm.

She stared at the castle, a dark smudge against a sunny sky, and finally spoke. "Picnic dinner aside, you understand there won't be a repeat of last time."

Shawn laughed, sunshine breaking through his concern as it always did. "You don't want an encore of *Mashed Potato?*" Things had worked out well with the orchestra. He'd win Amy back, too. "Anyway, the last time, for me, was with Niall in 1314. We stopped here on our way home from Jura."

She looked at him with interest. "Just how many battles did you fight?"

He shook his head, gazing across the small road to the water. "What do you count as a battle? Each raid? Or only against soldiers fighting back? Either way, I quit counting pretty fast."

James squealed. Amy threw open her door. "He needs to be nursed," she said.

Shawn, too, climbed out, and leaned on the car roof, watching her lift James. James kicked chubby legs, and let out another happy screech. She kissed him, laughing, and lifted him to her shoulder. Shawn opened the back door for the picnic basket. Straightening, she called to him across the car, "Tell me about the battle of Jura."

He heaved the basket out, and slammed the door. "Need help with the diaper bag?" She shook her head, the bag hanging over her shoulder, and James pulling at her hair. Shawn headed down a narrow road to the beach, and she fell into step beside him. "The battle of Jura. Weird to give it a name. To us, it just was. John of Lorn was being difficult, playing admiral of the high seas for Edward in England. Except they were our high seas. So we paid him a visit."

"On the high seas?" Amy raised her eyebrows.

"Yep." At the small slope down to the beach, he offered his hand. She hesitated briefly before taking it. Damp sand sank beneath his feet.

"On *water*. How did Niall like that?"

Shawn laughed. The afternoon breeze blew his hair, leaving a taste of salt. "By some chance, he happened to get sent off with a message and we left without him. Or rather, Brother Andrew got sent off."

"Brother Andrew being...you? We figured that out."

"Both of us." Shawn grinned. "In this instance, Niall. So they think Niall was on the galleys with them. But it was me."

"You sound rather pleased with yourself." As if suddenly aware of it, she looked down at her hand still in his, and pulled it away.

"I don't bite," he said. But the few moments she'd left her hand in his sang in his heart. He couldn't stop smiling.

"So you've said."

Even her acerbic tone couldn't dim his happiness. *I'm home!*

"I'm betting you had something to do with Niall being sent off. Does he know?"

Shawn laughed, loving the sun on his face and the sea air. "He guessed and he was pretty ticked, but he got over it. It was for the best, though. He was really in no shape to be on water." He swung the basket, enjoying the feel of the soft sand under his tennis shoes. He stopped as they neared the ruins, looking up at the hulking stones. He'd first come here two years ago with Amy; had slipped away from her when his phone vibrated, and sent the text to...Debra? Jo? He couldn't remember, two years later, who wrote for the magazine in New York, just that her apartment was all stark, bold slashes of stark, bold colors. And she'd worn her black hair short and spiked. He'd hated it, the one time he'd actually thought about it.

"What was it like?" Amy asked.

He jumped, thinking of Debra—or whatever her name had been. But Amy didn't know about her. He promised himself he'd tell her the truth, issue the full, complete apology she deserved. But she hadn't asked. Maybe she didn't know. Maybe there was no reason to hurt her, and they could just start fresh. He thought guiltily of Dana. That would hurt her. Badly. He felt guilty, too, that he hadn't contacted Dana since coming back. She'd be frantic.

Amy cocked her head to the side. "When you were here with Niall," she clarified. "You looked—startled. What did you think I meant?"

"Nothing." He started walking again. "With Niall. Yeah, well, for one thing, we rode. The tide was just coming in, and we had to hurry, like fifty of us, and the water coming in around the horse's feet. We were all pretty tired. Lachlan got sliced up pretty bad at the battle." He stopped to pick up a shell, fanning out in delicate shades of coral and pink, and handed it to her.

"Who's Lachlan?" She took the shell, smiled, bit her lip, and looked away.

"A friend. He and Owen were like a pair of drumsticks, you know, best friends or cousins or something, always together. Lachlan got married while I was there. And there was Red...." He was aware he was drifting off on a tangent. They approached the grassy slope running up to the black stone walls. "Give me your hand. You don't want to lose your footing with him."

The breeze gusted, flattening the tall grasses on the hillside and whipping her hair around her face. She turned her shoulder against it, sheltering James. He gasped and squirmed in the stiff wind. Shawn tugged her up, getting her into the shelter of the walls. "There won't be any breeze inside," he said. They rounded the heavy walls to the barred entrance. A grin stole across his face, remembering.

She turned away, refusing to meet his eyes, and once again pulled her hand from his. "Picnic, then home. I'll be watching the tide this time." Last time, it had come in, shutting them off from the mainland, trapping them in the castle overnight.

Shawn pushed the basket under the bar, squeezed through, and reached for James. Moments later, they stood in the abandoned, overgrown courtyard, the sun dimmed by the high walls, looking around. Shawn walked to a far wall. "Here's where the armory was," he said. Nothing remained. "And the stairs. Remember how they were overgrown? Almost more dirt than stone?"

"They still are," she reminded him.

"But they weren't then." He walked farther down the hall till he found them. "Christina MacRuari lived here. Fascinating woman, and anyone who thinks medieval women had no power never met her."

"I imagine nobody today has."

"I have." He looked around the ruin, the walls crumbling at the top, scrappy green plants pushing through the cracks in the stones, the courtyard empty but for the wild growth. "It was all brand new then, the stairs cut sharp and fresh, fires in the hearth, tapestries everywhere, a thousand candles. I was Brother Andrew that night, and walked up those stairs, thinking of you. It's so like it was...but different."

"Like you," Amy said.

He turned, hoping to see warmth in her eyes. But she turned, busying herself laying out a thick blanket for James. "Tell me about your visit here with Niall."

Relief surged through him. He wouldn't have to tell her about the women.

She lifted her eyes. "Then you can tell me the whole truth about everything— before you left."

He swallowed, feeling irritatingly like Rob. Maybe he should start with the confession and get it over with. Maybe he should tell her about the battles, about Niall, about all the good he'd done; put himself in a better light so she'd be more likely to forgive. Or he could stretch out the stories so they'd run out of time, so she'd forget.

"You two spent a lot of time together?"

Shawn nodded, staring at the picnic basket. He had no desire to sing about mashed potatoes. A sudden emptiness engulfed him. "Lots of time. He was like a brother." He pulled the plastic container of roast beef sandwiches from the basket. He'd never had a brother. Niall had had six who had died, and a best friend who had betrayed him. In a flash, he saw from Niall's perspective; Niall who had seemed never to need anyone. "I think I was like a brother to him, too," he said softly. *And I left him. I left all of them.* "It's strange," he added. "In some ways, they're more real to me than anything here."

She reached into the basket for a six pack of Coke, and spoke softly, staring at the picnic blanket. "Maybe because what you did there mattered."

"What I do here matters." But even as he spoke, he wasn't so sure.

"Nobody lives or dies because of what we do." Amy stared at the heavy garnet ring on her finger.

Shawn swallowed again. The Interloper flashed into his mind. He'd asked Rob a few questions. The man did mountain and water rescues. He saved lives. Shawn couldn't bring himself to ask if that's what she really wanted. He bit back pathetic, pleading words: *My house is nicer. I can take you anywhere in the world. I'm Someone.* And Christina drifted into his mind, a lovely, silent siren. He'd been none of those things in her world. But Christina would have had him as he was, without any of it. Maybe Amy didn't care about the house and the trips and the important personage, either. Which meant he didn't stand a chance against the Interloper—a man who did *Things That Mattered.* Like he had done with Niall, seven hundred years ago.

Glenmirril, 1316

In his cell, three stories up in the tower, MacDougall steadily pushed and pulled on the rain-spattered bars at his window, staring down as his men filed from the gray courtyard, past the body of his kinsman, lying in the drizzle. Taran kicked disdainfully at Somerled's head. It bumped across a puddle and landed, staring up into heavy clouds, the black beard and face smeared with blood and thick mud.

Anger. It was Taran's weakness. The Laird's was mercy. Red—he was naive and trusting. Gil—MacDougall wasn't sure yet. And Niall himself—his family and his over-confidence could be used against him.

But there was something else. MacDougall frowned, staring into the courtyard, thinking about the battle the previous night. There had been a monk in a gray robe. Men had spoken, in the past years, of the gray friar who accompanied Campbell.

Nobody seemed to know who he was, or from which monastery he hailed. He hadn't seen the monk this morning.

Below, Red led the last of his garrons, his beautiful animals, into the southern bailey, to the stables. Anger seethed in MacDougall. They were *his,* bred from prize stock, the finest animals in Scotland, and MacDonald had taken them! Only one remained in the courtyard—Duncan's, with the blaze of white on its nose.

At that moment, Hugh, Malcolm's giant of a brother, emerged from the northern tower, a linen-wrapped body slung over his shoulder. Hard, cold fury burned in MacDougall's gut, watching the ogre so careless with his only son, the son Niall had killed. Hugh tossed the body atop the garron. His voice carried up through the drizzle, as he addressed MacDougall's men.

Roger, MacDougall's steward, hastened to tie the body in place. Hugh wiped his hands against one another, as if brushing away filth. MacDougall's hands tightened on his bars till his knuckles turned white. *How dare he! How dare they!* His stomach knotted with anger. And he recognized something beneath the anger, as Roger took the garron's reins, and led his son away: *pain.*

It hit him with fierce trembling. He was seeing the first time he'd watched Duncan, a child of four, led around the ring. Duncan had sat straight and proud, even then, his chin lifted, ordering the riding master to hand over the reins, determined to ride by himself. MacDougall had watched the boy with pride. Now, he watched his son on another horse in a rain-spattered enemy courtyard, taking his last ride.

"Be thankful they're allowing him to go home for a Christian burial."

MacDougall jumped at the voice behind him, spinning to see Gil setting a basket of bread and a jug of ale on the small table.

"Be thankful they killed my son?" he demanded.

"Your son is not the only one being carried out in a linen cloth today." The lad backed up to the doorway, his hand on the knife in his belt. "You attacked us, yet you find your son's life worth more than our own man, dead in our kirk? We've a boy left fatherless, thanks to you. And still, our Laird grants him a Christian burial. Yes, you ought thank him." He shut the door, locking MacDougall back in.

MacDougall returned to his cell window. Below, the garron with his son bound across its back plodded through the gatehouse behind two of his men. He watched through the gray drizzle, until they emerged from the shadow of the gatehouse, at the far end of the drawbridge he'd crossed so many months ago with Christina, returning her to Glenmirril.

He watched the garron fall into step behind his long line of men heading south into the forest, back to Creagsmalan. He watched, his heart heavy with grief, as Duncan's body grew smaller and finally disappeared into the damp, dripping greenwood. Niall would pay dearly.

Castle Tioram, Present

Shawn wolfs down a second sandwich, and adds, "I pulled Lachlan out just on time. I saved his life."

I pull my hair to fall over my shoulder as I lean back. With raised eyebrows, I say, "You seem to have saved the lives of half of Scotland." As I say it, my words come to me. Nobody lives or dies because of what we do. *Shortly after, he started the many stories of courageous rescues.*

"I like to think I made a difference." He flushes.

I lean forward, studying his face to be sure. "Are you blushing!" He is! I laugh. "I've never seen you blush." I'm amused by this new Shawn. I like him, with this hint of vulnerability, even more than I liked the good I saw in the old Shawn.

"I'm not blushing," he snaps.

"Okay, you're not." But I can't wipe away the smile, try as I do for his sake. "It's just warm in here without the wind." I lean forward to rub James's back. He's drifted to sleep on his blanket, one fist pushed into his mouth.

Shawn, too, leans forward, running a finger over his son's thick, black hair. "Just like yours," he says. "He's beautiful." His eyes meet mine; glowing with their golden flecks set in the brown.

My mind flashes to Dana. I want to be angry. But that was a different man, a lifetime ago. He's here with me, not with her. Everything lurches inside me. I look away, feeling the heat rise on my own cheeks.

He laughs softly. "You're right. It's just warm in here without the wind."

I bite my lip, staring at my hand on James's back, Shawn's fingers a hair breadth away. None of this is fair to Angus. I wonder what he's doing. But he walked away and told me to work things out with Shawn.

"Amy?"

I swallow. It would be easy to be mad at Angus for walking away, to walk back into my old life with Shawn. It might also be disaster. It's been four days, and the other women haven't been mentioned. I pull my hand away. It's a pleasant day. I don't want to spoil the mood. But I have to say it. I clear my throat. "We're not just picking up where we left off." My voice is tight. He has laid out a sparkling, manicured path for me to walk back to what we had, lined it with every good thing in life, tempting me to enjoy it, and not ruin it by demanding answers. I can't look at him. My eyes lock on a wild flower, pushing its way up between two stones that were once Christina MacRuari's floor." You need to tell me the truth. About everything."

He doesn't respond. Even the sound of his breathing seems to drop a dynamic level. I lift my eyes. His jaw is tight. He stares at the picnic basket. "You already know," he says. Pianissimo. Barely audible.

"I need to hear it from you." There is a strong, accented tenuto on you.

He says nothing. Afternoon sun skims over ivied walls, across the tree sprouting in the abandoned courtyard, and glances off his hair, flashing glints of copper.

Anger rises at his hesitation. "You made a fool of me," I say. "You made me mistrust my own senses and perceptions. You made me question my own sanity with your lies. This time, you're going to tell me the truth."

Still, he says nothing.

His manicured path is but a painting—fake and insubstantial. Disappointment stabs. I wanted to know I was worth it to him, worth enough to come clean. Heat stings my eyes, and echoes in my voice. "Some things are too big to be set aside as if they never happened, no matter how much you've changed." *I grab blindly for empty Coke cans, jamming them in the basket.* "If your own comfort is still more important than the pain you caused me, it's time to go home, because you haven't changed enough." *I almost wish he'll prove himself the worst things—make this easy for me.*

"Wait!" *His head shoots up, his eyes wide.* "It's not that my comfort is more important. It's...."

I pause, a can half in the basket. I'll call Angus, tell him it's over with Shawn. When he doesn't speak, I prompt, "It's what?"

He lifts his hands in resignation. "I don't know. I'm sorry I hurt you."

"How many were there?" *My heart speeds up. What if it's worse than I already know? What if he tells me more names? More of my friends?*

He mumbles.

I scoop up the container that held sandwiches, and reach for James's diaper bag.

"A few," *he says more loudly.*

"How many in the orchestra?"

"What good does it do to know that now, Amy?" *he protests.* "It's never going to happen again, I swear."

I fold a corner of the blanket over James, preparing to scoop him up. "You're right, because I'm leaving."

"Just two!" *He scrambles to his knees, a hand on my arm, staying me.* "Caroline and Celine."

I pause, my heart pounding, a tremble beginning in my hands. "Let me be clear. All this lying in the name of not hurting me is garbage. Being lied to hurts, and the truth always comes out eventually. Was it only two in the orchestra?"

He nods, his eyes wide in earnestness. "Two."

The trembling climbs up my arms. My cheeks feel cool despite the warmth of the day. And I realize as much as I want my life to become simpler, I also want desperately to believe that he is all the good things I always believed. After everything, I still want to believe that. The apology on the rock convinced me. I want James to grow up with a simple life, his father there with him at dinner each evening, and tucking him into bed. Shawn's wide eyes, the look of guilelessness almost convince me I misunderstood Dana's tone, her words, her flurry of calls.

I give myself a mental shake, jarring myself from the fantasy he's trying to weave. I didn't misunderstand anything. I throw the last can into the basket. "It was your chance, Shawn."

He bolts to his feet, pacing across the dirt and stubby grasses and scattered flowers that make up the floor of the ancient courtyard. "Why do you want details, Amy? Can't you just accept that I'm admitting I cheated on you, I lied to you, and I spent two years regretting everything I've done and swore I would never do it again, and I kept that promise?"

I rise to my feet, too, my voice swelling on a crescendo. "How can I believe you kept that promise or will keep that promise if you're still trying to live by the creed that what I don't know won't hurt me? If you don't tell me the truth now, bit by bit, you'll slide back into thinking as long as I don't find out, it won't hurt. I'm not spending my life like that." I stoop to gather up James. I march toward the barred entrance. Behind me, Shawn paces. A bird screeches and beats its wings in the air. I wiggle a leg through the grate, leaning to squeeze through.

"Three!" he shouts.

I breathe out. The trembling in my arms eases. I stand, one ankle through the bars, facing him across the courtyard. A raven swoops over the wall and nestles in a tree, letting out a shriek. "Who?"

"Amy, please." He whispers. His eyes plead. "It's over. I'll never go near her again. I'll never speak to her again. I don't want to hurt you."

"Who?"

He turns his back. His hands rest on his hips, his shoulders tense.

I lean again, working myself and James under the grate.

"Dana."

I stop. It hurts—surprisingly, it hurts to hear him say it. But he's been honest. I straighten, clutching James to my chest.

Shawn stands in front of the solitary tree, staring at his feet. "Now it's over, isn't it? I told you you didn't want to know."

Overhead, a raven shrieks.

Glenmirril, June 1316

Outside, a raven screeched. The Laird glanced out the window, to heavy clouds overhead. "Our prayers are offered." With a grunt, he pushed himself up from his knees in the dark kirk.

Niall, too, rose, his eyes on the empty spot where Taran's father had lain. His eyes felt dry and scratchy with the exhaustion of the last days, with emptiness and Shawn's leaving, and grief for Taran and his father, laid to rest in the kirk yard. "Our prayers are offered," he repeated, hearing the flatness in his own voice. "May Shawn find peace. May Scotland find peace. May I have a few days with my wife and son."

The Laird clapped him on the shoulder. "You lack faith, Niall?"

Niall smiled. "'Tis hard to have faith contrary to what I see."

The Laird guided him past the few pews, through the lingering smell of incense, and out to the porch where Shawn had stood beside Allene, pretending to be her new groom. MacDonald stared up past the castle walls, to dark clouds, scuttling across the sky, promising to bring more rain soon. "I don't see the stars," he said. "But I know they are there, for I've seen them many times. My ancestors traveled by them for centuries. I know I will see them again."

Niall stared up silently, willing himself to believe the same.

MacDonald squeezed his shoulder. "Go to your wife, Niall."

Niall nodded, heading across the courtyard to the tower entrance. He glanced back at MacDonald standing on the kirk porch, looking up to the sky, before climbing the tower stairs. At the second floor, he turned, treading softly through the silent halls, beneath the flicker of the torches. Outside the windows, rain began trickling down, as it had all day, as it had for months, destroying crops, salt, firewood.

As he opened the door to his rooms, Allene spun from the window. Torch light flickered against her white shift and caught the copper highlights in her hair. A faint glimmer of moonlight eked through the clouds, turning her white gown to something floating and ethereal, and showing the first gentle swelling of her stomach. He caught his breath inadvertently, and hurried to her.

"You've been gone a long while." She touched his cheek, and his injured arm. "Is it well?"

"Aye. Your father bid me stay a wee bit with him in the kirk." He looked out at the black clouds against black night, at faint silver rain once again streaking down. MacDonald was right. The stars were still there. He was too quick to lose faith. MacDonald had prayed, and who knew what blessings would come on the morrow. He pressed Allene's head to his chest, kissing her hair. "Come to bed. We'll have some time together, aye?" Smiling, he took her hand, and led her to their chamber. He dropped to the bed, lifting one boot to his knee, working at the lace.

As he did, a knock sounded on the outer door. "Niall?" Hugh called in.

Sitting on the edge of the bed, one boot half unlaced, Niall looked up. He shook his head. Allene was already back in the solar. He waited, his fingers still on his lace, knowing what was coming, even as he denied it.

"Niall." She stood in the doorway. "A messenger has come. You must go at once."

Niall closed his eyes, swallowing the anger rising in his chest. It flooded his head, burning as strong and hot as the wound in his arm had, just days before.

"You know you must go." Allene touched his shoulder.

Niall wanted to scream. He wanted to be far away, where he would never be summoned away from his home, his wife, his children, never sent to possible death. He nodded. "Of course I'll go." He laced the boot back up. "From whom does the messenger come?"

"I don't know, Niall. But he awaits in the great hall. Hugh bids you hurry."

The boot tied securely, Niall pushed himself off the bed. His arm twitched with pain. He rubbed it, before tucking his shirt back into his breeks.

He crossed the bed chamber and dim solar, and found Hugh waiting, none too patiently. They said nothing, as they passed through torch-lit halls, down twisting stone stairs to the great hall. Niall's eyes fell first on his mother, standing near the fire in her warmest surcoat, her hair as perfectly done as if it were midday. The fire cast planes over her smooth cheeks. The Laird sat at the long wooden table with a man in Bruce's livery, who rose as Niall and Hugh entered. The man bowed, and looked to MacDonald.

"Niall." MacDonald's voice was heavy. "The Bruce summons you."

Niall looked to his mother, his eyebrows raised in question.

"I've asked your mother to bring you something." MacDonald's voice rumbled heavily, struggling out from under dozens of cares.

Niall's mother stepped forward. She held out a sword, larger than his own, resting across both her palms. Its smooth polished metal threw off flashes of firelight. "Your father's sword," she said. "You have made us all proud."

Niall bowed low. His heart kicked up a notch, pounding harder and faster. Nobody had to tell him he would be raiding with Bruce. He took the sword, feeling its solid weight. It would serve well. He drew in a deep breath, holding back a sigh.

Hugh clapped a hand on his shoulder.

"The Bruce bids you bring your harp," the messenger added.

MacDonald placed beefy hands on the scarred table and pushed himself up, like a bear rising from winter sleep. "Choose thirty men," he said. "You leave at dawn."

Niall raised one eyebrow in his best imitation of Shawn. "Stars?" he asked.

MacDonald sighed. "Faith, Niall. The clouds grow heavy, but the stars are there."

Castle Tioram, Present

"I told you it would be better to tell the truth," I say. "It would have been over if you'd lied."

He stands, tense, by the far, crumbling wall, as the light dies.

"Come and sit down." Compassion wounds my heart for his discomfort, though it hardly should. I wonder if he has the same compassion for the pain he caused me, or only compassion for his own pain, of guilt gnawing at his insides.

He turns, looking like a boy smeared with the chocolate he's been told not to eat, his mouth turned down, his eyes unable to meet mine. But he comes, slowly, as if wary of stepping into a trap, and sinks down beside me, his back against the stone wall. Starlings wheel in the sky above, a great cloud adding their voices to the evening symphony of birds and insects.

"How many when you flew out to talk shows?"

His voice halting, his eyes locked on a train of ants crossing Christina MacRuari's ancient floor, he tells me all I knew, plus one more, a horse breeder in Kentucky. I close my eyes. He never went near a horse for me. Why that should hurt more than that he slept with her, I don't know, but the knife saws in my gut, almost physically doubling me over.

But even more than wanting to stop the pain, I need to know. James stirs. I lift him off his blanket, comforting him on my shoulder, and question Shawn, while the tree in the courtyard casts ever longer shadows, while its leaves turn from green to charcoal-silver to black, till it's too dark for shadows, while the tide comes in, a soft swishing in the night, and closes Tioram off from the mainland.

I nurse James, feeling sickness rise in my throat, as Shawn answers, asking myself the whole time, Why am I doing this to myself? Swallows and swifts flock overhead, and perch on the castle walls. With James tucked under his blanket in my arms, safe from the midges, to the stuttering accompaniment of a turnstone out on the shore, I ask plaintively, "How could you do this to me? You said you loved me."

He hunches against the wall, his knees drawn up, his back half to me. "I did love you. I do love you. I never did it to hurt you."

I scramble up from my patch of ground. "I get that you didn't do it to hurt me, but you did it despite how it would hurt me. I just didn't matter at all." James squirms and sighs.

"You mattered a lot. I told them I would never tolerate you being hurt."

"Meaning, you forced them to cover for you." I shake my head in disgust. "Thanks. Anything else?"

"Haven't you heard enough?" Shawn huddles miserably against the wall of Castle Tioram, not even a shadow of the great Shawn Kleiner who struts across stage with girls screaming his name.

"Enough details, yes." I pace the dusky courtyard, James on my shoulder. I rub his back. "But why?" The steady rhythm of my hand soothes me, too. "I gave you everything you wanted, because I loved you. Why wasn't I enough?"

He shrugs. "It had nothing to do with that."

"How could it not? Why did you say you loved me if you didn't?"

"I did!"

"How could you love me and do that?" If I wasn't holding a baby, I'd throw my hands up in frustration.

"I don't know!" He sounds as frustrated as I feel. "I know I loved you. I do love you. I spent two years missing you. Anything you want. Marry me, Amy. Whatever wedding you want. Wherever you want it. I'll buy you a horse. The orchestra's leaving in a few days; soon as we get back to the States...."

I turn, my hand to James's head on my shoulder. "Shawn, I have students here. I have a life here. What made you think I'm going back to the States?"

Inverness, June, Present

The dwelling was hardly Claverock, Simon thought as he let himself out the back door into a small, unkempt garden. But it was empty—a place to regroup, retreat to after replenishing his money in dark alleys, sleep, resume training with the sword he'd retrieved from Brian's house, and prepare meals—though it was a sad descent that the Lord of Claverock must do so for himself. As long as he kept quiet, the villeins who dwelt in the attached homes remained oblivious to his presence.

Glancing across the row of empty gardens, each with its own walls, he slipped unseen across his own, and climbed the low wall to the street behind. He set off for the town, in search of more talk that would lead him to Shawn Kleiner, recently arrived from the fourteenth century. The *bus*, when he'd journeyed to Oban for his sword, had been abuzz with talk of Shawn's reappearance.

"Wild stories!" an older woman had murmured to her friend, in the seat beside him. "Time travel! Claims he fought with the Bruce!"

Her friend sniffed. "As if the Bruce would have the likes of him!"

Simon stared at her curiously, wondering if she might be quite soft in the head, or if *time travel* was perhaps more common to these people than he'd known. She glared at him. He smiled at her, and settled back in his seat, deciding she was merely mad.

It had taken him a full day to find a case in which to hide the sword. When he returned, Inverness was even more full of gossip. Time was short, he learned. Shawn was expected to leave for the far away country called *America.*

"Across the *ocean,*" a girl drawled when he asked where it was located. She twirled a finger in circles by her temple, and ran off, laughing. Simon seethed.

As he continued his walk into town, he helped himself to an apple at a market. Chewing the fruit, he headed for his favorite spot, leaning on the rail looking across the river to the jail, where girls congregated. Two of them ran up, giggling, shortly after he planted himself there, and stood gazing across, as two lasses at a bold knight.

One of them sighed. "He was *there.* I'd've *seen* him if I'd switched shifts like Jimmy asked me to."

"He's playing tonight," the other said. "I got a ticket!"

"Go *on!*" exclaimed the first. "How d' ye know?"

"Me friend Sara works at Eden Court. She heard and texted me straight away!"

Simon turned to the girls. "What is Eden Court?"

His question cut their chatter short. They stared in surprise, as the river slapped, silver-gray, against its banks below. Then one of them laughed. "You're not from around here."

Simon smiled. "I'm not. I'm from *America.*"

The glanced at each other, their faces doubtful. But one girl launched into an explanation. He didn't grasp all the words. *Movies?* He had no idea what that was. But it seemed to be a great courtyard for entertainment. And Shawn Kleiner would play there with a hundred musicians. Simon could hardly fathom a gallery large enough to hold so many minstrels.

"They've a rehearsal this morning," the girl said, eager to talk about him. "And the concert tonight. Ticket sales will be through the bleedin' roof! Just wait and see."

Simon smiled. "I will indeed. Can you point me toward this courtyard?"

The girls glanced at one another again and giggled. But they pointed him in the direction.

CHAPTER SIX

South of Scotland, 1316

Niall's troops, with MacDonald's banner flapping from the standard Lachlan carried, streamed up the ridge above Bruce's camp. They'd ridden hard, more than fifty miles a day in steady rain, stopped rarely, and slept little, till they paused the third evening at the top of a mountain pass. Niall was eager to shed the weight of the sword and harp on his back. In the glen below, more than a thousand men, small at this distance, bustled among tents and campfires. Several looked up, shielding their eyes against the sun blazing in the west, at the same time one of Bruce's guards emerged from behind a tree.

Niall bowed. "I am Sir Niall Campbell." The words came uncomfortably off his tongue, knowing Shawn's deeds, not his own, had garnered the title.

Bruce's messenger, at Niall's side, spoke. "He brings the men of MacDonald, at Bruce's bidding."

"Go, then, and make haste," said the guard. "They are even now preparing to depart at dawn on the morrow." He peered more closely at Niall. "Bruce wishes to see you anon." He pointed. "See where he is?"

"Aye." Niall nodded. The prancing lion banner snapped proudly over one tent. He nudged his garron, and thirty animals and men rustled into motion, descending the rocky path to the glen below.

"Why d' ye think he wants to see you?" Hugh asked.

"My comely face," Niall suggested. "My delightful personality, charming wit, and great wisdom."

"To kick you in the arse for your vanity, more likely," Hugh scoffed.

Niall grinned. "We both know I'm not the vainest of the two of me."

Hugh chuckled. "I pray he fares well."

"How could he not?" Niall asked. "He is in a time of peace. No war. A warm bed in his own home every night. Plenty of food in *stores* on every street." He cast an eye to the sky. It was a rare dry evening. But the wisps of white cloud had taken on a gray hue. The rain would come again, soon enough.

"A store is a market, aye?" Hugh asked, and at Niall's nod of confirmation, said, "I find it difficult to conceive of markets on every street. It defies imagination."

Niall laughed. "As does all he told us. But I saw it myself."

"I still wonder at times if 'twas not an elaborate jest."

"He never came down from the tower, did he?"

Hugh shook his head, giving the impression of a beast of prey about to dig in to its dinner, but for the wrinkles of good humor around his eyes. "He did not. And I think even you and he would not carry a jest so far."

Their ponies stepped daintily down the muddy path, to the base of the glen. A stream ran through its center where Niall suspected none ran in drier years. They followed Bruce's messenger, splashing across it one after another, and with a wave of his hand, Niall sent his men off with Hugh while he proceeded to Bruce's tent.

"He's had a bad time of it." The messenger spoke quietly. "His daughter died in childbirth."

"God have mercy," Niall breathed. "After losing her mother the same way? The child?"

"They cut him from her body after she'd died. They saved him."

"God be praised for that, at least." Niall crossed himself. Allene's time was coming. He prayed she would not give life with her own death. "Our realm sorely needs one less hot-headed than the king's brother."

"Aye, He is to be thanked," the messenger agreed. "Great hopes rest upon this child. Bruce is grateful. Still, he mourns her short and tragic life and suffers great guilt that his doings caused her to spend so much of it in captivity."

"And to end this way when she finally tastes freedom," Niall said.

As they neared the tent, they fell quiet. A guard stepped forward as Niall swung down off his hobin. "Sir Niall?" he queried.

"I am," Niall said.

The guard lifted the flap. Niall entered the dim tent to see the king at a table, with James Douglas, and his nephew Thomas Randolph, the Earl of Moray. They leaned over a hide map depicting the Cheviots and Lammermuirs, and the English landscape stretching into Northumbria. They all looked up as the raised flap shot a bolt of light across the map. Dark circles etched the king's eyes. His auburn hair had more streaks of gray than when last Niall had seen him. James Douglas, ten years the king's junior, looked strong and robust beside him, his black hair and beard bristling like a lion's mane. His blue eyes wrinkled into a smile at sight of Niall. He turned to Bruce. "I believe your tonic is here."

Niall dropped to one knee, bowing, holding the harp to his back. He rose, meeting Bruce's eyes. "My apologies, Your Grace. I bring no tonic. Only my men and sword."

Thomas Randolph rolled up the map, smiling. "I believe you've brought one more thing his Grace values as much as men and swords."

Niall frowned as Randolph and Douglas left. "Your Grace?" he inquired.

"You've heard, surely," the king rubbed his forehead, "of my daughter's death."

"Aye, Your Grace. I offer my condolences."

"I've been fighting more than ten years without cease. I've brought death and ill fortune on my friends and all whom I love."

"Your Grace," Niall objected. "None have forgotten the slaughter at Berwick or the hanging of our three hundred nobles in the barns of Ayr. You've given all for Scotland. How many more would die at England's hands had you *not* led us against their tyranny?"

Bruce removed the circle of gold from his head, and pushed his hand through his hair, a gesture laden with weariness. "I pray you speak truly, young Campbell."

"Still, I've no tonic," Niall said.

"You miss the value of your own gifts," said Bruce. "My fortune has turned since the early years. I've men and swords aplenty. You will fight, aye, but I want music for my men's spirits." He propped his elbows on his table, his hands clenched. "Play for me."

"Aye, your Grace." Seating himself, Niall removed his harp from its oil cloth, and tuned it. As his fingers brought a poignant old melody to life, his eyes traveled the tent. Bruce's head bowed against his clenched hands. A crucifix stood on his bedside table, beside a silver casket. Niall guessed it held St. Fillan's arm bone, that had miraculously appeared at Bannockburn. As his fingers moved over the strings, his mind wove with the melody in and out of his king's life.

He'd been hot-headed in his youth. He'd killed John Comyn before the altar. There was not a man among them who didn't know it. Yet, he'd sought absolution, and spent the last decade atoning, seeking God, living in faith, and serving his country and his people. He'd been stricken with illnesses, lost the best years of his marriage, lived hard, watched those he loved suffer and die, and had now lost his young daughter, only nineteen. Through it all, he'd remained faithful, humble, and self-sacrificing.

Why, God? Niall asked, as his song skipped up a trail of quick notes. *Why does a good man suffer so?* It was bold. But hadn't Moses himself questioned God? Hadn't Job? It seemed an unrelenting God who would let so much evil befall such a man.

As the light outside waned, at last Bruce raised his head.

Niall let the last notes drift away.

"Thank you," Bruce said. "You have given me the peace I begged from Our Lord tonight. I am blessed."

Inverness, Scotland, June, Present

Simon found the place easily, though it looked like no court he'd ever seen. It was large, certainly, but there was no courtyard at all. And the clothing! None of Edward's court would be seen in such atrocious garb! Tickets were *sold out*, the wisp of a youth behind the counter told him. Men with the stance of guards watched him. Simon headed outside, where he circled the place, a lion pacing, seeking prey. Just as he was about to leave, a huge silver *bus* arrived behind the misnamed court. It puffed smoke from its tail, and ground to a stop. Men and women poured out, wearing more of the hideous blue leggings so common here. They opened the belly of the bus and pulled out cases. "Where's Shawn?" someone called.

An elderly man stepped gingerly from the beast. "He's coming with Amy."

At that moment, a red car slid smoothly into the lot. Simon backed under a tree as he recognized Amy inside. Both doors opened. Amy climbed out one, while the man, Shawn, emerged from the other. He wore the same trews and *leine* he'd worn in the prison, though they were now clean. He lifted a hand, smiling and calling greetings. People flocked to him, men raising hands to slap his, women pressing in. Shawn was a man with whom to be reckoned, Simon decided. He drew people. He carried power.

Simon turned his attention to Amy, taking a black, rounded case from the car. Shawn, pushing from the crowd, pulled a large case from the car. He slammed the door, and slid his free hand around Amy's waist, under the thick, black hair. Simon watched. She edged away from him, rather than leaning in. Her *boyfriend,* her *beau,* Helen had called him. Was she his mistress, but unwilling? And where was Angus? He had seemed, in the hills, to be her husband. Did he know of the two of them?

Simon licked his lips, watching dozens of men and women engulf the two of them, swarming, chattering like magpies. Finally, Shawn edged through, pulling Amy with him. He lifted his hand in farewell, grinning, and saying, "I need a few minutes. See you inside."

The crowd milled toward a small door at the back of the Court, with talk, peals of laughter, and excitement. When the last of them had gone in, Simon circled the building, returning to the front entrance.

"Still no tickets, sir," the same boy said. He leaned forward, winking. "But I could get you in to see the *rehearsal*." He held out his palm. "If you like."

"I would," Simon dug in his pocket and put a bill in the boy's hand.

He looked at it, his eyes widening, and broke into a smile. "Give me a minute." He winked and disappeared.

Just as Simon began to wonder if he'd been played for a fool, the boy reappeared, beckoning. "They're getting started," he said. "No one will notice you now." He led Simon up a flight of stairs and down a long hall, through a door. Simon found himself high in a gallery, looking down into a large chamber, where workmen bustled among dozens of chairs on a stage. The elderly man from the bus spoke to a tall youth with a shock of white hair. They traversed the stage, pointing to the balconies on either side. Simon wondered if that was where the minstrels would sit.

He sank into a cushioned seat as men and women filed on stage, carrying strange lutes, viols, shawms, and silver flutes. Simon frowned as more and more of them appeared. Twitterings and rumblings and bits of melodies gathered and filled the air. These were the minstrels? There must be a hundred! He hadn't believed the girls when they said so. And why weren't they sitting in the gallery? And—he leaned forward, scanning the dozens of faces intently—where was Shawn?

♫

Trills and scales of every timbre met Shawn's ear as he eased open the auditorium door. The crack of light at the door attracted one or two, who lifted hands to eyes, but couldn't make out who had come in. That suited Shawn.

He set his trombone case on end and took a seat beside it in one of the plush, blue ranks of chairs at the back, wanting—needing—time to adjust. *Nothing we do here means life or death.* Everything he'd done, back there with Niall, meant something. It mattered deeply that he got Niall, Bessie, and Christina out of Creagsmalan. That meant he mattered.

A man he didn't recognize strode across stage with a rose brass trombone—an Edwards like his own, he guessed, with the slender F attachment rising in a second graceful curve—laughing back at something someone said in the wings, and lifted a hand in greeting to Jim. They leaned together, speaking like old friends, as the new trombonist sat down. Shawn had never spoken like old friends with Jim. He wondered why he'd treated the man with such disdain. He seemed friendly enough. He'd always cared for Amy.

Shawn frowned, closing his eyes in sudden, painful realization. *That* was why! Jim cared for Amy. Like a father. Jim disapproved of Shawn's treatment of her. A heavy knot, like an iron mace, sank cold and hard and sharp in Shawn's stomach. Why had he never seen that? It was the same reason he'd disliked Peter. In Niall's time, they would have been the men to beat Shawn senseless for his treatment of her. Here, now, their hands were tied by law and propriety, letting Shawn laughingly scorn their impotent disapproval.

Jim snapped his fingers, one, two, three, four, and he and the unknown man began a duet, something from *Carmina Burana.* It had Amy's stamp all over it, something in the chord structure and rhythms. A frown creased his forehead. Her life had gone on without him.

Rob strolled across stage, adding a trumpet part, spinning to dizzying heights and skipping in joyful sixteenth notes over the trombone duet. Zach looked back at the three, smiling. In the wings, Zach's wife squatted behind one of the small, blonde daughters, holding her hands and clapping them in time to the music.

These people were happy without him. He closed his eyes again, letting the cheerful music spin his mind around. The sweet tones of the trumpet danced heavenward. He could walk away. They didn't need him, hadn't missed him.

Or...he could repair the damage.

Amy wasn't leaving Scotland, anyway, and as Zach pointed out, he could earn his living without the orchestra. But Amy would want him to repair the damage.

Christina would want him to.

"People, people!" Conrad's voice broke into his reverie. "Let's tune. Peter, an A, please."

A perfect A 440 hummed from Peter's violin. Shawn opened his eyes. Amy had come onstage, dressed in denim capris and a garnet red sleeveless top. Her hair hung to her waist in a thick braid, and happiness flushed her cheeks as she spoke quickly to one of the women behind her, before leaning into her own A. Her eyes would be closed, he knew, from watching her tune many times. He'd always loved the intense concentration on her face as she played. But he'd teased her about it. She reached for one of the small pins at the bottom of the strings, making a minor adjustment, and once again drew her bow across the A. The violas joined, then the cellos and, finally, the rumbling of the basses, stretched across stage left.

"Where's Shawn got to?" Conrad shielded his eyes, searching the rows of blue velvet seats.

Shawn raised one lazy hand, in a short wave. "Right here." He rose, reaching for the leather handle of the trombone case. Musicians paused in their tuning. He picked out Celine, glancing at him and burying her head again in her harp strings, plucking chords. Dana clutched her horn to her chest, one hand in the bell, her eyes on him. Did he imagine it, or could he really see hope light her face from this distance? He broke the contact, and strode to the stairs on stage left. It felt good to have the familiar weight of his trombone swinging from his hand again. It was part of him.

Back in the brass, Jim lumbered to his feet, clutching his instrument against his big belly. "Welcome home, Shawn!" he shouted, his white mustache quivering, and hung the trombone over his left arm to clap, slow and steady. Behind the timpani, Aaron joined the clapping as Shawn climbed the three stairs. Then Zach, and his wife; Shawn's mother, cradling James in the wings beside Zach's wife, beamed. The cellists shuffled and stamped their feet, many of them smiling.

Something stung in Shawn's chest. He looked to Jim, and Aaron, the last men who should be cheering him. He looked to Amy, sitting in her old place behind Peter, beaming and clapping, along with Peter and the rest of the orchestra. Maybe there was hope for his future, if they could forgive him. Only Dana sat, staring, her hands still. His gaze swung to Caroline, pumping her hands enthusiastically, smiling ear to ear. She'd be disappointed, he thought.

Conrad raised a hand for silence. "Welcome home, Shawn." He shook his hand and gestured to the podium. Shawn understood they wanted to hear from him —something, anything.

He stepped up, setting the case beside him. Silence settled. All eyes focused on him. Leave or make amends? His heart pounded. His mind went blank as he scanned a hundred pairs of waiting eyes. Usually, hundreds of eyes didn't faze him.

This was not *usually*.

"Where were you?" someone shouted. A couple others hushed that voice, but others took up the question. Amy met his eyes, a frown creasing the bridge of her nose. He smiled, almost laughed, at the thought of telling them, and held up his hand. Silence fell again.

"I've talked to those who need to know about where I've been. Contrary to what some think, it was not a stunt, it was outside my control, and you wouldn't believe me if I told you. It's quite the story."

Laughter rippled through the orchestra. Shawn always had *quite the story.*

The memory came to him of Niall in the arched window seat, playing the harp, and Christina sitting sedately with Allene, sewing altar cloths, or drawing at her easel. He didn't smile, and their laughter died away. He clenched the sides of Conrad's podium, staring at the score full of tiny notes. Amy would want him to; Christina would want him to. He raised his head, swallowing, scanning the orchestra once again. His eyes lit on Celine, behind her harp, on Caroline, Jim, Aaron. Dana. He cleared his throat. "I did a lot of good for this orchestra."

Someone clapped.

He held up a hand to stall it. "I made a lot of mistakes, too. I hurt a lot of people." He stared at the notes dancing between his fingers, hearing the music in his head. "I'm sorry." His voice cracked on the word.

Silence hung around him. They needed more.

He lifted his gaze to Amy, and the room narrowed to just her, her cheeks flushed, her long, thick braid hanging shining and dark, and her eyes, cobalt blue, giving him strength. He was intensely aware of Dana's eyes on him, of Celine's. "Amy, I'm sorry. For everything. All of it." He looked around the orchestra. Some met his eyes. Some stared at their stands or wiggled fingers on keys and valves. "To all of you I bullied to keep secrets, and lie for me, I'm sorry." His eyes swept quickly over Celine and Dana. "I hurt other people, too. I apologize to them, too."

It felt like a splinter, embedded deep in his chest, being ripped out; more like a sharp, jagged stake. It hurt horribly, it stung and tore, and it felt good to be rid of it. He felt a sting of tears in his eyes. He blinked them back fiercely, and forced his voice out in solid bass tones. "Some of you have extended the hand of friendship and second chances, and I hope—no, I plan—to be worthy of that." He thought of the Earl of Ross, granted mercy by Bruce, showing himself worthy. He could do it, too.

A murmur arose, and then, once more, the sounds of applause and shuffling, stamping feet, scattered, then growing. Jim stood up in the back. Rob stood. The woodwinds stood, except for Caroline. She polished her flute, giving him a little smile and toss of her head.

A smile burst over Shawn's face. "Let's get this show on the road," he said, and stepped off the podium.

England, July 1316

"Like old times, aye?" Lachlan asked. Their horses ambled under the July sun, climbing yet another steep path to yet another pass, with hundreds of Bruce's men before them and hundreds more behind. Niall had played late into the night for Bruce, but the music had refreshed them both, and he rode happily under blue skies. It would rain soon enough. He would enjoy the sun and the soaring purple-heathered hills while he could.

"Very much." Niall gazed up the slopes. "What was the hardest battle won?"

"Douglas says sure an it was Coldstream, and you in the thick o' it, swinging like a madman," Lachlan remarked. "I was well glad to be your friend that day, an not ha' ye standing agin me."

Lachlan, on his one side, and Owen on his other, as they'd so often traveled with Shawn, refreshed his memory, with their reminiscences of stories Shawn had long ago told him, filling in details Shawn had forgotten or not seen worth mentioning. Shawn had argued with Edward Bruce about the war-like penchant for rape. It had largely stopped.

"Ross of Kintyre was not so happy with ye after St. Bee's," Owen chuckled.

"Seems he felt ye were looking at him wi' scorn."

"Aye, I recall," Niall said. It had been Ross whom Shawn had seen emerging from a house in the town of St. Bee's, the sound of a weeping woman trailing him.

Niall smiled, seeing a man very different in their telling, than he'd heard of in his time with the orchestra; a man different, even, than he'd seen at Glenmirril, where Shawn did his share of the work running a castle, and played harp, recorder, and chess, becoming a steadily more canny opponent.

As Owen and Lachlan chatted, he fell to wondering what Shawn was doing, if Amy had forgiven him. Or had she found someone else in the years he'd been gone? It was a long time for her to be left unknowing. Shawn would go back to playing for the orchestra. No more killing for him. He would be relieved to be back. He'd soon forget all of them. Niall thought of the parchments they'd promised to write and store away deep in the Bat Cave for Shawn to find. 'Twas a fool's game. They wouldn't last seven hundred years. And how could Shawn possibly care, anyway?

Niall glanced from Lachlan to Owen, on his either side, and for a moment, loneliness hit him hard. That had been him and Shawn. It had been him and Iohn and William, farther back. And maybe, had any of them lived, it would have been him and his six brothers, riding together for their king.

"Not that their priests appreciated it." Owen's voice broke through his thoughts.

"Appreciated what?" Niall rubbed his injured arm. It ached a fair bit. He supposed he should be grateful MacDougall had only injured his arm, rather than hang him as he'd hoped to do.

"Ye're gathering wool," Lachlan complained. "He said 'twas hardly a surprise you kept the men from desecrating the church, though the priests hardly appreciated what ye did for them."

"Aye, well." Shawn had told him he'd been assigned the pillage of the churches each time. "Why me?" Niall had demanded angrily, stalking across his chambers. "Of all the things Douglas could have me raid, why kirks?"

"He knows you'll respect the church," Shawn said. "At least, I think that's why."

MacDonald and Hugh, looking up from their game of chess, nodded in unison. "Aye, Lad," Hugh had rumbled. "He's the right of it. Douglas is not one for petty vengeance. He's a job to do, and he knows you'd be the last to harm a man of God. Even an English one." He spit onto the flagstones to reinforce his opinion of the English.

"Oh, look at you now!" Allene had fussed. "Must you spit on our floor!" And the discussion had been over.

"I doubt their priests know what's been done to our priests," Niall said to Owen now, as they rode. He sighed, thinking of the speed and comfort with which a car could cross the country, and the public houses everywhere that would dispense food in minutes, rather than the need to stop, make fires, and cook their own. Yes, Shawn was no doubt happy at home, not thinking of their parchments at all. He turned his eyes to the glen below, yet another in the long maze of glens and hills that would take them into Northumbria for his first raid.

Shawn had his life. This was his.

Inverness, Present

Simon watched, through the apology, and as the performance unfolded. The young man with white hair played a cornetto like instrument, while Shawn played a large, cumbersome version of a sackbut. The music was powerful, splendid. He would command his minstrels to write something like it when he returned.

But, Simon thought, he had to revise his opinion of the man himself: Shawn was a minstrel. Nothing more.

He was popular with his own kind, but no man of power, and therefore, easily dealt with. Still, Simon thought, as Shawn lowered his instrument in the middle of a piece, and issued directives to the orchestra, he *had* emerged from the fourteenth century, and therefore was important.

Simon's eyes cut to Amy, at the front of the dais with the lute-like instrument under her chin. She, too, knew things that would help him. Did she now reside in Inverness instead of Bannockburn? And how would he follow them to find their homes when they traveled in a car? She'd been wary of him, last time he'd met her.

The rehearsal came to an end, and Simon slid from his seat, into the shadows. He edged out the door, unseen, calculating his next move.

England, Summer 1316

The first raid came as something of a shock. It shouldn't, Niall reprimanded himself. Shawn had painted a vivid enough picture. Still, despite years of cattle raids, clan feuds, and all-out battle against the English, he'd never stormed townfolk, women and children, priests. Though Shawn had described it, actually thundering down the town's cobbled street to the church was something different altogether. The wind whipped his hair behind him, Lachlan and Owen on either hand, driving their hobins and, with wild swings of their claymores, and fierce Gaelic shouts, scattering the few Englishmen who made weak efforts to block their path. Most scurried as fast as they could down dark alleys. White nightshirts flapped in the scramble. One man gripped his nightcap tight to his head, dragging a child, who howled in fear as Niall lifted his sword. Shawn would be onstage right now, Niall thought, lifting the golden *tromboon*, spilling golden sound from it.

Niall leaned tight over his pony's neck, urging it on, till it skidded to a stop, hooves scraping cobbled stones, before the kirk. He threw himself off the animal. His feet slipped, he caught himself, and charged with his men through the front doors. A grand cathedral it was, with five arches narrowing in to huge wooden doors studded with big brass rings.

Inside, massive granite pillars supported a beamed ceiling. Niall scanned the interior. As his eyes adjusted to the dim light, he saw a priest crouched in a shrine. The flames of dozens of tiny candles flickered shadows and light over him. He clapped his hands atop his head as if it would hide him. He looked up fearfully, his eyes large liquid orbs in the night church.

Sickness gnawed Niall's stomach, staring at the altar, at the candles glowing beside the tabernacle that held the Presence of Christ. Barely glancing at the priest, he barked a command at Lachlan and Owen, and strode to the front of the church, falling on his knees with a thud that jarred his kneecaps. Anger consumed him.

Why? he demanded of God. It was how Shawn would speak to God—bold, not the least aware of his own position as a mere mortal, God's creature. *I'm to respect the authority You place over me, yet You place an authority over me who tells me to pillage Your very house!*

He jabbed at his forehead, chest, and shoulders, asking forgiveness for pillaging, for his own anger. His eyes fell on the three slashes on the stair below the altar. Shawn's mark. He closed his eyes, fighting demons within. Shawn would be sitting, even now, at a place like the Two-Eyed Traitor, somewhere peaceful, calm, with a full stomach rather than Niall's own, rumbling with nothing but the bannocks and oats he'd eaten hours ago. Shawn would be strutting across stage, as Niall had one night of his life, feted and cheered by multitudes. Never again would Shawn kill or pillage or fight his own conscience to do what must be done.

"The gold is in the cellar," the priest babbled behind him. Owen and Lachlan dragged him by his elderly arms, half falling over his feet in his effort to keep up with their strong young legs. There was a crack, the inadvertent breaking of a frail bone. The old man winced, gasping, "Take it and leave us!" Owen and Lachlan released him. He dropped to his knees, in pain rather than prayer.

Niall leapt to his feet, turning on the man. "Think ye I *don't* want to leave you!" Rage throbbed through him. He wanted to be home in his own chambers with Allene and his bairn. "Curses on your Edward!" Grabbing the man's cassock, he yanked the priest to his feet. "Think ye I like this?" he demanded. "You think I *asked* to raid a house of God!"

"'Tis none of my doing," the priest protested. "Don't kill me!"

Niall gripped the old man by the front of his black robe. "Think ye any of us want any other than to live in peace! 'Tis your Edward, your own king, who denies us that and inflicts us on one another year after year. You go to your Edward, and tell him to recognize Scotland as the independent nation it always was, and ye'll have seen the last of us!"

"Niall." Lachlan laid an uneasy hand on Niall's shoulder. "Don't hurt him. We are not the English."

"Hurt him?" Niall turned to his friend. "Have I hurt priests on other raids?"

"Never." The worry did not leave Lachlan's face.

Niall's eyes dropped from the man's terrified face, to his own fist bunched in the garments of a man of God. He released the priest, horrified at himself. He was less than Shawn—Shawn who made no pretense of following God. He took an inadvertent step backward.

A moan crawled from the old man's throat. He held his arm. Niall stared, noting the awkward angle. Never in his life had he harmed a priest. He should feel guilt. But it had been unintentional. The old man looked up, pleading for sympathy. Outside, a woman screamed.

"'Tis more than broken arms for our Scottish priests," Niall said softly. "'Tis crucifixion, nailed to the door of a burning church. Pray for the souls of our priests, aye? Now give us your gold, that we might sooner stop this war."

The old man limped into the sacristy, Niall behind him, and indicated a trap door in the floor. Owen knelt, pulling the door to reveal a hidden chamber, where treasure had accumulated in the two years since their last visit. He gathered it, reaching in up to his shoulder to scoop out chalices and tapestries and rings.

"It's all there," the priest whispered. "Take it. Spare our church, I beg you do not defile the house of God."

Niall looked around the sacristy, and at the jewels and chains Lachlan lifted admiringly from the sack, letting them spill back like waterfalls of gold and gems. He scooped a handful of coins himself. He would trade it all to be with Allene. But wouldn't that defeat the purpose, he thought. Bruce used the plunder to finance the war. Candles flickered off the gold that would finally allow him to live in peace, forever with Allene.

He thought of Shawn, in a place called *The States,* across an ocean so large no man had crossed it. A corner of his mouth twitched up. Had he not seen the wonders of Shawn's time himself, he'd hardly believe it. The jewels and gold clicked softly, rattling together in his trembling hands. He dropped them abruptly, snapping, "Let's get it back to the hills."

"You always have us look in the priest's house," Lachlan whispered. "What ails you, my Lord?"

Niall cast him a sharp glance. "Yes, his home." He reached into the hole to help Owen gather communion plates and rings. "Was I not here last time? They always hide more there, do they not?"

Lachlan and Owen nodded, not looking convinced, as the priest fell to his knees, weeping into his hands. "Please, my Lord, spare us aught to feed our children." Flames from the burning town outside flung blood red shadows, raging at the high arched windows.

"As Edward spares our children?" Niall stuffed the last of the hoard into his own bag. "Two of my brothers died a most awful death on Edwards' orders. Perhaps you'd care to discuss children with my mother?" He turned and followed his men to the living quarters outside the church. A fat housekeeper keened at their entrance, burying her face in her hands as if they'd killed someone.

"Where have we found it before?" Niall asked.

Lachlan looked at him strangely. "'Twas under the housekeeper's bed. Check his, too, and around the hearth for loose stones, mind ye."

With the woman's high-pitched wail cutting through their ears, and the crackling of flames outside, they searched the small house until they'd collected another bag of precious goods.

From outside came the shrieking of women, and crying of children. The smell of burning—wood and flesh and crops—reached him, along with the roar of flames, and a huge crash as the walls of some building, not so far off, fell in.

He and Owen ripped food from the priest's cupboards, a tapestry from the wall, anything of value they could find, and the whole time, he thought of Shawn, dining in leisure and peace of mind at the Two-Eyed Traitor. Bitterness seeped deeper, thinking of Iohn's betrayal. A restaurant in his memory, bah! It had been two years since he'd thought of it. But it filled his mind now.

"The horses," Owen reminded Niall.

Anger reared full blown, as he and Owen passed into the small stable behind the rectory, releasing the lone horse from its stall, and gathering the fine saddle hanging on the wall. The flames outside cast red, dancing shadows on the stable walls. Sweat flowed freely down Niall's back in the heat. The horse whinnied and reared, skittish of the fire. When, in Shawn's life, would his best friend ever try to kill him for land? For a title? When would he be forced to do things that appalled him? Or anything less pleasurable than playing music?

Owen pulled on the horse's reins, whispering to it, soothing it, till it danced back to earth, whickering. Niall hefted the saddle onto its back, buckling it underneath as the animal sidestepped again. The Scots had few horses, tending toward the small, tough hobins that could maneuver their rugged Highland hills. But a horse had uses, and Douglas would be pleased. Outside, a woman let out a piercing wail, keening a descant over the roaring drone of the flames and ostinato, arrhythmic shouts of men. His own personal orchestra, Niall thought sardonically.

He knotted the bag of gold to the pommel, as flames licked in around the window, and turned the horse over to Owen. "Take it up the hill," he ordered. He let himself back into the church, shutting out the worst of the cries and screams, the worst stench of burning, and dropped to his knees before the altar. He trailed his fingers over Shawn's three carved lines; his mind swam with images and hatred and resentment. It wasn't fair that Shawn—Shawn who sneered at God—got a life of ease while he spent every day grappling with death.

A wraith glided up beside him, breathing deeply. He looked up at the priest. Pain etched the papyrus skin over his emaciated skull. They stared at one another as flames cast waving shadows across the stained glass windows. "I wish 'twas not this way," Niall finally said. "'Tis sorry I am—for your arm."

The priest laid his good hand on Niall's shoulder. "In another time and place, we might be friends, aye?"

"There's a prophecy." Niall laid his own hand over the frail bones of the priest's, where it rested on his shoulder. "One day England and Scotland will live in peace." He rose to his feet, and touched the withered cheek. "Would that day comes soon." His voice cracked. "I'm sorry."

CHAPTER SEVEN

Inverness, Scotland, Present

In the narrow hallway, Shawn tugged at his cuff, even as he gripped the trombone, trying to hold it away from the press of black- and tuxedo-clad musicians flowing around them, toward the stage. The jacket clung irritably after two years in bell sleeves. A percussionist slapped him on the back. "Good to have you back."

"Hold *still*!" Amy tried to tie his bow tie.

"It feels like a noose," he grumbled. But he let go of the cuffs and lifted his chin. "How in the world did I play in this stuff?" Another group jostled past, offering Shawn congratulations and good wishes.

She laughed, leaned close, and whispered, "Niall felt the same way."

"Yes, they're still talking about his solution." He chuckled. He'd watched the video of Niall, in his own medieval clothing, telling the audience, *Tonight, I am Lord Niall Campbell, born in 1290.* "That took some chutzpah."

"Something he doesn't lack." She looked around the hallway, nearly empty now, and spoke softly. "Just remember, they think it was you." She gave the tie one last, sharp tug, and patted his cheek. It wasn't a pat he wanted. "Break a leg."

He laughed again. "I said that to Niall once. He said he'd rather not." He lifted the trombone and blew a high B flat, sliding easily up to the note above it.

She smiled, picking up her violin and bow off a table. "I imagine." It had been in this hallway, after a concert, that she'd kissed Niall. She didn't want to think about it. "Ready to play harp for an audience like this?"

He lowered the trombone. "I was born ready."

"A truer thing was never said."

They looked at each other for a moment in silence. He placed a hand on her black sleeve. The curtain of nervousness fell immediately, shading her eyes. She swallowed and looked away. "I don't think...."

"I told you everything in Tioram. I apologized for everything."

Amy glanced at the far end of the hall, and gave a small, sharp shake of her head.

Shawn turned. Caroline came toward them, her silver flute glinting back fluorescent lights as it swung from her hand, her black sweater as tight as it had always been. He realized he was frowning at her. He turned back to Amy, her head down, her shoulders tense.

Before he could speak, Caroline stopped next to them. Her fingers, with red oval nails, crawled up his arm. "Welcome home, Shawn," she cooed. "I can't wait to hear you play again." She raised herself on her toes and kissed his cheek, though he backed away. She gave Amy a wink, and left.

"Forget her," Shawn said, as she disappeared down the hall. "There's still a place for us here. Come back to the States with me."

Amy twisted under his grip. "I, um, you know, I have to go. They've all left. The big stars can wait, but the peon musicians need to be out there like now."

"Amy, what else do you want from me? What else can I do? I'll buy you a house and a horse...."

Her head snapped up. "You can stop the mind movies for me, okay?" Anger burned in her eyes. "Can your money do that? And restore my faith in people after you showed me how easy it is to lie? Pulling the knife out is a good start, but I'm still bleeding. Did you entirely miss what Caroline just did? The results of your actions don't stop just because you said you're sorry." She pulled away from him and pushed out the door behind Caroline.

He stood, staring after her. Still bleeding... He'd deal with Caroline, let her know she'd be out if she didn't stop. He leaned against the table, working his slide up and down, like a boat skimming over a glass lake, and shook his head. No. That would be his old, bullying ways. And he had no say in the orchestra anymore, anyway. Maybe the answer was not to play with Conrad, even for guest appearances. But he'd already signed the contract. He could honor that and the other gigs he'd already arranged, and move to Scotland himself. He'd almost never see Caroline again, or Celine. Maybe it would put Amy's mind at ease.

Over the speakers in the hallway, he heard Peter's A 440. The rest of the orchestra joined, one by one, working their way down the score order from the bright, sweet tones of flutes and oboes down to the low, dark sounds of tuba, trombone, and bassoon. He lifted his own instrument, sliding to second position and pouring warm air through. His eyes closed listening to the A over the loudspeaker. Perfect.

The door from the green room opened. Zach entered the hallway, tall, blonde, and good-looking in his tuxedo. His trumpet dangled from one hand. He stretched out the other, shaking. "It's going to be good," he said. From the speakers above came the first shimmering notes of *Benedictus*. They sparkled on Shawn's brain like the snowflakes dancing in the forest as he'd ridden through with Niall. Conrad had been shocked Shawn had no memory of the piece. "It's Alexander Campbell MacKenzie, a Scottish composer!" he'd ranted.

Shawn didn't admit the name meant nothing to him. But *Campbell* jumped out at him. Campbells had survived at Bannockburn, thanks to Niall's intervention, and this Campbell had been born when, in Shawn's life before disappearing in time, the man's ancestors had likely been killed. It hurt his brain to think about it.

"Trombone, harp, what else can you surprise them with?" Zach pulled his attention back to the present.

Shawn grinned, glad for an easy question. "I've gotten pretty good at recorder, the last couple years." He caught his mistake immediately, but Zach didn't react. Presumably he thought Shawn had been playing it since before his disappearance. The violins pulled out long chords. He could see it, as if he stood before them, the bows swaying like nymphs above the sea of the orchestra. Amy would be leaning into her violin, her face a mask of concentration.

Shawn and Zach smiled at each other, at a loss for words. Shawn wanted to ask, *How did you manage to do it all right when I messed up what I had so badly?* He didn't know the man well enough, not like he'd known Niall. He supposed Zach had led a different life, one where his father wasn't murdered for drugs.

And he supposed that was an excuse.

The flutes came in on cue, piping over the loudspeaker. The look on Amy's face, when Caroline kissed him, stood out in stark, bold colors in his mind's eye, and he understood: his apology didn't erase the past. An apology was barely a start.

Zach nodded toward the door in invitation, and they headed down the white hall to the dark wings of backstage. Kristen, Zach's wife, with her flounce of soft brown hair, holding a blonde daughter on each hip, leaned forward to give Zach a kiss, and they stood back, whispering to one another, smiling, their eyes alight, wrapped together in their own private Heaven.

Shawn looked away, feeling powerfully the presence of Christina, as she'd last stood with him in the Bat Cave. Was it just a week ago? She was long dead. He wondered if she looked down on him from her own Heaven, standing in these dark wings right now, if she waited eagerly to hear him play in his own world with the orchestra behind him. It made him happy to think she did.

England, Summer 1316

Day followed night and night followed day, the only certainty being uncertainty —except for the certainty of rain. He might sit around the campfires many more nights, Niall thought, under drizzle or downpour with Lachlan and Owen, playing his harp and speaking of home, of Margaret, Allene, and all they knew and loved. He might, as easily, be burying any of them, as singing around a campfire with them.

Or they might be burying him.

They hit Berwick on midsummer's day, with no more luck than in previous attempts, then stormed south, burning and pillaging, shouting fearsome cries that sent the English scurrying for the hills while the Scots looted their towns. Charred and devastated land trailed them all the way to Richmond, where a contingent of clerics hastened to meet them, trembling under a damp, white banner, on the drizzly road. Bruce, Moray, and Douglas entered the castle there with a strong guard, and came out with news they would sleep indoors that night. Men whooped with glee.

Food was scrounged from somewhere, despite heavy rains, and placed on the tables before Bruce's thousand men by young boys daring brave glances at the Scottish devils. *The Black Douglas!* they whispered. The gentle Jamie Douglas scared the English with the mere sound of his name.

Niall played and sang while the men ate, and the rain beat a harsh staccato against heavy lead glass in the windows high above. At his side, Conal harmonized in his soft tenor, though not as well as Iohn or Shawn, singing of lost love, battles heroically won, and battles tragically lost. Around them, men smiled for the first time in many weary weeks, as they sang the choruses.

Niall was able to forget, for a time, the image of the elderly priest, his face etched in pain. Drafts of ale kept his voice going as servants moved about the hall pouring wine and clearing bones, as English hounds sniffed for scraps. Niall thought of the days he and Iohn had sung in the great hall, and two years of music in the Bat Cave and solar with Shawn. Life marched on, claiming one friend after another.

He closed his eyes, searching for the gratitude that had once been so natural. *God,* he prayed as he plucked the wire strings, *make me a better man tomorrow than I was today. I seem to be going backward rather than forward.* But all he could see, in the dark of his mind, was Shawn's luxurious suite in twenty-first century Inverness. What wouldn't he give for a hot shower right now? He smiled, thinking of the sweet lattes that had jolted him awake each morning.

It had been a pleasant dream, no more, he reprimanded himself. He was lucky to have sweet memories, but this—cold nights on wet ground, skirling, fire, sacking churches—this was real life. He sighed. Try as he might, he saw little for which to be grateful, and wondered what he'd once been so darn happy about. Good food, a warm roof, he reminded himself. Good friends.

Only Conal at his side stayed his urge to snort. Tough dried meat and hard bannocks were hardly good food. Stars were not a warm roof. His brothers were dead, Iohn had betrayed him, Lachlan and Owen knew him so little that they weren't even aware they'd been friends with two different men these past years, and Shawn had disappeared into the mists of time. Even Allene was beyond his reach, many days' ride away behind Glenmirril's walls.

When even the ale could not keep the scratchy sound of exhaustion at bay, when the gaunt English hounds, starving like the rest of Europe, wolfed down what few scraps the Scots failed to devour, when the men rolled into their tartans in the rushes, with the eternal rain pattering on the windows, Niall lowered the harp and took his place, with his men, next to Hugh, who guarded the main doors to the great hall.

"Well done," Hugh whispered. Speaking softly was an accomplishment for him.

"Is it?" Niall tucked his father's sword under his tartan. "It seems but little in the face of starvation and war."

"Do you disregard your king's words?" Hugh asked. "Healing men's souls is the greatest good a man can do. You've become discontent, Niall. 'Tis unlike you."

Niall's breath slid out, unbidden, in a heavy sigh. The men were several feet away, sleeping soundly. Still, he chose his words with care. "He lives in peace, with those he loves, sleeping safe and warm between silken sheets, eating what he chooses, when he chooses. Yes, I am discontent knowing how good life can be, having once tasted that life. I think on all the Laird has read from Holy Scriptures, year after year, and I see what great fault it is in me, the envy. You need not tell me."

Hugh chuckled softly, a rumble in his large frame. "You're not the first man to feel it, and sure ye'll not be the last."

"That doesn't make it right." Niall stared out rain-spattered casements, to a sky fading to twilight.

"It makes it human." Hugh murmured the words like a giant's snore. "Our Lord has His reasons." His elbows resting on his knees, Hugh stared up at the dark clouds glowering in the window. "I've not always liked being the size of a bear, but God had Scotland in mind when He gave me size and strength, and I'll not tell the Creator of the Heavens I've other ideas."

"You've never seemed discontent with aught." Niall settled himself on his tartan, head pillowed in his clasped hands.

"We're all discontent with summat. Find the reasons, Niall, and discontent melts like snow in May."

"Tell me what reasons you see." The edge of bitterness that crept into his voice surprised Niall. "Why was I shown something beyond my grasp? Something that only makes me see how bad our lives really are? I never saw it before."

"You've the gift of leadership. But you grew up in this war. Malcolm and I, we remember peace, traveling freely, living freely. The young men of Scotland have known naught but war. They need the vision of freedom you were given. And the promise it will come."

When Niall said nothing, Hugh leaned forward, his bushy beard nearly scraping the floor. His eyes burned. "I've spent *twenty years* fighting England, Niall. D' ye not think I lose hope? We routed them at Bannockburn, and still they fight. D' ye know what it does for me, knowing peace *will* come? It puts power in my every step and every swing of the sword. It tells me if I die on the morrow, 'twill not be in vain. Men need to know their lives—and deaths—are not in vain. You and I, though we can't tell them, we know we will win peace, and our men see it in the way we fight. Because we *know* how the story ends!"

"You've great wisdom, Hugh." Niall smiled at last.

The corners of Hugh's eyes wrinkled. His beard lifted with his smile. "Aye, well, don't bandy it about. I've managed quite well till now playing the fool, aye?"

"Tell me," Niall said, "does the story, before it ends, include me spending time with my wife? Ever?"

"Raids last but so long," Hugh said, "and we'll be back in our Highlands. You'll be with Allene and your bairns." He clapped a hand on Niall's shoulder. "Get some rest. Dawn comes quickly."

"Aye." Niall stared out the window at the dark clouds blotting the sky.

"Niall," Hugh rumbled insistently.

Niall rolled his head to look at the man who had been there from his earliest childhood memories, the giant of Glenmirril, who always smiled.

"*You* cannot lose faith," Hugh whispered harshly. "Our men look to *you* for their own faith."

Niall said nothing, but turned his eyes back to the window, seeking even a single star behind the thick, rolling clouds.

Inverness, Present

The stage blazed with flood lights and the energy of the audience, cheering and shouting for Zach. Shawn stepped out, doubling the cheering. Girls screamed his name. He turned to Amy, behind him, giving her a smile and a wink. He wouldn't be seduced by it this time. He closed his eyes, listened for his cue—a flurry of fifths from Aaron on the timpani—and jumped in, the slide flashing, notes tripping out the end of the bell. Two years of fighting beside Douglas slipped away, as he swam once more in his natural habitat. The concerts in the Bat Cave and every other concert swirled around him, becoming one with the present, filling him with Joy.

Music and applause and speeches and the shouts of his own name spun around him like the colors of a kaleidoscope, until suddenly, it was over, musicians ambling to the wings, some squatting at the stage edge talking to audience members, others chatting among themselves.

"Got a party going, Shawn?" The young clarinet player clapped him on the shoulder as they headed into the dark wings.

Shawn glanced at Zach. He'd invited Shawn and Amy to join him and his family at a pub. He could meet them there after a quick party.... Shawn stopped. He'd just get drunk at a party; maybe do something stupid. "No, no parties. Maybe Rob wants to organize something."

He turned, with a smile for a fan, an older gentleman with thinning hair and a receding jaw. "Thank you, Sir, yes, I'm very happy to be back."

"Ye'll no say where ye've been?"

Shawn laughed. "Isn't it more fun reading the wild stories the papers come up with? This must be your beautiful wife? How did you enjoy the concert, Ma'am?"

"Marvelous," gushed the elderly woman beside him. Her blue-rinsed hair bobbed in enthusiasm. "The way you and Zach played together! Amazing!"

As the crowd thinned, Zach waved at him over the remaining heads. Shawn waved back, excusing himself from a young woman. "Where's Amy?" he asked, reaching Zach's side.

Kristen stood beside her husband. "I think she stepped out to get a little air." She fanned herself with a program, and blew in her daughter's face with a little laugh. "It's hot back here."

"Thanks." Shawn turned back for the heavy, steel door that led to the parking lot behind the theater. He pushed it open, onto a narrow metal catwalk in the cool June evening. Stars winked down from a sky of deep dusky blue. The soaring stone walls of the Bishop's Palace met the theater's modern magenta cement at the corner where he stood. The cat walk dropped, a few short steps, to the parking lot.

Somewhere in the dark lot, a man spoke. "I'm sorry. I shouldna have come. I thought you'd not see me."

There came a soft, indistinguishable murmur of a feminine voice. Shawn scanned the lot and saw them: two dark shadows, one in a flowing skirt, a hair breadth between them, by the Bishop's Palace.

"I only wanted to see you play. I promised I'd let you work it out, no pressure."

More murmurs. Shawn became still, wary of jarring the metal walkway. Amy hadn't mentioned Angus all week. She'd refused to answer questions, and he'd dropped it, confident he'd won her over, despite her continued insistence that he sleep on the couch.

"But how do you feel?" It was the Interloper. The glow of the performance faded. Except...maybe the man would see what he was up against and go away. But then...Amy seemed to value other things these days. *Nothing we do here means life or death.* He listened to soft murmurs and intimate laughs, like Zach and his wife backstage. The shadows met, his hand on her face, and melded.

Shawn's fist curled. She'd let *him* kiss her only once, in the tower, and though her heart often glowed in her eyes when she looked at him, she kept him at arm's length. He strained forward, wanting to hear her answer. How *did* she feel? And why hadn't he asked her himself?

Her voice rose, agitated. "I thought he was dead, or I never would have let myself fall in love with you and put us, put *you*, in this position."

"'Twas my own fault," said the Interloper. "'Twas no time to bring you coffee."

There was a laugh, they came together again, with more of the soft sounds that made Shawn want to kill someone. He turned, numb; careful of the chinking of the metal walkway, and eased the heavy stage door open, sliding back into the riptide of people who loved him.

♫

They had arrived in throngs, the men in black outfits or tartans about their waists, the women in gowns that shimmered, as if adorned by the stars of heaven. They flowed, with laughter and chatter as sparkling as their clothing, into the Court. Simon watched. Everything about them spoke of riches. If he couldn't get in, he would wait behind the Court to help himself to money afterward.

He rounded the building, choosing a spot under an oak, as the sky turned dusky. Finally, his wait was rewarded. A man came down the narrow street. Simon drew back behind his tree, watching for his chance. The man came closer, and with a start, Simon recognized Angus.

He melted farther back.

Angus passed by, unaware, stopping only feet from Simon and staring toward the back of the Court. There came a soft metallic clanking from the building itself. Simon peered cautiously around the great trunk, into the night. A shadow crossed the lot in a dark dress swirling to her toes. Long hair swung across her back. She flew into Angus's arms, hugging him tightly. They spoke softly, foreheads touching, his hands on her face, stroking her hair. He kissed her.

Simon frowned, trying to sort it out. They'd been hiking together, they had a child. What did Angus know of Shawn and Amy?

Angus pulled back abruptly. "I shouldn't have come," he said huskily. He took Amy's elbow, and directed her back toward the building. She went halfway, stopping to look back. Angus shook his head, and she turned, going up the clanking steps.

Angus stood motionless, staring after her. Finally, he turned. Simon pulled back. Angus scanned the trees for a long minute, before going out the narrow path on which he'd come. When he reached the end, Simon emerged from the trees. He'd hoped to replenish his cash with whatever hapless fool came this way in the dark. Instead, he would take his chance to find Angus's home. He smiled. That was also knowledge that might serve him well.

Glenmirril, Summer 1316

Under dusky twilight skies, Allene found her father on the parapets, in the perpetual drizzle, staring up at the black clouds that shrouded the western hills. He turned as she approached, and slipped his arm around her waist.

"What are you doing here, Father? The guards are on duty."

"Waiting to see the stars," he said.

"You'll not see them this night."

MacDonald smiled. "I see them there, behind the clouds." He looked down at her. "Is the bairn well?"

Allene laid a hand on her stomach. "Very well, Father."

"And you? You're well, lass?"

"Aye." She laid her head on his shoulder. "Apart from worrying about Niall."

"Father offers every mass for our men's safety," her father said.

"And as often as not, there are new widows when they return."

He squeezed her shoulder. "There will be better days, Lass. Shawn told us so."

"How many men must die before that time?" Allene asked. "He couldn't tell us when it happened."

"Then we must wait and see."

In the distance, above the tree line, three riders appeared. Allene recognized Christina's blue cloak. "And hope Niall is still alive when that time comes," she said.

"Faith, Lass."

Allene and her father watched from the parapets as Christina guided her hobin, picking its delicate way down the steep, muddy slope, pawing now and again as a stone slipped under its hoof. She disappeared under the trees, re-emerging minutes later, followed by an older man and the boy Niall and Shawn had brought with them from Carlisle.

"Red is quite devoted to her," she said, watching them.

"Aye," her father agreed. "The poor lad has been through a great deal in his short life. He's taken Shawn's leaving hard."

"As have others." Allene watched the riders silently for several moments before adding, "I'm grateful she *took* an escort this time."

"Has she not been doing so?" Her father rubbed his chin, under his big red and silver beard.

Allene shook her head. "Red, in fact, has chastised her for it." She sighed. "She is changed, Father. She is once more the woman who came to us from MacDougall. She smiles and is serene. But 'tis a mask."

"She was not harmed in their attack?"

Allene shook her head. "She was in my chambers, quite safe. Perchance it is the realization they may attack at any time. Or MacDougall being here."

"Should his confinement not give her peace? He has been a model prisoner."

"Which ought to give us pause," Allene said tartly.

"Aye, so it ought," the Laird replied. "But I talk often with Taran, I look in on him myself, and he remains quiet. He is no threat to Christina, and Duncan is dead."

"I know not, Father. She is pleasant, but says naught of importance. Summat is amiss, but she'll not say what."

MacDonald sighed. Christina and her escort descended to the drawbridge. She lifted her eyes to Allene and MacDonald on the tower, but gave no acknowledgment beyond a nod of the head.

"There's little to be done," MacDonald said, "If she'll not say. I'm sorry, lass."

Allene sighed, wanting more, needing to talk. She squeezed her father's hand, and turned for her chambers, where the wall sconces burned against coming night. There, she pulled out a roll of parchment and the quill with which she had tutored Shawn in correct penmanship, and seated herself at the desk near the window. She would talk with quill and parchment, and leave letters for Shawn as they'd promised.

Inverness, Present

The crowd, flooding from the Court as Angus reached the main road, made it easy for Simon to follow him, unobserved. But Simon doubted he needed the crowd. Angus stuck his hands in his pockets, his shoulders hunched, as he headed north along the river, and crossed onto a white, lacy bridge. Simon waited, not wanting to expose himself. But Angus stopped in the middle, his arms leaning on the white rail. He gazed into the water, motionless. A couple passed behind him. A pair of girls ran up onto the bridge, gushing. "His *hair!*" the tall one squealed. "I just want to run my *hands* through it!"

Simon rolled his eyes.

On the bridge, Angus glanced at them, and turned back to the water.

The evening crowd grew, as more people left the concert. Angus crossed the bridge, disappearing among them. Simon hurried after him, through the throngs. Water slapped on the river's banks as he pushed between two men wearing more of those plaids wrapped around their waists. "Watch yourself," one of them called after him. Simon threw a glare over his shoulder and turned in pursuit of Angus.

He stopped, staring into the night, the crowd.

Angus was nowhere to be seen.

Simon gave up on subtlety, bolting for the corner. He turned, looking first one way and then another. There was no sign of Angus. Simon chose a street and ran to the next corner. Only two girls walked in the dusk, between rows of houses.

Simon swore a medieval oath. He closed his eyes, tamping the anger. As his battle calm took over, he realized it didn't matter. Much as he guessed Angus had knowledge, he *knew* Shawn did. He was as well known as the great knights of great courts. He would be easy to find.

CHAPTER EIGHT

Inverness, Present

"It's quiet here tonight." Zach looked around the dim pub. His girls bounced up and down, excited by their concert dresses and being out late in the city. Following the waitress, he carried Emma on his hip, while Kristen led Sophie by the hand to a booth at the back. A few people looked up and gave nods of recognition as they walked through, still in their tuxedos, Amy in her black skirt and blouse, a diaper bag slung over her shoulder. Shawn carried James, sleeping now, in one arm.

He'd taken Amy's hand, and she hadn't objected, though she frowned, apparently deep in thought, whenever she looked at him. He should just admit he'd heard, he thought. She'd volunteered nothing about Angus being there. He'd ask her later, when they got back to the hotel.

"There ye are, then!" The waitress slid menus onto the table, and stood back. The little girls clambered onto the seats, bouncing with excitement, while Kristin slid in after Emma, settling them into something more mannerly with soft words. "Can I get ye something to drink?" the waitress asked.

With orders placed, the group settled in.

"You really turned this orchestra into something amazing," Kristin said to Shawn. His attention was less on her words than on Zach helping Emma sip from a glass of water too large for her. He glanced at Amy, leaning close to Sophie to say something. The little girl giggled, shaking curly blonde pig tails. Shawn's mind jumped like forked lightning from one thought to another. Did the Interloper have children, nieces, nephews? Did he like watching Amy with children as Shawn always had?

"The music you and Amy put together gets the audience so enthusiastic."

He could really lose her. It had never crossed his mind as a real possibility. His heart pounded a little harder, and his arms wrapped more tightly around James.

"After the last concert, we had four requests for the quintet arrangements. Are you thinking of publishing those?"

Emma finished sipping the water, and Zach lifted the glass back to the table. In his action, Shawn saw the centuries-gone ghost of Ronan stooping his gaunt frame to help one of Adam's children gather eggs.

"You're quite talented," Kristin added.

"*Tapadh leat*," Shawn murmured. The child had tripped, breaking the eggs. Ronan took the blame when Adam's widow stormed into the bailey, berating the unfortunate boy.

"*Tahpa*, what?" asked Kristin.

Shawn jolted back to the present, confused. A pub surrounded him—a modern pub. *Ronan's gone!* He laughed, drawing Amy's attention from Sophie. They both looked up at him. "*Tapadh leat*, thank you in Gaelic."

"You speak Gaelic?"

Amy stared at him, waiting for his answer.

"A little."

"He's fluent," Amy said. "In both modern and medieval Gaelic."

Zach looked up from the glass, smiling. "Say something."

"*Tha mo cridhe beubanaichte, tha mi briseadh-cridhe,*" he said. It was a line Christina had quoted. *My heart is torn, I am broken-hearted.*

Emma bounced on her seat, delighted with the sound.

"What does it mean?" asked Kristin.

He hadn't lost his knack for thinking up stories. He clapped his hands, rubbed them together, and grinned. "I'm hungry enough to eat a horse!"

Amy stared at him, not smiling like the others. "You must have said you have your heart set on a horse."

The waitress appeared, sliding plates across the table, with a cheery warning they were hot. Under cover of Kristin and Zach leaning in to divvy a meal between the two girls, Amy added, "Except the word horse was not in there."

Shawn's smile slipped. "How much Gaelic do you know?" he asked.

"I learned quite a bit with Angus while we looked for you."

He bit back the words, *He speaks Gaelic? To you?* It had been something between them, the words whispered in Gaelic. He didn't want to give the Interloper time or thought.

"Why is your heart torn?" she asked.

He looked from James, stirring in his arms, to Amy, unable to answer. He hadn't been accustomed to telling her his deepest thoughts. He hadn't been accustomed to looking at his own deepest thoughts, and wasn't sure himself of all the ways in which his heart was torn.

"Tell Mr. Kleiner what you think of Scotland," Zach was saying to Emma.

She gulped a mouthful of fish pie, and said, "It's cold. I like the dancing. Daddy said you dis-peared."

"Now, Emma, how did...?"

"Can you make yourself inbis-bul now, Mr. Finer? I want to see!"

Zach and Kristin stared at her, flustered. Heat climbed up Kristin's face. "I'm sorry. She heard us saying you're back...."

Amy laughed, breaking the tension. "Emma, invisible means you *can't* see him."

"I can make a quarter disappear," Shawn offered.

Emma clapped, bouncing and encouraging him. Zach and Kristin relaxed.

Amy handed him a coin, smiling, even as he shifted James to her arms. Her nephews had loved the trick and begged him to do it over and over. Her face lit with the look in her eyes that always made him melt, made him feel he could do anything, *would* do anything, to keep her.

He smiled at her. *Take that, Interloper. I bet you don't know a coin trick.* Leaning across the table, he pressed the coin to Emma's right ear, and palmed it. Her eyes grew wide. It was easy to slip the coin under a napkin while she shook her head, and turn up his hands, showing her his empty palms.

"But it's in my ear now!" She frowned. Sophie, squeezed between Zach and Kristin, laughed out loud. Shawn slid the coin from under the napkin, unseen by the girls, and put his hand under Emma's left hear. He tapped the right side of her head, and showed her the coin in his palm. She took it, studying it incredulously.

Amy's hand crept into his, under the table. He turned to her, smiling. But she looked as if her own heart was torn.

Shawn watched them through the evening, as he gradually relaxed. A hot toddy helped, with its lemon floating in hot amber liquid, but it was more than that. Zach and Kristin either knew nothing of his prior reputation—which seemed unlikely in the sense of impossible—or didn't hold it against him, despite the fact that they were clearly not among those who would have found his antics amusing. Needing to make up for the missed months, he held James, except for the brief time Amy threw a blanket over her shoulder and nursed him. He retrieved him to rest him on his shoulder and rub his back.

"Watch your tux." Amy slid a cloth over his shoulder. As she did, James gurgled and spit out a stream of white. Shawn thought of the last baby, the one he hadn't wanted, and wondered, would it have been a boy or a girl? Black hair like James? Or his own ginger? Would they have been like Kristin and Zach, each holding a child, whispering secrets, and smiling in the wings?

It would start now, he promised himself. It already had, with her hand on his shoulder, and the two of them smiling at each other over their child.

"They both try to play the piano," Zach was saying. "Sophie's started lessons."

Niall's hopes for his son had been survival, peace. "You want them to go into music?" Shawn asked.

"I want them to be happy. I want them to be good people."

It had been his father's answer, when people asked. The little girls worked on their mugs of hot chocolate, Emma on Kristin's lap, while Kristin tried desperately to prevent hot chocolate dripping on her daughter's concert dress. Images of his own family, himself and his parents, surrounded him, going to dinner one night years before his father's murder; of Niall and Allene in their chambers, standing over their own James in a bassinet. This is what families were. It's what he and Amy could be; what they could have been already, had he been wiser.

"That should be what we all want for our children," Amy said.

Shawn rubbed James's back. He wanted that above all for his son, and he saw with a jolt, that he himself had failed his father, by letting The Boy undo all his father had given him. James twisted his head into the curve of Shawn's shoulder, his breath warm and damp on his neck. Shawn smiled.

"You never quite get over your own children, do you?" Zach said.

"I know I won't," Shawn said.

Zach cleared his throat in the sudden awkward silence. "You're flying home with the orchestra tomorrow?"

Shawn glanced at Amy. She turned her attention to her food. Any hope he'd had that she would change her mind at the last minute disappeared. "Yeah, my things are packed," he said. He thrilled to the soft, warm weight of James on his chest, wrapped in his arms. He didn't want to leave him, either. "Lindsay's got interviews and talk shows set up for me. Ben's got a concert lined up for me, and has started planning a tour. I'll make sure my house is still there, play the concert, and...come back here."

Amy turned to him, questioning.

He didn't say it in front of Zach and Kristin. *Do you want me back?* He'd have to assume. He'd have to change her mind if she didn't. "I should be able to take care of everything in a couple of weeks. My mom's staying with you, right?"

Amy nodded. "I don't know what I'd do without her at this stage."

She made no objection to him coming back. She gave no encouragement.

He held James more tightly. It would have to work. He'd promised himself, and he still saw the look in her eyes that said he had a chance. A good one.

England, Summer 1316

"Not so energetic as ye once were," Owen said. They waited at twilight, several dozen men on a forested ridge, looking down a wooded slope into the English village of Furness. Evening damp dripped off leaves. Mist curled through the forest ferns, around the trunks of trees. Their horses danced under them, ears pricked forward to the smell of smoke rising from the glen below.

"What do you mean?" Niall asked.

"These last years, it seemed you were everywhere, doing everything, yet never tired. Now, you look as though you'd rather go to bed for a good long time."

Niall grinned, hiding the shock Owen's words sent through him. Before Shawn, he'd been respected, admired, even a little feared. Shawn's secret presence had launched him beyond that, to legendary proportions. Without Shawn, he felt, somehow, less than he had been.

He glanced down the ridge. Hugh was too far away to be any use. He shrugged and asked, "Do any of us want to be attacking yet another town?" He himself wanted more than anything to be with Allene, with James, to be there with her in childbirth, in case he lost her. It tore at his heart, knowing he might already have seen her for the last time on this earth, if things went poorly. "Do the blood and fire and screaming of women and children not make you want to go back to bed?"

"Aye, at times," Owen said.

From his other side, Lachlan spoke. "It makes me want to strike harder, faster, and more often, so they'll the sooner give us peace, and let me go home to Margaret."

"Where you'll go to bed," Owen said with a sly wink.

"Aye." Lachlan smiled pleasantly. "For a good, long while."

They fell silent, listening to the steady *drip drip drip* trickling down off the leafy canopy, landing on foliage, and metal helmets. Niall tried to say silent prayers, as the glen below grew darker. But the words slipped away into the distraction of the men around him, townsfolk moving in the village below, mist rising on the fields, watchmen setting torches aflame. Finally, with dark swallowing the land, Niall gave up on prayer, and spoke. "'Tis time."

Drawing his sword, raising it to signal the men lining the ridge, he gave the reins a sharp snap across his pony's neck—Shawn's pony, he corrected himself—and threw himself into a headlong race down the wooded slope, dozens of men and beasts flying beside him, around him. Their animals strained, hooves flying over rough ground, skimming over boulders and around trees and brush.

They'd done it often enough, Niall thought with anger. He leaned low under summer leaves flashing over his head, night wind blowing in his face. As they burst from the treeline onto rocky hill, dozens of men let loose blood-chilling skirling. Shouts of alarm exploded from the town.

They hit the bottom of the hill, speeding into a wall of chaos, of screaming, women in ghostly white nightdresses grabbing terrified children, men in nightshirts swinging scythes, or women rushing bairns to protection behind wooden hovels. Some tried, senselessly, to race for the town already flooded with raiding Scots.

As he did in each town, hating it more each time, Niall took gold from the kirk. As he, Lachlan, and Owen emerged onto the church steps, into the night drizzle, laden with heavy bags, he peered down the cobbled streets. What he saw made him stop so suddenly that Lachlan bumped into him, sending him stumbling down the first step as Hugh appeared beside him, a large bag in one hand.

"Look, Hugh." Niall pointed down the rain-smeared street, to a small squat complex. Smoke poured from the chimney of one thatched roof.

Hugh spoke one word. "Iron."

Lachlan breathed out slowly. "'Tis a foundry!"

"What wouldn't the Bruce do for so much?" Owen asked.

"Call Randolph and Douglas," Niall said. "There'll be iron aplenty on the homes, too, if there's a foundry here." He turned to Hugh, excitement lighting his voice. "Set the men to searching the town!" He whooped suddenly. "We've a great gift for our king and our country!"

"Praise God," Hugh said, and winked.

♫

Hours later, they melted into the dark peaks and misty glens, mingling with a stream of retreating Scots, moving silently under the drizzling night sky, with fifty cattle, dozens of prisoners, and horses stumbling under the weight of swords, axes, spears, knives, plate, bars of unprocessed iron from the foundry, iron fencing and grating torn from houses and the abbey, plating torn from doors, nails, arrowheads, scythes, and plows. Behind them, flames danced against dark clouds. Smoke drifted in black trails across the face of the silver moon, its pungent smell following them deep into the hills.

Niall half-dozed in his saddle, with Hugh at his side. Rain water dripped from the hood of his cloak, and rolled down his face. Sacks of iron bumped against the rump of his horse with every step. Prisoners stumbled along on either side, hands tied, with now and again a harsh word from Owen to keep them moving.

"What are you going to do to us?" one man, shivering in nightshirt and nightcap, demanded.

Niall's head jolted up, rousing him from a half-dream to the cloudy night and dark hills. "Ransom," he said. "Be glad we don't copy your king's ways, or we'd be mounting your heads on pikes around our walls."

"Do you not mind Longshanks' butchering our people at Berwick?" Hugh asked.

"That was years ago," the man snarled.

"Wasting our land," Niall snapped. "Starving our children, nailing our priests to church doors, burning our towns, invading our country, killing our people, monks, nuns, stealing our cattle, executing our men, year after year." He wiped a trickle of rain running down his face. "We wish only for it to stop. We will wage war til Edward grants the easiest of terms for which we asked: that England leave us alone."

The prisoner glanced up at him, and lowered his eyes, trudging along silently.

It was many cold, wet hours later that Douglas, far away at the head of the slow-winding column, called a halt. Pearl-gray streaks of dawn peered tentatively over the crests of the eastern hills. Hugh, Lachlan, and Owen helped Niall settle the cattle and prisoners in a large bowl hidden among the hills, and Niall, having dozed, took the first watch with Conal, and a dozen of Douglas's men. After a brief search of the animals, he found his harp, and sat on a rock, overlooking the three dozen prisoners.

As his fingers caressed the strings, his mind drifted to Allene, to his solar in Glenmirril, where he'd so often played harp and recorder with Shawn. He scanned the hidden valley as he plucked. Apart from prisoners rustling, seeking comfort on the hard ground, or guards perched on stones around the perimeter, watching, nothing moved. His music drifted out into the warm summer dawn, a soft ballad. Conal's voice lilted into a higher register, singing the sad chorus, and dropped again.

Minding Hugh's words at Richmond, Niall searched for something good. He'd be going home soon, perhaps before Allene's time came. He and Allene would have a second bairn to join James in the nursery. He reached the end of the piece, and slid effortlessly into a new one. Conal stopped singing, frowning at him. Fifteen feet away, one of Douglas's men called, "What piece is that, Campbell?"

Niall realized with a start with a start what he had done. He kept playing. "One of my own making," he answered, unable to tell them it's twenty-first century name. He added a snap to a note, finished the piece, with his mind firmly on a twenty-first century stage, with crowds watching and clapping, and cheering, and moved into the *Falkirk Lament,* praying that Shawn, at least, had found his peace.

Inverness, Present

Simon stood at the far end of a long path, peering through a tunnel of blossoming cherry trees to a castle. The *hotel* up the road, the man had said. Simon had not questioned the word, understanding only that it was where Shawn was to be found. Colorful pennants fluttered atop its stark, stone walls. Was it Shawn's home? Was he lord of this manor? Maybe *hotel* was their word for castle.

He looked again to the parapets. There were no archers. The front door, up a wide flight of steps, stood wide open. He would simply walk up as if he was expected, he decided, and inquire after Shawn.

He strode up the path. Shells and stones crunched pleasantly under his feet. A wide and well-groomed lawn stretched to either side. A wall rose farther out, with trees and blossoms spilling over the walls. Shawn must be a man of wealth and power, after all, despite being only a minstrel. Of course he was, if he could command time! Simon pondered, as he approached Shawn's castle. With such wealth and power, he would be a worthy ally. Perhaps, they could rule together. If he got out of hand or demanded too much, Simon would simply kill him. He climbed the broad stairs, looking for guards. There were none. He entered a broad foyer.

"Can I help you, Sir?"

An esquire looked out over a half wall. Simon hesitated, unsure how to title Shawn, to his servants. He went with the way he heard others refer to him. "I wish to speak to Shawn Kleiner," he said.

The man smiled. "I'm sorry, Sir. You just missed him."

"Summon him back anon," Simon commanded.

The man laughed. "Sir, I can't do that."

Simon frowned.

The man's laugh slipped. "I'm sorry," he said. "I thought you were messing with me. But I really can't."

"Why not?" Simon demanded.

"They fly out this morning."

Simon's brows furrowed more deeply. "And why do they fly?"

The man looked puzzled. "Well, Sir, 'tis the only way across the ocean, sure."

Simon frowned. So he had left on this journey to *America* already. "Why such haste? Was the tide going out?"

The corner of the man's mouth quirked up. Then it dropped. "They're flying, Sir, on a plane. To America."

"Ah, yes, a plane." Simon wasn't sure what a plane was. But it could cross great bodies of water, so it was a ship of some sort. And sea voyages took a great deal of time. "He'll be gone for many months?"

The servant spread his hands. "I dinna ken, Sir. He travels a great deal. You can check his website to find where he'll be playing next."

"Web sight?"

"On the internet?"

"Of course," Simon said. Brian had spoken of the internet, as had others. He'd thought it something to do with Brian's *computer*. It seemed odd that anything of Shawn's would be in the box on Brian's desk. And he had no access to it. The house had been empty when he'd returned for his sword. "He's gone for many months, though?"

"I'd think so," the servant said.

"I wish to speak to him. How do I embark on a plane?"

The servant drew back visibly. "You buy a ticket."

"Where?" Simon reached in his pocket for wads of money.

"On the internet. Or call an airline direct. However you like, really."

Simon noticed the man's growing discomfort. He'd made a misstep somewhere. He thought better of his plan, and withdrew his hand, empty, from his pocket. "Thank you," he said. "I'll look at his web."

Edinburgh, Present

The plane rumbled to life, vibrating the seat beneath Shawn. The metal walls around him hummed. Happiness hung around him like mist, remembering Amy's good-bye at the airport, and her promise. He'd won! *Take that, Interloper!* He smiled.

"Seat belts on!"

The voice snapped him from his happy reverie. Flight attendants marched down the aisles with skirts hiked to their knees. The women he'd seen in his week back had largely worn pants—strange enough after two years in medieval Scotland, but the sight of bare legs left him feeling a wee voyeuristic.

With one of Zach's daughters beside him, he stared at his datebook. Ben had sent him a list of proposed tour dates and locations. Lindsay had e-mailed him his itinerary of performances with four orchestras on the west coast, over the next three weeks. He pulled out his phone to dial the manager of the San Francisco Symphony.

"Hey, Mr. Finer!" Emma tugged at his sleeve.

"Emma, Mr. Kleiner is on the phone." Kristin leaned across the aisle.

"Cell phones off, please," spoke the captain over the loudspeaker, and the usual safety instructions began. Shawn snapped the phone shut with a sigh, leaning back on the headrest.

"Mr. Finer," Emma said again. "Why is your shirt so strange?"

"My shirt?" He glanced down at the *leine* Christina had sewn for him. White homespun linen, laced with a thin strip of leather at the throat, and sporting belled sleeves, it looked like what all the other men of Glenmirril wore. But she didn't know the other men of Glenmirril. "It's comfortable," he said.

The answer satisfied her. "Can you put the quarter in my ear again?" she asked.

He looked down at her earnest face, her blue eyes bright and blonde pig tails bobbing as she nodded to encourage him. A smile spread across his face. He'd done the trick for the smaller children at Glenmirril. He hoped he'd remembered to show Niall. It had been such a small detail of the day, something Amy's young cousins had loved, a trick his own father had loved. The television screens were down now, with diagrams of the safety exits, and the flight attendant in her insanely short skirt pointing helpfully. Another smile quirked Shawn's mouth, imagining a diagram of safety exits for Glenmirril in case of attack.

"Sure," he said to Emma. "Quarter or dime?" He suspected she didn't know the difference.

She bounced on her seat, wiggled her legs, and shouted, "Dime!"

"Listen, Emma." From across the aisle, Kristin laid a calming hand on her knee.

As Shawn dug in his pocket for a coin, a purring voice interrupted him. "Could you stop yelling and kicking my seat, Emma? That'd be great, thanks!"

He looked up to see Caroline leaning around the seat, a Cheshire smile as false as it was white plastered across her face. He barely had time to wonder what he'd ever seen in her before she rose from her seat, plucked Emma from hers, and switched places, leaving Kristin gasping.

"That's my daughter!" Kristin snapped. "Put her right back!" She started to rise to do so herself, when the attendant strode forward.

"Now, ladies, the captain has requested seat belts on. Everyone stay where you are, and we'll sort this out once we're in the air. She'll be fine, ma'am."

"This is not fine!" Kristin objected.

From his window seat, Zach gave Caroline a hard stare. "As soon as the plane takes off, Kristin," he said, and to Caroline, "Don't *ever* touch my daughter again."

Caroline tossed her head. Even seeing only the back of her blond bob, Shawn knew the smirk on her face well. "Sorry," she said. "I need to talk to Shawn."

The attendant looked warily from one to the other, and, deciding things would be okay, returned to her safety instructions. The plane began its slow roll from the gate, the airport sliding away.

Shawn dropped his head against his headrest, his eyes squeezed shut. *What have I done?* He opened them and rolled his head to stare at Caroline. She smiled, like a smoky speakeasy. "I missed you," she cooed.

"Yeah, well." He tried to think of the right thing to say. No need to be rude. She'd hardly begged him to take her to that party at the Blue Bell Inn. "It's been two...a year. You ought to realize I'm not really worth missing."

Her red nails settled on his thigh. "That's a matter of opinion on which we differ."

He lifted her hand off his leg, though he drew in a deep breath at the jolt it sent through him. He spoke softly. "Uh, you know I'm not renowned for faithfulness. Why would you want that?" Christina would not have tolerated it. The plane cantered smoothly onto a runway. Scotland's hills showed purple and green through the small window. He gazed down, wondering what had become of Christina.

Caroline ran a finger down his arm. "You'll change for me."

He smiled, seeing James's soft black hair and pink face. "I've already changed," he said. "For Amy." *And for Christina.* The thought popped into his mind, almost causing him to jump. Before she could reply, words came from his mouth, words he hadn't planned. "I owe you an apology, too, Caroline. I shouldn't have...." The thought came to him, too vividly, of swinging the tin pail full of money between them, laughing and sauntering drunkenly down the shore along the River Ness. And all that had followed.

He lowered his eyes, unable to look at her. And again, words came to him he would not normally have thought of himself. "I owe you an apology because maybe if I hadn't misled you—there was never going to be anything between us, you need to know that—maybe you would have seen someone who really loves you, somebody who would have treated you well." He forced himself to meet her eyes, bright blue under thick, black lashes.

Her lids drooped seductively. Her red mouth curved up invitingly. "You treated me *very* well."

"Oh, for God's sake." He rolled his eyes. Across the aisle, Kristin and Zach whispered over Sophie's head. The flight attendants moved with calm efficiency to their jump seats, smiling at one another and chatting as they buckled in. The plane revved its engine, swung right, and gunned its motor, catapulting down the runway. The heathered hills outside Edinburgh raced along beside it. Niall and Allene filled Shawn's mind. He stared out the window, feeling his heart was being ripped out, leaving them behind, not knowing what had happened to them.

He turned back to Caroline, glancing at her blood red nails resting on his arm. "That's not treating you well," he said softly, hoping the minds around them were on the plane even now lifting its front wheels off the tarmac, hoping they were too busy, feeling the lurch of their stomachs as he did, to listen in. "I never intended anything more than a fun few nights. It's called using you, Caroline." He turned his right palm up, tracing the faint scar from Allene's knife with his left finger. On one of his first nights in medieval Scotland, he'd found himself alone in the hills with her, and expected her to react as Caroline would have, to his advances. She'd stabbed him.

He dropped his voice even lower, missing Allene and Niall, Red and Taran and Brother David, and whispered, "Have some self respect."

She said nothing. Her hand fell from his arm. With a last grunt of its back wheels scraping the runway, the plane lifted like a giant eagle, wings spread against blue sky. The hills of purple grew quickly smaller as they rose, tearing at his heart as he left Niall and Red and Hugh behind, abandoning them again.

He turned to her. Her make-up stood out like a mask over pale skin. He'd never seen her without a seductive and inviting smile on her face. Without it, she looked older. The mask gone, he saw beneath the polished exterior. She was Joan's twenty-first century counterpart. Joan, the washerwoman in Dundolam, was heavy and rough and red and blunt, pleading for someone to love her.

Joan was nothing like Caroline. Caroline was everything like Joan.

"I said I'm sorry," he whispered, "and I meant it. It was as wrong to you as it was to Amy." And yet, it was still more wrong to Amy, he thought.

Across the aisle, Zach and Kristin glanced at them, and turned away, Kristin burrowing in a bag for a children's book. Caroline drew a breath, big enough for a long, slow phrase of *Greensleeves*. Overhead, the seat belt light flashed and beeped. "Maybe you should let Emma have her seat back," he said softly. "I'm sorry."

Their eyes met. She didn't smile, and in the lack of one, he saw her humanity. She nodded, and unbuckled her seat belt. "Hey, Emma, your boyfriend wants you back." Her voice dripped with acid.

"That's a disgusting," Kristin said. "You make yourself small."

Caroline tossed her familiar smirk back at Kristin, and dropped into her seat.

Emma bounced back beside Shawn. "Did you find the dime?"

Shawn smiled. "I keep finding more and more things." He pulled the coin from a deep pocket of his trews and pretended to push it into her ear.

Glenmirril, August 1316

Three hundred. Stretching his aching arms, MacDougall climbed to his feet after numerous floor dips, and glanced at the cell door. The window that covered its bars kept him in the dark about what his captors might be doing outside. It also protected him, giving him warning to stop his exercises before they should see. Watching it carefully, he moved on to the day's next task—removing a slat from his wooden bed, and filing it against the stone walls. It was as poor a weapon as his exercise was poor substitute for his usual training. Both were better than nothing.

Continuing his daily regimen, he returned to exercise, pulling and pushing with all his strength at the bars on the window that looked down into the bailey. At worst, he stayed strong. At best, he might finally loosen them. Three stories up was too far to climb out, unless he could craft a rope. He'd used a meat knife—the one time they'd left him one—to cut long strips from his blanket. It would be a long, slow job, acquiring enough material to make a rope, but it was one more possibility for escape.

Besides giving him hope, his self-imposed schedule helped pass the dull march of time. He turned next to sharpening the top of the table leg against the stone walls. When the sun shone high in the sky, he fit the weapon back in place under the table, and strode to the window that looked into the courtyard, watching. They would, as always, only see him staring out complacently. He knew a great deal of Glenmirril from doing so—stables, armory, chapel, kirk, kitchens. The Laird disappeared often into the maw below the great hall—so there must be something there in addition to dungeons. Christina rode out daily with a basket, always up the hill to the north.

Behind him, the window in the door opened. He turned. The youth, Taran, peered through. A moment later, the key clicked in the lock, and the boy entered with the day's meal.

MacDougall eyed the bread he knew would be hard and stale, the thin slice of cheese, and small bit of meat. "A fine meal to go with my fine abode," he said with what he hoped was gentle humor.

"Better this than the dungeon." Taran slid the trencher onto the table.

MacDougall gave a taut smile. "Aye. And ye're better company than rats. You'll still not speak to me? It seems we'll be seeing a great deal of one another."

He was but a boy, MacDougall thought. Boys were full of bravado, and quick to believe what they saw. Too sure of their own initial impressions.

Taran dropped the flagon of ale with a jarring thud next to the trencher, and gave a hard look that warned MacDougall not to underestimate him. "My father is dead, thanks to you."

"Men die in war. My own son was killed."

"You and your son had a choice. My father did not."

MacDougall studied the boy, from his shock of carrot hair past his pale face to stick-thin arms jutting from a tunic waiting for him to grow into it. He was tall, still gangly with youth. He would be easily overcome.

Taran laughed. "Surely ye don't think I'm alone? There are two men outside."

MacDougall glanced at the door. Through the bars, he spied vibrant red hair and the taller lad. Not men at all, he thought. Taran had two boys outside. MacDougall said nothing.

"You'd do well to remember," Taran added, "that despite my youth, I learned from the best."

MacDougall smiled, appreciating the boy's intelligence. He'd have been smarter still to play dumb and let MacDougall underestimate him. But he addressed the matter of invasions. "Your Lord Niall was in my son's castle. I'd every right to reclaim my prisoner."

"Nay. Ye'd a wandering minstrel in yer dungeon. My Lord Niall was with Jamie Douglas in England."

MacDougall frowned. It was difficult to explain why so many men would lie, even James Douglas, claiming Niall had been there, if he hadn't. The incident in the town, just before Bannockburn, niggled at him. They'd been on Niall's trail, hard on his heels as he raced into the town. Yet the man who looked like him wore different clothes than Niall had worn in the forest. How he could have acquired new clothes so quickly was a mystery, but a small one; the larger one was that whoever they laid hands on that day played sackbut with a mastery of which Iohn swore Niall was incapable. Moreover, the man had none of the marks which Niall Campbell bore.

"Taran." The tall lad looked through the door's bars. "'Tis our place only to see he doesn't leave. Sir Niall needs no defense."

Taran cast down a look of smug superiority.

MacDougall took a quick step forward. Taran's knife flashed up. MacDougall stopped, holding up a placating hand. "I only meant to ask...."

"You've no right to ask aught."

MacDougall cleared his throat, swallowing his pride. "I had hoped for reading material. Perhaps the Scriptures. Or...." He lowered his head, the humble repentant. "...to attend Mass."

"You'll not leave this cell," Gil said.

MacDougall allowed himself a moment of looking, he hoped, sorrowful, before asking, "Might your priest come to me, then? For absolution and Eucharist? The monk who attends...." Again, he had to choke down pride. "...Sir Niall? Might I speak with him?" He had not seen the monk in gray since the battle. He had not been at Niall's side, last Niall had ridden out.

Taran's eyes narrowed. "Open the door, Gil," he said.

MacDougall gave a bow. "I thank thee nonetheless for aught better than dungeon fare and the rats' thought-provoking conversation." He'd planted a seed.

Taran backed out of the room. The key scraped, metal on metal in the lock, as the tumblers slid into place. MacDougall sat down to his meal, his mind twisting through the maze of riddles Niall had left. Could it have been Fionn of Bergen, traveling minstrel, playing sackbut in the town? Clearly, there was a man somewhere in Scotland, who looked like Niall. *Is that such a wonder, with your clans inter-marrying?* he'd asked Iohn that hot June day in the town, as they watched the man play, a gypsy dancing before him.

MacDougall dug his teeth into the meat. It was tough, old, and tasteless. But what did he expect? Outside, the murmur of voices drifted through the door, two deep voices and one straining to escape boyhood. He returned to the puzzle of Niall. What were the odds Fionn of Bergen had been in that town at the same time as Niall, and later, at Creagsmalan, where Bruce had sent Niall? Even a betting man wouldn't lay odds on such a coincidence. So there *was* a man who looked like Niall.

And Niall knew it.

MacDougall frowned, washing the dry meat down with weak ale. It must have been Niall at the wedding, for the man on the kirk stair had shown the same scar about the waist that Niall had shown after Bruce's council.

But something bothered him about the man at Allene's side that day. MacDougall searched his memory. Just after he demanded to see the scar, Niall leaned close to MacDonald, whispering, and MacDonald stepped forth, proposing the deal about Christina. It had been Niall's idea. *Niall* thought of Christina. *Niall* wanted Christina. His eyes, the tension of his shoulders, the way he leaned forward, away from Allene, waiting for MacDougall's answer, were all those of a man who cared far more for another woman than he should, as he stood outside the kirk with his new bride.

"Jura," the deeper voice outside his door spoke. MacDougall paused, his fingers halfway to his mouth with the tough meat. "Fought like the Fenians, running around the ship like a born sailor. Our Niall's something else, Taran. He needs no defense."

Anger burned in MacDougall's gut. Duncan dead at their hands. His kin, John, defeated in the sound of Jura and barely escaped to London. He shoved the meat in his mouth, and wiped his beard. It had been Niall at the kirk last October. The scar proved that. All who knew Niall spoke of his love for Allene, his faithfulness and loyalty. So why had he leaned forward so intently for news of a woman he'd barely known? Was Niall perhaps not so faithful after all? What that meant, MacDougall couldn't guess. But he intended to be out of this tower, and every piece of information helped. He set aside the puzzle of Niall, certain he'd solved at least part of it: There were two men.

He swallowed the last of his ale, his thoughts going back to Christina. He returned to his small window, where he spent the next hour doing presses against the stone frame, strengthening himself for his escape. As he did so, he peered out, hoping for a glimpse of her. She hadn't come to the gardens in all this time, but he sometimes saw her in the northern bailey, leaving the castle on her small palfrey, her cloak flowing over the rump of her horse. The sight of her never failed to stir his heart and fill him with dreams for the future.

Inverness, Present

In the front room of the empty house, Simon swung his sword, spun, and lunged. Air whistled across its blade. He would need his skills sharp when he returned to his time. He slashed the sword through the air, feeling its weight, again and again, until sweat rolled down the side of his face, driven by anger.

It had taken careful questions, wary of disturbing anyone, before he fully grasped it: This land he'd learned of from Brian, across an ocean—it had once taken ships weeks to make the voyage, but *planes* traveled the sky—through the clouds!—in mere hours. He couldn't get on a plane without a *credit card* and identification. He could find a *credit card* in the wallets these men carried. He would find someone to forge documents.

But *America,* he understood, was a vast continent, hundreds of times larger than England and Scotland combined. Bigger than all of Europe. Shawn was as famed as a great knight. He *could* find him even in such a vast expanse—but what kind of *time* would it take?

He rested the sword hilt against the wall, wiping his face with his sleeve. Strength was not the only thing. With a *pen,* he outlined a man on the wall, a circle for the heart. He eyed the heart carefully, as he pondered the problem. He had only until Christmastide. Less than six months. Shawn was *not* the only person who knew what had happened.

Simon lunged. He stabbed the heart, tearing a chunk from the wall, smiled, and yanked back. Amy and Angus knew something. He drove at the wall again. Eamonn knew something. The sword dug deep in the heart, cleaving a hole. But his recent altercation with Eamonn meant it would be unwise to hunt for him so soon. Amy was wary of him. Angus...he might also be wary.

Simon lunged a third time, struck the heart a third time, and let the sword come to rest, studying his work. He did *have* until Christmastide. He might learn more of Edward's near future, before heading back, or of these people's planes and weapons—things he could use against the Scots.

And there was still the matter of killing James. Amy and the child, people said, had stayed here. He guessed that meant Shawn would be back. He sketched two more men on the wall, this time with smaller hearts. Taking no time to think, he drove at them, one after the other, back and forth, six strokes in as many heartbeats, and jumped back, studying six perfect strikes, three in each heart. He smiled. He would seek out Amy.

She'd been alarmed, last time he saw her. He'd scared her, rapping on her window. But he'd ever been good at charming women. He *could* convince her to talk to him. But he must find her first. He knew where to find Angus, at the police station, and Angus would lead him to Amy, who would lead him to James.

Yes, he had plenty to do between now and Christmastide, he mused. He drew a fourth man on the wall, the heart a mere point, and lunged.

CHAPTER NINE

Glasgow, Present

The plane will be over the Atlantic by now, almost to the east coast. My fingers prance on the strings, tapping and sliding, as my bow flashes. I lean in, intent on the flurry of black notes, trying to drive from my mind the thought that Caroline is with Shawn for twelve hours, from Edinburgh to the Midwest. I was grateful for the call this morning to sub, and the hope of keeping my mind off it all for a few hours.

The music collides to a stop, my notes the last to jump out into the silence, with my head still all but up against the stand. I look up, startled and embarrassed.

"Trumpets, a little life in those notes!" Dave is young to be a conductor, only a few years older than me, with the black hair of his ancestors and vivid blue eyes; his calm is the antithesis of Conrad's sturm und drang. "Lighter on the staccatos."

I breathe out in relief, whispering to Sarah, "I can't believe he didn't hear me."

"Violins," he adds, "keep your mind on the music."

I glance sheepishly at Sarah, who grins back.

"We're dragging a wee bit," says Dave. "Measure one-twenty-nine, trumpets." He lifts the baton. The trumpets flash the spotlights off their bells in splashes of gold, and a stream of music burbles out, as full of life as any I've ever heard. I try to study my notes. It's a new piece with a bit of bi-tonality I don't care for, but my part isn't particularly difficult, just runs of chromatic scales. My thoughts turn to Shawn's early morning departure.

I drove him to the airport before dawn. I didn't miss that he left my house, lugging the suitcase and trombone he brought over a year ago on the orchestra's first tour, but wearing the bell-sleeved shirt and loose-fitting trews—cleaned and mended—in which he'd arrived in Glenmirril's tower. "They're comfortable," he said, shortly, when he caught me looking. Then he cocked his familiar crooked grin and said, "Be grateful I didn't wear the vest. I'd really stand out in that."

"Standing out has never bothered you," I replied. I didn't add that it looked good on him—disturbingly appealing, in fact—and he wouldn't be alone in his choice of clothing within a week of being photographed in it.

He kissed and hugged his mother, held her close, saying, "I'll be back in a few weeks." He kissed James, sleeping in Carol's arms, his fingers lingering in the soft black down of his hair, and the smile fading away. "I'd say take good care of him, but I know you will."

"It's only three weeks." As I said it, it struck me that this time, three weeks in his son's life matters greatly to him. Before, an entire lifetime had not. I filed it away as evidence. He's really changed.

Still, he hung back, his hand on his son's head, till I said brusquely, "You can't be late."

He kissed James again, and snatched up his things, tossing them in the back of my red Renault. Out on the dark highway, leaning against the headrest of the passenger seat, he asked, "You'll wait for me?"

I didn't answer immediately; a twinge of guilt nagged me about being behind the theater with Angus. More than a twinge. I heard the soft click of the heavy metal door. My gut tells me it was Shawn, but he hasn't said a word.

"You're not going to run straight back to that guy?"

My guilt flashed away in loyalty to Angus, and anger at Shawn's disregard of all Angus did for him. "*That guy*, as you call him, has a name," I snapped, "and he got you out of 1316." I took my eyes off the road for the briefest moment, scanning his square jaw. The carriageway lights reflected in his golden eyes, hungry for the right answer. My anger died as suddenly as it rose. "I don't know what I'm going to do."

"He's nothing," Shawn said. "Just someone when you thought I was gone, aye?"

I swallowed the anger, trying to speak in a way he might actually hear. "I broke up with you for good reason. But I never wished ill on you." I drove silently for another mile, before saying, "I still hoped to someday see the man I thought was there, and seeing you go down under that sword, it ripped something out of me. I spent months grieving what could have been, and grieving your death."

My fingers hurt with clutching the wheel. "And in that time, he showed up. I fell in love with him, thinking you were gone forever." I threw a pleading look at him. "Can you understand that? He did everything for me, and for you, too, you might want to remember. And now you want me to just toss him aside."

"James needs his father."

I said nothing, remembering Angus holding James just minutes after birth, hearing his words in the abbey at Monadhliath—*I have been a father to James since he was born.* And he has been—holding him, loving him, providing for him, even.

Shawn added, more softly, "You need me. You always had faith in me."

"Doesn't that mean *you* need *me*?" I asked. But a tremble crawled up my arms, from my fingers on the steering wheel to my shoulders. More than a week has gone by with no clear answer to my heart or mind, just daily life with Shawn, remembering everything I loved in his broad shoulders and quick laugh and passion for life, thinking on Rose's words—*Shawn brought you to life*—yet missing Angus, his steady nature, his humor more subtle than Shawn's that crept up on me and made me laugh with the realization of a joke hidden like an Easter egg in a clever place.

Shawn turned away, looking out at the dark road and black fields zipping past.

"Tell me more about it," I said. We passed the time with his stories, of Niall and Allene and Hugh and Red. I listened intently, not to the facts of battles and people and landscapes and castles—although every detail fascinated me as a museum exhibit come to life—but for the things that had changed him; for proof he *had* changed.

"Violins!" I jump as Dave's voice yanks me into the present and Sarah pokes my arm. The early morning in the car fades away. I am in the glare of spotlights on a stage in Glasgow, my eyes fixed unseeing on a swarm of locusts disguised as notes; and Shawn is flying into JFK. I feel disoriented with the switch.

"Gathering wool, are we?" Sarah jokes.

I smile. "And lots of it. Sorry."

"Lots of shocks for you recently," she sympathizes. "Your boyfriend and all." She stares at me, waiting, I guess, for some explanation. I give none. "Coffee after rehearsal?" she asks.

Thankfully, Dave finishes his instructions. "Same place, measure one-twenty-nine." His arms swoop out, up, down, and thirty bows down with it, swirling up the chromatic scale in the fits of ecstasy the composer expressly requested.

"Good, good!" Dave cuts us off, calls for the orchestra to join us, and starts again, letting us go fifty measures, with exhortations for ecstasy.

"Composers." Jack, sitting on my other side, mutters as his bow flashes up and down his strings. "Fits of ecstasy! Why can he not just say fast or loud?"

I hold back a grin, concentrating on my music. My eyes flash to the trombones. They lean together, talking among themselves. My mind drifts back to Shawn. Sixty measures pass in ecstatic sixteenths, with the kettle drums pounding out heavy fifths, and the harp fluttering runs of arpeggios over it all. The trombone players sit up quickly, pointing at their music. This is their big entrance. As one, they become serious, lift their instruments, and draw breath.

"Stop!" Dave calls. The trombonists wilt in defeat as the music machine grinds to a halt. "Back to one-twenty-nine."

The trombonists groan and shake their heads. I chuckle.

"Funny now, is it?" asks Jack.

"Shawn," I explain. "He swore conductors do it on purpose."

"Shawn, that was your boyfriend? What do they do on purpose?"

"Cut the orchestra off just as the trombone players take a breath to come in after a long rest."

"Aye, well, why wouldn't they?" Jack asks with a wink and a grin.

Dave's baton slashes down, and Jack and I leap back into the fray. The trombonists begin a three-way game of rock-paper-scissors. Chromatic scales, flashing out under my fingers, slide to the back of my mind, and Shawn steps again to the front of the stage.

His stories fell silent as I pulled into the airport's parking ramp and shut off the engine. He made no move to get out. Ramp lights spilled through the window like a halo. He finally spoke, taking my hand and meeting my eyes. "Give me a chance, Amy. I'm the man you always wanted. I'm the one you believed in. Let me make it all up to you."

Shivers shot up my arm like a tremolo, spreading out from where he touched my palm. I said nothing. Every good moment with him sang through my memory, along with a flood of guilt and pain over Angus for even considering it. I shouldn't have kissed him, behind the theater. It wasn't fair to Angus, or to Shawn. And it didn't help me, either.

Shawn lowered his voice in the way that always got me, turned my insides to molten liquid. Especially in the semi-dark. "I thought about you always, the whole time I was gone."

"Easy to say," I shot back. But my voice shook with wanting him, wanting what we had that first year.

His hand moved up past my elbow. I swallowed, thinking of Angus, but didn't pull away from the thrill his touch sent racing up and down my arm. He had shown himself, for a week at least, to be all I ever believed of him, spending every moment with me, no unexplained absences. He confessed everything I knew and then some. He apologized. His behavior at rehearsals and the concert has been impeccable. I've fought for a week against throwing myself into his arms, torn between desire, hope, guilt, and Angus.

"I never wanted to be in this position," I said. "This is not fair to Angus."

Shawn's fingertips inched higher up my arm; slid around my back, running his hand down my hair, and returned to my shoulder, leaving a trail of sparks. "You and I, we were together almost three years."

"Two and a half." I breathed deeply, trying to ignore the flutter in my stomach.

"We have a child together."

"I'd never keep you away from him, even if I'm with Angus."

"We have a future together."

"I never agreed to that."

"But you never stopped loving me." His hand crept to the back of my neck, massaging.

I swallowed. "How do you know?"

He smiled, a slow, sultry smile, and his voice dropped. "I can tell by the way you're breathing right now."

I drew in a rough breath. "I'm not breathing any differently."

He laughed softly, running his finger down the line of my jaw; slipped his other hand to my cheek and pulled me in, kissing me, touching his lips to my brow, my cheek, my lips. "Still not breathing any differently?" he whispered.

I pulled back, explosions of pleasure bursting in my head. He was back! He was everything I always believed he could be!

And Angus was in Inverness, in pain. "Love and...this..." I objected, "are two different things."

His hand snaked around the back of my head, his hand pressed in my hair, whispering, "I love you, I've always loved you."

Tears ran down my cheeks. He came back from the dead. How could I even think of saying no? The words *I love you, too* came from my mouth, driven by a year of grief and memories, as he kissed me again.

He stopped, holding my face, forehead to forehead, nose to nose, the ramp lights spilling through the window, turning the ginger in his hair to strands of gold, and picking out the gold flecks in his irises. "You're glad I'm back?"

I nodded, swallowing, trying not to cry. "I thought you were dead. I couldn't stop thinking about all the good things between us." I tried to tell myself not to be stupid, not to forget the bad things. But those were over and done. He'd changed. He'd confessed everything.

"I tried for two years to get back to you." He brushed a finger against the streak of tears on my cheek. "Never again, we'll never be apart, and I'll never hurt you again. We'll get married as soon as we can. Life is going to be good."

I nodded, nodded hard, wanting it all, saying, "Yes!" and kissing him back, giving in to all I've felt since he came back, tears rolling down my face, clinging to him, not wanting him to go.

He finally disentangled himself, pushing my hair back, leaning his forehead against mine. "I'll see you soon, okay? I'll be back soon."

He climbed out of the car and took his suitcase and trombone from the back. I got out, too, watching the familiar scene. Rounding the car, he wrapped me tight in his arms. "You coming in?" he finally asked. I nodded, not wanting the moment to end. Nothing else mattered.

"That was good, now!" Dave's vigor breaks into my thoughts.

"Where've you been?" Jack lowers his violin. "You look a wee bit disoriented."

I lower my violin, grinning sheepishly at Jack. "I've done too many chromatic scales in my life. My mind is a million miles away." More like three thousand some, I think wryly. I glance at my watch, do the math, and figure they might be landing about now. Caroline preys on the edges of my mind. She'll take full advantage of the situation. I stubbornly remind myself it's Shawn's actions that matter, not Caroline's.

But that's the problem. Eight days of good behavior in my company doesn't tell me how he'll behave three thousand miles beyond my sight, apologies and confessions and loving moments with James notwithstanding.

I went into the airport with him, shy of being seen by the orchestra once again holding his hand. Several of them looked harder; but I suspect most expected it. Dana stayed away, casting sad glances our way. Caroline gave me a sultry, half-lidded gaze, making her disregard for me, and her plans for Shawn, clear. He hugged me one last time, piercing my soul with his gaze, before being sucked away into the security system. "I'll be back soon," he called over the arch of the x-ray machine.

"Let's move on to Loch Lomond. Wind quintet to the front." Dave studies the score on the podium as he speaks. He glances up, scanning the orchestra. The five

wind players, the flutist short and plump with fly-away brown curls, nothing like Caroline, rustle their music and instruments, and squeeze between and around stands, laughing and talking with one another about a false entrance on the last try.

I pull out my part, trying to ignore the familiar twist in the gut, of worry, jealousy, of flat out pain, that he might lie and cheat again. There's nothing I can do about it now, I tell myself sternly. The quintet settles around an arc of stands. They lift their instruments, waiting. I do likewise. Time will tell. The platitude does nothing for the itch in my fingers, wanting to reach for my cell phone and call, find out if he's with Caroline or any other woman. Not that he would admit it if he were. How did I let myself get sucked back in this morning? Dave's baton comes down, my bow with it, and I slip, at last, into the stream of music, away from worry.

England, Autumn, 1316

The trail of pack horses carrying pillaged treasure grew with each town; with each town, too, grew the string of noble prisoners, following from raid to raid until they could be brought back to Scotland to be held for ransom. Some towns rushed to meet the hundreds of invaders, safety payment in hand, begging to be left in peace. Some dragged their feet, handing it over only with threats. West Riding and others resisted, hoping for rescue from the nearby castles, and were made examples of, with fire devouring crops and towns alike, and more hostages led off for ransom.

With each raid, with each night of standing on a ridge watching crops burn, with each dawn that found him once again riding beside Hugh, Niall forced his mind to the prayer that had once come so easily. *May You grant us the peace we seek. Will You please bring me home soon to Allene?*

Along with Douglas, whose moniker, The Black Douglas, had become a warning to disobedient children in Northern England, Bruce himself led this raid. His good-son, Walter Stewart, widower of the deceased Marjorie and father to Scotland's heir, rode at his side. Bruce had once again been subject to a wasting illness. Determined that action was the way to fight it off, he had risen from his sick bed to lead the raids.

High on a hill overlooking another burning town, Niall stood by the evening campfire, as Bruce, in his tabard with the rearing lion, Douglas, with his shield of three blue stars hanging from his arm, and Stewart—barely older than Niall—discussed the next step.

"We've gone as far as Richmond," Bruce said, "with hardly a sign of resistance."

"Edward Carnarvon has peculiar ideas on governing a nation." Douglas sank onto a log, laying down his shield.

"'Tis to our benefit," Walter Stewart said, "or he might have a notion how to defend his country, rather than allow us to march across it unhindered."

Douglas cast a glance at the town and fields burning in the glen below. From the hills, they could see townfolk and farmers running, and hear faint screams. "If he cared a whit for good rule, he'd see his country is in chaos, and treat for peace."

"Perchance the time has come to push on to London," said Stewart.

Bruce considered before speaking, looking out over the crowd of soldiers, cattle, hostages, and pack horses loaded with gold, all filling the hollow in which they took refuge, some climbing the hills to find a bit of ground for sleeping. "Unhindered though we be," spoke Bruce, "we're burdened by hostages, treasure, and cattle, all of which slow us greatly. 'Tis best we turn and head north. What say you, Campbell?"

"You speak wisely, Your Grace." Niall, too, scanned the camp. The Scots traveled light and swift. They were breaking their own rules, so burdened, and risking becoming overly bold. He knew, too, that Bruce worried about his queen, due to give birth to her first child soon. Bruce's first wife had died giving birth to Marjorie; Marjorie had died giving birth to his grandson. Bruce said nothing of his fear for Elizabeth, but the men fully expected him to hurry home, as September wore away. "We've done well; I see no need to take greater chances."

Bruce turned his gaze from the southern hills, purple in the dusk, crawling with Scots returning from the burning town, to Niall. "I believe you await a bairn, too."

Niall smiled, thoughts of Allene warming his heart. "Aye, Your Grace, though not so soon as you." He wanted to hurry all the same, for though she was young and strong, women did die in childbirth. Shawn had said it hardly ever happened in his time. *Make the midwife clean her hands, boil the water, it cuts down on infections.* Niall sighed, staring out over the mist curling over the charred remains of the field below.

"I think," Bruce said, "we'll send one more message asking Edward to treat for peace. My Lord Campbell, where is that Brother Andrew who was so oft with you? He writes a fair hand, does he not?"

Niall jumped at the name. "Brother Andrew?" In the months since Shawn had left, Niall had barely thought of their alter ego. Shawn, to these people, had never existed. But Brother Andrew, whether it was Shawn or Niall beneath the hood, had been at the side of Niall Campbell—whether that was Shawn or Niall—for two years.

Bruce watched him. "The monk who never quite managed his vow of silence."

"Aye." Niall cleared his throat. "I believe he's gone back to his monastery."

"Which one is that? He did Scotland a fine service, running that message to Douglas just before Jura."

The irritation at Shawn finagling the switch still niggled on that one.

"I'd fain give a gift to his monastery in thanks," Bruce added.

"Aye, well." Niall's brain spun, seeking an answer. "I believe his monastery is a wee trek and quite self sufficient. I dare say they'd be glad to have the gift sent to the border cathedrals. They've suffered a fair bit and could use help re-building." His heart pounded; he schooled his face to remain calm and impassive, hoping Robert would be more concerned with his message to Edward of England. "I write a fair hand myself, Your Grace, if 'tis a message you're wanting. Who will carry it?"

Bruce arched his back and scratched irritably at the tabard and chain covering his chest. He peered intently at Niall, but his words were, "We'll send one of the men. Yes, write it, Sir Niall."

The writing case was brought, and Niall set quill to parchment, recording the words of one king to another, once more seeking peace.

"Easy terms," Douglas murmured. "Why must he subject the people of two countries to such misery?"

Niall finished the message. The lad waiting nearby sprinkled it with sand, and handed it to Bruce.

"Pride goes before the fall," Bruce replied, re-reading his words. "'Tis but a shame so many must fall with him." He nodded approval at the message, folded it, and called for his seal. With the wax setting, he looked for a messenger. His eyes settled on Niall. Niall's breath became still. *Please, no.* He wanted no part of Edward, London, any of it. He wanted only to be home with Allene.

Bruce's gaze moved on. "Walter," Bruce addressed his son-in-law. "Send one of your men forthwith."

Walter Stewart accepted the missive, bowing to his king. "Aye, Your Grace."

Niall let his breath out slowly. He'd be going home to Allene.

"There's much to be done. I'm going ahead." Bruce turned to Niall. "Wait here for his answer and bring it to me at Melrose."

Niall's heart sank, even as he bowed to his king. Knowing Edward Carnarvon, it could be a long wait. Neither peace nor his family looked to be any closer.

Midwest America, Present

Aaron pulled through the high iron gates onto Shawn's twenty acres, glancing around as he did. He'd asked, hours ago on the plane, how Shawn was getting home, and offered a ride. "You have a key?" he asked.

Shawn nodded. His stomach was finally settling. Two years away from high speeds on the highways had left him closing his eyes and fighting nausea most of the drive from the airport. Not that he'd ever admit that to Aaron. He'd pretended it was exhaustion. "Right in my jacket pocket where I left them last year."

They wound down the long paved driveway, under an arch of summer-green trees lifting graceful branches far overhead. Aaron sang softly. "The hills are alive...."

Shawn chuckled. "It does look a wee bit like the Von Trapp driveway, aye?"

Aaron cast him a sidelong look.

"Sorry," Shawn said. "It's become natural. At least I seem to be sticking to the right language now."

Aaron laughed. "It's a good start. I don't think anyone will object to the occasional *aye*. Whenever you have time to kill, I'd love to hear the story."

"No pun intended?"

"Huh?" Aaron's brow wrinkled.

"People do a lot of killing there. Then." Shawn leaned back against his seat with a heavy sigh. His house, a Tudor revival, came into view around the bend of the driveway, a beautiful two story jewel of brick and half-timbered beams and leaded glass windows, looking dusty and dim, on a cloth of wild green lawn, untended during his absence. He remembered, intensely, seeing it the first time. His father would have loved its flavor of the past. Dana had loved it.

But it would be empty. Glenmirril had never been empty. He turned to Aaron, not wanting to go in alone, not wanting to face so many memories alone, not yet. "I've got nothing to do now." He glanced at his watch. "In about fifteen hours, that's going to change dramatically. I'm sure there's still something to drink inside."

Aaron pulled around the circular patch of grass overgrown with weeds and wild flowers. It was where the water fountain was meant to go, right in front of the house. Shawn had run out of time to look into that. Maybe later. Right now, it didn't seem important. The low hum of the engine stopped. "Yeah, love to," Aaron said.

Shawn had the disturbing feeling Aaron was giving a favor, more than accepting one. An insightful man, he thought. Shawn let himself out of the car, grateful to be away from it. It would never love him back like his horse had, not even two weeks ago. A rush of longing for the animal swept over him, and a desire to buy apples.

He and Aaron simultaneously opened the back doors, Aaron taking his suitcase, and Shawn the trombone. He'd been glad to return to that, at least, even if he missed other things left behind in Niall's time. A minute later, they stood in Shawn's gray granite foyer soaring to skylights two stories above.

He set the trombone case in his studio, opening off the foyer on the right. The room's official name was den, and shelves lined its walls, but he used it to practice. Two electric keyboards waited under the diamond-paned windows for someone to make music; a half-finished score lay on the table beside them. A grand piano took up a good part of the floor space. Two black Manhasset music stands stood in the piano's curve where he'd left them, the night before the orchestra flew to Scotland. He and Amy had played duets, transposing off a score intended for flute and clarinet. He smiled, remembering. It had been a good night. He'd grilled hamburgers out in back for just the two of them. One of her polishing cloths lay, a puddle of bright yellow, on top of the piano where she'd forgotten it.

"You want this in your room?" Aaron asked.

Shawn turned back, disoriented. "Yeah, sure. Ahead on the right." His mind traveled through the bedroom, large and spacious, a king sized bed covered in deep forest greens, and a fireplace opposite its foot. It featured his and hers bathrooms and dressing rooms.

He followed Aaron down the short hall, but went ahead to the great room, with its cathedral ceilings, floor to ceiling fireplace rising two stories, and huge glass windows flanking the chimney piece. A large white fur lay before the hearth. A gray film of dust covered the white leather furniture. He made a mental note to call his house cleaners, first thing in the morning. He turned to his left, to the kitchen with its modern appliances and huge slabs of gray granite counters, an island with copper pots hanging above it. "Ostentatious," he said softly.

"Excuse me?"

Shawn turned, not having heard Aaron come in behind him, and laughed, with no humor. "I said it's ostentatious."

"It's beautiful," Aaron replied. "Anyone would love living here."

"Yeah, it's beautiful. I did love living here. But it's ostentatious. Who needs such huge counters?" He thought of the grimy, sooty brick fireplaces, big enough to hold ten men, with which Bessie and the cooks at Glenmirril worked, and wondered how Bessie's life had played out, if she and Christina had continued to walk the gardens for years after he left. He moved to the kitchen, running his hand over smooth, cold surfaces, touching the glass front of the big oven set in a brick wall.

The silver refrigerator hummed. The bills had been on automatic payments. For that, he supposed, he was grateful. He opened the door, bracing himself for a waft of spoiled food. None hit him. The shelves were bare and clean.

"I think your mother came down sometimes," Aaron said. "Before she went to Scotland to be with Amy. She'd have cleaned that out for you."

Shawn reached for the bottle of wine in the door. "I've got wine, bourbon, scotch, whiskey." He opened a cupboard, studying the array of liquor. "Rum—a bottle of Angostura bitters, vodka, some pretty good cognac I picked up just before I left. What do you like?"

"Bourbon."

Shawn reached into the cupboard above the counter, finding the bourbon among the many glittering bottles of alcohol and liqueurs. From the adjoining cabinet, he pulled two low balls, swished them with cold water, and filled them with ice and liquor. He and Aaron chinked the rims together, giving awkward smiles.

"If you want stories, come on and settle in." Shawn moved back to the great room. He chose the white suede recliner, his favorite, and sank back in it, setting his drink on a coaster on the side table.

Aaron relaxed into the matching chair opposite Shawn's. "I met him. Amy told me about the scars on his back. It's unreal, but no matter how I go over it, it's impossible to have set this up as a prank."

Shawn gave a short bark of a laugh. "Don't take this the wrong way." He stood, and lifted his shirt, edging the jeans down. The thick red scar stood out across his stomach and circled his side. "Real enough?"

Aaron gave a brief intake of breath, then leaned forward, studying it.

"Courtesy of an English knight, 1314. I'll spare you the sight of dropping my pants, but there's a scar down one leg from a wolf." He leaned to tug up one pant leg, revealing the row of black knotted threads the Scottish doctor had left, like angry insects crawling up his calf. "MacDougall's knife. Not sure how he got me down there. I wasn't exactly taking notes at the time."

"I guess most people won't believe you."

Shawn dropped his pant leg and sank back into the chair. He took a long, slow sip of his drink, relishing the ice. He hadn't had ice in two years. "I guess not. Why do you?"

Aaron shrugged. "I keep asking myself if I'm a gullible fool. But I saw it. He was nothing like you. Amy told me about the coins—he had a handful from medieval times he sold at the pawn shop. I saw how intense he was about Bannockburn. Nothing else mattered. The look in his eye when he told me about Glenmirril. It sent chills down my back, and I believed him. It mattered *intensely* to him what happened to those people." He paused, taking a drink. "Amy told me how he talked about Glenmirril and his life on the train. He knew too much. He knew it too well. The clothes he had, the way he couldn't be without his knife at first. It all fit too well with what he said, even though..."

Shawn nodded. "Even though it's crazy and impossible." He stared at the floor to ceiling stone fireplace. It called to mind those at Glenmirril, blazing and keeping the people warm. It called to mind each of their faces, the widow Muirne, short and plump and smiling; Ronan, tall and gaunt with his stringy red-gray beard; Niall's mother, elegant and gracious with a neck like a swan and long, slender fingers. Christina. He shut his eyes. "I fought with James Douglas. Imagine that. I raided churches in England." He gave a harsh laugh. "I plundered churches, stole their gold." He paused, taking a long pull on his drink. "You understand I had no choice? They thought I was Niall. They told me to do it. It's a world where you don't say no."

"Tell me about it."

Shawn told him, of Glenmirril, of James Douglas, of Lachlan and Owen. Aaron refilled their drinks, clinking in new cubes of ice from a bucket. Shawn told of the Morrison twins and Niall's wedding to Allene, breaking Niall out of Creagsmalan, chasing a wraith through the woods outside Roman ruins only to discover he was fighting a shivering, hungry boy, and meeting Christina MacRuari at Castle Tioram when it was new. The summer light shining in the windows on either side of the great hearth lost some of its power. He told of the trick played on MacDougall, telling him Niall could walk through walls. The shadows lengthened.

"Tell me about Niall," Aaron said. The bottle sat between them on the coffee table, empty.

Shawn stared a long time at the darkening windows. "He was like a brother," he finally said. "We did everything together. We were one person, and it's disconcerting to be myself again. To hear my own name." He swallowed another draft of his bourbon, a pleasant contrast to two years of ale. He wondered why he'd just divulged such a personal thought to someone he barely knew. And the thought hit him again: Aaron, drinking his expensive bourbon, was the one doing the real favor. Somehow, Aaron knew he needed to talk.

Shawn studied the percussionist for a minute, his narrow face and lock of black hair drooping over his forehead, and set his glass down on the coaster. "I was a shit to you," he said.

Aaron chewed on his words, nodding, before saying, "Yeah, you were."

"Why are you doing this for me?" Heat burned in his throat. It was just the liquor making him maudlin, he assured himself.

Again, Aaron took his time. Shawn was surprised to feel his heart kick up a notch on the metronome. What he could possibly fear from the man's answer, he didn't know. There was nothing to fear in his world, no maiming weapons, no lawless nooses waiting to snag the unwary throat.

"Were. You *were,* past tense. I've never been one to hold things against people."

Shawn cleared his throat, unsure what to say. "I owe you an apology all the same." He stared at his stockinged toes, propped on the coffee table. "I *was* a jerk, and I *am* sorry. I shouldn't have said those things in—in the...." His jaw tightened. The thought of his ugly, sardonic words while on their tour in the south shamed him. "I shouldn't have said any of it."

Aaron fell silent. Shawn's face washed alternate shades of heat and ice, unable to look up. When he did, Aaron regarded him, swishing the melting cubes in his bourbon. "It's over and done," he said. "You're a new man. But I will say, Celine has borne the brunt of it. Everyone in the bathroom that day knows things she wouldn't have volunteered. That idiot put that information on those stupid trading cards, put it out all over the world."

Shawn's jaw clenched and unclenched. "I'll make it up to her somehow." He couldn't look up.

Aaron gave his glass another swish, clinking the cubes against the side, set it on the coffee table and leaned forward. "Nothing will ever change this for her."

"I'll get her a recording contract. I'll write pieces that will make her famous."

"And have people jump to conclusions about why you're doing all that for her? Don't you see, you can't make this one up."

Shawn's lips tightened. "I apologized, back in Scotland," he said. "Maybe you and she and I and Amy could go out sometime. She and Amy are friends."

Aaron looked dubious.

"Has she forgiven me?" Shawn asked.

Aaron shrugged. "She's very forgiving, except with one person."

Shawn looked up. "Me?"

"I wish." Aaron shook his head with a harsh staccato laugh of anger. "Herself."

"Meaning what?"

"Meaning she's probably long since forgiven you, but she feels gullible and stupid. She can't forgive herself, and she can't look at you because of what it makes her see in herself. Don't you get it, Shawn? There are songs you can't un-play."

Scottish Borders, Autumn 1316

September ground into October, one rainy night after another, while Niall waited, with thousands of clansmen and hostages, in the wet hollows of the Annandale Hills. Gorges rose on all sides, giving some little protection from the wind; still the men idled about campfires, hands stretched over warming flames, as often as their duties allowed. Niall chafed at the delay, wishing he'd been sent ahead with the cattle and treasure. But he'd been held back to write letters and play music. He volunteered for hunting whenever possible, to escape the dull duty of guarding English hostages.

By day, the men played cards, dice, and chess under dripping trees and dripping tent flaps. Around the fires at night, they played music. Niall stuck with harp, not volunteering that he could play recorder. It had proven useful, having secrets up his belled sleeve, as Shawn would say. He sang with the men, and told stories after the evening meal, when purple streaked the sky above them.

"Tell about the hound and the great wind again," said Lachlan, wolfing down charred deer meat.

Niall smiled, thinking of the venison and fine sauces at Shawn's castle-hotel, and told again of the great wolfhound and his lady, blown away on a fantastic wind, to a place where incredible things happened.

"Their clothes are of every hue in the garden and more," Niall told the men. "They've devices that copy a dozen parchments in a minute."

The waiting is hard, Christina had once said. He himself had snapped at Allene for complaining of the waiting. He gained wisdom with age, he thought with a sigh, not liking at all what he was learning. The waiting was very hard.

"Go on," Owen prodded.

"They've wagons of metal that fly down the road faster than an arrow from a bow. And over the rainbow, into this world, a wind blew the lady and her wolfhound, where she met a man named Shawn." Night after night, he wove together life in Shawn's world with ancient Celtic tales, the *munchkins* from Shawn's original story, and his own imagination. "The lady searched her reticule and found no gold," he went on. The fire crackled with the juices of deer meat dripping in it, off long sharp sticks. "But Shawn, with a wave of his hand, took gold from walls."

"Shawn—why is a man called *old?*" asked one of the Gaelic Highlanders.

"Because his life spanned seven hundred years. 'Twould make him very old, though he remained young and strong those many centuries."

Over the nights awaiting Edward's reply, Niall worked himself and Allene, James, and the new bairn, all with different names, into a tapestry of the histories Shawn had told him.

"'Tis more fantastic than King Herla," said Owen. "Where d' ye come up wi' sich stories, Niall?"

Niall smiled. "We must think on summat, while we wait on Edward, aye?" He rose from his seat on a lichen-covered boulder at the side of the fire. "I'll be checking on the prisoners, now." He wandered to the northern end of the glen, where several of Glenmirril's men circled the prisoners' tents.

"All's well," Hugh reported, as Niall approached.

Niall checked each tent, nodding to each lord and town magistrate. At the last, he lifted the flap, soaked with the day's rain, and entered. "A game of chess, my Lord?"

The young Northampton looked up from where he sat on a cot, wearing once-fine garb much the worse for wear after days on the road with the raiding Scots. His lean young face was drawn with cold and boredom. "If you've a board available, my Lord. I thank thee."

Niall produced a small set lent him by Walter Stewart. They set out the pieces and began, by the light of a candle, sliding pawns, rooks, and knights in silence. Northampton pushed a pawn into the square occupied by Niall's knight, smiling. "You're usually a better player, my Lord."

Niall chuckled softly. "Usually. I've a great deal on my mind."

Northampton grinned. "Shouldn't it be me as has a great deal on his mind, seeing as I'm the captive in enemy hands?"

Niall dismissed his concern with a wave of his hand. "You're well fed and housed better than my men out there. In a month or two, your father will pay your ransom and you'll be home. 'Tis naught but an excursion in lovely Scotland, aye?"

"An excursion in Scotland, anyway," the young lord replied. "Does the mist and rain here ever stop?"

"But of course. We've a few clear days in July." Niall jumped his remaining knight over the ranks of pawns.

Northampton studied the move briefly before grimacing.

"Or," Niall added, "your king may grant our terms and ye'll be home anon."

Northampton withdrew a rook from danger. "Think you we like Edward any better than you? He's mismanaged England from the start, more interested in Hugh Despenser and thatching roofs than running a kingdom. Had his father lived, we'd never have lost at Bannockburn."

Niall smiled, pushing a pawn forward. "You'll understand we see it as a blessing his father didn't live."

Northampton laughed easily. "I do. Still, to be on the receiving end of the Scots raids, with our king unwilling to help, yet unwilling to treat so you'll stop...." He spread his hands. "It's not a position I wish to see my children in, God willing I live long enough to have any." After a moment's consideration, he lifted a bishop between delicate fingers, moving it along the diagonal to face Niall's pawn. "Have you children, Lord Campbell?"

"Call me Niall," Niall said.

"Call me Charles."

Niall moved his rook, claiming the unlucky bishop. "I'm surprised you didn't see that. I've a young son, and a bairn on the way. Are you married?"

"Aye, just last month."

"Is she bonny, then?"

Charles shrugged. "Her dowry is. It appealed greatly to my father. She's fair enough, though young. She's hardly said two words to me." He smiled. "I may find my time in Scotland pleasant after all, with no fear of scaring young women."

"Our lasses don't scare so easily." Niall fell silent as Charles's hand hovered over first one piece, then another, and finally settled on a pawn, moving it two spaces. Niall's thoughts drifted to Shawn. He'd found arranged marriage a horror. In his time, England and Scotland no longer fought. *Haven't for a long time,* Shawn had said. *Why would they? They've joined and become the United Kingdom.* People traveled back and forth freely, as they had before Alexander's death had prompted Longshanks to reach out his hand for another bauble in his crown.

Niall moved his bishop into play, careful to keep it out of the grasp of Charles's knight. "Imagine a time when we live in peace," he said. "A time when we visit one another as guest and friend rather than captor and hostage." The candle flickered in a draft, throwing shadows of knights and kings rearing at one another.

"I hear you tell stories of such a time and place," Charles said.

Niall sighed. "It passes time. I like being here as little as do you."

"Perhaps less if you've a wife you'd like to go home to." Charles slid his king.

"Aye, I'd very much like to be home with her. On Edward's whims hang all our lives. D' ye think he'll give us peace, now we've struck as far south as Richmond?"

Charles shook his head, the game forgotten. "He'll not care until you tear his palace down around his head, until you affect *his* life."

Niall pushed his queen out, threatening Charles's king. "An unlikely thing."

Charles stared glumly at the pieces. "I believe that's stalemate."

Niall studied the board a long while before agreeing. "I believe it is. An unsatisfying conclusion, aye?"

"Most unsatisfying."

Niall sighed, and leaned back in his chair, studying the young lord. "Are you a praying man?" he asked.

"For what those prayers are worth, aye, I am," the captive responded.

Niall smiled. "Is it safe to guess you pray for peace?"

"But of course!" Charles laughed. "Not that I don't appreciate the games of chess, but still I should prefer my castle to your tent."

Niall smiled more broadly, but then sobered. "If the English pray for peace and Scots pray for peace, then to whose prayers does God listen, that we don't have it?"

Charles lifted his hands in resignation.

"Do you ever doubt the worth of your prayers?" Niall asked.

Candle light flickered over the young man's face. It took a moment before he answered. "Suppose I did. What then? To whom else would I turn?" He began resetting the pieces. "Perhaps that you and I can play chess together is the promise that our prayers *are* being heard, but it is simply not yet time."

Niall considered that, as he set up his pawns. "To think so at least renews hope."

"My Lord Niall!"

Niall started at the sound of his name, and excusing himself, went to the tent flap. Owen waited there, dark circles under his eyes in the moonlight that had risen since Niall had entered the tent, his hair damp from having been under a chain hood all day. "My Lord Douglas summons you."

They both glanced at Charles, Lord of Northampton. "Pray you 'tis good news," Niall said, aware he spoke as if the young man himself were to blame.

Charles smiled tightly. The candle threw shadows over his face. "I've done little else, this fortnight in captivity."

Midwest America, Present

Moonlight glowed through the floor to ceiling windows on either side of the soaring fireplace. The bourbon left a sweet, warm glow on Shawn's insides. It only increased his wonder that he and Aaron could be friends, to discover the man he'd once scorned had worthwhile things to say. He sprawled back in his leather chair, a new bottle on the table at his side. "Why do you think it's so hard to say you're sorry?" His feet crossed one another on the coffee table, black-stockinged toes swaying back and forth. He hadn't been drunk, not really drunk, in two years, and didn't intend to become so now. He was by far sober enough to realize that, without the drink, he wouldn't ask such a question. Especially not of Aaron.

"It's admitting we failed." Aaron leaned forward to pour himself another glass.

Shawn nodded, noting the way Aaron said *we*, not *you*. Diplomatic, he thought.

"We all screw up," Aaron said, as if reading his thoughts and correcting him.

"Really?" Shawn couldn't keep the sardonic note from his voice. "When have you ever screwed up, Altar Boy?"

Aaron laughed, a low, dry sound that seemed to understand the epitaph was aimed at Shawn himself, a scathing criticism of himself for having once used it. "If you'd known me before...."

"Go ahead. You know every ugly thing I've ever done. Tell me what you did."

The fire burned low in the grate between the tall, dark windows. "I grew up in the projects in L.A." Aaron swished his drink in slow circles, staring into the dim room. "You grew up in a posh suburb. I guarantee you haven't done anything, even now, that I wasn't doing when I was fourteen."

The words hung, with no elaboration, between them. The silence was comfortable, something Shawn had only experienced with Niall, Amy, Christina, and Allene. Shawn watched his toes a moment before asking, "How does a kid like that end up in classical music?"

Aaron stared into a world of his own. "Talent, luck," he said. "A band director who wouldn't take no for an answer." He laughed again, suddenly, a short, sharp bark. "Altar boy, huh? You know I have two kids?"

Shawn shook his head, still working on absorbing the last images, a fourteen-year-old doing things he himself hadn't done, into the framework of the man he'd scorned as disgustingly chaste. "How old?"

"Jonathan was born when I was fifteen. He's eleven, and I've just convinced his mom to take my offer to get him out. He'll be here in a couple of weeks."

Shawn coughed. "How's Celine with that?"

Aaron smiled, a slow, private smile that touched things Shawn knew he'd never tell, not with the best bourbon in the world. "She has a heart as beautiful as she is. She's the one who made me keep trying. My daughter, Irena, she's eight. Cutest thing you ever saw. Her mom—she's more interested in drugs—decided to send her to me. She'll be here before school starts in September."

They sat in silence. The moon rose, a silver, glowing orb, in the window. The fire crackled, casting shadows on the leather furniture. Aaron leaned forward, topping off his drink. "Apologizing to people was the hardest thing I ever did. It meant saying I'm a fuck-up, you know. Nobody wants to believe that, let alone admit it to someone else. You don't know what they'll do with that piece of you.

It's not like they don't already know, but when you admit it, you hand them a weapon and then you can only pray they won't use it against you."

Shawn nodded. "Yeah."

After another comfortable silence, Aaron spoke again. "As long as you don't admit it, you hope you can keep bullshitting them and they can't pin anything on you, you hope you can keep convincing them the problem is them, and then you'll be safe. When you apologize, you cut away your safety net."

And you promise to change, Shawn thought. That promise had kept Caroline emboldened throughout the plane ride, working her way in next to him again, laying her hand on his knee, suggesting she give him a ride home. She had no fear of him, as she might have before.

"Why did you do it?" Aaron asked.

Shawn brought his bourbon-pleasant gaze back to Aaron. "Do what?"

Aaron stared into his drink. "Celine."

"Oh." Shawn didn't know what to say. The glass sagged in his hand, coming to rest on the arm of the recliner. He tried to remember why. "She's so much like Amy used to be," he said, almost to himself. That was it! "Amy was mad. Didn't trust me." He knew the rest. He couldn't say it.

"You tried to recapture what you had with Amy. Before you blew it."

Shawn nodded, and dropped his head back against the chair's pillow, hating himself for admitting it; sober enough to know that if he was just a little more sober, he wouldn't have. If he'd been a great deal more sober two years ago, he would have seen what fairy dust he'd been chasing, trying such a thing. And still expecting that somehow, things would get better with Amy.

"Maybe it's time you step to the other side of the fence," Aaron said.

Shawn opened his eyes. "What's that supposed to mean?"

"You don't like apologizing? Asking forgiveness?" Aaron rose, going to the dark floor to ceiling window, with the golden moonlight pouring through. At last, he turned. "You also have forgiving to *do*, and it's going to set you free."

Scottish Borders, Autumn, 1316

Silent prayer ran through Niall's mind as he made his way through the dark and drizzling camp, winding among tents, and guards, and men sleeping around camp fires. *Let this be the end. God, let there be peace.* His heart raged with hope.

He arrived at Douglas's tent, to be ushered in by a guard. Inside, two large candles gave more light, by far, than had been in Northampton's tent, flickering on canvas walls. Douglas sat at the table. Walter Stewart marched back and forth across the small space, gripping his heavy riding gloves. "He refused even to *see* our envoy," he fumed. He stopped only a moment, glancing at Niall, before shouting, "He left us waiting three days—*three days!*—before sending word he would not see us, that he would accept no terms. He never even *looked* at the terms."

"He knows the terms," Douglas sighed. "They've not changed. They could not get easier."

Niall's hopes and heart fell. "What now, my Lord?" he asked.

Douglas raised tired eyes to Niall. "Get some sleep," he said. "I leave at dawn to make haste to Bruce. Bring the hostages, cattle, and iron, and meet us in Melrose."

Niall bowed. "Yes, my Lord."

He took his leave, winding back through the camp to where the men of Glenmirril slept, to find Hugh on a rock, keeping watch. He lifted his great, shaggy head as Niall approached, asking, "What word?"

"He'll not accept," Niall said tersely. "We bring the cattle and hostages to Bruce in Melrose."

A broad smile spread across Hugh's face. "God be praised! Did I not tell you ye'd be home soon enough?"

"I may be home within the month," Niall replied, "but without Edward ready to negotiate, I'll soon be leaving again."

Hugh clapped Niall on the shoulder. "The war *will* end."

"Aye, but when?" Niall asked. They stared at the low embers, before Niall spoke again. "The Bruce questions if God is punishing him, still, for murdering Comyn before the altar. But if that be true, then how long does God punish, and why does he not punish Edward? Surely he has lived no better a life."

Hugh shrugged. "We cannot know, Niall. But if our king can remain faithful through his trials, so can we."

"Is our cause not just?" Niall persisted.

Hugh stared into the embers. "It is just, Niall. To fight tyranny is always just. You'll see. It'll come aright." After another moment, he smiled. "Get some rest. Ye've a long ride to Allene."

Her name brought a smile to Niall's face. "Aye," he said, rising from the boulder.

"And Niall?"

Niall stopped, waiting.

"You must continue praying."

"Aye," he said flatly. Leaving the soft glow of the embers, Niall crawled into the small tent he shared with Conal. Pulling his tartan over his shoulder, he thought of Shawn, home in his own bed, happy with Amy and his son. He was on his way back to Allene. *God,* he prayed, *thank you. Forgive my ingratitude. Help me do better.* He rolled over on his side, fixing his mind on Hugh's admonition to keep faith, and the promise of home, as he settled into the dark of sleep.

Midwest America, Present

Hatred railed in Shawn as he realized what Aaron was saying. He set his bourbon down hard on the end table. "Forgiveness doesn't even compute with murder. The two don't connect in any way." His voice rose. "Are you saying I should be friends with that little piece of...."

"I'm saying...."

Shawn burst from his chair. "Who told you about it anyway? Did you get some mixed-up story? Do you *get* that he stabbed my father a dozen times? For *drugs?*"

"I'm saying...."

Shawn strode the length of the living room, his shoulders bunched in fury. "A fit of anger because he couldn't have drugs, that's what he killed my father for. And ruined my life for."

"Listen to yourself," Aaron pressed. "Ruined your life. Did you ever make that connection?"

"No, that's not what it's...." But Shawn stopped, looking back over the years. He shook his head. "How can you see that?" The drinking had started days after the funeral, the women not long after.

"It's easy to see from the outside." Aaron stood by his chair.

"Why should I forgive that? What he did—it just keeps spreading."

"Spread it the other way. You know you didn't have to do any of what you did."

"I kept seeing it over and over!" Shawn shouted.

"Your mother had just as bad a loss," Aaron said. "What does *she* do with it?"

Shawn glared. He had no answer. He spun, planting his hands on the stone fireplace, leaning his head into his stiff arms. "Drinking stopped the nightmares."

"Being with someone stopped the hatred and emptiness for awhile," Aaron shot back. "I *get* it. But you used them, every single one of them."

"What was I *supposed* to do?" Shawn asked. "I kept seeing it."

"Didn't anything I just told you about my life sink in? Don't you think I *know* something about hatred and emptiness?"

Shawn shook his head. "Saying it's okay isn't the answer."

"You think that's what they're saying when they forgive you? Is that what you want from Amy, to say it was all okay?"

Shawn shook his head again, staring down at the floor.

The clock on the mantel ticked, loud, slow ticks.

Finally, Aaron spoke softly. "When you can forgive him, you'll understand how they can forgive you." When Shawn didn't answer, he said, "Just go see him. I'll go with you if it'll help. Just think about it. Let me know if you want me to do that."

Shawn stayed, braced against the fireplace, head down. The image of the boy filled his mind, ragged, rat-like, and malicious, in a way it hadn't done in two years. "No," he snapped. "I don't want you to do that. He needs to rot in prison."

CHAPTER TEN

It's early morning in America. I do the math as I open the cheery blue door of my home, as I've done it all morning, through another rehearsal, my mind caught in Shawn. "Hello? Carol?"

The house is quiet.

I step inside, looking down the hall, into the front room, glance up the stairs. It's silent. Carol must have taken James to the stores. Uncharacteristically, I feel only relief at being alone, no Carol, no James.

In the thirty some hours since Shawn's departure, he's barely left my mind. I wonder how he's handling being back in his own home, if anything happened with Caroline. And I'm flustered by my reaction at the airport yesterday, at the more or less promise that slipped out, that I hadn't decided to make.

No Shawn.

I kick off my shoes, drop my violin on the coffee table, and prop my feet up beside it, pressing the heels of my palms to my eyes. Thoughts of him distracted me throughout rehearsal again today. This is my profession, my livelihood, my reputation. And I did poorly.

I drop my hands. My eyes fall on the picture of Glenmirril Angus gave me. Indecision and guilt, I think. They are exhausting, demanding companions. I'm not happy with my decision at the airport yesterday. Shawn is quite capable of appearing exemplary for a week or two. I know that. Yet I let myself be sucked in, let him draw emotion from me again, as easily as he always has, as easily as he weaves magic with his music.

I want what we once had—working together on music, playing duets, stolen weekends away, his quick smile and joyful laugh. I miss it all, and I miss Angus. I miss Angus standing beside me at the battlefield holding out a coffee as he clutched his blue knit hat. I miss sitting side by side in archives with him, and climbing hills hand in hand; I miss the jokes he sent in his e-mails.

I'll never be happy with either decision, not entirely.

I glance at my phone, on the coffee table. I want to hear Angus's voice. I drop my head back against the couch, re-living memories—driving to the Highland games, excited about the classical music station he'd found; the intensity of his eyes that always felt as if he saw into my soul and found it good. Kissing him on the small patch of rocky shore behind Glenmirril, when I believed Shawn was dead; and in the pub, knowing he was alive. Racing to Iona, not even two weeks ago, plunging across what Angus claimed were not rough seas, and flying back across the country to Glenmirril; knowing his actions that night were not for himself, but for me and James.

Love is not self-seeking.

And now, suddenly, it's over, with no warning. Angus removed himself, without consulting me. Shawn is swirling me back into rehearsals and concerts and runs to the airport.

I touch the phone. Irritation rises. Angus could have tried harder. He didn't have to just walk away. I lift the phone. He's right, wanting me to sort it out with Shawn. I press the phone to my lips, thinking if he's at home or work—and wondering what I can say to him. I kissed Shawn again, swept in emotion. Angus wants my heart, all of it, and he's right to want that, but I'm caught in between. If I talk to Angus, will it make things clearer or murkier? I drop the phone to my lap, staring at it as if it will tell me the answers.

Glenmirril, Autumn 1316

"Please thank your laird for the book." MacDougall indicated *The Golden Legend* lying on the table.

Red set down the daily meal and picked up the book, without a word.

"Ha' ye read it?" MacDougall asked.

"No."

MacDougall doubted the boy could read at all. "I can teach you to read," he said.

Red's eyes lit up, but he said nothing.

"I'm particularly drawn to St. Francis. He was close to the birds and beasts."

"Aye."

"They say you are, too," MacDougall tried.

"Aye." Red backed toward the door.

"I'm grateful one such as you is caring for my hobins."

"They're fine animals!" A broad grin appeared on the boy's face.

"You're only recently come to Glenmirril, are you not?" MacDougall asked.

"Aye, Sir Niall brought me."

"Where did you meet Sir Niall?"

Red merely stared.

MacDougall tried another tack. "I'd hoped to talk with Sir Niall's monk."

Agitation crossed Red's face. "Brother Andrew's gone—back to his monastery." He backed out the door. It slammed, locking MacDougall back into isolation. He turned back to the window, musing as he strained on the bars—pushing and pulling in a steady rhythm. His instinct, that first day in the cell, had been right. There was something unusual about the monk. In these months in his cell, he had not seen him, or heard of him. And why should a monk returning to his monastery—a monk he could hardly have known well—cause the boy agitation?

MacDougall searched his mind for anything he knew of the boy. He knew only that he was not of Glenmirril, that Niall had brought him from somewhere—and the question of the monk caused him agitation.

Midwest America, Present

Shawn woke with two thoughts on his mind. Amy. The boy. He'd won Amy back. He'd call her immediately—it would be early afternoon in Scotland—and build on it, keep the momentum going. The boy, well—he wasn't visiting the louse in prison, that was that. Aaron had been crazy to even think such a thing.

The smell of coffee drifted in. Shawn smiled, loving being back. A punch of a button last night, and his coffee was waiting for him! Sitting up in his king-sized bed, he looked around his expansive bedroom, remembering all he'd loved about it, especially the morning sun pouring in the tall leaded glass windows. He smoothed his hand over the soft, forest green comforter. Damn, it felt better than sleeping on the ground with Hugh snoring in his ear!

Swinging his feet to the plush carpet, he grabbed his phone off the nightstand, stabbing *call* at Amy's name, as he crossed the marbled foyer, to the kitchen. He waited through the rings while he poured coffee, breathing deeply of hazelnut.

As he sipped, her voice came over the line. "This is Amy. Leave a message."

"Hey, where are you?" he asked. "Give me a call, okay? I love you, I miss you. Call me." He hung up, disappointed. She was probably in the bathroom, or nursing James. She'd call in a few minutes.

Aaron's suggestion crept back in. He pushed it away irritably. There was work to be done. Work always kept things at bay, and he was eager to resume his life and re-establish himself. Going to his office, across the granite foyer from the music room, he settled himself at his polished walnut desk, taking out a legal tablet and his Cross pen. It felt light and insubstantial after the quills Allene had pressed on him. He quickly filled a page with the elegant medieval script she'd made him learn, listing all he wanted to accomplish. A long to-do list always kept thoughts of the boy at bay. It would today, too.

Inverness, Present

"Tickets for the Edinburgh Festival." Claire, the new young secretary, dropped an envelope on Angus's desk, her pony tail bouncing, her red cardigan vibrant against her freckled face. She grinned, her head tilted to one side. "I'd hate to go alone."

Angus glanced up, his pen poised over his report. He was sure his attempt at a smile came out more as a grimace. She was nice. He hated watching her do this, when he'd shown no interest. "I work that day," he said.

"No, you don't." From his desk, Clive scribbled at his own report, not looking up. "I just gave you the day off. Freddy will do your beat."

Angus studied Claire's hopeful smile. He *was* lonely. "Freddy's useless on the water," he said. "What if we get a call?"

Clive slapped his pen down, glowering across the narrow space between their desks. "What if we get a call on your day off?"

Angus stared at his report, the words swimming before his eyes. Claire *was* nice. Pretty. Cheerful. Never a bad word to say about anyone. He fought with himself. It wasn't fair to her.

"We've these things called mobile phones," Clive snapped. "Go."

Angus's grimace relaxed into something more like a real smile. He'd been accused of taking dating too seriously. It was just a day out, no more. Surrounded by crowds. "Sure, Claire. It'll be fun. I'll pick you up."

She beamed, and bounced off, her ponytail swinging.

"You're a fool," Clive muttered.

Angus's cell phone buzzed in his pocket. "I'm not a fool," he said, reaching for it. "I'm trying to do the right thing."

"Any of the lads out there would love to have her drop tickets on their desk," Clive responded. "She's lovely."

Angus glanced at the caller ID. He drew in a quick breath. A smile flitted across his face, before he saw Clive frowning at him. He tamped it down, hit *talk,* and said with professional detachment, "Inspector MacLean."

"Since when do you answer your *personal* phone *Inspector MacLean?*" Clive muttered. "'Tis Amy, is it not?"

Midwest America, Present

In a long morning of fast dialing and faster talking, Shawn connected with Ben on the tour plans, arranged three more appearances with orchestras around the Midwest, talked with a publisher about putting out a new collection of his—and Amy's, he reminded himself—arrangements, scheduled two recording sessions, and hired the necessary musicians.

Midday, he called Amy again, once more getting voice mail. He dialed his mother, finding her at a park with Ina and James. "Amy had rehearsal," she said. "Sometimes she has coffee with Sarah afterward. Maybe she forgot to turn her phone back on."

He spoke instead to James, who gurgled and cooed and spit ear-splitting shrieks of glee back to him, bringing a smile to his face. On hanging up, he booked flights to Scotland and back to the States. He'd have a few weeks with Amy. He hoped it would be enough, with the promise he'd return again.

He glanced around the office, pulling out large envelopes and addressing them, before crossing the granite foyer to the music room to get parts for the musicians. They'd go in the mail first thing tomorrow morning. It all kept his mind off Aaron's urging to visit the prison—and off Amy's silence. He pushed music into envelopes—double checking parts and player names—and did another quintet arrangement, before looking again at the silent phone. It would be late in Scotland.

His jaw tensed, wondering how she could be so late, why she didn't return his calls —if she was with Angus. But the man lived two hundred miles away. He was being ridiculous. Besides, she'd promised him.

Hadn't she?

He frowned, trying to remember her exact words.

But he'd called three times. He'd send her an e-mail, he decided. Leaving the score paper for his laptop, he pulled up his account. Maybe a virtual card, something telling her all the wonderful things women loved to hear. Make sure she knew he was thinking of her. Too bad he couldn't send one to Niall, Allene, and Christina. He paused, trying to remember his password. The writer in New York— or the woman with the horses? It didn't matter which one, he knew the name. He tapped it in.

Blood-red letters popped up: *This password is invalid.*

He stared at the words, confused. It had been two years, but he'd been using her name, *Debra*, long before his disappearance. He typed it again, more slowly.

The letters jumped out at him again.

He tried a third time, changing the spelling, with the same result. Panic fluttered in his chest. There were details in those e-mails that he and several women did not want made public. Had someone changed the password? Amy? Had a reporter or fan hacked in? He pressed a hand to his forehead, trying to think. "Damn," was the only thought that came to mind. He paced a length of the office, aware he was behaving distressingly like Conrad, and succeeded in dragging up a second thought. "Shit!"

Right about now, medieval life, having a visible, tangible opponent, looked good.

"Damn!" He looked at the phone. Amy already had multiple voice mails from him. After all his lies, she just might not think his concerns were good enough reason to bug her again.

He did another lap of the office. It wasn't big enough for the serious pacing this required. He burst into the hall, nearly running its length, trying to think who he could call. He dashed back to the office, checked the orchestra roster, and punched in a number. Aaron answered immediately.

"Amy would have told Celine," Shawn burst out. "Celine would have told you. Did Amy get into my e-mail?"

Silence came back over the line.

Shawn's heart hammered. It *had* to be Amy. Those e-mails *couldn't* get out. "Come on, Aaron!" Panic flooded his voice. He marched down the hall to the great room and the window-flanked fireplace. "Help me out here! What do you know?"

Aaron chuckled.

"What are you laughing about," Shawn demanded. His old self descended firmly over his shoulders. Aaron would be looking for a new job! Across the country, back in the projects! His eyebrows drew down in a ferocious scowl.

Aaron laughed out loud. "Well, look who's back. Haven't you ever had a friend? A real friend?"

Shawn paused; feeling as he did coming out of a drunken stupor, trying to make sense of what was happening. Past and present swirled around him, like the aftereffects of a hangover. "Niall," he said. "Niall was a real friend. A brother."

A sound somewhere between a snort and a laugh erupted over the phone. "Then you know he'd laugh at you, too. And tell you you got yourself into this mess."

"Yeah." The anger shot back out. "Then he'd help me."

"Don't forget I met Niall. He'd have fun watching you squirm first," Aaron said, a broad grin in his voice. "Know what I like about cell phones?"

"They can't be hacked into?"

"I can turn off the ringer." He hung up.

Inverness, Present

Angus pushed away from his desk, and hurried out of the small office, as her voice breathed over the line. "Is it okay to ask how you are—*Inspector MacLean*?"

She was laughing at him. He smiled. He passed Claire at her desk, flashed a guilty smile, and moved faster, through the front doors to the street outside. "I'm fine." His voice fell. "He's back in America. Why are you calling?" Afternoon sunshine fell on his dark uniform.

"I miss you."

He swallowed, torn. He stepped back for a woman pushing a pram with two babies bundled inside. They were the size of James. He wanted to say, *I miss you, too.* He missed her so badly it was a physical ache. The woman hurried past. He drew breath and forced himself to speak gruffly. "Does Shawn know you're calling?"

"No." She hesitated, before adding softly, "I think you knew that."

"Then we're doing what he did to you." His voice dropped, and he hated the plea he heard in it. "Unless you've decided."

"How can I," she asked, "when you walked away? You didn't leave me many options."

A bird trilled from its perch overhead. A car honked in the street. "I left you with the space to decide what you really want."

"You thought walking away would just erase everything between us and leave me back at square one to deal with him in a vacuum?"

"I don't know!" he said in frustration. "I'm trying to do the right thing. For you. For me. I can't go on like this, Amy." He paced the sidewalk before the police station. A flock of gulls fluttered to scraps of bread at the corner. "You have to leave me entirely, or take him out of your heart."

"I'm trying."

"Trying which?"

"I don't *know*," she said in frustration. "I can't make myself feel and not feel on command. I didn't want any of this to happen."

"I'm not blaming you," he said softly. He stared at the shimmering sunlight on the River Ness a moment before asking, even as he told himself not to, not to set himself up: "You love him?"

"I'm so confused right now, I hardly know what the word means anymore," she said.

"Love is patient, love is kind." He wondered, at her silence, if she thought he'd been unkind, or less than patient, to walk away. "It's because I love you that it hurts so much," he said softly, "waiting to see if I'm door number one or two."

"I shouldn't have called," she said, and a moment later, "I just need to know, Angus, was it really that easy for you to walk away from me?" Her voice broke. "Because if it was, then I'm torn for no reason. I may as well embrace all the good in Shawn, give James his father so he never has to grow up asking questions, and save myself this heartache."

His mouth tightened. It would be best to tell her it *was* that easy. Set her free. A middle-aged couple walked by, hand in hand, smiling at each other. He drew in a breath, his throat tight; he tried to say it: *Yes, it was that easy.* "No," came out instead, on a ragged sigh. The couple glanced at him. He fought to keep the words in, but they tumbled out. "I feel like I'm being crucified. Every day hurts. But it hurts, too, knowing half your heart is with him. I wish I could make it easier for both of us, Amy."

She said nothing. He turned, and walked the other direction, passing the station again. "Amy?"

"I'm sorry," she whispered. "I just wanted to hear your voice."

He hesitated, at the station door. "Give it time," he said. They were meaningless words, he berated himself. "Amy, if you're with him, you can't call me."

He pushed *end.* He stood for a minute, listening to the traffic, watching the cars crowd the city street, and people hurrying by, laughing, scowling, thoughtful—all the colors of emotion swirling by him.

Bannockburn, Present

I sink into a chair in the small walled garden, the silent phone pressed to my lips. Clothes flutter from the line, snapping cheerfully in the breeze. I want to be angry, but Angus is right. Love is patient, love is kind. He's been those things. I have to be kind and leave him alone unless I can walk away from Shawn entirely. A part of me hopes Shawn will do something stupid, make the decision easy. But it's impossible not to fall in love all over again, seeing him live out everything I always believed him to be, deep down.

"Amy?" Carol's voice comes from the kitchen.

I jump from the chair. "I'm in the garden." With the phone clutched in my hand, I plaster on a smile for Carol, already opening the door.

Carol hesitates in the kitchen doorway, looking out into the small patch of walled yard. "Are you okay?"

"Fine." I slide the phone into my pocket. I give a laugh. "I can't believe how much laundry one baby can create." James's bibs and blankets and onesies flutter from the line.

Carol smiles. "I'm just back from the store. Stew or fish?"

"Fish. I'll be in to help in a minute."

Carol shuts the door. I lower myself back into the chair. The breeze dies and the sun suddenly becomes warm on my hair and shoulders. I should go to Angus. I stare, unseeing, at the clothes fluttering like banners, trying to imagine walking away from Shawn. He's become the man I always believed was there. I want to be with him. I want to be with Angus.

What I need, I decide, is time away from both of them. Now is the time, with Shawn gone. From the kitchen, I hear Carol's voice, chirping to James. My mind made up, I jump from the chair, ready to go in, eager once more to see James.

Inverness, Present

A hand touched his arm. Angus turned.

"Are you all right?" Claire's freckled face stared up at him in concern.

He nodded.

"Is it Amy?"

"How can you ask that?" Angus said. "'Tis not exactly a secret, about her. You and I are going to the Edinburgh Festival next week. Are we not supposed to at least pretend she's not here in my heart?"

Claire bit her lip. The gesture reminded him of Amy. "Ye've not noticed I'm not much good at pretending? I don't see the point."

Angus smiled, touched by her straight-forwardness, thinking of the times she'd left his favorite donut on his desk. "I guess I did notice," he admitted.

"I know I'm young and maybe naive, but I see you don't feel for me as I feel for you. It's okay, Inspector. Maybe some day you will, and if not, I'll know I didn't sit around pining and maybe pass up a chance. Maybe at least, I can put a little happiness back on your face, like I used to see."

He studied her, trying to fathom it. "You understand she's all I think about?"

Claire nodded vigorously. The black ponytail bounced. "I'm asking nothing of you. You demand too much of yourself." She held out her hand, a wordless offer.

His face relaxed into a genuine smile. "Maybe I am."

"Take a break from saving the world, Inspector, and enjoy the Festival."

He let her take his hand and lead him back into the station.

Midwest America, Present

"Damn you!" Shawn glared at the phone as he stabbed *end*. This was hardly funny. He marched up the hall again, into the great room, where he glared out one of the floor to ceiling windows, his fingers pressed to his temples, trying to think.

Celine's e-mails were in that account. Aaron would know that. His breathing slowed. Celine had been deeply humiliated by the bare bones on the trading cards. His heart slowed. Aaron would not be laughing if there was an Englishman's chance against Douglas that real details were out there floating to who knows whose desk in cyberspace. He took a deep breath.

If the details were out there, they'd have already hit the news stands.

So why hadn't Aaron just said so?

Shawn stared out across the broad expanse of yard, into the pine and oak wood beyond. A stream ran through his property, with a small waterfall. He'd walked there with Celine. Aaron probably knew that. And more. His breathing slowed. What would he have done, had Aaron walked through the woods with Amy, and more, and then come to him for help?

He trailed slowly back, from the great room to the office. With a deep, steadying breath, he tried one more password. And a second. The third one worked. He stared at the inbox, thick with unread e-mails, from a dozen women he could barely remember. Shame washed over him as he stared at them, at all he'd done to Amy, at the last of Celine's pleading e-mails. Aaron must have some idea of those, too, and of Shawn's cold responses.

He picked up the phone with unwilling hands, and dialed. Aaron's voicemail answered, cracking a joke and beeping in his ear. Shawn drew a breath. "Thank you. For a few things. I deserved that."

He set the receiver down, and leaned back. If he'd been in Aaron's place, he'd never be friends with someone like himself. He'd never offer himself a second chance. Maybe Aaron was right about seeing forgiveness from both sides.

He sat down at his desk and, with shaking hands, looked up the number for the prison.

Inverness, Present

Simon watched from across the river as Angus turned back into the jail house. He'd helped himself, at the indoor markets, to several hats to pull low over his eyes, and waited, watching the station from across the river, listening the while, to talk around him. With the excitement of Shawn's return fading, he heard nothing of use. He watched as men and women entered the jail in the morning, came and went throughout the day, and left again. But as afternoon wore into late evening, it became apparent he'd missed Angus's departure.

It didn't matter. Sieges took time, and he had that. Angus would be here every day. Sooner or later, Simon would be able to follow him to his home.

He smiled, sure of his success, and headed back to his new home to prepare food, and train. He had to be fit and ready to fight when he returned to his own time.

CHAPTER ELEVEN

Scottish Borders, Autumn 1316

"Feeling better?" Hugh beamed with pleasure, as their horses trotted under the morning sun, through the mist that rolled over the autumn hills, almost a week later.

"Reaching Scotland helps," Niall said. His harp bumped along his back, and his sword at his side. With Hugh and Conal, Owen and Lachlan, a host of fighting men, and several lads, he nudged fifty cattle, and horses loaded with gold, plate, jewels, and iron, up into the border hills. His spirits rose, his senses sharpened by the brisk chill and bright colors of October. "I've but to deliver cattle and prisoners to Bruce and be on my way home!" He raised his hand to his eyes, scanning the misty hills. "Though these cattle seem aggravatingly unconcerned about English pursuit."

"Let me see if I can get the men to hurry them along." Hugh slapped his reins, and rode ahead.

Wind blew cold down the glens, gusts yanking his cloak and chilling his fingers, and the lads, no more than sixteen, huddled miserably in their poor gear. Niall thanked God the physical demands of the day warmed him, though only just. The cattle plodded in their shaggy coats, now and again giving a lowing that echoed up the hills, sending nervous glances darting among the men. Niall, too, looked behind for signs of pursuit.

Owen gave him a curious glance. "Ye've done this more'na dozen times, Niall. There are so many glens the English will never find us. This is the stream ye usually have us stop at. Will ye no stop this time?"

"Aye," muttered Niall. For all the details Shawn had given, it was impossible to be completely accurate. He called the men, his voice carrying down the narrow ravine. The cattle shambled to the stream's rocky shore. Niall looked up to the clouds scudding across the sky. They were barely into Scotland.

"Be quick," he called. "We've a ways still until Melrose." Being so close to England made him nervous. He squatted on a flat, gray stone at the edge of a stream as gray as an old warrior's beard, and scooped cold water into his mouth. Shawn would be drinking fine wine. He'd be warm. He'd be with Amy. It had been more than four months since Niall had seen Allene. *Why, My Lord Savior?*

The question burned, despite his attempt at gratitude. *If I could only understand,* he thought silently to God. Why could there not be peace? Why, for all his prayers and devotion these many years, could he not be granted time with his wife and son? Why did a man like Shawn, who ignored God, merit a life of peace and ease?

Niall tried to bite back the thought in shame. Who was he to judge? Hadn't Shawn done a great deal of good here? But it persisted. Why did a man who scorned God get every blessing in life?

The cattle lowed. Niall rose, calling his men. "Up a ways, as fast as they'll move." Checking to see that all had heeded, he swung back onto the great bay liberated from England, and, bullying the shaggy cattle, they started on their way.

Niall drove the herd on, faster than they wanted to go, driving away his own thoughts. God ordained as God saw fit. He would think on God's words to Job. He'd do the task given him, and be grateful that, despite the delay waiting for Edward's snub, he *was* on his way home. The people of Shawn's time *weren't* all happy. He fooled himself, thinking Shawn's life was now perfect. It was not only wrong, but foolish, to envy what he didn't truly know, he reprimanded himself. He smiled, thinking of the fine horse beneath him, his homecoming, and the new bairn on the way. A bolt of sunshine shot through the gray clouds brushing the tops of the stark hills. They'd be at Melrose by nightfall. A few days, and he'd be home. In truth, life was not so bad. He smiled, thinking how near he was to seeing Allene.

Glenmirril, October 1316

Christina rode through the tunnel of pines, her back straight, and head high, a genteel half-smile curving her lips. Snow sprinkled her heavy blue cloak, flowing across the rump of her horse. "'Tis no better a fall than it was a summer," she remarked to Allene. "The Laird has done well providing for his people when so many go hungry."

"Aye." Her hand resting on her rounded stomach, Allene cast an eye to the late October sky, heavy with steel-gray clouds. She thought daily of Niall, far away in England, praying for him at Mass each morning, hoping he was not as miserable as she imagined he must be—and praying he would come home soon. "'Tis another miracle for Glenmirril, perhaps," she said, "that our crops and animals have done as well as they have." She turned to Red, riding behind them with Bessie. "We've left wood enough for the widow?"

"As much as we could carry, Milady," Red replied, drawing his horse alongside hers. "I'll chop more tomorrow."

"Then we'll take it to her next week," Allene said.

"My Lady," Red said, "you should not be riding even now, in your condition."

"I am fine, Red," Allene said. She glanced at Bessie, and lowered her voice. "Shawn assured me the women in his country carry on as normal while with child."

He responded, equally firmly, "My Lord Shawn is not here, Milady. Your father *is*, and he shall have my head if I allow you to ride out again."

She looked at him in surprise, realizing he was growing quickly into a man. Only months ago, he'd not have spoken so firmly.

"Taran and I will take it Friday week when our work is done."

Allene nodded, her mind sliding back to Christina. The autumn chill would explain the heavy cloaks she forever wore. But none of the other women seemed so cold even within the castle walls, even in the great hall with its four roaring hearths and the warmth of many bodies at meal times. She'd pressed Christina subtly, hoping for answers, as they stitched baby clothes, as they supervised the replacing of rush mats in the great hall and hanging of tapestries, as they carried food to the poor. But Christina's mask stayed in place, only making Allene more certain.

"Will that suit, Milady?" Red's tone suggested he'd asked once already.

"Aye, very well," Allene said. And to Christina, "Will they be needing more flour for the winter?"

"More can't hurt," Christina answered. "Though we'd best assure the castle stores are stocked ere we do so."

The horses clopped down the packed dirt path, coming out from among the pines, to Glenmirril's towering walls, slate gray against a blue gray loch. Wind whipped through Allene's cloak. She tugged it close, turning to see how Bessie fared in her patched garments. The girl's face was white. She wondered if Christina might speak to Bessie. They met in the gardens several times a week, walking hand in hand, heads leaned close talking in low voices. It might be Christina would feel safer confiding in a cook than in the daughter of a pious laird.

Their horses' hooves echoed back off the drawbridge. She wondered again what had passed between Shawn and Christina. Perhaps they'd all been too trusting in how he'd changed his ways. As they passed through the gatehouse and crossed the courtyard into the southern bailey, her eyes drifted up to the southern tower. Three stories up, MacDougall's bearded face filled the small window, gazing down at them. A shudder crept through her. She glanced at Christina, who stared straight ahead.

Melrose, Scotland, October 1316

Niall entered Bruce's chambers at Melrose Abbey, having been summoned the moment he arrived with the cattle. It would surely be something quick his king needed, and he would be home in a week or two, maybe even before the bairn was born. A fire roared in the grate, heaven-sent warmth after the chill outside. Niall loosened the collar of his cloak. He wanted to hold his chilled fingers to the fire roaring in the brazier, but he bowed low before Bruce. "Your Grace."

Bruce looked up from the desk where he and Douglas studied maps. "My Bard of Bannockburn!" He broke into a smile. "Finder of iron. A man of many talents. 'Tis glad I am to see you."

Niall smiled. He admired Bruce and Douglas greatly. But everything in him longed to be home with Allene. "As am I to see you, your Grace. 'Tis an honor." He sent up a prayer it would be a quick honor Bruce had in mind.

Bruce turned to Douglas and a cleric who sat over a pile of correspondence, his quill resting on the lip of an ink jar. "You've the papers from Edward?" Bruce asked.

"Peace?" Niall spoke in a quick breath, aware he was out of line, speaking so freely to his king.

But Bruce smiled. "Negotiations. Edward has requested talks after all."

Niall's brow furrowed. "But he refused to see us."

"He must have sent his man almost on their heels," Douglas said. "He arrived here shortly after I did."

"We must hope and pray," Bruce said gravely.

Emotions warred in Niall: anticipation, wanting to be in the thick of it, wanting to stride into this moment in history and leave a victorious letter for Shawn in the kneeler. *I did it, Shawn! I was there when the peace came about! I was there!* And he wanted to mount his pony and ride hard, ahead of the billowing winter clouds, back to Glenmirril.

Bruce held out a hand, into which the cleric laid a thick sheaf of parchments. Bruce scanned them, folded them, and sealed them, while Niall waited in silence, grateful at least for the fire's warmth. Bruce tapped the letters on the edge of his desk. "These are safe conduct papers. I need you and your men to escort the abbot safely that he might deliver them to Robert Hastings and Edward's new clerk, Robert of Baldock, in London." A smiled spread across the king's weary face.

"London, Your Grace?" Niall repeated, aware he sounded foolish. It was a week's ride or more with winter coming on. He added in waiting on Edward's whims, the likelihood of having to escort the negotiators, the ride back, reporting to Bruce afterward—if he didn't end up with his head on a pike—possibly staying for the negotiations, which could last who knew how long, and the long trek through the cold hills and glens, white with snow, to Glenmirril. The days spun through his head. It could be a month, or two, before he got home. The hills might become impassable.

Bruce beamed. "Aye, London. They are coming to Jedburgh to treat for peace."

Niall bowed. "Aye, Your Grace." He might be caught here until the raids started again in the spring. He might not see Allene, James, or the new child, until next fall. More than a year. His heart sank. He'd barely recognize James. "Very good tidings, Your Grace," Niall said, though his deeper thought was, *Why me?*

As if in answer, Bruce leaned forward. "I want you, as before, to get me any additional information there is to be gotten." He winked. "It would be unseemly for our abbots to befriend young women."

Niall bowed in acknowledgment. "What brought about his change of heart?"

"Perhaps," said Bruce, "our efforts here and in Ireland are swaying Edward."

"Then perhaps we will all be with our loved ones for Christmastide," Niall suggested hopefully.

Bruce shook his head. "Not so soon. Carrickfergus has fallen."

"The Irish castle your brother was besieging?"

Bruce nodded. "A stroke of luck. The ships sent to re-supply the castle were blown off course by a storm. They surrendered in September."

Niall had heard rumors—nightmarish tales—of the starvation in Ireland, of people eating their own horses. One story had made its way around the campfires that the desperate men holed inside Carrickfergus had eaten eight of their Scottish prisoners when they'd died. One did poorly to speak such rumors to a king. They couldn't possibly be true, anyway.

"My brother has need of more men," Bruce continued. "I sail with another two thousand in December."

"But if there's to be peace, Your Grace...."

"We've treated with the English before," Bruce said. "And it has come to naught. We will hope for the best but prepare for the worst. I sail in December. I need you and your men with me."

"To Ireland, Your Grace?" Niall asked weakly. The black memory of the loch's inky waters swirled up around Niall, bringing with it Alexander's bloated face. He swallowed against the darkening of his vision and forced himself to stand upright.

"Your skill as a soldier and your music are both of great value to me," Bruce said.

Niall bowed low. He'd just been handed more months of separation from Allene, more opportunities to die on the wrong end of a sword, and an order to cross the Irish Sea. "I am honored, Your Grace." He spoke truth. The Bruce honored him greatly. He just wished it didn't carry such a heavy price.

Glenmirril, November 1316

Taran's voice sounded outside the door. MacDougall tore his eyes reluctantly from Christina, riding into the courtyard below. As always, she kept her face averted from his tower. The key scraped in the lock, and the sullen youth entered, carrying a basket and a jug of ale. Outside, Gil watched, his sword at the ready.

Despite the boy's animosity, he believed he could sway Taran. Boys were naive and gullible, no matter how well trained. Training and life were simply two different teachers. MacDougall watched him set the meal on the spindly table. Day after day, through summer and deep into autumn, he had thanked him, playing the humble, self-effacing prisoner. Day after day, Taran scowled, making it clear his father's dead body outranked humble and self-effacing.

"Come now," MacDougall tried, as Taran set the ale on the table with a thud. "We've months, perhaps years, to see one another every day. Can we not be civil?"

"Would ye'd desired civility before ye killed my father."

MacDougall sighed. Stressing his right to retrieve his prisoner had been worse than useless. Taran idolized Niall. "I grieve my son, as you grieve your father," he said. "Let us be one in our grief."

"'Twas your decision to attack that took your son's life—and my father's." Taran's face flushed with anger. "This makes our grief separate things." He spit at MacDougall's feet and turned his back—not smart, MacDougall thought. Taran became careless in anger.

The door slammed. The key clicked in the lock, sealing MacDougall into boredom. He rose, pacing the cell, flexing his arms behind his back. He would be strong and ready, when his chance came.

Outside, Taran spoke, low and angry. At the door, MacDougall listened.

Jedburgh, November 1316

Niall rode at the head of the small army, with the abbot of Melrose on one side, Lachlan on the other, and the English negotiators behind them, their ponies climbing ever higher into Scotland's rugged hills. Their banners snapped overhead in the strong November wind, sending sharp *cracks* across the air. The breath of horses and men billowed out in the cold, frosty white puffs hanging briefly in the air and dissipating, quickly replaced by new ones. Niall buried one hand, chilly despite leather gloves, inside his cloak, leaving the other to guide the pony.

The English women had again been enthralled with Highlanders in their court, and beds had been a welcome change from sleeping under the stars. But seeing the luxury in which his oppressors lived did nothing to bolster his flagging faith.

"Good to be home, aye?" Lachlan echoed his thoughts.

"The very air feels different," Niall replied.

"Colder," said the abbot with a laugh. "Poorer."

"Free-er," said Niall.

"Aye, one day." The abbot glanced at Hastings and Baldock riding behind, absorbed in their own conversation. "It remains to be seen if this is the day."

"Surely they can't continue to refuse," Niall murmured.

"Edward is stubborn and I've heard stories of his new clerk." The abbot, too, lowered his voice. "Not so holy as one might hope from a man of the cloth."

Niall raised his eyebrows in question.

Lachlan nodded. "The whole Catel family has a reputation. I'd not raise my hope with him."

The abbot, with another glance behind, leaned closer yet. "They say that Edward, even as he sends negotiators, gathers men for another assault."

Niall thought uneasily of Bruce, doing the same. He wondered if they were equally guilty, or if Bruce was wise to know his enemy. "Pembroke has just dealt with another revolt in Wales," he said. "And Edward's nobles are none too happy with him. How does he find the strength to continue this war?"

"Pride gives strength," the abbot sighed. "And he imbibed pride aplenty with his father's ale."

The wind whistled around them, sloughing down the glen. Ahead, the route narrowed. "We're near Skaithmuir," Lachlan commented.

Niall looked at him. His voice carried weight. Shawn had fought at Skaithmuir against de Caillou. Shawn's report had been bare facts. Niall had no idea if he was supposed to have some reaction to the place. Bravado? Pride? Horror? "Quite the battle," he said noncommittally.

Lachlan chuckled. "You were a demon."

"Aye." Niall lapsed into silence, pondering the civilized world of Shawn's, that he had so briefly known, and the shock in Amy's eyes that he had wielded a knife and not hesitated to slice a man's arm with it. Shawn had done far more than draw blood. He'd killed men in battle. He'd driven his dirk deep into Duncan's gut in the tower, fully intending to kill.

Niall wondered how Amy was accepting a man who had done those things. Or whether Shawn had told her. Or how he fit in with all those civilized men in *tuxedos,* who wielded their music with such grace and power, but wouldn't last two minutes in a fight—men who were horrified by killing.

Soon, Niall thought, he might live in such a world, himself, if these negotiators agreed to Bruce's easy terms. But it would be different. He would still live among men who thought like himself, who understood the brutal need, at times, to kill, to defend, to protect. For just a moment, he wondered who really had it better—himself in a rough, hard world, but one in which he fit, or Shawn, trying to sleep in his silk sheets with blood-stained and battle-worn hands.

Midwest America, Present

Shawn stood in the prison's waiting room, a gray, dank place, in strong contrast to the warden's comfortable office. A row of chairs sat at a multi-stationed counter, with a glass barrier rising from counter to ceiling. Phones waited at each station, one on either side of the glass. Beyond the glass at each station were a chair and a metal door. He wished Amy would have answered her phone. He wished he could have talked to her before walking into this waiting room to see the boy.

Clarence.

His mind twisted around the name, feeling it. He'd forgotten the boy's name, all these years. Who named a kid Clarence, he thought.

"His mother's current boyfriend at the time he was born." The warden, a tall man with a broad chest and bristling handlebar mustache of jet black, had answered his question when he'd arrived. They'd given him coffee in the warden's office, a place of leather chairs and plants and family photos on the shelves, and offered a cookie, which he'd declined, and the warden had spent half an hour talking with him.

"That's not to say his father, you understand. This boyfriend showed up a few weeks before he was born, claimed naming rights, and in a fit of alcohol-induced maudlin, decided to honor his grandfather. He was there a couple months before the next boyfriend moved in. I think you can imagine a bit of what Clarence's life was like—a string of drunken, drugged-out men he was supposed to treat as loving stepfathers, while most of them ridiculed him for being small and weak and having a name like Clarence, among other things. The one at the time of your father's, uh, demise, thought it was great fun to call him Claire and give him hair ribbons for Christmas." He rolled his eyes. "I often think it's people like that who ought to be in prison beside some of these men. They played their part in what happened."

Shawn's lips tightened. He'd hated the nameless Clarence for years. The emotion would not so easily slide into blaming someone else.

"And of course, a fair number of those men were raised no better than what they passed on." The warden shrugged. "What can you do?" He tapped a manila folder on his desk, his eyes narrowed thoughtfully for a few seconds before saying,

"I imagine this isn't easy for you. I commend you for coming." He cleared his throat. "You know your mother's been in touch with me these nine years?"

Shawn swallowed, disliking the sensation of things being kept from him. For nine years. His words came out tight as a bowstring. "No, I didn't know."

"I imagine she worried about your reaction."

"I imagine she did." He took a strong gulp of coffee, and refilled the cup. Nerves thrummed up and down his arms. He wasn't sure *what* he would have been upset about, particularly. But anything remotely related to his father's murder had tended to send him into rages. His jaw clenched. He had every right to be angry.

"You know she visits him quite regularly herself?"

His jaw tightened further, till his teeth hurt. He swallowed hard against the taut muscles of his neck. "No."

The warden said nothing. Shawn knew he was resisting the urge to repeat himself. *I imagine she worried about your reaction.*

I imagine she did, Shawn finished their unspoken conversation. Blind rage climbed inside him, bit by bit, up his stomach, burning through his chest, into his throat. "So what are they, like best friends now or something?" He sounded small and mean, even to himself. "I guess her own son didn't need to intrude on the special little something they had?" He pushed out of his seat, trying to fight back the rage. "You know, that's really nice, the two of them keeping secrets from me." He turned his back to the warden, squeezing his eyes shut, seeing his mother in the blue-doored entry of Amy's home in Scotland, holding James. He tried to push down the anger. But the boy, lousy childhood or not, didn't deserve visits from his mother.

He became aware of the silence behind him, and turned, opening his eyes. The warden tapped his Bic on the manila folder.

"Mr. Kleiner, I understand this is hard for you." His eyes were large and sad— much as Shawn's father's eyes had looked on many occasions. Something softened in Shawn. But only a little. "I give you a great deal of credit for coming. Most people never do. I'll go with you, if you like."

Shawn had stood stiffly, angry at his mother, angry at this man, angry with Aaron for suggesting the whole thing, and angry with himself for, in a moment of stupidity, getting into his red Jaguar, and in more moments of stupidity, continuing to aim it toward Minnesota. He'd had chance after chance, as the prairie gave way to southern Minnesota's rocky bluffs, and rocky bluffs gave way to Minneapolis rising out of the plains, and he hadn't turned back. He wondered why. Because now he was here, the whole thing seemed the depths of insanity on all their parts.

Still, he *was* here. He'd given a one-shouldered shrug, an attempt at devil-may-care, and said, "Whatever."

Now, after a walk down steel-gray halls of concrete and iron bars, he stood in a holding pen, more steel and concrete and glass and guards and the big warden at his side. The boy—Clarence, he reminded himself—had lived here since he was eighteen. Nine years. His entire adult life. He tried not to think of that child, no different from James to start with, coming into the world, saddled with a name and a situation like ten pound weights on each ankle.

He tried to concentrate on the scruffy teenager, with lithe body and stooped shoulders, with greasy black hair hanging in spiral curls in his face, and sullen attitude, who had been in and out of his home for two years, since he'd been fifteen, and Shawn barely fourteen.

They'd gotten along well, Shawn remembered now. Despite the prison walls around him, he saw the bunk bed they'd shared, in Shawn's room, Clarence leaning over with a flashlight shining up under his face, turning it ghoulish, telling ghost stories, and the two of them laughing until his mother rapped on the door, reminding them school started early. They'd once cooked a meal together, when his mother had been held late at a meeting with a social worker, laughing till their sides ached as they'd thrown onions, carrots, peas, mushrooms, cheese, anything and everything they could find, into the meatloaf recipe she had told them to use. Oysters. Shawn smiled. They'd found a can of oysters, chopped them up fine, and mixed them in.

He hadn't thought of these things in years. They'd had fun.

He turned to the warden. "Do you know why he kept leaving our house? He seemed happy with us."

The warden shrugged. His big handlebar mustache seemed to move with his shoulders. "It's a messed up world. He went to you when his mother and her boyfriends had no use for him. He left when they threatened to complain to the law and social services. When she wanted help around the house, when a new boyfriend decided they'd play happy family, whatever."

A metal door scraped, behind the glass barrier. Shawn took a step backward.

"Do you want me to stay or leave?" the warden asked.

Shawn swallowed. He saw the boy—Clarence—as he'd looked at the trial, hunched and glaring at the world, wiry curls dangling over his eyes, a barrier between himself and the world.

"He calls me Claire and thinks it's funny to leave earrings on my dresser where my friends find them," he'd once confided to Shawn, deep in the night, quietly because his mother had already ordered them to stop talking and go to sleep. "Now they're calling me that at school."

The door swung open.

A tall man stepped through in a prison orange jumpsuit, his hands pinioned before him. His shoulders were broad and straight, his eyes dark and direct and pleading, his hair a neat dark cap, shiny over his head. His mouth moved. Shawn recognized his own name in the motion of the embouchure. He saw the plea in the eyes. He saw his father dying of multiple wounds in his truck in a parking lot, alone.

"Are you okay?" Shawn heard the warden's words echoing down a hall as long and dark as the tunnels to the Bat Cave.

He turned, pushing at a heavy force, feeling blindly for the door, gripping, tearing it open, feeling blindly down gray walls closing in on him, talking just to say something, *I'm leaving*, to guards in green, *I'm fine* to the warden, *this was a bad idea* to himself, pushing out into the open air beyond the prison, drawing in fresh air from the summer trees ringing the parking lot, stooping with hands on his knees, wondering if he was going to throw up, like he had at Skaithmuir, breathing deeply, drawing in breath, drawing in enough air to pick a high E out of nowhere, slowing his breathing, standing up finally, the spinning in his head slowing, till the trees once more stood straight and tall before him.

His red Jaguar waited in the parking lot, the top defiantly down, just beyond the grasping fingers of thieves and murderers. Shawn looked back at the gray block that housed his father's killer. He could go back in. His mother had gone in, how many times? She'd spoken with Clarence. How many times? What had they said? Aaron had offered forgiveness and friendship, hadn't he? Despite Shawn's crimes against him?

He closed his eyes, shook his head. He hadn't committed murder. He wanted nothing to do with the boy.

He got in his Jaguar, backed it out with a grinding of tire on pavement, and a squeal as he shot out of the parking lot. A double cheeseburger with everything on it and a large Oreo shake from McDonald's, a double tall mocha from Starbucks, Led Zeppelin in the CD player, something hard and fast, and he hit the open road for home, leaving it all behind. The bourbon in his cupboard would taste good right now.

Passing through the bluffs of southern Minnesota, he picked up his cell phone, blindly punching Amy's name. Talking wasn't what he wanted, but he'd promised her. It rang, over and over, and finally went to voice mail. He hung up, and, his hand shaking, thought who else he could call.

Jedburgh, November 1316

"Edward will not recognize you as King of Scots." The English negotiator, Robert Catel of Baldock, announced, his voice bouncing back from the high stone walls of Jedburgh Castle's great hall. He lifted his chin high, his eyes spitting fire at the assembled Scots, daring them to defy him.

Leaning back in his seat beside Hugh, Niall watched silently, fighting the knot in his stomach. War would continue. He wondered if it was worse to have had that brief hope.

From his throne, with the circlet of gold on his head and his gold-threaded livery worthy of any king in Europe, Bruce rose, his face betraying no emotion but for the tension in his jaw. "Scotland has ever been an independent nation with her own king," he replied levelly. "England has never had the right to come into our land and terrorize our people. Return to your king. Tell him that until he accepts our terms, until he recognizes me as king of Scots, and agrees to stay out of Scotland, he will have war. My Lord of Moray, escort them out."

With an arrogant toss of his head, and a swirl of his heavy cloak, Robert Catel followed Thomas Randolph. Robert Hastings hurried behind him, his head high, leaving no doubt what he thought of the Scots. The Englishmen slammed through the massive doors of the great hall. Bruce turned to Niall and gave a slight nod. Niall rose, and his men with him, to follow and make sure there would be no trouble. His father's sword swung at his side, a solid weight speaking of safety.

Outside, Hasting and Baldock flung ugly looks over their shoulders, but gathered their men to themselves without a fight, mounted their horses, and rode away.

"The gates," Moray said softly.

Niall, Hugh, and Lachlan bolted the gates behind the departing Englishmen.

"That didn't go well," Niall commented, on his return.

"Not so well as we'd hoped," Moray returned. "But no worse than we expected. Edward is, unfortunately, as stubborn as his father."

"Though fortunately," said Niall, "without the military skill to see it to the end."

They returned to the great hall. The lords, bishops, abbots, and king sat silently, as if waiting for their return.

"We sail to Ireland," Bruce informed the gathered men, when Niall and Moray had seated themselves.

Niall's insides turned green at the words, at the thought of water.

"Gather your men," Bruce added, "and meet in Ayr as quickly as possible. Sir James will be my authority in Scotland until my return. He will continue persuading England to acknowledge us."

Niall looked to Hugh. Their men were already here. Glenmirril was the opposite way from Ayr. There would be no chance to see Allene. Hugh leaned so close his beard tickled Niall's ear. "Surely someone must race to Glenmirril for men or supplies?"

"And bring more of our men to face death in Ireland so I can see Allene for a few hours?" Niall felt tension rise in his face and throat.

"Is there not some message desperately needing to be sent," Hugh returned in his lowest rumble.

"What message could be so important?"

"Should you become ill," Hugh hinted, "Conal would need to take your place."

Niall's jaw clenched till it ached. "You mean well, Hugh, and I'm grateful, but I won't lie to my king." He stopped, seeing the Bruce approach him. *Please, my Father in Heaven,* he found himself praying, *I know he has honored me greatly with his faith in me, but please...no more honors!*

Hugh and Niall rose, giving respectful bows. The king acknowledged them before placing his hand on Niall's arm, steering him away from Hugh. Shawn's irreverent streak gripped Niall by the throat, and he choked back what he knew Shawn would say: *Hey! God! Yeah, You! You're not a very good listener!*

At the far end of the hall, apart from the knots of men clustered at the fires in each of the big hearths, Bruce leaned his graying head close. "They tell me your wife's time is near."

Niall swallowed shame for having aimed such disrespectful, ungrateful thoughts at God. Hope leapt in his heart as high as the flames in the braziers. "Aye, Your Grace. It is past. She'll have given birth already."

"I wish I could spare you," Bruce said. "But our need is too great."

"Yes, Your Grace." The flame of hope wavered and died. Niall kept his face impassive. Disappointment was not his to show. It was the king's right to command, for the sake of a whole country.

"However, if you ride hard and fast, you can reach Glenmirril and return to Ayr, and have two days with her."

Joy at the regained opportunity squeezed Niall's heart with emotion. He blinked, something hot prickling his eyes. "It is said you are a man of compassion and mercy." He sank to one knee. "Thank you, Your Grace. Thank you!"

"Take Hugh and ten of your men and go anon," Bruce said. "The mountains are a poor place to ride this time of year. Give yourself plenty of time to reach Ayr. Let nothing short of death stop you being there by the eighteenth. I need you."

Glasgow, Present

Amy sat in her car outside Glasgow's concert hall, watching traffic and waiting for her chance to pull into the heavy flow. From her purse came the stirring tones of *Ride of the Valkyrie*—Shawn's ringtone. She glanced in the mirror, reminded herself she was on the opposite side of the car, and twisted the wheel, slipping into an opening.

The phone continued to sing. Her fingers tightened on the steering wheel. He'd called a few times, leaving voice mails she hadn't listened to. If it was important, he'd call his mother. She'd hoped a few days of no contact with either of them would tell her where her heart wanted to be. But it was impossible to escape them. James called to mind both Shawn and Angus. Her kitchen and front room, her car, playing the violin, the paint brushes and canvas Angus had given her, sitting in her front room—everything in her life called them both to mind now, each with good memories that left her feeling warm inside, wanting to see them again. Even sitting in church the last few mornings, hoping for peace or insight, reminded her of both of them.

The phone stopped, thankfully, as she reached the first stop light. Her fingers danced on the steering wheel, still feeling her violin strings, still jumping in the patterns of rehearsal. She harbored irritation at each of them—at Angus for walking away. The light turned; she eased her foot down on the gas. It was far more than irritation with Shawn, she thought, her eyes trained on the taillights ahead. It was pain and doubt. He was there with Caroline and Dana; he was traveling to California, where one of the women lived. And it was easy enough to fly anywhere he pleased.

The city streets passed quickly, and she eased onto the M80, northeast to Bannockburn. Shawn had told her everything, at Tioram. What he couldn't answer, was why. And that meant when temptation raised its head, teeth bared and snapping for him, he might do it again. It was his father's murder of course, feeding his demons, but he refused to see that. She checked her rear view mirror, and wondered what else impacted his cheating. Loneliness? Anger at her? Not getting his way? He might be experiencing all three right now.

A feeling of illness twisted, a heavy fist in her stomach. She'd looked up the magazine writer on the internet, telling herself not to, even as her fingers tapped on the keyboard. The woman's face filled her mind now, a stiff cloud of jet black hair, elegant high cheekbones, and smoky dark eyes with charcoal shadow sweeping gracefully to the corners. She'd posed in an outfit business-like and sexy, a button-up shirt not terribly buttoned up, bangles on her arms, as she perched on the corner of a desk piled high with important work. Her right hand held her left elbow; her left hand, resting against full red lips, dangled glasses from thumb and finger.

The traffic thinned as Amy reached open fields. The crease deepened between her eyebrows. The woman was everything Amy wasn't—important, someone like Shawn who made things happen, suave, sophisticated, reeking of sex appeal and adventure, undemanding; not a two-bit musician in jeans playing one tiny part that no one even heard, withholding affection, and angry and doubting. Not that Shawn hadn't given her plenty of reason, she reminded herself. Still, it must have been all good between them, no stress, no fighting, just fun.

The roundabout loomed ahead. With a deep breath, she launched the car into its swirl of traffic. Moments later, she shot onto the A80, alive and in one piece, and let her breath out. It hadn't been so bad. She must be getting used to it.

Back on a straight highway, she glanced at her purse. Maybe she should at least listen to his messages. She reached for the purse, fumbling inside for the slick casing of the phone. Maybe her lack of contact was driving him away. Her fingers closed on it. She gave her head a sharp shake and yanked her hand back, dropping it firmly on the wheel. After all his crimes against her and their relationship, if he couldn't wait patiently a few days, he didn't deserve a second chance. She picked up the phone and turned it off.

Midwest America, Present

The phone shook in Shawn's hand as he hit *call*. The wind ripped through his hair, as his Jaguar flashed in and out of traffic, inching past ninety. A horn squawked as he flew by. The phone rang. A voice of reason tried hard to shout in his ear. *You promised Amy!* But the wind was strong. It snatched the voice away, fluttering away behind the speeding car, bumping into windshields and flipping away between the cars behind him. The phone rang again.

What about Amy?

Somehow, the voice had crawled back, pulled itself up over the edge of his door, bellowing at him.

But Amy hadn't answered his phone calls. She hadn't returned them. She hadn't answered his e-mails.

"Hi, Shawwwwwn." Caroline's purr filled the phone. "I knew you'd call."

The shaking grew in his arms. He had promised Amy. He swallowed.

"Shawn?"

He didn't want to go back to his empty house. He couldn't face the night alone, taunted by nightmares and images and filled with his own hatred.

Her voice lost its purr, and climbed a notch. "Are you there, Shawn? What do you think you're doing?"

"Yeah. Yeah, I'm here." The path branched before him. Nightmares and fighting the hatred—or cheating on Amy.

"You want to talk? I could come over."

"Uh, yeah. I want to talk." He shut his eyes a second, remembered he was speeding down the highway at ninety-five miles an hour, and opened them in a panicked flash. He twisted the wheel, veering around a yellow Cabriolet, missing it by inches. The driver gave him the finger. He scowled back.

"Okay, so yeah, what do you want to—*talk*—about?" The resumed purring left no doubt what she expected his answer to be. "I can be there in fifteen minutes."

"I, uh, yeah, Caroline." He drew in a deep breath. He'd promised Amy. He swallowed. Christina would be horrified. He'd just drink a lot. He'd be fine without Caroline. "It was about that piece we played in Scotland."

"*Benedictus?*" Disbelief and disappointment etched her every word.

"Yeah, that one." He wracked his brain, trying to think why he'd call a flutist about *Benedictus*. It wasn't too late to shift gears. He had talent. He could save this conversation; if anyone could turn *Benedictus* into a come-on, it was him. He'd get drunker than he'd ever been, and then it wouldn't be his fault.

He flashed by another car; a woman turned, surprised, from the driver's seat, long, glossy black hair over her shoulder. Christina! She looked just like Christina.

"Okay, soooo...." Caroline dragged out the word.

Christina had been dead for seven hundred years. If anything she and Niall believed was true, she was in Heaven, frowning down at him, disappointed. *Ye'll be a good husband and father.* She'd believed in him, sent him away from herself, to do the right thing. She hadn't sent him away to return to his old ways. *What sort of man were you?* The disappointment in her voice had cut deep, touching vulnerable white bone.

"What about *Benedictus?*" Caroline's petulant pout came over the phone.

"Just getting input from all the orchestra members. That's all. Did it work with that concert?" He twisted the wheel again, leaping into the right lane as he raced a white Ford Focus. With a deep breath, he eased his foot a bit off the gas pedal. "Cause you know, I thought it was really out of place with everything else we did."

"It was all Scottish composers!" She sounded irritated. "How could it possibly be out of place?"

"Well, yeah, you're right, but, uh, were there pieces that would go better with it? Maybe pieces from that same era?"

He swallowed, cursing Christina and her damn faith; that included her damn faith in him. Where was she going to be through the long night when he couldn't sleep? When images of his father, fending off the blows of the knife, of the bloodied blade, assaulted his mind? But he felt her, almost saw Christina, sitting beside him, staring at him in that sad, quiet way she had, reprimanding him without saying a word.

"Well." Caroline gave a little laugh. "I'm thinking maybe a little *Bolero.* I've got a great recording. A few, in fact." Her voice dropped a perfect fifth. *Very* perfect. "How about I bring them over. I've got this great bottle of wine I want your opinion on. I could bring it, we could kill two birds with one stone."

Shawn glanced at the speedometer. It had dipped to eighty. He pulled back into the left lane, inching around a long, red church van full of children bouncing up and down, a woman driving, and a teenage son next to her, moving his head to the sounds of his iPod. It wasn't too late to salvage this with Caroline.

"That sounds really good." He smiled, slipping into his Barry White purr.

Don't think on it, Shawn Kleiner!

He glanced, startled, at the passenger seat, into the rear view mirror and into the back seat. It was Christina's voice. The woman driving the huge van shot him a glance. The children in the multiple seats behind her waved. He gave a weak smile and waved back. He'd clearly heard Christina's voice. Damn her!

"But you know," he said into the phone, "I don't think that would be a good idea. You and I, well—I told you on the plane." He kicked himself, figuratively. *Liar!* He'd just led her on, and now he was blaming her for knowing exactly why he'd called. "I'm sorry," he said. "I shouldn't have called." He hung up quickly, as he eased his Jaguar ahead of the big van. He sighed, and, sliding back to the right lane, in front of it, slowed to just over the speed limit.

The bluffs of southern Minnesota flattened out. His heart flattened with them, terrified of the night ahead. His fingers itched on the phone, still hanging in his hand. He could call Dana. She'd understand. She'd come over and just talk. He inched his thumb around the phone, seeking her name. But he'd promised Amy, and Christina seemed determined he'd honor that promise, no matter how long she'd been dead, no matter what lousy kind of day he'd had. He scowled. It's not like Amy would ever know.

He felt, though he neither saw nor heard, Christina's disapproval, emanating from the seat beside him. He gave the empty seat an equally disapproving sneer of his lip, then sighed in irritation as much at himself as at Christina or Caroline or anyone else. He eased his foot off the gas pedal, dropping to a mile under the speed limit. He had plenty of bourbon in the cupboard. And vodka. And liqueurs and wine and beer. He'd be fine. Really, he would. He'd be fine.

CHAPTER TWELVE

Glenmirril, December 1316

"A game of chess to pass time?"

It had been weeks since he'd tried. He was nothing if not patient. But then, MacDougall thought dryly, he'd all too much time to practice patience.

Taran glanced to Gilbert, who shrugged.

The key clicked in the lock, and Taran entered, no friendlier ever. MacDougall considered offering condolences for his father's death, and as quickly decided against it. The boy was proving less gullible than he'd hoped, and would see it for the maneuver it was. Their lives were tied together for some time. There was no need to press yet for any real liking from him. He set out the chess pieces silently. They were roughly carved wood, nothing like his own fine set of stone. They were better than nothing.

Taran watched silently, and made his opening move, sliding a pawn forward, without a word. The game proceeded in silence, broken only by Gilbert bringing the mid-day meal at the same time Taran said, "Check."

"The high point of my day," MacDougall said with what he hoped was a gently self-mocking smile. "Stale bread and ale."

Taran stared sullenly, and made no reply, as Gil plunked the basket and jug on the table's edge.

MacDougall tore a piece of bread with his teeth, studying the board as he chewed. Taran had made an error. But he was more intent on glaring down MacDougall than checking his move. Ignoring the opportunity, MacDougall pushed his queen into danger, between his king and Taran's rook.

Taran barely glanced at the board. His rook slid across the board, taking MacDougall's queen, and facing down his king. "Checkmate."

"Indeed." MacDougall shook his head, feigning surprise and disappointment. "You're a fine player."

With a look of smug satisfaction, Taran rose.

MacDougall cleared his throat hurriedly. "Might I ask a favor?"

"You'll get no favors," Taran returned.

"Only that I might write to my steward," MacDougall said hurriedly.

"No favors," Taran repeated.

"For the women and children of Creagsmalan," MacDougall added. "Can you not allow this small thing—for *their* sake?"

Taran left the cell, with no further answer. The key scraped in the tumblers. Outside, he murmured angrily with Red. He never looked back in. It was one thing MacDougall had learned of the boy's habits.

He went to his window. As always, he scanned the courtyard first. The vegetable patch, three stories below, lay under a blanket of frost. Though he looked out frequently each day, it had been weeks since he'd seen Christina. He sighed and lifted his eyes to the hills. From the trees above Glenmirril, a light flashed, rays of winter sunlight reflecting in a steady pattern. MacDougall smiled. He had no way of answering back, but he felt less alone, knowing Roger was about, and watching, too.

Midwest America, Present

The moon had risen high in the sky, a sleek white-silver crescent, by the time Shawn eased the Jaguar through tall wrought iron gates, and down the driveway under the dark arch of trees. He sat in the car, staring at the Tudor house, a dark shape in the night. He didn't want to go in; didn't want to spend the night alone. There had always been someone in Glenmirril. With a sigh, he tried Amy again. In between business calls to Ben and Lindsay, mainly to keep his mind off things, he'd tried her three times on the long drive, always getting her voice mail. It would be early in the morning, in Scotland. She'd turned her phone off for the night, he assured himself. That was all. He hesitated, and, pushing the end button, collapsed against the head rest.

His mind traveled through his years with Niall, even as he considered what to drink first. Red would look at him sadly, uncomprehendingly. Christina would be no more pleased to see him drink himself silly tonight, than to see him with Caroline. Nor would Niall, or Amy, or his mother. Why had he been okay without those things in Scotland? In medieval Scotland, he corrected himself. He'd been busy there, exhausted with hard work. So what, he thought. He kept busy here, too. He'd just spent a full day driving, with a very draining visit to the prison. He *should* be exhausted. But he knew the signs. He wouldn't sleep tonight.

He tried to think what he could do with the time. He had to quit calling Ben, but he could practice; do arrangements; book his flights—no, his flights were booked. Arrangements could take up the night easily. He'd brew coffee and get to work.

Inside, with the coffee machine burbling and lights illuminating the granite foyer, the soaring brick fireplace, granite counters, and newly-cleaned windows— the cleaning woman had been eager to get back to work for him—he set up a large sheaf of paper, lined with multiple staves. He paused only minutes before jotting the first notes as he heard them in his head, a flurry of sixteenths right from the start, in the flutes, six measures of it before the string basses entered on a drone. Four more measures, and in came the whole orchestra.

The notes flew from his pencil almost as fast as they'd fly from the instruments; the faster he wrote, the farther he outran the images of blood and murder and hatred. He went back to measure one, jotting in whole rests for those not yet playing, reached measure 25, and began a slow and beautiful violin solo, concentrating on his feelings for Amy, remembering the first time he'd walked down the hall to his audition and seen her—smooth, pale skin and jet black hair he wanted to run his hands through. She'd been laughing at something the man at her side said. He wrote the laugh into the solo, a quick little flurry of thirty-second notes skipping up an arpeggio and sliding into a scale fragment.

The coffee maker let out a trill and burst into *Ride of the Valkyrie*. He smiled. Amy never had told him where she'd found such a thing. When he stopped writing, he felt the cramp in his hand. It had been two years since he'd put such demands on it. And the images came rushing back, without the steady flow of notes—images of the boy stabbing and stabbing and stabbing at his defenseless father, who had done everything for the kid.

He stalked the coffee machine, bursting upon his prey, backed into the oak paneled corner of the counter, and flushed it, pouring his coffee with a vengeance it didn't deserve. It sloshed, burning his hand. He ran cold water on it. Back in the music room, he finished Amy's solo, and jotted in chords for the brass, leading into a recap of the violin melody, a virtual explosion of her solo from the whole orchestra. That's what would happen next. Everything they'd had would explode into a beautiful life together. He'd show her he could be all she'd believed of him! He'd buy her horses.... *The image of his father in the truck, dying, gripping his chest, would not leave him.*

Shawn slapped the pencil down and sipped the coffee. It wasn't too late to call Caroline. She'd come in a heartbeat. Or Dana. She lived but five minutes away. She'd been hurt when he'd chilled her attempts at renewing the friendship. He didn't blame her. He'd managed to hurt everyone he cared for.

He sighed, as he turned back to his question: why had the bloody images and nightmares disappeared in his time with Niall? What had been different? The coffee slid down his throat, pungent and bitter. His mother, Amy, Christina, Niall —all of them would be pleased he'd opted for coffee instead of whiskey. He set his mind free, roaming the halls of Glenmirril with Niall, Hugh, Allene; following Christina down the hall, down stairs, to the chapel. He saw the Laird's life-sized carving of Christ, in the Bat Cave. He wanted to be there, feeling the peace that always came to him when he crept into the back pew of the chapel, the hood of Brother Andrew shrouding his face, and watched Christina.

Slowly, he drained his coffee, considered trying to sleep, and knew he wouldn't. With a last glance at the half-finished score—he knew exactly what he'd do with it on the morrow—he fished in his pocket for his keys. There was a church nearby that stayed open all night. Perpetual Affirmation, they called it. Permanent Adornment. Or something. To him, it meant the doors were open. Maybe he'd find the same peace there he'd found in Glenmirril's chapel.

He let himself out of the house into the warm July night, with a huge moon blooming on the horizon, and his Jaguar with the roof still down, and headed for Personal Arrangement. Or whatever it was called.

Glenmirril, December 1316

Niall sank with gratitude into the steaming tub, luxuriating in scented water that eased his tired and aching body. He'd ridden across Glenmirril's snowy drawbridge hours ago, as the sun sank in the west. Leaving the great bay for Red to tend, he went with Conal and Hugh to meet with Morrison and Darnley—the Laird had retired, they said—discussing the poor harvest, and reporting on politics in England, before hastening to his chambers. He'd found the solar empty, but for Bessie snuffing the candles. "She's retired," Bessie had said, when he asked after Allene. "My Lord, she sleeps but poorly these days."

Niall had fought with himself, hearing the plea a servant could not voice. *Please don't ask me to wake her.* He wanted to see her, hold her, talk with her. There was so little time. She could sleep for months while he went to Ireland. "Let her rest," he had whispered. He would see her soon enough.

When the water cooled, he climbed out dripping, dried off, and, in a nightshirt smelling of fresh lavender, slipped into the bedroom. He twitched the curtains apart on the far side, where moonlight wouldn't disturb Allene. She lay on her side, facing him, her hair spilling around her face. He eased under the sheets. She sighed. Her eyelids fluttered. Niall watched, smiling. The past months faded. He was here now—nothing else mattered. He would walk the hills again with her, see his sons, maybe take James to the shore as Shawn had.

The fire in the hearth crackled, casting dancing shadows over the bed hangings. Allene's hair tickled his nose; she breathed evenly on his chest. Her eyelids fluttered again, and this time opened. Her eyes rested a moment on Niall. She blinked, then gasped, and struggled to sit up. "Niall? You're home!"

He nodded, smiling, wrapping her in his arms, burying his face in her curls. "For a wee bit." He pulled her down, kissing her.

After a minute, she pulled away. "We've a braw bonny laddie! The most beautiful bairn ever!"

"Aye, Bessie told me. And you're well!" He buried his face in her hair, inhaling the scent of herbs and heather. "Do you know how I feared I'd never see you again?"

"Aye, I know well," she said. "Are you not at war? Do you not think I fear each time you leave that I've said good-bye for the last time?" Tears glistened in the corners of her eyes. She brushed at them, laughed, and said, "You're home. We'll not spoil it with weeping, aye?"

"No!" He laughed out loud, and pulled her close, his hands in her hair, kissing her more deeply.

Midwest America, Present

The massive front doors of the church didn't budge. Shawn tugged, staring up their great, wooden height, like the churches he'd raided, thinking he'd been wrong.

"Can I help you, sir?" He turned, wondering for a moment, how this old woman behind him knew he'd been knighted; then blinked, remembering he was in twenty-first century America, where it was a meaningless title.

She blinked up, tiny and white-haired, from the bottom of the great flight of stairs leading to God. Leading, rather, to the doors to God—which happened to be locked. "Uh, yeah, I'm here for Personal Adornment. Are they not doing it tonight?"

Her mouth twitched. "Perpetual Adoration. It means it's perpetual. All the time." Her voice carried surprisingly well for one so small and old. "Come around the side." She waited, her hand resting on a honey-wood cane, while he descended the stairs. She squinted up at him, and, as he descended the last stair, lifted a pair of eyeglasses to her eyes. She let out a gasp. "Shawn Kleiner!"

He smiled a little. "Yeah. That's me." The smile faded. It wasn't why he was here. He didn't want to talk about his concerts or music. "I'm just here for, what was that called again?"

"Oh, my!" She reached out a blue-veined hand, clutching his before he could respond. "My granddaughter said you were back. We have prayed and prayed and *prayed* for you!"

"Really?" It wasn't what he usually heard, when people said they'd been thinking about him.

"Oh, my, yes, in every way! Gladys will be so thrilled! You're really here for Perpetual Adoration?"

"Well, just to go and sit, yeah. I don't have to *do* anything, do I?"

"Come along!" She towed him, moving with a speed that left him wondering if she was really supporting an old and weak cane, rather than the other way around. They rounded the side of the church, past a row of stained glass windows, to a steep flight of stairs. She torpedoed up them, almost dragging him, and flung the door open. They passed through a dim foyer, into a cathedral-style church. The red candle—he remembered it from years ago—burned behind the altar. Pews of highly-polished, honey-colored wood marched to the back of the church. A white marble altar dominated the front.

On the left, a ten foot arched niche held a life-sized statue of the Virgin Mary. She stood atop the world, a snake crushed under her bare feet. Her blue and white robe flowed around her, and she held her hands in serene prayer. A crown of twelve stars glowed around her head. Peace reached out to him. To the right stood St. Joseph with lilies in one hand and the Christ child in the other.

Over the altar between the two, hung a gigantic crucifix. It was what he'd come for, remembering hour upon hour before the crucifixes, in the Bat Cave and in the chapel with Christina, kneeling irritably, morning after morning, with Hugh, the Laird, Niall, and Red. He stepped forward, dimly noting the old woman dipping her hand in holy water, and easing arthritically to one knee, before rising and hissing, "Gladys! He's *here!* Shawn Kleiner we prayed for! He's *here!*"

He turned. Another old woman, tall and elegant, stared at him. She reminded him of Niall's mother, but for her age and modern clothing. She rose from the kneeler, inclined her head, and came to grip his hands between hers. "It's good to see you here," she said. "How are you?"

Shawn stared at her. The whole world *knew* he'd disappeared for a year. *Apart from multiple wounds and resulting ugly scars as a result of two years in medieval Scotland,* he wanted to say, *and apart from stupidly having just looked at the man who murdered my father, I'm doing well, thank you. And you?* "Fine," he said.

"I imagine you're here for peace and quiet," she said with a smile. "Not to chat with old ladies." She released his hands, and returned to her spot, joined by the smaller dynamo with the cane. Shawn wandered across the front of the altar, choosing a seat across the aisle. His first impulse was to look for a spot to carve his three lines. But there was no more need to leave his mark. He pushed back the instinct, the itch in his arm to carve, the *need* to leave a cry for help. He was home, safe from killing and fear, back home, making music, job offers and requests for interviews rolling in.

He sank down to the pew with a heavy sigh, not sure what he'd expected to find. Christina would not be here. Yet warmth and peace settled on his shoulders, the same peace he'd always felt in her presence. He wondered where she had been during the battle; wondered as he had before, if she'd been in danger. For all he knew, she'd died that night, while he skited off to safety.

And what if she had survived? He stared up at the crucifix behind the altar. What of the rest of her life? Had they married her off, like cattle sold at market, to another lord? He liked to think maybe they'd adjusted some of their thinking, too, in consequence of knowing him, as he had his own; that maybe they wouldn't do that—at least—not to *her.*

He found he cared even less for the thought she'd married another man for love. He heard a small snort, and realized it was himself. He cast a guilty glance at the two women; they stared at him curiously, averting their eyes quickly when he looked their way. "Sorry," he whispered across the aisle. "Just thinking about things." Thinking, he told himself sternly, that he hardly had any claim on her. He'd spent their year and a half together telling her he was going back to Amy. Yet he wanted her to spend her life pining for him and lonely? Of course not. Not in his mind. But in his heart, he didn't like the thought of her with someone else, *loving* someone else.

Do you know so little of what love is? Christina had asked him. He stared at Christ on the cross, and it dawned on him, that was love. If it had ever really happened. But it seemed far less real than the Arabian Nights, to think a man had lived, claimed to be God, and died so he, Shawn, could get into Heaven. God was love. He'd told Niall so. There was no danger to the eternal soul.

No, love, to him, showed in his father's actions, something he could see, not in a fable about someone who may or may not have lived two thousand years ago, whose actions had no discernible effect on him. The warden's words came back to him. Clarence had been at their home only when his mother and her boyfriends had allowed it. And as Shawn stared at Christ, he remembered a Christmas with chicken for dinner, a piece of music and new pair of jeans under the tree. He shut his eyes, trying to remember that day, trying to remember what his parents had given each other. Nothing.

He frowned; opened his eyes, studying the altar, wondering why that memory came to him now. But no matter how he rolled the memory around, poked it from every angle, he couldn't think what significance it had.

The scent of candles drifted to him—hundreds of jewel-toned candles set before Mary. It brought him back to Glenmirril's chapel. He leaned his forearms on his legs, hands clasped together and head hung down, and let the peace of those mornings wash over him.

Glenmirril, December 1316

Niall lay in the dark womb, inside the closed bed hangings, relishing the feel of her in his arms, thanking God for Bruce's kindness in the midst of war. After months on horseback, sleeping in soft moss, being pelted and drenched in unending rain, it felt unreal—as distant and dream-like as his time in Shawn's world. He wanted to pull her closer, re-live their reunion over and over again, assure himself it was she and James and the as-yet unseen William that were real, not the fighting and flames and hunger, and screams of women.

He closed his eyes, pressing his face into her hair, breathing deeply, wishing it real forever—never wondering when disease, childbirth, war, famine, or enemy attack might tear him from his family.

She stirred. In the new rhythm of her breathing, he knew she'd woken. "Did I disturb you?" he whispered.

"I often wake at night," she whispered back.

"When did that start?" They'd spent little enough time together since their marriage two years ago, what with parliaments and missions for the Bruce.

"When you left. I worry on a great many things."

"MacDougall?" he asked.

"He is a model prisoner." Tension clenched her throat, despite the words.

He hesitated a moment before saying what they both knew. "'Tis unlike him."

"I have said so to Father. He says 'tis grief over his son."

Niall snorted.

"You sound like Shawn," she whispered.

"He had, at times, a certain eloquence beyond words."

"Aye, at times. But MacDougall remains locked in the tower. What could he possibly do?"

"Who guards him?" Niall watched her in the dark, seeing little more than her shape against the pillow.

"Taran, Red, and Gil. He'll get no help from any of them."

Niall nodded. "Taran will never be turned by MacDougall, as long as his father lies dead in our crypts."

"Turned, no." Allene relaxed on his chest.

Niall weighed her words, before asking, "What, then?"

"Deceit." She twisted her head to look up at him. "Trickery."

"Taran is quick-witted," Niall said. Inside the enclosing curtains, the dark faded to gray as dawn approached.

"I know not, Niall." She sighed, and he heard in the sound the months of worrying. "But Taran, for all his loyalty, courage, and skill, has an innocence about him. He is hard and wary, yet knows so little of the wiles of men. The lad has barely been beyond these walls."

"Even so," Niall admitted. Perhaps he should take him, and leave another as a guard. "Still, he'll do nothing without your father's consent."

"My father is hardly to be seen," Allene said. "His spirit seems to have left him since June. He disappears for hours at a time to the Bat Cave."

"Does he?" Uneasiness stirred in Niall's gut.

"Aye. Morrison and Darnley fret on his neglect of Glenmirril. They take charge as they can. Ronan takes Taran under his wing, where my father ought to step in."

"Give him time," Niall murmured. "Life has changed a great deal for all of us."

"Aye." Allene sighed. "Though he grumbled so, I believe he enjoyed Shawn a great deal, impertinence and all."

Niall's heart twisted. "And Christina?" he asked.

Allene curled closer into him. "She is withdrawn and pale. I worry for her."

"She is too sensible to pine after him." Niall said.

"Perhaps we all believe her facade too well." Allene boosted herself up on one elbow, looking down at him. "Perhaps we should stop expecting her to forever be stoic." She gripped his nightshirt. "Tell me, Niall, are you as strong as you seem? Or does the loss eat at you, too? Do you not feel grief? Do you want what can't be, and feel your spirit grow anxious?"

"It does no good to talk of such things." Niall took her fingers from his shirt. "He never belonged here."

"Does he belong there? He seemed happy here, and a better man than the one I first met. Why would God bring him here if he didn't belong?"

"I know not, Allene. They were good years, but 'tis done. What use is pining?"

Allene's head bowed. "Is that what I say to Christina, when she sits in the window where he sat, staring listlessly across the water?"

Niall squeezed his eyes tight, pressing a palm into them. Home was supposed to be a respite from cares. "Go with her to the chapel. Encourage her to feed the poor as she's always done. Help Muirne and Adam's widow with their bairns. Walk in the gardens with Bessie, which comforted her. Shall I speak to your father of finding a husband for her? Perhaps 'tis what she needs." He snapped his fingers. "Hugh! Has your father not said 'tis time for him to take a wife again?"

"'Tis not so simple, Niall." Allene hugged herself in the warm cocoon of the bed. "Don't marry her to Hugh."

"Why not? He'd be good to her. They've affection and respect for one another."

She shrugged. "Something inside me says 'tis not the right thing."

Midwest America, Present

A hand touched Shawn's shoulder. "Sir?"

Shawn's mind spun. Was it hard ground he was sleeping on? Why weren't his men calling him Sir *Niall?*

"It's morning."

Shawn squinted, opened his eyes, only to be stabbed by a ray of jewel-red light bursting through the stained glass robe of Jesus in the window high above. He pulled an arm over his eyes, fending off the light, and peered up. Stiffness covered his back like a cloak; a crick in his neck stabbed a sharp pain through when he moved too quickly. The man above him wore a black robe with a white collar. "Sorry, Father MacDonald," he muttered.

"Father Pat," the man corrected. "Mass will be starting soon."

"Oh." The cloud of sleep lifted from Shawn's mind, and he realized he was in Midwest America, twenty-first century. He felt refreshed, he thought with surprise. "I guess I'll head out. I came for Perpetual...what's that called? I didn't mean to fall asleep."

"No problem." Father Pat was young and dark-haired, like Father MacDonald. Except, Shawn reminded himself, Father MacDonald was long dead. It hurt to think so. The corners of Father Pat's eyes crinkled into a smile. "If you find enough peace here to fall asleep, that's a good thing, right?"

"Aye." Shawn found himself smiling. He hadn't made a habit of smiling at priests. "It's a good thing." He cracked his head to the side, working out the crick.

Father Pat held out his hand. "Come back anytime."

"I might." Shawn shook his hand, and with a genuflection before the altar— more a tribute to Niall's sensibilities, and an apology for all the pillaging he'd done than any faith in God—he left the church, into the early June morning. He stared at his red Jaguar, sitting alone on the black tarmac, between two bright yellow lines. McDonald's for breakfast, he thought. First, he pulled out his cell phone and hit Amy's name. It rang endlessly, finally dumping him in her voice mail. He hung up. He'd left too many messages already.

It was seven, his phone told him. He had an appointment in one hour with his publisher, and after that, a rehearsal with a brass quintet, followed by a flight to California for his first appearance with an orchestra there.

The car's black leather seat, when he climbed in, was warm from the sun. He glanced at the church, as he backed from his parking spot. If he'd known he would sleep so well, he would have just stayed home. He arched his back again, trying to loosen the stiffness, and pulled out of the tarmac lot, trying to remember where to find the nearest McDonald's.

Glenmirril, December 1316

Niall woke in the morning, the bed dark with the curtains pulled, and the sun sleeping late, in December. He felt disoriented, finding himself in Glenmirril, rather than London, Jedburgh, or a dozen abbeys along the way; in bed with Allene, rather than on the hard, cold ground with dark clouds overhead and his tartan clasped around his head against rain. He watched Allene, smiling in her sleep as she curled into his shoulder. He brushed a copper strand of hair off her face, wondering if he'd wake up to find himself in Jedburgh with Hugh shouting for him to get moving, or Conal calling him for the next watch, or Bruce wanting him to play his harp.

But it was real. He smiled, curling a strand of Allene's hair around his finger. There would be two whole days with good food, no burning fields, no barreling through towns of screaming women and children, no racing for the gold of England's abbeys and churches.

He watched Allene sleep another minute, thinking on his uncharacteristic discontent with life, these last months. Really, he had a great deal for which to be thankful. He smoothed her hair from her forehead, and decided he'd go to the chapel before she awoke, and ask God, there, to forgive him his grumbling.

He eased himself from the warm cocoon of the curtained bed, moving silently across the furs on the stone floor to stare out the arched window to the loch. The thick mist swirling over its surface had a pink tint in the pearly dawn finally struggling up over snow-crested eastern hills. He'd seen a time of peace, a time when he'd never wonder who might be lurking beyond those hills, waiting to attack, though Shawn had been unable to tell him when that peace would begin. The next raid might be the turning point, the thing that convinced Edward he must withdraw and give Scotland the peace they'd long sought. Then he'd beat his sword into a plow and spend his days with his family, working hard, doing the things he loved in the peace of his own home, as Shawn did.

Without training the men for war, he wondered, what would he do? Hunting and hawking? Supervise the workings of the castle? Pray, feed the poor as Christina did, teach music to the castle children? Such a thing had never been done, not in the way Shawn spoke of in his time. And certainly not by the laird of the castle.

For now, he thought, he'd break his fast, maybe walk on the shore and sit on the rock there with Allene and James. He could play his harp in his own warm halls, play the recorder, take James to the stable, and cradle William in his arms. *Two whole days!* He smiled, thinking of it. But first, he'd go to the chapel and give thanks.

The halls were quiet, early in the morning, but for a lad or two scurrying about lighting fires. They bobbed bows at him, and hurried about their business. He opened the chapel door. The smell of incense and wax drifted out. He stopped, soaking in the familiar site of the stone floor and arched beams supporting the ceiling, the small altar at the front with a crucifix above it, tapestries, and altar cloths embroidered in silver and gold and a palette of rich colors by Allene and the women of Glenmirril, and the rows of pews, polished to a high gleam.

He'd spent countless hours here since he'd been barely able to walk. It filled him with memories of his father and older brothers kneeling around him, towering above him, as tall and strong and safe as the walls of Glenmirril; and later with his mother and Finola making sure he sat still; through the years of his youth when he wanted nothing more than to turn and watch Allene, sitting beside her father; and into the years with Shawn at his side, cloaked as Brother Andrew and irritably scratching his ear. Niall smiled.

As his eyes adjusted to the dim interior, he saw Christina kneeling in the front pew. Her glossy black hair spilled from under a white barbet, over her blue cloak. She glanced over her shoulder. She gave a sudden start, her eyes flew wide. Then her face fell. She nodded, and turned away. Niall frowned. It was unlike her.

He entered the chapel, pulling the door behind him. Christina knelt, frozen, though he swore he saw her shoulders stiffen under the heavy cloak. He moved down the narrow aisle, his leather boots silent against the stone floor, till he reached her pew. She looked up.

Niall stared in shock. It wasn't that she looked pale and drawn, rather than fresh and happy as she had just months ago, before Shawn's leaving. It was her eyes. She stared at him wildly, like an animal in a trap.

"Christina?" He glanced at the Crucifix, conscious of ignoring Christ in His chapel. "What is amiss?"

The mask of peace and calm he had seen in Creagsmalan's great hall slipped over her face, as surely as if another had taken her place, here in the pew. She smiled. "All is well, Niall. What joy to see you home safe." But she remained on her knees, even as she raised her pale, slender fingers for the customary greeting.

Niall dropped to one knee at her side, and kissed her fingertips. "And great joy to see you in good health." His words came out flat. He studied her face. She held the mask firmly in place, gazing placidly at him. "Christina," he murmured, "something disturbs you. If you'll not tell me, then confide in Allene."

She smiled, peaceful as an angel. "All is well, Niall."

"Clearly 'tis not." When she continued to smile blandly, he added, "I'm going to the Bat Cave. Perhaps you'd like to visit?"

She shook her head. "'Twill be chilly there."

"Okay, then." He started at the sound of Shawn's modern English slipping from his mouth, then sighed in relief, remembering Christina would not ask questions.

"I thought you'd returned to your own time, Shawn." Her smile thawed into something genuine, and the tension sagged from her shoulders. As suddenly, her lip quivered, and her mouth turned down. She buried her face in her hands.

Still on one knee, Niall pulled her against his shoulder. He couldn't think of a single, comforting thing to say. He closed his eyes, trailing *Aves* through his head. Her voice came to him, muffled, from his shoulder. "'Twould have been all right, had he stayed."

"He wasn't at peace...." Niall stopped. He felt the roundness of her stomach at the same time she yanked back, turning abruptly to the altar, and tugging her cloak tight. Her face became impassive, as pale and still as a statue, gazing at the Crucifix.

"Of course he had to go." She bowed her head.

"Christina...."

Her forehead touched her folded hands. "I was praying, Niall. Allene will

Laura Vosika

surely be up by now and looking for you."

"Shawn?" he asked.

She turned to him, staring, neither confirming nor denying, not speaking at all.

The chill of the floor bit into his knee. Gripping the back of the pew with more force than needed, he pushed himself to his feet. "The Laird needs to know." He turned, raking his hand through his hair, feeling blindly for the next pew. He'd trusted Shawn, almost as much as he'd trusted Christina.

"Please don't." Her words brushed his ear as softly as a butterfly.

He stopped, unsure whether he'd heard them or imagined them. "How do you plan to hide it?" he whispered harshly, his back to her. He squeezed his eyes shut, scanning the days, searching for any time Shawn had been alone with her, ever, for more than a minute. It hadn't happened. But who else was there? Their affection for one another had blazed brightly for all to see.

"I've hidden it so far," she whispered. "Help me, Niall. There must be a way."

He turned back. She stood in the aisle, her cloak clutched about herself, hiding the truth. "You're asking me to lie to my Laird."

"Not lie. Only to say naught."

She stood on his left, beseeching. Years of duty and fidelity to MacDonald hovered at his right, pulling him toward the chapel doors and the Bat Cave. He looked to the Crucifix, hating the choice before him.

CHAPTER THIRTEEN

Inverness, Present

It wasn't possible to watch the door every minute. He needed to sleep, or at times find food. Standing around too long attracted attention. It was anyone's guess when Angus arrived or left. And, Simon realized after a week of the siege—there was a back door.

It took days—days of circling the building, keeping his distance from the men who had hauled him in weeks prior, trying to watch either door through which Angus might enter or exit—before his efforts were rewarded. But finally, as he watched from across the river, Angus stepped out from the front door accompanied by the girl with jet black hair.

But he went back in, and despite hours of watching, never re-emerged. He'd left through the back door, Simon realized, as even the long summer day began to paint streaks of sunset across the sky.

It took another week, moving around to avoid notice, listening to the conversations around him for anything he could learn of Shawn—which was mainly that he had beautiful hair and many women wished to run their hands through it—before he had a sense of Angus's hours. It took several more days, including two in which Angus didn't appear at all, before Simon managed to be at the correct door when he left.

Tugging his newest hat over his eyes, Simon fell into step behind him, careful to keep the crowd between himself and his prey. Angus stopped at a pub. Clive came out the front door, two pints in hand, greeting him in loud welcome. Simon fell back, drifting across the street as they seated themselves at an outdoor table. As sunset gilded the clouds hovering over the city, they went inside. Simon waited, and waited, until a sheriff approached. "You waiting for something?" he asked.

Simon thought of the weapons they carried, and the jail that might hold him longer this time. Going home and taking power mattered more than putting this simpleton in his place for speaking so to a great knight. He smiled tightly, bowed, and went on his way.

The following day, Simon watched the back door that appeared to be Angus's choice. But as the hour of Angus's departure approached, a screech of inhuman sound split the air. Men erupted from the station as knights would pour from the armory on their way to battle. A boy stopped beside Simon, watching. "Some day that's going to be me," he said.

"What are they doing?" Simon asked.

The boy nodded at the equipment they carried—ropes, picks, and more, that Simon couldn't name. "They go up there prepared for anything. One of them may be hanging off a cliff in midair, held up only by those straps, trying to reach yer man."

Simon watched as they ran, pushing gear into the vehicle. Their shouts carried across the street, the wagon doors slammed, and with a squeal of tires, siren screaming like a wildcat in heat, the thing tore into the road and disappeared.

Simon filed the information away and returned the next afternoon to watch for Angus's departure.

Glenmirril, December 1316

Niall stood in the doorway of the Bat Cave, breathing in the oil of flickering torches, and the wax of dozens of candles glittering under the life-sized crucifix. Even as he watched MacDonald kneel under the crucifix, swathed in his fur-lined cloak, his conscience raged. Tell or not? Allene's father would be furious. He was already spending his hours hidden in the Bat Cave, carving and praying, neglecting his duties—one of several things Niall must speak to him about. Who would it hurt to keep Christina's secret? He and Allene could find an answer. He said his own prayers, as he watched MacDonald across the dim cave, for wisdom and guidance.

MacDonald turned. His eyes lit. He pushed himself to his feet, grunting. "Niall, you're home, Son!" He lumbered across the cave, past his wood-working bench, where the skeletal pieces of a harp rested, another attempt to re-create the harp of the twenty-first century of which Niall had told him.

Niall watched, arguing with himself the whole time. It was his duty. MacDonald held high standards. But he was known, too, for mercy and compassion.

MacDonald threw his arms around Niall, nearly squeezing the life out of him, and slapping his back. "Can you bide a wee bit? Were the negotiations successful?"

Niall shook his head, stepping out of the embrace. "Bruce gave me leave to see the wee bairn."

"A fine braw laddie he is, too!"

"I've two days before I must leave for Ayr."

"Why does Bruce want you in Ayr?"

Niall stared at the ground. He hated to say it. He hated leaving MacDonald and Allene worrying, as much as he hated his own immediate future.

"Why are you going to Ayr?" MacDonald demanded sternly.

"Bruce is going to Ireland to fight with Edward."

MacDonald's shoulders sagged. "Then the peace talks came to naught."

Niall sighed. "What Edward Carnarvon lacks in military skill, he makes up for in stubbornness. He'll not recognize Bruce as king."

"So 'tis more war." MacDonald turned, pacing the room. "Does he not have enough troubles with the Welsh and Lancaster and Ireland?"

Niall watched silently, his own problems churning in his mind—how he was going to walk away from Allene and his sons; how he was going to get on that ship; how he could deceive the Laird and hide information, or ignore Christina's pleading.

MacDonald turned under the crucifix and re-traced his steps. "You're quiet, Niall. Are you worried?"

Niall shook his head. Then he nodded. "Not worried as much as a great deal weighs on my mind."

"Crossing water?"

Niall's jaw tightened. He'd done quite well with all of them pretending they didn't notice.

"You must remember all Shawn told you. Play your harp on the shore."

"'Tis a wee bit chilly for that just now." Niall spoke more sharply than he'd intended.

"Then think on it, as Shawn told you to. His time may have faults, Niall, but what he suggests is better than aught we've had to offer you. Think about getting on that boat with your harp, and playing and being at peace. You must at least *try*."

"'Tis not the crossing that weighs on my mind." Niall consoled himself it was not exactly a lie. The crossing was not the *only* thing that weighed on his mind. Did one omitted word make for a lie? He glanced at the crucifix.

MacDonald dropped a heavy hand on Niall's shoulder. "I'll pray for you, lad."

Niall bit back the words that prayer didn't seem to change much, settling for a tight, "Thank you, my Lord."

MacDonald frowned at him. "You doubt?"

"My Lord," Niall said, "'tis only that I've seen but few answers, of late."

MacDonald chuckled. "Perhaps your expectations are unrealistic. Your head has been turned by grief, loss, by tales of Shawn's world."

"No," Niall said. "I *saw* Shawn's world. 'Tis all he said. Women go about at night with no fear! They've no guards at their doors!"

"They've problems and heartache, same as all men." MacDonald crossed the room to a large log propped against the wall. "I shall offer prayers regardless of your present doubt." He searched among the tools on his workbench before lifting a plane.

"We've much to discuss." Niall hoped the hint was strong enough MacDonald would put down the tools and listen.

"Discuss it, then." MacDonald lowered the plane. But instead of turning to Niall, he circled the wood. He touched it, like a physician feeling bones. "A Madonna, do you think?"

"Yes, my Lord. 'Twill make a good Madonna." Niall didn't see it. It was more a testament to his faith in MacDonald's gift. "Darnley and Morrison hope you'll soon be back in the great hall running Glenmirril."

The Laird's eyes didn't leave the thick oak column. "Darnley and Morrison fash themselves overmuch. I've a great deal to think on, and I think best here. 'Tis time well spent. What else did you wish to discuss?"

Niall thought of Christina's eyes, pleading in the chapel. His insides knotted. He couldn't lie to his lord. Nor did he wish to betray her. "How do you fare with MacDougall?" he asked. "Allene worries."

"MacDougall is locked and guarded more closely than the spices." MacDonald ran his hands up and down the column. His shaggy eyebrows puckered.

"His mind is sharper than the tartest spices, and he's a fair bit more crafty."

MacDonald lifted a chisel and hammer, and circled the column one more time. "Aye, he is that. I'm fully aware of all that passes with him. Was there more?" MacDonald stopped in his circuit.

He *had* to say something, Niall chided himself. He couldn't lie to his laird. "Have you thought on giving Christina in marriage again?" A feeble hope flickered in a corner of his mind. Allene didn't like the idea, but it would solve the problem.

"Aye." MacDonald touched the wood one more time before setting the chisel to it and raising the hammer. "I've seen little of her since the attack."

Niall held his tongue, wary of saying the wrong thing.

"We knew she would be distraught when he left." MacDonald sighed heavily. "Perhaps 'tis indeed time to think of another husband for her."

"Of a better ilk than Duncan MacDougall this time," Niall said.

"Och, Niall, we must think of the good of the clan."

"For once, we must think of the good of the one," Niall replied. "She married once for the sake of the clan, at great personal cost to herself. Nor did it give us the alliance and peace we'd hoped."

"True. Still, for her sake or the clan's, I believe you're right. We must choose another husband for her."

"In Shawn's time, they choose for themselves."

"'Tis neither here nor there."

"'Tis there." Niall kept his face straight.

MacDonald glared. "I'm none so enamored of his time. They're *impertinent*."

Niall smiled. "In general, nor am I. However, I think there may be a time—forgive my choice of words, my Lord—and a place for some of his ideas. Perhaps this is one, if we could allow Christina some say in the matter."

"I'll think on it, Niall."

Niall knew he wouldn't. It was perhaps as well, if it meant he might consider Niall's idea. "Would she and Hugh not suit one another well?"

MacDonald grunted. He lowered the hammer and finally looked at Niall. "Aye, now, not a bad thought. He's in need of a wife. He's been alone long enough, since Elizabeth's death. And we could hardly want a better woman for him than Christina."

Allene's misgivings fretted at the edges of Niall's mind. He pushed them away. She had the luxury, in the safety of a castle, to think with her heart. He must be practical. A husband was what Christina needed. "Will you speak of it to Hugh?"

"I think I will." He lifted the plane, forced it along the curve of the wood, and smiled at the shaving that curled, thin as parchment, off of it.

Niall relaxed. Hugh would help Christina, and take the child as his own.

"Was there more?" MacDonald asked.

Niall hovered on the edge of speech. Shawn would have spoken. Shawn would have had no qualms about saying, *Look, I don't care if you're the Pope, you have a castle up there waiting for you to take charge! Do something about MacDougall! Do something about Christina!*

But he wasn't Shawn. And there was nothing to be done about MacDougall other than what MacDonald was already doing.

"No, my Lord." His insides resumed their nervous dance. He was lying to his laird.

"'Tis interesting you mention Christina." MacDonald set the plane on the tool bench and crossed the cave to Niall. "Allene was quite worried for her, when first Shawn left. I believed her grief would let up. But she appears more ill at ease now than before."

Niall swallowed, and stared at the floor. He clasped his hands behind his back. He couldn't betray Christina. He couldn't lie to his lord.

"Niall."

Niall raised his head, meeting MacDonald's eyes. They had become stern.

"You know summat, d' ye not?"

Against his will, Niall nodded. He swallowed hard, praying that by some miracle, Allene's father would simply walk away, not pursue the matter.

"Tell me what you know."

Niall closed his eyes, the image of the crucifix and the dozens of flickering candles burning behind his lids. He had never been one to lie. And he wasn't at all sure now was the time to start. Malcolm MacDonald was known by all to be a man of mercy. It was his right as Laird to know what transpired in his castle, among those for whom he bore responsibility. He needed to know, before he went out and made a marriage arrangement for her. He opened his eyes and looked directly at MacDonald, feeling sick as he betrayed Christina. "She is with child."

Midwest America, Present

It was impossible to miss the large pink envelope stuck in the crack of his door. If Shawn hadn't seen it, he would have smelled it. The scent of roses wafted down his front steps. It would be Caroline. Dana would never be so ostentatious, or feminine, or perfumed. He stared at it, tempted. Amy hadn't returned his calls. She clearly didn't want to speak to him. Didn't that free him from his promise?

His jaw tensed. It was unfair to blame her. Maybe she was busy. She was subbing again, with a lot of new music. She'd be practicing, and caring for a new baby. He took the card between two fingers, fumbling with the lock. Holding the powerful smell at arm's length, as soon as he'd let himself in and passed through the granite foyer and into the kitchen, his foot hit the lever at the base of the shiny silver garbage can. The lid lifted, and gulped down the card, swallowing some of the scent. "Couldn't get it all?" Shawn muttered.

He took a five minute shower, still relishing daily shampoos, and, towel around waist, stuck his head in his walk-in closet. Nothing appealed. He didn't have time.

It was a ten minute drive to the publisher. He wanted to be comfortable. He grabbed his breeks and the *leine* Christina had sewn—the cleaning lady had washed them on his return—and pulled them on. He stuffed the pants legs into soft leather boots, twins to Niall's own pair back in the 1300's, brushed his hair and tied it back with the same leather thong that had held it the night he left—left what? He hadn't left Scotland that night, only a certain time.

There was no time to worry about it. With his briefcase stuffed full of his proposal and copies of scores and parts, he set off into the warm day, enjoying the wind rippling through his hair as his convertible sped down the highway, a bright red flash among the duller cars on the road. The publisher gave his medieval outfit a once over, before smiling, shaking hands, and ushering him into a luxurious office of deep pile carpet, framed and signed photos of musicians, and heavy, mahogany desk vibrating with its own importance under a pile of important papers to and from important people.

The deal was soon done, with healthy percentages going each to himself and Amy, and an agreement to publish five more editions as soon as he could have the parts and scores ready.

The musicians in the quintet, likewise, said nothing about his outfit when he met them at his house. They welcomed him home, offering well-wishes. They couldn't restrain curious stares, but his reputation prevented any comments. He dealt their parts out, like playing cards, onto the stands, and an hour later, lifted to a higher plane of life with the warm air flowing in and out of his lungs, and the golden flow of the music spilling over him, wrapped up the session. "Monday, three weeks from now, ten a.m. with the sound engineer. B sharp." He missed Niall.

They laughed at the old joke, shook hands, and twenty minutes later, he was back in his car, his tuxedo in a garment bag, an overnight bag on the back seat, and his trombone propped on the floor of the car, leaning against the passenger seat like a friend, the seat belt stretched around it, speeding toward the airport. A good day's work so far, all of it keeping his mind off Clarence, and a rehearsal this evening with the San Francisco Symphony. He glanced at his cell phone, lying on the passenger seat, and thought about calling Amy. She didn't seem to want to hear from him. Maybe he'd call Dana once he got through security.

Glenmirril, December 1316

Christina pulled deep into herself as the argument raged, hotter than the fire blazing in the Laird's grate, the Laird shouting, and Niall raising his voice, pleading for calm.

She had retreated from the chapel in panic, up to the third floor hall, from whence she watched MacDonald storm into the courtyard, Niall scrambling at his heels while MacDonald shouted for Hugh. The three of them had disappeared back into the tower, and she'd been left, trembling, for well over an hour, before Niall had appeared, looking pale, to summon her.

In the Laird's chamber now, she gripped her hands together against the shaking, till the effort of clutching her hands caused her arms to tremble. He might send her away from Glenmirril.

"'Tis Shawn's child, is it not?" MacDonald demanded for the third time.

She stared at him blankly, hiding behind the frozen mask that had protected her from the worst of Duncan's rages, letting him think she didn't comprehend, and wondering why she couldn't speak the truth. Would he send her back to Creagsmalan? They wouldn't take her. She was no longer kin to them.

"Is it Shawn's?" Niall pressed, though with less volume.

"Who else's could it be?" MacDonald's face darkened. "I *trusted* him! How could he do this to us, to *her*?"

"We don't *know* it's his!" Niall rounded on MacDonald.

Perhaps those whom she'd shown kindness would take her in, Christina thought. That would not include the jailer. Or maybe he could tell his wife the truth, now that neither Duncan nor his father was a threat, and maybe they would take pity on her.

"We *know* there was no one else," MacDonald raged. "She is not one to throw herself about. Surely it could only be Shawn. I thought he'd changed!"

No, Christina decided. As long as MacDougall lived, he was potential danger.

"He changed a great deal," Niall insisted. "Perhaps entirely. We've no evidence this is his doing."

Not that she'd wish ill on him, Christina thought. He was a conflicted man, believing himself better than he was, perhaps even genuinely trying to be. Though he certainly blinded himself enough to miss the mark and do as he pleased, regardless.

"He took advantage!" MacDonald rose from the table, his hands clasped behind his back, his great shaggy eyebrows furrowing in anger and frustration. "He *knew* our ways and went against my word!"

The words pounded in Christina's mind, rising up like the dull, all-consuming thunder of the waves pounding the rocks outside Creagsmalan, till she couldn't think, till Niall and the Laird became blurs of sound and color around her.

"She hasn't said...."

She should tell them. She tried. She formed the name in her mind, but it choked her.

"Did he not *think* what he was leaving her to face alone!" MacDonald slammed his fist into his palm, emphasizing the words. "Did he leave here *still* not comprehending what it is for a woman *here and now* to be unwed and pregnant?"

She didn't know why she couldn't say the words. Humiliation rose, threatening to turn her cheeks bright pink, and she guessed shame must be the reason.

"It would have happened just before his leaving." Niall defended Shawn. "He wouldn't have known he was leaving her with child."

MacDonald would surely kill him, Christina decided. She didn't want to bring about more death, a newer and deeper feud. Things were bad enough. It was reason enough not to speak.

"Are they fools in his time?" MacDonald roared, jolting Christina from her brooding. "Surely he knew it *could* happen, and still he left her!"

Who knew what MacDonald would do, Christina thought. He *was* the father of her child, and she *had* lied to him—twice.

"If he turns up," MacDonald fumed. "I'll pillory him! I'll flay him. I'll...."

"He's not coming back," Niall said heavily, and grief welled in Christina's heart.

"I'll disembowel him myself and burn his guts before his eyes!"

Christina lifted her head, tried to speak, but no words would leave her mouth.

Niall and the Laird both stared at her momentarily, before MacDonald erupted again. "How could he leave her to face the shame alone!"

Christina felt the frown of a question cross her face, and smoothed her features back into the safety of non-expression that had served so well with Duncan. But Niall had seen.

"He's safe in his own time," he assured her. "And the Laird will do none of that anyway."

"I certainly will!" MacDonald roared. "And I'll mount his head on a pike over the gatehouse! Then he'll marry her like an honorable man!"

"Aye, a fine husband he'll make with his head on a pike and his intestines in the hearth," Niall said dryly.

"His impertinence and disrespect have badly affected you," MacDonald thundered, "and that will be the end of it!"

Niall inclined his head in a respectful bow. "My apologies, my Lord. But we must still decide what to *do*."

MacDonald dropped heavily into the chair at the table, his face a mask of fury. "*Do?*" The word erupted as something close to the angry snarl of a lion, the effect heightened by the quiver of his bushy red and white mane. "There's naught to be *done*. She's with child and soon enough 'twill be impossible to hide."

"Marriage," Niall reminded him.

From her seat on the couch, Christina's head shot up. Red rimmed her eyes. "Oh, no!" she breathed. "No."

MacDonald looked at her in shock, as if she'd risen in wraith-like curls of smoke before him. "*No?*"

She lowered her eyes quickly to her hands, clenched in her lap. "My apologies, my Lord. I did not mean to speak out of turn."

"Christina, *think*!" Niall crossed the room to her and dropped on his knee. "You marry—a good and kind man this time, I promise." He cast a hard stare at MacDonald, knowing he was pushing his luck. "We say you've taken ill. You take to your rooms. You are saved the shame, the child has a name."

The tendons in Christina's neck tightened. Her knuckles turned white. She stared resolutely at her hands. "By the time I can claim to have a newborn baby, the child will be six months old. 'Tis not possible, Niall."

He touched her hand. "Are you not even interested in who you'll marry?"

She lifted her head slowly, her eyes wide. "You've already arranged it?"

From the table, MacDonald spoke gruffly. "We've discussed it. He's kind, Christina. He'll treat you well. 'Twill be a good match."

Christina looked from the Laird to Niall. "I've no wish to marry," she whispered.

"Christina, you *must*. Unless you wish to go to a convent." He watched her dark blue eyes, thinking she couldn't possibly expect Shawn to come back. "You can't wish to live your life alone."

"'Tis not what I wish." Her eyes pierced his.

He felt, in the instant, what it must be for her to look at his face and see Shawn, to be looking at him even now and seeing Shawn. "You know you can't have what you wish," he said softly. "None of us can. If I could make it so for you, Christina, I would. But he is gone."

"I wonder often," she whispered, "if he comes to these rooms, as the man from his time did, and tries to speak to us."

"Even if he did, he'd not hear or see us." Niall squeezed her hands. "Christina, even if he could, he's no more than a ghost to us now. You cannot build a life on hoping for a glimpse of a ghost."

She hung her head. "I know, Niall. Just give me time."

"We *haven't* time," he insisted in frustration. "You're with child *now*. Do you not even care to know who we've chosen?"

She shook her head. "It matters little."

"I should think it matters a great deal." He rose, turning to MacDonald, waiting.

MacDonald rose from the table. "Christina."

She looked up, her hands gripping one another in a death lock.

"Hugh was honored to accept you as his wife. He'll be good to you. You've affection for one another already."

"Does he know?" she whispered.

MacDonald nodded. "He says you are an honorable woman, and he'll accept the child as his own."

"When is the marriage to take place?" She asked with the lackluster tone in which she might inquire about her own execution.

"Tomorrow."

She didn't answer, her head bowed over clenched hands.

MacDonald rose from his chair, going to her and dropping heavily to one knee. He prised her hands apart, taking them in his own, and spoke gently. "Christina, in time, your grief...." He stopped, Shawn's name sour on his tongue. "Your grief will pass. And you'll have a good man at your side."

She lifted her eyes. "Please don't make me do this."

He shook his head, a flicker of the anger returning. "You must."

West Coast America, Present

"Good rehearsal." Tessa, the singer, sidled up beside Shawn in the green room as he polished the bell of his trombone, quick, circular motions of the cloth until the brass gleamed, flashing the fluorescent lights back from its curve.

Shawn looked up, into wide golden-brown eyes and honey-brown hair, round pink cheeks and a narrow, little chin, that all gave her a fragile look—and something else, too, that he recognized instantly. Amy hadn't returned his calls. "Hate to let it end so soon." He detached the bell from the slide and lowered it into the case, a slow smile curving his mouth. Amy would never know.

He could evade Clarence's face for the night. It had played on the edge of his mind all day, no matter how busy he kept himself, the clean-cut face of yesterday, above an orange jump suit and shackled wrists, morphing in and out of the face he'd known in high school, the scruffy, long-haired boy who hung over the top bunk, shining a flashlight up under his eyes, laughing and telling ghost stories. He'd wondered, leaning back in first class on the plane, why he'd forgotten those nights. But he wanted to forget. Hate was easier than compassion or forgiveness. Far easier. His hand paused a micro-second in the act of polishing the slide, wondering if that's what Amy felt about him.

Tessa boosted herself onto the table, her thigh grazing the edge of the case. She twirled a finger in the leather lace at the throat of his *leine.* "It doesn't *have* to end so soon." White teeth flashed. She'd obviously played this game before.

Shawn studied her, returning to polishing the slide. Comparisons to both Amy and Christina jumped to mind. They were both taller, thinner, both with long, black hair compared to the soft brown waves curling around her face. "You don't even know me," he said. Why beat around the bush? They both knew what was going on.

Dimples deepened in each of her cheeks. "I know *of* you."

His eyes narrowed. Two years ago, he would have taken it as a compliment. Now, it twisted in his gut, remembering the shock and horror on Christina's face. *What kind of a man* are *you?* He fit the slide into the case, his fingers brushing the plush, brown lining. *I know* of *you* sounded different, far different, after knowing Christina, than it had before. It left a sour note in his ears now.

"Maybe I can get the secret out of you where you've been for a year." Her slender legs crossed one another, inching her short skirt higher. Her palms braced on the table, she leaned forward, letting her eyes run from his shirt to his boots and back.

He laughed, suddenly. He could see it all clearly: feeling warm, safe, loved, for an hour, maybe three or four, and knowing in the morning she didn't really know him or love him. Hell, he couldn't even tell her where he'd been without her laughing. Christina, Amy—they knew him, knew his life. He could be honest with them.

"I've been in medieval Scotland." He dropped the lid of the case and snapped the bronze latches with a satisfying click. "I fought at Skaithmuir with James Douglas. Funny how people don't believe me."

She smiled more widely. He had no doubt she'd mastered the deepening of those dimples in a mirror as carefully as she'd mastered her arpeggios, and knew full well their impact. And they had an impact. His insides stirred. He wavered. He hadn't turned her down yet. It made no difference if she knew him or not. A good night was a good night, a night away from the image of the boy stabbing his father. And Amy had hardly rushed to forgive and accept him back.

"Seriously," Tessa purred. Her fingers crawled up on top of the fawn-colored case, inching toward his hand. "Tell me where you were."

His resolve flapped in the wind, like the Laird's pennants on Glenmirril's ramparts. She didn't have Christina or Amy's dignity. They'd never throw themselves at a man who didn't know them or care for them. He leaned forward. She did, too, her soft brown bangs tickling his forehead, her eyes wide in anticipation. "Can you keep a secret?" he whispered.

She nodded eagerly.

He moved back, swinging the case off the table, out from under her hand, with a grin. Oldest line in the world, and so easy. "So can I. Do you have a ride home, or do you want me to call you a taxi?"

Her face fell. He hated himself and dreaded the night ahead, sure to be full of insomnia, full of ugly images. Damn Christina, anyway, for deciding to be his conscience. He hoped she was happy, wherever she was, because he sure wasn't.

Glenmirril, December 1316

In the courtyard, Hugh lunged and parried with Red, skipping and dodging the boy's attempts to strike him back. A flock of chickens dodged around the edges of their practice space, squawking angrily at having their feeding interrupted. Three of the castle children, in brown and beige tunics and leggings and thick cloaks, sat against the castle wall, watching. Taran stood beside them, leaning in and shouting. "To his right, Red! Quick now!"

"Hugh!" From the tower doorway, Niall shouted over the racket.

Hugh, his face streaming with sweat despite the chilly day, held up a hand to Red. He retrieved his cloak from the girl, no more than seven, who held it for him, as he pushed his sword back into its scabbard. As he climbed the stairs, wiping his brow with a kerchief, he asked, "What has she to say?"

"Come to the Laird's chambers, Hugh." Niall glanced up the tower stairs. He had not gone to the top since the night Shawn had disappeared. He wondered, if he took Allene up, if he held her tight, would they disappear together into Shawn's time? Or might they disappear to some other time, centuries ago, or somewhere beyond Shawn's time? He wondered if he could appear in the days his own father had been alive. He squelched the thought. He had duties. There was no time for daydreams.

"I get no answer?" Hugh rumbled.

"I fear she dreams of Shawn returning." Niall stopped on the second floor, at the Laird's chambers. As he raised his hand to knock, the door swung open.

"Enter." MacDonald handed Hugh a mug of ale. "Tomorrow, Hugh."

Hugh accepted the cup, but didn't drink. "You look haggard, Malcolm," he said. "Did your talk with Christina not go well?"

"Very little has gone well these many months." Malcolm sighed. "Christina has no wish to marry. Still, you'll speak your vows on the morrow."

"Will I, now?" Hugh set his ale on MacDonald's table and went to the window, looking down through the shining glass panes at the winter-gray loch. "What is her objection?" He turned, grinning. "Perhaps I'm not comely, or too small of stature?"

Malcolm smiled, though it was a tired smile that didn't light his eyes or ease the creases of worry in his forehead. "'Tis not you, Hugh. She simply does not wish to marry. I believe Niall will have told you as much, despite my orders to the contrary."

"Would our Niall do things his own way?" Hugh turned to Niall in mock surprise. "Certainly, Niall, you always follow your Laird's orders."

Niall shrugged. "I try."

MacDonald snorted. "You told him, then?"

"A word or two may have slipped out," Niall said.

"'Tis only our guess, you understand," MacDonald said to his brother. "Niall says she holds hope of Shawn's return."

"She objects strongly?" Hugh asked.

"Her first word was *no*," grumbled the Laird, "as was her second, before she remembered to whom she spoke. Had she dared a third and fourth word, they also would have been no. She is the saddest looking bride-to-be I've yet seen. But 'tis not you, Hugh."

"Then perhaps for the time being, we should respect her wishes," Hugh said. "'Tis all very recent for her."

"She is a *woman*," MacDonald argued. "She needs a husband. Especially now, with a child on the way! Have I not always arranged the marriages of our people? 'Tis the way it is done."

"In his time, 'tis not...."

"We're not *in* his time!" Malcolm thundered. His bushy beard quivered. His eyes shot fire.

"I'm only saying he knows how to swim," Hugh said mildly.

"What has *that* to do with Christina and her child?" Malcolm demanded. The scar on his cheek stood out, stark white against his flush of anger.

Niall stepped back against the wall, his lips tight, torn between amusement and desperation to see Christina cared for.

"Only that his time is not all bad," Hugh said. "They've a decent idea or two, one or two things we might learn from."

The Laird shook his head. "We'll do things as they're done in *this* time."

"Maybe not this time," Hugh said, then lowered his eyes to the floor, murmuring, "Forgive the choice of words." Heaving a sigh, he stared once again at the loch.

"You are perfect for one another," MacDonald objected. "Surely, Hugh, you've not had your head turned, too, by Shawn's tales of marrying for *love*! Surely you'll not object because she suffers from grief. You've affection and respect for one another. Did you expect more? Love will grow."

Hugh turned from the window. Sunlight shone behind his bristling mane. "I'd take Christina to wife as quick as an arrow flies, Malcolm. On no account of my own would I say no. But she has had one awful marriage, she grieves Shawn's going, she is with child, and we don't know whose or how. Do we push this on her, too?"

"She needs a husband *because* she is with child. She needs someone to claim it."

"Surely we can think of another way to handle it. Give her time, Malcolm, and if you still wish me to marry her in a year, when perhaps she is more at peace and has come to accept that he is not coming back, I will abide your wishes."

MacDonald pulled himself up taller and straighter. His red and silver beard quivered. His eyes narrowed. "I am your Laird. I didn't ask your opinion. You'll marry her on the morrow."

Hugh laughed. He took three giant steps to the table, downed half the ale, and clapped MacDonald on the back. "How d' ye plan to make me?" He lifted a hand to Niall, and walked out of the door.

CHAPTER FOURTEEN

Bannockburn, Present

I let myself in the cheery blue door after a morning walk. From the front room comes James's cooing and chuckling, and Carol's voice. Only as I enter the room, the soothing fawn and beige decor and a basket of boughs and pine cones in the hearth, do I realize it's not the voice of a woman speaking to a baby.

Carol holds out the phone. Her eyebrows lift in silent plea. "It's Shawn," she says, needlessly. "Please?" She bounces James gently in her other arm.

The phone hovers between us. I fancy, for a minute, I can hear Shawn's breath, hanging in suspended animation, waiting. The good and the bad—concerts and writing music and the hit-in-the-gut feeling of each lie—all twist around me like a spiderweb, clinging, tightening more as I struggle to get free.

"Please," Carol whispers.

I nod mutely, and take the phone, heading numbly up the stairs. I drop onto the peach cover of my bed, waiting.

"Amy?" His voice cracks.

"I'm here," I say.

"Amy!" His voice strengthens. "I'm in my hotel room in San Francisco. I've been calling you."

His voice is warm, a rich baritone with velvet harmonies, as golden as the flecks in his brown eyes. I find myself smiling, clutching it around myself like a fleece blanket on a chilly night. "How was your flight?" I want more of his voice. I close my eyes, hating the equally strong feeling of fickleness and betrayal. I wanted space—from Shawn and Angus both. But I couldn't look his mother in the eye and refuse to speak to her son whom she missed and loved and mourned, whose return has brought her so much joy.

"Good. The flight was good."

I swallow, gripping the phone in both hands. "Caroline didn't hit on you?"

Silence falls like an iron curtain. I know. I hold my breath, waiting to see if he'll tell the truth.

"Yeah." A small sound comes over the line. "Yeah, she did."

Relief floods me. He's being honest! I smile a little, laugh a short bark of a sound. "She did? You're admitting it?"

"It was on the plane, Amy. I told her no. She left a card in my door at my house. I threw it out." He laughs, a short bark. *"I almost choked on the perfume before I reached the garbage can. I didn't call back. I haven't seen her since I got off the plane."* He sounds eager, pleased, his voice rising, like a child proud of himself.

I hesitate, my hand clenching the phone. My voice comes out barely above a whisper. *"Were you tempted?"* This time, the silence stretches. My mouth tightens. I close my eyes, shutting out the sunny bedroom, seeing Caroline all too clearly, in various of her tight sweaters. *"You were tempted, weren't you?"* I ask.

"Not on the plane." His voice, too, comes out softly, hoarsely.

"When? You said you haven't seen her since then." The familiar unease fills my stomach; the familiar dizziness of conflicting stories spins in my head. My back tenses, ready to stand my ground when his story changes.

"Later," he says. *"I almost called her yesterday."*

"Why?" I open my eyes, swallowing over the knot in my throat, as I stare at the dresser where our picture once stood.

"I'm trying to start over." His voice rises in agitation. *"I'm trying to be honest. I was upset. I tried to call you, first. You didn't answer."*

"Don't you dare blame anything on me!" I shoot up from the bed, pacing and forcibly stopped myself at the window.

"I didn't mean to," he says hastily. *"I didn't mean it like that. I'm just saying."*

I lift a hand to the lace half-curtains, looking out at the sunny day. The boy and girl next door race down the street, shouting and laughing, followed by a woofing, black dog pounding on their heels. I draw in a steadying breath. *"How did you mean it? Why were you upset?"*

"I went to see...uh...I went to...the boy...."

The children fall in a heap at the far end of the street, the black dog flopping all over them, its tail wagging furiously, its head lifted in joyful barking. *"The prison?"* I guess.

A choked sound comes over the line, and he says, *"Aye."*

"Oh." My hand falls from the curtains. *"Shawn."* Outside, the boy bounces up off the ground like only a child can, and, shrieking with laughter, runs from the dog. Carol told me once how Clarence loved their dogs. I wonder if he and Shawn chased a dog together like these children. I've never thought much about the days when he lived with Shawn. Shawn never mentioned it. *"Are you okay?"*

He makes a choked sound—not a laugh, not a cry. *"I called her."*

I turn from the window, back into the bedroom, feeling sick. *"You called her?"* A photograph of Glenmirril sits on the dresser. Angus gave it to me. I pull my eyes away. He'll be at work now, in his office, maybe, unless a call for a rescue has come in. I wonder if I'll even hear about it, if he's injured, up there in the mountains, if he would call and ask me to come.

"I was upset!" Shawn's voice snatches me away from Angus. *"I thought better of it. I told her I wanted her opinion on* Benedictus. *I hung up, Amy, I swear I hung up, and I didn't see her at all. I wasn't thinking straight."*

I take a deep breath. He went to the prison. He'd have been upset. "Okay. I understand. This time you hung up." I take another breath. "Next time you won't call her in the first place, right?" He hung up on Caroline. I can live with that...for now. "Are you okay? What happened at the prison? Did you talk to him?"

For a few seconds, in which I put the photograph of the castle in the drawer, I think he isn't going to answer. But as the drawer slides shut, he says, "No."

"Why not?" I hesitate. "Were you angry?"

"I don't know."

My fingers dance on the dresser top, nerves shooting through my arms. He's never said so much, not when he's sober at least. "I would have been," I say.

"Yeah, I guess. I don't know."

I hesitate, not sure where to go. "So if you didn't talk to him, did you see him?"

"Yeah, I saw him."

"And?"

"And, uh, my mom's been visiting him. I left."

"Just left?" I drop back onto the bed. "Did he look like you remember?"

Again, he pauses, long enough that I think I've asked the wrong question. I pull in my breath against the tightening of my lungs. But he answers. "No. His hair was short. He hated long hair, and his mother wouldn't let him cut it. How's James?"

It's my turn to pause, unsure whether to let the change of subject go. But he's said more than he ever has. "He's good," I whisper. "His smile is just like yours."

Shawn chuckles. "That's a good thing, right?"

"It's good," I say. "He smiles all the time." Like you, I think, but don't say. It's one of the things I loved about him, his unfailing cheerfulness. "How's San Francisco? How was the rehearsal?"

"Great! It was great. Kept my chops, thanks to MacDonald's sackbut."

"You're ready for Sacramento next week?" I ask.

He laughs. "Is Sacramento ready for me?"

I smile. "Is anyone, really?"

I hear his soft chuckle over the phone, and he adds, "Sacramento, Portland, Seattle, and I'll be home the second week of July."

I say nothing. I should say I can't wait. *But I wanted space, in which I might suddenly know what I really want.*

"I came straight to the hotel," he says.

I realize he thinks that's what my silence is about. My mind fills in the blanks. "Alone? No offers?" My stomach flutters. He'll get angry if I keep questioning him. My spine stiffens. Let him get angry. I have every right to ask.

"Uh, yeah."

"Yeah there weren't, or yeah there were?"

"The singer." His voice suggests his head is hanging, eyes averted. "I called a taxi for her and came home alone."

"Was she mad?"

"Yeah." He laughs a little. "Ticked. But it's not like I started it."

"Are you glad you did it?" My fingers knead the lace overlay of the bedspread, my stomach knotting.

"Yeah. I was. I am."

I glance at the clock, subtract the hours, and realize it's the middle of the night for him. He went to the prison. He has insomnia. My heart aches for him. Downstairs, James lets out a squeal of joy, and Carol laughs in turn.

"Are you mad?" he asks. "I didn't ask her to hit on me."

"Did you consider it?" The lace rolls into a knot between my fingers. I let go of it, not wanting to ruin the bedspread. The question burns in my heart. I wanted to hear he didn't, not for the space of a thirty-second note. But I wouldn't believe it.

"Yeah, I considered. I don't want to see Clarence tonight."

I let out my breath. "You know it's about him?"

"It's what went through my head when she sat there, all dimples and cleavage, Amy. I'm trying to be honest. I spent two years missing you. I want to do it right this time. I don't want to hurt you, but I don't want to lie. I was tempted. But I didn't."

"Okay." I swallow, hurt that he was tempted at all. But can I really expect miracles? My hand strays to the crucifix at my throat. "I'm glad you told me." He resisted. He chose insomnia over the singer, chose insomnia over hurting me. The pain in my heart eases a little.

"You're not mad?"

"You didn't do it," I say. I don't add that if he'd been a different person, she wouldn't have even tried. He's a different man now. It will take other people time to learn that.

We slide into easy conversation, talking for an hour, of San Francisco, of his rehearsal and trip to the publisher, the music he wants to arrange, of Niall and Allene and James, and I hang up, missing the sound of his voice already.

Glenmirril, December 1316

"Now what!" MacDonald slammed his fist on the table. "Never has he defied me! Never! Do I send him away? Exile him from Glenmirril? Put him in stocks?"

Tension inched up Niall's neck. This was supposed to be his time with Allene and his bairns. Instead, he'd barely seen her, and his sons, not at all. He sorely wished to respond as Shawn would. *Perhaps you ought burn his intestines before his eyes, mount his head on a pike, and then make him marry her.* But he didn't want to spend what wee precious time he had at odds with his lord and good-father. "May I speak?" he asked.

"You always have," MacDonald grumbled.

Despite the annoyance, Niall's tension ebbed away. "He has defied you once in all these years. Perhaps it means 'tis time to listen rather than command."

The Laird glanced at him, appearing for a moment stunned, then launched into a fit of pacing, ignoring his words. "She needs a husband! He will take her mind off Shawn and the grief of the past years."

"Maybe in a year or two, he'll do that."

"How do we explain her pregnancy?" At the window, MacDonald spun.

"She was going to take to her rooms, anyway."

"That was when we had an explanation for the *child*." MacDonald lifted the flagon, swirled what was left of the ale, and tossed it down his throat. "Have you forgotten we have not merely a pregnancy to explain, but a *child*?"

"If we are correct about the timing," Niall said, "we've three months to figure this out. Surely if we were clever enough to pull off Shawn's presence for two years, we can think up a story for a new bairn."

MacDonald glanced at his empty cup, glowered at it, and slammed it on the table. "How?"

"We'll try to think what Shawn would say."

"Shawn!" MacDonald exploded. "Shawn, Shawn, *Shawn!*" His hands flew into the air. "I've had enough of Shawn! 'Tis Shawn who left us with this predicament!"

Niall bit back a smile, thinking of Conrad. Perhaps it was Shawn who had driven that poor man to such pacing and ranting, after all. "Perhaps I'll think of aught before I leave."

"'Twill have to be passed off as another woman's child," the Laird said.

"Such a woman would have to hide herself for many months, too. She and her husband would both have to be trusted with the secret." Niall shook his head. "There must be a better way."

MacDonald gave a snort of irritation. "Marriage to Hugh is a better way. Bull-headed bollox! I should throw him in the stocks!" MacDonald paced the room, and stared out the window, shoulders hunched and hands clasped behind his back.

Niall cleared his throat.

MacDonald turned.

"My Lord, I beg your leave. I've seen Allene but briefly, and my son not at all. Might I go to them?"

"Go." The word came out a sigh, and Niall was glad, suddenly, that he did not yet bear the full responsibilities of the castle. He bowed low, and let himself out before MacDonald could change his mind.

West Coast America, Present

Early in the morning, in his hotel room, Shawn pushed *end*, and dropped back against the pile of hotel pillows, smiling, his stocking feet up on the bedspread. He should have tried this talking thing thing long ago. It felt good. Warm. Safe.

The smile grew, thinking of James with his dark hair and toothless grin. He'd heard him, laughing those baby belly laughs, when his mother put the phone to his ear, and he'd talked to his son. He set the phone on the nightstand. His fingers curled around the remote. But he didn't want to watch TV.

He dropped his head back against the headboard, letting his mind drift from the rehearsal, the sea of new faces, the way he'd reveled in once again meeting and greeting, being toasted and celebrated, working the crowd; in the swell of the orchestra behind him making everything he did twice as glorious. But he smiled more broadly, still, thinking of his concerts in the Bat Cave, the deepest reaches under Glenmirril, solo sackbut, or sometimes Niall playing along on harp or recorder. Laughter—they'd been happy, the Laird, and Hugh, Niall, Allene, Christina, and himself, far below the castle.

He felt the familiar insomnia, the restlessness that kept him up nights. He'd forgotten his practice mute, out of the habit of packing for these trips. He turned on his phone, fiddling with the buttons. He could pull up internet on it, Google their names, see if he could find out. He was surprised he hadn't thought of it before, but then he'd been back what, a month? And running from one thing to another the whole time, with no chance to think. It was usually better that way.

He frowned, his fingers still for a largo measure. Did he really want to know? Maybe find out that, in addition to everything other rotten, lousy thing he'd done in his life, he'd abandoned them, scrambling up the tower stairs to safety in Amy's twenty-first century arms, while they fought his battles and died? He shut his eyes suddenly, breathing in deeply. What if he found *Christina* had died? He couldn't live with that. He may as well have killed her himself.

He shut the phone off, and turned to his suitcase for his big pads of score paper. He had to have arrangements ready before he got to Seattle next week.

Glenmirril, December 1316

Niall stopped in the chapel on his way back to his rooms. The candles flickered as they had that morning; the incense hung, faint on the air, as it had that morning. But he stood at the back, the peace and gratitude of several hours ago gone. He stared at the crucifix feeling only dull anger. *Why Christina?* he asked. *What has she ever done to deserve this? What have I done, God, that You should constantly tear me from my family? What has Scotland done?* He'd watched Edward live in luxury, untouched by any consequence for his many atrocities. He'd watched the courtiers in their finery spend their days at dancing, drawing, and idle gossip, with no concern for their people, dying and starving in the north. *Why, God?* He glared at the crucifix, wanting answers.

His audacity overcame him. He lowered his eyes. But the anger remained. He had a day and a half left. Heaving a sigh for the lost hours, he let himself back into the hall, determined to spend his time with Allene and his sons, in happiness.

He found Allene on the couch in their solar, holding William in his swaddling clothes. Her hair flowed in a waterfall of red curls down her back. On the floor under the window, a thick fur spread beneath him, James played with a wooden horse. Niall guessed the Laird had carved it.

He kissed Allene, and joined her, taking William in his arms. In the swaddling clothes, only his tiny pink face showed. Niall smiled, his heart exploding in wonder. "He's bonny," he said, in awe.

"Aye." Allene glowed with pleasure.

On the floor, James looked up. Sunlight slanted through the window, turning his hair to shining copper. He smiled, showing a full set of teeth, and said, "*Eich!*"

"Yes, horse." Handing William back carefully, Niall joined his son on the fur. He raised his eyes to Allene. "Has he been on one yet?"

"Shawn used to set him on the hobins' backs. But he's not old enough to ride."

"A Scot is always old enough to ride." Niall grinned at her, remembering a long-ago journey to Stirling, when they'd both been quite young. He felt the months of warfare melt away in the sunshine.

She smiled. "A Scot is always too quick to think his son should be on a horse."

"It was the *Ame-erican,*" he stretched the word out in the twang he remembered of Amy's speech, "who put him on a horse. Though I can't say I disagree with him."

"He did enjoy it," Allene said. "He'd be happy if you took him down again."

"Then I will. And we'll have a horse saddled up for young William, too." Niall laughed at the grimace on Allene's face, then turned back to James. He picked up the wooden knight, its shield painted with the rearing red lion of Robert the Bruce. "See, James, this is our king. See his shield with the lion? Even now, he's fighting for us."

"King?" James squinted up quizzically at Niall. "*Athair?*"

Niall's heart sank, gazing into his son's blue eyes. Shawn's son would not be asking. "Yes, I'm your father." He touched his James's red curls. "And one day, I'll be home long enough you won't need to ask." He spent a few more minutes on the floor, prancing the wooden horse and king around their furry landscape, before re-joining Allene on the couch.

"Finally a chance to sit down." She leaned into his shoulder.

"Finally. I've not yet had a chance to see my mother, Finola, Gil."

"They're well," she said.

"Red?" he asked. "He's settling in?"

"He seems happy here with Taran and Gil." Allene sighed. "Though he misses you and Shawn something fierce, and I cannot answer his questions."

"It cannot be otherwise." Niall reached to take William, admiring him anew. He touched the wisp of black hair peeking from under the wrappings, and raised his eyes to Allene's, in amazement. "How can one grasp that he didn't exist, and now he does? Surely 'tis a miracle every time!"

She smiled. "Two of them we've been blessed with. I thank God each morning." She twined her fingers in his. "Had you business to attend to so early?"

Niall studied the face of his new son, unsure how much to tell her. But she was his wife, and Christina's closest friend. She was worried, and would hear from her father soon enough, or catch the cruel whispers that were sure to arrive any day now like December's gusts. "I went to the chapel," he said. "Christina was there."

Allene became still. "She goes nowhere else these days, but the chapel and her rooms. It kept you away for hours, and she has not returned. It does not bode well."

"It does not," he agreed. "But your father is a man of compassion and mercy. He'll be kind, though he is even now railing against her and Shawn in his chambers."

Allene's head drooped. "She is with child, then."

"She is."

"'Tis Shawn's?"

"She'll not say." He stared out the window, not wanting to spend their precious hours on difficulties.

Allene pushed herself up off his shoulder. When he didn't look at her, she touched his chin and turned his face. "Then perhaps it isn't."

"So I told your father. But he says, and I have to agree, who else?"

"There was a battle here," Allene said. "Surely you are not so ignorant of the ways of enemy soldiers?"

"She was in the Bat Cave with the women." The same thought that had refused to show itself, as he'd gone from the chapel to the Laird's rooms, showed itself again.

Allene tilted her head. "I told her to go with James. I watched her go."

"Then it can't have been the MacDougalls. The women didn't come up until after they were rounded up. Was she with the women then?"

"I sent Hugh. I came straight away to tend your arm."

"And Christina helped you. So Hugh must have brought her up from the Bat Cave." Niall tried to think back, and finally shook his head. "'Tis no good, Allene. I could barely stand, let alone think, when Christina arrived." After a moment, he added, "But something seemed wrong about it, from the chapel to your father's chambers, though I couldn't say what. Did she come in too soon to have been in the Bat Cave? Might she have left and been up here during the battle, or before?"

"'Tis possible, Niall. I've never thought to ask her."

"Then it may be she was up here. When she was told to be in the Cave."

"Not doing as she was told," Allene mused. "Perhaps she follows your example."

"Or yours." Niall gave her a sour look. "I'm home but two days, Allene."

"Not so much time to poke fun at ye," she returned. "I'd best keep at it."

Her words brought a wry smile to his face. "Perhaps warfare has made me forget how to laugh at myself."

"You'd best not," said Allene. "'Tis a skill you need often enough."

He laughed this time.

But her next words lacked humor. "What will become of Christina? Will my father turn her out?"

Niall sighed. In his arms, William stirred. His eyes fluttered and opened. He stared at Niall with large, unblinking eyes, as dark blue as the loch outside. "I think not. 'Tis not in his nature." He handed William back to Allene and lifted James off the rug. "Shall we go see the horses?"

"Horses!" James repeated. "*Uisge!*"

"Water?" Niall looked to Allene.

"My father takes him to the shore." Allene hesitated, looking uncertain, then leaned forward, over William in her lap, and said in a rush, "Take him, Niall! He loves going down."

With James in his arms, Niall glanced out the window. "'Tis a wee bit chilly."

Rising, Allene laid William in his cradle. "He's a warm cloak." She disappeared into the sleeping chamber, returning with the clothing. "Come along, Niall."

Bannockburn, Present

I sink back against the pillow, James on my shoulder, asleep after nursing. I stroke his hair, downy as the fluff on a new chick. He draws in a shuddering breath, and blows it out, warm against my neck, as warm as Shawn's voice against my ear through the long phone conversation. The rich timbre of his voice has always touched something deep in me.

But the name Tessa hangs over my shoulder. I try to picture her; I dropped a question or two, trying to sound casual. I've seen him backstage often enough with women. I try to see it—Shawn swinging the case down and walking away, taking her outside and hailing a taxi. It conflicts with all I've ever seen of him.

I rise carefully from the bed, laying James in his bassinet. He squirms, threatening for a moment to wake up, but he tucks his arms under his chest, his cheek pressed tight against his fists, and settles back to sleep. I pull the blanket up over his neck, against the black curls, and cross the hallway to my office.

I stare at the computer, considering posting on a forum. He's doing all the right things. He walked away from her. Why don't I feel reassured? But I know why—I have only his word, and he's lied to me hundreds of times. Yes, he's been great for a couple weeks, but he's always been able to do that. What's changed?

I stare at the computer, playing out the unwritten conversation. I can hardly reply, He spent two years in medieval Scotland fighting for his life, under Niall's influence. That might really change a man.

He proved at Tioram that he's changed. Never before would he have told me everything. Never before has the cocky grin left his face; never before has the cajoling and wheedling and protesting his innocence left his voice. Never before has he hung his head in shame and refused to meet my eyes, or let slip the wounded boy cringing behind the man's ego.

Still, images haunt me: Shawn and the writer in New York with her business-white blouse unbuttoned dangerously low; Shawn and Caroline. I squeeze my eyes shut, willing them away. I want to be with Angus, never wondering. My fingers tingle with the urge to call him, hear his calm words, his cool logic. But I've moved forward with Shawn; given him promises, even. Time, I think. It will take time. Forgiveness. Second chances. I twist Bruce's ring on my finger, remembering the determination on Shawn's face as he threw it, more than a year ago, and turned back to rescue a child, at great personal cost. He's a new man.

But Angus has been true all along. And I can't tear myself away from Shawn. The memory of his voice over the phone, his soft laugh, warms me. He's coming home, and I find I'm excited, about following his tour, the videos that will spring up on YouTube, the interviews. He's always funny in his interviews, making the crowd laugh, making me laugh so hard, sometimes, I can hardly breathe. Whether I want to admit it or not, Rose is right. Something in Shawn brings me to life like no one else ever has. And it's with growing excitement that I think, he could be coming home to anyone. And he's coming home to me.

Glenmirril, December 1316

"'Twas naught but a dainty fence, in Shawn's time." With Allene holding James at his side, Niall gazed up at the great wooden doors of the water gate, that would hold off any army that sailed in by way of the loch.

"How did...?" She stopped. "They've no need of stopping armies, have they?" A shadow crossed her face. "'Tis nigh impossible to comprehend a world without need of these great doors. Nobody attacks Glenmirril then?"

"You've forgotten, Glenmirril is half in ruins in his time." He pointed. "The southern half is broken down. Our northern half was broken down, but they repaired a great deal of it." He pushed one of the mighty doors. A strong breeze gusted through from the loch. "Nobody lives here anymore."

"'Tis sad to think." Allene clutched his arm with her free hand, even as James let out a gasp at the shock of wind, and buried his face in her shoulder. They pushed against the breeze, down the pebbly path, to the shore. Slate-gray waves pounded the rocks, splashing up to the boulder. A bird screeched overhead, flapping its wings against a charcoal sky.

"Just the place for a bairn," Niall muttered.

Allene clutched his arm more tightly and smiled up at him. "Aye. He's happy to be here in all weather." Even as she spoke, James turned from her shoulder, and reached his hand out as if to touch the bird before it wheeled away toward the hills across the loch. When it disappeared, he turned his attention to the water, stretching his hand out and straining to escape Allene's arms.

"Hugh said he should learn to swim," Allene said tentatively, holding tightly against his squirming. "How was it Shawn taught you?"

Niall laughed, soft and low. "You'll not give up, you and Hugh and your father."

She shook her head vigorously. A tight hood against the cold kept her hair from flying around her face. "Oh, no, Niall. Ye see plots everywhere. We but think Shawn perhaps had the right of it, knowing how to survive in water."

Niall pulled her tightly against his chest, squeezing James between them, and kissed the top of her head. "You make a poor conspirator, and a worse liar."

"Come now, Niall, just tell me how he taught Hugh." At James's insistent screech, she let him down. He tumbled to his knees on the rocks, but picked himself up immediately, clinging to Niall's leg to steady himself, before toddling to the water.

"He made him put his head in the water," Niall said.

"And how did Hugh breathe with his head in the water?"

James crashed to his knees again, his fingers inches from the loch. He turned to Allene, with glee, slapping at the stones, and reaching for the water.

"Shawn had him sing. He said if air is going out, water can't go in." He sighed. "Allene, please. I've but a day before I must leave again." He dropped to the boulder, staring at the water that thrashed in the winter wind, as the storm of problems at Glenmirril thrashed in his mind. He wanted them all to go away. "What have we had, then? Six months, seven, of the two years we've been wed?"

"Edward will see reason soon." Allene dropped to the boulder beside him. "We'll forget these days and live in peace. Did Shawn not say 'twill be so?"

"Aye." The rest of the thought came out now. "But I don't know whether that be in our lifetimes, Allene." He watched James squat on the rocky shore, picking up pebbles, and wondered how long their lifetimes would be. Shawn fully expected lives to stretch into decades, for himself, his children, Amy, all whom he loved.

"What if we could go to Shawn's time?" Niall turned to Allene. "He asked me one night, if I could take you and James and your father, would I go. I laughed at him then. But now I would, Allene. After these past months, I would. We could go to the tower and walk out into a world with no war."

She stared up at him, her brows furrowed. The wind tugged at a long red curl straying from under her hood. "There's no world without war," she said.

"He said..."

"He said in *his country* there's no war."

"That's where we'd go." Niall grasped her hand, wanting her to see, to agree. "We'd get on a *plane* and fly to his country. What d' ye think it's like, flying above the clouds like a bird?"

"I'd not like it," Allene said. "I prefer to stay here on earth with you and James and William and my father."

"James and your father and I would be with you. Then we'd come down in his country. There'd be naught but making music all day." Excitement glowed in his eyes. "I *lived* it, Allene, for almost two weeks."

"You've forgotten all else ye've told me of his time." She gazed up at him. "Loose women, all of them so angry and unhappy about one thing or another."

"I'm well beyond caring about that," Niall said. "Could we not still be who *we* are? Need we become like Caroline and Rob?" He leaned down to kiss her.

She became still, pulling back from his kiss. "Ye said 'tis dangerous."

"Perchance I was wrong. There are different kinds of dangers." Niall sighed. "My arm still hurts, at times, from MacDougall's blade. I never hurt there."

"You said yourself they hurt in different ways. And you were there but days."

"I'd never again worry about you dying in childbirth. I'd not be forever going to war. Would ye not like to raise James in peace, no fear of diseases nor the English? Think, Allene! Amy will never hide her son away in a dungeon, waiting and praying for her bairn's life. *Never!*" A wash of hatred for MacDougall surged over him.

She was silent, her lips pressed together, staring down at her hands.

A gull cried over head. James held out a stone to them, saying, "*Balbhag?*"

"Aye, James." Allene smiled, taking his offering. "'Tis a bonny pebble."

"Allene?" Niall whispered. "Would you not give our bairns peace?"

"This is where we belong, Niall." She stared at the stone in her hand, a white

stone veined with black. "Would ye leave Wat the smith to fend for our people?
Or Lachlan and Owen and Ronan to fight for themselves?" She raised her eyes to
his. "Would you leave the widow Muirne and her poor fatherless children to their
fate? Your mother? What of your sister Finola and Gil, and Taran without his
father? Or would ye crowd us all into the tower?"

Niall said nothing.

She laughed softly. "Imagine the lot of us appearing in the tower of their time.
Would we look to them like ghosts, as the man from Amy's time did to us?"

"We'd be solid and alive, as I was when I was there."

"Where would we live?" she asked. "What would we do? He said people
flock to see Glenmirril, hundreds of them each day. We couldn't live here."

"We would find something." He touched the side of her face, leaning close.

"Regardless, you can't take me or our bairns." She pulled back from him. "Or
my father. 'Tis only you and Shawn can cross. You'd not leave us, would ye?"

"Never." Niall pulled her back, smoothing the escaped strand of hair, kissing
her temple. "But think on it, Allene. What if I went to the tower and held you
tight, would we cross together?" His voice rose in excitement. "Would you at least
try?"

She pulled back more sharply. "What of our people? Ye'd leave Christina and
my father?" Her voice rose. "*Red,* Niall, ye'd abandon *Red*? Has the poor lad not
had enough losses?"

"We'll take them, too."

"Oh, 'tis a foregone conclusion now we're going?"

Niall dropped his hand, deflated. "Your father has spent his life protecting
everyone, Allene. He's scarred, he limps from injuries. Does he not deserve a few
peaceful years, in a *cabin* fishing?"

"What's this *cabin?*"

"A small house on a loch."

"A *hovel?* Are you mad!" Allene flung a hand out, indicating the great walls
rising above them. "Why would my father be wanting a hovel on a loch when he's
a *castle* on a loch? And why would a laird fish?"

"*Iasg?*" James looked up at them, his brow furrowing.

Allene took a deep breath and lowered her voice. "That's the lads' job. I
thought ye far too sensible to take a fancy to Shawn's strange notions."

Niall laughed, out of frustration and sorrow rather than humor. "Is it such a
strange notion to want to be with my wife and bairns? To live in peace and know
death is not wandering our halls choosing whom to take next? Hoping 'twill not be
those I love?"

She stared at James, at the water lapping close to his toes. "Have you forgotten
'tis not forever, Niall?" She lifted her eyes, laying feather-light fingers on his arm.
Her breath brushed his cheek. "My mother and brother, your father and brothers, I
feel them all around us. They've but gone for a wee bit, and we'll join them one
day, aye?"

"Have you become so good at waiting?" He let her touch smooth away some
of the frustration. But a part of him wanted the old Allene back, the one who railed

at waiting, who had connived to make a dangerous cross-country trip with Shawn rather than wait. Because, he knew, he had no desire to become good at waiting. He wanted, rather, to be rid of the waiting and danger altogether. "My whole life has been war," he said. "It's taken my father, my brothers, Adam, Iohn."

"Iohn chose his own way."

"He'd have chosen differently in a different world. I killed the best friend I ever had."

"Hush now." She dropped her head against his shoulder. "He was one of us. He lived and thought as we do. But in the end, 'twas Shawn who was ever loyal to you. *He* is the best friend you ever had."

"And he is gone."

"Aye, I've learned some patience," Allene said. "It helps to have bairns to care for, to have Christina here, altar linens to sew, the poor to feed."

Niall sighed, wrapping his hand through hers. Maybe he'd needed, just for these few minutes, to believe he could walk away from it all. But she was right. He couldn't leave his people. He would continue to fight for his king.

James scooted forward suddenly on his knees, as a wave splashed out of the loch, over his hand. Niall rose to scoop him up. Water sloshed over his toes. He jolted back, glanced in shame at Allene, and forced himself not to move, despite the ill feeling swirling in his stomach. The memory of trying to load the boats for Jura flashed over him like a summer storm. This time, Shawn was not there to get him out of it with a dirty trick. There would be no running away to Shawn's time. Allene was right in all she said. Short of death, he'd be boarding Angus Og's galley to Ireland.

He lifted James high in the air, feeling the icy water swirl around his foot, and smiled at the boy. "You've become fond of our loch, have ye?" James smiled, reaching for Niall's face, and leaning down to plant a sloppy kiss on Niall's cheek.

He'd think of this, Niall decided, as he climbed on the galley, days from now. He hugged James tight, wishing he could stay. But maybe, just maybe, God would heed the prayers of Malcolm MacDonald, and the crossing, maybe, wouldn't be so bad.

West Coast America, Present

Shawn smoothed the large score paper, not so rich and creamy as the monks' vellum, over the large draft table hotels provided him. It felt good to touch—so smooth, so different from the rough parchment that had erupted with texture under his fingers.

He filled his black mug, the one adorned with a gold trombone, up to the rim with pungent black coffee, and paced the large room once, twice, humming a U2 piece. The next album, after the Broadway hits, would feature music from European musicians. The permissions had been acquired shortly before he'd gone to sleep in the tower, a lifetime ago. He hummed it again, trying it in his mind first with a brass quintet, next with a jazz combo; he hummed again, hearing it accompanied by full orchestra, maybe heavy on strings—or would it work with a strong brass section?

No, lighter, he decided; very light on the accompaniment, maybe a little theme and variations on the original melody, only briefly, and back to something more like the original. Opening his eyes, he flung himself into his chair, lifted his favorite pencil, eyes almost closed, and the notes flew, danced, skipped, from the pencil, fluttering from the staves like a hundred tiny black and white leaves rustling with life, with only the soft sounds of swallowing coffee, and the faint scratch of graphite against the cream-colored score.

His phone emitted a *ka-ching* as he placed the final tonic chord at the end. He glanced at the window. Pink dawn showed through. The night was over. He hit talk, cutting off the cash register. "Yeah, Ben."

"Hey, Shawn, a couple details on those pieces you sent."

"Let me grab mine." Shawn reached for his briefcase, and pulled out his music.

An hour later, with the questions answered and a dozen more details ironed out, Shawn returned to the manuscript. He started at the top. His forehead furrowed, deeper and deeper as he read it, realizing what he'd written.

CHAPTER FIFTEEN

West of Scotland, December 1316

"Keep moving, Niall."

Niall stood at the bottom of the gangplank leading onto Angus Og's galley, a dozen men before him, and more behind. Icy winds blew in from the sea, billowing his cloak out around his legs. The Laird was praying, he reminded himself. Still, the galley bobbed on inky black seas that resurrected Alexander's bloated face. Men pushed onto the boat, with griddles and sacks of meal. They jammed the gangplank. Niall carried his own sack, his sword, and his harp. Behind him, Hugh urged him forward with hushed whispers. "Get to the front and beat the drum. You'll forget you're on water."

Niall took a deep breath, as the man ahead of him jolted into motion, and space opened up. He swallowed, focused on James by the shore, as he'd promised himself he'd do. He saw it in his mind, the rocky bit of land behind Glenmirril, Allene and James, slate-gray water washing the rocks, and James laughing big belly laughs, straining for the water. The gangplank swayed under his feet, rocking his stomach.

"Go to the front," Hugh urged. "You'll beat the drum and forget all else."

"Yes." Niall nodded, not because he believed it, but because he *wanted* to believe it. He reached the top of the gangplank, and made the mistake of looking down. Water sloshed below, in the gap between the board and the ship, where iron hooks clamped it to the sides. Alexander looked up at him from the water smashing against the side of the galley.

"Move, Niall!" Hugh spoke firmly. "There are two dozen men behind ye waiting!" He pushed Niall's shoulder, and Niall toppled over the edge, landing with a buckling of one knee, between two benches. Heat flashed up his face. Years flew quickly—one day his own son would be beside him, witnessing such humiliating failure. So much for prayer! Hugh caught him under the elbow. "Go to the front," he whispered harshly. "Look at naught but the drum."

Niall did as ordered, walking through a haze, Alexander's face floating before him and around him, and his stomach revolted, chiding himself to be strong for the day his sons might sail by his side.

"'Tis naught but sea-sickness." Hugh pushed him to the front of the galley, and thrust the beater into his hand.

The wind tore around the ship, even where it sat scraped up against the shore. Overhead, Angus Og's banners snapped, with sharp cracks, in the wind. Niall closed his eyes, fighting the rocking of the ship and his stomach, to stand upright. He braced his legs and gripped the edge of the drum. The wind pushed the harp against his back, and blew through his coif.

He focused his eyes on Hugh, sitting in the third bench. The last of the men settled themselves, gripping their oars with hands swathed in three-fingered mitts of heavy wool. Some shouted in enthusiasm. Some looked grim. All looked to Niall. He pushed away the feel of Alexander clinging to him. With his jaw tight, hating the distance opening between himself and Glenmirril's decked halls, hating Edward of Carnarvon for pressing his false claims, hating his own weakness, he lifted the beater and smashed it with all the force of his hatred, on the skin stretched as tight as his nerves, across the drum.

Seattle, Present

Shawn wondered, as he strode into rehearsal for the Seattle recording session, what the group would think of the arrangement. He hummed the melody, pleased with his work, unplanned though it had been. He was half an hour early. He smiled as he fit his trombone together, thinking of the whirlwind weeks of touring, crowds, reporters, Ben calling to tell him there were a million hits on YouTube videos of his concerts, and money was rolling in. Yes, he was back! Recording today, the big Fourth of July deal with the Seattle Symphony, the *1812* and fireworks, and he'd be on his way home to Amy and James.

He lifted the trombone to his lips. It was easy, closing his eyes, and hearing the echo off the multi-million dollar acoustically-engineered ceiling and walls, to slide back to the Bat Cave. If he opened his eyes, he'd see Allene and Christina, sitting on the Laird's workbench, shoulder to shoulder with torchlight playing over their faces, watching him, entranced. He slid into *Don't Cry for Me, Argentina,* remembering the last day, just a month—and seven hundred years—ago. The poignant minors bounced around the hall, sending out lonely cries. In his mind, they were all alive, Christina waiting, waiting, watching.

The truth was, he *had* left her, them, all of them.

The words sang with the liquid motion of the slide. Niall had sung it with him sometimes, in a warm bass. His wild days were behind him, he wanted to tell Christina. He was keeping his....

"*...promi—ise.*"

His eyes shot open. Disorientation flooded him. He recognized the weight in his hand as a trombone, not the lighter, smaller sackbut.

"Don't stop. It's great." Kieran, the French horn player grinned at him. "I never expected *Don't Cry for Me Argentina* in medieval garb...but it works."

Shawn laughed, covering the shock of being yanked between two times and places; covering the grief of Niall, Allene, and Christina slipping back into the cold ground that now held their dead bodies. "Gotta think outside the box," he said.

"You need a sackbut to go with the outfit."

Shawn glanced down at his trews stuffed into leather boots, and bell-sleeved shirt. "They're comfortable," he said. "Are the rest of them coming?" He blew some lip slurs.

"Yeah." Kieran scratched his ear and turned his back, taking out his French horn.

Shawn lowered his instrument. Kieran was stiff—the way MacDougall would be, just before he pulled a knife. Shawn's hand dropped to his belt in a heartbeat, before he remembered he had no dirk. And a twenty-first century horn player was unlikely to pull a weapon on him. "Something's wrong," he said.

Kieran turned, the golden snail of an instrument swinging in his hand. His eyes darted from the floor to one of the acoustical sound boxes to a music stand. He cleared his throat. "Yeah, Don and Leon are coming."

"Suzanna can't make it?"

"She asked Derick to fill in for her." He scratched his ear again, staring at the music stand.

"Okay." The old, familiar anger started its slow burn in Shawn's stomach. "Why wasn't I consulted?"

"Derick's really good," Kieran assured him.

"But I *hired* Suzanna." Shawn took a step closer, knowing he was intimidating the man. "*Not Derick.*"

Kieran cleared his throat and swallowed. Then he met Shawn's eyes. "You know Suzanna and I are seeing each other."

"So? Makes for good playing."

Kieran cleared his throat again. "She wasn't, uh." He stopped, his eyes flickered over the walls, and then said abruptly, "She had a family emergency. If Derick's not okay, I can get you any of a dozen other trumpet players."

Shawn recognized the lie. His mind skipped from one fact to another—the last time he'd recorded in Seattle—with Kieran—the drummer that day—his girlfriend. She'd been easy to lure away from the drummer. Kieran had watched him do it.

Shawn understood. Suzanna didn't want to work with him. Kieran didn't want her working with him. The shock hit him like Loch Ness in winter. His power, his money, his influence, his talent—they all meant nothing. She would turn down the opportunity to work with a great musician to avoid him personally. He revolted her. Rage rose in him as his eyes locked on Kieran. He'd fire him! He'd get him black balled! He'd....

Christina's sad eyes looked back at him through the music, the song he'd played for her in the Bat Cave. *What kind of a man* were *you?*

They went over me! he argued with her. *I didn't hire Derick!*

What kind of a man are *you?* she whispered. *'Tis your own fault, sure, they'll not have her near the likes of you!*

His shoulders slumped. He turned his back, fumbling with the extra parts waiting on the piano, the piece he'd been so proud of, looking busy. "Derick's fine," he said. "I'm sorry. I mean, about her family emergency." He set the parts on the stands, not looking at Kieran. "Tell her—I'm sorry."

Carrickfergus, Ireland, December 1316

Land had never looked so good.

Niall spent the first hours of the crossing pounding the rhythm of the rowing with the cudgel. The ghastly green illness never left his stomach as wind tore at his hair and cloak where he stood at the prow pounding the cudgel. As the ship sped over the winter gray seas, spray mingled with eternal drizzle, blowing salt into his mouth. It tasted of death, of white, bloated faces. When Owen took over pounding the rhythm of the rowing, he slid, sick to his stomach, into his rain-soaked seat on the bench beside Hugh, heaving the mighty oar and swinging it back out over the white-capped water, while Hugh chanted, under his breath, with the beat of the cudgel, "Harps. Harps. James by the sea," till Niall would have smiled if he'd been capable of anything other than holding back panic. He threw himself into rowing, into James's smiling face. It kept the worst of the images of drowning black water and Alexander, reaching and pleading, seawater streaming from his hair, at bay.

The skies opened up, the drizzle becoming a torrent, blinding them, till it was impossible to know if they rowed over the sea or under, impossible to do anything but pull the oar, with the smell of salt water all around, with water streaming down his beard, over every inch of exposed skin, numbing his fingers, dripping from his hair, into his eyes, soaking through his cloak, chilling him, pulling him under. He closed his eyes, felt himself sway, and suddenly, felt Hugh shaking him, and shouting, "A victory song! Niall, play for us."

"Niall, Niall, Niall!" the men chanted, and seemed not to notice him stumble as Hugh pushed him from his seat, as he slid from his place at the oar, felt the boat master pull him through the torrent, down the swaying, lurching aisle, and shove the harp into his hands. He collapsed on the bench beside Owen, who grinned at him.

With rain in his eyes, he plucked out the melody. He thrust his energy into watching his fingers on the strings, watching the strings tremble; anything that distracted him from the sloshing, pounding, driving, killing waves scratching and biting at the small ship, so close; from the thought of sliding, drowning, in the dark, snarling waves that snapped and lashed for his life, that would spit Alexander's white face out at him, and found himself emerging from the damp underwater world, drifting into the world of song, forgetting, finally, all but his fingers moving over the strings, as he led the men in a prolonged vocal outburst somewhere between a war chant and song. He moved from one piece to another, till their throats gave out with the singing and the fierce December wind that billowed their sails and slung icy rain and sprays of salt water across their faces.

At long last, the rain let up, and through the misty world, a long line of black appeared, smudged across the western horizon. A ragged shout went up from the men. It grew as the evening sun burst through the clouds, shooting rays of sunlight down onto calming waters; as Carrickfergus Castle rose, its solid square keep and sprawling walls a bulwark against the setting sun. Niall ran his fingers through one more song, his eyes locked on the shore speeding at them through the spray of salt water and pounding of Owen's cudgel, and his mind fixed on his music and James's smile. Under the powerful strokes of dozens of strong arms, the galley raced up onto the beach, scraping and jolting Niall where he sat.

On the castle wall, Scottish banners waved. Edward Bruce's troops looked down and cheered. In the galley, men threw down their oars and rose on their seats, shouting back with victorious pumping fists, and soon they were streaming off the boat, leaping over the sides onto the sand, or jostling for the gangplank even as other men wrestled it into place. Niall stumbled into line behind them, his harp bumping his back, his sword beating his leg. He reached the sand, dropped to his knees, and vomited. Around him, everything went black.

Seattle, Present

"Interesting. I never would have thought to set *With or Without You* to this sort of accompaniment." Derick, Suzanna's uninvited replacement, set his trumpet down after they'd played Shawn's arrangement.

Shawn grinned at Derick, forgetting the churn of emotions he couldn't even name over Derick being there at all. He was a good player, after all, and a friendly sort. "Ironically, neither did I. I didn't realize what I'd done until I came back and looked at it with a fresh eye."

The other players leaned forward, studying their parts in the wake of the first read-through. The second trumpet, Leon, tapped his fingernails on the bell of his trumpet, a light ringing sound. "I like it. It works. We should try it with period instruments. It would be even better, because that's really what it's written for."

Don, the tuba player, peered around his instrument. "I never heard you had any real specialty in medieval music. What brought this on?"

"I've listened to a lot of medieval music the last couple of years." Shawn smiled at his understatement.

Gazes darted around the small group of stands. There were dozens of YouTube clips with millions of views, of Shawn smiling arrogantly, telling reporters he'd been in medieval Scotland, along with the clip from the concert Niall had played, apparently of Shawn Kleiner telling the world, *I am Niall Campbell, born in 1290 on the shores of Loch Ness.* They looked anywhere but at Shawn, standing before them looking like he'd escaped from a SCA weekend.

Kieran stared at his feet. He hadn't met Shawn's eyes since he'd broken the news about Suzanna, simply played his part, looking as if he expected a Welsh archer to shoot him in the back at any second.

Leon cleared his throat. "It's great. Let's try again, and see if we can borrow instruments from the consortium for tomorrow, or have them record it."

"I'll play the sackbut myself on this piece," Shawn said.

Christina drifted to his mind. *With or without you....* She would be proud of him. He smiled, remembering her in the chapel, the day she'd learned of her annulment from Duncan. She had been happy at Glenmirril, with him and Niall and Allene, in their chambers, in the Bat Cave when he played the sackbut.

"Shawn?"

His attention snapped back to the practice room, and four musicians staring at him. "I'll definitely play on this recording," he said.

Carrickfergus, December 1316

Niall jolted upright. Alexander's hands touched his face and hair, damp and clammy. They pulled at his clothes, at the leather lacing the throat of his shirt. He looked wildly around in the dim room. A pale white face stared at him. He bolted from the bed, backing against the wall, trying to slow his frantic breathing.

"'Tis but me, Sir Niall," came a soft, feminine voice from the shadows.

Niall drew in another, slower breath, and let his eyes focus. It wasn't Alexander. It was a maid, looking as scared of him as he must look of her. Her rounded stomach told him she was with child. A cloth hung from her hand. Droplets of water fell, one by one, to the floor, from its edge. On the bedside table stood a bucket of water.

"I'm sorry." The tension drained from his arms. He'd fainted on the shore. Heat climbed up his face. "I thought...." It didn't matter. One didn't say such things to servants. Or anyone. "Thank you for your care."

"There's food." She lowered the cloth, and he realized she'd been as tense as he. "If you'd like. Sir."

"Yes, thank you."

She disappeared out the door. Almost immediately, Hugh entered, bearing a jug, and a basket of bread and cheese. "'Tis not much to be had." He laid the offerings on the table. "But they tell me we're fortunate to have anything a' tall. The famine has hit especially hard here. The last thing Ireland needed was more rain."

"I passed out." Niall poked at the basket. It held two slices of bread and two of cheese. He wondered if this was his meal. Or if it was for himself and Hugh to share. "Will the men ever follow me again?"

"Always, Niall." Hugh lifted a stone flagon from the table, and tipped the ewer of ale. A stream of pale amber liquid flowed between the two. "They've always respected you. Many were sea sick. You didn't see it, so busy were you about your own fears. Remember, they saw you fight like a demon on the ships at Jura. They whisper that you've taken ill and are concerned for your health." He poured ale for himself, handed Niall a cup, and raised his own in salute. "You did it, Niall!" He beamed through his bushy beard. "You crossed the Irish Sea!"

"Aye, so I did," Niall said, though collapsing, vomiting, and blacking out didn't quite qualify as success, to his mind. "The question is, will I ever bring myself to cross it again to get back to Allene?"

"You will." Hugh downed the ale and wiped his beard. "You've had a good sleep. Now eat." He left, leaving the whole meal. Niall hoped Hugh had gotten more than two slices of bread and cheese. He wouldn't last long on such scant fare.

Niall wolfed the food, wondering how he would face the men, despite Hugh's reassurances. He swished it down with the ale, and dropped to his bed, hands dangling between his knees, to stare at the crucifix on the wall. The Laird would joyfully say his prayers had been answered. Niall wasn't so sure. *How am I any use,* he asked God, *when I can barely survive a boat ride?* He dropped his head in half-hearted prayer for the coming days and battles, and, rising, left the sanctuary of his room.

Seattle, Present

Shawn hunched in a pew in the first church he found, after a long day of rehearsals. His trombone rested in its case at his feet. He stared, half seeing, at the altar far away, an ornate white marble affair, under a massive ribbed dome. The walls, nothing like Glenmirril's chapel covered in tapestries, were as white as the daze that hovered around him. Someone didn't want to work with him—*Shawn Kleiner, world's foremost musician!* She wouldn't work with him!

He stared at the altar. He'd been knighted by Robert the Bruce. He'd behaved with decorum for two years, worked hard, protected women and children. And she wouldn't work with him.

What kind of man are *you?* Christina's words stung.

With a sigh, he rose and swung the trombone case up off the floor. He had a rehearsal with the orchestra in the morning and a concert in the evening. He should at least try to get some sleep. He headed through Seattle's streets, to his hotel, mulling on the difference in how Suzanna, Amy, and Christina viewed him. He wanted to talk to Amy. It would be the middle of the night there. He wanted to talk to Christina, but his expensive cell phone, with the most up to date technology, couldn't do that for him.

He passed through streets coming alive with the first street lamps and earliest party-goers. They held no interest for him—a dramatic change from his last visit here. He only wanted to be back in his hotel room. But there, the restlessness grew. He wanted to be home with Amy and James. He wanted to be in Glenmirril, playing harp in the great hall, or playing chess with Hugh. He pulled up the internet, and started a game online with chessislife in Indiana. A clever opponent, quick, and creative, just like Hugh.

It wasn't the same.

He missed Hugh's bear-like eyebrows furrowing in thought, and the roar of laughter at a clever move.

Shawn pushed his queen across the virtual board, straight into a trap not as subtle as chessislife likely thought. Hugh had used a similar trick until Shawn learned it too well to be caught. Minutes later, he worked his opponent into stalemate, and signed off. It was too early in Scotland to call Amy. He didn't want to play another game.

He stared at the computer. Pulled up Google.

Don't do it, he told himself. *What if you find out they all died?*

What if I find out they didn't? he argued back. *All this guilt could be for nothing.*

Don't say I didn't warn you, he warned, as his fingers rose to the keyboard.

He typed in *Niall Campbell*. And he stopped, staring at the name. He was torturing himself. He had to just find out, one way or another. He hit *enter.* Up popped page after page of realtors, doctors, lawyers, an actor. He tried again. *Niall Campbell 14th Century. Niel Cambel. Nel Cambul Glenmirril.* A dozen pages gave him little information. He wondered if and when Niall had become laird. He smiled.

But the smile faded quickly. Niall would only become laird when MacDonald died. Shawn didn't want to think of it. He'd seen death at Glenmirril. MacDonald would lie all night in the chapel, with dozens of candles flickering. Shawn didn't like to think of Allene or Niall kneeling by his side through the night. Allene's eyes would be red and swollen with crying. Niall would be stoic. Bagpipes and drums would lament the fallen warrior.

Nothing would ever be the same without Malcolm MacDonald.

Shawn clicked quickly on a link, but immediately closed his eyes, afraid to look. In the dark cocoon, he slipped into the world of long ago. Niall might have become laird on June 9, 1316. He didn't want to know. He didn't want to find out he'd left Malcolm to die. But not knowing was killing him.

He opened his eyes slowly to a page in bold slashes of blue and white, Niall's colors, with a brief two-line summation of Niall's life. *Fought for the Bruce. Knighted in the raids following Bannockburn.* It gave no dates. In the relief that washed over him, he realized he didn't want to know when Niall died, or how. He could do nothing about it. He clicked back to the search engine, where his fingers hesitated on the keyboard, thinking of Christina.

He got up, agitated. Coffee. He poured coffee, strong and black, from the coffee maker, and paced the room, drinking. He forced himself to pull out his score paper. The pencil scratched, leaving a trail of notes fluttering on the trumpet staff like spring leaves. The tuba soon hummed a rich drone below. He didn't want to find out she'd married someone else. He filled in a long, sweet counter melody in the French horn and swallowed the last of the coffee. He wanted to know she'd been okay the night he left. He set the mug down, with a sharp crack on the desk.

It would torment him forever, not knowing. He type in the search engine: *Christina MacDougall.*

A list sprang up. Facebook. Linked In. A doctor in California.

He shook his head. He had a concert tomorrow. He had to put this out of his mind. He couldn't handle knowing something bad had happened to her that night. He snapped off the coffee maker, pumping out its pungent smell. He'd look another day. He left his pencil and staff paper, took three sleeping pills and climbed into bed.

Carrickfergus, Christmas 1316

The feasting lasted three days. Someone had hung sad, scanty boughs of evergreen. They were poor substitutes for Glenmirril's gaily decked halls, though their scent mingled tantalizingly with hundreds of wax tapers, and roasted venison carried in by streams of servants to the thousands of Scots filling the hall. He could almost forget the rain streaming down the windows and pattering in the courtyard, as the dishes kept coming, each smelling better than the last.

"I thought there was famine here." On the third day, Niall stood in the doorway of the great hall with Hugh, Owen, and Lachlan, wanting to be home, with one bird roasted inside another, a dozen sauces, fruits and nuts, and, most importantly, Allene and her father beside him. He surveyed the crowd of bearded men at Carrickfergus's tables. Gil Harper sat before Robert and Edward Bruce at the head table, singing lauds to the Scots. Candle and firelight flickered off the gold threads of the prancing lion on Bruce's tabard, and off the thin circlets of gold on the brothers' heads.

"There's famine indeed." Beside them, the servant girl who had cared for Niall spoke softly in an Irish brogue. "We'll see it soon enough."

"We?" His eyes flickered from the dozens of tapers back to the girl. Her skin was pale, with a smattering of freckles. Her red hair was pulled back into a braid as thick as a man's arm. "You're coming with us?"

"Aye, my Lord."

"Aren't you a wee bit young to be following an army?" Lachlan asked.

"I'm nearly eighteen." She lifted her chin. "Sure an I'll be helping with the cooking and laundry."

"What is your name?" Niall tried to keep his eyes off the girl's rounded stomach. It was unthinkable that Christina might travel with an army, cooking and doing laundry, in her present state.

"Roysia, Sir."

"Where are your parents? Where is your husband?" Owen asked.

"My parents died last fall from famine. My husband died."

"You're a widow," Owen clarified.

The girl nodded. "He was sent in with the thirty, last summer during the siege, to talk about their surrender. Instead, they took our men hostage. He died."

"I'm sorry." Words escaped Niall. Even if he died, Allene would be safe at Glenmirril, protected and cared for. Worse, he thought of the rumors, that the eight men who had died had been eaten by the half-starved English inside the castle. He hoped she hadn't heard the same stories. Her passive face gave him hope she hadn't. He hoped they weren't true. It was too ugly to think of such things going on, perhaps right here in the hall where they now celebrated the nativity of the Lord.

Her gentle words cut into his dark thoughts. "'Tis grateful I am, Sir, to the Bruces. They've given me safety."

"Traveling with an army is safe?" Niall resisted the urge to snort in his best impression of Shawn. Gil Harper's music drifted over a lull in the conversation.

"Safer than being alone in my father's croft," she said. "I've food and a warm, dry place to sleep."

"Aye, that you do." Sadness filled Niall's heart, dragging it down with heaviness.

"Sir Niall," she said, "His Grace summons you to his table."

Niall thanked her. Hugh, Lachlan, and Owen drifted off to find seats while he made his way to Bruce's table. His mind stayed on Roysia. She had nothing. No parents, no husband, nothing but to travel a famine-parched land serving an army of thousands in the last weeks of her pregnancy. And for that, she was grateful.

He felt the unwitting reprimand to his own ingratitude.

CHAPTER SIXTEEN

Inverness, Present

Once more Angus emerged from the door Simon had chosen to watch. Once more, Simon followed, tamping frustration at the time it was taking to find his home, irritable with the possibility he might again join Clive for an endless evening at a pub, as he had several times now, or get lost in the crowd as he had after the concert.

Instead, this time, he wove through the streets steadily nearer Simon's own dwelling. Simon's heart sped up. Angus couldn't know, could he? Simon slowed, letting the distance between them grow, wishing for cover of darkness. But the sun remained stubbornly bright.

Angus turned down Simon's own street. His heart speeding up, Simon followed cautiously, tensed for a trap. At the corner, he stopped altogether, watching. Angus paused before the empty house, chatting with a boy. Simon's heart pounded. The boy pointed at Simon's home. Angus laughed, and shook his head. Simon backed up. Angus waved to the boy, took another few steps, and climbed the stair to the house beside Simon's.

Simon's heart slowed, as Angus entered. Slowly, his smile grew. God favored him. He'd led him to a house right beside Angus's. He could watch him carefully. Pleased, Simon made his way down the back of the row of houses, a hat pulled low to shield his face. He slipped over the wall into his own back garden.

Upstairs, he took up his station at his window. Angus came out his front door some time later, in new clothes, carrying a bouquet of flowers. He glanced at Simon's house. A frown flitted across his face, before he climbed into his green *car* and backed into the street. Simon's brows furrowed. There would be no following him when he used the *car*. As quickly, his brow cleared. It made but little difference. It was a matter of time before Amy came, and with her, James.

Glenmirril, January 1317

It was four weeks and ten games of chess—seven wins to Taran, and a stalemate—before the boy progressed from *Checkmate* to a grunted agreement that it was a nice day. It took another two weeks before he volunteered the observation that it looked like rain. Breaking his defenses was a slow game, MacDougall thought, even as he gave grudging admiration to MacDonald and Niall for the discipline and caution of their men, even the boys. Had it been him, though, he'd change the guards more often to prevent such a thing. They were still over-confident.

Another three weeks, and MacDougall left Adomnan's *Life of Columba* on the table. It took a week before Taran commented, "Not done yet?"

MacDougall shrugged. "Daylight is scarce; I've been given no candles."

"Don't think ye will be."

Eight words: the most the boy had spoken in months.

"I'd not ask," MacDougall said. "I've time aplenty, aye? Ha' ye read it?"

"No."

"Are you acquainted with Columba?"

"We know him well at Glenmirril."

"So I've heard." When it elicited no further comment from Taran, MacDougall tried again. "I find the question of why he left Ireland particularly interesting."

Taran volunteered no opinion. But neither did he scowl. MacDougall leaned forward. "I, myself, think 'tis no great mystery, but that the reasons are all one. He copies the psalter, an argument ensues, a battle results, he prays God give victory to his side, three thousand men die, and he flees Ireland in penance for those deaths. No one event excludes the others, aye?"

Taran merely stared at him; whether from lack of understanding, lack of opinion, or continued malice, MacDougall didn't try to guess. He pressed on. "The real importance of the man, regardless, is what he did for Alba, aye?"

"Aye. He was a great man of God."

He'd handed MacDougall another tool; MacDougall used it. "A miracle worker. Forgiving. Compassionate. They say your laird values such things."

"Aye."

MacDougall remained wary of the boy's intelligence. It was too soon to follow up on those ideas. He turned to a discussion of Columba's encounter with Brude, and the boy listened, though his eyes remained narrow with suspicion.

At last, he rose, without a word, once more locking MacDougall into his small world. MacDougall stared at the door. How many times had he listened, to hear no more than boys' idle talk? But he was a man of war. He would persist until he escaped or died. He rose and moved quietly to the door, listening. He caught the tail of a sentence.

"...lady Christina," Taran murmured. "She's not been the same since the attack."

"Ye know naught," Red returned.

"There are *rumors*," Taran whispered darkly.

"There are *always* rumors," hissed Red. "Only a fool pays them heed."

"She's taken to her rooms," Taran insisted. "Count the months, Red. *Count the months*."

In his room, MacDougall counted the months.

Seattle, Present

Shawn sank into the leather couch in his hotel suite, his eyes closed in enjoyment. He ran a hand over the cover, luxuriating in the soft suede. His cummerbund and bow tie lay on the table by the door. At his ear, his cell phone rang, summoning Amy across the ocean. He felt good. The concert had gone well. They'd cheered him, loved him—saved him from the wound that someone wouldn't work with him.

"Hello!" She came on, a little breathless.

He smiled. "You answered."

He heard a quick intake of breath, a pause, and she said softly, "Yes."

His grin grew, despite the wariness in her voice. Warmth flooded his insides. "I'm back from the concert and the after party."

She didn't answer immediately.

"Symphony sponsored," he added hastily, sitting forward abruptly on the couch. "A charity deal for the big donors, meet the musicians. It wasn't...."

"I know," she said softly. "We watched. It was great."

Shawn smiled, remembering. The energy, encores, applause, the perfection of the orchestra behind him—it had been beyond great, leaving him energized. He rose, pacing the room, turning on the coffee maker, stopping at the score he'd worked on earlier. "You watched?" It meant everything to him that she had. "It was the middle of the night for you."

"It was on BBC," she said, and her voice dropped further. "You were amazing. You're really amazing."

Shawn's smile grew. "You like the arrangements?"

Again she paused. When she spoke, it was slowly. "They sounded...medieval."

He laughed. "Didn't they. I didn't realize what I was doing." His mind lit on Christina, her eyes glowing softly as she listened to him play in the Bat Cave; her eyes lowered, avoiding his, when he posed as Niall, playing harp in the great hall after dinner. "I wrote them down, got a call, and when I came back and looked again—there it was. Medieval."

She laughed. Not with the happiness he remembered from their first days together. Just a soft laugh that left him feeling she was sad. "Tell me more about Allene," she said.

"Allene?" Something stilled inside him, like the internal warning just before de Caillou's troops had appeared, the quiver of hairs on his arms, in response to unseen and unheard ripples deep in the forest. "Why?"

There was a silence, in which he imagined her giving a shrug. Then she said, "I'm curious. Niall talked about her. You knew her. What was she like?"

Shawn closed his eyes, sinking into the fawn suede couch and memories. He saw Allene ministering to her people in the courtyard despite her own torment waiting to see if Niall had come home from battle; sewing in her chambers with Christina embroidering beside her or drawing at her easel. "She was good," he said.

"*Good?*" Disbelief rang in Amy's voice. "Good how? I know what the old you would have meant by that."

"No!" Shawn sat up abruptly, surprised at the strength of his denial. "No, I mean, really, genuinely *good.* She always took care of everyone else first. She saw the good in people. She worked hard for other people."

"What did she look like?"

"Not too tall. Red hair, lots of it, freckles, lots of energy." He relaxed more deeply into the couch, his eyes closed, as they came to life around him, flowing into words and across the ocean to Amy. Gangly, awkward Ronan. Taran and his one-eyed father, so proud to have fought beside William Wallace, and of his son learning under Sir Niall.

"Niall's mother," Shawn said, "was beautiful, thin and elegant. His sister Finola and her son Gil—always seeing the humor in life. Margaret Morrison, she married Lachlan the night before Allene's wedding." He saw them each in technicolor against the gray backdrop of Glenmirril's stone walls, the colorful tapestries warming those walls, with the life of Amy's breath warm over the phone, helping them live by her very listening.

He wandered the room as he spoke, looking out the window to the city lights, running his hand over the smooth score paper dancing with graphite notes. He frowned, looking at them, and suddenly stopped.

"Shawn?" she asked. "What about Margaret?"

"Just a sec." He studied the notes, recognizing them. "Hey, Amy," he asked, "do you remember *Laughing Brass,* the piece by...."

"The 14-year-old. Of course I remember it. You loved playing it."

"Are you near a computer?" he asked. "Look him up."

It was a moment before a small gasp came over the line. "Shawn, he's gone! That was the greatest piece!"

"Yeah." Shawn's voice came out tight over the knot in his throat. "He never existed. I'm just looking at my score. I just re-wrote it. But it's not my work."

Silence came back over the line for a moment before she said, "You know he's not the only one."

"I know," Shawn said. "What about all this great music that never exists now, because Niall and I changed history?"

"If you'd had any say in the matter," Amy said, "would you change it back? Leave them to die in exchange for that music, for all the people who have never existed now?"

Shawn swallowed. He stared out over the city, the Space Needle floating like a giant spaceship—he wished he had told Niall about it. A life was a life. Objectively, Niall and Allene and all who lived because of the change didn't count for any more than Jason and Ethan and all who had winked out of existence when the English died at Bannockburn instead of the Scots. "No," he said. "I know objectively there's no way to balance it out, but I'd do everything, all over, to save them again if I had to. Is that wrong? Because it means other people never existed."

"Who knows anymore what's right or wrong," Amy said. "But I'm glad Niall and Allene lived."

"What about all this music?" Shawn said. "Who's here to put it in the world?"

"You are," she said without hesitation.

The lights twinkled below him. He thought of the millions of views of *Laughing Brass* on YouTube, the many comments about how it had brightened someone's day, lifted their spirits. It belonged in the world, it belonged to the people who smiled because of it. "But it's not my work," he said.

"Figure something out," Amy returned. "You can re-write any piece you've ever heard. Give that music back to the world."

Shawn laughed. "Do you see the irony here?"

"You more worried about ethics than me?" A smile sounded in Amy's voice.

Shawn could see her, maybe looking out her own window at Bannockburn in the morning, maybe with mist on the ground. He laughed. "Yeah. I guess having Niall and Mass inflicted on me day after day has messed me up a little." After another moment, he said, "I wonder how many pieces I remember that no one else does."

"Start a list," Amy said. "I don't even want to sort out the question of whether it's plagiarism when it never actually existed."

"It existed in my life and yours."

"I say put great music back into the world," Amy countered.

"I'll be home soon." He turned back to the table, running his fingers over the graphite notes as if they would give him an answer. By home, he meant Scotland, her small house cramped with her, James, Carol, and himself, rather than his spacious and luxurious mansion. He liked it that way. "Maybe we could go somewhere together? Do something?"

It took her a few seconds to answer, in which his insides twisted, wondering if she'd talked to Angus.

"I'd like that," she said. "Wherever you want to go."

"Iona." The word came out without thought. "Let's go to Iona."

Silence fluttered between them, before she said, "Why Iona?"

"I don't know," he admitted. "It popped into my head. Curiosity. Peace. It's meant to be peaceful there."

"Okay," she said softly. "I liked it."

He hung up in the small hours of the morning, looking forward to seeing Iona that had been such a mystery. Contented, he turned to his computer, and began running searches on every piece of music he could think of. He had a list of several dozen that no longer existed before he noticed the tab still open to a search on Christina. He pulled it up, staring at her name, and wondering why he hadn't mentioned her to Amy. Iona had been important to her. He shrugged it off. No big deal. He'd never touched her. Nothing more than kissing her fingers, nothing but social convention there. Then.

He set up a fresh pad of score paper and began writing one of the missing pieces, a madrigal by an English composer, Thomas de Clare, of the late sixteenth century whose family, Shawn recalled, had run toward knights and earls—exactly the sort who had died at Bannockburn. He turned to his computer and searched *de*

Clare Bannockburn. Gilbert de Clare, Earl of Hertford, Earl of Gloucester, had died at the battle, shortly after his twenty-third birthday. He'd never gone home to father Thomas de Clare's ancestors.

Inverness, Present

"Nice evening with Claire?" Clive slid into his desk, a pen in one hand and a chocolate donut in the other, a minute before nine.

Angus jabbed at the X in the corner of his screen, shutting down the video clip of Shawn's sell out concert in Seattle, and the 20-something video blogger gushing about his hair. "Did I say I want to talk about it?" He jotted a note on the report in front of him, and brushed a hand over his own shorn curls.

"You never *say* so." Clive bit into his donut, and spoke around bulging cheeks. "But you always do."

Stabbing at the computer keyboard to bring up his e-mail, Angus muttered, "Only because you'll not shut your trap till I do." He scanned the inbox: A request from a scout troop to speak on water safety. A notice from the drum and pipe band.

"We've been at this ten years now," Clive said. "You may as well tell me. She's persistent, is she not?"

"Not as persistent as you." Angus scanned the scouts' dates, and accepted.

"'Twas was a good idea on her part," Clive persisted, "Get to know each other a bit before you spend a whole day together at the Games."

"Mmhm." Angus typed an e-mail to the chief, telling him about the speaking engagement in September.

"A big band at Blackfriars, she told the girls out front. Nice place."

"Lot of history there," Angus murmured.

"I'm sure she knew that would appeal to you." Clive brushed at the donut crumbs on his uniform.

Angus opened the e-mail from the pipe band. A performance at Glenmirril. He'd developed mixed feelings about the place. But he'd always loved the castle, and he loved playing. *Sounds grand,* he typed. *I'll be there.* He'd have to get the kilt to the cleaners and practice a little. It had been awhile. It stung that Amy had looked forward to seeing him play, and now she wouldn't be there.

"She's a nice girl," Clive continued.

"So you said." Angus noted the speaking engagement and pipe band gigs on the calendar on his desk.

"Did you kiss her?"

"Ah, fer feck's sake, Chisolm!" Angus slammed the pen down. His head shot up. "I didn't kiss her, I didn't sleep with her, I didn't hold her hand. I didn't want to go out with her or anyone in the first place."

"Which is exactly why you should, instead of moping about. She's a nice girl."

"Which is why she should go out with Pete at the front desk and quit wasting her time on me."

"But you had a nice time with her."

"Yes," Angus snapped. "It had to be a big band playing. But we enjoyed it, and I almost forgot there were trombones parading in front of my eyes." He shook his head, the anger at Clive melting away. "You're right. She's nice."

♫

Now that he could track Angus easily, Simon used the hours Angus spent in the police station doing his own work. He found a public hall full of books—a *library*. He read by the hour, their peculiar form of English becoming ever easier. He studied Edward Carnarvon's life, so that he would appear a seer like Thomas the Rhymer.

He learned of their powerful weapons. He studied a book on the construction of a mighty *cannon*. It could shoot giant lead balls that would tear down castle walls and rip through Scottish armies. In the 1400s, a Scottish king called James of the Fiery Face would die when his own cannon exploded near him. Served the Scots right, Simon thought, as he studied diagrams of the weapon. He would build them before anyone else, and use them to conquer the world.

There was still the problem of getting home, however, and of killing the James in his own life. His high expectation of being led to Amy fluttered and died, like autumn leaves. Angus came and went on a predictable schedule. But though Simon watched from a window, night after night, Amy never appeared. Wretched urchins ran up and down the street, shouting hellacious noises. Curs barked. Wives left and returned with arm loads of food. Amy never appeared.

Simon ventured out by night to acquire more of this people's currency, and by day to buy—or take—food. He divided his days between training, watching for Amy, and strolling the town, seeking information. He found bearded, shifty-eyed men with Celtic designs inked up and down their arms, who promised they could—for a price—provide all the documentation he needed to get on a *plane*.

After many days, Simon slipped from the house before the sun rose, before the time Angus always left, and set out toward the police station. He leaned on a rail a ways from it, watching the river. When Angus came out onto the main street, Simon turned, raising his eyebrows. "Angus! What a surprise!"

The man stopped. He was taller than Simon, and broad. But without weapons, no one in this age could stand against Edward's finest knight. He'd bested many a strong man in tourney and battle. Angus was no threat.

"Simon?" Angus stopped. No look of friendly greeting crossed his face. "What are you doing here?"

"Visiting," Simon replied. "It's a beautiful city, is it not? And you?"

"Going to work," Angus said shortly, and made to move by.

"It's a stroke of fortune I met you," Simon's words snaked out, a rope, snagging Angus and reeling him back. Water lapped below, sparkling in the bright morning.

Angus turned, unsmiling, as he squinted into the rising sun.

"The translation," Simon said quickly. "Amy asked me about it. I found some items in my—research. Relating to that. I'd fain show them to her."

Angus's eyes narrowed. He took a step backward.

Simon wondered what he'd said wrong. "She had such an interest in it," he pressed. "Do you know where I might find her?"

Angus shook his head.

"Are you not...her husband?" Simon ventured.

Angus's lips tightened. He turned and stalked away.

Simon started to go after him. But a voice warned him he would only rile the man and rouse his suspicions. And he didn't want to get near the jail, where those who had brought him in might recognize him.

He'd best stay clear of Angus for a time, too. He wasn't her husband. So where was she? Back in Bannockburn, likely. Anger rippled beneath the surface. The time wasted! He hadn't found Amy, and though the man at the *hotel* said Shawn traveled frequently, there was no word of him returning.

But he hadn't wasted his time, Simon reminded himself. He'd met people who could do things for him. He knew Angus's schedule, which might yet have its uses. He was regaining his skills and strength.

He would seek Amy, he decided. He would simply have to be more careful about it this time than on previous attempts.

Ireland, January 1317

"Gratitude," Niall murmured to Hugh, who rode on his right. "I should have had it when things were good." Edward Bruce and Thomas Randolph rode ahead of them, and thousands more behind.

"Aye," agreed Hugh. Soft drizzle trickled from his big beard. "We see but afterward how good we had it."

Niall glanced at his companion, disturbed by how gaunt he'd grown, and snorted. "'Tis a sad comment that things are now so bad that mere warfare looks good."

They rode in silence for a time. Over the weeks since they'd left Carrickfergus, they'd ridden entire days, up green hills, and through lush glens, mile after mile, with little sign of the English. Those that did appear watched silently from ridges before melting away, unwilling to give battle. They had seen, instead, more than Niall had ever imagined of emaciated peasants, of men fallen from starvation in water-logged fields, and at the sides of roads.

They passed through villages of miserable daub and wattle huts with thatched roofs, and rain-soaked chickens squawking in their yards. Sometimes, gaunt, skeletal women stood in doorways, holding gaunt, skeletal hands of children clothed in damp rags, watching with silent, starving eyes, as the thousands of men passed. Each dead body, each hollow-eyed child, each rain-soaked night in the open, ate away at Niall's faith.

The entire army had grown steadily more quiet, till the sound of Gil's and Niall's harps, and the steady *chink chink chink* of thousands of coats of mail, and the jingle of stirrups and creak of leather were the only sounds to accompany the steady *drip drip drip* of the eternal rain.

"Evening's coming," Hugh murmured now, as they rode. "It looks to be another wet night."

"Just one dry night," Niall murmured. He did not speak the rest of his thought: *And I could believe God still cares.* He gazed the length of the glen through which they rode, soaring hills on either side, like a hundred others, hanging with white mist turning pink and purple at the far western end as the sun began its descent. He shivered in the clammy winter evening.

"Shelter!"

The voice jarred him. Hope stirred in his heart. He snapped to attention as he pulled the reins of his shaggy garron. The animal plodded to a halt, its head drooping, as Colin Campbell, son of the deceased Lord of Lochawe, cantered down the lines. "A village ahead," he called. "A town almost! We may find shelter!"

"Not for thousands," Hugh murmured.

"Perhaps for Roysia," Niall returned. "There may be a kirk that can at least keep the rain off the sickest of our men."

"If the English aren't waiting to ambush us," Hugh said darkly.

Colin Campbell scanned the men. His eyes fell on Niall. "Sir Niall," he called. "Bring ten of your men to scout the village with me."

"Hugh, Lachlan," Niall called. He glanced at Owen, and moved on, choosing eight others.

"My Lord?" Owen questioned.

Niall gave his head a shake and moved away with the others.

"Why have you left him?" Lachlan asked, as they joined Randolph's men.

"Roysia," Niall answered curtly. When they'd huddled over their rain-drenched attempts at campfires, these past weeks, Hugh slipped bits of his meal to Niall; while Niall, Owen, and Lachlan found ways to slip bits of theirs into Roysia's bowl, fearful as she, along with the army, grew steadily thinner, but for the swelling of her stomach. Niall spurred his mount, riding ahead, unwilling to elaborate: If the English waited in ambush, they would not be returning. She must at least have Owen.

Thomas Randolph nodded a terse greeting. "Take the main road," he ordered. "We'll take the south, Colin the north."

Niall raised his hand, hailing his men forward. "Pray there are no English," he said softly to Hugh. He touched his helmet, securing it.

"The Lord has already had a few words from me." Hugh grinned. "Sure an He'll tire of my voice ere we reach the first house."

"Then promise Him he'll hear a great deal more of you, should I not make it home to Allene." Niall spoke grimly. His thoughts wavered between hope for a dry night and fear of an ambush.

Hugh chuckled, as they rounded a twist in the glen and saw the first, miserable hut. "You've returned, Shawn?"

Niall grinned. "Aye, 'twould be his way of prayer, sure. Perhaps I ought watch my tongue."

They fell silent as they approached the village. It was, as Colin had said, almost a town. Niall held up his hand, stopping his men at the head of the street, just before the first house, a one-story hut adjoined to several more, before they joined a long row of two story daub and wattle houses, pressing close to the mud street. At the far end, a kirk rose, its bell tower standing boldly against the setting sun.

"It's unearthly still," Lachlan whispered. He drew an arrow from his quiver, nocking it. The other men drew swords, and knives, as they stepped into the mist rising with the evening.

"Aye." Niall nodded. "'Tis a bad omen." He watched water drip from an eave, and scanned the narrow street, the houses, windows, for any sign of life, before riding forward. "Spread out," he said softly. "Let's not make ourselves an easy target."

As he and Hugh passed further into town, the long row of half timbered houses closed in on either side, the upper stories hanging almost above their heads. The chill and damp grew. A rough *caw, cawwww* drew his attention upward. A black bird lifted from a roof, shouting down at them, and wheeled away. "There is death here," Niall whispered.

Several more steps, and the stench hit them: a heavy, moldering odor that turned his stomach. He slid from his pony. Hugh did likewise, and they continued down the silent street, aware of their men behind them, guarding their backs.

The sun sank lower behind the church's tower. Niall stepped up to a house, rubbing its window with his mist-dampened sleeve. He peered into the gloomy room. Eight men lay on the floor, side by side, little more than skeletons stretched over with skin. Niall closed his eyes, grateful for the evening. He suspected he would not like to see the remains in strong light. The stench assured him they *were* remains.

"What is it?" Hugh asked from the street.

"Famine." Niall backed away, his hand over his mouth and nose. Hugh took a step forward, but Niall shook his head. "You've no wish to see. Trust me. They've put the bodies there."

"You're sure 'tis...?"

Niall nodded sharply. "'Twould have been a waste of an arrow to kill a man so close to dead as these were. Aye, 'twas famine took them."

Hugh's jaw tightened. "That doesn't mean there *aren't* English here." He looked across the narrow street, where Lachlan was stepping away from a window, his hand likewise pressed to his nose.

"We'll see," Niall said.

They continued through the village, as the shadows lengthened in the puddle-spattered street, as the mist rose. His men entered one house after another, weapons ready. Niall's despair grew with each report of emaciated victims, until they reached the last house on the street, standing before the church. The soft hoot of an owl sounded from its roof.

Lachlan looked up with startled eyes, and crossed himself.

"'Tis but an owl," Niall said. He thought of Shawn, laughing at their beliefs about owls. *In my time, they're a symbol of wisdom,* he had said.

"They're poor omens," Lachlan returned tersely. And then, "Look, Sir Niall." He pointed to the house beside them. A bone-thin woman sprawled on her stomach in a small patch of grass. An emaciated dog, as large and shaggy as the Laird's hunting hounds, lay at her feet, its chin resting on one leg, looking up at them.

"Are you guarding her?" Niall asked, touched by the dog's loyalty.

"I suspect there's naught more you can do for her," Hugh said.

Her fine gown of sapphire blue suggested she had been a merchant's daughter or wife. A thick braid of curling red hair reminded him of Allene and Roysia. It trailed the length of her back to fall in the muddy patch of lawn. Niall took a step closer. Her face was turned toward him, a blank death mask. Her lips and chin were a ghastly green. One hand clenched a tuft of green grass. The dog growled.

"I'll not hurt her," Niall said.

The dog gave a woof, as if understanding, and, lifting its head, dug its teeth into her already well- gnawed leg.

Niall froze in horror.

From the street came the sound of one of his men retching.

Niall felt dizzy, sick. He covered it with anger, scooping up a rock, and throwing it viciously at the animal. "Be off!" he shouted. The dog growled, but scrambled to its feet, backing up. Niall brandished his sword. The dog tucked its tail and ran.

Niall lifted his eyes to the bell tower. "*Where are You?*" he shouted in fury. "Give me *some* cause to keep faith! Anything!"

"Niall...." Hugh touched his shoulder.

Niall shook him off.

"Sir Niall! What have you found?"

Niall lifted his eyes to see Colin Campbell.

"Naught but famine," he snapped.

"There are no English," Hugh said. "No one in his right mind would stay in this God-forsaken town."

"We've found the same," Thomas Randolph called, emerging from another street to join them before the church. He and his men held their hands to their noses. "An attempt at a mass grave. They couldn't even bury their dead anymore." He turned to Colin. "Send men to tell Bruce. We need to bury the bodies. But there are houses for all of us." He wheeled his pony and rode away.

Niall stared at the dead woman, with her mangled leg. The odor of death filled his nostrils, churning in his stomach. The dog peered around the corner, whining.

Hugh touched his shoulder. "There will always be bad times," he said. "Come to the church. Let us give thanks we have survived to protect our people, and pray for these poor souls."

Niall nodded, turning blindly. The church—yes, there he would find hope. He climbed the few stairs, and pushed open the wooden doors, staring for a moment into the darkening church. A candle burned on the altar. He walked toward it, still smelling death. Then he saw him, sprawled on the stairs to the altar.

In his rough brown monk's habit, he'd been at first invisible in the shadows. As Niall's eyes adjusted to the dark, he saw the robe-covered emaciated shoulders. One hand stretched as if in plea toward the altar. Niall approached warily. The monk didn't move. Niall let out his breath. *God, if You've spared just this one man, I could keep faith. Just one.*

He knelt, rolling him over. The body was warm, the mouth smeared in green; the eyes stared. And underneath, cradled protectively in one arm, was the baby, with a cap of red curls. Like his James. Perhaps like Roysia's child waiting to be born.

Niall knew, as if he'd watched it happen. The monk had taken the child from the dead woman, taken it into the church, the last sanctuary, praying to Heaven, crying to God, for help. Help had not come. The baby, too, stared blankly at the rafters.

God had forsaken even this innocent child; had ignored even the prayers of this desperate monk. God had let them die even here on the very stairs to the altar. No good and loving God could allow this, even as a man of God climbed the stairs to the altar itself, begging for the life of an innocent child. Prayer was useless.

Niall wept, for the townspeople, the woman, the monk, the child—and for the loss of his God.

Inverness, Present

Angus frowned at his computer monitor, his pen snapping a staccato beat on the edge of his desk, as he thought about the chance encounter with Simon. He pulled his keyboard out, but before he got farther, a light tap sounded on the door. He glanced up. "Come in."

The door inched open. Claire waited tentatively in the half-open door, a watering can in her hand. "I came to water your fern."

"Oh, aye, the poor thing needs it," Angus said. "I'm afraid I forget."

She squeezed through the space between his and Clive's desks, and stretched up to water the fern on the cabinet behind Angus. "The day's barely begun," she said. "What has you looking so worried already?"

Angus turned to study her. Her black hair bobbed in a pert ponytail. Freckles sprinkled the bridge of her nose.

She set the watering can on his desk, turning her cornflower blue eyes on him. "I'm sorry. Perhaps 'twas personal."

"Not particularly," he said. "I ran into someone on the way to work. The man who went up to the monastery with myself and Amy."

"And why should that worry you?" she asked. "Was he unfriendly or rude?"

Angus shook his head. "Something just seemed off about him."

Claire seated herself in Clive's chair. "And what was it?"

"His accent," Angus said abruptly. "Like none I've ever heard." He paused, then added, "Which is hardly a reason to think someone's off. 'Twas the way he invited himself along. And he seemed like two different people on the hike, friendly, then irritable." And he'd lied to Amy about the translation. But he couldn't tell Claire that. "It seems odd how he keeps turning up," he finished. "And asking about her."

"Perhaps you ought tell her," Claire said.

Angus shook her head. "I'd not want to scare her over nothing." And he didn't want to appear to be looking for reasons to call her. "He's really done nothing."

"Can you see if there are records on him?" Claire asked. "They trust your instincts here, so I say something's wrong if it's bothering you."

Angus turned to his keyboard, before remembering. "If he told me his surname, I don't remember."

"How did you meet him?" Claire asked. "There must be someone...."

The shrill of a bell cut off her words. Feet pounded in the hall outside the office.

"Angus!" Clive, breathless, skidded to a stop in their office door. "Two hikers, broken leg. Let's go!"

Angus jabbed a button on his computer. Simon would have to wait.

Ireland, February 1317

Niall's tired horse plodded, alongside Hugh's, with Lachlan behind them, through thick woodland. Drizzle rattled on the leaves overhead, turning the world around him gray and green. Mist floated along the ground. Ireland's gentle hills had rolled by endlessly in the weeks since leaving the nightmare village, a lush palette of greens. To the half-starved horses and men, it was little consolation. Cruel irony, thought Niall, how the same rain that brought hellish famine had painted the landscape every shade of heaven. At least the peasantry would starve to death amidst beauty. A chill shuddered through him.

"They say there are a hundred shades of green in Ireland." Riding at Niall's side, Hugh's voice did not boom as it had weeks ago. He'd lost weight, till he looked like a great bearded corpse astride his hobin.

"I'd only be interested in those shades that are edible," Niall returned. In the gray forest, few men looked any better than Hugh. The feast of Carrickfergus was a distant memory, in the desolation of the Irish countryside, gripped more tightly in the unforgiving fingers of famine, even, than the rest of Europe.

"The only edible thing is the horses, and I'd not care to eat them if they turn green."

Niall smiled. Hugh's humor took the worst edge off the nightmare—that, and the fact there had been little fighting. The English melted away ahead of them, so that the Bruces had marched the country from one end to the other, as had kings of old, unhindered, with Niall and Gil Harper playing and singing in the evenings around campfires. It would be pleasant enough, Niall thought sardonically, but for hunger, steady rain, and emaciated corpses along the road. As if to highlight his morose thoughts, several raindrops trickled from the overhead leaves, bouncing musically off his helmet. Ahead, thankfully, woodland gave way, and Bruce's vanguard emerged into an open glen.

"Lachlan looks like an unmatched oar riding alone back there," Niall commented, as they neared the edge of the copse. "Where's Owen?"

Hugh chuckled. "Where d' ye think?"

"With the women?" Niall guessed. Owen had been among the young soldiers finding reasons to spend time with the laundresses, though the Laird's stamp on his personality showed. When Niall found him with them, he was not trying to seduce any of them, but helping Roysia, grown ever larger with child, carry her heavy loads.

"Aye," Hugh confirmed. "He's quite taken with her." He rode silently for a time before saying, softly, "You mustn't lose faith, Niall."

"What makes you think I have?" Niall asked. He didn't want to talk about it.

For one of the few times in all the years Niall had known him, Hugh's voice held no humor. "D' ye think I've not noticed you no longer pray in the morning?"

Niall stared straight ahead, at the end of the forest trail, lined with explosions of lush ferns that thrived in the rain that killed everything else.

After a moment, Hugh said, "You've taken the faith of others for granted. Have you never stopped to think how your mother lost six sons, one after another, and then your father, yet she trusts?"

Niall said nothing. His thoughts fell on his brothers, what he could remember of them, and of his mother's acceptance of each death, kneeling in quiet grief before the altar, never wavering.

"What of the Laird?" Hugh pressed. "Has he not lost his wife and son? Have I not lost Elizabeth and lived in the forest? Has Bruce not suffered a great deal?"

"Yet men like Edward live in luxury." Niall spoke harshly, hating his weakness. "Life was good in Shawn's time. Life *can* be good!" He lifted his head, meeting Hugh's eyes. "Tell me why God lavishes blessings on *them*, and not on those who serve Him!"

"We're called to something different, Lad," Hugh said.

"If I could but understand *why*," Niall persisted, "I could be as unwavering."

Hugh smiled sadly. "Ah, then 'twould not be *faith*, would it? Do we not follow the Bruce, even when we do not know his battle plan?"

They passed from the wooded trail into a long, broad valley opening up between two rolling, wooded ridges. Mist crawled along the grass.

A bustle in the glen caught his attention. "The Bruce is coming!"

Niall started at the sound of Lachlan's voice, as his friend cantered up beside him. Through the weeks of hunger, Lachlan had spoken less and less. Niall had begun to fear that Margaret, waiting at home for Lachlan, would not see her young husband again in this world, if they didn't find more food soon. The next time Hugh slipped a morsel into his bowl, Niall vowed, he'd move it to Lachlan's. His mind turned, out of habit, to St. Bride, St. Columba, and St. Fillan. But prayer would not come.

The army parted ahead, and Niall's thoughts returned to his king as Bruce cantered up, and wheeled to ride alongside them. "How d' ye fare?" he asked.

"Well, Your Grace." In his saddle, Niall bowed. Bruce, he noted, looked no better-fed than his troops. Edward Carnarvon, he suspected, ate well enough, at the expense of his men if need be—which was why the Scots loved their king and would die for him, or ride through this hellish landscape, barren of food for him.

"Keep a close watch," Bruce said. "You are known as a man of prayer." Niall felt Hugh's eyes on him, as Bruce added, "I hope you'll join me in asking Columba and Fillan to storm Heaven for us."

Hugh smiled. "We will, Your Grace. Certainly they'll see fit to send a few stags our way soon."

Bruce's eyes flickered from Niall, silent on his horse, back to Hugh, but he laughed. "'Twill take more than a few to feed our five thousand." He glanced the length of the long column. "I've not seen the rear of my brother's troops for some time. I'd not like to think we'll face battle separated from the bulk of our army."

A cold wind soughed down the valley, stirring the mist. It floated higher.

"There have been none to stand against us," Hugh said. But he reached to his back, feeling his sword there.

Niall felt his father's sword bumping reassuringly against his own back.

"Your Grace!" All of them, even Lachlan with his lackluster eyes, looked up at the shout from ahead. Colin Campbell, rode furiously through the gray-green mist, driving his heels into the ribs of his half-starved pony. He waited, barely, for Bruce's nod of permission, before blurting out, "Your brother is more than a mile ahead. We are completely separated!"

Irritation flashed across Bruce's face, replaced as quickly by the decisiveness that made him a great commander. "Send messengers to tell him to slow down."

"Your Grace, I'm not sure 'tis wise. We've told them. We came back in haste, and on our way saw motion in the wood."

As if cued, a lone archer burst out on the hillside, men shouted, and an arrow whistled through the drizzle. Hugh grabbed Niall, yanking his head down over his pony's neck, as a second arrow shot overhead. To Niall's right, a horse screamed.

"Nobody engage!" Bruce bellowed. "He'll have support nearby."

On the hill, a second archer appeared, his arrow zinging into Bruce's army. All around Niall, shields flashed up, forming a wooden barricade against arrows.

"Battle positions!" Bruce shouted. "Soon we shall have more to cope with." His words echoed up and down the length of his army, *Battle positions, battle positions!*

"Battle positions!" Niall roared at his own men, wheeling his pony. In the chaos of horses spinning, pikes lifting, swords scraping from scabbards, he saw Colin Campbell shout *yah!* dig his heels into his mount, and charge the archers, sword spinning over his head. One of the Englishmen scrambled for safety, too late, as Colin's sword whirled into his body, felling him in a bloody heap. Bruce rode hard on Colin's heels, fist raised, and cuffed the boy sharply on the head. He collapsed over his pommel, immediately struggling to right himself, shaking his head.

"Pull him down," Bruce roared to Hugh. "Take him to the back!"

"We need every man, Your Grace," Hugh objected.

Bruce rounded on him. "Breaking orders leads to defeat! D' ye think yon wretches would dare attack, unless they had support nearby?"

Colin blinked fiercely, rubbing his temple.

Hugh lowered his head. "I only meant, your Grace..."

"We shall have much to do soon," Bruce snapped. "Let each man prepare."

As he spoke, a rank of English bowmen appeared on the ridge, arrows flying.

Niall's arm flew up, his shield covering his body and head. Beside him, Lachlan shouted. Niall twisted in his saddle to see an arrow quivering in Lachlan's arm. It had barely lodged; with a twist, Niall wrenched it out.

"Archers!" Bruce shouted. "On them!"

A row of Bruce's archers dropped to their knees, a second row standing behind them, bows pointing to the sky. Their arrows rippled through the winter drizzle, carrying a cry of pain from the English back to Bruce's army.

"Drive them back," Bruce called to his archers, even as he swung his great sword in an arc, sending the army onward.

Grabbing his own weapon, Niall shouted, "Get your sword, Lachlan. You'll fight hard, whatever is ahead!"

"*Look* what's ahead." Lachlan's voice scraped out raw and gray, as if he'd seen hell.

Niall lifted his eyes. Above the gloam, where the valley opened up, floated an army, stretching as far as the eye could see.

"God a' mighty," Hugh whispered. "There must be forty thousand."

With no conscious thought, Niall crossed himself, murmuring, *Ave Maria, St. Bride, come to our aid.* He broke into a gallop with the rest, gripping his own reins in one hand and Lachlan's in the other, shouting, "You'll fight your way through. You'll see Margaret ahead of you every step of the way, Lachlan, and fight to get home to her. Never mind that arm." His own exhaustion slipped away as the heat of battle rose in him.

Bruce cantered past them. A weak ray of sun flashed suddenly from the heavens, glinting off the circle of gold on his helmet, before gray clouds scudded across the sky again. The sight of the massive army slowed Bruce not at all. "Now, Lords, show who is to be valiant in this fight. On them, without more delay!" Bruce charged, his battle ax a blur of motion over his head. Niall bent low over his horse's neck, driving it on, behind his king.

One of the men let loose a skirling war cry. Hugh shook his sword, answering with one of his own, and the sound echoed in Niall's throat. Hunger fell away. As he drove his horse forward, he swung his sword, testing its weight, raising it, and with the first bone-jarring clash of Scottish horse on English, swung, pounded, stabbed, clutching the horse with his knees, wanting nothing more than to kill those who had invaded his country. The first enemy fell beneath his sword. He whirled on the second, slashing, his targe raised against blows, ducking, stabbing, and yanking his sword from a second body.

He glanced to Lachlan, swinging as if he'd never been touched by an arrow. Ahead, Bruce's ax flashed and spun, his face turned from gentle king to demon. Screams echoed across the glen. Fine winter mist drizzled from the skies. English war horses reared, kicking. Foot soldiers packed into tight schiltrons, bristling forward with spears out, charging the cavalry. No mace or sword could reach them.

Niall fought his way through the army before him, swinging, killing, always keeping near Lachlan and Hugh, refusing to think of the size of the army. *Just keep killing.* He hacked at a man in gold livery, sent him flying from his horse, kicked at him as he tried to pull Niall down, and backhanded his sword across the man's neck hard enough to crumple him to his knees. Lachlan leaned down, plunging his own sword through the man's chest, and yanking back.

Above the fray, in the gray Irish mist, Bruce's battle ax whirled, disappeared, and lifted again. "Fight, men!" Bruce shouted. "For Scotland!"

Niall raised his shield over his head as an English knight came at him. A blow jarred his arm all the way to his shoulder, and wrenched his back, but slid away. He twisted in the saddle, yanked his pony's reins, and spun back into battle, slashing at the knight's back, pounding with his shield and blade, till he knocked the man from his saddle. The horse slipped in dark red mud, its lips bared over massive teeth, ripping the air with its scream. Hugh appeared from behind, yanking the fallen knight's sword, and vaulting onto the animal even as it regained its feet. He charged forward, two swords swinging, into the thick of the fight.

"Come on, Lachlan!" Niall shouted, and followed Hugh in, slashing, hacking, closing his ears to the screams all around; hearing only the call of Scotland, crying for freedom. He did the math—eight to one. He'd kill eight English knights, as would each of his comrades, and come out the other side, and they'd go home to Scotland, free Scotland, and he'd spend his life at home with Allene and his sons.

A knight appeared in the mist before him, silver-gray armor blurring into silver-gray mist. Niall gripped his pony tight with his knees, raised his shield, and swung his sword, thinking of Allene, always Allene.

SECOND MOVEMENT

CHAPTER SEVENTEEN

Inverness, Present

The Court that was not much of a court—they might know about Amy. Simon crossed broad swirls of labyrinth-like grassy patterns, to entered the airy foyer. He was becoming accustomed to doors of glass. Light poured in through them, illuminating divans as yellow as bumble bees, and a pink post supporting the ceiling.

"Can I help you, Sir?" called a woman from the desk.

He took his eyes off the daffodil settee and approached her desk with an affable smile. "The American orchestra that played here...."

"They've long since gone." She looked puzzled.

"Yes," he acknowledged. "But a young woman played with them—violin—her name is Amy. She remained in Scotland?"

The woman twisted her face in thought, staring up at the ceiling. Her eyes darted back to him, and she said, "Well, now, aye. Now you mention it, I did hear that."

"I'm so very hoping you can help me find her," Simon purred sweetly. "She played like an angel."

"Sure an' she did!" The woman's eyes lit up. "That solo, that lovely dress! The one *before* yer man showed up again! I wish I could ever play so beautifully!"

Simon let his smile grow. "You play, do you?"

"Oh, aye!" Her professional demeanor slipped in this personal connection. "I played all through uni, and did quite a bit of playing for churches and some local musicals, but I wasn't good enough to get into the RSNO."

"A shame," Simon sympathized, having no idea what *aras-enno* might be. But clearly only the best got in.

She chatted on a bit about things musical. He smiled, nodded, and made the expected responses. The rapport she was building in her mind would help him get the information he wanted.

"This Amy," he finally said. "Now, I'm looking for musicians. You've had such experience, certainly you're a fine player."

She demurred, her eyelids fluttering just a heartbeat before meeting his eyes. "Well, not good enough for the RSNO, but I do play *well*. If I do say so."

"What if I could hire Amy and yourself?" Simon suggested. "Do you know where I might find her?"

The woman's lips pursed in thought, before saying, "It was at Bannockburn yer man disappeared last year. She moved there."

"She's remained there?" he clarified. "She didn't go to America? Or elsewhere in Scotland?"

"I did hear them talking after the concert." The woman dropped her voice. She glanced around, as if unsure she was supposed to say it, but added, "She had that boyfriend, you know, a police officer. But when yer man showed up again, she dropped the poor lad and skited off with Shawn. Yes, she stayed in Bannockburn."

"Thank you," Simon purred. He turned to leave.

"Well, I haven't her number to give you, you know," the woman called.

Simon turned back. "Her number?"

"You know, her phone number. Or her address. Sure you're not going all the way to Bannockburn and just hope you find her?"

"No," Simon said smoothly. "I've a friend in Bannockburn."

Scotland, Present

The day dawned with mist crawling along the ground, but the promise of warmth. By midday, Angus pulled off his sweatshirt, and Claire tied her sweater around her waist, revealing a baby-blue t-shirt that brought out the cornflower hue of her eyes. She kept her hand on her purse, away from any expectation that he hold it, though her eyes sparkled at the caber tossing and Highland dancing. It all distracted him for minutes at a time, from the recent news that Shawn had returned to Scotland.

"I used to be quite good," Claire said.

"Did you now?" He watched the girls onstage, dancing in their checkered dresses to the skirling of pipes, and thinking of taking Amy to the games less than a year ago. He wondered where she was now. "No more?"

She laughed. "I got busy. School, life. Though I think at times of applying to teach at a school. And you? You like playing pipes with the police band?"

"Very much."

They watched in silence, as the girls leapt from foot to foot, their skirts bouncing, arms arced gracefully over their heads. They filed off, making way for three girls in sailor outfits. The girl on the left had jet black curls and freckles. She flashed him a grin. It was a year since he'd seen her at the other Games, where Amy had been amazed that her violin student Sinead also danced; and only months since he'd seen her at the pub where Amy had discovered she was Siobhan, Sinead's identical twin. It had been the day that tossed him headlong into the world of Shawn's disappearance, which truth he could only discuss with Amy and Shawn himself.

"They say the hornpipe is part of the Royal Navy...." He stopped.

"The Royal Navy's training program." She smiled. "I know."

She knew, too, he could see in her eyes, that he'd been thinking of Amy. "I'm sorry," he said.

"You can talk about her, you know. I'm a good listener."

He stared at the dancers, at Siobhan hauling in the ropes while her feet kicked in and out with straight, pointed toes. "That would be unkind to you."

"Inspector MacLean, you spend your life rescuing others. Let someone take care of you the once. It's not so bad when you get used to it."

Angus laughed. "I suppose it wouldn't be." The dancers leapt and skipped, legs flying to the cry of the pipes, as they hauled on imaginary ropes and sails, and finally, saluted. They filed off, replaced immediately by a pair of girls in blue checked skirts and matching waistcoats and socks, each bearing a pair of swords.

"One of my favorites," Claire said as they laid the crossed swords at their feet.

The bagpipes started once more. The girls bowed stiffly at the waist, rose on their toes, and skipped into intricate footwork around the blades.

"I hope he's treating her well." Angus didn't take his eyes off the dancers. "It's what bothers me most."

Claire, too, watched them steadily. "I've heard by all accounts he came back a different man. You spoke with him that day. You drove him to your house to sleep before he went down to his mam in Bannockburn. What was he like?"

"Arrogant, rude. Tired."

The girls skipped over the blades of their swords. Their skirts bounced high.

"To her?"

"To me. He didn't seem aware she might have moved on, without him."

"He seems changed in his interviews."

"You've seen them?"

"They're all over YouTube Along with a great deal of talk about where he was for a year. The story he told that morning! Clive and the chief were livid! And Clive is surprised you weren't."

Angus turned to her. "He is?"

"Aye, he keeps saying of all who should be in a rage, him playing such games with the police, you'd more reason times ten than any of them." She, too, took her gaze off the stage. "He can't understand it." She watched him, waiting for an answer, and when he gave none, added, "It's all the girls in the office talk about. Where do you think he was?"

Angus shrugged. "What matters is, he's back." Her question brought a deep desire to be with Amy. He'd never in his life had to evade questions. He disliked having to do it now.

"*Is* he treating her well? Have you talked to her since he came back?"

Angus hesitated. But Claire was like a soft pillow, inviting him to sink in, offering comfort. "A couple times." He didn't mention Eden Court. "She called the day you came outside. We didn't really talk about him."

"Why is she calling if she left you?" The bagpipe trailed into a long drone as the girls finished their dance with the same stiff-waisted bow with which they'd begun.

"She didn't leave me." Angus watched the girls trail off stage, replaced by a similar group.

"You left her?" Claire turned to him in surprise. "Why?"

"She was torn."

Claire shook her head as she stared at the new group of dancers, poised with arms akimbo. "You left her, Inspector MacLean, and now you wonder why you're alone?"

"She's torn," Angus repeated. "She needs to see him for who he is now, not for who she thought he might be. And make a decision."

"It seems you made the decision for her by walking away," Claire said.

"Was I wrong? I meant to give her space. Not make it more difficult for her. I meant to let them work it out without interference. They've a son to think of."

Claire heaved a sigh. "Perhaps you're far too honorable."

"I want her whole heart, not half of it."

"Most men would feel the same."

"I asked her to marry me last April." Once again, Angus stared at the stage. "She said yes. You should know that."

"Yes," Claire agreed in a weak breath. "Then why...?"

"We both found out she was more torn than even she realized." He turned to her suddenly, speaking intently. "Do you see, Claire, why I had to walk away?"

"But last April, he wasn't back yet. What happ...?"

"Then when he came back...." Angus spoke quickly, unable to tell her Shawn had left seven hundred year old messages for Amy in an ancient monastery. "I guess I hoped she'd miss what she and I had. She tells me I'm a better man."

"You are. You've always been upright and good. Nothing like him."

"But she stays with him. I don't understand women at all."

Claire's mouth turned down. "Our hearts don't always co-operate with our heads. He's very attractive you know. I can believe it would be hard to walk away from him when he sets out to charm. Plus she's a child with him. That means a great deal to someone like her."

"Should I have set out to charm her, too, then?" He heard the tinge of bitterness in his voice. "Fought over her like dogs over a bone?"

Claire laid a hand on his arm. "'Tis not your way, Inspector MacLean. Don't try to be him. She loved you for who you are. And she may yet come back for that."

She hadn't in the weeks he'd been gone, Angus thought.

Claire touched his hand. "I hope, for your sake, that she will."

Angus studied her, her blue eyes gazing back at him in earnest. The pipes wailed to a *fine* and he heard the sound of the dancers tromping off stage. The words *love is not self seeking* drifted through his mind. "Thank you," he said.

Isle of Iona, Present

"This is it! Iona!" Waves crashed against rocks. James curled into his chest, shuddering in the soft breeze. He'd never imagined it would feel so good to hold his own child, better than the best party he'd ever thrown. "You like it here?"

Amy reached to tug the blanket more closely around James. "I love it. It's peaceful in a way I've never experienced before."

He glanced down. Her skirt twisted around her legs. Her hand retreated inside the pocket of her long cardigan. Suzanna leapt to mind, refusing to work with him. And Christina, who wouldn't have pulled away, who wouldn't have kept her hands tightly in her pockets, as if he might scar her with a touch. Still, Amy was here, she and James and him, walking Iona's sandy beach.

"Did you ever come here?" she asked.

He shook his head. The wind tugged his hair, tied back with a leather thong, and billowed his trews, held tight by his boots. "No. But MacDougall's daughter-in-law came every year to pray."

He wondered if Christina had continued to come every June. It had been MacDougall's land; but being on Bruce's bad side, it may have soon been given to someone else. He wondered why he'd called her *MacDougall's daughter-in-law.*

"The thieving MacDougalls?"

"Yeah, them." He hoped, for Christina's sake, that the land had been given to someone else, that she'd been able to continue coming. She'd found peace here. Of course, he mused, she had the chapel at Glenmirril, and not the same need to escape that she'd had at Creagsmalan.

"That wasn't Christina, was it?"

Shawn's stomach gave a violent start. "Christina?" He wondered if he imagined the heightened pitch of guilt in his voice.

"Angus and I—we read about her at Creagsmalan. Chasing her husband through the dungeons with a frying pan—figuratively speaking, of course— divorcing him, betraying him to his enemies. Not that the MacDougalls deserved any better, from what Niall said," she added quickly.

Shawn stared out over water as rich and blue as Christina's favorite gown. "Is that how she's remembered?" He worked for an even tone. When Amy said nothing, he turned to her. She watched him, much as she'd studied him, eyebrows furrowed, the first time he'd snatched his cell phone from her, when she'd asked who Jo was and he'd lied. He turned away. He didn't want to lie. But there was nothing to tell about Christina. Not really.

"You knew her," Amy said.

He nodded, not looking at her. A seagull screeched and wheeled against the summer sky. James squirmed against his chest, letting out a matching, high-pitched shout, and settled again. From under the blankets came the sound of him chewing on his fist. "It was Niall she supposedly betrayed Duncan and MacDougall to. Gave him their plans for attacking Bruce. Chasing him through the dungeons—it wasn't the shrew they made her out to be. There was a girl. Duncan took her down there."

Amy turned a little pale in the July sun.

"You get the idea." Shawn said.

"I've been down there. It's horrible. I don't *want* to get the idea."

"No." His voice was flat. "You don't. Christina was protecting Bessie. And she paid for it."

They stood, side by side, neither speaking, while Shawn's thoughts churned with the rhythm of the waves. Amy would notice he hadn't answered her question completely. She would assume. But nothing had ever happened between them.

"She divorced Duncan?"

He nodded. He couldn't look at her. He couldn't tell her how strongly the day was emblazoned on his mind, how Christina, in her garnet red gown, had received the news in Niall and Allene's solar with her usual calm, taken a neat dozen more stitches, and excused herself. He'd followed her at a distance, through gray stone halls to the chapel, and slid in quietly, watching from behind, while she knelt motionless before the Blessed Sacrament. She'd turned, finally, to face him, with red, swollen eyes, and let him hold her. *You have no idea what it was like,* she'd said. It was the first, last, and only reference she'd ever made to Duncan's abuse.

He turned to Amy. Questions burned in her eyes. *She was a friend of yours? How good a friend?* When he said nothing, she turned, crossing the beach, the wind twisting her skirt around her ankles.

"Amy."

She kept walking.

It was just as well, he thought, because he really didn't know what to say. He hurried after her, hugging James to his chest, slowed by his feet sinking in the sand. Anger burned in him, that she would jump to conclusions, thinking things Christina would never do. But then, he had to admit he'd given her every reason to think *he* would. He pumped his legs harder, clutching James close so as not to jostle him. "Amy, come back!" He still didn't know what he would say. But he hurried behind her, climbing the sandy hill, wary of hurting James, who lifted his head and gave his short, sharp cries into the wind.

As white sand gave way to stubby, wind-blown grass, she spun, face calm. "I get it. It was seven hundred years ago. You were gone for two years. I didn't exist then. But you lied to me, *here* and *now.*"

"I didn't lie!"

"You just didn't mention her. For how many weeks now?"

"But it wasn't like that," he protested.

"It was like *something.*" Her arms snaked around her body, hugging herself against the salty breeze. "We came all the way to Iona because you wanted to see where your girlfriend spent time. Although I must say it's a change, you being interested in someone who prays."

Shawn stared at the ground. "Nothing happened between us." His jaw tightened. "Okay, I kissed her fingertips. Social convention. It was expected, almost required."

"But we came here because she did. Your heart is with her." She walked away, across the grassy field, leaving Shawn to struggle after, hugging James close. She was on the road back into town before he caught up to her. "When's the next ferry?" she asked, not looking at him.

"We didn't come here because she did," Shawn objected. "I came here because I have a lot of questions."

"About her?"

He shook his head, staring at the rough road passing beneath his feet. "About

God." He stopped, waiting for her critical response. When he looked up, she waited, her face softening, tendrils of black hair blowing around it in the wind. He dared say more. "About right and wrong. Forgiveness." The wind cut through his linen shirt. He hugged James more tightly. "Iona seemed like the place for answers."

In the field beside them, a sheep bleated. Amy glanced at it and started walking again, down the long road. Shawn walked beside her for some time, taking in hills, boulders, cows, sheep, and the distant sea. James gave a weak cry and buried his face in Shawn's shoulder.

"Let's get him in from the cold." He touched her arm tentatively and quickly dropped his hand. They walked in silence, coming finally to the abbey standing strong against the breeze. He paid their entrance fee, and they walked in silence past the Abbot's Hill. At the small Columba Shrine, he ducked to enter, glancing around the minuscule interior, barely big enough for the two of them. It was where Christina had prayed, but it couldn't possibly look the same. Four chairs faced one another, two by two. The crucifix was polished wood, modern in design. A series of circles formed the vertical and cross bars. The door shut behind them, clipping off the sunlight and closing them into a cool, dim den of stone, with the cross before them.

Amy twitched the blanket off James. He squealed, laughed, and reached for her hair. Shawn lifted him out of the front pack, and handed him over. Amy loosened his sweater and hat, kissed his nose, and set him to nursing. "Tell me about her," she said softly, her eyes locked on James.

There was barely room to pace here. Shawn wasn't sure if that was better or worse. He dropped into one of the facing chairs, his knees only inches from hers, as restless as Niall must have been in his dungeon cell. "She saved Niall from hanging."

Amy breathed in. Her eyes fixed on him, with James cradled in her arms, nursing. "How?"

"She got MacDougall out in the glen, where he saw me, pretending to be Niall. She whipped him into a frenzy, shouting for his guards that Niall had escaped. While they were out chasing through the glen for Niall—which was me—she got Niall out of the dungeon."

"You admire her," Amy said. And a moment later, softly, as if in grudging admission, "I'm grateful to her for saving Niall."

Shawn touched James's toe, his heart lost between two worlds, between his own James, and Niall's son. He frowned, his mind drifting away. The James he'd last seen as an infant was long dead—grown, perhaps, to a strong young warrior fighting beside his father or Douglas or Bruce; or a tough, old man, as strong and wily as his grandfather. Or perhaps he'd died as an infant in arms, shielded by Bessie's body as she tried to protect him from the MacDougalls.

"Shawn?"

He started.

Her hand lay on his arm. "You're disappearing."

He jolted more strongly.

"Figuratively!" Her fingers dug into his arm as if she, too, feared he might slip away.

He forced a laugh. "I'm not going anywhere." But it unnerved him. He stared at the crucifix, his eyes drifting to another reality. "I killed men, with James Douglas. At Jura. Do you know what it's like to use all your strength to drive a sword through a man, to hear it scrape against his spine, to watch his eyes as he dies?"

Her fingers tightened on his arm. She said nothing.

"Does that make you sick?" He turned to her. "Does it make you hate me?"

She shook her head. But she swallowed hard, and he guessed she was seeing it. "Angus..." She glanced at him guiltily, but kept going. "Angus said, if you were raiding with Douglas, those things happened. He said we can't judge by today's standards."

"He's right." He turned his palm up, studying the faint, white scar from Allene's knife. His mind turned to Duncan, his eyes wide in shock. Shawn closed his own eyes, feeling the weight and warmth of Duncan's body against his own fist as he plunged the blade into his stomach. Duncan's blood pooled warm around his fingers where they gripped the hilt. He'd felt no gloating, watching Duncan's eyes. He'd felt justified, thinking of the hot poker on Christina's ankle. He'd felt relief, knowing Duncan would never hurt her again.

Christina and Clarence crowded his mind; he wondered what Clarence had felt, driving his knife into James Kleiner, what Christina, who believed so strongly in forgiveness, would think—had thought—when she found out he'd killed Duncan, what Christina would say about his own lack of forgiveness of Clarence. The three of them—himself, Christina, and Clarence—danced a Celtic knot of a moral pattern inside his head, swaying to a minor beat. He'd killed many men—Clarence had killed one. He'd killed for just reasons—Clarence had killed in rage. Duncan had harmed Christina repeatedly, deliberately, and she'd forgiven. Clarence had struck out once, in pain, against a man who had done all he could for him. Christina, he knew, could forgive. He couldn't.

And he didn't have the moral algebra to calculate who was right or wrong.

"What happened?"

Amy's voice brought him back to the tiny shrine. She touched his palm. The white scar came back into focus, alongside disjointed memories of two years ago, of who he'd been, of Allene's knife biting into his palm. "Nothing." He shook his head, turning his hands quickly, lacing his fingers together. "Tell me how I forgive. Is it what I should do—about Clarence?" He stared at Amy, but his heart prayed that somehow, Christina was in this chapel, sometime in the past, able to send her wisdom through time to him. He wondered why he'd never asked her, when he had the chance. He wondered if he could find her grave. A chill shot through him, imagining a cold and sterile effigy, lying atop a stone sepulcher; solemn-faced in death where she had laughed, or worn a smile, hovering gently on her lips and lighting her eyes, in life. He didn't want to see her in death.

He didn't want to see another stone effigy beside her in death, of one who had walked beside her in life, who had taken his place.

"Of course you should forgive," Amy said. "But that's easy to say, isn't it?"

His next words came out *pianissimo*. "Do you forgive me?"

She leaned forward, sliding one arm under James, and freeing a hand to lace her fingers into his, her palm against the scar. "Yes." Her head dropped on his shoulder.

He rested his own head atop hers, his eyes closed, his two lives swirling around him, Christina's black hair and Amy's, the warmth in Christina's eyes and the pain in Amy's. He hardly recognized the man he'd been, the man she'd known just a year ago. "How can you?" he asked.

It took her a long time to answer. "Because you've stopped."

"You don't hate me? You don't want to get back at me?"

"No."

"Why not?"

"Because it came out of your pain. I always knew that."

"So did what Clarence did." He could see it clearly, here in the quiet of the chapel, the lost and abused boy, with a cast of strangers parading through his life and home, insulting and shaming him. With the long, black cork-screw curls like the enemy he'd battled at Bannockburn, the one Niall had killed. The images painted by the warden's words pressed on Shawn's mind, a boy beaten down literally and figuratively. But the images didn't touch his heart. "I can't set it aside," he said. "I want his life to be the hell he made mine."

"Your mother told me a little. His life *was* hell. More than yours has been."

"I can't forgive."

"It doesn't happen all at once," she said.

His mind on Christina, he had an urge to laugh and ask, *What do you know of forgiveness?* It was different worlds, he reminded himself, different kinds of cruelty.

Amy stood abruptly, her arms wrapped around James. But there was nowhere to run in the cramped space. She turned away, her knees bumping the chair.

"What?" he demanded. He hadn't *said* the words.

She shrugged, her back to him. "You were about to make that snorting sound you make. I could feel it. As always, you come first, your pain is worse than anyone's."

He spread his hands, stung, and angry at the abrupt loss of the intimate moment. "My father *did* get murdered. I *have* just come out of a kind of hellish medieval life where people like to maim and kill."

"Nobody's been through what you've been through." She turned to him; her eyes burned with the same sarcasm that laced her voice.

"Well, nobody living today," he said.

"And to think it only made you more arrogant." She tore the chapel door open. A bright bar of light erupted in the cool, dim interior, casting a high sheen on the polished crucifix. She stopped, a dark silhouette against the light, her hair swinging at her waist like Christina's. Her voice dropped, soft and low, like Christina's. "You're old enough to start seeing there are different ways of killing and maiming."

He stared at her—a dark shape in the bright rectangle of sun bursting through the small door—tugged between two times and two women, disoriented. "What do you mean?" It was a stall. He knew what she meant. He'd lain in his fur-covered, curtained bed, in the fourteenth century, with Christina and Amy side by side in his mind and heart, knowing Christina would never allow herself to be bullied and pushed as Amy had. And knowing Christina had an entire society, most armed with deadly steel, standing behind her.

Amy had had no one.

"I wouldn't wish it on my worst enemy." In the doorway, she spoke, low and musical. "What your cheating and lies did. It changed people's view of me. It destroyed me inside. Left me feeling worthless and hating myself. Not sure of my own perceptions or sanity anymore. Unable to function. Less than what I had been. You *took* part of me. As surely as if you'd cut off my arm. People today— we hurt each other in different ways, but just as badly. Inside, where it's not so obvious." He said nothing, and she added, "Believe me, I know plenty about forgiveness."

She released the door, shutting him into the dim interior. He dropped his head in his hands, sinking deep in himself. He should go after her. He wanted to hear Christina's voice and wisdom, here in her cherished refuge. He drew a deep breath, eyes on the crucifix.

He knew he just had.

Glenmirril, 1317

"Will you not at least say why you'll not marry Hugh?" Poking a needle through the hem of a shirt for Muirne's oldest son, Allene lifted her eyes to Christina.

Christina gazed out the window, her own needle flowing as steadily as a shuttle through a loom, before her eyes darted back to Allene. "I can't say."

"Surely...."

"I don't know, myself." Christina bent her head over her work. "'Twas foolish. He's a good man. I could hope for no better."

Their needles flashed in and out for a time before Christina spoke so softly that Allene paused and looked up to be sure she'd heard. "I'm grateful to your father."

"My father spoke harshly to you."

"He did as he sees best. I'm with child without benefit of marriage. Hugh has disobeyed him because of me. And still, he allows me to stay."

Allene poked her needle twice more through the material, before dropping the shirt to her lap. "Will you not say whose it is! What can it hurt to say 'tis Shawn's?"

Christina lifted her eyes, staring through Allene as if she had not spoken, and lowered her gaze again to the shirt in her hands. "Has your father said what will become of the child?"

Allene's lips pursed, angry at the evasion. But she'd tried. Christina slipped away as gracefully as an eel in the loch, from answering. Allene lifted a hand in frustration. "He spends his time in the Bat Cave, praying. He has no answers."

Christina bowed her head. "I am sorry I have brought this on him."

"Have you?" Allene asked.

"I have." She knotted the thread and snipped it with a tiny pair of silver scissors. "I have been foolish and ungrateful. When Hugh returns, I shall marry him."

Iona, Present

I push through the salty breeze. James, tucked under his blanket, kicks his legs against me, gurgling at whatever thoughts go through his mind. I smile, relishing the sound. I feel strong. I have forgiven. I am unsure about the future with Shawn, but I have been strong enough to have compassion instead of hate—yes, it takes strength to refuse to hate—and that knowledge wraps around me like armor.

There's no ferry at the dock. I take James to the Argyll Hotel, to a table in the sun room, overlooking the sea, and order coffee from a heavy, grandmotherly waitress, who introduces herself as Finoula.

It feels good to be alone. No Shawn to beat me down. No Angus to rescue me. Just me—and God, I slowly realize. As if He followed me from the chapel, walking silently by my side, and slid into the chair across the table, waiting quietly—as real as Shawn beside me in the chapel—until I notice Him.

James, cradled in my arm, smiles up at me. One tooth shows its first white edges through his gums. He laughs, and pounds the table, reaching for the silverware.

Myself, James, and God, I think. If He were a real presence, I would say Thank You out loud, for the gift of my son. I wonder what his future will be: just me, or his father and mother together, or a step-father? Right now, it doesn't matter. Right now, at this moment, he is happy, and so am I. It felt good to walk away from Shawn.

Sun pours in windows that look out on gardens and the sea below. I hand James a spoon. He sets to gnawing on it, squealing intermittently. I think of the unknown Christina, so different, by Shawn's account, than the woman in Creagsmalan recounts. I wonder who she was. In a testament to how much he and I have both changed, I believe him when he says he did no more than kiss her fingertips. But I think—no, I know—he felt far more for her than he lets on. My hand drifts to the crucifix under my sweater. When I think of the woman Shawn described, saving Niall at great cost to herself, I can't hate her, as I hated those other unknown women.

"A beautiful bairn." The waitress slides coffee onto the table. Her apron billows over rolls of fat. Her eyes sink in a sea of wrinkles when she smiles. "Might I hold him?"

She looks as if she's held many babies. James turns to her, and breaks into a grin, screeching his happiness. He reaches for her. I can't help smiling. "I think he's asking the same thing." I lift him, spoon still in his mouth, to the woman.

Finoula accepts James into her arms, and they smile and coo at one another.

He bangs the spoon on her nose. She laughs, and taps it on his, too. "Such a blessing, bairns." Finoula looks up, not minding James tugging at her silvery curls. "God is certainly smiling on you."

"Do you think so?" I ask. The last years have been a roller coaster.

"Och, I know so. You've a beautiful child and ye're here on Iona, aren't ye?"

I smile, touched by the simple logic. Shawn would find it laughable. The unpleasant experiences of the years with him flutter away as if on a breeze, leaving me with a peace I haven't felt since he strutted onstage to take his place as lord of the orchestra. "It does feel like a world apart here," I say.

"Oh, 'tis." Finoula slides her bulk into the seat opposite. She cradles James on her shoulder, her attention on me. "'Tis a thin place, where Heaven and God and things we dinna ken come a wee bit closer, now."

I glance at my clasped hands, at Bruce's garnet ring, heavy on my finger. I don't even know the woman. There's no reason to spew my innermost feelings all over. Finoula's plump hand, with veins of robin's egg blue, covers mine. "What ye feel here, what you see. Trust it."

I look up, meeting eyes of bright blue, younger than Finoula, older than time. "What I feel here is that I'm forgiven and right with God again," I say softly, surprised at myself for saying this to a stranger.

"Perhaps because you've forgiven, you can finally feel God's forgiveness. But He never stopped loving you." She squeezes my hand, and stands, handing James back.

Ireland, February 1317

"Niall, stop!"

Panting, coated in sweat beneath his leather armor and chain hauberk, Niall came to himself, staring first at Hugh's hand on his sword arm, and then at the carnage around him. In the dying light, bodies littered the wide valley.

"There were forty thousand," he whispered in horror.

"Now there are five thousand," Hugh said. "Just us."

Niall's gaze traveled the battlefield. Dead, dying, broken bodies—of men, of horses—sprawled everywhere, shoulder to shoulder, one man collapsed atop another, limbs flung out, eyes staring at the darkening sky. Horror faded to numbness. There could be no god here. They were on their own.

"We must move quickly," Hugh said. "Find our own wounded."

"Owen and Lachlan?"

"Owen is fine. Roysia is helping him tend the wounded."

"Lachlan?" Niall's heart beat faster. He'd had no fear for himself. He'd known—*had* to believe—he'd come through the vast host alive. But he'd feared for his friends, the men he'd known since childhood, for their loved ones waiting behind Glenmirril's strong walls.

"Stripping the dead," Hugh said. "We've much to do, and night coming fast."

Mist curled, like chilly loch water, around Niall's ankles. He nodded. His heart slowed. Lachlan and Owen lived. Margaret would not be among the new widows. Through the mist, the Scots moved like wraiths, in and out among the dead, stooping to gather valuables, now and again shouting at the discovery of food in a dead man's pockets, or lifting an injured friend, helping him off the field of carnage.

An English knight sprawled at Niall's feet. Niall dropped numbly to one knee. He swiped his hand over the dead eyes, lowering the lids, before beginning the distasteful job of claiming weapons, gold, food, anything that would help Bruce's army and Scotland. "Dried meat." He held the treasure up, showing it to Hugh.

"Very...good." Hugh's words slurred. He pressed his hand to his side. Blood seeped through his fingers.

Niall tilted his head. "Hugh...your hand...."

"'Tis not...my hand." Hugh swayed.

Niall leapt to his feet, catching Hugh as he collapsed.

CHAPTER EIGHTEEN

Iona, Present

Shawn hunched on a chair in the chapel. He should go after her, he thought. He was sending the wrong message, letting her go—a message he didn't want to send—because she was right. He'd been an ass. Again. He *had* been about to snort. And he would have been wrong. She knew plenty about forgiveness. He thought of the e-mails he'd feared she'd read—Jo's florid praise, Debra's graphic reminiscences, Celine's tears at his silence. His face grew warm in the cool chapel. Maybe she hadn't read the actual e-mails, but she understood; she *knew.* How must it feel? Yet she didn't want to kill him, or make his life hell as he wanted to do to Clarence.

He stared, unseeing, at the modern crucifix, wondering what the chapel had been like when Christina made her yearly pilgrimages. He rose, touching the walls that had stood for centuries, the stones she had looked at, that had sheltered her, if only briefly, from Duncan. He touched the small lectern. Had there been an altar? The crucifix would have been very different.

She'd come as respite from Duncan. Had she come with hate in her heart? He couldn't imagine that of her. No, she'd no doubt prayed for him. Knowing her, she'd seen his rages as more of an eternal danger to himself than a present danger to her, and prayed for his sake more than her own. The urge to snort rose in him. He wrinkled his nose, tightened his mouth, and held it back. He pressed a hand to his forehead. He couldn't pray for Clarence.

He turned in agitation, but the cell was too small to pace. He dropped back onto the chair, wishing Christina could speak to him across time, wishing he could explain to her why this was *different*, why he couldn't be expected to do as she had done. Clarence had *killed* his father. Duncan hadn't actually killed her. Clarence had been shown love and kindness by the Kleiner family; he had no excuse. It was different. In his mind, it was all different. *It had to be!*

He rose again, taking a step to the Bible on the stand. If Christina were capable of envy, she would envy his ability to have a Bible, any Bible, dozens of Bibles, if he wanted. His fingers trailed the thick page, and he inhaled the rich smell of paper and ink, wisdom and leather, wishing he could give her such a gift, though he himself saw no value in it. *Forgive, love, don't do this, don't do that, yada yada.* What was its value?

He flipped a page, touching the letters as if they might seep into his fingers, and tell him something his eyes had missed. He slid his hand across, and the words underneath revealed themselves. *So likewise shall my heavenly Father do also unto you, if ye from your hearts forgive not every one his brother their trespasses.*

He yanked his hand away, burned. Christina would love to have such a thing, to treasure, to keep in Niall's solar where she and Allene could look at it, read it. He swallowed. That's all it meant to him, just something Christina would treasure, something he could give her and see the smile light her eyes.

He spun in the the small chapel, threw open the door, and pushed out into the salty wind.

Ireland, March 1317

In the candlelight in his tent, Bruce held up his hand. Niall's fingers stilled on the strings of his harp. He'd been playing for an hour, he guessed, as he'd played every night since the battle a month ago. He'd played since shortly after the moon rose, a huge silver orb across Ireland's sad skies. He'd played with his head bowed, seeking refuge from the memories of carnage that haunted him, while Bruce sat, motionless, chin on steepled fingers, staring at the small crucifix on the table.

Finally, his king spoke. "How does Hugh fare?"

Niall lowered the harp to his knees. "His recovery is slow, Your Grace. He's only this day risen from his bed."

"I doubted the wisdom of allowing him to continue with us." Bruce sighed. "'Twas but your pleading on his behalf that swayed me." When Niall said nothing, Bruce prompted him. "You may speak, Sir Niall."

"He'd have fared worse, left behind where he'd have less to eat even than what we are able to provide."

"More importantly," said Bruce, his eyes on the crucifix, "he finds purpose with us. I believe he may have refused even his king's command, in order to remain at your side. Purpose will keep a man going long past the day he would otherwise have died. You inspire devotion, Sir Niall."

Niall bowed his head, humbled. "I hope I prove worthy of that."

They sat in silence a moment before Robert said, "I've a job for you."

"Your Grace?" Niall inquired, with no enthusiasm. He wanted only to be home.

"The laundress, the one your man Owen is so taken with."

"Roysia."

Bruce nodded. "Aye, Roysia. When is her time?"

"Two months." Niall wondered, in truth, that she had made it this far.

Bruce stared for a time at the crucifix, while Niall waited. Finally, he spoke. "You are to watch for a town where she can stay in safety. You, Owen, and Hugh will escort her. Hugh can recover while remaining loyally at your side."

Niall rose, bowing low. "Your Grace." He stopped, willing his voice not to crack with emotion. "Thank you." He turned to go.

"One thing more, Sir Niall." Bruce spoke almost too softly to be heard.

Niall turned back. Bruce stared at the crucifix. "Your Grace?"

The king lifted his eyes. "You follow my battle plans, even if you do not know why I've chosen as I do."

Niall became still, waiting, wondering what Bruce knew.

"I believe your Brother Andrew, were he here, would back me up on this." Bruce raised an eyebrow, before adding, "As your king, I give one more command. Even if you do not see reason, even if your faith fails you, pray as you once did." He smiled. "Your king hears far more than you believe."

"Your Grace, I will always follow your orders." Niall bowed and left, wondering to which king Bruce referred.

Isle of Iona, Present

Amy had spread out a blanket, where James lay on his back, waving his feet in the wind. Shawn stood on the road above, watching. Her hair hung down her back. A flurry of tendrils escaped from the braid, whipping in the breeze. She leaned over James, and even at this distance, he could see their delight in one another and hear James's happy sounds. Niall's son had been a happy baby, looking up to Shawn with wide, trusting eyes, and smiling a similar, gummy grin, drooling in glee, when Shawn laid his hand on the rough hide of a garron in the stables, or took him to the shore behind Glenmirril, splashing his bare feet in the summer water.

Shawn sat down on the rocks, watching Amy and his son, enjoying the moment. A dozen little boats bobbed in the water, like a colorful spray of balloons lifting into the blue sky. The air smelled of salt. Christina had walked this shore, seven hundred years ago. He wondered if the breeze had whipped her hair from under her barbets, as it tugged at Amy's; if it had twisted her long, garnet surcoat around her ankles; if she'd stood on the shore looking out and reveling in the summer blues, and sunlight dancing on the waves.

You'll do what's right, she'd said, the night before he left. Was it only six weeks ago? Six weeks, seven hundred years, a killing in the tower, a police interrogation, a reunion with the woman he swore to love, a child held, ocean and countries crossed, eight concerts played, an album started, and fourteen talk shows later.

It wasn't six weeks; it was a lifetime.

She'd told him to go make it right with Amy. She'd trusted him to be the man she saw in him.

Slowly, the guilt faded; the guilt over staying in the chapel, thinking of Christina, when Amy turned and left. He swore he felt Christina's hand, light as the sea breeze, on his shoulder, knew she was telling him, *You needed the time alone. So did she.*

A seagull screeched overhead and dove for something in the sparkling waves. Amy turned. Her eyes fell on him, and the smile for James slid from her face. Neither of them moved. He studied her. Something had changed in the hour they'd been apart. Her eyes seemed calmer, her back straighter. Strength and peace hovered around her. She made no move to come to him.

Shawn rose, and picked his way over the rocks, to the sandy beach. She watched silently. He lowered himself to the sand beside her. She'd kicked her shoes off and tucked her legs under her skirt. Her bare toes showed at the edges. Her thick braid fell to her waist, collecting sandy sparkles in the ends of her hair. They stared at each other. He cleared his throat. "I'm sorry. I have a lot of learning to do."

"You're trying."

He'd hoped for more enthusiastic words.

"You need to find your own place," she said, "if you're staying in Scotland."

"*What?*" He blinked and stared in disbelief. "Because you thought I was going to say something stupid?"

"I know you were going to say it."

"I thought better. I knew I was wrong. I *didn't* say it."

"Anyway, that's not what it's about." Amy reached to let James grip her finger, and smiled at him.

"Is it Angus?" He bit back his accusation that she'd been with him, behind the theater.

She laughed and shook her head, as if she spoke to a slow-witted child. "It's got nothing to do with Angus. We never lived together before, you and I."

"I'm staying in my own room," he protested. "I'm honoring my promises. What have I done wrong?"

"Nothing." She stared out across the water, watching the ferry separate itself from the green hills of Mull. "But you came back, you needed somewhere to stay, and it turned long term."

"I'll pay rent," he said. "I'll pay all of it. We're a family, now."

She shook her head. "No, we're two people who once had something, back when we were both very different. We made a child together. I'm not sure what that makes us, but I never agreed to live with you, and all of a sudden, that's what I'm doing. The professor will be back soon. We both need to find our own places."

"I want...." He stopped. A pain as sharp as his own dagger stabbed his heart. Wasn't that the point? It wasn't all about what he wanted. Not anymore. He stared at the sand, drawing in deep, slow breaths, so he wouldn't suffocate. "Okay. Same neighborhood, maybe, same street? So we can still be together?"

"Same row of houses if you like," she said.

A bit of air seeped back into his lungs. "You're not breaking up with me, then?"

She scooped James up, wrapping the blanket around him, as the ferry scraped up its concrete landing. "Not today."

Inverness, Present

"Thank you." Claire stopped at the back lot of the police station, where they'd left their cars. Her hands stayed in the deep pockets of her cardigan. "I enjoyed it."

Angus smiled. "As did I." Her freckles and blue eyes and short, black ponytail had grown on him. But she felt like a sister, and he felt unkind, letting her hope. He was relieved she stayed inches away, not leaning close.

"Aren't you going to your car?" she asked.

"I've something to do inside," he said. "I'll see you Monday, aye?"

She smiled, looking as pleased as if he had kissed her, and turned for her car. He waited while she got in, though the evening light was strong, in July. When she drove off with a wave, he let himself in the back door, greeted the night dispatcher, and went to his office, head down, not wanting to answer questions of the men on duty.

He unlocked his office and turned on the light. It felt lifeless without Clive, but in the bright halogen lights, the fern on top of the filing cabinet looked brighter than he remembered. He wondered why he only now noticed what a difference Claire's nurturing made. But it wasn't what he'd come for.

Seating himself, he checked his work e-mail, knowing he was putting off what he'd come to do. He answered the chief's request for a copy of a report, confirmed he'd be at the pipe band performance on July 27, and opened his personal e-mail.

He closed his eyes, a shield against the list of names that didn't include Amy. Claire was right, he chided himself. He'd told her to work it out with Shawn. He'd reprimanded her for calling, told her to stay away, so now he was hurt she did? Shawn was back in Scotland. Angus had watched a clip on YouTube that gave the information, hating himself for wanting to know about Amy and James. Shawn was back, and she hadn't called and hadn't e-mailed. It was time to accept it, though it felt like sharp rocks in his stomach.

He unpinned her picture from his cork board. In it, her hair fell free to her waist, as she held James just days after his birth. He slid it to the back of his drawer, under some sticky pads. It only hurt to look at it every day.

He took out his phone, scrolled through the pictures, and stared long and hard at the image of the Glenmirril Lady that had moved from one phone to another since he'd first owned a mobile phone. Here, in the office where he'd first seen Amy on the telly, first been jolted to see the Glenmirril Lady in the flesh—here where it started—seemed like the place to lay it to rest.

He touched the screen, frowning, thinking of the medieval laird Niall Campbell, a man he'd seen lying in a hospital bed, a man he'd spoken to at the castle hotel on the River Ness. It had to have been Niall who had put a quill to parchment and drawn Amy's likeness. Had he done it for Shawn? Had he been in love with Amy himself? Rob, in his interview with the police, when Shawn—Niall —disappeared, had been very clear that Amy and Shawn—Niall—had been on very good terms when Niall—Shawn in the police reports and in Rob's mind—had disappeared into the forest, a year and six weeks ago.

Amy believed Niall had only been carried away by fear, excitement, being alone in a foreign world with only her at his side; that he truly loved only Allene. Angus believed Amy underestimated herself. It was no wonder, after two and a half years of Shawn tearing her down. His fingers tightened on the phone, studying the picture of the ancient drawing found at Glenmirril. It was Amy, holding her violin on her knee, her hair flowing down her back, smiling at the camera. It had caught her in a moment of complete peace and joy. It was what had captivated him from the first moment he'd seen it, years ago with his cousin in the Glenmirril archives.

Anger burned deep inside. Shawn didn't deserve a second chance. But then, even Claire said he seemed a changed man, and Amy had made her choice. He didn't blame her. They had a long history. Shawn had changed. There was James.

With a knot in his throat, he hit *delete.* It was better not to carry her image with him. A bar appeared across the bottom of the Glenmirril Lady. *Are you sure you want to delete this?* He stared for another few seconds. His fingers trailed over the small part of the picture where her earrings hung, the earrings she swore Niall had never seen. Of course he didn't want to delete it. He blinked hard, and hit *Yes.*

The picture flickered away into darkness.

Done, his phone told him. In his heart, it would never be done.

CHAPTER NINETEEN

Ireland, April 1317

"Your Grace." Niall stopped in the entrance of the tent.

The Bruces and their nephew, Thomas, leaned over a map. Bruce looked up from their deliberations. Three more weeks had left the king gaunter still, his hair more gray. Niall tried to tamp down his feeling that his prayers for his king, like all others, went unheeded.

"Speak, Sir Niall."

"We've found a place for Roysia."

Bruce breathed out a sigh. "Praise God," he said. "I'd begun to fear there was no such place in all the country. Who? Where?"

"A miller and his wife. They live on the river, where they've a way to feed her. A day's ride, near the route we're traveling."

"Excellent!" Bruce beamed, looking from Edward to Thomas. "Did I not say we'd find a place?"

Thomas smiled, already leaning in to the maps, his finger trailing the river, searching for the place. "You did, Your Grace."

Looking pleased, despite his weariness, Bruce added. "And you, Sir Niall? Did I not say have faith in your king's plans?"

"You did, Your Grace." Niall smiled despite himself, holding back his cynical thought that his own men and Bruce's gold—not God—had found the place. Despite following his king's orders these past weeks, he felt naught but dry silence in answer to prayer, where once he'd felt God close by. It felt even more pointless than it had a month ago.

"Tell Roysia and Hugh. We leave at dawn, and have her there by night."

"Thank you, Your Grace." With the closest thing to joy he'd felt since arriving, Niall bowed and turned.

As he reached for the tent flap, Colin Campbell burst through, nearly falling to his knees, as he shouted breathlessly, "A scout, Y' Grace! Edmund Butler's army fast approaching!"

"How many?" Thomas shot to his feet, letting the map snap back into a roll.

"Forty thousand!"

The Bruces and their nephew exchanged glances.

"Did we not clear the field of the bloody English last time they had forty thousand?" Edward smirked. "Then it was only you. Now, 'tis you and me both!"

"Neither did I deliberately engage such odds," Robert snapped. "Need I remind you?" He shook his head. "God was with us, but will we continually test Him to see how many times He'll rescue us from foolhardiness?"

Edward threw his head back, laughing. "We are *Scots.* 'Twould be foolhardy *twelve* to one, perchance, but we've overcome worse than this."

"No." Robert rose from the table, rolling another map. "Colin, my Lord Niall, rouse the men. We leave within the hour."

"Aye, Your Grace." Niall bowed, and strode out of the tent. He'd gone not a furlong when he heard the *whoosh* of the tent being taken down behind him. He mounted his pony and kicked it into action, shouting, "Prepare to march!" He rode the length of the camp, sending Lachlan and Owen to do the same.

At the far end, he sought them out, confirming they'd covered the full camp. He found Owen by the river, lifting wet shirts from the water for Roysia, wringing them for her. Her face looked strained. "Pack the shirts wet," Niall told them. "We've no time to lose. Forty thousand will soon be on us!" He wheeled his horse in search of Bruce. Everywhere he went, he saw Scots slinging bags across the backs of pack animals, and on their horses, ready to ride. He found the king with his brother.

"The latest report?" Bruce asked.

"Butler is a mile away," Edward replied.

Bruce turned to Niall. "We're ready to march?"

Niall gave a quick bow. "Your Grace, the men are mounted."

"Well done." Bruce grasped his pommel. As his foot touched the stirrup, a scream split the air. "What in the name of God is that?" Bruce's head whipped around, searching his vast army. "Is it one of the women?"

"Your Grace!" Owen's horse burst through the knot of men and animals. He slid to the ground, dropping to both knees before the king. "Roysia, the laundress. Her time has come!"

"'Twas her scream we heard?" Bruce asked.

Owen nodded furiously. His hands clenched in supplication, he looked up to his king. "Your Grace, she is terrified of being left. Grant me this, my Lord, give me two men to help hide her in the wood. I'll stay with her."

"You would all die," Bruce said bluntly.

"I know that, Your Grace." Owen bent his head. "But I cannot leave her. Please do not make me, Your Grace."

Bruce glanced once over his shoulder, to the crest of the hill where Butler's horde would appear, and back to the river, where the girl's cries continued. "What man among us would walk away from a woman in such a state?" he asked. "Edward, tell the men to take up battle positions."

"'Tis *folly,* Your Grace," objected Thomas. "They've *forty thousand*!"

"We'll not abandon a woman giving birth." Bruce stared resolutely at the hill. "Owen, take two men and the women. Get the laundress to the safest place you can find, until she is delivered."

"Aye, Your Grace, I thank thee, I thank thee with all my heart!" Owen's voice choked. He scrambled to his feet and threw himself back on his pony, driving it fast to the river.

"Sir Niall!"

"Your Grace." Niall's heart pounded. Thomas was right. 'Twas folly.

"I have possibly just committed thousands of Scots to death." Robert stared grimly at the pass, while his brother and Thomas wheeled away to rally their men. "Pray for a miracle. Pray for St. Bride's protection. Pray as you prepare your men for battle, and command them to pray, as well."

Niall bowed low. He swallowed. Edward Bruce was right, too. They'd won against worse odds. But then, they'd had food in their stomachs. Now, they were an army with barely strength to haul themselves onto their horses—what horses remained. A third of the animals had died of hunger and exhaustion. Niall pulled himself onto his pony, the one that had been Shawn's a lifetime ago, and drove it through the crowd, finding his men and calling orders.

From the river, Roysia's cries diminished. From all around, came the rustle of men changing course, turning to face the yet unseen enemy, the harsh whisper of steel on leather as they drew swords from scabbards. Archers formed ranks, bows at their sides. Pikemen clustered into schiltrons, spears pointing at the sky, waiting to kill.

Niall and the men of Glenmirril took their place among the hosts of Bruce's Irish and Scottish army. Men stretched across the wide swath of spring-green meadow, facing the gap between two hills through which Butler's army would stream. They stood, strangely quiet, so that the only sounds were the spring song of a lark, and beyond the river at their backs, the occasional cry from Roysia.

It was foolishness, Niall thought. But his king had ordered him. If nothing else, he thought, his men might die with hope, instead of fear. Covering his doubt from the men who looked to him, he fell to his knees, hands clasped. "Men of Glenmirril," he said, with more confidence than he felt, "Our king charges us pray for a miracle." Around him, his men, too, dropped to their knees, and folded their hands. "*Pater noster, qui es in caelis,*" Niall began.

Two dozen voices joined him. "*Santificetur nom en tuum.*"

His heart pounded so hard he could barely speak. Butler's forty thousand would flood over the pass at any time. *Adveniat regnum tuum; fiat voluntas tua.*

What had God done for the monk and the child, dead before His very altar?

Sicut in caelo et in terra, the men chanted around him. Shawn would laugh them to scorn, to see them falling to their knees as a military maneuver.

Panem nostrum cotidianum da nobis hodie, he intoned. Shawn was right. He should sharpen a sword, check the pike men's formation, convince Bruce to retreat, take Roysia in a litter.

Et dim itte nobis debita nostra. Beside him, Hugh, a giant, gaunt scarecrow, pale and shaking with the exertion of being out of bed, rumbled the words, his head bowed low over his hands.

Niall lifted his eyes. A glint of light winked in the gap between the hills. His heart hammered. The nerves up and down his arms screamed to *do* something, to *act*. He had to protect Hugh now, in addition to himself. But his king had commanded him to pray. *Sicut et nos dimitimus....*

Behind him, a woman's scream split the air. He swallowed, forcing himself to do as his king commanded. *Debitoribus nostris.*

Butler's army flowed into the passage. They grew on the crests of the hills, rising on either side of the passage, stretching for furlongs on either side, farther and farther, locusts blackening the earth.

Shawn hadn't done so well without prayer, Niall reminded himself. He wouldn't let Shawn's attitude sway him. He threw the words out more strongly. *Et ne nos inducas in tentationem!*

Any minute now, any second, the vast host would swarm down the hillside. His legs screamed to jump to action, to leap on his horse. He lifted his head higher, eyes closed, searching his heart for any sign of God's presence. *Sed libera nos a malo!*

He opened his eyes. Butler's army stared down, tens of thousands, cavalry, foot soldiers, armored knights, archers, covering the hills like ants on honey, six, seven, eight to one against the Scots in the valley and the helpless woman behind them.

Amen, he and his men finished.

"St. Bride," Niall shouted, and the men joined him in the prayer.

"Pray for us."

No matter what Shawn thought, Niall reminded himself, prayer was still the mightiest sword at one's side. Just for this moment, he had to believe it again!

Behind them, came another cry from Roysia, this one louder. Niall's blood curdled, wondering how long they could hold off the host before them, and what would happen to her and the newborn child when Butler's army broke through. What would happen to Owen, the last man between her and the enemy?

Before him, as the prayer came from his mouth, he watched Bruce, his back strong and straight, his garron pawing the ground, eager for action. Bruce's battle ax hung from his hand. Across the field, Thomas Moray waited, still as a statue, and farther still across the valley, a schiltron stood motionless, spears bristling.

Roysia screamed a third time.

Niall drew in deep breaths, telling himself to trust God, trust in prayer.

On the hill, motion rippled across the vast army. They began to move. Niall's heart kicked up its tempo, pounding, ready for battle.

"Amen," finished Hugh beside him.

Bannockburn, Present

"The beautiful girl who plays the violin," Simon said, for the tenth time that day. He stood on the edge of a field where children kicked a ball, with a short, stout woman he guessed to be their nurse. She looked up at him quizzically. "With the *American orchestra.*" He felt the way his speech slowed on the unfamiliar words, despite having practiced them softly, sitting alone on the train down to Bannockburn.

"I know all about yer man," the woman said. It had been a common response.

"Everyone knows about *him*, sure!"

"But where can I find *her*?" Simon asked.

Like the rest, she shook her head. "I'd not know. It's Shawn and Zach the telly talks about."

Simon smiled tightly, and left, heading down the street toward the shops. He passed another of the enormous parchment-like hangings that were everywhere. He stopped, staring up at the minstrels, dressed in garb that would have passed in his own time, and the words *The Best of Scotland* emblazoned under their feet.

"Did you hear them play?" a voice asked.

Simon turned, surprised to be addressed, and appraised her. She was young. And attractive. She smiled up at him with kohl-lined eyes. He let his own smile grow. "I did indeed. A woman played with them—violin. Long black hair." He used his previous story. "She plays gloriously. I wish to hire her. Do you know who she is?"

"That's his girlfriend," she said promptly, and laughed. "Like I wouldn't know *that!* Wouldn't I love to be in her shoes! His *hair!*"

"Would you?" Simon kept the pleasant smile frozen in place. "Amy, I believe. Have you her surname? How I could contact her?"

"Aye, Amy Nelson. She lives here in Bannockburn, you know."

"I do," Simon said smoothly. "Do you know where?" He cleared his throat. "So I can hire her."

"Oh, now, I don't know that," the girl said. "But I'm thinking sure you could check online."

"Online?"

She tilted her head at him, smiled uncertainly, and walked away.

The smile slipped from his face. He had a surname. *Nelson.* He turned slowly in the street, surveying the stores, planning his next move.

Ireland, April 1317

Niall barely remembered intoning the prayer, even as he scrambled to his feet, squinting up at the hills. "What are they doing?" he asked Hugh. He couldn't believe what he was seeing. He *must* be mistaken!

Hugh climbed unsteadily to his feet, clutching his pony's saddle with a shaking hand, and shielding his eyes to study the movement of Butler's troops. His voice came out in disbelief. "They're *leaving.*"

"Leaving?" Niall felt as shocked as Hugh sounded.

"Leaving," Hugh repeated.

"They're leaving!" Lachlan jumped to his feet, the most energy Niall had seen from him in weeks.

Niall watched, still doubting. But bit by bit, the thick black mass receded. "Why?" he asked.

"Did you not trust in your own prayers?" A smile spread across Hugh's face under the bushy beard.

"I expected something *different.*" Niall grasped the stirrup on his pony, and pulled himself to his feet. "A victory. Why would they *leave?*"

Ahead, Bruce cantered among the men, issuing orders, sending out scouts. "Stay in formation!" His voice rang out over the army, echoed up and down the line by Edward Bruce, de Soulis, Moray, and all the clan chiefs.

"Don't move," Niall called to his own men.

They waited while the sun peaked at the height of the sky. They waited while it crept westward. They waited while their stomachs rumbled and their legs shook with exhaustion, while the Bruces and Moray consulted and rode out again, till the scouts came back, and Bruce turned, victory lighting his face.

"Niall. Sir."

Niall turned.

Owen stood in his chain hauberk. He cradled a bundle in his arms, swaddled in a soldier's shirt, looking dazed. "I need to tell his Grace."

Looking at the child in amazement, Niall pointed across the field. "There."

"They didn't attack." Owen stood in the midst of the army, holding the child in as much bewilderment as if he'd been dropped into the middle of Shawn's world. "How could they not have attacked?"

"We've no idea," Niall answered.

Owen, his bemused gaze dropping back to the child, stumbled toward the Bruce, who cantered toward Niall and his men, meeting Owen halfway. "'Tis a boy," Owen said, and suddenly, tears rolled down his cheeks, big round tears. "Your Grace, God bless you, 'tis a boy. You saved her life and his."

The King of Scots slid off his horse, took the child, and lifted him high in the air. "God be blessed!" he shouted, for all to hear. "The child is born, and Butler has left. Now let us head back to Ulster, thanking God for the miracle that happened here!"

Cheers rose from the throats of thousands of men, all across the field. Niall closed his eyes, thanking St. Bride, and Columba, and Fillan for their intervention on behalf of this half-starved army and this new child. Around him, cheers resounded, while the shuffle of men mounting horses joined the symphony.

Roysia appeared at his side, helped by another of the serving women and Lachlan, at the same time Bruce joined him, still carrying the child, with Owen trailing in his wake. He passed the baby to Owen, kissed Roysia on each of her pale cheeks, and turned to Niall. "I saw the doubt in your eyes."

Niall fell to his knee, his head bowed, shame and joy and awe all washing through him till he feared tears might roll down his cheeks, too. "I'm sorry, Your Grace, for doubting." His voice cracked.

Bruce's smile grew. "Your King hears you. Rise."

Niall raised his head, lowering his voice. "But why did they leave?"

"Maybe one day we'll know." Bruce beamed. "Whatever the worldly reason, I name it a miracle."

CHAPTER TWENTY

Glenmirril, April 1317

"Edward Longshanks, you'd have to see him to believe how tall he was!" MacDougall had come to enjoy regaling Red with tales of his days in the Crusades. "You should have seen him the day he sailed into Acre."

"Tell me again about Baibars sending his men to get baptized," Red said.

MacDougall glanced at Taran, pressed against the wall in the cell grown dim with twilight, arms crossed over his chest, and eyes narrowed. The boy had seen little beyond Glenmirril itself. Over the past weeks, he'd inched closer, as MacDougall told his tales, finally coming into the cell itself, still pretending he wasn't interested.

MacDougall brought his eyes back to Red, telling the story for the third time. "Edward saw quickly that it was a ruse." He leaned forward, embellishing the story with hand motions. "They came at him out of the water, and quicker than a flash, he had his sword through one, his dagger through another."

"What's Acre like?" Red asked. "Bigger than Carlisle?"

"Much bigger! Walls a thousand feet high!" MacDougall stared up beyond the confinement of his own small cell. "The sea bluer than anything you've ever seen, so clear a man could see to the bottom, shores of sand finer and whiter than flour." He glanced out the window, to the rain pouring down from the evening sky. "The sun shone all the time." He resisted the urge to say the walls had been covered in gold. Sometimes, the sun had beat down so strongly, it seemed they were.

"You were there?" Taran asked.

Red and MacDougall both turned to him in surprise.

"You fought the Mamluks?" Taran asked. His curiosity creeping over his hatred, he took a step closer. "Did you *see* Baibars?"

"Not close up," MacDougall admitted. "Across the battlefield, maybe. Vicious man. Merciless, and prided himself on it." He liked the boy, he thought in surprise. He wished Duncan had ever taken time to ask about his crusading days with Edward, or play chess, or talk theology. But he wasn't biding his time in MacDonald's tower to find a replacement son. He studied Taran a moment, and took a chance. "I've concern for my wife," he said.

"Your wife?" Taran's eyes narrowed.

"Aye. I've hoped to send her a message."

Taran turned abruptly. "'Tis no concern of mine. Gilbert! Open the door! Red, come away now."

MacDougall sighed, watching them leave, wondering if he'd really undone months of slow and steady work that quickly. It didn't matter. He had time.

Ireland, April 1317

His Grace's summons reached Niall as the campfires dwindled to embers and the men rustled into tartans in the night dew. Bruce sat in a hard chair, one elbow propped on its arm supporting his chin, as he gazed at a silver crucifix shining in the candle light on the small table. "Play for me," he said softly.

Niall seated himself obediently, and pulled out his harp. He closed his eyes, losing himself in music with the poignant chords he knew would lift his king's mood. When he looked up some time later, Bruce heaved a sigh. "Think you on Butler's departure, Your Grace?" Niall ventured.

Bruce nodded. "We witnessed a miracle today."

Niall laid his harp across his knees. "Yet you do not speak with joy."

Bruce's brows furrowed as he gazed at the crucifix. "'Tis no lack of joy, but ruminations."

"On what do you ruminate, Your Grace?" Niall asked.

"I am thinking I would gladly know one day that God granted a miracle because He deemed me worthy to ask. But such was not the case today."

"Was it not?" Niall asked in surprise. "You are a God-fearing man, Your Grace."

Bruce lifted his eyes to Niall. "I killed Comyn before the altar at Greyfriars."

Niall nodded reluctantly. Bruce had been a hot-headed youth. There had been deep contention over the throne. Comyn had betrayed Bruce to Edward of England.

Bruce spoke again. "I've often thought 'tis the reason I've lived hard these many years. I've lost almost all whom I have loved. My friends, brothers, wife, and daughter have all died. I killed a man on holy ground. I've been ex-communicated more times than I can count." Bruce lifted his flagon from the table, swished it, and sipped. "Yet time after time, I see that when I act out of compassion and humanity for others, our Father smiles on us and blesses us with His protection."

They sat silently for a few moments before Bruce said, "Play a bit more. Your music gives me peace."

Niall lifted his harp, touching the strings, while Bruce slumped back into thought, staring at the crucifix. After a time, he lifted his hand. Niall lowered the harp. "Your man, Owen, is taken with the laundress," Bruce said.

"He is," Niall agreed, curious about the direction of such a statement.

"Hugh's recovery goes poorly."

"He tries to rise from his bed too soon," Niall replied. "He's near starvation."

Bruce studied him momentarily before saying, "You've not heard from Brother Andrew?"

Niall's heart jumped. He kept his face impassive. "I have not, Your Grace."

The edge of Bruce's lip quirked as if in amusement. "An interesting man, your devoted monk. I'd fain meet him again."

"I shall tell him, should I hear from him." Niall's heart thumped more loudly. He was lying to his king. He desperately wished the Bruce would say no more of Brother Andrew, whose existence he couldn't explain.

"A shame. I'd a mission for him." Bruce leaned forward.

Niall resisted the urge to back up, and fought to keep his voice even. "Your Grace, perhaps I can be of service in his stead?"

Bruce smiled. "I suspect you will do it as well as he would have."

"Your Grace?"

"I want you to take Owen, the laundress, her child, and Hugh, back to Scotland."

Niall's heart jumped in elation, disbelief, and relief. Bruce wasn't pressing for answers! He was going home! William would have grown a great deal in the months he'd been gone! As quickly as joy had come, panic shot through. It meant another sea crossing. With only a small group, it would be a smaller boat, nearer the gray, drowning waves that had claimed Alexander and spit him back out, white and bloated and matted with sea weeds. His head became light, seeing his brother's face.

Bruce was speaking. Words floated above Niall's head. He drew breath, trying to push away the image. "Your Grace? My apologies."

Bruce cleared his throat. "I said, I believe Owen and Roysia would both be pleased were I to issue a royal decree for him to wed her."

Niall smiled, thinking of a lifetime ago in the future, where Amy was shocked at the idea of being ordered to marry. The Bruce, he thought, was a man ahead of his time, to even consider Owen or Roysia's wishes. "He's a good man," he told his king. "He'll treat her well."

"Aye, 'tis clear. I saw him today beg to put his very life between her and harm. There can be no greater love. Tell your laird it is my wish. Send them to Glenmirril. You will take a message to Jamie Douglas."

"My Lord?" Niall's eyebrows shot up.

"Hugh and Roysia must get to Glenmirril," Bruce explained. "That leaves you. Would it were different, but I choose carefully whom I trust with messages. You and Brother Andrew seem equally trustworthy."

"Yes, Your Grace." Niall bowed his head, hiding the color that touched his cheeks at mention of Brother Andrew—Bruce knew—and hiding his disappointment that he would not go straight to Glenmirril. But Bruce had been separated from Elizabeth and Marjorie for eight long years, and spent more time than any of his men away from his family. He'd barely had a marriage; his small grandson was Scotland's only heir, as a result.

"Tell Sir James I'm returning to Scotland, and to summon the lords to a council at Scone in June. I want you there, too."

"Yes, Your Grace." It was the highest honor, for his king to summon him to council. It left no time to return to Glenmirril. The months since his wedding ticked through his mind, most of them spent far away. He thought of Shawn, with his family each day. Anger welled in his chest, joining the swirl of emotions that had swept over him since he'd stepped into Bruce's tent, on top of the emotions of the day, of watching an army mass, ready to crush them, yet inexplicably turn away.

"We've much for which to be grateful," Bruce said. "We have seen God's hand this day."

"We have, Your Grace." It was as if the king had read his mind, Niall thought. And Bruce spoke true. By all rights, he should be dead on the battlefield, not going home to Allene and his sons at all.

"We'd have fought bravely, but if we could defeat forty thousand in our present state, I know not."

Niall bowed acknowledgment before asking, "From where are we to take ship?"

"Carrickfergus. Take twenty of your men. You leave at dawn."

Never had those words sounded so good to Niall.

"Your Grace?" A voice called softly outside the tent. "We've found an English soldier in camp."

Niall and Bruce rose hastily, the harp left against the chair, and hurried into the cloudy night.

Bannockburn, Present

It was several days and dozens of encounters later, that Simon saw a slender boy with long, thin hair walking down the street, carrying a black case like that which Amy carried. Simon followed him. After several blocks, the boy turned into a store. Cautiously, Simon entered. Hidden by a shelf of cans and boxes, he listened as the boy chatted with a girl in another aisle. His irritation grew as they discussed the warm summer, her purchases, her sister's dance class. They moved down the aisle. On his side of the shelf, Simon followed, keeping out of sight. Their talk turned to a favored teacher.

"Can I help you, sir?"

Simon startled at the voice at his side.

"Can I help you find something?" an elderly man repeated.

"No," Simon snapped.

The man wiped his hands on an apron, frowning, but walked away. Simon glared after him, hoping he hadn't missed anything important. The voices on the other side of the shelf had grown softer. He hurried down the aisle, listening. "...said anything about him?" he heard. They rounded the corner, nearly bumping into him. He ducked his head and edged away, pretending to study a row of green bottles.

"I've not seen her since he got back," the boy answered.

"When's your next lesson?"

Simon edged around the shelf, once again separating himself from their view, but listening. A violin, lessons. Had he finally stumbled on a way to find her?

"I had to take the summer off. We're going on holiday."

"Did you hear what he's saying?" the girl asked in amazement.

"Aye, medieval Scotland!" the boy chuckled.

Simon smiled at the bottle in his hand. Yes, he'd found someone, finally, who knew Amy. Their voices drifted toward the front of the store. Simon set the bottle on the shelf and headed out into the bright sunshine, waiting down the street. When the boy came out, Simon sauntered up alongside him. "Is that a violin?" he asked.

The boy glanced over in surprise. Then his face broke into an easy smile. "Aye."

In Simon's time, the lad would be tending a knight's horse, learning to fight, perhaps going to his first battle. But he had the innocent eyes of a youth who hardly knew war existed, had never seen blood, never heard men cry in pain as their life ebbed away. Simon smiled. The innocent were the easiest to get information from. They thought all were just as they were. "Do you know Amy Nelson?" he asked.

The boy's eyes lit up. "Aye! I take lessons with her!" He spoke with pride. "Do you know her?"

Simon shook his head. "No, but I hope to. I've a boy who would like to study violin." Be careful not to appear too interested in where she lives, Simon warned himself. He put on an air of concern. "Is she a *good* teacher?"

"Oh, she's grand now, she is!" the boy exclaimed. "I've moved to first desk since I started studying with her."

"Have you?" Simon had no idea where desks came into anything. He asked a few more questions, playing the part of concerned parent, before asking, "Can you show me where she lives?"

The boy hesitated for half a heartbeat, before smiling again. "Aye, just around the corner." He led him another half block, before turning pointing down a street. "Middle of the street, blue door. That's hers."

Simon smiled. He gave a curt nod to the boy and walked toward the house. As he neared it, he saw the door partially open and heard voices. Her car sat in the front, one door open, and boxes in the back. Now, in broad daylight, was not the time. He glanced over his shoulder. The boy was gone. Simon strode past. He would return at night to deal with the child.

Bannockburn, Present

"So, that's it." Shawn lowered the last box to the kitchen counter of Amy's new home. "It's kind of bare."

Amy shrugged. "I like the space. James doesn't care."

"My mom took him out?"

"To the park." Amy opened a box on the far end of the counter and began lifting out dishes. "She said it's too nice a day not to take advantage of. She's picking up dinner, too." She set the plates in a cupboard. "I guess—I suppose it would be okay for you to have dinner with us."

"Thanks. Yeah. That'd be nice." He reached into the box for a handful of silverware, and glanced around before choosing one of two drawers to drop them into. "The beds were delivered?"

She shook her head. "Not yet."

"They're supposed to be here," he said.

Amy shrugged. "We still have a night in the old place, if they don't show up." She lowered her eyes. "Thank you for ordering them. I've been meaning to, and the days slipped away. The new quartet, the piece Conrad wants me to arrange, new students...." She'd also spent the last days preparing for a trip to the States to record an album. She'd put off mentioning it to Shawn. In the past, he'd have had some critical comment.

"You're busy. You're in demand. I'll have a table for you by dinner."

"We'll be fine, Shawn. You have your own house to get in order." She cleared her throat, staring at the floor. "I didn't give you much warning about finding your own place, back on Iona."

"No. It's okay. I'll get you a table. You know in my mind, I consider us...more. We have a child. I have responsibilities."

She gave a nervous laugh. "I can hear Niall saying that."

Shawn grinned. "Yeah, well, he might have rubbed off on me. A wee bit. Like a bad skin condition."

She smiled, meeting his eyes, with the gold flecks dancing in the brown depths. All the good feelings rushed back, all the flutterings of the heart and weak knees he'd always made her feel. "Have you tried to find out what happened to him?" she asked.

Shawn's smile slipped. He shook his head. His hand trailed over the box on the counter. "You have your tea kettle around here somewhere?"

She opened the box under his hand, aware of him less than an inch from her. Her stomach flipped. She pulled out the kettle and two mugs. Shawn picked up the one from Eileen Donan, studying the image of the castle. She didn't volunteer that Angus had given it to her.

Shawn cleared his throat. "No, I've been kind of, well...afraid...to find out. What if it's bad?"

Amy focused her attention on the crystal stream of water pouring into the kettle. "I don't want to think that."

"It matters to you?" he asked curiously.

She looked up from the water. "Of course it does!"

"You only knew him for two weeks."

"He's like you, Shawn. He makes an impact. He was good and kind. Even Allene left strong impressions on me, just from what he said of her. I can't stand to think of anything bad happening to them." Water burbled from the spout. She turned off the water and set the kettle on the stove top.

Shawn snapped on the burner. His arm grazed hers. "That makes two of us. Except if something bad happened that night, you're not guilty of leaving them."

"Oh, Shawn!" She turned to him, throwing off her concern about getting too close. Her fingers closed on the bell sleeve of his linen shirt. "You *wanted* to come back; they wanted that *for you.* Anything could have happened, good or bad, and it could have turned out either way, whether you'd stayed or gone."

He shrugged, turning away so her hands fell off him, and pulled the rose-covered china teacups from the box. "Where do you want these?"

"The cupboard, the shelf above the plates. Why don't you at least try? You might find something good and set your mind at ease."

Shawn lifted a cup gingerly from its wrappings, the paper crinkling loudly in the empty kitchen. "He was important in his own time. But historically speaking, not so much. There won't be much on him."

"But with the internet...?"

Shawn paused, his hand on a teacup, resting on the shelf. "I could," he said slowly. "How could I have forgotten?"

"Forgotten what?" Amy dug through a box looking for coffee.

He frowned, speaking as if to himself. "Because it's been seven months since they gave it to me. So much has happened. Aye, I can find out...maybe." His hand slid from the cup. "But I'm not sure I want to."

"At worst, your fears will be confirmed." Amy pulled out the coffee. "At best, your mind will be put at ease."

"I would need to go to Glenmirril." Shawn rested his hands on the counter, his head down. "I've had mixed feelings about that."

Amy touched his back gingerly. "Put your mind at ease, Shawn. Would it help if I went with you?" She wasn't sure she wanted to, either.

"You want to?"

She shrugged. "I'm sure you feel the same; even more so. Too many disturbing things happened there, and so many good memories, too."

He nodded. Steam billowed from the kettle in watery puffs. "It's disturbing to think I'll be so close to Niall and Allene, yet be unable to touch them and speak to them." The kettle whistled, a high-pitched shriek. "When do you have a day free?" he asked.

She pulled out her phone, studied its calendar, and said, "July 27."

He sighed. "Okay. July 27, Glenmirril." He glanced around the kitchen, blank as a new slate but for the boxes of dishes. "Well, we have food, dishes, blankets. Should we spend the night here or in the professor's house?"

"I don't want your mom having to sleep on the floor," Amy said. "If the beds don't show up, we'll sleep there."

Shawn glanced out the window, still light, and then at his watch. "They're running out of time. Come on. Let's find my mom and James and see about dinner, and then we'll have to make a decision."

Ireland, April 1317

"Your Grace."

In the glow of the flickering campfire, Bruce acknowledged the Highlander waiting at the edge of the circle. His hand rested on the arm of another man, wearing a surcoat with English arms. Around the campfire, men stiffened and lowered the meat or bannocks they'd been about to eat. Several held weapons. Niall's mind settled on his own dirk, in his boot; his thoughts turned to Hugh, once again taken to bed with fever.

Bruce studied the intruder.

His brother Edward circled the man. "How do you come to be in our camp?" he demanded.

"He comes freely," said the Scot, "asking to join us."

Edward looked the man up and down, studying his black beard and the helmet nestled in the crook of one elbow.

But it was Robert who spoke. "Why?"

"I'm Irish." The man's brogue gave evidence he spoke the truth. "I want them out of my country. I left as soon as I could." He dropped suddenly to one knee, bowing. "Please, Your Grace, let me fight with you."

Bruce came a step closer, studying the man. "Were you with Butler?"

"Aye, Your Grace."

Bruce glanced at his commanders, and at Niall. "Why did Butler leave?"

Niall felt his excitement rise at the question.

The man looked up. "My Lord, he said one as cautious and wise as the Bruce would not fight with so small a force; that if you stopped and waited for us, then sure an you had reinforcements nearby."

The king's smile grew. "Aye. We had powerful reinforcements." His eyes met Niall's. "My Lord Niall summoned them, did you not, Sir Niall?"

Niall smiled back. "Your Grace, it seems my men and I did. Your words, as ever, were wise."

"Wise enough only to know things come aright when one does the right thing for the right reason."

Inverness, Present

Angus hesitated at the front door of the police station, second-guessing. He should just walk out that door and leave for the night. It wasn't fair to Claire. But then, maybe, it was. He liked her company. They'd had fun at the Games. He had to let Amy slide into his past.

Claire looked up from her desk. Her eyes lit up. "Hello, Inspector! Are you off for home? How was the donut?"

"Grand, thanks." He smiled, thinking he should walk away and leave her alone. His heart wasn't in it, not really. But she *was* nice. He'd been entirely honest with her, and she still wanted to see him. He closed the distance between them in a few steps, and squatted down, arms on her desk. "I'm, uh..." He cleared his throat. It felt different, very different, from offering Amy a coffee. Everything had seemed natural and easy with Amy. "My pipe band is playing at Glenmirril." Amy had wanted to hear him play. It wouldn't happen. "Would you like to come?"

Her face shone. "When?"

"The twenty-seventh, in the evening."

Claire glanced at the calendar on her desk. "I'm off that day."

"I have to be there early," Angus said. "But we could meet in the coffee shop, before I start playing."

"I'd love to."

Angus smiled, and rose. He had the same sad, reluctant feeling he did, on waking from a good dream, and forcing himself to get out of bed and leave it behind, no matter how much he looked forward to the day. Amy had to slide into the realm of pleasant dreams that needed to be left behind. Claire was nice. "Thanks for the donut," he said, and headed out into the evening.

Bannockburn, Present

As clouds slid across the face of the moon, Simon boosted himself over the wall, and dropped stealthily into the small garden behind Amy's house. In the next yard, a dog barked. Simon slid his knife from his belt, and waited quietly, pressed to the wall. A child's voice called, and the dog quieted. Simon inched along the wall toward the kitchen door. He tried the handle and smiled. It was unlocked. He eased the door open. It swung in soundlessly. He put a foot to the floor, gently, testing. It was silent. He glanced around the tiny kitchen, lit only by a stray moonbeam. It was empty. A hall stretched before him, dark and silent.

He moved down it stealthily, to peer into the room at the end. Moonlight skimmed through lace curtains, throwing dappled shadows over a couch, low table, and wing chair. The small fireplace was cold and dark. A book shelf stood behind a chair at the far end of the room, stretching up to the ceiling. Simon turned for the stairs, moving slowly, wary of creaks. At the top, his knife drawn, he peered into the first cell. It was one of their bath chambers. Beside it was a bed chamber. Moonlight showed the covers stretched neatly, flatly, across the empty bed in the dark room. Frowning, he entered, checking the wardrobe in the wall. It was empty. He listened, but heard nothing. He moved down the hall. The room at the far end held a desk and tables, all bare. Simon turned to the room on his left. Its bed, too, was neatly made. The hair prickled on the back of his neck. She wasn't here. Had she left town for some reason? He opened the closet doors and the dresser drawers. They were empty. There was no sign of a woman or a child. There was no sign of anyone at all. *The place was empty!*

He spun, teeth clenched, and drove his knife into the wall.

Glenmirril, April 1317

"His bell is linked to miracles, too?" Red's eyes were round in wonder, shining in the candle light that warded off the dark of another overcast day. Rain came down in sheets outside MacDougall's window, leaving a puddle on the sill, in addition to the eternal damp chill.

"Aye, for pains in the head," MacDougall reminded him.

"They say our king brought his arm bone to Bannockburn!" Red said.

MacDougall smiled tightly. He shut the heavy book, and rose, handing it to Red. "Give your Laird my deepest thanks."

"Oh, aye!" the boy assured him.

"You're reading on your own?" MacDougall asked. Helping the lad read cemented the bond that existed in Red's mind.

The boy bobbed his carrot-top hair with enthusiasm. "Aye, my Lord, though little enough time is left after the horses."

MacDougall studied him. "They say you're quite good with them."

"Oh, aye, they're my brothers!" Red grinned broadly, and launched into a description of the Laird's stables, to the steady percussive beat of the rain, enthusiastic about the care given to the animals.

MacDougall listened patiently, scooping up any information carelessly dropped.

"My own horses were a great source of pride to me," MacDougall interjected. "I worry about them."

"Certainly your steward sees to them?" Red said.

MacDougall hung his head, just a little so as not to overdo it. "Aye, my fine hobins...." But his fine hobins were in MacDonald's stables. "Of course, there are few there now, but I worry, too, for my...orchards. My steward is not as familiar with them as am I. I wish I could speak with my wife on these matters."

"Do you think they'll have fared at all well with all this rain?" Red glanced at the downpour outside.

MacDougall sighed. "There are ways to tend them in such weather. Their fruit would help my people in this difficult time."

"Could you not write to her and tell her what needs doing?"

MacDougall looked up, surprise and gratitude stamped carefully on his features. "Why, Lad, could I? For the people of Creagsmalan? Would you ask your Laird?"

"Aye, I'll ask," Red said, and almost immediately switched back to his narrative about Glenmirril's hobins, and one that had been given to Sir...the boy hesitated, a soft *shh* whispering from his mouth, before saying, "...to Sir Niall. And my Lady Christina, now." He launched into a story regarding her horsemanship.

MacDougall leaned forward, as eager for news of Christina as for details of Glenmirril's operations.

"Red!" Gil appeared at the door. "Stop talking to him, and come out of there!"

Red stopped, mid-sentence about Christina's palfrey. "I was only after saying...."

Gil frowned. "Aye, and you ought not."

"He was reading to me about St. Fillan."

"I can read to you about St. Fillan, now, can I not?" Gil swung the door open, casting a disdainful glance at MacDougall in the gloomy cell.

MacDougall raced to the door as it swung closed. "You'll ask?" he called to Red.

The boy grinned. "Aye, of course."

"You'll do no such thing." Gil's key clicked in the lock. "He's up to no good."

His fingers wrapped in the bars, MacDougall watched the two walk away as Taran, watching suspiciously, took over.

Bannockburn, Present

Amy's house was empty!

Fury burned white hot in Simon, hotter than the stove before him, where a chunk of meat simmered in a pan. He'd found the cavernous, abandoned building on his return to Bannockburn. It had a small room at one side with a cooker, a few abandoned utensils and dishes, and a long table—a fine camp while he decided on his next move, and an excellent place to train. Its long walls were covered with dozens of outlines of men, lunged and speared over and over.

But he'd been foolish to let anger consume him, to leave damage to her wall that would surely raise alarms. It might be best to vacate Bannockburn for a time.

He shoved at the meat with a wooden spoon, and returned to the table, to the bound leaves of parchment waiting there. A *notebook,* the mistress at the market had called it. And a *pen.* In the midst of learning Brian's world, he'd barely thought about these pens until he had to seek one out himself. It felt strange in his hand, short and light. She'd looked at him strangely when he'd requested ink. "You've the ink *in the pen already,* Sir," she'd said, slowly and distinctly, as if he were perhaps touched. He'd smiled coldly, laid bills on the counter, and taken his purchases. He would find ink at another store, if this *pen* failed to do as she'd implied.

He'd vented his rage—at the woman, the monk, at Amy, James, her empty home—on a hideous looking youth in black leather, in the alley behind the shop. It had felt good to see the arrogance in the boy's eyes slide into fear, to sink his knife into flesh, take power. He'd replenished his money—the boy carried a great deal —and as he purchased a bottle of wine, savored the image of the market woman finding the body. She would know. She would take his warning.

Doubtfully, Simon set the *pen* to the clean white vellum—weak and thin compared to parchment, and white as bleached petticoats. It glared on his eyes. But his pen worked, ink flowing. He stopped, turning the *pen* to study it from every angle. It held so little ink. He wondered if he should have bought more. Perhaps it was his purchase of only one which had left her looking at him strangely.

It mattered not. He filled the lines, in his own familiar English, with his plans for his return. *Seize power from Edward. Fortify Berwick. Move more English lords north. Rebuild Northumbria. Regain Scotland.* Inch by inch, foot by foot, he would take back what that fool Edward had lost. He added another line, pressing hard.

Raze the land, destroy the Scots.

He studied the words. *Destroy the Scots.* He had until Christmas. He must learn more of the weapons of this time. He would use them to destroy any who opposed him. He would kill every last Scot, bring peace to Northumbria. The people would hail him for ridding them of the pestilence from the north. He would tighten his grip on Ireland and Wales.

It must be a long term plan, fueled with patience and deliberation.

With Scotland, Ireland, and Wales subdued—something even Longshanks had failed to do—his armies would sweep across France, Spain, all Europe. He would seek this land across the ocean, the vast continent where Shawn journeyed, and it would be his.

He studied his list, sipping wine. Yes, he had a great deal to learn about this time's weapons. But little good it would do him, if he couldn't learn how to move through time. It was still dangerous to seek Eamonn. The altercation was too recent, and he might find himself once again in jail. Shawn had disappeared across the great ocean. Amy's house was inexplicably empty. Behind him, the meat sizzled.

Simon frowned, tapping the pen on the eye-blindingly white *notebook*. Why? Had the boy lied to him, misled him? Had he given the boy cause for suspicion? He didn't think so. Had the boy simply been wrong? That seemed impossible. He studied with Amy. He'd been to her dwelling numerous times.

Simon rose, pacing. Did it matter? She was not there. Bannockburn was uncomfortably large for finding a woman, but small enough he was beginning to recognize people—and they might begin to wonder why he was still asking after her. Especially now, with damage to her home. He looked for a place to jab his pen, but remembered the ink didn't smear, and dropped it on the table as he returned to poke at the meat.

He had other options. Helen, the scholar with the snake-like hair, knew a great deal. The *library* he'd found—its thousands of books might hold answers. Still—it would be wiser to leave Bannockburn for a time.

He made his decision. If the monk spoke true, he had until Christmas. Five months still. The more he knew before he found Eamonn, the more power he held. So he would speak with Helen, pursue any ideas she had, and return in a few weeks' time to search the *library*, when people had forgotten the hole in Amy's wall.

Simon downed his wine, and snatched up his sword, whirling and piercing the hearts of the phantom enemies inked on his walls, a dozen neat, clean strokes that left the plaster in shreds, before the meat sizzled again. He smiled, satisfied, and poured another glass of wine.

CHAPTER TWENTY-ONE

Carrickfergus, Ireland, April 1317

It was a ragged group that stood on the shore, looking across crashing gray waves to Scotland, somewhere beyond the misty horizon. Home and Allene and his sons pulled Niall. Fear for Hugh pushed him. The sight of the long, low fishing boat, its stern scraped up on the shore, paralyzed him. Niall stared at it in dread.

Roysia stood on the shore holding her child, Owen's hand on her back. Salty sea wind blew her long hair in her face. She huddled over the baby, wrapped in a threadbare blanket. The boy lifted his head into the wind, crying with cold. Niall took off his cloak, wrapping it around Roysia and her bairn. He couldn't deny the miracle that had saved the boy's life on a battlefield. His king had ordered him to pray, yet he struggled to utter prayers that would bring no relief.

Hugh leaned on Niall as the first men climbed into the boat. "You did it once," he murmured.

"Angus Og's galleys are larger by far," Niall whispered back, feeling green. "I was farther from the water." But he closed his eyes, forcing out a silent, *St. Brendan, pray for me.*

"'Tis bigger than a currach," Hugh whispered. "Harps. James on the shore."

A ghostly smile slipped past Niall's mouth. He *had* made it across once, after all, even if not in Shawn's swashbuckling manner.

Hugh inched him a step forward. "Think on Shawn swimming, the day we went hawking with Christina."

The smile grew. Niall felt the sun of that day, bright despite the cold, bursting in flashes off the loch, and Shawn splashing in, and out again, flinging water from his hair, shaking with cold; Christina laughing as she watched, Brother David looking on in astonishment.

"Help me in," Hugh said.

Niall blinked, stunned to find himself at the boat, with no memory of moving closer. He closed his eyes, steeling himself against the vision of Alexander, forcing himself to see Allene smiling on the shore, and managed to lift one leg over the stern. He braced himself, but Hugh's weight was half what it should have been, and Hugh tumbled into the boat. The men who had already climbed in caught him, easing him to the floor of the craft, where he crashed and curled on his side, knees pulled up, breathing heavily.

"Sir Niall," Owen called.

Niall turned to see Roysia waiting, Owen at her side, for help climbing in as she bounced the crying baby.

"Get in, Niall," Hugh gasped from the bottom of the boat. "Harps. James."

Niall drew in a sharp breath, put James in his mind, laughing in the wind behind Glenmirril, and put one foot in the boat. Alexander hovered, pleading for attention. There was sand firm under his foot. He took the child into one arm and held out a hand to Roysia. The front of the boat swayed, rocked by the waves. Alexander's white face wavered before his eyes. His stomach turned. *Faith is trusting our king's plans, without demanding we understand them first,* Bruce had said.

"Niall?" Owen's voice reached him. "Sir Niall?"

Harps, James, Niall told himself. He could send them off, find an excuse to stay. He stared at Roysia's white hand in his, and helped her into the boat. He could pass it off as duty, courage, nobility. Roysia settled onto the bench over Hugh, leaning to touch his shoulder and murmur to him.

Owen sighed behind him, betraying impatience.

Hugh raised his head. "Get in, Niall." He reached for his hand, pulling.

Niall stumbled, his second boot dragging over the low stern. He hated lying, he reminded himself.

Roysia touched his elbow, looking up at him with concern.

"Something you ate?" Owen asked, and to Roysia, "You should have seen him at Jura, born to water, jumping from bow to stern, fighting like a madman sure as if he was on dry land."

Shame boiled in Niall. It had been Shawn. He hated lying, and he'd be lying most of all to himself, if he stayed, trying to pass it off as duty and courage. Staying would be cowardice, as it was only his fear of water that would induce him to do so. Besides, Bruce had charged him with a message to James Douglas.

He took up his oar, trying to think of the harp on his back, and Allene and his sons before him; of Shawn in the loch, swinging one arm after the other. The last of the men settled into place and lifted their oars. Niall closed his eyes against the bile in his stomach, refusing to look at the smashing, gray waves, throwing themselves high over the side of the boat. He threw the shaking of his arms into pulling the oar, seeing Shawn's arms swinging, his legs slicing the water, with each pull of the oar. A few hours, and he'd be on dry land again. He had to believe it.

Glenmirril, Present

"Things settled with the professor?" Shawn asked, as he angled her car into the last parking spot in the lot above Glenmirril.

"Mmhm." Amy studied the castle, its pennants snapping, and crowds thronging the gatehouse. It seemed unusually busy. "Although I can't understand how I never saw that hole. Even behind a door like that...."

Shawn shut off the engine. "Anything else out of place?"

"Nothing."

They fell silent, neither she nor Shawn making any move to leave her car. Neither spoke for some time. Finally, Shawn put his hand on the door handle. "I don't know what we're scared of."

"Not scared." Amy glanced at him, once again wearing breeks and a loose, linen shirt, his hair bound back.

"What, then?"

She lifted one shoulder in resignation. "I don't know. Just—a lot of memories, good and bad here. I feel like they might swallow me."

"Better to face it, huh? I told Niall that about water. Nothing's going to happen."

"You haven't told me exactly where we're going."

Shawn leaned back against the headrest. "There's a cave way down, through the dungeons. Only a few of us knew about it."

"Is it open to the public?"

"I hope not," Shawn said. "More chance everything's okay down there."

"What's everything?" she asked. "What is it you're hoping to find?"

"Listen, let's just look around. Enjoy the castle. There may not be anything there. I don't even know if the way is open to the Bat Cave."

"The Bat Cave?" she murmured.

He laughed. "Like Batman and Robin. Drove them nuts I called it that. They don't really get the concept of superheroes." He corrected himself. "Didn't get the concept. Wrong tense. They're gone."

Amy's mouth tightened at the sorrow in his voice. She didn't know how to comfort him. She looked at the floor, at her hands on her denim-clad knees. "Well, let's go, then."

They left the car. The sun shone brightly on Glenmirril's walls. Shawn leaned on the roof of the car, staring across the wide lawn below, over the castle walls into the two baileys, the northern one solid and strong, the southern walls half in ruins. He looked wistful. Amy studied the scene, trying to imagine what he saw.

"Last time I stood above Glenmirril like this," he said, "I was hiding in the trees with Niall and Lachlan and Owen, Gilbert, Red, Hugh, the Laird. We could see MacDougall's army on this side of the moat, and MacDonald's men on the parapets, waiting. I could smell the boiling oil all the way up here."

He painted a vivid picture. With pine trees scenting the air, she almost feared that if she closed her eyes, she'd be in the midst of it, feel the trees crawl back down the slopes to reclaim the parking lot and visitors center, feel their spindly fingered limbs brush her cheek and tug at her hair; smell the heavy scent of men in the woods, waiting to kill.

"Amy?"

Her eyes snapped open. Her breath came hard. "I'm sorry."

"I shouldn't tell you these things. It's outside our world."

She shook her head sharply. "No, it's okay. Talk, share, right? Without it, what do we have? Maybe we should get our tickets."

He rounded the car and took her hand. "But this is sharing too much. How can you cope with knowing I killed men? More than a few."

She tried to slow her breath. She wished he would stop talking. "Allene must know Niall...." She stopped. She couldn't say it. "It was a different world. You've come back kinder. What else matters? It's getting late. Let's go in."

They walked to the visitor's center for their tickets. As Shawn pulled out his wallet, Amy saw the poster beside the ticket booth. *Inverness Police Pipe and Drum Corp. July 27. 5 p.m.* They'd driven more than two hours to be here. Still, she touched his sleeve. "Shawn, could we...?" Her eyes fell on the tickets in his hand.

"Ready?" he asked.

West of Scotland, April 1317

"Stand tall," Hugh whispered in Niall's ear, even as Niall supported him. They clambered out of the craft together, Niall wondering who carried whom. "Harps, James. Don't puke now, lad, you made it."

Niall managed five steps up the damp sand, half-pulled along by Hugh, before he staggered, and dropped his hands on his knees, barely keeping himself upright. The sound of the waves slapping the boat's sides made him sick.

"Stand up, Niall," Hugh commanded.

At his side, Niall felt Hugh sway. He needed to find horses, get Hugh and Roysia to Ayr where they would receive care until they could make the long journey to Inverness, get messages to James Douglas. *Harps, James,* he told himself. He'd made it. There was no reason to feel ill now. He pushed himself up, hearing Roysia's bairn cry on the beach behind him—the child whom only a miracle had seen safely into this world—as Owen helped her out of the boat. *St. Brendan, I'm here,* he managed to pray. Maybe he was being demanding, expecting St. Brendan to deliver him to shore with the same elation Shawn would have felt.

At his side, Hugh crumpled. "Niall," Lachlan shouted, "help me!"

Glenmirril, Present

"Shawn, we really shouldn't!" Excitement and trepidation mingle in me as they so often do with Shawn, as we stand at the top of a dark, narrow flight of stairs.

Shawn grins over his shoulder. "There are no no-trespass laws in Scotland." He squeezes my hand.

I give a weak smile. Angus said the same thing. There are no no-trespass laws and no police anyway. Except me. *I don't want to go down, where maybe we aren't supposed to be.*

"We paid admission to the castle, so let's see it all." Shawn winks. "Not my fault I know more than the tour guides, aye?"

His logic is unassailable, his sense of adventure infectious. I find I want to see the underground cavern, perhaps undisturbed and unknown for centuries. I want to see where Shawn and Niall spent time. And I don't want to see the pipe band that will soon be parading in the bailey, not for my sake, not for Angus's. I'm unlikely to meet him deep in the dungeons, in a cave only six people knew, seven hundred years ago.

"Will you?" Shawn asks. I realize he's waiting for an answer. Another change — he never used to wait, but always pulled me along, assuming I'd happily follow.

I nod. "As long as we're not breaking through any locked doors. Your batteries won't give out, will they?"

"Doesn't matter. I can do it in the dark if I need to."

I give my head a sharp shake. "No. I don't want to be down there in the dark."

"Brand new." He pats a pocket in his baggy trews. "Plus I've got spares. You up for it?"

I nod again, this time with certainty, and he almost skips with glee down the rough-hewn stairs. As the gloom reaches out, he switches on his flashlight. It's beam slices the dark, illuminating earthen walls.

I squeeze close. "It's safe? It won't cave in?" I think of James, back home with Carol.

"They won't." He plays the light from the earthen floor to an arched roof overhead. "There were dungeons." He falls silent. I wonder what he's thinking about those dungeons. Suddenly, he shakes himself, and moves. Another hundred feet, and the flashlight illuminates a yawning maw on the right. Shawn swings the beam around the cell. The air here is colder and staler than in the passage.

I shudder. "Did they leave people to starve to death in there?"

"I'm sure any bones have long since been removed." Shawn steps in.

"That's not what I asked," I say.

"In MacDonald's time, I'd like to think not."

"Even though we can't judge by our own standards?"

"Yeah, even though." Shawn backs out of the cell. He shines the flashlight up under his chin, turning his face into a spectral mask, as he drags the last word out into a ghostly moan. "Th—ohhhhhhhhh!"

"Shawn, stop it!" I laugh, a nervous shield against the eeriness gripping my neck in an icy vice. "Let's get out of here."

He slips his arm around me, a comfortable feeling, and leads me deeper down the tunnel. "There should be six more." We squeeze together side by side in the narrow passage. Dirt walls brush my sleeve, but I don't want to be behind, not even with the safety of his hand around mine. His voice, counting off the cells, lights the pressing dark as much as the flashlight. "To the right," he says, and shortly after, "To the left. Same hand we wear a wedding ring on in my time."

A chill snakes through me. "You're in your time."

"So I am."

I follow, forced behind him, finally, as the walls narrow, trying not to squeeze his hand too hard, trying to shake the feel of long-dead fingers raking through my hair and down my back. "The bat cave was a happy place," I whisper. "We'll feel that, won't we?"

"I hope so."

"What did you do there?" I hate the pitch of my voice that betrays nervousness. But I prefer betraying my fear to letting silence close in alongside the dark.

"Played the sackbut, mostly." He falls quiet. I've come to recognize these times: he's drifting away to his memories, a place he only sometimes invites me to follow.

I squeeze his hand. *"You want a future, you and me. Then tell me about your life. Did Niall or the Laird come down with you?"* I find myself reluctant to say the name Christina.

"Yeah." He sounds distant, though I press against his back in the dark. *"Sometimes I played for them. Sometimes Niall played the harp."*

"You liked it?" I wonder if Christina watched him play. I feel a stab of jealousy, remembering watching him that first time at the jazz club, and the rush of excitement that it was me he was thinking of. Did she feel the same?

Shawn gives a short bark of laughter. *"It was hardly Lincoln Center."*

"Again, not what I asked."

"I loved it." His voice is husky, a world of pain and loss wrapped in three words. *"I loved playing for the monks of Monadhliath. I loved making people happy, no matter how small the crowd was."*

He falls silent, following the beam of light, and this time, I let him. His confidence has driven back some of the fear. Still, I tread on his leather-booted heels, as the tunnel narrows even more and the ceiling closes in, scowling just over our heads. *"We're not going to have to crawl, are we?"* I whisper.

He chuckles. *"No. Hugh had to stoop a little at the very end, but it doesn't get any smaller than this."* Seconds later, he stops. He swishes the light over the wall on his left, feeling it with his free hand.

"Shawn?"

His hand stills on what I guess is a door. He drops his forehead on it, shoulders bowed, and draws a deep, shuddering breath.

I lay my hand on his back, my cheek on his shoulder. *"We don't have to,"* I say.

"I want to." He lifts his head, and clears his throat. *"I just wish I'd see them on the other side."*

"If it hurts...."

"I'm fine." His words are sharp. He hands me the flashlight, runs a hand up and down the door, jiggles a latch, and finally, draws back and powers his shoulder into the wood. It splinters; the sharp stench of decay erupts into the dark tunnel. I gasp. Shawn braces himself against the wall and kicks. The door swings in on its hinges. So much for not breaking through locked doors.

"It doesn't matter," he says. *"No one's been here in years."* He laughs, though even he sounds a little shaky, and tries to make a joke. *"Probably still uses the same key the Laird did. It's long gone."* He holds out his hand and I place the flashlight in it. He offers his other hand. *"Walk in with me,"* he says.

Glenmirril, April 1317

"You've discussed dinner with the cooks?" MacDonald looked up as Allene entered his solar. At his side, Brother David fell silent.

She nodded. "I've checked the spices and set the menu for next week. I've looked over the stores of flour and meat."

"What of Conal?"

"He's working with the boys. Red is tending the new foal. Darnley is in the armory, and Morrison is looking over the estate accounts."

MacDonald sighed. "'Tis too much work for the few of us. Have there been no messengers?"

"None," she said. "I'd have come to you straight away." She crossed the solar to her sewing basket, selecting a half-sewn baby shirt, and taking out a threaded needle.

"Christina?"

"In her room, and looking happier than she has in a long while." She nodded at the easel by the window, which bore a half-finished drawing of two lords and a lady riding horses, with hawks on their wrists. The faces were startlingly life-like. "You see she's begun to draw again. 'Tis a good sign."

Her father said nothing.

"Though we must come to a plan soon." Allene pushed the needle through the shirt and lifted her eyes to her father. "The child is a month old. He cannot be hidden forever." They both turned to Brother David.

He cleared his throat. "I learned singing and theology, Milady. 'Tis sorely lacking in the practical art of subterfuge, I am. I cannot but think but Shawn would have an answer."

"Then we must think like Shawn." Allene poked the needle into the tiny shirt and drew it through.

"I've tried," MacDonald snapped. "Naught but impertinent remarks come to mind! 'Tis no help a' tall!"

Allene's mouth tightened against a smile that would only anger him. He missed Shawn as much as any of them, she was sure. Instead, she gave them her news. "Red says MacDougall is again asking to correspond with his wife."

Her father turned to the window, staring out at the hills to the north. "He's been in the tower for ten months. He's been a model prisoner."

"He's sly and deceitful." Allene said firmly. "We've lived at peace with the MacDougalls, without him and Duncan stirring up trouble."

"But can I hold him forever?" MacDonald wondered. "If a day comes I must release him, would it not be better to do so with the possibility of peace between us?"

"There never would have been peace," Allene said. "Not with Duncan alive and sure not now he's dead."

"He discusses theology and St. Columba at length with Red. Perhaps with time on his hands and an interest in his Lord Savior, he is as much changed as Shawn?" He glanced at Christina's drawing. His brow darkened. "As much as we *believed* him to be."

Allene's lips pursed, but no longer in amusement. "Shawn himself would not believe a man could change so much."

"Shawn had no faith in God. I do." MacDonald turned to the monk. "What say you, Brother David?"

Brother David stopped writing. "I say," he said, jabbing his quill into the ink jar, "that Glenmirril is known far and wide to be as innocent as doves. Your example to your people is commendable. But that is not all Scriptures say to be."

"Be wily as serpents," MacDonald mused. "Do you think I am not?"

"You are wise. But MacDougall is wilier by far. Why is he so concerned for his wife? He has until now had no use for her but for her lands and money."

"Perhaps he misses her. The loss of a son will often set a man to thinking on how he's lived his life and what is left him."

"I wish to see the best in others," Brother David said. "But 'tis not always wise."

"The question remains, however," said the Laird, turning from the window, "will it cause more problems in the future to deny a simple enough request?"

"Will it cause more problems," Allene asked, "to allow communication which he may use to plot against us?" She dropped the sewing to her lap. "Father, you *know* he'll direct his anger at Niall."

"You would read all communication, of course," Brother David suggested. "I think perhaps 'tis safe as long as you read carefully, well aware that all may not be as it seems. Perhaps you will even learn something of his true mind."

"You're not thinking of allowing it, surely!" Allene rose abruptly from the settee, the sewing hanging from one hand.

"Perhaps I will," said MacDonald. "Allene, send for Gil."

Glenmirril, Present

Together, we squeeze across the threshold. Shawn flashes the light high into the chamber. I gasp—a gasp of delight this time. "It must be fifty feet up!"

Shawn draws breath and lifts his voice. "Oh, come, oh, come Emma—a—an—uel." His song echoes off the high ceiling and bounces back from the walls, as if a Heavenly choir harmonizes his bass.

"It's beautiful!" I breathe.

He continues singing, drawing in great lungs full of air, as he leads me around the perimeter, a sea of darkness cut only by the flashlight's beam. He stops at the wall on the left, and the words Ransom captive I—i—is—rael die away. He puts a hand out, touching empty space. "The Laird's workbench—it's gone." The flashlight sags in his hand, pointing to the line where wall and floor meet.

I touch his arm. "It's seven hundred years, Shawn."

He laughs, a rough, ragged sound that doesn't convince me. "Yeah. Of course. But where did it go? It was huge."

I touch his arm tentatively. "Niall loved and admired him. Tell me about him."

"He was amazing." Shawn sags to the floor, his back against the wall where the workbench stood. The flashlight shines up into the ceiling somewhere high above. I hear him disappearing into the mist of memories, but this time, he offers me a hand to walk along. "Tough as nails. But he cared about people."

I think of Christina, wondering if she followed Shawn down these tunnels, clutching his hand as I did.

Shawn pats the floor, inviting me. I join him, leaning into his shoulder, liking the feel of his arm around me, and the vibrations of his voice as he talks. We're back in the best of our good days together.

"Allene came down here, and Hugh and Brother David. I used to argue theology with Brother David." He grins. "He got so riled."

I smile. "I bet you did, too."

Shawn laughs, a sound sad enough to call the dead to himself. The flashlight settles, sending a trail of light across the dark floor, and he talks, his words weaving to life Lachlan, Owen, Taran and his one-eyed father, the boy, Red, the Morrison twins, and Hugh, until they seem to be all around, the colors of the tapestries vivid, and fires blazing in the hearth. Any moment, the Laird's great hunting hounds might let loose with a big woof, and nose my hand for a scratch. Time disappears, as we walk together in the past.

And then, Shawn scrambles suddenly off the floor, leaving me disoriented and scrambling up after him. The flashlight springs to life, lifting to the walls. "The crucifix hung over there." It takes a moment for him to find a deep recess. He shines the light all over the walls, feeling them with his hands. He stops, frowning.

"What's wrong?" I ask.

"There were recesses on each side. How can they be gone?" He's agitated, angry. "They were carved out of solid rock!"

"Could they have been filled in over the years?"

He shakes his head. "No!"

"Boarded up?" I suggest.

"Yeah. Hold this."

I take the flashlight. He goes back to feeling the walls, probing like a master surgeon, seeking. Abruptly, he starts rubbing, scratching. "It's here!" His voice rises in excitement. "I found it!" As he did at the cave's entrance, he backs up and slams a shoulder into the wall.

I wince at the impact. "Is it that important?" I ask.

He doesn't answer, but backs up a second time, and a third. I think he must surely break his shoulder. "Shawn, stop it!"

He gives his head a sharp shake, and slams into it again, fierce determination on his face.

"What's in there?" I ask. A shiver trickles down my spine, thinking what ancient secrets might be boarded up in this hidden cavern. Maybe even bones.

The wood splinters on the fifth impact, shooting the smell of rotting wood through the air. I sneeze hard in the puff of dust and dirt. But I'm grateful, because I know this side of Shawn, the manic who won't stop until a passage is perfect, until his goal is accomplished. He grins, rubbing his shoulder. "It's here."

He tears at the remaining wood, ripping into it, tossing it like a madman. I back away against the opposite wall of the recess, wondering if this is the man he was on the raids with James Douglas. He stops as suddenly as he started, breathing hard. "It's here." *He speaks in awe, as if beholding a relic.* "It's still here after all this time!"

He puts a foot inside the wreckage, reaching in and heaving out something large and heavy. I stare in shock. It can't be. "A kneeler?" *I ask.*

He wrestles it out into the niche, looking as pleased as if a new trombone has just arrived. "Yeah. They made me a kneeler."

"A kneeler? Like what you kneel on in church?" *I ask in disbelief.* "For you?"

Shawn laughs aloud, his head thrown back. The sound echoes through the dim cavern, up beyond the reach of the flashlight. "Yeah. I know, right? That's what I said when they showed it to me."

"I'm still having a hard time imagining you in church." *I lift a hand to my nose. The stench of rotted wood is acrid.*

He doesn't crack the joke I expect, but says, "It got to feel kind of peaceful." *He drops the object in the middle of the floor with a thud. Ancient dust explodes up into the beam of the flashlight. He grins up at me.* "Not my normal fare, huh? Shine the light over here."

I shine it on the side. He drops to one knee, eyebrows dipping. His fingers skim the wood, up under the armrest. He exhales, smiling, and closing his eyes in what appears to be silent thanks. A panel slides off into his hand. I swallow, my body trembling with nerves. "They built it for me." *He pulls out a long, bulging roll.* "With a secret compartment so they could leave me letters."

Christina flashes across my mind. I feel her, suddenly, beside me, watching him.

He looks up at me. "What's wrong?"

"Nothing." *But the feeling is unnerving. She's here. Watching him. I wonder if he feels it, too.*

He scrambles to his feet, looking at the kneeler. "I guess there's no way to get it out of the castle." *He hands me the roll. It's oiled skin. It throws up a new musty odor as he leans to pick up the panel. Gently, as gently as he treats his trombone, he fits it back in its hidden compartment. He stares at it for a moment, then pats it, and turns brusquely.* "Let's go."

"Should we give this to the historical society or something?" *I lift the package.*

Annoyance crosses his face, visible in the flashlight's glow in the black cavern. "They're mine."

"How do you know?"

"They're in the kneeler they built for me. Specifically to leave me messages." *He snatches it from my hand, as he once snatched his cell phone.*

"Christina left you messages?"

"She was here that day. She might have." *He speaks nonchalantly, but he turns, not waiting for me, and strides across the cave.*

I catch up to him in the doorway. "Can I see them?"

He spins, the light in his hand wobbling drunkenly off inky walls. "She's seven hundred years dead, Amy! Are you going to accuse me of cheating on you with someone who's dead?"

I resist the urge to slap him. "The best defense is a good offense," I snap. "It's time you told me what happened with her."

"Nothing. Absolutely nothing." His anger slashes through me like a whip. "I kissed her fingertips once. Social convention. Are you going to hang me for that?"

"You were in love with her!" I slap him with the accusation. My own anger spins into the old, familiar dance with his. "She was down here with you, wasn't she?"

"Totally chaperoned. We were alone once for about half a minute. Even I can't get far in thirty seconds."

"You're far too modest." I throw as much acid into the words, into his face, as I can.

"Not something I'm often accused of." He glares down at me. The tendons in his neck stand out.

"You have no cause to be angry with me," I throw back. "It seems we're visiting places you went with Christina—here, Iona—not places I went with Angus. I deserve at least an explanation."

"I was there for two years," he snaps. "I never touched her. I came back for you. You understand I could have stayed there. I chose you.*"*

A pain digs sharply in my chest, a fingernail twisting and drawing blood. I could have anyone. I'm here with you. *It didn't mean much the last time he said it. I withdraw a step, half-turning away.*

He deflates before me, in the shadows thrown up from the flashlight that hangs limp in his hand. He hangs his head. "I'm sorry, Amy. I want to do it right this time. And I'm still screwing it up." He draws breath; rakes a hand through his hair, and addresses short, curt words to the wall. "She came down here a lot. I wonder if she's here even now."

I wonder, too. "You loved her." The words are no longer an accusation.

"I respected her. I admired her. I felt safe with her." He shrugs. "I don't know what I felt."

My anger drifts away into the darkness, in the face of this meek and apologetic Shawn. I touch his hand. "I think you felt love. You've never known what love feels like. Genuine love."

"I'm sorry," he says.

I'm not sure what he's apologizing for.

Then he adds, "That's not true, you know. Those other women, I know that wasn't love. But I did love you. I do *love you."*

"You admire and respect me?"

He nods, staring at the floor. "Somewhere along the line, I realized what I saw in her was exactly what I loved in you." His voice is soft. He's not accustomed to such raw, naked honesty. "And all the failings I saw in you later, what I saw as your weakness, was what I did to you myself." He lifts his eyes, finally, to mine.

I wrap my arms around myself, not knowing what to say to this new and humble Shawn. He's right. It seems unkind and unnecessary to say so, when he's admitting it. "It seems a little ironic," I say, choosing my words carefully, "that you're upset about Angus when you feel exactly the same about someone, yourself."

"I walked away from her." His voice is insistent, pleading. "I left her in the past, knowing I was walking into a time where she's dead. Would you have walked away from Angus for me?"

"No." I shake my head. "But you cheated on me. And I still did everything in my power to get you back. At the cost of hurting him."

Shawn pushes at the dirt with the toe of his leather boot. He turns his head, swallows. The flashlight, pointed at the floor, throws shadows across his face.

"I'm not happy about that," I add. "Just a reminder: I thought you were dead and never coming back."

"Okay." He stares at the far wall, at the floor, anywhere but me. "Yeah, I understand." He looks at me, finally. "I'm sorry."

I stare up at his shadowy face, deciding how important it is to read any messages Christina may have left him. She's seven hundred years gone, after all. "Tell me about her," I say softly. "Share that part of yourself. I won't ask to see the scrolls."

"Okay." He nods. "I can do that. I just didn't want...."

"To hurt me. I know." We've been down here a long time. The pipe band should be long gone. "Maybe we should get some light and air."

"Yeah." He pulls the remains of the door shut, tucks the scrolls under his arm, and slips his hand in mine, leading me through the dark, twisting labyrinth, back to light.

Stirling, Present

"Delightful to see you again!" Helen sang, as she slid into the booth.

Simon smiled, a taut drawing of his mouth that made the tendons in his neck stand out. Knowing what to expect this time did not make her snake-like hair less hideous, or the clacking of the ball in her mouth less disturbing. "And you," he lied smoothly. The door would open in December, and he needed answers.

Helen leaned across the wooden table, placing the glasses on her nose, and peered at him. "You asked what happened with Shawn. Did Amy not tell you?"

He shook his head. "Not entirely, and I've not seen her again."

"Oh, that, I'll call her for you."

"What I'd like," Simon said quickly, "is to know where she dwells so I might call on her myself."

Helen pulled out her *phone.* "I'll ask her now."

Alarm reared in Simon. He waved a hand nonchalantly. "As we're here, won't you tell me yourself what happened?"

"I told you some of it already," she said.

"No matter." Simon looked up as the waitress approached. "What shall I have the serving woman bring you?" He smiled, pleased with himself for learning the social conventions of the day.

Helen glanced at him with a frown, and turned to the waitress. "Haggis, please."

With their orders placed, Simon said, "Start from the beginning."

Helen leaned forward, forgetting whatever had caused her to frown. Her eyes lit, she launched into the story. He almost forgot her clacking tongue as she entranced him with a recap of the tale of Shawn Kleiner, a bard of fame and wealth, with a woman in every town, a love of good ale, and lucky at games of chance and Amy, his mistress, leaving him in Glenmirril overnight.

The waitress appeared with their food. "Och, that American!" she said. "Woke up in that castle calling himself Niall Campbell, did he not?" She rolled her eyes. "How my girls went on about it, fancying him as they did!" She slid a plate of chicken in front of Simon, and haggis before Helen, and set down their drinks. "Though I'd not mind running my hands through his hair, myself now!" She winked.

"Niall Campbell," Simon mused, when she'd gone. "A fourteenth century inhabitant of Glenmirril, was he not?"

"Aye." Helen stabbed a fork into her haggis. "How an American knew such an obscure historical figure was a matter of much speculation. His father, they say, loved Scottish history, so 'tis possible...."

"After he awoke calling himself Niall Campbell?" Simon cut off her blathering, not interested in her erroneous speculation. She'd no clue what had really transpired.

"After that?" She looked at him, her fork in her dinner. "His obsession with Bannockburn. They say he was *mad*, researching, printing up maps of the battle and grounds. Amy took him to the Trossachs. I don't understand why she'd have done, when 'twas so clear he wasn't right in the head."

"The Trossachs, rather than Bannockburn," Simon said. "Why?"

"To find a man named Hugh."

"Malcolm MacDonald's brother." Simon dug into his chicken. Juices ran down his chin. He wiped them with the back of his hand.

"Aye." Frowning, Helen dabbed at her own chin with a cloth. "You being a professor, it shouldn't surprise me you know that. But...." She tilted her head, studying him. The rope hair bobbed.

"But?" Simon inquired.

"Excuse me for saying, no offense, you don't *seem* like a professor."

Simon lowered his chicken, smiling. "Nor do you." The learned men of his time had been, well, *men*. And the wise women didn't behave with such levity.

Helen threw her head back and laughed. "Touche." They smiled at one another for a moment, before she resumed her attack on her meal, and added, "He came out of the mountains, straight to the re-enactment. He spent the evening before playing the harp...."

"Niall Campbell played harp."

Helen lowered her fork. "You *are* well versed on Niall Campbell."

Simon shrugged. "The story's been bandied about, hm? But Shawn plays the large sackbut."

"Sackbut? They're called trombones these days. But it seems he did indeed also know how to play harp." She took another bite, and resumed the story. "He took part in the re-enactment—odd thing for an American and a musician. 'Twas not planned as part of their tour here, sure, and there was quite the uproar as to what possessed him to go out on that field, and where he got medieval clothing."

"Did they ever learn where?" Simon asked.

Helen shook her head. "No. And when it was over, he was simply *gone.* Then he turns up, back in the tower of Glenmirril, wearing his re-enactment garb, carrying a sword, covered in filth, and making a joke of it all—after a *year* of being gone, after all the money and time they put into looking for him!" Helen, for the first time since Simon had met her, looked angry. "All he put Amy through, even hiking up to Monadhliath with a new baby, and what does he have to say for himself, but tall tales about fighting with the Bruce!" She harrumphed. "I can't believe she'll have aught to do with him!"

Simon's mind worked. There had been two men. If Niall Campbell had been in Helen's time, gone to the battle and disappeared a year ago, and Shawn had only just re-appeared, that meant Shawn and Niall had both lived in his time for a year. His eyebrows knit. Niall had crossed twice. So had Shawn. So there *was* a method. He leaned forward. "Let's play a game, shall we?" Excitement shimmered in his voice.

"Depends on the game." Helen set down her fork.

"You'd say Amy behaved out of character, taking him to the Trossachs when he was clearly mad?"

"Absolutely!" Helen declared. "Anyone will say she put up with his womanizing far too long...."

Simon raised his eyebrows. A man was entitled to his mistresses.

Helen went on, oblivious. "But she seems to me to have a decent head on her shoulders, for all that. Even women with sense fall in love and put up with nonsense in the hopes they'll change. So it never made sense, her watching him behave as they say he did, and taking him to the woods like that."

"But it *would* be rational had it been Niall Campbell," Simon suggested. "If in fact Shawn Kleiner is not telling tales, but the truth."

Helen's eyes grew wide. "What are you saying?"

"I'm saying," Simon said, "that if the two switched places in time, if Niall Campbell of fourteenth century Glenmirril was here, then his behavior—studying Bannockburn, trying to get Hugh MacDonald and his men from the mountains to fight—would be quite sane. So, too, then, would *her* behavior be quite rational."

"Aye, but...."

"Remember—a game." Simon smiled, lifting his mug to his lips. Ale slid, cool and pale, down his throat, as he watched her over the rim.

She pursed her lips, staring at the ceiling. "As a game..." Her eyes came back to his. "*If* this were true, then...?"

"How did it happen?" Simon finished. "If men moved across time, what, in your knowledge of Scottish history, could explain it?"

A smile grew on Helen's face. "Why, Simon Beaumont, you *continue* to surprise me! First, a sense of humor. Now, an imagination. If you don't mind me saying, you don't seem one to take flights of fancy, any more than you seem like a professor."

"Say as you will." He smiled. "But tell me how such a thing might happen."

"It couldn't," she said.

"*If* it could?" His smile tightened. She wore on his nerves. He modulated his voice. "If you knew it had *indeed* come to pass, how would you explain it?"

"Hm." She took another bite, chewing slowly. "Well," she finally said, "I'd look at Michael Scott, Thomas the Rhymer, and Lord Soulis."

"Lord Soulis." Simon stroked his smooth chin. "*William* de Soulis?"

"Certainly," Helen said. "With his reputation? If time travel is possible, it might involve some mystery or magic, aye? And who do we know in Niall's time who had such things?"

"Yes," Simon agreed. He should have thought of that. "They did whisper he knew the black arts."

"And learned them, they say, from Michael Scott. And you no doubt know Thomas of Erceldoune's claims."

Simon nodded. In his youth, he'd met the old and stooped Thomas, shortly before he disappeared—back to Elfland, many whispered. He knew William de Soulis well, from the years he'd been loyal to Edward. He'd admired the man, but been wary of him. He did carry a strength that defied nature. "What became of Lord de Soulis?" he asked.

Helen's brows drew together.

Simon understood this was something a professor ought to know. But William had been alive and well last Simon had seen him, ready to fight at Bannockburn. He frowned. Perhaps he'd died there? "A head injury." Simon pulled back his hair, revealing the scar, a reminder of that terrible day, the heavy armor, sweat trickling inside it, as he struggled to rise and defend himself against the sword flashing down. "I forget things."

"Of course!" Helen glanced at the scar, pulled her eyes away, and took a quick gulp of her ale. "Well, there's the official story and then there are rumors."

"Indeed?" Simon lifted his eyebrows. "The official story is?"

"Died in confinement at the castle of Dumfries, 1320 or '21."

"And why was he confined?"

"For a plot against the life of King Robert."

"It failed?" Simon asked.

Helen gaped. "Of *course* it did! Did Bruce not sign the Declaration of Arbroath in 1320?" She glanced at his temple. "I'm sorry. I...."

Simon smiled. "I do have unfortunate gaps in memory. What of the rumors?"

Her eyes lit up. "Oh, now much more interesting, those!"

"Rumors always are," Simon said dryly.

She threw her hands suddenly up into the air, rolled her eyes, and exploded, "Boil him if you please, but let me hear no more of him!" Her ropes of hair quivered.

Simon drew back in surprise. Around the tavern, heads turned.

Helen laughed, straightening herself. "So said the Bruce. There was a steady stream of complaints against Soulis's cruelty and tyranny."

"A man must keep his tenants in hand," Simon said.

Helen laughed. "Certainly an understatement. People said he was invincible, due to his sorcery."

"They did say that," Simon agreed, ignoring her misinterpretation of his words as jest. "Neither rope nor hemp could bind or hang him. Steel couldn't cut him. Water couldn't drown him." He leaned in. "So what did they do?" He would have power over de Soulis, too, when he got back, armed with such knowledge.

She lowered her voice, though it thrilled with the tale as she leaned across the table. "Three hundred sixty knights and squires gathered. They wrapped him in lead torn from Bruce's own castle, and boiled him alive at Nine Stanes Rig."

Simon's eyes narrowed. "*Which* knights?" He would deal with them! Or perhaps—lead them.

Helen drew back. "Well, I haven't a *list*!" She cleared her throat. "Of course, 'tis not the only version of the story. Another says 'twas the villagers who gathered. One says 'twas the Cout of Kielder and his party, invited to dinner and then murdered, that was the last straw, while another says 'twas Alexander Armstrong, Laird of Mangerton."

"*Armstrong?*" Simon asked. "William would not ask his inferior to dinner."

Helen tilted her head, studying him a moment before answering. "Soulis tried to carry off a young Armstrong girl to his castle. Her father tried to stop him, and Soulis killed him on the spot. A crowd rose up. Only Alexander Armstrong could calm them. Soulis was angry that the crowd had listened to his inferior, but not to him, so he invited Alexander to dinner and killed him."

They fell silent, Simon eating, and drinking his ale. None of it told him a thing about time travel. "What's left of Hermitage Castle?" he finally asked. "Are any of William's possessions still there?" He'd heard stories that possessions sometimes retained a person's power.

"They say a key of his was found in the 1700s." She shrugged. "But where that is, I couldn't say."

"You said if time travel were possible, you'd start with him. Was there ever any belief he did such a thing?"

Helen shook her head. "No. Only that he is said to have practiced dark arts."

Simon sighed. He was getting nowhere. "Thomas Learmonth, then. Did he move through time, and how?"

Helen laughed. "I doubt anyone today believes that."

Simon did not smile. "He was known far and wide as True Thomas, who could not lie. And he says he did."

Helen studied him a moment before answering soberly. "He also says 'twas fairies. The Elf Queen. So if you're looking to travel through time, and turning to him for answers, you'll need to find yourself an Elf Queen." She glanced at her half-eaten meal, dabbed her mouth with her napkin, and tossed it on the table.

"Excuse me. I find I'm not feeling well." She rose, leaving the tavern without looking back.

Simon watched her with narrowed eyes. The Hermitage, he decided. He would hunt through de Soulis's home.

Glenmirril, Present

My uneasiness returns as we climb dark stairs toward gray light above. There is no sound of a pipe band. But some of them might still be roaming the castle grounds. Another three steps, and I notice the quiet above. "What time is it?" I ask.

At the top of the stairs, Shawn glances at his watch, squinting as sunlight hits us after so long in the dark. "Past nine. It's closed."

"We were down there that long?" Uneasiness stirs, as if I, too, have been caught in a time slide.

"Looks like it." He looks around the empty courtyard, then grins at me. "Unless they changed the law since we went down, we're still free to go to the tower."

"That tower doesn't scare you?" I ask.

He shakes his head. "Niall won't go near it. And I don't think anything happens, except on the Feast of Columba." I hesitate, still. He tucks the oilskin inside his shirt, takes my hand, and says, "Come on. Last one there is an out of tune oboe."

A corner of my mouth quirks up, but I give my usual answer without enthusiasm. "That's redundant."

We walk hand in hand to the tower, not racing as we would have once, but climbing worn stairs curving up through the cool dim tower, past the last splash of sunlight pouring through the cross in the archer's slot.

In the tower, a cool breeze blows. Evening light shimmers on the surface of the loch far below. Shawn leans his arms on the parapets. I don't want to ruin the moment. But I don't want what we had—when fear silenced me. I speak softly. "Tell me about Christina."

He stares out over the wall for so long, I think he isn't going to answer. Then he points to the hills. "She'd ride over those hills, with Allene and Bessie to bring food to the poor. She spent a lot of time in church."

I hold my desire to make a sarcastic comment about the unknown Christina, who did nothing wrong, ashamed of my petty jealousy.

"She drew, she embroidered altar linens, she sewed clothes."

My hand hovers over his back, and falls away, realizing. "Like the shirt you're wearing?"

His shoulders tense. "And the pants," he says softly. He turns from the hills, studying my face. "You want honesty, Amy, I haven't forgotten she made them, but they're comfortable. The jeans felt so stiff the first night, I couldn't move. I've had extra pairs made since I came back. This pair I have on now isn't Christina's."

He knows exactly which pair she made. I bite my lip, trying to rein in pain, trying to have a conversation that helps us, helps me, trying to understand. "You were...." I search for the right word. "Friends?" I think of Dana. I think of his angry rejoinder that he only kissed Christina's fingertips. He would regard it as sullying Christina to ask, Friends like Dana?

"We talked. She accepted me with all my faults."

I draw back as if slapped. "So did I."

"You did." He stares at me, seeming disoriented for just a moment, and then says, "It was me. I was different by the time I met her and I was able to see what she gave. I understand now what you offered."

I bow my head, hating my jealousy. I didn't exist, after all. If I can believe him —and I do—he didn't touch her. But he gave her his heart. I realize, now, that's far more painful.

I give a little laugh, thinking of his feelings about Angus. "We're a fine pair, aren't we?" I stare at the flagstones. "Maybe we shouldn't be trying to fix this."

"I came back to fix it," he whispers, a white-hot blaze in his voice. "I came back to make it up to you and do it right. There's James."

I raise my eyes, studying his face, the face I loved, wanting it to be as it was in the early days. "Do you think we can really get through this?"

He leans back against the parapets, and pulls me into his waiting arms. His fingers push through my hair. "That's up to us, isn't it?"

His touch, in my hair, on my cheek, sends thrills through me. When he pulls me against his shoulder, holding me, I forget everything in the warmth of his arms, in the beat of his heart through the linen shirt rough against my cheek, a shirt made by Christina's centuries-dead hands. I close my eyes, telling myself not to rush, not to let emotion or fear rule, to think it through—for myself, for Angus, for James.

His hands caress my back. His lips brush my temple, and all thought melts. Overhead, a bird calls; in the hills, a sheep bleats. The glow of the sinking sun presses through my closed lids, turning my dark world rosy. "I've always loved you," he whispers. His hand slides under my chin; his lips press mine, soft, testing.

Everything else disappears but his hands in my hair, his body against mine, remembering everything I ever felt with him, and all I ever wanted.

And suddenly he jerks back, tensed for battle.

My eyes fly open, disoriented. His head is up, listening. The sky glows; streaks of pink and peach bounce off the silver stone walls around us. "Why...?"

He touches a finger to his lips.

I tense, too, as voices reach me, a woman's words on the stairs, light and playful. "Are you sure we should be here? I'd not want the police upset with me."

"You'll not upset the police," comes a gruff voice. He sounds impatient.

I yank back from Shawn. My heart trips over itself and then races to catch up.

"I'd want to be sure, now." The hint in the woman's voice is clear.

"I promise." He sounds amused now.

Their voices dip for the space of two largo measures. I bite my lip, avoiding Shawn's eyes.

"It's him, isn't it?" Shawn whispers.

I nod. A giggle drifts up from the stairs. I swallow, not wanting to hear it.

Then: *"Inspector!" followed by a quick gasp and a laugh.*

I stare at the flagstone floor of the tower, my jaw tight. The sounds from the stairwell stop. I desperately pray they'll go away.

"Wonder what they're doing?" Shawn raises one eyebrow.

The silence is broken by a sudden flurry of feet. I step away from Shawn, bracing myself. She bursts into the tower, laughing, turning to look behind her, not noticing us. Angus appears, his eyes on the girl, and reaches for her hand, smiling.

Then he sees us.

The smile drops instantly. In the dusk, red flares up his cheeks. His hand springs from the girl's. "Amy!"

The girl turns to us, still smiling. She looks to Angus staring at me, and back at me, as I stare at Angus. "Oh!" She opens her mouth to say more, then stops.

"Claire, this is Amy." Angus clears his throat. "Amy, this is Claire."

I blink hard, stung. I bite back the words he said to me not so long ago. Didn't take you long. *I swallow the ache, clamp hard the lip that wants to tremble, and hold out my hand. "Nice to meet you."*

Claire takes my hand. "And you," she says, but it sounds more a question than a statement.

Shawn slides an arm around my shoulder and holds out his own hand to Claire. "Shawn," he drawls.

She takes it, smiling uncertainly, and looks back to Angus.

Angus clears his throat again. "Have you, uh, been up here long?"

Shawn cocks a lazy grin at him. "No. You know it's a magic tower. We just dropped in, just now, from 1296. It was quiet on the stairs when we got here."

I glare at him.

The color deepens on Angus's cheeks. He looks at me, and his eyes slide away. Then he meets my eyes again. "Where's James?"

*"*My son *is home with my mother." Shawn emphasizes* my son.

"Give him my love," Angus says softly, ignoring Shawn. He takes a step forward.

I nod, blinking hard, staring at the floor. My hands grip one another.

"Claire, we should go," Angus says, and to me, "I'm sorry. I didn't know you were here. I'd not have...." He stops. "I'm sorry." He turns, reaching for Claire's elbow, saying, "Careful, now, it's dark on the stairs," and they leave.

We stand silently for a full minute, the dusk growing around us, watching the empty doorway. Then Shawn slaps his hands together. "Well. Back to our regularly scheduled kissing?" he asks sardonically.

My arms wrap around my body, seeking warmth. I want to run to the west wall and watch Angus cross the courtyard. I force myself to the east, looking out over the mist rising on the loch, straining my ears for any sound from Angus and Claire, for the sound of a car departing.

"Come on." Shawn drops his hands on my shoulders, trying to pull me around.

I shrug him off. "Just give me a minute," I say.

"You were only seeing him a few months. I'm back, we're working it out,

right?"

"You haven't wanted to hear anything I've said, these past six weeks. I love him." I stare at the dusky water below. Shadows swirl in its depths, beneath the mist. "I promised to marry him."

"No, you can't have," Shawn says. "Why would you do that unless you slept with him. Did you?"

I snort. "Seriously? Are we back to that? You can be the one to wonder for once. I'd agree to marry him because I love him. I love being with him. I love his voice. I love his humor."

"Then why...?"

"Why am I here with you?" I spin to him in exasperation. "Because I'm torn, Shawn! Why is that so hard for you to understand? He's a good man."

"Yeah, so am I. I'm a good guy now, too, remember?"

"Ugh!" I throw my hands in the air with an ugly grunt of frustration. "You are so clueless."

CHAPTER TWENTY-TWO

Inverness, Present

"I'm sorry, Claire." Angus stood by her car. She reached for his shoulders, rising on tiptoe to kiss him. His hands stayed at his sides, and she lowered herself again.

"I know it was recent with her," she said. "I know you still feel for her. I'm all right with that."

"You shouldn't be," he said. "You deserve a man who loves you above all. You shouldn't be second in anyone's affections."

She stared at the ground. Her hand lingered on his arm. "You've not enjoyed our time?"

"I have."

"Then we can have dinner, go to the cinema. It need not be serious."

He shook his head. "Claire, not now. Maybe in a few months. But now, you'd be spending your affection hoping for things that may not happen. I'm sorry."

"I'll still set aside your favorite donuts?" She looked up hopefully.

He shook his head. "Treat me like any of the others, Claire. Don't wait and hope. I'm afraid you'll be disappointed."

"Is that not what you're doing with her?"

He nodded. "And it's foolish and it hurts. Which is why I'd not want to see you do it to yourself."

"But when we kissed, I felt...."

He turned her to the car. "I was wrong." He wouldn't hurt her by saying he'd felt none of what he'd felt kissing Amy. He'd hoped he would. But he hadn't. It had been pleasant, nothing more, and he'd felt empty, missing all that should go with love. "I'm sorry, Claire."

West of Scotland, April 1317

With a large silver moon filling the open window, Niall sat by Hugh's bedside, gazing at the still, gaunt figure beneath the fur. His big beard rose and fell with his shallow breathing. A fire flickered in the grate.

"He's awake?"

Niall looked up to see Roysia enter with a large, steaming bowl, and a towel.

"Not now," he replied. "But he's woken several times. He'll not leave us."

"God be praised." She set the bowl on the bedside table, and touched Hugh's head. "I thank our good Lord that Adair has taken us in."

Niall smiled sadly. Yes, God had granted them refuge. A cool breeze blew through the stone casement behind him, into the stifling sick room.

"Will I pull the shutters?" Roysia glanced out at the stars twinkling against the black sky.

Niall shook his head. Shawn had been big on fresh air. In the bed, Hugh stirred, and opened his eyes. He gazed at the hangings for a moment, before turning to Niall.

"Roysia has brought you soup." Niall grinned. "But you'll have to stop lying about, and sit up."

With a groan, and some help from Niall, Hugh managed to pull himself upright against the pillows. But his hands shook so that Niall lifted the spoon for him. "I'm away to Douglas at dawn," he said, as Hugh sipped. "You and Roysia will bide here. My Lord Adair will care well for you."

"Where will he find food for two more?" Hugh whispered. Even his voice was weak and thin compared to his former robustness.

"We're on the Irish Sea," Niall replied. "It provides well."

Hugh's head sank back against the headboard, worn from his few words and effort to eat.

Roysia lifted the spoon, her hand under it. "There you are, Hugh," she murmured. "A few more bites, and we'll leave you be."

Hugh obediently opened his mouth, though his eyes remained closed.

Niall watched as she patiently fed him. "I hate to leave him," he said softly.

"Food and rest are all he needs." Roysia eased the spoon into his mouth, and wiped his beard. "He'll be strong as an ox ere you return."

"I pray 'tis so," Niall replied.

"You're leaving soon?" she asked.

Niall nodded. "At dawn. I came to say good-bye."

Hugh opened his eyes, looking from Niall to the girl. "Thank you, Roysia." His voice came out more strongly than it had just minutes ago, though he didn't lift his head. "I must speak to Sir Niall."

She bobbed a curtsy, and laid the bowl and cloth on the table. "Yes, sir."

When the heavy door closed behind her, Hugh struggled up off his pillows. "Promise me." His eyes burned with some of his old energy. "Stop at every loch and put your foot in."

Niall's lips tightened. His illness on the boat was bad enough. That he'd allowed Roysia to believe the lie of sea sickness only fueled the shame. "I've a mission," he said curtly.

"Put your hand in," Hugh pressed. "Move your arms. Think how Shawn swam. You must *try!*"

Niall said nothing. The memory of the nightmare boat ride, his stomach heaving with each swell of the waves, feeling sicker with each spray of sea water into the boat, had not loosened its grip. He'd woken with sharp jolts, the two nights they'd been here, seeing Alexander's face.

"Promise me," Hugh rasped. "Or I'll rise from this bed to go with you and *make* you. And that'll be the death of me." When Niall said nothing, Hugh reached for his arm, squeezing, saying, "Just a hand, Niall. You know you must do *something.* Anything. Promise me!"

Niall drew a deep breath. Just a hand, he told himself. A toe or a foot. He'd done that much on the shore behind Glenmirril. He sighed. "I will."

Hugh sank back into his pillows. But he smiled.

Niall gripped Hugh's hand. "Get strong, Hugh. I'll see you soon, aye?"

"Aye," Hugh agreed with a grin. "You canna be rid of me so easily as all that."

"God be with you, Hugh." Niall squeezed his shoulder, and took his leave, hurrying through the stone passages, and praying he'd see Hugh again in this life. He was eating, and that was good.

After a restless few hours' sleep, he arrived in the courtyard to see his men with Lord Adair. He had outfitted them with garrons to ride to James Douglas. With rest, and their stomachs full with the best meals they'd had since the Christmas feast at Carrickfergus, they mounted up. Owen hugged Roysia a long time, and kissed her child, before joining them. Niall swung up into his own saddle. They clopped over the drawbridge, a ragtag, half-starved group, but in better shape by far than they had been, leaving Hugh and Roysia behind, and rode into the sun painting the sky pink in the east, in search of James Douglas.

Glenmirril, Present

Amy saw Angus's mini, a small, dark shape at the far end of the dark lot, and her heart gave a lurch. She could see him, in the glow of the parking lot lights, leaned back against his seat. She guessed his eyes were closed and he hadn't seen them. Shawn glanced over, and turned for her Renault, gripping her elbow. She yanked her arm away, and they climbed into her car. The tension of the tower doubled in the tight space of the vehicle.

She stuck the key in the ignition, but made no move to turn it.

"Let's go," Shawn said.

"When I'm ready."

"What are you waiting for?"

She shrugged. "I don't know. I'm drained. Aren't you? Being here where so much happened? Being in the Bat Cave that meant so much to you? Finding their messages? What just happened in the tower? It doesn't leave you exhausted?"

"Yes? No? Right now, I'm still pretty happy just to be alive at the end of each day, and not worried about being attacked outside the castle walls."

She frowned. "Yeah. I guess that's a different way of thinking."

"*Did* you sleep with him?"

She sighed, dropping her head back against the headrest. "Why is that so important to you? You said yourself it never meant anything, with all those women."

"But it means something to *you.* Did you?"

"We've had this discussion." She crossed her arms, saying no more.

He leaned his head back, too, and they sat in silence. He rolled his head, finally, looking at her. "You know we can't go on like this."

She shrugged again. "Then maybe we shouldn't. You were gone for a year, I thought you were dead, and you left part of your heart with Christina, too." After another moment's silence, the parking lot lights casting shadows over the planes of his jaw, she added, "He's mostly responsible for getting you out of there, Shawn. He doesn't deserve your anger. He didn't deserve that snarky crack in the tower."

Shawn jerked upright and flung open the door.

Amy sat up abruptly. "Shawn, what are you doing?"

He slammed the door and marched across the parking lot. She pressed the palms of her hands to her closed eyes. She had no energy left. She just prayed he wouldn't do anything too stupid. With a last glance after him, storming toward Angus's car, she turned to Glenmirril, trying to see it as it had been, with Niall and Allene, the Laird, Hugh and Christina, coming and going, maybe watching from the battlements that stood even today.

Shawn had told her bits and pieces of the battle that night. Allene in the bailey, swinging a sword. "Women weren't taught to fight in those days," she'd said.

"Allene was. The Laird was straight-laced and conservative. He was also forward-thinking and unconventional."

Amy's hand drifted to the crucifix hidden under her shirt. She wondered, looking down from the parking lot, into the castle bailey, about the aftermath of that battle. About Niall, the boy—who had lost six brothers and a best friend, clutching the hand of his friend, sending him away—and Niall, the man—who had kissed her. What had awaited him at the bottom of the tower stairs? They knew he'd become laird. But what of Allene, fighting men larger and stronger than herself? What of Christina?

She could look it up. But research and archives now turned her heart to Angus. The answers might be there in the scrolls Shawn had just retrieved, but she'd promised not to look.

She leaned forward, suddenly, thinking she saw a light flicker, like candlelight, in one of the rooms. She blinked. It wasn't there. She was imagining things. She shut her eyes, not wanting to think about it, not wanting to think about what was happening at the other end of the parking lot, just wanting a normal life.

♫

A soft click told Shawn the Interloper had unlocked the door, though he didn't turn his head. Shawn opened the door and slid in, shutting the two of them in the dark womb of the car. Angus stared straight ahead at the castle, not acknowledging Shawn.

Shawn, too, stared at the castle he'd known so well. They sat in silence. Finally, Shawn spoke. "Did you sleep with her?"

Angus smiled slowly, winding Shawn's nerves as tight as a bowstring. "Now, if you're asking me," he said, "sure you're getting no answer from her." He rolled his head, grinning at Shawn. "I think I'll respect her wishes."

Shawn fought the urge to lash out, with fists, with words, to wipe the smug smile off the man's face, and the brogue—which he was sure Amy found *charming* —right out of his voice. His stomach knotted with the desire to loose the rage. With a deep breath, he asked himself why he'd come. "Why did you do it?" he asked.

Angus stared at him. The lights outside carved a shadow down one side of his face. "Do what?"

"Bring me back."

Angus returned his gaze to the castle. It was a full minute before he said, "Many reasons."

"You're not going to tell me?"

"Do you think you can understand them?"

"I have no idea," Shawn said curtly, "until you tell me. It's possible I'll surprise you with a little more intelligence than you give me credit for."

"Amy said you had your good qualities." Angus spoke as if he had his doubts.

"Amy's smart. So why'd you do it?"

"For Amy. For James. For your mother. Because I couldn't leave a modern man in such a world."

"Very noble," Shawn sneered. "Do you have a selfish streak in you like the rest of humanity?"

"Aye." A smile played on Angus's lips. "History is my passion. Especially Glenmirril. How could I pass up the chance to talk to a man who lived it?"

"What convinced you this insane story is true?"

"Everything fits." Angus tapped a finger on the steering wheel. "Right up to you appearing exactly where the prophecy suggested, in medieval garb with blood on your sword, telling us when and how Duncan MacDougall died."

"So you're hoping I'll tell you about it? Why should I?"

Angus shrugged. "Don't, then. But you've a captive audience. One who believes you. You'll not find much of that here."

"To hear about history," Shawn mused. "That seems a poor reason to risk everything you had with her. There has to be more."

"I thought for Amy, James, your mother, and general humanity were strong enough reasons," Angus said.

"Other *selfish* reasons," Shawn snapped. "I don't believe anyone is that selfless."

"More's the pity," Angus replied. "'Tis a sad place in your head, if everyone must have selfish reasons for doing good. But if it makes you feel better, I've known from the start I'm fighting a ghost, until Amy sees you again in the flesh and blood. With you back, I've a chance. With you gone, I could never compete against a man who became perfect in her imagination, the man who threw himself in front of a charging war horse to save a child."

"Huh." Shawn grunted, relaxing against his headrest. "She thought I'd come back perfect?"

"She thought you'd come back all she ever thought you were."

"Well, I don't know if she's right or wrong," Shawn admitted.

They sat in silence for a time, a silence like a warm, comfortable cloak, before Angus spoke again. "Why do you think Amy won't tell you if we slept together?"

"Let me know how it feels," Shawn said.

"How what feels."

"Wondering. Knowing maybe someone I love was with someone else." He stared out the window, and admitted, in a low voice, "It feels like crap."

"And you've not even thought beyond sex," Angus said.

"What the hell is that supposed to mean?" Shawn shot him an irritable glance. "Isn't that what we're *talking* about?"

Angus turned to him. "You never considered anything else that passed between us, did you?"

"Like *what*?" Shawn threw his full arsenal of belligerence into the two words.

"Like the moments that make up real love. Like seeing the good in someone, like noticing the way the sun shines off her hair, or the jokes she sends with her e-mails."

"She doesn't send jokes with her e-mails."

"Or rubbing her feet when she's had a long day and they're swollen. Do you know her favorite coffee?"

Shawn shrugged. "We tried loads of different coffees together."

Angus smiled. "You don't know, do you? Mocha with hazelnut."

"Yeah, well, I've been gone awhile. Maybe she decided that after I left."

Angus smiled, staring into the distance, and Shawn had the disturbing understanding that Angus had experienced a deeper intimacy with Amy, one he himself had never considered. He'd longed for her, wanted to possess her; but he'd never smiled like that, just thinking about her. "No," Angus said. "She ordered mocha hazelnut the first time she went to the Heritage Centre, right after Niall left."

"Yeah. Well."

"She's a talented artist. Do you know which artists she admires? Or who her favorite composer is?"

Shawn pounced on it. "The Russian composers! Mussorgsky, Tchaikovsky. They write the best trombone parts!"

Angus scoffed. "Those are *your* favorites. She likes Telemann. Pachelbel. Bach."

"Well, yeah, any classical musician would. That doesn't mean...." He stopped. "How do you know?"

"Because I listened to her instead of pushing her to go to bed."

Shawn cleared his throat. His jaw clamped tight, he stared down at the castle.

Angus pierced him with a gaze. "Do you understand there's intimacy in being there when a baby is born? In bringing a child home from the hospital together? In doing the washing up because she's knackered?"

Shawn had no words. He wanted to protest that Angus had had no business bringing his son home. But he knew the answer. He hadn't been there. Had he not disappeared, chances were high he still wouldn't have been there. He shoved the shame down with anger.

Angus seemed to read his irritation. "Would you rather she'd been alone?" he asked softly.

"No," Shawn admitted, with the same enthusiasm with which he'd agree to being drawn and quartered.

"Did you ever watch her sleep?" Angus asked. "And feel love, just watching?"

"No," Shawn admitted, more reluctantly still.

Angus's voice dropped to little more than a whisper. "She's beautiful, not just on the outside where I bet you saw it the first second you laid eyes on her, just like I did, but inside where you never looked. You may have felt it on some level. But you never pursued it. She was unhappy knowing you were in danger. I hoped that if you came back, if she chose you, she'd be happy. I hope if she stays with you, you'll treat her well."

Glenmirril, April 1317

It was dark outside, rain still trickling down, when Red set parchment, quill, and ink on the spindly table. "The Laird says you might write."

Taran stood, glowering, outside the door.

MacDougall thanked him, humbly, eyes lowered that the boy might not see the gloating there. MacDonald was wily. He'd use the lad, sending him with parchment and quills, and no comment. MacDougall knew his words would be read before they went out. But he'd had months to plan. If Taran or Red watched, they would see the ink flow effortlessly. He pulled the candle close, dipped the quill and wrote.

To my dearest wife, whose well-being has worried me these many months.

It had never been other than a marriage of alliances. Neither of them had ever pretended otherwise. She would take the missive to his steward.

I worry about you, alone in your chamber in your last illness.

She was quite well. He glanced up at Taran, watching warily, and continued.

My only consolation is that you have such beautiful gardens upon which to look. I pray they give you the same joy they always gave me.

Her chamber hovered high above the sea, that pounded on jagged rocks.

I pray you seek help that you may soon leave your confinement. Have you spoken to the physician? See that Roger assists you in every possible way. He is to use my men as he sees fit. I have been granted correspondence that Creagsmalan....

He stopped. He had meant to say that Creagsmalan not suffer. MacDonald would read it. MacDougall dipped his quill and returned it to vellum, completing the sentence...*Creagsmalan's women and children do not suffer in my absence.* That would appeal to MacDonald. *Tell Roger the orchards in the glen to the north are ripe. Opportunity abounds there.*

Roger knew the northern glen well. Roger would take his meaning.

In the flickering candlelight, he added a few endearments, and several pages of mundanities—that would give MacDonald plenty to look through, seeking clues—expressed concern for a few men in particular, and sanded the whole thing dry, before passing it out to Taran, who looked as wary as he had in the initial days.

Smiling, MacDougall returned to his window, searching the wooded hill for Roger's signals. On the hillside, a pair of lights shone through the trees.

Glenmirril, Present

When Shawn reached Amy's car, he saw she'd fallen asleep, leaning against the window. He stopped, his hand on the door handle. Heeding Angus's words, he watched her. She looked more at peace than he'd seen her in the last weeks. Her mouth curved in a smile. She'd looked like that, back when he started with the orchestra— calm, relaxed, always smiling. It had been part of what had drawn him. Over the years, she'd become tense and agitated. But not with Angus.

Mocha with hazelnut, he told himself. *Bach, Telemann, Pachelbel.* Irritation at Angus bridled in him. Sighing, he opened the passenger door. In the driver's seat, she jolted, her cheeks flushed, tendrils of hair curling on her cheek. Tension sprang back to her face. She gave a sharp twist to Bruce's ring on her right hand, and glanced out the window. Shawn turned to see Angus driving away. He slid in and pulled the door shut, studying her in the lamp light shining through the windshield.

"What happened?" she asked.

"Nothing. We talked."

"You were angry when you left."

"It's not important." He reached for her hand.

She let him take it, as if allowing a wild boar's approach. Her fingers lay stiff in his. "Yes, it's important. I agreed to let you read Christina's messages, no questions asked, and now you keep secrets with my friend, too?"

"How about I promise to tell you next week?"

"Promise, then."

"I do. If you still want to know, I'll tell you."

She studied him, eyes narrowed.

"I'm not playing word games," he said, realizing what she was thinking. "I've moved out, I've done everything you've asked. I know word games aren't going to get me back in."

"Okay. Next week."

"Who's your favorite composer?" he asked.

"Well, you think the Russian...."

"Yeah, they write great trombone parts. Who's *your* favorite?"

"Pachelbel. Telemann. Bach."

Pain stabbed Shawn's heart. He'd hoped Angus had been wrong. He could have salvaged some pride. "I'd offer you a mocha with hazelnut, but the coffee shops are closed."

Her hand relaxed in his. She laughed a little, as if she'd missed the joke and hoped no one would notice she didn't get it. "Who said anything about coffee?"

He grinned. "I did. Who's your favorite artist?"

"What is this, twenty questions? Why are you asking me this at ten at night?"

He laughed, delighted he'd brought out her smile. "Just tell me. Not Picasso."

She shuddered. "No."

"The *Pictures at an Exhibition* guy? The orange Gate of Kiev. I bet it wasn't him."

She laughed. "*No!* Mary Cassat."

"Mary who? Never heard of her."

"She paints mothers with children. Soft. Realistic."

He racked his brain, searching for another question, anything other than *did you sleep with him?* It took a full minute. "Why do you like paintings of children and mothers?"

Her shoulders relaxed. He realized he was so used to her tension he hadn't noticed it, till she sighed into a softer form before his eyes. "Because I'd like to think that's the kind of mother I'll be."

The next question came to his mind on its own. "Did you always want to be a mother?" He'd never thought of her as she might have been in college, or high school, or in any life besides with him. His own shoulders settled.

"Yeah. Always. I wanted to play in a symphony the first time I saw one when I was three. And I wanted to be a mother."

Her pleas, with the first baby, came back to him. He saw it, suddenly, differently: not an overly emotional woman who couldn't see her own best interests, but a woman mourning a baby she knew he'd push her to get rid of, a baby she'd always wanted. He couldn't bring himself to utter the heartfelt *I'm sorry* that erupted in his chest. Maybe she'd forgotten about it. Maybe it would be safer to not mention it and remind her. But his next words broke, thinking of it. "Why did you want to be a mother so badly?"

She shrugged. "Partly, I think it's natural. I wanted to be to a child what Rose was to me. I wanted, with my child, what I didn't have with my mother."

He stared at her in surprise. "What didn't you have with your mother?"

"You never noticed I spent every Christmas with you?"

He shrugged. "Well, yeah, I noticed, but—what's up with her?"

"Critical. Self-absorbed."

"I'm sorry." He tried to think back. He'd met her mother twice. He vaguely remembered her detailing a long list of medical issues and telling him Amy had been thoughtless to move so far away when her family needed her.

"So, the plane ticket...?"

Amy shrugged. "She's still my mother."

"Oh." They sat in silence. He tried to picture Amy in high school, winning her audition to Juilliard; at birthday parties as a child; with her first violin. He'd never thought of any of it. "Tell me about Angus," he said.

Tension snapped back into her shoulders. She yanked her hand from his, reaching for the keys in the ignition.

He touched her fingers on the steering wheel. "Amy, I didn't mean that. Tell me about *him*. How did you meet him? What did you talk about?"

"Why?" Her hand didn't leave the keys.

"Because I want to know *you*."

"You're not going to ask...?"

"No, I'm not. He did your dishes for you?"

She smiled, her hand sliding from the keys. "He did more dishes than any man without a wife and children should ever have to do."

"What else?"

"He likes Parcheesi. And Irn-bru. He knows history, and Gaelic."

"Is that how you knew what I said, that night with Zach and Kristin?"

She nodded. "He took me to Mass Christmas Eve, and two old women gave him the cold shoulder because I was pregnant. I've never known anyone to make a sacrifice like that for me."

The pains he'd been suffering multiplied. *Anyone* included him. "They gave you the cold shoulder, too?" he asked, trying to ignore his own pain.

She nodded. "They looked like two old lemons, pursing their lips and letting everyone know I didn't belong there." She stopped speaking.

The realization settled on Shawn that in their years together, she'd never spoken so much. He'd never given her the chance. As she watched him, he saw a question in her eyes: *Would you take that risk for me?*

He slid his hand into hers, knowing he would—now. "He was good to James?"

"Very good. He held him, fed him, played with him. He bought him toys and gave him his nephew's old books and read to him."

"What is it you love about him?"

Amy sank back against the headrest, almost as relaxed as when he'd come upon her sleeping. Light shone in her eyes, and her mouth curved in a small smile. "Why? You're not going to try to be him?"

"I think it's obvious I can't be him."

"And he can't be you."

Shawn grinned, a self-mocking grin. "Nobody could be me."

She laughed. "True."

They stared at each other for a few more seconds, while Shawn's insides turned watery, and his heart grew warm. He thought he understood what Angus meant about different kinds of intimacy, and wondered why he'd never noticed before what more there could be between them. "So what is it you love about him?"

"He's funny. In a different way from you. It sneaks up on you." Her smile grew. "Always clean humor. He's gentle. And generous—always sees the best in people. Always has compassion. Gives his all."

Shawn drew in a deep breath. His first thought lit on Clarence. Clarence had ruined his life. There had been no one like Clarence in Angus's life. His second thought was of Christina. She'd had someone as awful as Clarence, but remained patient, giving, and kind. He had no excuse. "You're tired," he said softly. "Do you want me to drive?"

She handed him the keys, and they switched places. She sank back against the passenger seat, her hand going to the crucifix at her throat. Shawn turned the key. The car lights flashed down onto the castle. His lips tightened, staring at it, thinking about the letters, and wondering what he would find.:

Glenmirril, April 1317

In MacDonald's candlelit chambers, with Brother David standing at the writing desk, Red bowed low, and handed MacDougall's letter to his Laird.

MacDonald unfolded the pages carefully, scanning them in the light of the candle on the table. He handed them to Brother David, who held them close under the flame, taking his time. He handed the letter back at last, saying, "I see naught amiss."

"Nor do I," admitted MacDonald. "And that is not the MacDougall we know." He dropped the pages on Brother David's writing desk. As the monk set to copying it, the Laird turned to stare out the window to the hill and trees, dark against the starry sky. "Tell me what you saw, Red."

"He wrote swiftly," Red reported. "He hesitated only once."

"My Lord." Brother David paused in his own writing, looking up. "If he wrote swiftly, 'tis that his words were well planned. When I write, I often hesitate, searching for the right words."

Malcolm nodded. "You speak wisely, Brother David." He turned to Red. "Watch him carefully. Be on your guard. Let Darnley and Morrison know I'll want to speak with them in the morning."

Red bowed and left.

MacDonald sighed. "Are we trapping the snake at his own game, Brother David, or are we stepping into his trap? I need not send the letter on." He turned back to the window. His eyes narrowed as a faint pair of lights winked on the hillside. He stared harder, unsure if he was really seeing anything. He frowned, thinking on how Shawn said the place would be in seven hundred years. There, where the lights seemed to glimmer among the trees on the hill, Shawn had said there would be a *parking lot.* "A place to park *cars,"* he'd explained. The speeding wagons made of the same steel as a sword. MacDonald smiled, wishing that somehow he was seeing the lights of Shawn's *car,* that maybe Shawn was, even now in his own time, looking down on Glenmirril. He was being fanciful, he told himself sternly. He sighed.

"My Lord?" Brother David inquired.

"Do you see a light on the hill?"

Brother David joined him at the window. He peered into the forest, and shook his head.

MacDonald frowned. "Nor do I, now. Perhaps I'm only tired." Then he smiled. "I do believe I miss him, impertinent though he was."

Brother David laughed, not asking to whom he referred, but said, "And I believe if there's deceit hidden in MacDougall's letter, he would be the one to find it."

"Write him a letter, Brother David," MacDonald said sadly. "I'll take it to the Bat Cave on the morrow. Give him my warmest wishes. Tell him my prayers are with him and Amy and his James." He sighed again, staring at the hill.

Bannockburn, Present

Wrapped in my peach robe, I twist my hair into a heavy braid down my back. In the small hours of the morning, I ponder the day's events. The talk on the long ride home with Shawn warms me as much as the peach and lace duvet I slide under. I hug the memory as close as the cover I pull over my shoulder, replaying each of his soft words, his deep laugh, the crinkle around his eyes and the light in them, each time he smiled; and feeling warmer, still, knowing he's downstairs now, cradling a sleeping James on his chest.

It's as good as the first night he came to my apartment with the plane tickets—better really. That night, we set our motif, talking about him, his plans, his music, his albums. Tonight, he asked about Mary Cassat and McTaggart, listening as I talked about their techniques. I enjoyed telling him, tonight, about my passions, and how Mary Cassat's paintings left me feeling I could step into a dream.

"Better than a magic tower," Shawn joked. We laughed, though there's nothing funny about disappearing into a brutal time. "Makes my problems here look good," he said when I said so.

"What problems," I asked, as we entered my home under the night stars. "We have a beautiful son. Your career's exploding. You're having to turn down offers. People are clamoring for our Broadway album. Ben's planning this big tour, and people are snapping up tickets. It's all good, Shawn. What's wrong?"

"No," he said, as he lit the fire in my small hearth. "Tonight I listen."

"It's a two-way street," I insisted. "What's wrong?"

He sighed, staring at the small blaze crackling in my fireplace. "There are those who can't believe I'm different. There are those who don't want me to be different."

In the warmth of my bed, I think who 'those' might be. Caroline. Dana. Fan girls. It doesn't matter. He seems happy with who he is now, only surprised that others don't accept it. "Forget it," he said. "Tell me about McTaggart." We talked softly until James cried upstairs, and Shawn took him, telling me to get some sleep.

Alone in my quiet room, I wonder again what Angus said to him. I think of Claire, giggling on the tower stairs. It's too easy to imagine the look on Angus's face, as he leaned in to kiss her, just before the laugh cut off with her last quick catch of breath. I throw myself flat on my back, staring at the ceiling. I'm happy he's happy, I tell myself. Memories fill my mind, of the day Angus drove me to Creagsmalan and asked me about my favorite music. Yes, Angus steered Shawn in the right direction. Is it because he found someone new and doesn't want me coming back after him?

His story of the Glenmirril Lady tells me otherwise. I sigh. Even now, he's being selfless, helping Shawn, regardless of the cost to himself. It warms my heart to Angus even more. It tears me even more.

With a sigh, I throw back the cover and swing my legs out of bed. Moments later, I stand silently in the doorway of the front room. The scent of wood smoke is warm and comfortable. A fire crackles low in the hearth. Shadow and light dance across Shawn as he sprawls in the arm chair, his head lolling back. His hair spreads across the cushion, the golden auburn I love. James relaxes on his chest, his light breath rising and falling with Shawn's deeper sighs. He sucks on his fist, smiling in his sleep. Moonlight outlines Shawn's square jaw, with a faint edge of golden stubble.

I cinch the belt of my robe, leaning on the door frame, watching. A smile touches my lips. This is what it will be, if I marry Shawn—raising James together in his half-timbered mansion, picnics on his land, splashing in the stream with James. I would cook dinner in his kitchen of granite counters, we'd have the barbecues he loves, and after the guests drifted away, it would be just us, talking softly on the fur rug in front of the fire place. Someday, James might play backstage with Sophie and Emma.

Shawn's lips curve upward. I realize with a start that he's woken and is watching me, too. My heart skips. I swallow. Warmth flushes my body.

"Are you coming in?" He uses the voice he knows will melt my bones.

I nod, slide into the room, to perch on the couch against the wall.

"I don't bite." His eyes dance.

He's laughing at me. I smile, but my heart won't slow; my nerves won't settle. "Biting wasn't really what I was afraid of."

"What are you afraid of?"

Angus fills my mind. I can't tell Shawn I'm afraid I've thrown away the kindest, most loving man I've ever known; I'm afraid of choosing Angus, if I still have that choice, and missing Shawn forever. Rose is right. He brings something to life in me like no one ever has. I can't tell him I'm afraid of spending my whole life missing one or the other of them terribly, with a sharp pain that never goes away.

So I evade. "We found a book from the 1700's with a chapter about Niall," I say. "It said he walked on the shore behind Glenmirril with his son."

Shawn's smile grows, changing from seductive to genuine. "I know I'd hardly be considered the fatherly type here," he says, "but their ideas on parenting seemed strange—nursemaids raising babies, fathers ignoring their children. I wanted James—Niall's James—to have something like what I had with my father."

I smile, touched by his love for a child. "What else did you do?"

The light in Shawn's eye shifts, moving from me to memories. He relaxes into a place happier than I ever knew him. "I took him to the stables. He loved the horses. I thought of you, and what our child might be like."

I smile as he talks about removing James's swaddling. He chuckles. "Bessie was shocked. Very unconventional, she said—he'd get cold or roll into the fire. Allene said he'd put things in his mouth, and didn't I have any sense? But he loved reaching for the harp strings, and having his toes dipped in the loch. He liked the horses."

I smile, seeing it all. "And what did Niall think?" I love the timbre of his voice as he tells of riding through glens and along rivers, of racing through the night after Carlisle with Niall and Red, of hawking, and their shock when he leaped into a cold loch. "You miss it," I say.

He laughs. "Yeah, I miss getting cut in half. I miss seeing people die and hearing new widows and orphans cry when we came home. Not!"

I study him. He cared about those widows and orphans. His eyes glow. "But it wasn't all bad," I insist. "You do *miss it."*

"It was satisfying." He rises abruptly, laying James in his bassinet in the corner. He adds kindling to the fire and turns, meeting my eyes. "I want to be here, with you and James." He touches his iPod, on the mantel. The Righteous Brothers glide from 1950's America into twenty-first century Scotland, crooning to the accompaniment of the crackling fire.

I stand up, bumping the couch. "No, Shawn. Turn that off." I back against the door frame. I don't want to get sucked back in. I'm not sure. I miss Angus terribly.

Shawn offers his hand. "Did you find the manuscripts I left at Monadhliath?"

I nod. The memory of that day hits me hard, of reading one manuscript after another with melodies of love and apology; of the tornado of emotion sucking air from me; of every good memory of Shawn reaching for me, touching me—of Angus finding me crying over the manuscripts and storming away in shock and pain, revoking his proposal.

"Did you remember?"

The Righteous Brothers croon, soft harmony to his words; the music and the smell of wood smoke call forth a night in his living room, slow dancing in front of his fireplace, just as seeing the melody in the manuscript called it up. Just as he knew it would. I swallow hard over the lump in my throat, nodding.

He smiles. "Every detail?"

I nod, resisting being pulled back in, resisting the memory, even as I savor it.

His fingers stretch for mine. "Remember Tioram? The first time?"

I take a step back. But I smile against my will. "You're not going to sing about potatoes, are you?" The words come out on a shaky laugh.

"No potatoes," he whispers. He takes another step forward, and touches my arm; soft strains beckon.

I squeeze my eyes, remembering the soft breeze over Tioram's ramparts, his hand on my arm, on my back, that night. "Shawn, don't." I miss Angus. But I stay, my eyes closed, as his fingers trail down my arm, electric through the peach robe.

"Do you remember the day we arranged Power of Love?*"*

I nod, remembering the walk along early spring roads, muddy with the last traces of snow, to the awning, and the rain dripping down, and his hands in my hair. His fingers touch my neck, and trace the outline of my ear. I draw a deep breath. "I told you...." I hate the way my words come out breathless, fluttering away on the crackle of the fire. The Righteous Brothers croon. I draw breath and speak sternly. "I'm not ready to take this further."

"I promised." The words whisper against my cheek. "I just want to be with you." His lips brush my temple. "I liked talking with you in the car. I liked holding James so you could sleep."

His arms wrap around me; his breath warms my neck. Excitement dances in my stomach, up and down my arms, prickling my neck. "Did Angus tell you to do those things?" My voice comes out as if a breeze might blow it away.

"Mm, I'll tell you next week." He massages my neck, under my hair, to the accompaniment of violins.

"He told you." I try to sound stern, but a laugh comes out. "Don't kiss me."

"I won't. Dance with me." He pulls me into the room, into the narrow space between the coffee table and hearth. "I just want to be with you."

I lay my head on his chest, relishing his cheek against my hair, his arms around me, his body swaying against mine. I close my eyes, and wrap my arms around his neck. I missed this so much. For tonight, nothing else matters.

CHAPTER TWENTY-THREE

Crossing Scotland, April 1317

Niall stooped at each loch they passed to put his hand in up to his wrist, though he had to fight his revulsion as the water writhed like a tub full of snakes around his wrist. He made camp by lochs each evening, and played his harp there, thinking of Shawn, James, and Allene, as the water lapped, soft harmony to his music. He removed his boots each night, rolled up his breeks, and stood in water up to his ankles. It turned his stomach, summoned Alexander's white face, his hair dripping with seaweed. He was sure Shawn's time had no idea what they were doing. But Hugh was right. His other choice was to do nothing. He could hardly make it worse.

And—there was Roysia's child, born safely under the very eyes of an enemy army. It was impossible to think of that wee bairn without feeling the power of the miracle that had granted him life. Bruce had been right. Therefore, he would do, too, as Hugh asked, praying silently, if hopelessly, as cool water swirled around wrist or ankle. *My father, help me.* And softly, head hung in shame, as water crept coldly around his feet: *Forgive my anger and doubt.* He was grateful when they left the lochs behind to push into Ettrick Forest.

As they approached Lintalee, a pack of shaggy hounds, nearly as tall as their garrons, raced through the trees, swift and silent as the wolves they hunted, surrounding them with affectionate greetings as Douglas's men burst from the woods, hailing them. A mile further, Douglas strode from his new home, beaming ear to ear as he crossed the courtyard. He slapped Niall on the back. "What news of our king?"

"Returning anon," Niall said, "and bids you meet him at Scone." He grinned, pleased to see Douglas, looking healthier than any of the Scots in Ireland's famished land. He was grateful, as Douglas led him and his men into the great hall, the hounds darting beside them, for venison, boar, and fish after months of near starvation in Ireland, grateful when the men once more asked for stories of the wolfhound and the wind, and grateful to go to work the next day, putting the last touches on the new manor. It took his mind off Hugh, half dead at a castle across the country, and Allene at Glenmirril awaiting news of him.

Owen and Lachlan worked beside him, sweating in the early spring, with birdsong lilting in the air. The nightmare of the Irish campaign loosened its claws, though he thought often of the men left behind, of Bruce, gaunt to the point of emaciation when last he'd seen him. He hoped—he *prayed*—his king would make it to Scone. He, by contrast, would do these few days of work, feast at Douglas's house warming, and head home.

"Awfully close to the border, aye?" Owen hefted a stone onto the wall surrounding the place, snapping Niall from his thoughts.

"A hundred Englishmen will run from the very name Douglas," Niall said. "Sure they'll not attack him on Scottish soil."

"And he's chosen his ground well as always," Lachlan added.

Within days, the house was finished. His heart light with the prospect of the night's feasting and entertainment, and heading home the next day to Allene, Niall entered the great hall with Lachlan and Owen. Serving boys poured in, setting out steaming platters of meat and bread. Douglas's men flocked to wooden benches, pounded trestle tables, and shouted for ale. A man juggled small burlap balls stuffed with straw, until he tripped over one of Douglas's shaggy hounds, and the balls showered down around him. He grinned at the laughter and ribbing showering down with them. The dog woofed, skittered in the rushes, and licked the man's face.

Amidst the laughter, the door crashed open. A messenger exploded into the ribaldry. "My Lord!" He paused, breathing hard, hands on knees, before looking up, in search of Douglas's height and head of black hair. "Arundel is coming to take down Jedburgh forest," he gasped.

The men fell silent, ales half-hoisted. Serving boys paused mid-step.

At the head table, Douglas rose, his face turning dark. As always, Niall found it hard to reconcile the peaceful, even gentle, man before him with the warrior who tore through armies like fire through Northumbria's fields. "How many?" he demanded.

"Ten thousand!"

Douglas scanned the fifty knights in his brand new hall. "Sir Niall." He spoke with no more excitement than if he were sending the cook for a platter of goose. "Assemble your men. Weave rushes together to close the end of the pass. Then take the left flank with me. Lachlan, Owen, your archers on the right. When they're done shooting, Sir Niall, we fall on them."

"Ten thousand to fifty," Niall murmured to Lachlan. He hoped he would see Allene again. Maybe even with all his limbs intact.

Lachlan grinned. "Gives them a fighting chance, aye? Another ten on our side, 'twould hardly be sporting."

Bannockburn, Present

As James babbled on the floor, Shawn set up his new keyboard in his living room. It wasn't his grand piano back home, but it worked. A table beside it held a dozen pads of staff paper, two dozen fresh new pencils, and an electric sharpener. He had arrangements to write for this tour Ben was putting together.

He smiled as he thought of the previous night. He'd held Amy, swaying to the music as the fire flickered, and it had been like their first year again. She'd fallen asleep on the couch, her head on his lap. It was another step forward. Shawn grinned ear to ear, humming as he sharpened his pencils to a deadly point. They were working together on the Broadway album they'd planned two years ago—a year ago, he corrected himself—at Tioram. He had a few hours, while she taught lessons, to work on it. He glanced at his son, gnawing with gusto on the ear of his rabbit.

Shawn watched. James kicked his legs and flipped over onto his back, the rabbit landing on top of him as he gripped its ear. He looked up at Shawn and gave a gurgling laugh. Shawn smiled, struck by the resemblance to Niall's son, who differed only in his ginger hair. He got down on the floor, on his stomach, and wiggled the stuffed animal in James's face. James laughed and grabbed for it.

"You like that?" Shawn asked. "I'll show you some horses. I'll take you to the shore." The album forgotten, he lay on the floor, talking with his son, showing him toys, and reading to him from his books. They were in Gaelic. Angus's. Shawn felt a sting of guilt. Angus had brought him back from medieval exile, and in return, he'd taken all Angus treasured—Amy and James. And Angus had given him yet another key to winning her back.

James gave a small smile. He sighed, and his eyes closed, his fist relaxing on the rabbit's ear. Shawn smoothed his dark hair off his forehead. "I should get to work, huh?" he asked the sleeping child. But he saw Niall's James, sleeping on a fur, months ago in 1316, a blanket clutched in one fist.

Shawn pushed himself up off the floor and stared at the staff paper. Amy would be back in two hours. He was supposed to have an arrangement started, and dinner in the oven. All he'd done was sharpen pencils. With the first song singing through his head as a brass quintet, he headed to the kitchen to sprinkle spices, onions, tomatoes, and mushrooms into a pan of chicken. He should write down the notes while they were fresh in his mind, he thought, as he slid the pan into the oven. But as clearly as he heard the music, he saw Niall's son, laughing with his toes in the chilly water behind Glenmirril. He stared, unseeing, at the oven. And he realized—he was scared. More scared than he'd been storming into battle against de Caillou's hordes.

The parchments were in his room. The oilskin had been thick. If they'd all died that night, there'd be nothing there. So there was nothing to fear. He would find out Christina was just fine. A quick look, he decided, and he'd start on the music. With a check on James, sleeping peacefully in the front room, he climbed the stairs.

Minutes later, Shawn smoothed the parchments out on the desk in his studio. Peace hummed around his heart like a rich chord—something with a low G, he thought, and a seventh—thinking of Amy swaying in his arms last night, with violins and crooning wrapping them together in soft, velvet ribbons of music. She'd let go of Angus. They'd be a family.

He was re-establishing himself. He'd set his mind at peace about leaving the battle, and get completely back to his own life. He'd do something really great for Angus, something to make it up to him.

Excitement tingled beside the peace, staring at the top-most parchment. These were seven hundred years old! And they'd been left *for him!* He could skip to the last one, find out how the story ended. He considered it, his fingers resting on the thick vellum, as if its lacy script might soak into his fingers and tell him. No, he decided. He wanted the whole story. He wanted to live it as they had, walk beside them, day by day, as they told the story.

He missed them, suddenly, with a vengeance. He wanted to be in the window sill, keeping time with his leather heels against the stone wall, piping on the recorder while Niall played his harp and Allene looked up from her sewing and Christina from her easel, with shining eyes. He wanted to be at the chess table with Hugh roaring in laughter at an easy capture of Shawn's queen. He even wanted to be there with the Laird grumbling that it was time he got used to daily Mass and quit complaining. Thick as the stack of parchments was, it wouldn't give him those daily details.

He studied the sheaf, and felt his eyebrows dip. Yes, it was thick, but not twenty or thirty years thick. He hoped it didn't mean there hadn't been long for them. Maybe they'd simply forgotten him quickly and quit writing. It would be better to think that, to let them live on into old age in his mind, than to find death had called quickly on the heels of his departure.

He moved his hand and let his eyes focus on the first curling words. It was Niall's handwriting, flowing, bold, and firm. Shawn smiled, as Niall lived again. His voice touched Shawn's ears with a Gaelic lilt, as the words touched his eyes.

June 10, 1316
Shawn, my brother,
The battle ended quickly in the wake of your leaving. By the time I reached the bottom of the tower, MacDougall's men had been rounded up.

Shawn's breath rushed out in relief, and he realized how scared he'd been, despite the number of letters.

Some were eager to mount heads on the parapets. The Laird stayed such hands, and after many hours in prayer in the Bat Cave, caused me to strike fear in them, letting it be known we might execute each of them. I did in fact strike the head from one man. I believe you'll not be dealing with men in such manner where you are.

Shawn stared at the words, torn between dark humor—no, he hadn't struck Dan's head off in the elegant conference room—and the striking, tragic difference in the lives he and Niall now led.

MacDonald's mercy, then, came as real mercy, and they were grateful and quick to swear on bended knee they should harm us no more. MacDougall was given leave to bid Duncan farewell in the tower, though it stretches my understanding, try as I do to see Christ in each man, to understand how anyone, even his own father, could grieve such a one as Duncan. Or that such a one as MacDougall possesses filial emotion at all. But grieve he did. He came down from the tower with his face drawn, his eyes red with unshed grief. In the only sign of humility I have ever seen from him, he fell to his knees before the Laird, begging leave to send his son's body home for proper burial.

It was easy to imagine it, as his eyes absorbed Niall's description. The Laird did not accede easily. He raged. He pushed the point of a sword under MacDougall's chin. He asked Taran, "Your father died today. Will I give his murderer a Christian burial?" Taran stared silently at MacDougall, his face tight. MacDonald spoke to the Widow Muirne. "Ronan, who has been so good to you and your fatherless children, who gave you his only sheep to see you through a hard winter, is even now in the chapel, infection raging through his body from clan MacDougall's sword. He mayn't live the night. Will we pay respect to those who have perhaps taken another good man from us, unprovoked?" The Widow Muirne stared stonily at MacDougall. Her youngest three clung to her skirts, weeping for Ronan; her oldest son held her arm, giving no quarter, in his hard gaze at the invader.

In the end, wrote Niall, *'twas left to me. I sent Duncan home with his men. MacDougall stayed in our southern tower. He was grateful, at the time, that his son would not feed crows on our parapets. I question the wisdom of mercy. Though my faith tells me 'tis right, 'tis hard to allow that respect to he who has caused us such grief and harm, who—my knowledge of men's hearts tells me—will continue to do so. He will soon forget the mercy of a Christian burial and dwell on Duncan's death, and seek vengeance.*

It was true, Shawn thought. He hoped they'd been wise and changed their minds. The thick roll gave him hope they had. There was no way to know—but to read on.

Red asks where you have gone. I know not what to tell him. We say you have gone home and are happy there. I pray, my friend, that you are happy in your peaceful time, that you will find our letters, which we will write, and that you find joy in Amy and your own James, as I find in Allene and my son. I pray all is—will be—well with you, and I wish you could send messages back, but of course it cannot be. My harp seems silent without your recorder singing with it. Give my love to Amy.
Your brother in Christ's love, Niall

Something hot pricked the corners of Shawn's eyes. He blinked. He'd killed Duncan. Niall would pay the price. Not that he'd had much choice.

He rose, fighting agitation, and went to the kitchen to make coffee, reflecting on the letter. It said nothing about the Laird or Christina. So they must be okay. It was too soon for Niall to have known Ronan's fate. Shawn took his coffee, in the

black and gold mug, back to his room, staring at the parchments. It hurt to think of
Ronan injured; Ronan with the hair-trigger temper that go him into trouble and the
good heart that got him out again. It hurt to think maybe Ronan had not left the
chapel on his own two feet, but had stayed, mourned by the castle, with Muirne and
her six children, who had come to see Ronan as a father, in the front rank of
mourners. It hurt to think of Muirne and her children left alone once more.

He couldn't face reading the next parchment to find out. The smell of chicken
reminded him he had a meal to watch, a son to care for. Blinking furiously, he
rolled the parchments and slid them into the oil skin. He had music to write.

Lintalee, Scottish Borders, 1317

Arundel led his men into the trap like a conductor following a score. They
tramped through the forest with a steady, percussive pulse while the jingle of
bridles and creak of leather added melody and counter melody to their ominous
symphony. His men swung axes, ready to tear down the forest that sheltered
Douglas and his merry men. Even now, those men waited quietly behind the trees
above either side of the pass, hidden by fresh green leaves, bushes, and ferns, their
soft breathing covered by birdsong and the chatter of a nearby brook as they waited
silently through their hundreds of measures of rest. Arundel either didn't know, or
had no concern, that the pass would narrow gradually from the wide trail they
tramped, to a small path. Niall's men had worked swiftly and well, weaving
foliage to block the pass entirely.

As Arundel's great host reached the woven blockade, they turned, perplexed,
for only a moment, before a hiss whispered through the air and arrows rained
down. The spring forest erupted into a chaotic melody of horses screaming, men
shouting, chaos as they tried to turn and run back through their own army, which
now hemmed them in. There was no enemy to fight; no escape from the monsoon
of arrows.

Niall breathed out an *Ave*. He leaned his head against a tree, awaiting his cue,
awaiting his entrance.

The arrow shower continued, measure after measure. A few men fought to get
shields over their heads, adding a percussive rhythm to the music of death, but most
had come armed only with axes. In minutes, bodies littered the glen. A last volley
of arrows rained down on the survivors, followed by a weak trickle.

"A Douglas!" James loosed his war cry, lifting his sword. His solo call echoed
through the forest.

Arundel, standing among his decimated army, looked about wildly, shouting to
those still standing. But Niall and Douglas and their men were on them, slashing,
hacking. The mild Sir James spun, struck, dodged, and bellowed like a Minotaur,
sending energy to Niall's own sword, till he didn't know what demon possessed
him.

It ended quickly. In the sudden silence, Niall lowered his sword, a conductor's
baton slashing down. There was no applause.

The glen ran red with blood. It stained his boots. It spattered his tunic and the rocks and ferns of the glen. Men lay at his feet, with feathered arrows protruding from chests and eyes, with deep gashes where Scottish swords had ravaged.

Neither Arundel nor his men would be going home. Panting, glaring between thick black brows, Douglas snatched a helmet off a dead man. A fur hat surmounted it. "Stay home!" he shouted into the blank eyes staring to the trees above. His breath came sharp and hard. "Leave us be!"

"Sir James." Niall touched his arm. "Let us return to Lintalee."

"Aye." Douglas jammed the hat on his head, and, seeming to settle into his usual, gentle nature, led his men, climbing over dead bodies, twisted and staring on the forest floor, from the glen of death. Several men nursed ax wounds; one limped between Lachlan and Owen, clinging to their shoulders.

At Douglas's doorway, Niall stared at a crowd of strangers, feasting and drinking, throwing back the ale intended for Douglas's housewarming party. His adrenaline mounted. His hand tightened on his sword.

Douglas's steward approached, bowing.

"Who is this in my house?" Douglas demanded.

"Arundel's rear guard," the steward said.

They watched silently, as Arundel's troops ate and drank, laughing and calling to one another, oblivious to their entrance. Servants trembled against the walls, running when the English yelled for more. In one corner, a dog whined, his head between his paws. Niall's eyes moved over the crowd, as the steward said, "My Lord, I've made sure your guests had their fill of your spirits."

Jamie Douglas smiled slowly. "Good man."

Niall, too, smiled, watching the uninvited company. One sang loudly and off-key in the center of the room. Several snored with their heads on the table.

James raised his hand to alert the men gathering in the doorway behind him. They paused, noting the situation, and spreading word to those outside. Steel hissed against leather scabbards as dozens of men drew their weapons.

Bannockburn, Present

"It's been over a week." Amy laid down her fork as she finished Shawn's meatloaf. He'd added haggis, and she would gladly have eaten the whole pan, it tasted so good. "What happened with Angus?"

"You like the meatloaf?" he asked.

"Leave it to you to outdo the Scots on their own specialty. What did Angus say?"

Shawn rose from the table, clearing his plate and hers. "Is James asleep?"

"I heard him playing in there. What happened with Angus?"

"Ben's got eight concerts lined...."

Amy raised her eyebrows.

"Does it really matter a week later?" He dropped the dishes in the sink and turned on hot water, his back to her.

She gathered glasses and silverware, bringing them to the filling sink. "It matters that you keep your promise. Did you ask him obnoxious personal questions?"

Shawn raised one eyebrow. "Me? *Me?* You think I'd do that?"

"In a heartbeat," she said. "Keep your promise or I go home."

"You can't." He circled a cloth around a plate in the hot water. "You have to work on the album."

She smiled. "Technology's great. E-mail me a copy. I'll work on it at home. Because if you break your promise, I leave. I'd assume you *did* ask that particular question, but you still have all your teeth. And I know Angus wouldn't answer it. So what happened?"

Shawn sighed.

"Is it that hard?" Amy felt a twinge of sympathy. "After all we've talked about?"

"Pretty much what you thought." Shawn handed her the plate. "He knew your favorite composers, your favorite coffee."

"And what did he say when you asked questions that are none of your business?" She ran the drying cloth over the plate.

Shawn stared into the soapy water.

"Shawn?" She lowered the plate, watching him.

He cleared his throat. "He laughed." His next words came with difficulty. "He said if I had to ask him, obviously you hadn't answered, and he'd respect that."

Amy smiled, amused at the thought of Shawn Kleiner not getting what he demanded. She wiped the smile away as he looked up. "And yet you haven't asked me again."

"No." He handed her another plate. "It seems he has a valid point or two, and maybe I should be more concerned about all the, uh, *foot rubbing* and, um, *talking* you two did."

"Hm. Yes, maybe you should." Amy dried the second plate and slid it into the cupboard. "Or that he always saw good in me. He was amazed when he heard *Damnation of Faust.*" She picked up James's small plastic baby bowl. "Speaking of which, I'm flying to the States next month to solo on an album."

Shawn lowered the glass he'd been washing. "We're not recording."

"But Mike Mansfield is."

"Mike Mansfield?" Shawn looked perplexed. "The guy who sells out every concert? The one who's always in the top forty?"

She nodded, waiting for his critical comment.

He frowned. "You're recording with him?"

The nerves tightened in her stomach, waiting for him to downplay it. It would give her a reason to walk away, go back to Angus. Of course, he might be happily home in his kitchen, serving dinner to Claire from his crock pot, on his blue tablecloth. Maybe Clive was even now sharing a Scotch with them, and all three had forgotten her. She slid James's bowl into the cupboard and picked up a glass to dry.

Shawn's mouth moved. The frown deepened.

"Just a fluke, do you think?" Amy found herself testing him, offering the put-down, rather than answering.

Color rose in his cheeks.

She'd never seen such a thing. She put the glass in the cupboard.

"Uh, no." He circled a cloth in another glass. "No. Just...how did he pick *you?*"

She slapped the drying towel on the table and walked down the hall.

"Amy! I didn't mean it like that!"

She spun, her hair flying. "How *did* you mean it? See, when I told Angus, his face lit up, like he was *proud* of me, he said congratulations. He said I play well."

Shawn stood in the narrow hall, the glass in his hand. "I didn't mean...."

"Guess what, Shawn, there are lots of people, *professionals*, who think I play very well. Conrad, Peter, the Royal Scottish National Orchestra, Mike Mansfield. That includes me, by the way. *I'm* a professional musician, and *I* like my playing."

"No, I *really* didn't mean it like that," he protested, the glass dripping *plink plink plink* on the linoleum. "Of course you're good enough to play on his album. I never should have said those things. I mean, two years ago...."

"*One* year ago. It's only a year to *me*, and that's not very long." She blinked furiously, and swiped a hand across one eye.

"...when I said them. I only meant, did you audition? Did you answer an ad?"

She drew in a sharp breath, caught in the claws of anger, not sure she wanted to free herself; not sure she believed him. "I spent the last year I was with you listening to your criticisms," she said. "Why should I believe you didn't mean it like that? Exactly the way you would have meant it then?"

He spread his hands, helplessly. "Haven't you seen *any* changes?"

She nodded, hesitantly.

"Don't they count for anything?"

She didn't answer.

"Have I criticized once since I got back?" he asked.

"No," she admitted. In the front room, James pushed himself up on hands and knees, the rabbit's ear gripped in one hand, and rocked back and forth, smiling at her. Some of her anger melted, watching him. But she turned back to Shawn. "But you know, it never occurred to you I might be recording for anyone other than you. You got back and it had never occurred to you anyone else might be interested in me."

"That's not true," he protested. "I spent the whole time I was gone thinking you might have married Rob."

"Rob?" she asked in disbelief.

"Well, it was always pretty obvious he liked you."

"But see, that's just it," Amy said. "You never once thought anyone other than your sycophant friend could have any interest in me. Did you really think my whole life revolved around you and I only had anything because you gave it to me?"

"No, I didn't think that. Amy, this isn't fair. I really didn't mean...."

She sighed. "No, okay, maybe you didn't mean it deliberately. Maybe you're completely changed and it'll take me as long to believe it as it takes everyone else." She entered the living room and sank into an armchair. "My friend Adam from

Juilliard played one of our CDs for Mike. He asked for me. I guess for a change you can drive me to the airport."

"Are you taking James?" he asked.

James gave a short, sharp squeal, smiling up at Shawn, and pounded his hand on the floor.

"I'll only be gone a couple days. Do you want him to stay with you?"

"I'll be practicing, making calls, working on music. Yeah, I want him to stay."

"Okay." She thought about apologizing for jumping to conclusions. She said nothing.

Shawn dropped to his knees in front of Amy. James looked up at him and babbled, rocking on his hands and knees. "You'll do great." Shawn took her hands in his. "Mike chose well."

South of Scotland, Present

Robin Redcaps, familiars, children abducted for bloody rituals! Hiding his irritation with a smile, Simon lifted his hand in the dim pub, summoning another round for himself and the men who joined him each night to tell local lore. He'd begun to wonder if they were making half of it up, to keep drinking his ale.

"They say 'twas Thomas of Erceldoune," one drunken lout said, much louder than necessary, "who told the people how to conquer him."

Simon leaned forward, pretending interest. He'd known William. He didn't doubt he dabbled in dark arts, and he'd certainly deserted England when it suited him. Still, the stories grew wilder. Simon waited as the man told of William's temper over some wench. Simon smiled, remembering. He'd been present at that event. He wondered how the woman in question had become so feisty. Umberland's daughter had, in fact, been quite meek. Nonetheless, he nodded. "Yes, true. But what I want to know is this." He looked at the three men, two voluble, scruffy, and fond of drink, the third tall, trim, and well-groomed, sipping his brew slowly. "Could Lord de Soulis control time?"

The ruffians glanced at one another. One wrinkled his brow. "Control time?"

The other shook his head. "He did nothing of the sort. Black arts, aye, but..." He scratched at the stubble on his chin. "You're talkin' time travel, now, are you?"

Simon nodded. "Yes. Like Herla, perhaps."

The first man laughed scathingly. "No, there's no stories like that. De Soulis was *real,* historical, you know. Not a myth like yer Herla."

Simon smiled tightly. He could always use more money. This man would pay for his insolence. "But you believe he dabbled in dark arts?"

"Well, it's what they say," replied the man, more doubtfully.

"And why would such arts *not* include control of time?"

The man looked baffled. "Well, now, no offense. It's just...I never heard such."

"You?" Simon turned to the quieter man. "What do you think?"

"Who's to say centuries later," he replied. "Though I never heard it."

"What if one wished to harness de Soulis's powers?" Simon asked. "What would one do?" He looked from one to the other.

One of the scruffy men shrank in his seat. The other looked away, then rose abruptly, saying, "I thank ye for the ale. My missus'll be looking for me." He raised a hand in farewell, and strode out.

Simon watched him go, and brought his gaze back to the table. The tall man pulled in his legs and leaned forward, his hands wrapped around his glass. "Well, now, if it's dark powers from Soulis you're wanting, you'd search his home for anything he's left behind. There's unlikely to be anything so many years later. But you stay the night there, perhaps you'll get the chance to ask him directly."

Simon raised his eyebrows in question.

The scruffy man explained. "They say you can still hear the screams of his victims at night." He looked at the floor, appearing nervous. "I wouldn't, meself. No reason to mess with such things."

Simon pushed his ale aside, and rose. He was learning nothing.

"He learned from Michael Scott," said the tall man, once again reclining. "He'd be the one who would know. Or go to the Eildon Hills and find if anything is left of Thomas Erceldoune."

Lintalee, 1317

His heart slowing, Niall dropped to his knee in the middle of James Douglas's new, blood-spattered hall of Lintalee. "Fools," he murmured, scanning the death. Did they really think the Black Douglas, the terror of the English, of whom mothers warned small children, would allow them to feast on his food in his new home?

He searched the great hall for his friends. Across the room, Owen pushed his sword into his scabbard, his face red with the fight. Lachlan, nearby, leaned to help one of Douglas's men to his feet. Englishmen lay broken and dead, near doors where the few sober ones had tried to flee, on the floor, one sprawled across the table, an arrow protruding from his head, his last drunken grin on his face. Niall wondered if the man had died unaware he was no longer at a party.

Several Scots dragged the dead from Douglas's new home. A dog nosed at one of the bodies. Niall thought of the wolfhound in Ireland. His stomach turned. Douglas, wearing the fur-topped helmet from the battle in the forest, waved the animal away. "You!" he shouted to one of the serving boys who crept, trembling, from the kitchen to stare at the scene. "Get these dogs out of here!"

The boy, barely bigger than the beasts, scrambled, shouting for the dogs, grabbing two by their ruffs, as the rest ran to him, following him out.

"Bloody Sassenach, go home!"

Niall spun at the outburst. At the hearth, one of Douglas's men brought his sword down on a corpse's neck. He grabbed the head as it rolled, raising it jubilantly by its hair. Angry Scots jeered at the blankly staring face. Blood dripped from the neck.

"What shall I do with it?" shouted the man, grinning.

"Where were their heads when they thought to eat Jamie Douglas's housewarming feast?" someone called out. Hoots filled the hall.

The man jammed the head between the corpse's legs. "Right there!" he shouted.

Ribald laughter filled the hall.

Niall's gaze dropped to the dead man at his feet. Anger and grief railed in him. These men would have killed him; left Allene widowed and his boys fatherless. He had done the same to their wives and children. But they had come into Douglas's home, with intent to kill. He had not gone to their homes. Still, he made the sign of the cross over the man, and closed his eyelids.

A hand fell on his shoulder. He looked up to Jamie Douglas.

The giant man stared solemnly down at him. "Help me take him out," he said.

They each grasped an arm, pulling the corpse through blood-stained rushes.

Only outside did James speak again. "Your men have great faith in you. They believe you when you say peace will come."

Niall stared at the man, laid in the courtyard with the dead. "It will," he said.

"They say you've seen it."

Niall looked up at James. "I have. There will be a day when the English and Scots live in peace. When they play music together and visit one another as friends. But I'm no seer. I don't know when it will come."

"Yet you speak as one who has seen. You know without a doubt, in a way I no longer do, that it *will* come."

Niall stared at the bodies at his feet.

"You've done remarkable deeds. Survived remarkable injuries, and been right back on your feet." James clapped him on the shoulder. "Do not lose faith, Sir Niall, for your faith keeps your men going. More than you know." He scanned the bodies lining his courtyard, flies buzzing around them. "We'll give them a Christian burial, aye? You *are* going home to your wife and bairns. Let us thank God."

Hermitage Castle, Present

Simon hiked across sheep-studded pastures and darkening hills to Hermitage Castle, seeing at last a dark block of stone against the gray evening sky. It wasn't the place Simon had stayed as a guest. It must have been built after William's time. Simon's nerves stretched taut under the heavy clouds. More time wasted!

Still, it was *some* connection to Soulis. Family items would have been moved to a new family home. He'd come all this way. He would search.

He descended the hill. The stream that had circled William's home bubbled alongside the new hulking monstrosity. Simon had never been one to be fanciful. But it did seem to cast an evil shadow out, reaching for him. He entered, looking up high, stark walls. There was little enough to search, but he did the job thoroughly, climbing what few stairs remained, searching the rooms, open to angry, leaden skies.

As shadows lengthened, he climbed a rail, lowering himself into a pit. It might have been part of the original dungeons, a place William might have stood. As Simon searched, digging at the walls, the jingle of keys reached him. He became still, fancying de Soulis's jailer, a wraith rattling ghostly keys.

"Anybody in here?" a woman called.

Simon relaxed, chastising himself for foolishness, even as he melted to the wall, in the shadow of the railing above. Footsteps sounded. She called again, her steps retreated. He heard the dry scrape of the wooden door over flagstones, and the short report as the bolt slid to. He was locked in for the night.

A chill shot up Simon's spine and down his arms. It didn't matter, he snapped at himself. He'd not feared de Soulis in life. He certainly didn't fear him in death. If the man showed himself, he could do no harm. He might even give him information.

Not that Simon believed for a moment in ghosts. Superstitious nonsense! He grasped the rail and hoisted himself up and over, landing on silent leather boots in the dusky ruin, its walls stark and high.

He searched again, until shadows filled the place, until it grew too dark to see. Finally, he settled in a corner, wrapped in a warm tartan he'd taken from a local shop. He stared up at the sky, a rich, dark blue overhead, with silver stars coming out. The stillness of the place pressed in on him. The stories of William's black deeds filled his heart. *Why, Simon!* Helen's words mocked him. *An imagination!*

The sky darkened to black. A moan echoed outside. Just the wind on the moors, he told himself. To think it was the screams of seven-hundred year dead victims was foolishness. Still, he sat up, peering into the gloom of the ruins, both seeking and fearing a glimpse of William. Maybe he would learn something. The moaning grew. He rose, prowling the roofless rooms, up and down moonlit stairs. "William!" he shouted. "Show yourself!"

The moaning ceased.

Simon shivered, and returned to his corner. Mist curled along the floor. The wind rose again—it *must* be the wind! But it sounded eerily like the cries of children. He wasn't sure he wanted to roam the hills in the dark of night, even if he could break through the locked door. Neither would he want to sleep at the ruined chapel, with its gravestones, or by the river, thick with bugs in the night. He rolled into his tartan, turning his back to the empty room, and tried to sleep.

♫

In the morning, when the woman unlocked the doors and disappeared again, Simon left through the soaring entrance, glad to be out of the evil place. He extended his search to the surrounding moors and hills, the chapel ruins and graveyard. He walked the Hermitage Water, through high grasses and flowers, searching, and stood at the stone marking the resting place of the Cout of Kielder, a giant of a man, buried outside the protection of the churchyard. He stared down at the smooth green grass for a long time, remembering the giant of a man, and feeling disoriented. Everyone he knew was dead. When he returned, they would spring back to life. And he would know when and how and where each of them would die.

But there was nothing here to tell him how to return. He had no idea what he could possibly be searching for, anyway.

As evening approached, the wind once again soughed mournfully—all too much like the cries of children. He thought of the woman in Berwick, the pregnant woman, and Longshanks' hand on his arm as he raised his sword, stopping him. But she was dead. Her child was dead. He hadn't thought of them in years.

He turned his mind from it. It was business, war, nothing more. He had places to go, Michael Scott's books to pursue, Thomas the Rhymer to track. But first, speaking of business, he had some to attend to. He hiked back across twilight hills to the village, killed the lout from the pub, and took his money.

Only then did he set out for the Eildon Hills. He would rather cross this terrain by night, than stay again in William's horrible home.

CHAPTER TWENTY-FOUR

Bannockburn, Present

The days passed in a flurry of calls and e-mails—from Ben, his producer, his agent, his publisher, magazines and TV shows wanting interviews. When Amy taught lessons at her home, Shawn cared for James, relishing every moment with the child he'd once lost hope of ever seeing. He cooked dinner with Amy, and spent hours writing arrangements for the album and tour, watching her as she sat at his keyboard picking out the chords, accompaniments, and counter melodies people thought of as his style. He saw, now, how very much 'his' style had always been hers, working beside him.

He relished his second chance, and the way she looked at him as she once had, the way her hand slipped into his as they walked to the market, and the moments she laid her cheek suddenly on his shoulder as they worked. It was only his fears, he was sure, that made him think sometimes she hung back.

He practiced and memorized the solos he and Amy wrote for the Broadway album. He relished being able to play for hours on end. He felt a deep, pulsing gratitude he hadn't felt since before his father's death—or, perhaps, ever.

"I haven't heard any of your old pieces," Amy said one morning as she arrived at his house with James. She dropped the diaper bag to the floor. "The Davison *Sonata. Blue Bells.* They'll want to hear it."

"I'll get to it," Shawn took James, who gave a short shout of excitement and strained from Amy's arms for him. "Hey!" He lifted his son high up in the air, bringing on giggles. "Who's that? Is that James?"

James kicked chubby legs, high up over Shawn's head.

"Careful," Amy said.

Shawn chuckled. "He's fine! This is what fathers are for!" He lifted James up and down, bringing on more laughter. James belched. A long green trail oozed from his mouth, landing on Shawn's face.

"He just ate." Amy grinned, handing him a cloth. "I have eight students. Your mom will be over in a bit." She touched his cheek, smiling. "I'd kiss you, but...."

He winked, wiping at his face with James on his hip. "I clean up well, and there *will* be a rain check."

He watched her head back to her own house, loving the swing of her hair, and the curve of her cheek as she turned to wave. It was good to be home. "Come on, James," he said. "*Blue Bells?* Davison?" But the thought of them called forth the Christina, Niall and Allene. James let out a soft questioning mewl, patting his face.

"Right," he said. "You've eaten. Diaper? Smells fine. Okay, toys. One piece, then I'll play *Blue Bells.*" He settled James, sitting on his blanket with his toys, and sat down to an arrangement of *Any Dream Will Do.* But the Bat Cave was in his head, Christina and Niall laughing there. He forced himself to write the melody in the flutes. The parchments were in his room. He added the verse in a nice woodwind quintet with strings playing harmonies. He could read another one. With clenched jaw, he added a roll in the timpani. He didn't want to read more. Ronan might have died. He put a rhythm in the snare drum. Something awful might have happened to Niall. He re-read the snare rhythm. It didn't fit. He glanced at James. He'd fallen asleep with one hand clenched in his rabbit's ear, and the other pushed in his mouth.

Shawn slapped the pencil down. They'd left the messages for a reason! He stormed the stairs, two at a time. In his room, he slid the ancient roll from the oilskin, and moved the first parchment to the back. Squinting at the faded words of the next missive, he recognized Allene's script.

10 October The Year of Our Lord 1316
My Dearest Shawn, Greetings

Shawn smiled. In his vernacular, such warm words might alarm Amy. In Allene's, they were nothing but a casual *Hey, how ya doin'?* He smoothed his hand over the sheet, fearing Ronan's death.

My father and Brother David send greetings and wish you godspeed.

That meant they were still alive.

I think about writing more, as do Christina and the others. But our days go as they always did. You know them well. James has grown a great deal. You will be pleased to know I could not bear to see him bound up and let him out of his swaddling. He walks. He says uisge and wishes to go to the shore, where you took him. There are those who fret, but it seems, as you say, that freedom and fresh air are no hindrance to a child. He is a braw, bonny laddie.

Niall was sent to England immediately after you went and has not returned. It is my way to ask for prayers. Yet by the time you read these words, you will be able to open the pages of your internet—Shawn smiled at her assumption that the internet opened like a book—*and know whether we got our peace, or if war continues*—continued?—*It is difficult to know which tense to use when I speak to you.*

Living it, waiting in fear, is so very different. My father speaks of Kenneth MacAlpin and Viking invaders, and I think how easy it is to hear the story now, knowing the ending. But it must have been equally hard for them, living it, not knowing what the morrow would bring. How I wish I could be in your time but moments, to read your internet, and know all will be well. Then could I wait patiently through these grim times.

It makes no sense to the mind of man to ask for prayers seven centuries after events, and yet I do ask, for it is all I know. I hope you have found peace with God and finally believe He waits on your prayers, too. Pray for us, for we so need it.

MacDougall remains quiet , giving no trouble. I do not trust him one bit.

As well you shouldn't, Shawn thought.

Though you drove Brother David mad, he seems a wee bit gloomy now. He has no one with whom to argue theology anymore, for we all agree with him.

Shawn smiled, imagining the lackluster discussion as they all vehemently agreed with one another.

I hesitate to tell you. Perhaps I should not. But I worry greatly about Christina. She has not been the same since your leaving. I thought her too practical to grieve so for what she knows cannot be otherwise, yet she changed greatly. She sits often in the window where you sat, but the room is silent without you and Niall playing music. Please pray for her, too.

Shawn read the words three times, his stomach knotting with guilt. But it did no good to read the words over and over. There was nothing he could do for her. He forced himself to move on.

I never met Amy, but feel I did, so clear were your descriptions of her. Give her my love, and your James. My father and Brother David are here, interrupting their argument over chess to say theirs, too.

Yours in Christ, Allene

Shawn touched the faded ink. Its dullness, sinking into the page, made him feel as if Allene herself was fading from his sight. Which was ridiculous, he told himself, because she was long gone, buried somewhere. He squeezed his eyes tight, not wanting to think of it. She said nothing of Ronan. Did that mean four months had erased yet another death from her mind, or that she simply hadn't thought to mention a man who had been hearty and hale again all that time? Nothing could kill Ronan, Shawn decided. It would have to do for now.

He counted the months: she would have been writing only weeks before giving birth to the child with whom she'd been pregnant during the battle in Glenmirril's courtyard. She said nothing about that. But then, that was her way. Sad, he thought. He'd have liked to have known.

But his deeper concern was Christina. Allene was right. She wasn't one to sit in a window and stare, but to smile peacefully and say others had it worse, that she was blessed while there were those who needed food, and she would do well to bring it to them. He wanted to stretch his hand across time, touch her fingertips once more, and tell her—tell her what? There was nothing he could tell her.

He'd left her, and he'd done it with her blessing. A fist sank in his stomach. He wanted her to be happy. He didn't want her sitting in the windowsill where he'd so often sat, mourning. He studied the parchments, torn. He wanted to read the next one, to find Christina was happy again, and Ronan dancing at a feast. But he might find out worse. *Just read it,* he told himself sternly.

He moved Allene's letter to the back, revealing the next. He drew a deep breath, fearing it. But it could be good news, he reminded himself. He lowered his eyes. He couldn't make out the date, except for a *17.*

To our Dear Brother in Christ.

That had to be Brother David. Shawn smiled, touching the words. The smile slipped. If a monk wrote, was it to report death? He had to quit doing this to himself! He splashed into the words as furiously as he'd thrown himself into the loch the day they'd gone hawking, the day he'd sat on the shore with Christina in her sapphire blue gown, grabbing her every word hungrily, devouring them. *...Red with the horses as if he speaks their tongue...he misses you fiercely.* Shawn's eyes stung. He missed the boy! *The Laird spends hours in the Bat Cave....*

"Do something," Shawn whispered. "Your people *need* you!"

No word of Christina. He reached the last line. *They move as if in a dream—a poor one—with Niall, Hugh, and so many of our men off to war in Ireland....*

Shawn squeezed his eyes tight. *This* was worse! Last he checked, Ireland lay beyond a sea. *God, you can't do that to him. You know how he is about water!* He pressed a palm to his forehead. God *had* done it to him. And there wasn't a thing he could do about it.

He rose irritably, pacing. He had to *work.* He should go through that list and finish calling musicians—twenty of them still to look over and talk to. But Niall had been sent to Ireland. He *needed* to know he was okay. Not only was there this crossing water business, but there was war going on there. People could die! *Niall* could die! But there was nothing he could *do.*

He forced himself to pick up his phone and call Elinore Stanfield, pianist. She answered on the fourth ring. Children babbled in the background.

"Hey, Elinore!" Shawn used his jovial business voice, trying to push away thoughts of Niall. "Shawn Kleiner here!"

She gave a quick gasp. "Shawn! I heard...! How are you?"

"Good. Great! Got talk shows and gigs lining up. Listen, Ben's putting together a tour, big band music, great stuff from the 20's, some old Jack Teagarden. He recommended you for my rhythm section. What do you think?" He gave her recording and concert dates, and soon had her confirmation. He hung up—one more call taken care of—and turned to the laptop.

He'd take a look—just a quick one—find out what happened in Ireland. Even if it had gone badly, certainly *someone* had gotten back to Scotland, and that someone was more likely than not to be Niall. He had to believe it.

It took a few search terms, a dozen pages, before the information began to sink in. All of Europe, in 1316, had been in the stark skeletal grip of famine. Shawn remembered well the concerns over the rain rotting crops in the fields. Ireland was hit especially hard, the people reduced to eating grass—and their own dead.

Shawn swallowed, looking away from the words. It didn't help. He forced his eyes back. If Niall had to live it, he could at least read it. Bruce's troops had suffered along with the Irish people. Their horses had slowed with hunger, and they'd resorted to eating the gaunt animals as they died off. They had not been welcomed.

He slammed the lid of the laptop. He didn't want to read any more of Bruce's army crossing the devastated land, fighting hunger and the English all at once.

And Niall and Hugh were in the thick of it.

There was still a stack of parchments, Shawn assured himself. Niall and Hugh had both gone home; otherwise, someone would have told him and quit writing. He chose to believe that. With their safety assured in his mind, if not in truth, he forced himself back to the list of musicians. He glanced at the clock. Three hours had passed while he searched for news of Niall and Hugh. Exhaustion washed over him. He laid his head down on the desk. He'd get to the musicians...in a minute.

Glenmirril, April 1317

"Father." In the dim candlelight of the Bat Cave, Allene addressed his back as he knelt before the crucifix, on the kneeler he'd made for Shawn. "A party approaches."

MacDonald turned, his eyes sunken, looking thinner than he had in years past. The famine touched them all, though the pigeons in the dovecot had managed, and the loch gave them fish. "Who?" he asked.

"They fly the banner of Adair."

MacDonald grunted as he pushed himself to his feet. "They're a ways from home. What would they be doing up here?"

"A letter for Shawn." Allene handed him a rolled parchment. "We can be assured they come as friends. They were riding over the ridge even as I came down to tell you."

MacDonald slipped the panel from the kneeler, and pulled out the oilskin bag. He slid the parchments out and rolled the new one around them, before replacing it all and snapping the panel back into place. "We'd best be meeting them, then. How big is the party? You've let the cooks know?" He crossed the cave, snuffing torches as he went, and locked the door behind them with a clink of his great key ring.

Fresh air hit Allene as they climbed the stairs and emerged into the courtyard. Men flowed through the gatehouse, thirty or more. Castle children danced around the incoming crowd. Allene surveyed the group riding in, worn from the long journey, but smiling. One tall man, gaunt as a skeleton, riding beside a girl clutching a child, grinned more broadly than the rest. His eyes lit on Allene, his smile growing behind his bushy beard. She backed up, her eyes lowered.

A laugh boomed out across the courtyard. *Hugh!* Her head shot up, searching for him, before her eyes settled on the skeletal giant. "Hugh?" she whispered. Her hand flew to her mouth.

He laughed, jumping from the horse, and crushing her in an embrace. "You didn't recognize me? And to think I've put two stone back on!"

She pulled back, fear shooting through her heart. "Where's Niall? Lachlan and Owen?" Surely, he'd not be so happy if anything had befallen them, she told herself.

"In Jedburgh with Douglas. They left me off at the nearest castle with strict instructions to eat and sleep till I was well enough to ride home. He'll be back anon." He turned to MacDonald, clasping him, too, in a bear hug.

When they separated, MacDonald said gruffly, "And why did you not stay in Ireland or go to Jedburgh yourself?"

"A wee disagreement with an English arrow," Hugh said. "It almost got the better of me." He looked around the courtyard, and lowered his voice to a mere shout. "Where's Christina?"

"She's ill," Allene said. "Though she's on the mend and will be down soon and back to her old ways." She turned to the unknown girl. "Will you not introduce us?"

Hugh turned, reaching for the child, and helping the girl down. She was as thin as Hugh, though over a foot shorter. She dropped a deep curtsy to the Laird, her eyes on the ground. "Roysia," Hugh introduced her. "She was widowed in the siege of Carrickfergus. Bruce sends orders that he wishes her to marry our Owen."

MacDonald smiled. "Then she shall do so." He clapped his hand on Hugh's emaciated shoulder, pulled him into a long, tight hug, and when he released him, lifted his leonine head, and shouted joyfully to the castle courtyard, "My brother is home! We've a new child and a new bride! Tonight we will feast and thank God!"

Bannockburn, Present

"Shawn, we're leaving."

Startled from sleep, Shawn shot to his feet, grabbing for his dirk in his boot.

Amy jolted back, alarm in her dark eyes, her hand pressed to James's head, as he let out his own shriek.

Shawn's breathing steadied quickly, his eyes traveling from the small modern living room, to the shock on Amy's face, and to his own hand. "I'm sorry." He lowered the knife, embarrassed. "It was...a dream." Another week of researching the Bruces' war in Ireland had steeped his sleep in battle, famine, corpses, and the horrible images of Niall and Hugh in the middle of it.

"You're falling asleep a lot, this past week." She swayed, holding James to her, shushing him. He turned his head to Shawn, studying him with doubtful eyes.

"Busy week." Shawn gave a laugh that he was sure she knew was forced, but he clung to the excuse. "Three more concerts set up. Six more arrangements."

She bit her lip, not answering, as she soothed James. She was being nice, he thought, not pointing out that *she* had pounded out six more arrangements, while he mostly nodded and agreed to phrases he never heard her play, his mind lodged on a long night's reading, or falling asleep in the easy chair when he sat back to listen to her try out chords. Just now, he'd walked beside Niall, through a village street of corpses, as Niall played *The Falkirk Lament.*

"Look, I just...I was just tired," he said.

From the kitchen came the sound of water running, and Carol singing.

Amy lifted her eyes. "Tell me what's going on. It's the parchments, isn't it?"

"They're fine," he said. "They're great."

Her lips tightened. She gave a quick nod, tried for a smile, and said, "I'm glad."

"Really, it's just a lot of work," he insisted.

She nodded again. "I need to get James home for his nap. Dinner tonight?"

"Yeah." He nodded, too. He gave a laugh, knowing he wasn't fooling her. "I'll have something nice. A bottle of red wine."

"Please talk to me," she whispered.

"I will," he promised. "Just...there's nothing to tell. I will."

She blinked furiously, nodded hard and fast, saying, "Okay, yeah, that's fine. Maybe next week. You'll finish the arrangement?"

"Yeah." He glanced at the score sheet covered in her notation. "I'll have it."

"You remember your meeting with the publisher at four? I'm leaving my keys for you. The car's in front."

"Yeah. I'll be there."

The concern did not ease off her face.

He laughed. "I'm *fine*. I haven't missed a meeting yet."

"Okay." Looking doubtful, she turned for the door. James looked at him over her shoulder, his mouth puckered, eyebrows drawn together.

As the door shut behind them, Shawn dropped down at the table in his front room, picking up a pencil. But the music in his head fell silent. He stared in frustration at the notes skipping over the cream tablets. They were black jumbles of butterflies in widow's weeds, swaying to Niall's *Falkirk Lament.*

He slapped his pencil down on the table. It did no good to avoid it. Leaving the papers like fallen leaves, he bolted up the stairs to his bedroom, and eased the parchments from their oilskin, flattening them carefully across his comforter.

January, the Year of Our Lord, 1317
My Dear Shawn

He recognized Allene's handwriting and relaxed into her brogue, seeing her at the desk in her solar

Peace talks failed again. Niall came home but long enough to kiss his new son. Our William was born in November, a fine, braw laddie like his brother.

It is quiet, with you and Niall and so many of our men gone. The great hall seems morose of an evening. The women and children fell unnaturally quiet for a week, in the wake of the men leaving. Only gradually do the children leave their mother's sides and play again with one another, but quietly, as if their noise might bring disaster upon their fathers. The women smile a wee bit again, and talk. Those whose husbands and sons and brothers are gone gather together amongst themselves.

It is too soon to have word how Niall fared on the sea voyage. I pray that all you tried to tell him helped, but I'll not know for months. The waiting is hard. Praying, not knowing whether God hears, is hard. A blot of ink marred the paper. Her words continued beneath it. *Again, I hesitate to tell you. But you wished news of us. And you cared for her.*

Shawn's muscles tensed. *No, God! Not Christina.* His throat hurt. He drew a deep breath, telling himself it was better to read and find out, than sit here worrying. He touched the words.

Christina is heavy with child. Her time is in March.

He felt as if a tornado ripped him off his feet, slammed his head into a brick wall, and threw him to the ground. He read the words again. The math was easy. There had been someone immediately before or after he'd left. He didn't believe it of her. She wouldn't. And that left only one answer. Feeling sick to his stomach, he read on:

She'll not say whose it is. She is less withdrawn, perhaps in relief that she need no longer hide this from us, but keeps to her chambers and we've yet to decide how to explain the child's presence when her time comes. Father is in a rage, but still, he'll not expose her to shame, nor take her chance for a good husband. He blames you, despite Niall's cautions. He is in a fury that you left her to face this alone, not giving her the shelter of your name and marriage.

Shawn's jaw ached with his own fury. "Didn't I do everything you asked, from the first day!" he shouted at the parchment, at the long-dead Laird so quick to doubt him. "How dare you assume!"

I told him even if it is yours, you'd not have known in June. He says you knew you took the chance. I wish not to believe this, Shawn, and I struggle to understand what it was for you to come from a time so very different to live among us and change your ways. Perhaps in the end, knowing you were leaving her, this was your way.

'Tis hard for me to reconcile that with the good and true man you showed yourself to be these two years, so changed from what I first knew of you, and who Niall said you had been in your world. Perhaps as you read this, you know you are innocent. Only you and Christina know what passed between you. I worry in that case even more, for then it was not the wanton behavior that Father believes.

Shawn slapped the parchment down, heedless of its age. *Who?* The women should have been in hiding. MacDougall's men had been rounded up after the battle. Could one have escaped and hidden in the castle? No one from Glenmirril would have assaulted her. He wished, with a force so vicious he felt it would tear him in half, that he could be there, for just ten minutes, to talk to Christina, find out who had done this, destroy the man and mount his head on a pike, grab the Laird by his arrogant, self-righteous tunic, slam him against a wall, and demand to know how he could be so quick to accuse. He raked his hand through his hair, and forced his eyes back to Allene's words.

I can but ask again for your prayers for Niall, for Christina, though it makes no sense to do so centuries after our lives are lived. Surely God in His goodness might carry prayer across time as He carried you. It gives me hope to think so.

Prayers! Shawn snorted, pacing his chamber. Christina was pregnant.

"Shawn?" his mother called up the stairs. "Is everything all right?"

He stormed down the stairs, stared blankly at her, standing in the hallway, wiping her hands on a towel.

"Shawn?"

He saw Niall's mother; the centuries swayed and collapsed in on one another.

"Shawn," she whispered. "What's happening to you?"

He stared blankly at her. Christina was pregnant! Someone had done this to her. He stormed out the front door. He wanted a quintain to charge, a wide moor to mount his garron and storm across, a tree to chop, an enemy at whom to swing a sword, *anything*, to release the beast. A dog raced into the street, barking, and stopped dead at sight of him. It tucked its tail and turned, bolting back for its own yard. Shawn scowled. He stopped, staring at Amy's car. Glasgow.

"Shawn, what's going on?" His mother stood on the step.

"I'm fine." He gave his head a sharp shake, staring at her. It was his mother, not Niall's. No medieval gown. Soft brown hair curling around her face. No braid. But Christina...he felt disoriented, stumbling between two worlds. He drew a breath. "I'm just getting in the car. I'm going to my meeting."

"Are you sure?" She started down the stairs. "Shawn, let me call Amy."

He was in the car, key twisting, engine humming to life with a throat that would never eat an apple from his hand. He backed out, telling himself to watch the road, watch for children, put himself firmly back into this century. The town gave way to fields. He pulled carefully onto the highway, almost tiptoeing, compensating for the agitation that battered the gates of his mind, flaying him, assaulting him. Christina was pregnant. *Who?* There was nothing he could *do*! He couldn't *help* her!

The fields streaked by, till he arrived, far too early, in Glasgow. A glance at his clock told him he had time to kill. He snorted in dull humor—no, *Niall* had time— to *kill*. He parked the car and got out, determined to walk off the agitation. His cell phone rang. He tore it from his pocket, spoiling for a fight, hoping for someone to bite into. It was Ben. He took a deep breath, forcing down the fight or flight adrenaline, pushed talk, and smiled into the phone. "Hey, what's up!"

Bannockburn, Present

Simon fumed as he marched across twilight fields, back into Bannockburn.

Hermitage—nothing! Nine Stane Rig, the desolate few stones in waving grasses where de Soulis would die—nothing!

The Eildon Hills—nothing! He'd climbed all three, slept on their slopes for nights on end, and searched every side. Of course they hadn't taken him back in time, despite Thomas's story of an elf queen. He'd visited Michael Scot's haunts, returned to Melrose, where people said he was buried, and trekked from Glenluce Abbey to Burgh-under-Bowness in England, on a fruitless chase after his books. Nothing!

He learned nothing that might move him across time. People grew uneasy when asked how Thomas or Michael might have do so. It was a month wasted, no closer to finding answers, Amy, or the crucifix; no closer to killing the monk or James!

A spatter of drops on his face pulled him back to the present. He looked up. Rain trickled from a sky grown cloudy while he mused. He stopped, taking his bearings. A creek flowed before him, small enough to step across on a stone or two —the Bannock Burn. *They fell in the water with their heavy armor and couldn't get up,* Helen had relayed with gusto. *Thousands of English drowned there.* Once again, he stared at a place where those he'd known had died. He wondered who. He wondered if he could return to just before the battle, so he could turn their fortunes.

He snorted in disgust. He didn't know how to get back at all, let alone choose the day. Maybe he'd reappear at the moment he'd left. He had much to learn. He would *have* to chance going after Eamonn again, or hunting down Amy. Or Angus. But he must tread carefully. He started up the slope.

There was still the hall of books. He would see what they might tell him of time travel. The lights of the town twinkled against the darkening sky. Yes, he would do some reading, put a bit more time between himself and the events with Amy and Eamonn. Then, with greater knowledge, he would seek them out again— if he still needed to. Satisfied, he headed into town, to the abandoned hall he'd made his own.

On the first street, he saw the torn, damp vellum stuck to a post. He glanced at it, then stopped, looking more carefully. A picture showed the hideous black-clad youth from the alley. The words below read: *Wanted. Information on the death of Graham Dromond.* Simon glanced up and down the street. It was deserted. He tore down the picture and continued to his home, finding it as the sky became black.

He entered cautiously, lest anyone had moved in. But a quick search told him he was alone. His sword was safe in the floorboards where he'd hidden it, along with his *notebook* and *pen.* He pulled them out, choosing his next steps. Information, and then—James. He smiled, thinking of the moment. Months had passed since he'd spoken with Angus or asked after Amy. Their guard would be down.

But this time, he would seek the child through Shawn. People here knew Shawn the way people in his own time whispered of a famed knight or a great lord. Yes, the library, and then the child.

Glasgow, Present

The call ended in front of a church. Shawn stared blankly at the heavy doors. Ben wanted more—more arrangements, more talk shows, more interviews. Allene's letter played through his mind; anger and concern for Christina chewed at him. He stared at the church. Allene wanted him to pray. He didn't have *time*. It would do neither Christina nor Niall any good. The alternative was to do nothing, he chided himself. The sun beat down on his shoulders as he stared at the cathedral before him. There was something familiar about it. *He didn't have time!* It came to him, as he worked modern and medieval maps together in his mind. He'd been here with Niall.

He moved like a man in a dream to the cathedral. He told himself Niall would not be there. But a slice of his heart expected to walk through the narrowing arches, zeroing in on the huge wooden doors, and see Niall on his knees before the altar, as he had been that day. He opened the door and slipped in.

Stone columns soared to a vaulted ceiling high above. It was what he'd known with Niall—but different. Wooden chairs now circled the base of each column, as if waiting for the laughter of children playing musical chairs in this sacred chamber. They seemed, in his mind, to be there, waiting to burst through time's veil, the same way Niall seemed to hover just out of reach. Age and silence hung all around. Summer light poured through tall, narrow arches of stained glass. In Niall's August, there had been raiding in Northern England, followed by a summons to a sea journey and warfare in Ireland. Shawn walked through the empty nave, his leather boots silent on the stone floor.

He entered the quire, staring at row after row of pews the color of dark cinnamon. The smell of wood polish hung in the air. Light danced through the windows, a bright sheen on dark wood. In the front pew knelt a figure in a gray robe. Shawn's heart hammered. He glided forward on silent feet, his mind wavering between centuries. There had been no red cushions on the pews when he came with Niall. The windows were different. He knew that.

Still, the kneeling monk drew him. He'd seen Amy at Monadhliath. There was no reason he couldn't see Niall here. At the front, he slid into the pew across the aisle from the monk. A cowl hid the man's face.

"Niall," Shawn whispered.

The man turned, staring at Shawn quizzically. His face was narrow, almost gaunt, his hair sandy and thin. "I *am* kneeling."

Shawn's mind reeled. He smiled. Niall would be amused. "I'm sorry. I thought you were someone else."

The monk smiled, and bowed back over folded hands. Shawn dropped to his knees. The people he'd left behind danced like reels of old celluloid through his mind. He wondered if William, the new baby, had the same rich auburn hair as his brother—Allene hadn't said—if Bessie continued to grow more cheerful, if Conal would return safely from his battles, how Allene fared, waiting, and waiting, and waiting, for Niall's rare and brief returns. Mostly, he pondered Christina's fate, unwed and pregnant and the Laird displeased with her.

It was a ridiculous request on Allene's part. But he bowed his head and prayed for them. Especially Christina. With the cathedral's strong stone walls rising all around him, the stained glass shining down, he sank inside himself, feeling the echo of hundreds of years and millions of people through history, on their knees beside him, around him, before him, felt Christina on her knees in Glenmirril's chapel, felt the hundreds of hours of Niall and Allene, the Laird, Hugh, and Brother David in the chapel, and felt himself part of a great army stretching across history.

Peace settled in his soul. God would hear. God would help Christina.

CHAPTER TWENTY-FIVE

Bannockburn, September, Present

In the library, Simon leaned back in his chair, legs outstretched, staring up at the high windows. Rain dimpled the glass. There were books enough to keep him busy for a year. He'd been at it for weeks, his nervousness growing as the days passed. Though he was learning a great deal, Christmas was less than three months away.

"I found more on Michael Scott!" The irritating *librarian* approached with another pile. She'd not tired of it, but rather took greater delight each day in his endless searches. He'd added to his knowledge of Edward's life in the years after Bannockburn. He'd continued his study of weapons, filling an entire *notebook* with diagrams. But he'd learned nothing useful of Michael Scott, or Lord Soulis.

Last week, he'd cautiously broached the subject of time travel. Contrary to the wariness it had roused in others, she'd eagerly brought him a set of thick books on events that would transpire between England and Scotland four hundred years in his own future. He read eagerly. Though the historian seemed more interested in a woman's trysts with a certain Jamie, he did learn that standing stones carried her across time.

As the woman added three new books to the stack already teetering on the edge of his desk, he pointed to one of the volumes. "Where are these stones?" he asked.

She looked taken aback for a moment, and then burst into laughter. "Oh, you *are* funny!" She sobered in the face of his hard stare. "Oh, no, sir, that's *fiction.*"

"Fiction?" He gave her the cold gaze that sent his page scurrying.

"Fiction." She frowned. "Not real."

"Not *real*?" Simon demanded. "The Jacobites are real." He'd come across them in the previous week's reading.

"Well, yes, Sir...I mean no, Sir." She took a step back. "The *history* is true, but the rest...'tis a *story*." As his brows drew together darkly, she hastened to say, "You *asked* for time travel."

"I did not ask for *stories!*" Simon barked.

She bobbed her head, though she looked confused—and as if she pitied him. "Right, Sir. We've plenty of non-fiction." She scurried away, and as Simon stared out the rain-streaked windows, re-appeared, waving another book. "If 'tis non-fiction you're wanting, here's another on Edward!" she enthused. "He was murdered at Berkeley Castle, now!"

"September, 1327. By his wife," Simon recited.

"Well, now, she didn't do the deed herself."

"I should think not."

His gaze dropped to a leather-bound tome before him, detailing the doings of Michael Scott. It told him nothing helpful. Despite all his journeys and reading, he still had no ideas beyond the crucifix and castle, or waiting until next year's re-enactment, about how to return. Perhaps he needed to just settle in and wait until June, and cross back into the actual battle. He'd walk off the field into his own time. He'd save the battle, and destroy the Scots there, as they would have been, had the English had a competent commander. And that left him plenty of time to kill James.

♬

"You'll be okay?" As Amy folded a blue tunic into her suitcase, she glanced at the rain spattering the window.

Shawn flopped back on the bed, pulling her down on top of him. "He'll be with me and my mom."

She laughed, trying to pull off him, protesting, "We have to leave in two hours."

He rolled, pinning her beneath him. "You're packed, you're fine." He pressed his hand in her hair, kissing her. She relaxed. She returned the kiss. His heart soared. Her lips and hair were soft. She loved him! He was with her, his son, building a family, making right all his mistakes! He lifted his head, soaking in the sight of her eyes warm on his. "I've been taking care of him every day for months. Are you really worried?"

"No." Amy sighed. "I've just never been away from him more than a few hours. You're busy."

Shawn twisted a strand of her hair around his finger. "A meeting with the publisher after I drop you off. Then it's just *yadda yadda* with Ben about the tour, and practicing."

"*Blue Bells*, maybe?"

"Yeah, of course." Shawn rolled away abruptly, sitting on the edge of the bed. He didn't want to play it; didn't want to be sucked back into the Bat Cave and the helplessness of knowing he could do nothing for those he'd left behind. He'd stayed away from the parchments for weeks, leaving Christina in eternal limbo.

Behind him, Amy climbed to her knees. Her hands fell on his shoulders, her cheek rested against the back of his neck. For a moment, she said nothing. He was grateful. He suspected she knew.

Then she said softly, "I felt...them. In the Bat Cave. I wish I could help you."

He turned suddenly, needing her, wrapping his arms around her, sinking his head against her warm neck. She stroked his hair, his cheek, as if she knew of the tears he held back as forcibly as he'd once fought off de Caillou's Gascons at Skaithmuir. He pushed them out of his mind, thought of all the good in his life, of Amy, of James, of people who wanted to hear him play, of people who left his concerts smiling.

He became still in her arms. After a moment, he cleared his throat. "James will be fine." He broke into a smile, and lifting his head, kissed her again. He pulled away at last, saying, "I'm glad I'm back. Thank you."

She laughed. "For what?"

"Everything." He squeezed her hand, as he jumped up from the bed. "Let's go for a walk!"

She shook her head, but another laugh came out. "It's raining!"

"We've walked in the rain before." He pulled her up from the bed, wrapping her into a slow dance, and whispered against her ear, "And it ended very well."

♫

"Did you want that book on Edward?"

"Hm?" Simon raised his eyebrows.

The gray-haired woman nearly danced before him in excitement. "'Tis the best book on him! I can...."

Simon glanced at the pile of books. He knew enough of Edward. "I want time travel," he clipped off. She wore on his nerves. "Something *real.*"

She stopped her jittery excitement, cocking her head. "Time travel? *Real* time travel?"

"Yes," he said impatiently. "You've nothing to tell how it's done?"

She blinked at him. "Well, Einstein had some ideas."

"I wish to speak to him." He hoped the man wasn't in *America* like Shawn.

She blinked at him. "Well...he's....he's *dead* these many years. I meant...I meant a *book*, you know."

Simon sighed. He'd dearly like to kill her. He was through with her. But only this morning, he'd seen another tattered post stuck to a shop window, showing that insolent girl from the store. He questioned, as it was, whether he'd been wise to return here.

"Get me the book," he commanded.

"Well...you know...don't get the wrong idea," she said hesitantly.

Simon rose, glaring down at her.

She backed up a step, but persisted. "You know it's not as if Einstein *could* travel through time. He only...."

"Get it," he snapped. He headed for the door, leaving her to deal with the dozens of books she'd removed from the shelves. He would read what she brought, but sooner or later, he must give up this path, and try to find the crucifix and Eamonn. He flung open the door, blinking in the bright sun that had replaced the recent rain, and heard a short, sharp squeal. He froze. He squinted into the light, peering down the street. There, not a dozen paces ahead, was Amy, carrying the horrible spawn. Beside her, shaking out a tartan umbrella, walked Shawn.

With a smile, Simon fell into step some distance behind, trailing them block after block until they turned into a house. From the shelter of trees in a small, grassy park just across from his door, Simon noted the house number and street. As he watched, the door opened again. Shawn emerged with a case. Amy followed, wearing a long sweater and carrying her violin. Shawn opened the back of her car to heft the case in. Amy turned to the house, where an older woman stood in the doorway, holding the child. She lifted its hand, making it wave. The thing let out one of its ugly squeals.

Amy put her violin in the car, and returned to the doorway to lift him in her arms, and hug him tightly. She spoke to the woman, kissed the baby, and handed him back. Shawn, with a hand on Amy's back, led her to the car. He backed it out, and they drove away.

Simon glanced at the sky. Evening would fall soon. They were clearly leaving on a journey. Perhaps to *America.* The child and woman were alone. He studied the windows, upper and lower, guessing at the layout inside, before smiling, and heading back to the hall of books. He would deal with the child after dark.

Glenmirril, 1317

Malcolm entered the room, trailed by Brother David, to find Hugh sitting in the window, much as Shawn had once done, though Hugh, even emaciated as he was, filled it more than Shawn had.

Hugh turned, showing a broad grin. "Malcolm!"

Malcolm glared at him. "Adair's men tell me you said you were well enough for the journey."

Hugh winked. "Clearly I was, for here I am! Still on this side."

Malcolm didn't smile. "Clearly you weren't. You collapsed on the stairs before you reached your rooms. Would it have killed you to wait till you were truly well?"

Brother David opened the writing case on the desk under the window.

Hugh laughed. "The man who threatened to burn my intestines and mount my head on a pike—concerned for my well-being?"

"'Twas *Shawn's* intestines I threatened to burn. And 'twas no idle threat." His bushy eyebrows furrowed in anger. "Did you not *think* that we've need of you? Did you not *think* of the good of Scotland and Glenmirril?"

Hugh sobered. "I've thought of naught else, these twenty years, Malcolm. My life has been devoted to them." He threw a deliberate glance at Brother David, writing at the desk. "And it seems you've something to discuss with me. So 'tis a grand thing I've come to your rescue yet again, rather than lie abed."

Malcolm snorted.

"Careful." Hugh's mouth quirked up. "Someone might take you for Shawn."

At the desk, Brother David lifted his head, with a grin. Malcolm glared. The monk quickly forced it back.

"I gave MacDougall permission to write his steward." MacDonald dropped a bundle on the table. "This is his first letter, and his steward's response. MacDougall will not acquiesce to his imprisonment, or give up revenge for Duncan's death." He indicated the packet angrily. "So read them and tell me what's hidden here that I'm not seeing."

Hugh swung his long legs down from the window, grinning at his brother.

"'Tis grand I came home."

"I've just finished copying Roger's reply." Brother David rose, and the three of them studied the originals together, searching for anything amiss, words that might have alternate meanings, codes woven in. "Every other letter, every third letter?" Hugh studied the ten pages spread before them.

"Last letter of every line?" Brother David offered.

They found nothing.

"Perchance we're wrong and he simply cares about his orchards," Hugh said.

"Is there no hope for his redemption?" Brother David asked. "He's reading a great deal on the saints and the faith."

Malcolm frowned. "He asks for the books, at least."

"And discusses them with Red," Brother David said. "He's also asking Roger to send him a monk."

"A Franciscan," Hugh said. "He's quite particular on that. Any reason he'd be drawn to Franciscans?"

"He talks a great deal with Red about the horses. Perhaps 'tis Francis's way with animals?" Brother David suggested.

"Give it to MacDougall," Hugh advised. "What he writes in return may help us put the pieces together. Then we'll decide again how to proceed."

Bannockburn, Present

From the moonlit flower-lined path leading to the red door, Simon heard the child's cries. Night had fallen, leaving the air cool, and stars bright overhead—though not so bright as in his own time. Women and children had disappeared behind doors, leaving the street deserted. The child's cries stopped. Simon touched the knife at his waist, and turned the knob.

The door opened silently. His eyes barely had time to adjust to the light inside, before he heard a sharp voice from above. "Who are you?" Simon lifted his gaze. The woman stood at the railing in the hallway above, cradling the child in her arms.

"It's James, is it not?" Behind his back, he twisted the latch, locking the door.

Fear flickered over her face. "Who are you?" She took a step, backing down the hall above.

He moved slowly to the bottom stair. Best not to alarm her. "Is Shawn home?"

"Get out." Her voice shook. She backed up another step.

Simon launched himself at the stairs. She spun, running. Simon scrambled up the steps, rounding the rail at the top, to face two closed doors at the end of the hall. Thumps and bangs came from the one on his left. He smiled. Their doors were weak. He glanced at the narrow hall. It gave no room to back up and ram the door, but he wouldn't need much. First, he thought, he should make sure Shawn really wasn't here. He backed down the hall, watching the door. The thumping and pounding continued. It didn't matter. There was nowhere for her to go. She couldn't stop him breaking through the door.

He inched down the stairs, wary of creaks. Let her imagine him outside the door. Let her fear. He caressed the hilt of his knife, as he reached the bottom. The lower level held only the front room, clearly empty, and the kitchen down the narrow hall. If Shawn was here, he'd have come running by now. Simon climbed the stairs again, and stood outside the door. "Come out," he said softly. "I mean you no harm."

No sound came from within. He leaned close, his head to the thin wood, listening. The distinctive short squeal erupted. Simon twisted the knob. It was, as he expected, locked. "I brought the child a toy," he said.

"Get out," the woman called. "The police are being called."

Simon backed against the opposite wall, and rammed the door, hard. She screamed. The wood splintered but, surprisingly, did not give. His eyes narrowed. From behind came the sound of something heavy being pushed. She'd barricaded it. He threw himself at it again, and again. The wood gave just above his shoulder. Inside, James yelped. Simon rammed the door again. It splintered with a loud crack. A thin stream of light broke through. He smiled. Whatever she'd jammed against the door couldn't cover the whole thing.

He backed against the wall, raised one booted foot, and kicked, connecting with a satisfying crunch. More light burst through. James wailed. Simon kicked again.

"Call the police!" she shouted.

He peered through the splintered door, to see her leaning out the window. In a crib against the far wall, James writhed and shrieked.

Simon's fury bubbled. The woman would die, too, and slowly, for causing trouble. He reached through the broken wood, wiggling the door handle, feeling for whatever blocked it.

Something slammed into his arm. He ground his teeth. Blood oozed from a long scrape. She would pay! She hit him again. He yanked his arm back.

"Call the police!" she screamed.

He backed against the wall, and kicked, and kicked again, tearing a gaping hole in the upper half of the door. He saw her through it, holding a drawer from the bureau that blocked the door. She'd pay for her defiance; she'd pay dearly!

She backed up a step, the drawer raised.

Suddenly, from below, came a pounding. Simon swore, launching himself at the broken door. Outside, a man yelled.

She glanced at the window, shouting, "Hurry!" In the crib, James shrieked.

Simon yanked his knife, pounding at the splinters, shoving, pushing through over the dresser. She came at him, swinging. He flung an arm up. The drawer jarred his elbow. But she was no knight. Her weapon was no mace. He lifted his knee, trying to get through. At the bottom of the stairs, the front door crashed open.

"Protect James!" roared a man.

Simon spun, flinging himself down the hall. He reached the top of the stairs when Shawn was halfway up, wearing breeks and a *leine*.

Shawn froze, watching, waiting.

Simon's eyes flickered over him. Shawn had no weapon. Simon's lips curved up in a slow smile. "How was 1314?" he whispered.

"The police are coming." Shawn backed down the stairs, gesturing to the open front door, and the night beyond. "Walk out before they come."

"Oh, no." Simon lifted his dagger. "*You* walk out. Close the door behind you."

Shawn laughed. "I'm not impressed by your knife. There's a lot worse where I've been."

Simon's smile grew. Knowledge was power. Though wary of losing the upper hand, he took a step down the stairs.

"He has a knife, Shawn," the woman called, her voice high with tension. The child screeched.

"Find more to block the door." Shawn's eyes never left Simon.

"Did you fight with Bruce?" Simon asked. "How is he?"

Shawn backed down another step. Sounds came from the bedroom. Suddenly, a bright blue object hurtled out. It missed Simon by a good length, but in the split second distraction, Shawn lunged up the stairs, shouting, "I told you to block the door!"

Simon raised his knife.

Grabbing the rail, Shawn skidded to a halt, three steps below, tantalizingly just out of reach. He backed down a step again, suddenly smiling. "Throw more," he called, his eyes locked on Simon.

"Don't be a fool," Simon whispered. "When I'm through with you, I have my fun with her."

"But you're not *going* to be through with me." Shawn's smile faded. "Come on." He lowered himself step by step, watching Simon.

James shrieked, a steady, percussive siren.

Another projectile launched from the room. Simon ducked. Shawn dove in, and jumped back, as Simon recovered. Anger swished a lethal tail in Simon's gut. A book sailed through the ruined door, grazing his shoulder. His lips tightened. He glanced from the door, to Shawn on the stairs, and came down two steps. Another book sailed over the railing, glancing off his back. He swore, and lunged. Shawn skipped down the last stairs, and spun, racing down the hall. Simon bolted after him, eager for the kill, to plunge the knife into Shawn's back, feel its blade grate on bone.

James's screams pierced the air.

As Simon skidded to the bottom of the stairs, Shawn burst from the kitchen, a knife in each hand. Simon froze.

"You didn't really think I was running, did you?" Shawn moved forward, muscles taut for action.

Simon backed up the stairs. Shawn inched closer, his eyes as sharp as his dual blades. Simon licked his lips, and backed up another step. Another object sailed from the room, round and glassy. It struck the railing. Glass shards exploded around Simon's head. He raised his arms, protecting his eyes, and Shawn was on him, knives flashing.

The child screeched, short, sharp reports, that pierced Simon's head.

In a heartbeat, Simon pinned Shawn's wrist to the wall, squeezing with the hand that had crushed throats. The press of his body trapped Shawn's other arm between them. But Simon couldn't reach his own knife, caught in his hand that pinned Shawn's wrist. He squeezed harder, trying to shake the weapon from Shawn's grip. Shawn's lips tightened, turning white. He strained against Simon's weight. His fingers trembled.

James wailed like a spirit from Hell.

Sweat broke out across Shawn's forehead.

"Call the police!" the woman shrieked upstairs.

With a grunt, Shawn wrenched himself sideways. Simon stumbled, caught himself, and slashed his knife up. Shawn sucked his stomach in, barely avoiding the blade, and threw himself forward. Simon skipped up two stairs, dodging. Carol's face and arm appeared in the broken doorway, a small gray object in her hand. Simon glanced between the two of them. The thing flew over the rail. He jumped up a step, stumbled, scrambled up another as Shawn came at him, slicing at his legs from below. Simon swiped, but Shawn grabbed his legs, and the two of them rolled down the stairs, locked in a furious embrace. They tore apart at the bottom, scrambling to their feet, panting, circling one another in the tight space. Shawn dove. Sirens split the night. Simon glanced from Shawn to the open door, and bolted into the dark.

THIRD MOVEMENT

CHAPTER TWENTY-SIX

Bannockburn, Present

After checking their badges, Shawn let the cops in.

"Hold on," he said, as they pushed into the narrow hallway. "Just let me get to my son and mom."

"We need to look for him *now,*" an officer barked.

"Medium height," Shawn snapped. Upstairs, James screeched. He tried to get through the mass of officers.

"Mr. Kleiner, we need...."

"Stocky, swarthy," Shawn said, and half a dozen officers dispersed into the night, flashlight beams swinging in white arcs across gardens and cars, across the sleeping faces of the row homes, across shop fronts and the church in the next street.

"He's gone, Mom!" Shawn climbed the stairs, over the shattered lamp, exercise weight, and books, calling, "Are you okay?" James shrieked, one sharp staccato sound of agitation after another.

"I'm fine," she said. But her voice shook. He came down the hall to the sound of the dresser being tugged away. He could see through the destroyed frame, James screaming in his crib. He wanted to reach out, wanted to take his son in his arms. His mother's face was pale, her lips white, tears spilling from her eyes. Her hands shook as she tugged at the dresser.

Outside, lights flashed.

"What happened here?" An officer appeared at his side, surveying the wrecked door.

Shawn reached through the hole, pushing at the dresser. "Mom, go get him. We'll get this."

She sagged in relief, turning. Shawn's heart ached. He'd seen the same look, the shock, on the faces of dozens of women as he raided medieval English towns with James Douglas. Such horror should have stayed in the fourteenth century. He and the officer, wedged side by side in the small space, alternately shoved at the door, and reached through to push at the dresser, as Carol gathered James up, comforting him. His cries diminished, till he let out only small shuddering breaths. The officer gave one last push on the door, and Shawn squeezed through. He wrapped his arms around Carol, around his son, and where James's cries stopped, hers began, shaking in his arms.

♫

Black anger swirled in Simon, hiding in walled gardens and darting from bush to bush, with wailing, demonic lights flashing all around, beams of light sweeping in arcs, and the calls of one policeman to another.

In brief respites of darkness, he threw himself over walls, creeping from one walled garden to another, finally emerging cautiously at the far end of the row of houses. He stopped there, catching his breath after the fight and flight, chastising himself. It was a *woman and child!* It should have been *easy*! Had one of his men failed so miserably, he'd have him flogged!

It *would* have been easy, he reminded himself, had Shawn stayed away. And now Shawn had seen him, it became impossible to speak with him. He would have to get information by threat to Amy and the child.

"Any sign of him?" a voice called close by.

Simon drew back into the bushes outside the garden wall. A beam of light swung within inches of his feet, and the man came so close, Simon could, if he chose, reach out, wrap his hand around the man's mouth and slide his blade through the blue uniform, past his spine, into his heart. He lifted a hand, inching the branches down, while the other tightened around the hilt of his knife.

But the goal was to return to his own time. He couldn't stay in Bannockburn. He would deal with James when Amy returned to Inverness—she surely would, as long as Angus was there. Failing that, it didn't matter, really, if the child died now, or as a young man. He knew, from the snake-woman's archives, that James was coming. He'd not be taken by surprise. In fact—Simon smiled—it might be more satisfying to kill him *then*, to stand with his knife in the boy's gut, watching a lifetime of hope and expectation flicker and fade in his dying eyes.

Yes, it would be *very* satisfying.

"No sign of him," the man called. "He must have gone the other way. Have they seen anything down that end?"

Yes, the goal was to return to his own time, Simon thought. There were more places to get answers. He would go there—as soon as he retrieved his *notebooks* that held the key to building formidable weapons. His hand relaxed on his knife. He watched as the beam of light, swinging in wide arcs, moved slowly away from where he crouched.

♫

"You've no clue a' tall who he was?" the officer asked for the third time. The two cops, a man and a woman, perched on the edges of chairs in Shawn's front room.

"I didn't the first two times you asked," Shawn snapped, "and you notice no carrier pigeon has brought me new information in the last ten minutes."

In Carol's arm, James startled in his sleep. She touched the back of Shawn's hand. "He's just doing his job."

"Yeah, well, he's doing a crappy job," Shawn barked. "A guy broke in and hammered down your door trying to kill you, and his bright idea is to ask fifteen times in a row if I know who he was? How the hell would I know who he was?"

"Shawn, please." She handed James to him, and rose. "Officer, can I make tea for all of us?"

"That'd be lovely," said the woman.

"But he knew the child's name?" the man asked Carol.

She sighed, and for the third time, said, "Shawn's talked about him in his interviews. Everyone knows his name." She headed to the kitchen.

The woman turned to Shawn. "You say he was one point seven meters?"

"I don't know," Shawn said irritably. "Shorter than me. Five eight, five nine. I didn't stop to ask, while he was trying to kill me."

"Build?" she asked, jotting in her notebook.

"Strong." Shawn frowned. Not that he'd gotten into many fights in his own time, but he'd grown strong in Niall's, and hadn't expected any difficulty fighting anyone off. "Very strong," he added.

"Do you mean stocky?" she asked.

He blinked at her. The thought of the damage to Amy's wall flashed through his mind. James stirred in his arm, curling into his body with a small sniffle. He looked at him, seeing for a moment Niall's son.

"Sir, Mr. Kleiner." The man leaned forward. "Are you all *right*?"

Shawn looked up at him, disoriented. Past and present mixed in his head. "Yes, stocky," he agreed. It had felt like fighting on the ship at Jura, taking every ounce of strength he possessed. "Muscular."

"Shall I get you water?" the woman asked.

He shook his head. "I'm fine."

"Any mannerisms you noticed?"

"Yeah, a mannerism like he wanted to kill me."

The male officer heaved a heavy sigh. "Mr. Kleiner, we'll not get far with comments like that."

The scent of licorice floated into the room. Carol set a tray of tea cups and a tea pot on the coffee table, saying, "His speech."

Shawn looked up at her, as she poured tea into a cup. "His speech?"

"His accent." Carol offered the cup to the woman, who took it and sipped.

The man jotted in his notebook. "What sort of accent?"

Carol picked up another teacup. "It was like nothing I've ever heard. You didn't notice it, Shawn?"

Shawn shook his head. "No, he sounded normal to me."

"Normal?" She tilted her head, the pot poised in her hand. "How could you *possibly* think he sounded *normal*?"

Monadhliath Mountains

Simon trekked through the night, farther and farther from the lights of Bannockburn, into fields and hills, where stars exploded overhead in their black sea. He'd given himself away, he reflected, as he stepped over a small stream.

Shawn now knew his face, and they would be looking for him. There might be portraits of himself on posts, as there were of the boy and girl he'd killed. He couldn't go back to Bannockburn. Ever.

He pushed himself harder up the slope, angry at his failure. But at least he had his notebook, with the precious diagrams of powerful weapons, safe against his body, under his shirt. And it felt good to feel the earth beneath his feet again, though his muscles protested after many miles of the rough terrain. A month with books had made him soft and weak. He must return to his own ways, if he wanted to be a force to be reckoned with.

A shaggy long-horned cow, lying in moonlit shadows, its legs tucked under it, mooed at him. It was bigger than any cow in his time, by far. But his knife would take care of it. He considered killing it simply to vent rage. But he had business. A knight in the King's service did not stoop to such pettiness and lack of control.

The pasture inched upward. As he climbed ever higher through the night, into the Monadhliath Mountains, he reviewed all he knew—the birth dates of Edward's children, world events—with which he would appear to prophesy. This was a test like no other. He must know these things. He planned his words to Edward, how he would take control of the weak monarch, and how he would subdue the Scots, once he had power. There would be nothing left of them when he finished.

He turned, scanning north and west, piecing together all he knew, from the times he'd come through in his own century, from his hike with Amy and Angus, and the positions of the stars, Inverness, and Bannockburn. He had plenty of time for the monastery. He smiled to himself. Yes, time was his.

Bannockburn, Present

"We can't tell Amy." Shawn made the announcement with finality as he set his and Carol's suitcases down on the blue carpet and looked around the brightly lit hotel room. It would do for the night.

Carol slipped the diaper bag to the floor, and carried the sleeping James to a cot against one wall. She laid him down gently. "Shawn, you *have* to tell Amy. He's her son, too."

Shawn shook his head strenuously. "She's recording tomorrow. You *know* what she's going to do if I call her right now and tell her."

Carol sighed, her eyes shut for just a moment. She opened them again, looking as exhausted as he felt, after battling with the man on the stairs. "Okay," she said. "You're right. He's fine, we'll tell her as soon as she's done. But I'm not sure this move is necessary."

"Lindsay's already on it."

"If it was someone looking for you," she objected, "won't he find you again, wherever you move us?"

Shawn gave a grunt in lieu of an answer. He had no answer. He strode to the window, staring out into the lights of the city. Far away, Stirling Castle shone on its hill. It seemed like yesterday he'd stood in a battlefield, shoulder to shoulder with Hugh and Adam, right here where the motel sat, ready to die to prevent the English reaching it. Now, it was just a place people visited to look at tapestries. Yet he'd once again put his own body between evil and those he loved.

As he stared out the window, the image of the damaged wall in the professor's house came back to him. His eyebrows furrowed, not wanting to believe it. But his gut told him: the man who had attacked his mother had also been in Amy's house, looking for her. Why?

"Shawn?"

He turned. His mother's face was drawn with fear. He couldn't tell her.

He spread his hands. "What's my other choice? Do nothing? I think, though, you and Amy should fly home with James. Come with me when I start my tour."

In his cot, James let out a heavy sigh and rolled onto his back. He blinked up at them, frowning as if about to start crying.

"Turn down the light," Carol said softly. She went to James, pulling a blanket up under his chin, as the lights winked off in the room. He rolled over again, letting her rub his back. "You have to decide that with Amy," she said.

"Of course she'll bring him back," Shawn said. But his words came out irritably as he threw himself on a bed and began unlacing one leather boot. He wasn't as sure as he'd like to be. He'd have to make her see the sense in it.

Carol sat down on the other bed, removing her own shoes. "The thing is," she reminded him, "if someone's looking for you in particular, going to the States does no good." She paused, her hands on the lace of one shoe. "You no doubt made more enemies there than you have here."

Shawn's jaw tightened. He stared out the window into the starry sky above the far-away castle.

"I'm not criticizing," she said. "You've come back different. But you can't undo the past. And racing James off to the States isn't the answer, if it was a random attack. And you certainly have to make that decision *with* Amy, not for her."

"She's not going to want to leave," he admitted. He pulled off his boot, dropping it at the foot of the bed.

"She did have a life here with Angus," Carol pointed out.

"Yeah." Shawn barely restrained a snort, as he loosened the laces on the second boot.

"He was good to her and for her," Carol said.

Shawn pulled at his boot, muttering, "Even my own mother."

"He's a good man, Shawn," she said. "He got you back. He took care of your son and loved him like his own." She opened her suitcase, rummaging in the dark. "Have you considered calling him about this? He might be able to help."

"I don't need his help," Shawn said stiffly.

"But maybe James does." Carol opened the bathroom door, standing in the bar of light. "Maybe your son should come before your pride." She closed the door, swamping the room once more in dark.

Shawn snorted. It had *nothing* to do with pride, he assured himself. He just didn't need the guy's help.

Monadhliath Mountains, Present

As dawn broke, Simon stopped on a barren crest, peering with raised hand into the rising sun, where it laced the undersides of clouds, gold and pink. He gazed down in satisfaction over the orchards spreading around the ancient monastery. The rising sun lit the church tower and the great stone walls that had stood for eons. Their bell tolled, low and mournful, great slow swings of the huge beast, its voice sounding a deep cry of anguish on every fourth beat.

He would get a good meal from them first, and then get to business. They were alone, a few men, old and weak. If Eamonn had returned, the old monk would tell him, this time, where the crucifix really was. If he hadn't, the other monks would tell him what they knew. There had been a dozen of the crucifixes. Perhaps they all did the same thing. Perhaps they held other powers that would be useful.

He set off down the hill, rounding the monastery to the front gates.

Bannockburn, Present

The phone jarred Shawn awake as dawn peered through a sliver-thin gap in the curtains. He fumbled for his phone, hoping it didn't wake James.

"Sergeant MacGowan," a deep voice barked, when he answered. "We've found nothing. We believe 'twas a random attack. There's nothing more we can do."

"Yeah, thanks for that nothing." Shawn muttered. He hung up and stared irritably at the ceiling in the gray light, wondering what else he could do. *Random attack* didn't sit right with him. The man had been violent, too determined—too *personal*.

But he had no proof. A hole in Amy's wall proved nothing. He had no idea where to turn. He glanced at James in his cot. His mother was right. He had a responsibility to his son. But Angus was the only answer that occurred to him.

Outside, an early morning bird let out a peal of joyful song, despite the gray. Picking up his phone again, Shawn pulled up Amy's name. He could ask her for Angus's number. She would ask why he wanted it. He wouldn't upset her before her big moment. He swung his legs to the floor, and raked a hand through his hair. He went to James's crib, touching his son's soft, black curls as he slept. Decisions had been simpler, when he only considered what was fun. Maybe he could just tell Amy they were all moving home. He gave his head a sharp shake. No, he couldn't. He had promised himself and Christina he was going to be better. In her bed, Carol rolled over and let out a heavy sigh.

Shawn paced the dim room. He could look up the number to the Inverness police station. He kept forgetting he had internet. But Bannockburn said it was a random attack. What was Angus going to do about that? His phone rang while he stared at it, showing Lindsay's number.

"Hey, Lindsay," he said softly, not wanting to wake up James. "You found something?"

Yeah," she said. "You need to call them to go look at it. Got a pen?"

"Yeah." Shawn grabbed the pen and notepad off the nightstand. James stirred in his sleep as Shawn took down the information and thanked her.

"You never used to thank me for anything," she said.

"I'm thanking you now." The tension of the night whipped through him. "I was a screw-up, okay. It'd be nice if people could quit reminding me. Maybe just for a day or two."

"You're being a screw-up now," she said.

"Forgive me," he snapped. "I've had a rough night."

James squirmed in his bed and let out a high-pitched yelp.

"So sad," she said. "Like no one else in the world ever had a rough night. So did I, but you notice I'm still up at midnight doing your work for you?"

"I pay you well!" At the sharp report of his voice, James let out a whimper.

"Not well enough to snap at me in the middle of the night. We all got used to being treated with respect while you were gone, and realized we didn't actually need your money." She hung up on him.

He lowered his phone with a sigh, and rubbed James's back. Carol stirred in the pearly light pushing through the crack in the curtains. "Is he awake?" she murmured.

"Not yet," Shawn answered. "Lindsay just called. We have a new place." As he spoke, his phone emitted the *ka-ching* of a cash register. He hit *answer,* moving away from James's cot. "Hey, Ben." He let himself out into the hotel's hallway, as Carol rose from her bed. "What's up?"

"I got the last confirmation on your tour appearance today," his manager said. "The list is in your e-mail. Twenty concerts through October, November, December. Everyone's booked, ready to go. I have you on thirty talk shows—TV, radio, internet—and interviews with thirteen print publications. I need you home mid October."

"The first concert isn't until...."

"You need to be home, Shawn. If you want to rebuild your career, you need to *be* here! You know you can't just fly in that morning and walk onstage!"

Shawn's irritation inched upward, warring with Lindsay's reprimand. He drew a harsh breath, and tried to speak calmly. "I *told* you I wanted to do these by phone. Amy's not ready to leave." And he could hardly leave her and Carol alone with this freak show on the loose, not knowing if it was really random.

"Shawn, you know how this business works," Ben shot back. "I got you on all the major network stations. That's what you *said* you wanted. Some of them tape early. You want me to cancel? There go hundreds of thousands of dollars in ticket sales, and there slides your reputation into the pit of unreliability. People are going to be less inclined to work with you or give you interviews in the future. Tell me what you want me to do, Shawn. I'll do it, but you better be aware of the consequences."

Shawn sighed. "Let me talk to Amy," he said. "Uh, Ben?"

"Yeah?"

"Thanks." Shawn cleared his throat. "Thank you."

He ended the call and leaned against the wall. Down the hall, a door opened.

A man and woman emerged, pulling suitcases behind them. The woman glanced at Shawn in his trews, bell-sleeved shirt, and bare feet, and looked away. Humility and meekness settled uneasily on Shawn's homespun-clad shoulders. He stared at the ceiling, thinking maybe he could grab this moment of uncomfortable humility, and call Angus.

He lifted the phone, staring at it. "You need to," he muttered. He shut his eyes tight, seeing his snide crack to Angus in the tower. He'd taken everything Angus loved. Besides, he didn't *want* Angus being the hero and winning her back. There was nothing Angus could do anyway. It had nothing to do with all that other stuff. Really, it didn't. It was just there was nothing Angus could do. He put the phone back in his pocket and returned to his room. He'd deal with it himself.

Monadhliath Mountains, Present

The gates were closed. Through them, Simon saw a lawn lush with autumn rains, and a garden with green curling vines twisting around wooden stakes. Beyond it rose the monastery, with arched Gothic windows on either side of the sharp point of the Gothic entrance. Simon pushed black, iron bars. They didn't give. He shook them, sending their rattle into the crisp autumn morning. A flock of birds lifted off, screeching, from a tree just inside. The gates were locked tight.

Simon searched for the cord hanging by the cool stone wall that arced over the iron bars. He pulled it. Deep in the abbey, a bell tolled, brighter than the previous bells. He waited. The birds settled back into the tree branches, scolding him. His lips tightened.

"Open up!" he called. Nothing moved inside the gate, save vines swaying in a breeze, and leaves rustling. The scent of honeysuckle rose around him. He leaned close, trying to see around the side of the building. The place seemed deserted.

He yanked the cord again. The bell called out, faint and distant. No one came. Simon shook the bars. "Open up!" he shouted. The birds screeched and shot from the tree in a dark cloud, disappearing into the blue sky. Simon yanked the cord again, and again, and again, and again. The bell cried out. Simon leaned into the iron bars, searching the grounds. They couldn't all have left. He gave it one last, angry yank. From around the church, tottered a bent old monk, carrying a basket against his brown robe.

"You!" Simon called.

The monk continued to the garden, dropping to his knees and pulling a spade from the basket.

"You!" Simon shouted. "The Lord of Claverock summons you!"

On hands and knees, the old man dug in rich loam.

Simon shook the gates, shouting a medieval oath. "Come here anon!" he demanded.

"He's not heard a sound these three years. He'll not hear you."

Simon jumped at the voice murmuring nearly in his ear. Brother Fergal stood, a shadow against the wall, on the other side of the gate, his arms tucked in his sleeves.

Simon forced a tight smile. "Surely you've hospitality for a weary traveler. You remember me?"

"Aye." Fergal smiled. "Brother Eamonn had peculiar notions about you. We've oft accused him of being overly fond of Brother Jimmy's special brew."

Simon's smile brightened. "I believe he was a bit mad."

"He'd the most preposterous story." Brother Fergal smiled up into the tree's leafy branches. From their midst came a single chirp. "A knight of Longshanks' retinue, he said." Fergal met Simon's eyes. "Where do you think he comes up with such ideas?"

"The brew, naturally." Simon's face relaxed. Nobody would believe anything else. "Let me in, Good Brother. I have journeyed a long way, and am hungry."

"I imagine." Brother Fergal lifted a long, slender stick.

Simon glanced from it, back to the monk. "Open the gate, then."

Fergal rested one end of the stick on his shoulder, the other on the iron bars.

Simon glanced at it. It was no ordinary stick, but polished smooth, with bits of metal glinting off it. Simon laughed. "Do you intend to beat me with your stick? What have I done, Good Brother, that you should wish to harm me?"

Fergal smiled. "See the orchards?"

Simon glanced over his shoulder at the trees, and back to Fergal. "You wish me to bring you apples?"

"Aye, we'll have fruit for breakfast." Fergal hefted the stick.

Shrugging, Simon turned. As he did, Fergal spoke, his first word swallowed. "...didn't exist in Edward's time."

Simon glanced back at him—the man was madder than Eamonn—and continued to the tree. He plucked a low-hanging apple, wondering what game the man played. But it was a small thing, to make his way in amongst the monks and get the crucifix.

"Stop." Fergal peered down the length of the stick. "Hold it out."

"Do you not wish me to bring it to you?"

"To the side." Fergal hefted the stick on his shoulder. "Turn around."

Simon's irritation mounted. "What game is this?" he demanded.

"Do it," Fergal said, "or I'll not open these gates."

With pursed lips, Simon turned his back to the monastery. The man would pay for his insolence.

A sharp report sounded behind him. The apple exploded in Simon's hand, bits of sticky, juicy apple flying everywhere, spattering his sleeve. Simon spun in shock. Fergal stood as he had, the walking stick on his shoulder. "What is this?" Simon demanded. He looked from the mess in his hand to the tree behind him, to the clouds above. "What kind of apple is this?" he asked.

Fergal watched him, unmoving.

Simon shook the mess off his hand, storming forward. Fergal stood motionless behind the portcullis. Simon drew breath. He needed to get in. He walked the last steps to the gate calmly, a smile plastered on his face. "Some trick?" He gripped the bars, the walking stick an inch from his chest. He paid it no heed. "Very clever. I've done as you asked. Now give me a meal."

Fergal lowered the stick, eye to eye with Simon through the grate. "You've never seen a gun."

"Gun?" Simon smiled. "What is *gun?*"

"Perhaps Eamonn is saner than we thought," Fergal murmured. "I will heed his warning. My Lord of Claverock." He sketched a half bow. "Brother Wallace will leave food for you." He indicated a small wooden door which allowed things to be passed through the wall. "But I cannot allow you to enter."

Anger flashed across Simon's face. He shook the bars.

"You would do well to believe me." Fergal's eyes locked on Simon. "Now that I understand Eamonn, I shall pass on his message to you, though I questioned his sobriety when he gave it to me."

Simon glanced from the stick to Fergal's sharp, brown eyes.

"He awaits you in Inverness," Fergal reported. "He said you should know where to find him, and he will give you that which you seek." Turning his back, Fergal walked away.

Simon shook the bars in fury, watching helplessly as Fergal disappeared into the monastery. In the garden, the elderly monk dug and scraped.

CHAPTER TWENTY-SEVEN

Bannockburn, Present

Full morning brought assurance from the police that they would watch the new place closely in the coming days. By ten, Shawn and Carol stood in the front room of their new home. By two, he'd moved in their few belongings, and set up his keyboard, their beds, and James's crib. At three, Carol announced, over Shawn's objections, that she couldn't live in fear, and would go out with Ina.

"At least take a knife!" Shawn exploded in frustration.

"A *knife*?" Her eyes flew open wide.

He raked a hand through his hair, trying to cover his mistake. "Aren't guns illegal here?"

She looked at him strangely, and left.

Shawn checked on James, asleep in his new room. He locked the bedroom door, went down to check that the front door was locked, and pushed knives into each of his boots, and into the waistband of his trews. Satisfied, he called Ben, checking that advertising was moving along, and set to work on some arrangements.

When James woke up, he changed his diaper, made him toast and warm mashed carrots, and, with the phone on speaker while he supervised his eating, talked to his publicist about promotional posters. "I need them about yesterday," he said. "Get them straight out to the people who need them." He thought guiltily of Lindsay's comments, and added, "I mean, I'd really appreciate that."

"Right on it," the man said.

Thanking him, Shawn disconnected. James smashed his hands in the carrots, sending spatters of orange across the table. "What next?" Shawn asked, reaching for a cloth. James squealed and chortled. Shawn glanced at his watch. Amy might only now be on her way to the studio. It would be hours before he could call her. It left plenty of time for worry to plague him. "You think the police are right?" he asked, as he wiped the table. James squealed. A frown creased his forehead as Shawn swished the cloth over his hands.

His mother thought it might be someone he'd angered in the past. Shawn had to reluctantly agree he'd given several people cause for anger. The angry husband, though—he was in the States. Jimmy, the big Scot he'd given counterfeits to? Could it have been one of his friends?

In the front room, bare but for the keyboard and a kitchen chair, he set James on his blanket, and put toys around him, including the white rabbit. He should call Angus, he thought. But it only made it more galling to think maybe his own actions had endangered his son. How could he face admitting that to Mr. Perfect? He sank onto the chair.

Clutching his rabbit's ear, James crawled the few feet to Shawn, grinning at him.

Shawn smiled back, trying to think. What would Niall do? What would Christina want him to do? She'd remind him he *had* cheated the man, regardless of his intentions or justifications. She'd want him to make amends. He sighed. He didn't even know the guy's last name.

He watched James, reaching for his knee, climbing to his feet, trying to think how he could find out. Maybe he should figure out, first, if it even had anything to do with Jimmy. He closed his eyes, listening to his son chatter. Christina would say it didn't matter, that he should make amends, anyway. Okay, fine, he would. But how? *How?* It had been at that place in Inverness...the Blue Bell Inn.

Opening his eyes, he grabbed his laptop. In a minute, he had the Blue Bell's number, and shortly after a squeal erupted in his ear from the woman who had tended bar the night of his party, so long ago. "I heard you were back! When you coming to see us, Love?"

Shawn smiled, remembering her well. But he had a problem. "Hey," he drawled, in his most wheedling—and always successful—Barry White register. "I can't wait to get up there. Soon as I'm not so booked up." He imagined Christina frowning down from above at the white lie, and decided it was not a lie. He'd drop by. He would. *Soon.* Then it would be true. "But I need your help. Remember Jimmy...?"

"Oh, aye!" She sounded aghast. "Was he in a rage over you! He says you gave him counterfeits! Tell me you didn't!"

"I did." Shawn sighed. Remorseful. Self-effacing. It always worked. "But it was an accident. Someone gave them to me." Again, he thought of Christina, hearing the words come out of his mouth. She wouldn't approve half-truths any better than lies, but, he consoled himself, he was trying to make it right. "Look, that's why I called. I want to make it right. Do you know how I can reach him? I don't even know his last name."

She hesitated a moment before saying, "He's still steamed. Especially about that night in jail over it. He'd as like kill you as see you."

Shawn felt the blood drain from his face. "He went to *jail?*" he asked weakly. *He'd as like kill you.* He didn't dare ask if the man would send a friend to try to harm a woman and child.

"Oh, aye. He tried to pay his entrance to a poker game with those bills and got caught. He'd been trying to clean up his life, see, he'd had a wee bit of trouble before, and they didn't believe him at first."

Shawn pressed a hand to his forehead. It got worse and worse. "So now he wants to kill me?"

"Not that I blame you—he *did* attack you first—but nor has his arm been quite the same since you sliced him behind Eden Court."

"I did *what*?" Shawn asked in surprise. "I never...!" He stopped. Niall had done it. Yes, Niall had mentioned that, two long years ago. "Okay." He drew a deep breath. "I don't blame him for attacking me. I want to make it right. How can I reach him?" Maybe, if he could sit down and talk with the man, give him enough money...maybe he would find out if Jimmy knew anything about the attack. Maybe, he thought, he should call Angus.

He shrugged the feeling off. Guilt clung to the edge of his thoughts on Angus, along with embarrassment. Angus had had to clue him in how to win Amy back— he, Shawn Kleiner, who had never needed any help with women! No, the Bannockburn police were dealing with it. He'd call Jimmy himself.

"You'll come up then?" asked the woman.

"Sorry, come up where?" Shawn asked.

"I said Jimmy will be here tonight. Maybe it's best to meet him in a public place, you know, Love?"

Shawn made a quick calculation. It would mean leaving his mother alone for hours. But he always worked best with people face to face. He could ask Ina to stay with his mother. The police were watching the house. And certainly the man couldn't find the new place so fast. "I'll be there," he said.

He hung up, texted his mother, and glanced at the time. Amy had left her car keys. He had a couple hours until he needed to leave. In the meantime, there was work to do—when wasn't there? James patted his knee, saying, "Baa! Baa!"

"Books?" Shawn guessed. He dug a book from the diaper bag, and flipped it open. *To Hamish*, it said on the inside cover. *Love, Uncle Angus*. Another twinge of guilt shot through Shawn. Pushing it away, he got down on the floor to read the story, in Gaelic, about a horse. James listened intently for ten pages, sitting on Shawn's lap, before trying to chew on the book. Shawn thought, as he wrested it from his mouth, of Angus reading to James, of taking Niall's son to the stable....and of Christina, alone and pregnant.

James drifted off in his arms. A glance at his watch told him Amy would still be in Mike Mansfield's studio in New York. He laid James on his blanket, wrapping it up over his shoulder. Christina played on his mind. He'd hadn't read the parchments in over a month. But now he was alone, he had nothing to keep his thoughts at bay. He should read the next one. Maybe he'd find good news.

The front door flew open. Carol and Ina bursting in, laughing. "I'm here," Carol said breathlessly. "Are you ready to go?"

His conscience quivered again. "You're sure you'll be safe?"

Carol's eyes fell on the knives at his waist, and in his boots. Her smile fled.

Ina, too, became serious. "'Twas a random attack, the police said. If not, he'll not have found you again so soon. We're fine."

Shawn took a deep breath. It was time to drive up to see Jimmy. What did he fear, he asked himself? He'd fought far worse than Jimmy. No...he feared asking a man in humility for help. He feared finding he could do nothing to protect his son.

Carol touched his arm. "Shawn...leave the knives.

Inverness, Present

"Take a look at this." Lacking his usual easy going cheer, Clive tossed a report on Angus's desk. Angus looked up inquiringly. "Chief saw it just now." Clive's mouth was tight. Lines etched the corners of his eyes. "He said to show you."

With his gut stirring, Angus lowered his eyes, scanning the report. The unease grew as words jumped out at him. *Kleiner. Home intruder. Broken door. Stocky, swarthy.* He looked up. "Amy was on the plane to New York by then."

"Aye, only just." Clive nodded grimly, indicating the report. "Kleiner drove her to the airport. Carol and James were in the home. Yer man was vicious. Ripped out the entire upper half of the door."

Angus's eyes strayed to the cork board where Amy's photograph had hung. "They're all right?" he asked softly, staring at the empty spot.

"Shaken. But not hurt." Clive sat down heavily in his own chair.

"Kleiner fought him off?" Anger and gratitude grappled. Shawn had taken James and Amy away. Shawn had protected his son.

"I called Bannockburn straight away," Clive said. "'Tis not in the report, but I spoke to yer man who talked to him last night. He said Kleiner was very clear that the man was unusually strong."

"Was he now?" Angus re-read the report, not surprised by the information. "What's this about?" he asked. "Carol says the intruder had a peculiar accent. Shawn disagreed."

Clive leaned forward, studying the words, and shrugged. "I suppose he's been here this past year and a half and is more acclimated to our speech."

"Could be," Angus said. "They've not found the perp?"

Clive shook his head. "But Kleiner took his mum and son to a hotel for the night. Found them a new place already. MacGowan says he went overboard. Says it was a random attack. But I thought you'd want to know." He rose. "We have the talk at that school in an hour."

Angus nodded, as he slid the report into a folder. "Aye. Just give me a minute."

Clive left, shutting the door behind him. Angus drummed his fingers on the folder, staring at the cork board. It had happened last night. Shawn would have told Amy immediately. But she hadn't called him. It hurt. He wondered if the description jumped out to her as it had to him, and what she would do about it. He wondered if it was his place to follow up and learn more about this intruder, to confirm whether it was Simon and start digging into who Simon was. Amy hadn't asked him to. It was technically none of his business. But it unnerved him to do nothing, with his gut screaming. Shawn had taken James and Carol to safety, he told himself. He had this talk at the school, and then he would think about what he should do—what he *could* do.

But it hurt that Amy had not confided in him. James was like his own son, and she hadn't even *told* him. He opened the drawer in the cabinet behind him, and added the folder to the file on Shawn. Snatching his hat off the cabinet, he headed out to talk to school children.

Inverness, Present

The Blue Bell was much as Shawn remembered, full of dark greens and heavy mahoganies, laughter and happiness. As if he stepped into a memory, cheers erupted when he entered the place. "Shawn Kleiner!" shouted the woman at the bar. She leaned forward, grabbing him on each side of the face to plant a kiss on his lips.

He laughed, but in shock, and pulled back. It had been two years since anyone had done such a thing.

It took only a minute, even in the dim interior, to spot Jimmy. His eyes locked on Shawn, he rose to his full height, shoving the table from him. It scraped three feet, knocking chairs on their backs and sending two men scrambling out of its path. For a fleeting moment, Shawn wished he'd kept his knives.

But that wasn't why he'd come, he sternly reminded himself.

A hush whispered over the Blue Bell's patrons, a silent wave. Faces turned to Shawn, as they did at his concerts. But these faces held fear, and—he knew it from medieval life—an ugly desire for blood.

Shawn's mind flickered back to two years ago, when he'd actually feared Jimmy. Now he saw a giant with no weapons and no real fighting skills but his size...and a man he had wronged. He saw a man who had been wronged by life, most likely born into a rough neighborhood. It was disturbingly easy to imagine Jimmy, lumbering toward him, as a child growing up with an alcoholic father, a boy, fearful in a corner.

And Shawn had wronged him again.

Enough to make him send a friend after an innocent woman and child?

Shawn strode forward. He knew Jimmy wouldn't take his hand. "I'm sorry," he said. "I want to make it right. Can we talk?" He glanced at the bar crowd staring silently at the two of them. "Out front?"

Jimmy looked around at his audience, with a big grin. "He disnae want tae be seen gittin a tankin."

Nervous laughter skittered around the room.

Shawn glanced at the scar running down the man's forearm. He wondered that Jimmy was so confident. But something told him it was bluffing, bravado—trying save face in front of his friends.

"Ye'll fight fair this time," Jimmy informed him. Around him, his friends nodded. Three of them rose, arms across chests. "No knives."

"I didn't come to fight." Shawn glanced at the three men who had risen, all shorter than himself, two of them slight and wiry. They were nothing compared to medieval warriors coming at him on horseback. He held back a smile that would only antagonize them, and said to Jimmy, "I came to apologize. Let's talk out front."

He turned his back, heading to the door. In a heart beat, he heard the rush, and spun, catching Jimmy around the neck, twisting, and throwing him to the floor. His three friends stopped, mid-stride, caught in shock at how easily Shawn had thrown the giant down.

"I didn't come to fight," Shawn said steadily, meeting each of their eyes. The two slighter men took steps back. The third came no nearer.

Shawn pulled a large bundle of cash from his pocket, as Jimmy pushed himself, dazed, from the floor. Eyeing him, Shawn counted out the bills onto the counter in front of the woman who had kissed him. "Ten times the counterfeits I gave you," he announced. "Six hundred pounds."

In all the crowded pub, no one said a word.

Jimmy scrambled to his feet, glowering, but keeping a safe distance from Shawn. "Money disnae buy ye back a night in the the pen, or gittin accused ae sumhin a nivir done!"

Shawn stared at his toes. "If I knew how to buy that back, I would. I panicked when I saw someone had passed them on to me. I never meant a thing like that to happen. I just thought it wouldn't matter, that you'd have more than you had before. I'm sorry, Jimmy. I want to make it right."

The crowd stared at him.

Jimmy stared at him.

Niall, and his prayers, flickered through Shawn's mind. There was no hope of getting answers from Jimmy, even if he knew something. *God, if you're half what Niall thinks you are, give me some help.* "I'll be outside," he said. He turned his back again, and walked out the door. He passed between the tables on the porch, down the stairs, and waited on the empty street.

A full five minutes passed, in which the noise slowly rose again in the pub, in which Shawn kept his back steadfastly to it, listening, waiting, thinking of his mother sobbing in his arms, of James, of the man on the stairs—and wondering if his own actions, his own carelessness of other people's lives, had indeed brought that on two of the three people he loved most in this time.

God, he thought, *I'm sorry. I made excuses. I didn't think. I never meant to hurt him. Please, do you think you could convince Jimmy to come out?*

He thought about the money he'd just thrown on the bar, and Jimmy's angry words. *Money disnae buy ye back a night in the the pen, or gittin accused ae sumhin a nivir done!* Even driving up here, even walking into the Blue Bell Inn, he had still failed to understand what he had really done to the man. And throwing down so much money, so carelessly, he saw, had only been another blow to Jimmy's pride: *Look what I have that you don't. Look who I am, that you aren't.*

Please, God, he thought, *that's not what I meant.*

From afar came the gentle ripple of the River Ness. A couple passed hand in hand. Footsteps fell on the stairs behind him. The hair rose on the back of his neck. His senses heightened. He didn't turn.

Jimmy stood beside him.

They glanced at one another. Jimmy held out a hand, offering Shawn a Guinness.

Shawn took it, not saying a word.

"Lets go tae the Caledonian," Jimmy said.

They walked silently, side by side.

In the pub, they took a quiet seat in the back. "You want something to eat?"

Shawn asked.

When he'd ordered two more Guinnesses and a meal for each of them, he sat back, waiting.

"Why'd ye dae it?" Jimmy asked.

"The counterfeits?" Shawn replied. "I was stupid, I was scared. I realized just before you came—I mean to my room, two years ago—that they were there. I was afraid of my girlfriend finding out, I was afraid you'd beat me to a pulp. Mostly...." He laughed bitterly, thinking of the irony. "Mostly, I was afraid if you beat me up, she'd find out what I'd been up to and dump me. Which she did, anyway. But you want a why, that's it."

Jimmy shook his head. "A dinny git it." He held out his arm, showing the scar from Niall's knife. "This. Whit ye jist did in there—but ye thought a'd batter ye?"

Shawn stared at the table, his lips tight. "I was a different man. That really wasn't me behind the theater."

"Aye, ye said at the time."

Shawn lifted his head. "It really wasn't. His name is Niall—was Niall—and yeah, he looks just like me."

The waiter slid their drinks onto the table, and disappeared.

Jimmy grunted, took a gulp of his brew, and set it on the table with a jarring thud. "But I meant, why dae ye give a feck noo?"

Shawn stared at a spot on the wall behind Jimmy's head, trying to put it into words. "I've spent the last two years with Niall," he finally said.

"Ye were only gone a year."

"Yeah, a year." Shawn heard the irritation in his own voice. He had to remember it was only a year. "Everything's changed. *I've* changed. I was wrong. But I never meant for anything bad to happen to you. I was just looking out for my own skin, not thinking. The money, repaying what I owed you—consider it a start. What else can I do to make it right?"

Jimmy stared at him, his big face sullen. "A lost ma *joab* because o' it! Yer money, noo...." He took it from his pocket, tossing it disdainfully on the table. "It disnae cover months ae bills a couldny peh."

"Tell me how much," Shawn said. "I'll pay them."

Jimmy glared. "Big feckin star! Ye think ye kin jist throw money at it aw? That wiz ma *name!* A wiz tryin tae dae better, show folk a could be counted oan noo. A wiz gonny yase the winnins fae that poker game tae pay aff ma bills, get a fresh start, dae better. Noo look at me, right back where a started an naebody will gie me the time o day noo; sayn am jist the prick av always been!" Resentment shot from his eyes. "How you gonny fix that fur me?"

Shawn's jaw tightened. He stared at the colorful bills lying wrinkled on the table.

"There you go now," a voice said, and a plate with a hamburger slid into his view.

"Thanks," Shawn muttered. He heard the soft clink of Jimmy's plate touching down across the table.

The man didn't move, didn't say a word.

Shawn looked up. "A job?" he suggested. "Can I find you a job?"

Jimmy snorted. "Daein whit? Playn yer horn wi ye?" He laughed scathingly, an eruption of sound that reddened his face and drew the startled attention of several diners. He waved his arm, and added, "Mibbe a could lead yer orchestra?" He looked around at the growing number of people looking his way. He laughed harshly, calling to his new-found audience, "Kin ye see me conductin' his American symphony, aye?"

They laughed.

Shawn's lips tightened. Irritation boiled inside. "What do you do?" He forced himself to stay calm, to remember Jimmy had cause to be angry.

"Construction. *Did.* A *did* construction. A was guid at it, too."

An idea sprang on Shawn. He might make amends and get the information he needed. "Can I hire you to fix a door in my house? This door—it's torn apart." He watched the Scot carefully.

Jimmy's eyes narrowed. "Hows that gonny set me up fur a real joab?"

"It happened last night. Someone broke into my home, attacked my mother."

"Aye well…am sorry tae hear aboot yer maw, bit what's that goat tae dae wi me gittin a real joab?" Jimmy gazed at him steadily.

Shawn frowned. He read people well. Jimmy knew nothing of the attack. He turned the information over.

"So, aye," Jimmy demanded. "Ye gonny git me a joab?"

"I'll give you recommendations," Shawn said. The idea grew. "Can you run a business?"

Jimmy didn't answer.

"How about I have a web site made for you," Shawn suggested. "Business cards, get you started?"

Jimmy continued to glower.

"Say something!" Shawn exploded. "Even *Go to hell,* but *say* something!"

Jimmy slugged back a third of his pint, and slammed it on the table. "You grew up in yer posh American scheme did ye no?" he snapped. "A goat Pollock, you goat yer uni. A goat the streets, naebody is iver gonny take me fur anythin but the halfwit av been."

Shawn became still. Aaron, Dan, Duncan, Christina, Allene, Amy, himself, Tessa, Suzanne—and forcibly pushing his way into the group—Clarence—all danced a stately reel of ghostly emotions and memories: People who had changed. People who hadn't. People who accepted changes. People who didn't. People who gave second chances. People who didn't.

He bowed his head. He took a deep breath, almost shuddering. "Jimmy." He raised his eyes. "We aren't so different. I had a reputation, too. There are people who won't let me be someone new. I have to decide, too, if they're going to force me back into that box, or if I'm going to make my own decisions." He glanced at his watch, and subtracted five. Amy would be finishing her recording soon. He looked back to Jimmy. "I took something from you. More than I ever meant to. I *owe* you this. Don't throw it away because of a few jerks who want to hold you down. Be the man you're trying to be, and screw anyone who doesn't believe it."

Jimmy stared at him. It was no longer a glower.

Shawn flipped his business card onto the table between their untouched meals. "I have to call my wi—my girlfriend—about the attack. Say the word, and you'll have all you need to start your own business. Anything else I can do, give me a ring." He rose, dreading the coming call.

New York City, Present

"That's a wrap!" Flashing a triumphant grin at his sound engineer, Mike makes the announcement as he removes his headphones. He turns to me. "Perfect!"

I smile, the thrill of a strong performance singing through me as I lower my violin. "I can't wait to hear it. When is it coming out?"

"January." He puts a hand on my shoulder, guiding me to the edge of the room, away from the keyboard and guitar players. "I'll be doing a tour to promote it. Can you join me to play live?"

I hesitate. There's James, Carol, Shawn. My students.

"I pay well." He leans closer, giving a charming smile.

He's perfected that look, I know. I smile self-consciously, drawing back. There's Angus. Not that he'll miss me—because there's also Claire. Still, I recoil at the thought of leaving Scotland, and I know it's Angus I don't want to leave.

"Can we talk about it over dinner?" Mike's dimples deepen. I know he knows their effect. And they are having an effect.

Still, I hesitate. Behind him, the keyboard player, chatting with the drummer, lifts his instrument off its rack.

"Hey, Mike." The guitarist hails him. "That gig tomorrow...."

"Can you hold on?" Mike touches my arm once more, waiting for my nod, before leaving.

I pull my phone from my pocket, turning it on. I'm waiting to hear from Rose about getting together while I'm here. I'm hoping Carol will text, tell me how James is. The phone beeps, and a moment later, sounds Ride of the Valkyrie.

"That dinner?" Mike asks, returning.

"I'm sorry," I say. "I need to get this. It could be about James."

He smiles, nodding, as he opens the studio door and lets me out.

"Shawn," I say almost breathlessly, as I answer. "How is James?"

"Great! Great," comes Shawn's voice over the phone, as I cross a lounge of soft carpet, deep leather sofas, and potted plants. "I talked to Ben, you know, just this morning, and it turns out...." He laughs. "He's got me set up on all these great talk shows, you know, lots of great promotion, lots of things I can do for you and James, and the thing is, it starts soon, so you know, I thought we could take him back to the States. My mom, you know, she'd love to go back, and...."

He's rambling. My gut stirs. "Shawn," I interrupt. "What's going on?"

"What?" There's a heartbeat of silence in the wake of his shocked question. Innocence rings from his voice—the exact innocence that always makes me the most suspicious.

"What's going on?" I demand more firmly.

"Why are you so suspicious?" he counters.

"I don't need to talk to you," I remind him. "Your mother will be more than happy to tell me how James is doing." I glance over my shoulder. The others are still in the studio. "And just so you know, Mike Mansfield just invited me to dinner."

"Look," he says hastily, "Don't go to dinner with him. I just meant...I mean, we should think about moving back, you know? I have this big tour coming up. And James should have both of us, right? And you've got this recording, and he'll want you to play live on a tour, right?"

"Yes, he just mentioned that," I say.

"So what do you think?" he asks.

The studio door opens. Mike and his band come out, the pianist swinging his heavy workstation at his side in its leather case. "Everything okay?" Mike asks.

I force a smile, nodding. He stops, a frown creasing his forehead, and then gestures for the other three to leave with him. "Shawn," I say softly, "when you ramble, it's because you don't want to tell me something. I'm not agreeing to anything until you tell me what's going on." He takes a deep breath. I wait, noting the orchids and coffee pot on the sideboard, and the tension creeping into my back.

"Just...." He stops. He clears his throat. "Just that I want us to be together. I have to start taping, and I don't want you and my mom staying here alone."

"We were fine alone before you came back." I sink down onto a leather couch, my mind whirring. Is it protectiveness on his part? Does he doubt my competence? Is he trying to pull me away from Angus?

"Um...yes. Yes, you were," he agrees. "Um...are you...are you done recording?"

"Yes," I say slowly. "What does that have to do with me moving back?"

Mike returns, gives me a quizzical look, and moves to the sideboard, pouring coffee, as Shawn clarifies his question. "You're totally done? The whole thing? No more recording today or tomorrow or next week?"

"Totally done." My nerves begin to itch. Mike pours in creamer and sugar, stirring the coffee. "What's going on?" I glance up, thanking Mike as he hands me the Styrofoam cup, and leaves again.

"Okay, don't freak out," Shawn says.

I suck in breath. "First, don't accuse me of freaking out. Second, the very fact you think I might is scaring me." I stand abruptly, setting the coffee on the counter.

"It was nothing," Shawn says.

"Obviously it was, or you wouldn't be minimizing and avoiding." I bite back the words, Who was it this time, *reminding myself that won't help, and all I care about now is James.*

"Okay, well, it was just this little thing, you know...."

"Just tell me!" I blurt out. "Some woman? Just a little slip?"

"Someone broke into the house. I finished the arrangements, Ben has the tour..."

My breath slips out, anger submerged under a wave of fear. "Someone broke into the house?"

"It was nothing. Everything is fine." His words tumble over one another. "So, you know, really, I just wanted us to be together. You could live in my house. Your own room, you know. Or we could find you something new, or...."

"James is okay?" I sink weakly to the couch. "Your mother?"

"They're fine," he says.

"When did this happen?" I do the math. It's evening in Scotland. "Today? In broad daylight?"

"Um..." He clears his throat. "When I drove you to the airport."

I shoot up off the couch. "Last night?" I press a hand to my forehead. "This happened last night and you didn't tell me?"

"See," he says, "I knew you'd freak out!"

My eyes narrow, though he isn't there to glare at. "Someone broke into your home where my son was, and you didn't bother telling me. I'm a thousand miles away and he was in danger! How dare you use the words freak out with me!"

He says nothing.

"Shawn?" I hear him draw breath.

"Would you have gotten on the first flight home?" His wheedling is gone. This is the real Shawn.

"Of course!"

"He was okay. They're perfectly safe. I wanted you to be able to play and not be upset or worried."

My heart slows, considering his words.

"Amy," he adds, "I'm trying to do the right thing. He was perfectly safe. So I'm sorry if I did the wrong thing, but I wanted you to be able to do your recording."

I sit down again, glancing at the untouched coffee.

"I wanted Mike to have the very best on his album," he says softly. He's once again wheedling, flattering; just this once, I'm not sure I care.

I force myself to speak calmly. "They're perfectly safe. But you want me to uproot my life and move, which makes me think you're still not telling me something."

Again, the silence. Then he says, "Really, Amy, it was just a random break-in. The police said so." His voice becomes softer. "But I have to be in the States for a long time, and it would mean a lot to me if you would be there, with James. I'll keep a place in Scotland for you to go back any time you want. Please?"

I lift the coffee, swirling it softly in its cup. "I'll think about it," I say. "But there has to be a place for me to go back there."

"There will be," he says hastily. "I'll make sure."

"And I'm not promising anything right now," I say.

"The sooner, the better," he says. "I wish you would."

The door opens, Mike looking in with a question stamped all over his face.

"Shawn," I say, "I have to go." I end the call, turning to Mike. "I need to get back to my son," I say. "There was a break in. I'll be booking the soonest flight out that I can."

"I'm sorry," he says. "January?"

"Can I have a few days to think about it?"

He smiles. "Of course."

I smile back, half-heartedly. My mind is on James, on Shawn—on leaving Angus.

CHAPTER TWENTY-EIGHT

Glenmirril, May 1317

MacDougall watched the cell door, as he finished the last of four hundred floor dips—ending a long night of strengthening exercises, sword maneuvers, what agility training he could with the leg of the table he'd separated, and resting each foot in turn on the window sill to stretch and bend. It kept his mind occupied while waiting for Roger's confirmation that plans were moving forward.

Now, as the sun rose, he watched and listened. At the first sound from outside, he turned to the window, standing complacently, as they always saw him standing, staring placidly into the courtyard, as they always saw him staring. Christina emerged from the northern tower in her blue riding gown. He smiled. In the last weeks, she had begun to come out again. She never looked up. She never laughed.

There was no sign of the rumored child. The one time his guards whispered of it, as he stood pressed to the door listening, they seemed content that the gossips had simply been mistaken. "She is, after all, a woman of virtue," Gil had informed the other two loftily. "'Twas the words of small, jealous minds."

Gil spoke true, MacDougall thought, watching her pass through the gate in the stone wall that divided the courtyards. Everything in her drew him. He cared not if it was virtue or beauty. She simply drew him.

She disappeared into the stables below his cell. Even as he worked through his codes to Roger, his plans for escape and for Niall, he delighted in watching her emerge again on her palfrey, her sapphire gown flowing across its rump. Soon, they would be together again. Surely, she dreamed of it, too. Surely it was why she walked under his tower each day, letting him know she'd not forgotten.

She rode back into the northern bailey, where Allene and a few guards joined her, carrying baskets. He watched them ride out over the drawbridge, following their path as long as he could see them beyond the walls, until they disappeared up the wooded hill, going north—as they always did. As his letter had told Roger.

The keys clicked in the lock. MacDougall turned, complacent as always, giving Red a humble smile, as he set food and ale on the table, its leg carefully fit back into place. "I thank you," MacDougall said.

"Have you more stories of the Holy Land?"

MacDougall smiled, the gentle smile of a father for a beloved son. "I believe I've told you all of them—some several times."

"Tell about Baibars again," Red seated himself at the table.

MacDougall laughed, hiding his irritation. After all, the boy might be of further use. He sat, telling again about Baibars, as he ate his bread. "And have you news of the outside world," he asked, when he'd finished.

Red shrugged. "War, famine, disease."

It was his usual answer, under MacDonald's orders, no doubt, always followed by rising from the table. MacDougall placed his hand on the corner over the removable leg, making sure Red didn't jar it loose and learn his secret. "*Nihil sub sole novum.*" He quoted Ecclesiastes, translating for the boy raised by a farrier. "*There is nothing new under the sun.* So our good scriptures say." He smiled in what he hoped was a beatific imitation of the saints. "However, the weather seems improved."

"Aye," agreed Red enthusiastically. "There is great hope in Glenmirril that we shall once again have abundant harvest."

MacDougall smiled. The boy played nicely into his hand. "So true. Speaking of which, has my steward written? I've great concern for my own fields and herds. For my people. The *children.*"

Red shook his head. "I'll bring his reply when he does." He grinned again, a comical look under his shock of bright hair, and backed out the door.

MacDougall sighed. Eventually, one of them would turn his back. It didn't matter. It had taken months of building trust just to gain communication with Roger, and he did not have the gray robe he wanted. But on pondering Niall, the monk who had traveled with him, and the man who thought of Christina on the kirk stairs, he thought he knew where to find one.

Inverness, Present

A donut and a steaming mug of hazelnut mocha waited on Angus's desk. He glanced at the fern. Its leaves burst with green vitality. He smiled. He should tell Claire to stop, but she didn't ask for more, didn't seem to expect anything from him. Indeed, he'd heard Pete boasting, out front, that he was taking her to a *ceilidh.* He sank into his chair, sipping the hot brew. It felt good to be taken care of, especially after a rescue, hard on the heels of the talk, had kept him out well into the night.

But questions about the attacker had spun through his head, leaving him staring at his dark bedroom ceiling for hours, despite the climb into the hills that should have left him sleeping like the Fenians.

He stretched out a foot to kick his office door shut, and retrieved the file on the attack in Kleiner's home. He scanned it four, five times, but there was nothing to suggest it was anything other than the random attack MacGowan called it. His eyes lingered on the note that Carol had mentioned the man's accent. Was that so odd, Angus wondered. Clive was right. She was American, after all.

He leaned back in his chair, kicking his feet up on his desk, and locking his hands behind his head. His eyes closed, he tried to imagine the voice Carol had heard. His eyebrows drew together. She'd been here for months. She was accustomed to the Scottish accent. So the man might be from England, Wales....

The shock hit him like cold waves when he had to dive into the chilly North Sea on a rescue. He dropped his feet to the floor, grabbing the file. He scanned it. Yes. Shawn had shrugged off his mother's comment, saying he'd noticed nothing unusual. It was too mad, Angus warned himself. But he could think of exactly one accent that Carol would find peculiar enough to note, yet would seem normal to Shawn.

Pulling up YouTube, Angus entered a search term. Dozens of results popped up. He turned on a play list, listening to one after another, his eyes closed, soaking in the sounds. He didn't like the implication. It couldn't be. And yet...it all fit.

But what, he wondered, as a man recited Chaucer, was he supposed to tell the Chief? He'd already pushed his luck, commandeering that ferry, and having no explanation as to how he'd known Kleiner would be at Glenmirril. He'd lose his job. He be placed on medical leave and told to 'see someone.'

That hem hath holp-en whan that they were seek-uth, Chaucer finished. Angus opened his eyes, watching the next video load. As the voice began an old English poem, his eyes closed again, soaking in the vowels—*When the nyhtegale singes, The wodes waxen grene*—and returning to his musings. *Lefant gras ant blosme springes.*

He could give the information to Shawn, let him deal with it. *In Averyl, Y wene.* His mouth tensed in a grimace. He didn't want to talk to Shawn. *And love is to myn herte gone.* The very name, the thought of his face—*With one spere so kene*—the memory of Amy getting in a car—*Nyht ant day my blod hit drynkes*—and driving away with him, turned his stomach sour. *Myn herte deth me tene.*

My heart causes me death. His days in archives translated the line for him easily.

The door crashed open, jarring him. His eyes flew open, his feet shot to the floor.

"What's that you're listening to?" Clive demanded.

Angus fumbled with the mouse, shutting it down. "Nothing."

"'Twas something." Clive insisted.

Angus spun his chair, pulling a file from the cabinet, and tossed it on Clive's desk. "We need to re-open this case. New information came in. Better look it over before the Chief comes to talk about it."

With a snort of irritation, Clive took the file. They fell to work, jotting notes, making calls, tossing questions across the small space between their desks. When Clive left for lunch, Angus returned to YouTube. His certainty grew as he listened to more videos. It couldn't be true, he insisted. *But you've already accepted that it can happen*, he argued with himself, *and has happened. So why not?*

Because it's too much, he shot back.

Because it was too frightening, he admitted. Because he couldn't report it to the Bannockburn or Inverness police. But he couldn't sit on it, either.

He could call Amy. He picked up his phone—and stopped. He could be wrong. He didn't want to alarm her. But he could be right—in which case, he couldn't say nothing. He *had* to call Shawn. Shawn was equipped to deal with someone like Simon. Angus's lips tightened. He didn't want to talk to Shawn. Amy could tell him herself.

He turned the phone on, staring at the *dial* screen. He'd seen the attack on his news feed this morning, and had scanned several reports, one of which mentioned Amy had taken an immediate flight back from her recording in America. He smiled, thinking of the first time he'd seen her, the stunning shock of her dark eyes and long, thick hair—and of realizing she was the Glenmirril Lady in the flesh, his medieval drawing come to vibrant life.

The smile fell from his face. She'd made her choice. She didn't want him. Still, he couldn't abandon her and James to danger. He made a quick call, using his title to get her flight's arrival time, and hung up, drumming his fingers on his desk. Her plane would land in thirty minutes. He'd give them time to get home, and then call.

Glenmirril, May 1317

"The most glorious May in two years!" Lachlan trotted on Niall's left, lifting his face to the fresh green leaves above. Owen rode on his right. Behind them, the tack and swords of their men jingled.

"'Tis indeed glorious to see green and sunshine after so many gray months," Owen said. A bird trilled overhead in the thick leaves. "And to hear birds sing. I'd begun to think we'd never hear them again."

"And Glenmirril just over the rise," added Lachlan. "There can be no more beautiful day." He glanced at Niall. "Yet you seem forlorn."

"Only tired." Niall looked up into the green canopy. He lowered his voice, not caring to have the men behind them join the conversation. "Are you not worn with a marriage spent fighting?" Memories swamped him of riding over the same rise with Shawn. He'd felt closer to Shawn than he did, even now, to Lachlan, Owen, Conal, or anyone but Allene.

"Aye. But the thought of Margaret just beyond the hills lifts my heart. I'll not think on what's over and done." Lachlan leaned to look across to Owen on Niall's other side. "I believe Roysia will be waiting, too."

"Aye, Hugh will have brought her," Owen said, and to Niall, "Certainly you'll not let the past months steal the joy of coming home."

"I'll not," Niall replied. "Still, I wish there were less *coming* home, and more *staying* home."

"When has anyone had such a life?" Lachlan chuckled, as he nudged his pony up the steep slope, along the winding path through the trees.

Niall said nothing. Lachlan spoke true. Few men in history had had such a life. And he could hardly tell Lachlan that one day, they would, that he had tasted such a life. After riding another mile through the forest bursting with spring, with the sound of birdsong and creaking leather, and quiet talk behind them, Niall asked, "Is it good to see that a better life is possible and have hope, or does it only make us discontent?"

"'Tis a hard question." Lachlan lifted his gaze to the leafy canopy, as if seeking the answer there. "I suppose as in all things, 'tis what one makes of it, aye?" A moment later, he asked, "When have you seen a time when men live at home in peace, seeing their wives and bairns every night?"

"In the stories he tells," said Owen.

"But where did such ideas come to you from?" asked Lachlan.

"Hope, perhaps," Niall said. "Dreams of what I wish life were."

"Yet we've never known different."

"Under Alexander, we had peace. Our fathers stayed home. More than we do, at least." His heart lifted as the ponies climbed the crest of the last hill. Any moment now, he would see Glenmirril below, solid on the shore, its banners fluttering in the breeze off the loch.

"And under Bruce, we will have peace again," Lachlan said. "Of all Glenmirril, Niall, you were once the most full of hope and life. What has changed?"

Niall shrugged. "Life is not what it was. I have become disillusioned. Surely 'tis no good thing."

"Surely 'tis a normal thing," Lachlan returned. "You choose different men each time to accompany you. But 'tis always you leaving. If only you could be two men to share the burdens you carry."

Niall laughed, thinking of Shawn. Yes, he had once had someone to share the burden. Now it was only him. And he had to acknowledge, he'd been making it the worse for himself by imagining Shawn living a carefree life, somewhere out there in the centuries ahead. He must think on the good in his own life. He must remember the miracle on the battle field.

His pony skidded on a stone. It kicked, stomped, and bolted the last two steps to the top of the hill, regaining its footing. Niall stopped, staring down on Glenmirril and a lifetime of memories: playing in the courtyard with Alexander; carrying stones together to the men on the ramparts the day Longshanks came through; kissing Allene behind the oven, and being chased by the Laird; leaving for his foster family in the south, and the day of his return; waking up in the tower and coming down to find Amy and Rob on his shore. He smiled. Life had been good. Really, he had no cause for complaint.

Glasgow, Present

"James is safe?"

Shawn stared, uncomprehending, at Amy, pushing out from the crowd, hurrying toward him with her carry-on rolling behind her and her violin swinging at her side. Her tunic top flowed over leggings, and a hat highlighted her cheekbones. "James?" she asked again, as she reached him.

"I haven't read...." He stopped. She wasn't asking about Niall's son.

She dropped the handle of the carry-on, her hand flying to his. All around them, people hailed one another, kissed, and hugged. "Shawn?"

"Yes," he said abruptly. "He's fine!" He blinked down at her, settling himself in the present, remembering the first day he'd seen her, remembering...he was home! He'd won her back! She'd forgiven him! A smile broke across his face. He swept her into his arms, hugging her tightly, and laughing. "I *missed* you!"

She pulled back with a weak half-smile. "James, Carol? You left them alone?"

"Ina's with them." He grabbed the handle of her suitcase, took her hand, and wove deftly through the crowd, around a burly man with a guitar strapped to his back, past two college girls in university sweatshirts. "It was just a random thing, that's all. I moved them to a new house. Do you have luggage?"

She shook her head, hurrying to keep up with him.

"Shawn *Kleiner*!" The scream split the air around them.

Shawn tightened his grip on Amy's hand, pulling her along, but the girl caught up to them, grabbing his arm. He stopped, plastering on a smile.

"Could I...." She looked up adoringly, hopefully, digging in her purse. "Could I get my picture with you?"

"Sure." The smile stuck in place, Shawn waited impatiently while she stretched her phone out, leaning against him and mugging for it. "I'm sorry," he said, as soon as it flashed. "She's had a long flight. We need to get home. Nice to meet you." He pulled Amy along, hearing *Thank you* shouted behind him, and, *I love your hair!*

"You missed the chance to sell another twenty CDs," Amy said dryly.

He stopped, looking down at her sadly. "I came back for *you*. Don't you believe anything has changed?"

She looked at her toes for a moment, and started walking. "I'm sorry, Shawn."

Glass doors swooshed open, ushering them out into a drizzly day. Shawn smiled, remembering the awning, the dripping rain, the first time he'd kissed her. He glanced down at her. She, too, stared at the rain pouring from the overhang. Her face softened. She smiled, a small smile, a faint blush climbing up her cheeks.

Laughing, he took her hand, and they ran through the drizzle to the parking ramp, with the rain pattering above, and trickling down the open sides of the ramp.

Glenmirril, May 1317

With Red gone, MacDougall returned to the window. The sun had passed its apex. MacDougall braced his hands on either side of the casement, doing presses as he scanned the courtyards. Allene, returned from alms-giving, spoke with a servant in the courtyard, and disappeared into the tower. He was disappointed Christina was not with her. A tall, slender monk in a brown robe crossed the bailey. In the gardens below, two men knelt in the rows of brown earth with small trowels. Across the southern courtyard, smoke puffed from the blacksmith's shop, and a steady *clang clang clang* rose on the spring air.

On the castle walls, one of the men gave a shout and pointed. MacDougall studied the hills. Motion rippled under the trees. From the parapets, one of the men shouted down into the courtyard. Children burst from the great hall, followed at a more sedate pace by a colorful bouquet of castle women in bright gowns and barbets. Niall's mother followed, slender and stately. MacDougall smiled. He could twist the screws on Niall by killing his mother.

In the southern bailey, men flowed from the armory into the northern courtyard. Allene and Christina emerged from the tower, Allene holding a red-headed child on her hip, and Christina carrying an infant—Allene's new bairn—in swaddling clothes. Niall's sons. MacDougall's smile grew. They would serve even better.

A cheer rose on the parapets, and moments later, a line of men appeared on the hill above the castle, riding out from under the trees. MacDougall's eyes narrowed, recognizing the banner. He wasn't ready yet. He preferred being left alone with only the Laird's decisions regarding his actions, for rumor whispered that the old man disappeared often, losing interest in the goings-on of his castle. On the other hand, MacDougall thought, as he watched the banner flutter on the spring breeze, it might be the opportunity to move his plans forward, regardless of the robe.

Niall was home.

Road to Bannockburn, Present

"How do you know it was random?" I press.

Shawn stares straight ahead at the road unrolling from Glasgow's grip. His hands tighten on the wheel. "I don't," he admits.

Stocky, swarthy, Shawn said. Simon flashes through my mind, but the attack was in Shawn's home, not mine. I wasn't even there. I glance at his hands, his knuckles white on the wheel. But it has to be asked. "Could it be someone who's mad at you?

His jaw tenses. "I guess." His words are taut, an E string ready to snap.

"I'm just asking," I placate. "Because if it's random, it's over. But if someone is that angry with you, James and Carol aren't safe."

"That's why I moved them," he says. "We'll be careful about anyone knowing where I live."

"What are the police doing?" I ask.

"Nothing. They said it was random."

"That's good enough for you?"

Tension grips his shoulders. "What do you want me to do?" he demands.

"Call Angus." The words slip out. He stares straight ahead as the carriageway slips from suburban sprawl into fields. I see his anger rising. My own climbs. This is my son. Shawn's ego can step aside for once. "He has resources," I say. "He might be able to find out something. Why wouldn't you, if it's to protect James?"

"I didn't think of it," he says.

I sigh, leaning back against the seat, not believing him for the flutter of a trill. The faintest whiff of deception lingers on him, the unwillingness to talk about it that always told me he was holding back. What would he want to hide from me? This is my son, after all, our son. Someone he angered? Because nothing is random with someone so well known as Shawn, still dominating headlines and hash tags.

I'm uneasy with the police brushing it off as random. Angus loves James. He would look harder. I'm uneasy about dragging him back into my life, asking him for help when I can't give him what he wants. It's not fair to him. But isn't James's safety more important?

Shawn reaches for my hand, over the gear stick, drawing me from my thoughts. "Right now, he's fine. But you know...." He glances at me, and his eyes flicker back to the road. "This is why I want you to move back."

I gaze at the hills rolling by, reminiscent of so many hills I drove through with Angus. My heart aches with missing him.

Shawn's fingers twine in mine. "Why wouldn't you, if it's to protect James?"

Touche. I don't want to be across an ocean from Angus. I swallow. "I just think we need to know one way or the other." *Almost as quickly, I add,* "If I had to, for James, yes, I'd pick him up right now and turn right back for the airport."

He glances at me again, his eyes lingering this time, while I stare resolutely ahead, pretending I don't notice; wishing he'd put his eyes back on the road. Angus stands between us, a silent ghost, as once Shawn's silent ghost stood between me and Angus. I change the subject. "Did you read more parchments? Are they okay?"

Shawn shrugs. "As okay as you can be in a war-torn, famine-ridden world. What do you think? Burgers on the grill tonight?"

I look at his face, seeing his exhaustion, the strain. I touch his hair, smiling at the girl calling back, smiling as I remember Niall's enigmatic comment about French shampoo. "You've had a couple of sleepless nights," *I say.* "You're tired."

He grins, the Puckish smile that always makes my heart flop over. "Yeah, I've been tired before."

"Get some rest," *I say.* "We don't own a grill. Maybe you can sleep while I see what we can find."

Glenmirril, May 1317

The men crowded behind him as Glenmirril came into view below, cheers rising from their throats. Niall himself felt only worn. But he smiled, heartened by their energy. Lachlan lifted high MacDonald's banner, letting the breeze snap it out. On the parapet, guards pointed and shouted, and the men on the hill called back, waving.

Niall's smile grew, lifted by their enthusiasm, and he nudged his horse, Shawn's horse. It, too, knew Glenmirril, and the warm stalls waiting there, and skipped down the hill, whickering and tossing its head as its hooves struck the drawbridge. The men on the parapets shouted down greetings. Through the gatehouse arch, Niall saw women and children rushing into the courtyard.

He stopped, letting his men ride ahead to find their families, while he scanned the crowd for Allene's red hair. It was harder to spot, now that she wore head coverings as befit a married woman. He saw Christina, wearing the remote smile that masked her pain and fear. Slender in her blue gown, she showed no sign of having been with child. She cradled William on her shoulder. Then James's auburn curls jumped out at him, and there was Allene.

Allene saw him at the same moment. She hesitated, scanning the crowd. He knew her well. Duty came first. She'd be looking to see if they'd brought home injured men, or tidings of more widows and orphans at Glenmirril. He slid off the pony, assured himself the men were all in and finding their families, and went to her, wrapping his arms around her. "There are no new widows," he whispered in her ear.

"God be praised!" Her eyes shone. "Let us thank Him."

"Yes, let us." Niall spoke gravely, powerfully aware how his view of life had changed. In Shawn's world, no one would think to thank God for a safe arrival home. It was expected. He must remember the miracle on the battlefield, he chided himself; quit comparing or trying to understand, but be grateful Allene was here, grounding him, reminding him of all that was good in his life. He must thank God she had given birth twice and lived. Neither Bruce's first wife nor daughter had survived even once. "I've much to be thankful for," he told her. "Where's your father?"

"I'm here," came MacDonald's deep rumble at Niall's side. He spun Niall, and embraced him in a tight grip. "Welcome home, son. We've prayed day and night." He lifted his leonine head and shouted into the joyous crowd in the courtyard. "Our prayers are answered!" The people of Glenmirril cheered.

Red bounded to his side, clapping his shoulder—more a man than the boy Niall had left behind—and hugging him, before taking Shawn's pony.

Hugh appeared in the doorway of the tower, not so robust as he had been, and hugged Niall, too, slapping his back with nearly his previous strength. "Welcome home!" Roysia followed him, holding her son wrapped in swaddling clothes. He'd grown a great deal since his birth on the battlefield, and twisted in the tight bindings to peer with bright eyes into the crowd and noise. Roysia saw Owen, and glanced up at Hugh. He nodded, and she hurried to Owen, who embraced her.

"Come to the chapel," MacDonald said, "and let us give thanks."

Niall kissed James, on Allene's hip, who looked hesitantly at Allene.

"'Tis your father," she told the boy. "Give him a kiss. He'll be home for a time."

"For a wee bit," Niall hedged. He didn't have the heart to tell her he was due back at Scone. "James, do you not remember playing with your horses and going to the shore with me? Do you not remember I played the harp while your mother held you?" A deep ache throbbed in his heart, desperately needing the child to remember.

James's eyes lit. *"Athair?"* He reached for Niall. Niall took the boy into his arms, his heart squeezing in pain and joy. He'd be leaving again. Bruce did no less, he reminded himself. In fact, he did more, serving all of Scotland. Niall buried his face in James's ginger hair, smelling the heather soap Allene used.

"Come, we must go," Allene whispered. She tugged his arm, and he joined the people flowing across Glenmirril's courtyard to the kirk. He took Christina's arm, wanting William close, and they took their seats in the front pew of the kirk. Niall's weariness washed away in the familiar scents of incense and beeswax polish that had been the backdrop of his life at Glenmirril. The old priest came out from the sacristy, as the last of the men and their families shuffled into place and settled in pews.

Niall's hand twined with Allene's as Latin words of thanks drifted over him. He closed his eyes, thinking of the child in his arms who didn't remember him, and another boy, three pews back, delivered to life in the valley of the shadow of death.

Allene squeezed his hand. He wanted nothing more than the feel of her, even as he thanked God for bringing him safely home, for delivering his children and wife safely in childbirth, for giving him this time with her. For a moment, behind closed lids, her hand warm on his, he felt God all around him, as he had so long ago.

The priest finished at long last, jolting him from the peace of thanksgiving into hope for the future. He leaned close to Allene, his eyes twinkling. "Give the children to Bessie."

Allene's cheeks burned pink. Her eyes shone.

Monadhliath Mountains, Present

Simon wasted the rest of the day and a good part of the night seeking a way into the monastery, circling it, searching the walls for any entrance. The fool monks didn't even post a watch! Free to search, he would catch them sleeping, unawares, in their cells. He would deal with them, and *then* pay Eamonn a visit, letting him know his brethren were dead. The old man would tremble in terror!

But the walls were thick, high, strong, and sheer. The doors and gates, what few he found, held fast. As the sun rose, spreading blood red rays behind silhouetted hills, Simon dropped to the ground under an apple tree. Breaking his fast with the sweet, dripping fruit, he studied the stone walls rising above the morning mist. Eamonn awaited him in Inverness. He would use Eamonn to get into Monadhliath. Yes, he would simply deal with them in a different order than he'd intended. But in the end, they *would* regret defying him. They would plead for mercy! Fergal would beg for the lives of his men, and finally, for their quick deaths, at least. How he would beg!

Smiling as though the vengeance were already complete, Simon wiped sticky juice from his chin. Suddenly, a sharp report jolted him. From the branch above, an apple exploded, spewing pulp onto his head.

Simon leapt to his feet, his eyes shooting across the misty lawn toward the sound, his heart slowing to the deadly calm that carried him into battle. Fergal stood atop the monastery walls. The walking stick in his hand pointed at Simon, smoking.

Simon backed away, horror dawning. The *walking stick* was the gun Fergal spoke of! *It* had destroyed the apples! It was some form of those weapons he'd so carefully diagrammed. These men were not defenseless.

"Leave us or my gun shall do to you what it did to the apples!" Fergal shouted.

Simon wiped pulp from his head. Unfamiliar fear stirred, realizing he hadn't even begun to understand what he'd read in the books.

"Surely you're satisfied after a night of searching, there is no way in," Fergal called down. He moved the stick on his shoulder, its smoking end pointed at

Simon. "Eamonn awaits you. 'Tis time for you to go."

Simon backed away, helpless and raging that he, Lord of Claverock, should be cowed by monks. *Monks!* He would destroy Monadhliath in his own time, he vowed. Satisfied with the vengeance he would wreak before these men ever existed, he whirled and stormed down the mountain. Eamonn was waiting.

Glenmirril, May 1317

"We must solve the problem of Christina's child." Allene stood in her shift at the window of the bed chamber, looking out on the loch as dawn's first rays shimmered over sparkling sapphire waters. "He is nearly two months. We cannot hide him much longer, and the strain is telling. Though she wears the mask well, while we sew with the women, I see it when we are alone. It is only she and I and Bessie to care for the child, as no one else can know he exists. We are all exhausted, with caring for three bairns, nursing Hugh, and running a castle."

Niall rose from the bed, and joined her at the window. "'Tis much too late to pass him off as Hugh's child, even if they'd agree to marry one another now."

"She has said she will," Allene reported. "She has nursed him these past weeks with great devotion."

"But she'll still not say whose it is?"

"She looks right through me!" Allene threw her hands up in agitation. "If she's confided to Hugh, he'll not say."

Niall's eyebrows furrowed. He didn't want to think about whose child it was. Maybe it was better for all of them to simply accept the boy's presence and not ask questions. "Your father has come up with nothing?"

"Oh, aye, he's come up with another bench, a drum, and a box large enough to hold ten pounds of turnips. His dilemma is proving a great source of new items for Glenmirril. Including a cradle for the source of all his turmoil." She leaned against the window frame, staring over the loch.

Niall tightened the corners of his mouth against the smile that threatened. It wasn't funny. In fact, it saddened him to see the Laird, who had always been so in control, at a loss for answers. He supposed life was not what it had been, in his younger years. "And Hugh?"

"Hugh was far more ill than he let on. He made it to the tower and collapsed. He's in no shape to sort out a child whose presence needs a story." She turned from the window. "Shawn was ever good at thinking up stories. For this purpose, now, 'twould serve for good. Can we not think what he would do?"

The idea jumped to Niall's mind as if Shawn himself had appeared and dropped it there. "I have it!" he exclaimed. The idea grew, and his excitement, as he told her.

Allene's look of dismay grew, too. "Niall, this is *not* a good idea."

"Have you a better one?" Niall grinned. It would work. Shawn himself couldn't have thought up a better plan!

Inverness, early October, Present

Time moved slowly, with paperwork, phone calls, and an interminable meeting about caring for their rescue equipment. The busy season was coming, things must be in order, Mick O'Shaughnessy from the Mountain Corp reminded them. Angus sighed. They'd been doing their job for years. Did they really need the reminder from a kid just out of uni? Still, he jotted a note on his calendar to check over his own equipment, make sure it was in good order, and ready to go.

An afternoon meeting filled time. As soon as he could extricate himself from it, he returned to his office, pulling up Amy's name on his phone. Still, he hesitated, pulling up the last video he'd watched on YouTube, wanting to hear it one more time. As he listened, Claire entered with her watering can.

"Middle English?" she asked, resting the can on the corner of his desk.

"Aye." Angus nodded absently, watching the man on the screen recite poetry. "Chaucer. Fourteenth century."

"You understand him?" Claire asked. "What's he saying?"

"'Tis the Knight's Tale from *Canterbury Tales.*"

Claire gave a small shake of her head. "Hard to believe that's English."

"If you saw the spelling," Angus said, "you'd see a great deal of similarity."

Just then, a loud voice erupted in the hall, drowning out the video. With a sigh, Angus hit pause.

Claire rolled her eyes, and stepped to the fern behind Angus. "Him again."

"Him who?" Angus asked.

"He was brought in just before you got here this morning, his knickers in a knot!" She glanced over her shoulder at him as water streamed into the fern's rich loam.

Out in the hallway, another rush of unintelligible words raked the air.

"What the devil is he saying?" Angus asked.

Claire shrugged, lifting the can, stopping the flow of water. "Who's to say. 'Tis an old man from the Hebrides. No one could make out a word." She left, pulling the door behind her. It dimmed the shouting from the hall, and Angus hit *play* again. But he frowned, as he watched the man reciting. It was one man's interpretation of what Chaucer *may* have sounded like. And Chaucer was one speaker of Middle English, which spanned centuries and countries, each region and decade with its own accent.

He jabbed at the mouse to shut down the tab. "What am I on about?" he muttered. Carol thought the attacker had a strange accent, and therefore it must be a time traveler? Angus thumped back in his chair, arms across his chest, and stared at the place on his board where the picture of Amy and James had hung.

If he was right, he had to call her. But maybe he was looking for reasons to call. Did he really want to send her into a panic over nothing? Clive was right. Carol was unaccustomed to UK accents. Maybe the attacker was from Ireland. Maybe he was from Eastern Europe and English was his second language. Shawn wouldn't have noticed an accent either way. He'd been *fighting* the man, not chatting over tea.

Angus shook his head, irritated with himself for not thinking through the obvious explanations first. His mouth tightened. He would check a few more things, he decided. It couldn't hurt to look. But he wouldn't alarm her with this story when there were too many other—and more reasonable—explanations. The question, he thought to himself, was where to even begin researching whether an unknown attacker might be a medieval madman posing as a modern professor.

He let out a snort uncomfortably reminiscent of Shawn. Even the words to pose the question made him sound mad. Yet his gut burned, screaming that this was not the random attack Bannockburn PD said it was.

But where to begin? An idea came to mind. He glanced at the clock. When he finished work, he decided, yes, that's where he would start. He would do this one more thing, before calling Amy or Shawn. To be sure. It was preposterous, a needle in a haystack. But it was a place to start. And far better than throwing everyone into panic over a wild, unsubstantiated guess.

CHAPTER TWENTY-NINE

Glenmirril, May 1317

"Are you mad?" Christina asked with ironic calm. Her eyes strayed to the cradle, beside her easel, where her son slept.

Allene spoke true, Niall thought. Though Christina sat in her usual peaceful pose in the solar, her charcoal stick against the vellum on which she drew, morning sunlight fell on the thinnest of lines etched around her mouth, betraying a great deal of tension these past months.

Hugh sat at the chess table. He'd regained most of the weight he'd lost in Ireland, and color had returned to his face, though Niall noted streaks of silver in his beard that had not been there, and the circles under his eyes that had appeared in Ireland had not faded. Allene and her father stood together by the window on whose sill Shawn had so often sat. MacDonald stared out across the loch, his hands clasped behind his back. He'd said little so far.

"How can you ask this of me?" Christina lowered the charcoal to her lap.

"He'll be alone but minutes," Niall promised.

"A great deal can happen to a child in mere minutes." Though she spoke with the melodious peace that had so drawn Shawn, the lines deepened around her mouth. "And will it not look suspicious if one of you finds him?"

"We won't," Niall said. "We'll ignore the cries until Lachlan or Owen hears."

"Ignore his cries!" Christina's mask slipped. "You cannot possibly...."

Hugh spoke gently. "It must be this way, Christina, for your own protection. The Laird has been generous and merciful. You'll not say whose the child is, and it will become steadily more difficult to hide a bairn."

"He'll be in *danger*!" she objected. "This is my *son!*" The charcoal convulsed in her hand. "You can't really mean to *do* such a thing!" She looked frantically from one to the other, as she laid her hand on the hood of the cradle.

"Christina, you must." Allene came to her side. "We need *some* explanation for his presence." Her hand, too, fell on the cradle. "He'll be safe!"

Christina lifted her eyes to Allene. "Then allow William to go in his place."

Allene looked at the floor.

Christina turned to Niall. "Will you substitute your own son?"

Meeting her terrified eyes, Niall's confidence that Shawn would be proud of this plan wavered.

Before he could answer, Hugh rose from his seat at the chess board, and came to her, kneeling beside the cradle. "Christina, all our people have seen William." He took her hands between his. "All will see James Angus when we bring him in. They are not even the same size. 'Tis not possible."

Niall stepped closer, hating himself for inflicting this on her. "I shall be with him to the last moment," he said. "Any wild animals will have to go through me first."

"Except," Christina said, "for that last moment." She lifted one eyebrow. "When you are not there to be gone through."

Niall stared at the floor.

"My word is law." MacDonald turned from the window, his voice filling the room. "It is this or send him away entirely."

Christina drew in a deep breath, her eyes closed.

They watched her silently, waiting.

She opened her eyes, fixing them on her son. She pulled one hand from Hugh's to stroke James Angus's black curls. He sighed in his sleep.

"We'll all be there with him," Niall said softly.

Christina bit her lip, and blinked her eyes hard, before saying, "Assuming this works, and Lachlan finds a child—a *live* child—what then? You must give him to one of the women to care for. Will I ever see him again, but in another woman's arms?"

"You will be several days without him," MacDonald said. "A month, even. I will take my time, lest anyone conclude, from too hasty a decision, that I have just returned a child to the woman who was ill and out of sight these past months."

Christina bowed her head. "Yes, My Lord."

"Tomorrow morning, before dawn," the Laird said heavily.

Allene slid her arm around Christina's shoulders. "'Twill come aright, Christina. James Angus will be safe."

Inverness, Present

The house next to Angus's remained empty. After strolling down the street, and down the back lane to assure himself he was alone, Simon slipped over the garden wall and let himself in his own back door. It was late enough—and Angus's house silent enough—that he took his station at the upper window, staying back, despite the cover of lace curtains. The waiting dragged on interminably, but finally, at the far end of the street, Angus appeared, a bulging canvas bag swinging from each hand, leafy vegetables sticking out. He climbed the steps of his house and disappeared inside.

Simon moved silently down his stairs, and pressed his ear to the wall adjoining Angus's home. Footsteps paced the hall, a door opened, and something heavy dragged across the floor. Simon glanced around his own narrow hall, at a cupboard tucked under the stairs. Angus must have pulled something from his own cupboard. Simon followed his footsteps back to the kitchen.

Once again, he pressed his ear to the wall. Water ran and stopped. A door opened and closed. It would be the outside door. Simon moved to his kitchen window, to peer cautiously over the low wall into Angus's garden. The blooms that had been colorful throughout the summer had wilted into sad browns in the beating autumn rains. The past days had been sunny, if cool, leaving the brown stalks dry. Angus stood in his small patch of grass, holding a black bag. He glanced up at the sky, a phone to his ear. Simon inched the window open.

"Busy season coming at us." Angus's words floated over the fence, clear as a bell. He dropped the bundle to the ground, opening it with one hand as he listened.

"Young Mick's on our backs." Angus laughed and added, "Aye, now it's finally dry." He fell silent, the phone to his ear, as he spread out a web of what looked like rope, but flat and black.

Simon pressed close to the glass, watching. Angus nodded now and again, and glanced twice at the fading sunlight.

"A pint sounds grand," he finally said.

Simon's hopes soared. If Angus went out, there would be time to look around his home, maybe find some scrap of paper with Amy's whereabouts on it, or Eamonn's. Maybe a device or some writing that would tell Simon how to control time, or lead him to Shawn.

"But I've things to do at home," Angus said.

Simon's irritation sprang back. But he stilled himself. Patience would win. A few more words, too muffled to make out, floated from the other yard. Simon pressed his ear to the screen, straining to hear.

"Tomorrow, then." Angus stowed the phone in a pocket, and bent his dark hair over the straps and gear, running his hands over each piece, studying, twisting, adjusting, while Simon watched. Sooner or later, he thought, Amy would come with James. Until then, he would train, continue his study of weaponry—he would learn to build a *gun* like Fergal's—and seek Brother Eamonn. Tonight, he would watch through Angus's windows, and see what he could learn. He waited until dusk became night, until Angus gathered his equipment and headed back inside, before letting himself out his back door. He disappeared into the dark, making his way to the far end of the row of homes, and back, to the bushes in front of Angus's home. Rising carefully on his toes, he peered into the window.

Glenmirril, 1317

"Best to keep moving," Allene murmured, guiding Christina through the kitchens after dinner. "Keep your head up. No one must suspect."

"Amy didn't have to hide her child," Christina whispered back.

"Amy does not—won't—live in our time," returned Allene. "Saying it will be different one day does us no good now." She stopped abruptly as a cook came around a corner. A bright smile flashed across her face. "Berta! I've come to check the kitchen stores. What of the dinner scraps? You've packed them for the poor?"

The girl bobbed. "Aye, Milady. 'Tis done."

Christina followed mutely, as Berta showed them around the kitchen pantries, and Allene inspected the spices, picking out the laudanum. Christina gathered up the food basket, covering the bottle with two loaves of bread, and they left the kitchen. She leaned close, hissing, "There *are* wild boar in the forest, and they're quite vicious. There are wolves."

"Hush, Christina." Allene gripped her arm. "Have faith in Niall." They stopped talking as three serving boys hurried toward them. When they'd passed, Allene added, "Shawn and Niall spoke of you as a woman of great courage in the face of Duncan's rages."

"What mother does not fear more for her child than for herself?" Christina's voice trembled. "How am I to have faith when I can do naught for my own son?"

Inverness, October, Present

With his gear replaced in his upstairs closet, and chicken baking in the oven, Angus returned to his front room. He glanced through the lace curtains at the window. Outside, the bushes swayed against the window in an evening breeze. Street lamps spilled light on the road in a pale, yellow puddles. Children called to one another in the dusk. A dog barked. Angus opened his laptop, checking his e-mail first. There was nothing from Amy. He hadn't expected it, but his heart sank a little, as it did each time he saw nothing from her. He'd walked away, he reminded himself. He'd hoped she'd see that she wanted him. He still hoped she'd come to him about the attack.

He sighed, missing her, even if it *was* his own fault, and opened YouTube His search turned up only a short list. It was a mixed blessing. Less chance of finding anything, but at least he wouldn't be at it all night.

He clicked on the first, an amateur filming of the Bannockburn re-enactment the previous summer, two minutes long. He watched carefully, and ran it again, but it was only a fragment of the blind old abbot of Inchaffray giving absolution to the troops. The next video was fifteen minutes. He kept his eyes locked on the screen, backing up now and again, pausing the action several times, and reviewing sections.

There was nothing.

The aroma of baking chicken filled the room as he turned on the third. After the fourth, he took his dinner from the oven, leaving it out to cool. He glanced around his small kitchen. Irritation filled him, imagining Shawn's kitchen. It probably had acre-long slabs of shining granite counters, and gleaming, elegantly arched faucets, and slate floors, like he'd seen on movies of American homes. Of *course* she hadn't come back. Why should she? Grabbing a Guinness from the small refrigerator under the counter, Angus returned to the front room, and pulled up the final video. If he found nothing here, he had to think up another idea.

Something rustled outside the window. He looked up. Dark night stared in blankly above the lace. There was no more sound. Angus sipped his beer, and started the video. Re-enactors filled the screen. "We're at the re-enactment of the Battle of Bannockburn," said a man's voice. In the background, a man and woman spoke unintelligibly. It was another amateur effort. But those often gave the best results, with their lack of editing. Angus glanced at the lower corner of the video. Fifty minutes, it told him. He sighed. It increased the chances of finding something, but it was a lot of watching. He might have to break it up, if his eyes got tired.

On screen, with laughing and excited chatter unlikely to be found in a real battle, the re-enactors gathered into lines. A call sounded somewhere unseen, and their smiles slipped. They donned the personas of medieval fighters, as surely as they had donned their authentic medieval *braies* that morning. They turned their backs to the camera. It zoomed in on the English, facing them across the field, closing in on a horse draped in emerald green trappings, tossing its head.

"Here comes the Abbot of Inchaffray," the man's voice whispered in awed tones. He panned back, and a monk, more portly than the average medieval monk, moved along the line of Scots, his hand raised in benediction, his feet bare.

Angus sipped his beer, watching intently, scanning every corner of the screen, trying to make out the faces of the English across the way. The video dragged on predictably, Scots marching forward in tight, prickly *schiltrons*. The English charged. The picture became a mass of bodies. Angus tried desperately to watch every face, English and Scottish, trying to guess what would make a genuine medieval fighter stand out among a crowd devoted to being authentically medieval.

But they *couldn't* be totally authentic, Angus reminded himself. There was too much unknown of the time. The same processes, plants, and tools were not available. Anyone genuinely medieval would stand out.

Anyone genuinely medieval would be genuinely killing.

Angus's eyes flickered across the cavalry as the cameraman panned them. They all looked roughly the same. Angus glanced at the time in the corner. A half hour had passed. He wondered if he'd already missed something. More likely, there was nothing to be found. He sipped his beer.

"What's that over there?" a female voice asked off screen.

"Hold on, now," said the man. "I'm filming."

"No, there's a woman...."

"Look over here." The man returned to his narrator's voice, speaking more loudly. "We've a knight fallen from his horse." He zoomed in on a man in a blue and gold tabard struggling on the ground. Angus watched. The coat of arms flashed tantalizing into sight as the man tried to push himself up.

"Look over there, get that," said the woman. The camera slid away, giving Angus only the briefest glimpse of the action that followed. But it was enough. It bolstered what his gut had told him.

He backed it up, watching again, stopping it, trying to focus on the tabard—the clue that would confirm who the knight on the ground had been. He watched a third time, and sat back, torn between frustration and satisfaction. It was enough—except that he couldn't make out the arms, no matter how he backed it up and replayed it, or enlarged it to fill the computer screen. He should send it to Shawn, he thought. Keep things neat. Let him deal with it.

He opened a new e-mail, inserting the link. But his fingers paused over the addressee. He was grateful to Shawn for protecting James. But he was angry it had been Shawn. *He* had been there for James since before birth. It should have been him. He wanted nothing to do with the arrogant piece of shite. But he needed to leave Amy alone. He hesitated, second guessing his choice to send it to Shawn. He should find out what he could about the man pulled off the field first. He had resources Shawn didn't.

"You're avoiding him," Angus muttered. Still, it *would* be better to have real information. Maybe it *was* just an injured re-enactor.

Professors, he decided. Historians. His cousin was a professor of medieval languages. He would have answers. Angus pasted in the video, added his questions, and sent it to every professor of medieval history and historian he knew, including half a dozen friends. He stopped at Brian's e-mail. He hadn't heard back from him about his previous questions. He should give him a call. The time on his clock told him it was late. He'd call tomorrow, after that meeting.

He shut the laptop and rose to turn off the lights. Outside, the bushes scraped against the window. Angus stopped, looking back. All was silent. Frowning, he opened the front door. Clouds scuttled across the moon, leaving the night dark but for the street lamps. He peered into the bushes. All was silent. He smiled. The neighbor children's dog had taken to burying bones there. That's all it had been.

Glenmirril, May 1317

Hugh elected himself to spirit the box out of the castle, saying, "Shawn taught me to swim." He stared hard at Niall. "Knees straight. Fingers together."

Niall scowled. "We're discussing getting the box out."

"I'll take it through the secret tunnel tonight, take it up the loch a ways, and hide it. Then we need only hide the baby under my cloak when we leave in the morning." Niall and MacDonald took guard duty on the wall overlooking the loch while Hugh slipped down to the Bat Cave and made his mission with the box.

Short hours later, with dawn still gray, they donned hunting gear and gathered the bundled, sleeping child from Christina. She barely breathed, her face drawn in fear as she kissed him, and handed him over.

Allene wrapped an arm around her shoulder. "They'll care for him well, sure."

"You gave him laudanum?" MacDonald asked. "We canna have him cry as we pass the guards."

Christina nodded, blinking her eyes furiously.

Allene squeezed her shoulder. "'Twill not harm him, Christina. He'll come back safe, you'll see, and soon you'll be raising him as your own, no more need to hide."

Christina nodded mutely, as one locked in a nightmare.

"I'll be with him till the last moment," Niall reassured her. "No harm will come to him."

"Can I not come with you?" she asked suddenly, raising desperate eyes.

Niall and Allene exchanged glances. "'Twill be nigh impossible for you to play the part," Allene said. "An hour, no more, and they'll be back with him. Until then, you and I will see to the gardens."

The baby sighed and settled into Hugh's big arms. Allene rose, kissed the baby, and twitched Hugh's cloak together, pinning it with a large, gold brooch over the child. "God go with you," she whispered.

Niall and MacDonald strode through the torch-lit halls before Hugh, shielding any glimpse of the bulge under his cloak. MacDonald went to the great hall to rouse his hounds, while Niall and Hugh headed for the stable. Hugh handed the baby to Niall while he climbed on a horse. Niall looked down at the tiny, sleeping face. The child seemed barely to breathe. Christina's fears crept under his own skin, as he wondered if they'd inadvertently hurt the boy, trying to salvage the situation. But the child gave a gentle sigh.

"*Gratias*," Niall whispered. He lifted the baby into Hugh's waiting arms, and re-settled Hugh's cloak.

When MacDonald arrived with his hounds, they rode out on either side of Hugh to shield his awkward seat on his horse. His prolonged illness would be explanation enough, they hoped. The dogs loped at their sides.

"We saw a boar, even from the ramparts!" MacDonald shouted at the guards. "Send someone to rouse Lachlan and Owen!" One of the dogs gave a deep woof, as if to emphasize the Laird's words.

"Aye, my Lord." One guard bowed, as the other hastened to do his bidding.

They crossed the drawbridge, each clomp of the horses' hooves jolting Niall's nerves, fearing the guard stopping them, calling them back, for any reason, for the baby to be revealed. But they passed into the field beyond the moat without incident, riding past the pell and the stretch of grass where the boys trained. Mist floated over it, rosy tendrils in the first rays of dawn. They climbed the hill, Hugh awkward in his attempt to keep the child hidden, and Niall and MacDonald riding close by his sides, up through the wooded path, to the ridge where only two days before Niall had looked down, anticipating his homecoming. The dogs galloped ahead in the cool, spring dawn, down the other side, into the fertile hunting grounds, which even famine had not completely destroyed.

"Take the child," Hugh said. "I'll get the box and meet you at the tree." He passed James Angus between the ponies, to Niall's arms, and, unburdened, shot off.

Niall and MacDonald rode to the tent-like fir tree high on the ridge. Bluebells made a thick carpet through the forest, softening the sound of their passing. They waited only minutes before Hugh cantered up the hill, clinging with difficulty to the box. He slid off his pony, and he and Niall wiggled under the lowest boughs of the tree, while MacDonald wheeled his horse to see if Lachlan and Owen had managed to come up so quickly.

"Here, next to the trunk, hurry!" Niall whispered, fearful of the two appearing too soon. Hugh, bent double in the small, dark space under the thick branches, pushed the box up against the trunk. He opened the lid, patting the blankets. Niall nestled the baby down into them. "Are we doing the right thing?" he asked.

"Have we any choice?" Hugh whispered back.

"In Shawn's time, Amy went about pregnant and unwed. 'Twas clear she would raise her child openly."

"I canna fathom it," replied Hugh. "Is there no social order? If one does it so freely, will not others?"

"I think they did." Niall touched the boy's cheek, wondering if it was Shawn's son. He liked to think he was looking at the son of a man who had been a brother to him, though the implication left him uneasy.

"And who cares for all these women who are as good as widows, with no husband, no father for their child?"

"She was paid to play her violin." Niall stroked the baby's cheek. "She cared for herself."

Hugh shook his head. "I can't grasp these things. Women living alone in castles all to themselves. Who protected them? Who guarded the walls at night?"

"He told you over and over there are no ramparts, and no need for guards."

"I cannot fathom it." Hugh too, gazed on the child. "D' ye think 'tis Shawn's?"

Niall pulled his finger from the box. "Was she in the Bat Cave with the women when you went for them?"

"I can't remember." Frustration edged Hugh's voice. "We'd been up all day and all night, we'd fought a hard battle. I thought only on getting back to the courtyard."

"If she was in the Bat Cave, it must be his."

"I'd not like to believe it of him." Hugh edged the blanket higher under James Angus's chin.

"Nor would I," Niall said, "though I try to remember our ways were so foreign to him. Nor do I prefer the other explanation. If this isn't Shawn's child, one of the MacDougalls found her."

A short whistle sounded outside their leafy cocoon. It was the Laird's signal that Lachlan and Owen were leaving the castle. "Go," Niall told Hugh. "Lead them away. I'll wait here until he stirs. Make sure they're nowhere near when I come out. I'll find you and we'll make our way back."

Nodding, Hugh backed out under the boughs, and disappeared, leaving Niall alone with the sleeping child. Outside the piney hideaway, MacDonald shouted, "Hugh, have you seen it? Where has it gone?"

"Farther up," Hugh called. "Tell those sluggards to make haste!"

Their voices held the peculiar echoing quality of early dawn. Mist crawled across the ground, hovering around the tree trunk in wispy tendrils. Niall reached into the box and tugged the blanket more closely around the baby, hoping he was warm enough. They'd argued the point, MacDonald insisting there could be only one threadbare blanket, for any woman so poor as to leave her child in the woods would not have warm blankets for him. In the small space, for a short time, the boy would be fine. Christina's mouth had tightened, deepening the lines around the corners, but she had known better than to argue.

As Niall watched the boy sleeping, he knew MacDonald was right. There was no point in the elaborate ruse if they left such obvious clues as wrapping the child in thick swaddling clothes worthy of a laird. Still, he hated it as much as Christina. It went against every instinct crying for him to protect the helpless. He inched the blanket back again, studying the face, trying to see any resemblance to Shawn or his own James.

The light, filtering through the branches, took on a rosy hue. Outside, Lachlan called, "How big was this boar?"

"It must have been some fine size to be seen from the ramparts." Owen sounded doubtful.

One of the dogs woofed. Garrons thundered past the tree. The baby in the box gave a little whistling breath, and his eyes fluttered open. Too soon, Niall thought, as their eyes met in the dim light. If he cried now, Niall would be caught here with him, and the game given away. "Sh," he whispered, stroking the boy's cheek. He strained his ears, trying to judge how far his friends had gone. Not far enough. He could still hear them. He should leave now, but he'd promised Christina he'd stay until the last moment, until the boy cried.

"*Ave Maria,*" he whispered. "*Gratia plena.* Protect him."

The clod of hooves faded. Niall breathed more easily. The boy watched him with bright eyes, the same golden brown as Shawn's. From outside the boughs came the padding of heavy feet. Niall listened, and suddenly, his spine stiffened. In place of hoof beats came the sound Christina dreaded most: the distinct, guttural snuffling of a wild boar.

CHAPTER THIRTY

Bannockburn, Present

As well as you can do in a war-torn, famine-ridden world.

Shawn's flippant words haunted him through a false facade of grilling on their new grill, through a restless night, and through preparing the big band parts, the next morning, for printing, until he gave in and slid the parchments, once more, from their oilskin. *The Year of our Lord 1317. The Feast of St. Augustine.*

Shawn recognized Niall's bold, firm hand. He did an internet search to find the date of the feast of St. Augustine, and translated. May 27, 1317. He smiled. Niall had come home from Ireland! "Thank you, God," he whispered. It meant, somehow, he'd crossed water—twice!

Greetings, my Brother,
Allene will have told you I've had no chance to write, these many months. I'll not repeat all that has kept me from e-mailing you. This parchment and quill will not have so much slachran. LOL.

Shawn frowned at the word *slachran.* "Battering ram?" he murmured. Suddenly it hit him. *This quill and parchment have not so much RAM!* He laughed aloud at the modern parlance flowing out of elegant script via medieval Gaelic. It was easy to see Niall riding his shaggy garron under spring trees, talking about Toto and Kansas, laughing easily. He wondered how a year of warfare had changed Niall—if he still laughed at life and looked for pranks to play and kissed his pony on its nose when he thought no one was looking.

I reached Ireland. I'll not say easily. Lachlan spoke of the difference from the Niall who fought at Jura, as if born to ships. Hugh passed my green face off as sea sickness. I played my harp, as you told me, and forgot about the water below. Almost. Coming home was worse, in a smaller boat. You know I dislike admitting such weakness to any man, but as I owe you a great debt, as you've a right to know the results of your efforts, it seems I must. So I thank you, my friend, for all you have unwittingly done for me, despite your general ineptness in all areas of character, weaponry, combat, and fourteenth century life in general.

Shawn smiled, as he knew Niall had been smiling as he wrote those words.

Who got you knighted, he would have shot back, had he been there. *Who earned you a reputation as Superman? If you'd been quicker, I wouldn't have had to rescue the kid myself, and I'd've been home a lot sooner.* There was no one, in his twenty-first century life, with whom he spoke that way, with whom he felt so at ease. It had been good, the late night confidences with Aaron. But it wasn't *brothers.*

I find Allene and the bairns in good health. Hugh took an arrow in one of Edward Bruce's overly-confident battles, but is recovered and makes sport of it. On the matter of Edward's hot-headedness, he is less amused. As are we all.

I have oft thought of your talk of your old men fishing. But it seems to me, as I return and see more white than red in the Laird's beard, that he stays vigorous and strong in his work. Though he takes delight, as did you, in spending time with James and wee William, people find it odd to see the Laird holding an infant, so he does so now only in Allene's solar.

You will want to know about Christina. She has returned to her former self, perhaps as much as she ever will. She feeds the poor and prays and aids Allene in overseeing the kitchens, maids, gardens, sewing, and all that must be done. I was not certain of Allene's wisdom in telling you Christina bore a child, yet she did tell you. 'Twas a boy, whom she called James Angus. You'll want to know of our plan to explain the child's presence....

Shawn read with growing horror. He didn't need Allene's prodding this time. "God, you have *got* to give him a better idea. He's going to get that kid killed!"

Glenmirril, May 1317

Niall closed his eyes, praying harder. Suddenly, the Laird's wooden box looked flimsy, sitting amidst the curls of mist. What had he been thinking! A boar's tusks would tear through it straightaway. Even if it merely tossed the box around, the bairn would be badly hurt. He couldn't leave the child now. In the dim space under the boughs, his fingers tightened around his dirk, ready should the animal push through the low-hanging branches. He hoped it wasn't as big as the imaginary boar they'd created to lure Lachlan and Owen to the hunt. God, he feared, had a sense of humor. A rather dark one. It would serve him right for lying.

Niall pressed his back to the massive trunk of the entwined pines, breathing deeply, as he listened to the boar snuffle at the drooping boughs. It must certainly smell him. He edged the baby behind the trunk, trying to be silent. Calling for help would bring on the boar. And it would reach him long before help did. He waited, dirk in his left hand, sword in his right, praying.

The snuffling turned to a deep grunt. The boughs trembled. Niall's fingers tightened on the dirk. He raised the sword as a tusk appeared. Niall hesitated. It had no reason to push through the wall of greenery. He could rush it, fight with momentum and surprise—or wait and hope it left. If it came in, he lost momentum and surprise. And he'd be caught in a tight space with its slashing tusks. If he made too much noise, Lachlan and Owen would find him here under the tree with a baby, and with tongues still wagging about Christina's illness, they'd figure it out.

The branches shook; the snout appeared. Instinct erupted. Niall rushed it, arcing his sword through the boughs, and jabbing up with the dirk. The branches slowed his swing, but still it connected forcefully, his dirk tearing through hide and muscle. The animal let out a dull roar, thrashing its tusks. Niall yanked back, dancing out of the way.

He had to keep the boar away from the baby. He barreled through the drooping branches. They scratched his face, tore his shirt, and grasped his cloak, but he burst out into the forest. "Here, I'm here!" he shouted, drawing the boar's attention.

Blood flowed from the animal's left shoulder. It turned, sizing him up with beady eyes, and lowered its head. Niall crouched, knife and sword up. "Hugh!" he bellowed. "Owen!"

It charged. Niall lunged aside, barely avoiding the jagged tusks, spun, and swung his sword down, slashing the animal's back. Blood trailed down its side. It gave a vicious snort, wheeled, and thrust its tusks up.

Niall skipped back, narrowly avoiding goring. He danced to the side, but the animal rounded. Niall backed away from the tree, drawing it, shouting, "Lachlan!"

The thing pawed, grunted, and inched forward.

"Hugh!" Niall shouted. The beast took a step. Niall leapt, hoping to get around the tusks, but it spun, and charged. Niall lunged aside. One tusk scraped his leg.

A wail erupted from inside the pine. The boar turned to the sound. Niall dove, jabbing his knife up into its throat. Bristles scraped his hand. Blood flowed down his arm. The animal bellowed, rounding on him. He skipped back, staying at its side, while it thrashed its head, trying to reach him. He crashed his sword down on its neck. One front leg buckled under the blow. It shook its head and scrambled to its feet, charging, unaffected by the blood streaming into its eyes.

"Hugh!" Niall roared. He jumped back again, stabbed with his knife, catching it in its shoulder, twisting with the boar as it forced him back toward the tree.

From within, the baby's cries rose. Niall glanced back, and in the second's distraction, the boar twisted, facing him. He couldn't let it charge him here. The momentum would carry it straight into the tree, into the baby. Niall roared, lifted his sword like a spear, and launched himself between the tusks. He landed on its back, grappling for a hold, as his legs dangled over its snout. The pig bellowed, shaking its head, while Niall clung on, trying to sink his knife in. The baby's cries rose. Niall stabbed again and again, as the boar snapped at his legs, flopping over its snout. "Hugh! Owen!" he screamed. He drove the knife in deep, aiming for the lungs, the heart, anything that would slow the monster down.

With a toss of its head, it dislodged him, flinging him into the pine's drooping boughs. He crashed on his back in the middle of a limb. His sword flew from his hand. The boar snorted, lowered its head, and charged.

Bannockburn, Present

The *ka ching* of his phone jarred Shawn, jerking him from a vivid dream of Christina's son, crying alone under a tree. He knew the one Niall meant: two pines grown close, till they'd become a single monolith, their boughs spreading like a circus tent, to the ground. James Angus would be safe in the green paradise inside —*if* no wild animal pushed through. He dreaded reading further. The ring tone *ka-ching*-ed again. Shawn fumbled at the phone, his thoughts on Christina's son. "Yeah, it's Shawn," he mumbled.

Ben's voice erupted with a curse. "Tell me you're not drinking again, Shawn!"

"What?" Shawn squinted, rubbing sleep from his eyes, and fending off the glare of sun shining in his window. He sat up straighter. "What are you talking about?"

"It's barely noon there, and you're mumbling."

Shawn rose, snapping back into the present. "I'm mumbling because you woke me up from a nap, you bampot."

"What the hell's a bampot?"

"An *eejit!*"

"What the...forget it. I'm still trying to decide, wherever you were for a year, if I prefer dealing with your previous incarnation or this new one that spouts off bizarre words and dresses like Renfest every day."

"They're comfortable," Shawn snapped. "What do you want?"

"It's more what you ought to want, which is to get that final list to me. I've got people waiting and no names. You promised you'd have it to me yesterday. Even when you were drunk all the time, you always had everything together a day before deadline. What's going on?"

"It's on my computer." Shawn opened his laptop and had his e-mail up in seconds. "I'm attaching it now." He smiled, thinking of Niall's comment about ram. He doubted Niall had ever grasped that the tiniest chip could hold thousands of pages of parchments. He added Ben's address, and hit send. "On its way," he said.

"Yeah. Hang on. Refreshing. Refreshing again. Yeah, it's here. Hang on while I look it over."

Shawn heard the click of keys over the phone line. His mind strayed to Niall. *He* had survived to write about it—but what of Christina's son? He'd *kill* Niall if he'd hurt Christina's son!

"You don't want to tell me what's up?" Ben asked.

"Huh?" Shawn's mind jolted between times. "What's up with what?"

"Not having this list! Look, I'm not asking in a critical manner. But you disappeared for a *year* with no real explanation, you came back like you'd matured ten years—and I mean that in a good way, it's great to see the last of the obnoxious college party boy—but you're not on top of things like you used to be, even when you were a personal wreck."

"Thanks. I wasn't..." Shawn stopped.

"I'm asking as a friend." Ben's voice dropped. "If you need to talk, you know?"

"Yeah, just a lot on my mind. I've got a kid now. I'm trying to spend time with him, be there for Amy. I just lost track of time, is all."

"You know how this business works." The irritation came back to Ben's voice. "You *can't* lose track of time. Okay, I'm looking at the list. Let's run through this together and double-check." They talked through each of Shawn's choices.

"I'm really liking this 20's focus and Jack Teagarden," Ben said. "You'll have that last part to me today?"

"Don't worry, Ben. It's going to be done." Shawn thought of the baby under the tree. "Don't sweat the small stuff," he said, "and it's all small stuff, right? Not like we have to hide our children with wild boar on the loose." But as he hung up, he thought of his own James. Whoever had been on the stairs was far worse than a wild board, and Amy had said no more of going back with him. His thoughts wavered between Amy, work, and Christina's son. He had to get his work done. But the parchment pulled him.

Glenmirril, May 1317

Niall scrambled to his knees amidst the boughs, and jumped back. Under the branches, the baby screeched. A tusk scraped Niall's calf. He threw himself across the boar's back, driving his knife into the boar. Its bristles scraped his cheek raw. He drew the knife from its thrashing body and stabbed again.

"Hold on, Niall!"

He only dimly heard the voices. Beneath him, the beast's motions slowed. It tumbled to its knees, flung its head and let out a roar, a dull bass accompaniment to the baby's high-pitched wails. Niall drove the knife in again through thick hide. His arm trembled with the effort.

"We're coming, Niall!"

He heard the dogs woofing. They bounded from the woods into the clearing.

The boar's hind legs crumpled. It swung its head, trying to reach him, before it collapsed to the forest floor, rolling onto his legs and pinning him to the ground. The dogs danced around it, darting in and out. It grunted, thrashing its tusks at them. Above him, Lachlan blotted out the rising sun, his spear raised high over his head.

"Please don't," Niall whispered with the last of his strength.

The baby's screech split the air.

Lachlan froze. Perplexity crossed his face.

"I'm under the boar," Niall said slowly. "Do not drive that spear through me."

Owen raced up the hill, panting. "What is that sound?"

Lachlan lowered the spear. The boar dropped its head; its breathing came in deep gasps. Its heavy musk filled Niall's nostrils. Niall dropped his head on the ground, assured Lachlan was not going to skewer him, and willing the crushing weight off his legs. The boar's bristles dug through his trews. "I think it's a baby," he rasped.

"A baby?"

The smaller dog barked at the dying boar, while the larger one darted at its throat. The animal swung deadly tusks, and the dog backed up, circling.

"Get this thing off me!"

"Why is there a baby in the tree?"

"I'll never walk again," Niall said irritably, "if you don't get this thing off me."

Hugh cantered up the hill, sliding off his pony before it stopped. "Help me," he ordered the cousins. He grasped the creature's back legs. It twitched, raised its head and warned Hugh off.

"Watch yourself!" Hugh snapped at it. "Haste, Owen!"

Niall closed his eyes, fighting the awful pain. The baby screeched in short, sharp wails, each louder than the last. "I found the boar," he said. The bristles clawed across his legs as they tugged it, inch by inch, the animal fighting even in its dying moments. Finally, the weight slid off Niall. He didn't move.

"Now what is that sound?" MacDonald came up the path. His dogs barked and raced to him, leaping all around him.

Letting go of the pig's legs, Owen studied the tree, as if it would give him an answer. Then he dropped to his knees, shoving aside the heavy boughs. One of the dogs raced after him, barking, nosing through the limbs.

"Are ye alive, Niall?" MacDonald asked.

"Barely," Niall whispered.

"He's bleeding."

Niall felt the ground tremble as Hugh dropped to his knees. Giant hands probed his leg. He winced.

"I've seen worse," Hugh announced.

"It's a baby!" Owen shouted from inside the tree.

The boar drew in a deep, shuddering breath, let it out, and made no more sound.

"A baby," Niall sighed. "How bad is it, Hugh?"

"I need a bandage."

Niall threw his arm across his eyes, hearing the sound of cloth ripping. His cheek stung from the scrape of boar's bristles. "Wash it," he said. "Shawn said."

"*Old* said?" asked Lachlan.

Niall chuckled. Shawn's name sounded like the Gaelic word for old. "Old saying," he told Lachlan. "Can you get water?"

The limbs near him rustled. Owen swore, and suddenly another thump jolted the ground near Niall. He opened his eyes and rolled his head. Owen sat on his rump, the box between his legs, tangled in the tree limbs. Pine needles clung to his hair. From the box came a long, drawn-out wail.

"Take it out." Niall barely got the words out before he winced at the pressure of Hugh's hands, tightening a bandage around his leg.

"We'll wash it at home," Hugh said. And to Lachlan, "Tie this monster up. A fine feast tonight, aye?"

"I can't hold a baby," Owen objected.

"You *delivered* one," Niall pointed out. "Pick him up!" He grunted as Hugh gave another jerk on the bandages, knotting them tightly.

Owen stuck a hand in the box, and yanked it back.

"It's just a baby." Niall held back a laugh. "It *is* just a baby, isn't it?"

"Who would leave a baby here?" MacDonald recited the lines he'd prepared for himself. He glanced at Lachlan roping the boar's legs, then strode forward and dropped to one knee by the box he'd built. "One thin blanket," he announced. "It must be a poor woman. From very far away."

Niall groaned, dropping his arm back over his eyes. He hoped the Laird's words sounded more genuine to those who didn't know the truth, than they did to him.

"We must find out who did this!" Owen sounded outraged. He lifted the baby from the box. It wiggled in its bindings, its face red.

"No!" MacDonald jumped to his feet, shaking his great mane. "No! That is what we will *not* do! D' ye think whoever left it would be so foolish as to leave it close to home? No doubt it was someone traveling, a long way from home so they'd not be found out. And if a woman left her child, certainly she was desperate, aye?"

"Perhaps." Owen sounded doubtful. He held the baby at arms length, looking as worried as if it were a snake.

"Can ye not cuddle the thing?" Hugh demanded. "It won't bite ye."

Owen settled it close to his chest, rocking it awkwardly. Its cries settled, bit by bit. The worry did not leave his face. One of the dogs stretched its head up, sniffing at the bundle in his arms.

"What would Roysia have done?" Niall opened his eyes, commanding Owen's attention. "Were it not for Bruce's goodwill? What if this woman had no one?"

"Aye, you speak true." Compassion crept into Owen's voice. "Will we bring it to Glenmirril?"

"What a grand idea, Owen!" MacDonald heaved something between a grunt and a sigh. "If someone left it so close, sure an she *intended* someone from the castle to find it and take it in."

Lachlan gave the ropes around the boar's front legs a last jerk, tightening them, and looked up. "Perhaps she's near, even now, waiting to make sure it's cared for. Like Delilah waiting to see that Moses was rescued from the river."

"'Twas not Delilah," MacDonald grumbled. "D' ye not listen when I read?"

"I try," Lachlan said. "Shall we look for her?"

They all paused, Lachlan gripping the rope, Hugh's great hands on Niall's leg, Owen becoming still. Even the baby in his arms fell silent. MacDonald looked around the forest, as if a woman might appear. After a moment, he spoke slowly. "We've been through the wood, and have seen naught. If she'd been around, she'd have taken the chance to run while we fought the boar."

"We?" Niall heaved himself halfway to sitting. "*We?* Why do I not remember the rest of you fighting the boar with me?"

"And if she's here, she clearly does not wish to be found. We'll care for her child, which is *certainly* what she wished."

"But..." Owen looked from the baby in his arms to MacDonald.

MacDonald's eyebrows lowered, storm clouds over angry eyes.

Owen stopped.

"Can you stand?" Hugh heaved himself to his feet and reached down to help Niall up.

Niall winced as his weight landed on the injured leg. He lifted it immediately. "I'll be fine on my horse."

Hugh looped an arm around Niall's back, and led him to his pony, helping him up, while MacDonald issued orders about the baby and the boar. Soon, they were riding down the hill, the baby mewling in Owen's arms, and the boar dragging over dirt and pine needles behind the ponies straining to pull its bulk. The shaggy hounds bounded ahead, woofing in glee.

At Niall's side, with the others ahead, Hugh grinned. "Well now, a giant boar in the forest. Convenient."

"Not the word I used when I saw it," Niall muttered.

Hugh chuckled. "Well done, Niall. You've made the story look truer than we ever could have hoped for."

"I do my best," Niall muttered. His entire body hurt. "I but hope I'll walk again."

"Naught but a scratch. Ye'll be fine."

Niall thought of Shawn. He'd be prancing across a stage with a sackbut—a trombone—entertaining screaming women. Going home to silk sheets, luxuriating in the roiling waters of a *hot tub*. Eating his fill of exotic and delicious foods. Not feeling the sting of a raw cheek and gored leg.

The risen sun shone down through the leafy canopy, dappling the dirt path. The scent of pine filled the air, giving a burst of life and energy to Niall's lungs. He was among friends. He would feast on boar tonight. The story would go around the castle of how he'd fought the monster single-handedly, and the legend that had started with MacDougall's arrow and grown with Shawn's deeds would continue. Christina's secret was safe, and he had a few days with Allene and his precious boys.

Niall laughed suddenly, thrilling to the beauty around him, and Glenmirril sprawling below, as they reached the top of the hill, its stones shining silver in the morning sun, its banners flying. "Yes, I'll be fine," he said.

Bannockburn, Present

It would only take minutes to finish the letter, Shawn decided. He flattened it on the desk and leaned in, concluding Niall's account. *And so we brought the child home safe, Owen in a wee daze as he once again carried a child across Glenmirril's bridge.* Shawn smiled at the image. *Though I have some injuries and am in a great deal of pain.* "Serves you right," Shawn muttered. "Teach you not to take a stupid chance like that again!" But he breathed easier, knowing both Christina's son, and Niall, were safe.

Whether Lachlan's Margaret suspects and said so to him, or if by the grace of our good Savior, I know not, but Lachlan himself suggested Christina raise the child. She has her son, yet her name remains pure. She has said she shall marry Hugh.

Shawn's emotions swung back. "Don't do that, Christina!" he whispered. Much as he liked Hugh, Christina did not belong with him. But then, he admitted, he wouldn't think she belonged with anyone. Disturbed at the intensity of his own reaction, he forced himself to continue:

She has asked me to teach her the harp, and is quick to learn. You will be pleased to know that the music of Toto continues to sound in Allene's solar. The band. Not the dog.

Shawn smiled, though his heart remained stuck on the thought of her married to Hugh. They didn't belong together. Really, they didn't.

MacDougall continues to be a perfect prisoner, giving no cause for concern. He plays chess with Taran, discusses his reading with him, and gives us no trouble. But MacDougall is not one to accept defeat. The Laird is allowing him correspondence with his steward. The first exchanges seem innocent. It worries me, nonetheless, and I dislike having to leave again, knowing he is here, with those I love.

But then, neither would it reassure me to have him elsewhere. I struggle with the theological virtue of mercy, as opposed to the hard truth of living mercy. I should feel safer with MacDougall's head on a pike on our walls, where his brain can no longer scheme against us. It does no good to write it, when there is no way for you to respond. Yet I feel better having told you, much as we once talked.

I have but days before I leave for the Bruce's council at Scone.

In the absence of any way of knowing, we imagine you happy with Amy and your son, and playing your trombone on the great stages of the world. Give my love to them. May God be with you, my friend. Though I know you doubt, I myself look forward to the day we meet again in His kingdom.

In Christ's love, Niall

Shawn re-read the last words. The problem of Christina's son was solved. Thank God. And, he realized with surprise, he *meant* that. *Thank you, God.* But his gut told him the problem with MacDougall was only starting.

CHAPTER THIRTY-ONE

Glenmirril, May 1317

The sun touched Glenmirril's parapets as Niall rode across the drawbridge with the rest. Owen cradled the crying baby in one arm, gripping his reins with the other hand, and protesting. "Why am I carrying it? I know naught of bairns!"

"You carried one all the way from Ireland," Hugh said. "You know best."

He, MacDonald, and Niall had judged it best for the baby to be seen as little as possible in their company, to avoid any association that might lead back to Christina.

The guards in the gatehouse gaped—at the boar, at Niall's scraped-up face and bandaged, bloody leg, and most of all, at Owen. Owen himself looked stunned to find himself riding back from a hunt with a screaming infant instead of a deer. "I dinna ken," he said over and over, raising his voice above the howls of the baby, when they questioned him. "'Twas in a tree."

The guards looked at one another. "A *tree*?" one queried.

Another pressed forward, as if to verify it was really a baby, while the first jibed Owen about returning to Glenmirril a second time with a bairn in tow. "What will your new wife say?" he asked.

The bewilderment on Owen's face grew. "I dinna ken," he said again.

"Move along!" the Laird barked. "Have you naught better to do than rile the man? You!" He rounded on the guard poking fun at Owen. "Find a nursemaid. Can you not see this bairn needs feeding?"

The man looked affronted to be sent on such an errand, but had more sense than to argue. The other guard snapped to high military form, not wanting to be demoted to hunting nursemaids. In the courtyard, people turned from their duties, straining to see what was shrieking in the gatehouse.

"Lachlan, get this boar to the kitchens," MacDonald continued. "Send the physician to Niall's chambers."

Conal appeared at the top of the stairs from the great hall, across the courtyard, and raised his hand. He hurried down the stairs, to the gatehouse, giving a quick bow to MacDonald and a quicker glance at Owen with the screeching child, now thrashing in its bunting. "My Lord, MacDougall's steward has come."

Still on his pony, Niall turned to MacDonald, one eyebrow raised. "Surely you're not allowing him communication?" he whispered.

"I check every missive that comes and goes," MacDonald hissed back.

"And MacDougall knows that. Let Roger care for Creagsmalan as he sees fit."

"I'm allowing it thinking I may see what he's up to. And to build goodwill for the day he leaves."

"There will never be goodwill from MacDougall," Niall objected.

"The first letters are harmless," the Laird said. "Check the orchards. Feed the cattle. Watch the ale mistress, for she tastes the ale a wee bit more than necessary."

Niall's eyes narrowed. Something sat wrong. "Will it be delivered by our own men, not by one who will pass messages not written in the letter?"

"That's why Roger comes to me." MacDonald glanced around the courtyard, at the growing crowd. "This is naught to discuss with a gathering audience."

"Yes, my Lord." Niall gave a bow. The first guard emerged from the great hall with a short, round woman hastening after him, wiping her hands on her apron. MacDonald led the dazed Owen into the courtyard, where the castle folk edged closer, eager to see the spectacle. More appeared at the windows of the halls on the upper floors. Niall studied the casements on the third floor. Christina waited and watched there, beside Allene.

The nursemaid bustled to Owen's horse, clucking and reaching for the child. She gathered him into her arms, shushing him. "There, now," she soothed. "Let's get you fed!" She bobbed to MacDonald. "I'll take good care of the wee bairn, my Lord."

"Feed it and bring it to my chambers." MacDonald turned to Conal.

"He awaits you in the great hall, my Lord."

"Very good. Niall, go to your chambers."

"Immediately, my Lord. As soon as we've spoken to MacDougall's steward."

MacDonald lowered his eyebrows. Niall smiled placidly. The power had begun to shift, and they both knew it. He nudged his horse with his good leg, riding to the stairs of the great hall. There, Hugh helped him down, and he limped up the stairs after MacDonald's stiff back, fighting a grimace of pain. He followed MacDonald into the hall, where Roger stood near a wall, looking impatient and uncomfortable as two of MacDonald's men guarded the door with pikes and swords.

When MacDonald entered, Roger strode forward, giving no bow. Niall stayed by the door, not only because his leg screamed with pain, but to watch. Roger took no notice of him. With his torn clothes and scraped up face, Niall thought he might well look more like a servant than the next laird. Being overlooked suited his purposes.

"I was promised correspondence with my Laird," the steward began, failing to give MacDonald the courtesy of an address. "I've been waiting more than an hour."

MacDonald's eyebrows beetled over his eyes. Without a word, he stalked past the man, and seated himself on his throne-like chair at the head of the hall. He lifted a hand, summoning his own steward, waiting by the door to the kitchens. The man rushed forward and dropped to one knee, head bowed. "My Lord?"

"Bring me ale and meat. Is the boar being slaughtered?"

"They've begun, my Lord. 'Twill be ready for the evening meal."

"Very good. The head on a platter, and tell my minstrel to compose a song. Sir Niall fought it single-handedly. Be quick with the ale."

Roger stomped forward. MacDonald's men jumped, barring his way with their pikes. "MacDonald!" he shouted. "You made a promise."

One of the guards thumped his pike on the floor. "Show respect," he thundered.

MacDonald said nothing, merely steepling the tips of his fingers together, and watching the man steadily until his steward returned with a tankard of ale and a flagon, which he set on the table next to the chair. MacDonald waited while he poured, and drank slowly, all the while watching MacDougall's steward. Niall watched the tension rise in the man's shoulders.

Finally, the Laird set down his flagon and drew the back of his wrist across his lips. "Now." He addressed the man with something only slightly less threatening than thunder in his voice. "I made no promise to be treated like your servant in my own castle. Will you try again, or will my men escort you out?"

MacDougall's man stiffened even more. Niall guessed he fought between pride and duty. Duty won. He bowed his head, though his shoulders were still stiff. "My apologies, my Lord. It was only that...."

MacDonald rose from his chair, his face as angry as the loch on a stormy night. "It was only that you had the mistaken notion you could come into my castle and behave with disrespect. Was it perhaps that I showed mercy, letting your people go home in peace, even after you attacked my home and my people, after you killed a good man and left a boy fatherless?"

"No, my Lord..."

"Is it perhaps that I have allowed your laird to live, despite his unprovoked attack and his multiple attempts to kill my good-son?"

"No, my Lord. I was wrong."

"Would it perhaps help you show proper respect if I depart from the Bruce's ways and behave, instead, like those MacDougall has supported in the past? What would his friend Edward of Carnarvon do, if I attacked his castle and killed his people? Would I be in a comfortable cell with books to read, or would my head be rotting on a pike for all to see?"

Roger bowed his head, not answering.

"We both know," the Laird answered for him, "that had I attacked Creagsmalan, my head would be rotting on a pike. Gregor!"

One of the guards snapped to attention.

"Tell Conal to prepare the beheading block in the courtyard. MacDougall will look out from our parapets, since my mercy has been misconstrued as weakness."

MacDougall's man jolted. "No, my Lord!" He dropped abruptly to one knee, stretching out imploring hands. "My Lord, I was *wrong*. 'Twas not my Lord MacDougall's fault. Please, my Lord."

The Laird stood motionless, his hand clasped in those of the kneeling steward.

Tension crept into Niall's back. His leg ached. Worse, he suspected he'd been wrong, too—wrong to believe the balance of power had shifted. MacDonald was an actor of the highest caliber, one to rival Shawn's genius at playing roles. Even knowing him as he did, Niall wondered if he would carry through with beheading MacDougall. It would set Allene's mind to rest.

Gregor waited at the door, frozen, transfixed by the scene.

Slowly, MacDonald raised his head, meeting Niall's eyes. His face was hard. He turned to Gregor. "MacDougall will wait at the beheading block on his knees while I speak with his steward."

"Yes, my Lord." Gregor hurried past Niall, his tabard swishing.

"I only wanted..." The steward's head came up.

"Silence!"

Roger's head dropped quickly into a deep bow. He released MacDonald's hands, but stayed on his knees.

They waited, Niall, the stewards, the guard, and MacDonald. The sun rose higher, shooting a thick bolt of light through the window. Dust motes trembled on it, sliding down to the steward's heels.

Conal returned, bowing low. "My Lord."

"Is MacDougall on his knees before the beheading block?"

"Aye." Conal stepped back to wait at Niall's side.

The Laird returned to his seat, where, with a nod of his head, his steward poured him more ale. He drank slowly, regarding the man on his knees. When he finished, he spoke. "Rise."

Roger did so, trembling.

"Speak."

"My Lord." The words came out barely a whisper. "I came to speak with MacDougall as I was promised."

"You were *granted* communication regarding Creagsmalan. You were promised no meetings."

"My apologies, my Lord. I misspoke."

"I think not," MacDonald said. "I think you and MacDougall believe you can play me for a fool."

"No, my Lord!" The man's voice rose in agitation. "I misspoke. Forgive me."

"Ah, forgiveness, mercy." MacDonald downed another draft of ale. "Mercy is misunderstood by your people."

"No, my Lord. I crave your mercy. I shall be always grateful."

"Where is the letter you wish to give your laird?"

The man fumbled in his tunic, drawing out a sealed letter with shaking hands.

MacDonald gave a barely perceptible nod of his head. His steward crossed the room, reaching for the document. MacDougall's man hesitated.

"Something you wish us not to see?" MacDonald asked. He raised his voice. "Conal."

Conal stepped forward.

"No, please! Take it!" Panic rang in Roger's voice. He thrust the letter at MacDonald's steward. "Mercy, my Lord."

Something about MacDonald's brief report of MacDougall's letters had bothered Niall. Roger's behavior increased the uneasiness. He met MacDonald's eyes, as the steward placed the missive into his hand.

"Please, my Lord," Roger whispered, "spare his life."

"Conal, send MacDougall back to his cell." The Laird tapped the letter in his palm, regarding the man on his knees. "You," he finally said, "will wait in the chapel for MacDougall's reply. Guards, take him. Some time with our Lord is always a good thing."

The man scrambled to his feet, shaking off the guard's hands. They ushered him out of the great hall.

MacDonald waited until he was gone before downing the rest of his ale in a gulp, re-filling the tankard and bringing it himself to Niall. "You're shaking," he said.

"I am not." But even as the words came out of Niall's mouth, he realized how badly his leg hurt. It was indeed shaking. He accepted the ale, downing it in three gulps. It would take the edge off the burn running up the wound.

"You were told to go to your chambers," the Laird said. "Perhaps since you object to doing as you're told, you ought go to the chapel with MacDougall's man and spend time on your knees, yourself."

Niall lowered his head. He knew what Shawn's insolent response would have been. *I spend plenty of time on my knees, but thanks for offering.* He'd only aroused the Laird's genuine anger once in his life. He'd no wish do it a second time. He'd been wrong to disobey, particularly in front of everyone, and arrogant in his manner of doing so. "My apologies, my Lord," he said.

"Wait here."

Niall swallowed. "Yes, my Lord." He guessed he'd be waiting a long time on the trembling leg, and there would be no second tankard of ale.

MacDonald frowned at the letter in his hand, and marched out of the great hall, leaving Niall with a guard. Niall heaved a sigh. He'd been foolish to think the Laird's hours in the Bat Cave meant he was losing his command of the castle. He steadied himself on his good leg and figured he might as well use the time to pray. He could certainly use some wisdom, in general, and about MacDougall in particular. He clasped his hands behind his back, thought about the miracle on the battlefield, and began a *Pater.*

Inverness, Present

Simon woke with energy. He had learned something, last night, of Angus's life and home. Today, he had a plan for finding Eamonn. He splashed water over his chest and under his arms, in the bathing chamber. He left through the back door, climbing garden walls, and headed into town. There, he paid a barber to shave him, and got directions to local churches. Eamonn wanted to play games, did he? He would be easy to find. A monk would be in a church, or some place associated with religion—to which churches could lead him.

"Brother Eamonn?" At the first one, the woman screwed up her face. "How would I know any Brother Eamonn?"

"An old man," Simon explained. Still, she had no idea.

At the next, he elaborated. "Frail, tall, thin. From Monadhliath."

"Why don't you ask them?" she asked quizzically. "Sure an' they can tell you where one of their monks is."

"I'm unable to climb the hills," Simon explained with a smooth smile.

"Hm." She peered into space, before announcing, "Yes, I've heard they make themselves difficult to reach." She shrugged, indicating she couldn't help him.

At another church, the receptionist cocked her head at him as if he were simple, and said, "Sir, we're not *Catholic*. Why would we know where a *monk* is?"

His eyes narrowed at her insolence. The cross was right there, on the wall behind her. What did she *propose* a church was, if not Catholic? A large man walked in, arms folded across his chest. "Can I help you?"

Simon smiled. "Perhaps later." In a dark alley, he promised himself. One or both of them would pay. He noted the place, and moved on. His irritation grew as the afternoon wore away, dusk falling early and bringing with it a chill.

It was only at the sixth church that he found a woman capable of something other than staring blankly. "Why do you want to find him?" she asked.

Simon let his smile slip into place. "I met him some time ago. He was so helpful to me. I would fain repay his kindness. He is ill, and I hope to look in on him. Bring him...." He wasn't sure what one brought an ill monk. He had a vague memory of his mother bringing food to women in the village. "Food," he said. "And a gift."

"How kind!" She tilted her head, looking at him admiringly.

"So where would an elderly monk go?" Simon pressed, more interested in information than adulation.

"Well," she said, "I can think of a few places. Give me a day or two to ask around, and I'll get back to you. Have you a number I can call?"

"I'll come back tomorrow."

She waved a hand at a chair. "Oh, sit down! I've time now." She proved eager to help, dialing the hospital, dialing the nursing home to which they'd sent him, explaining she was trying to help a man who'd met him long ago. Simon studied a *magazine*, listening to her chatter on the phone. After the fifth call, she beamed. "Well, now it seems I've found something. I'll know tomorrow. Can I call you?"

Simon smiled. "I'll come back." He turned to go, then abruptly turned back. "Remind him, please, he has something he promised to me."

Bannockburn, Present

"I have to leave soon." Shawn lifted his head from the large pad of score paper. "Have you decided?"

Under the long window where they worked, Amy sat back, from three hours of arranging. She shook her head. "I've been doing the arrangements, practicing, teaching." She stared out the window. "I hate the thought of leaving my students."

Shawn suspected it wasn't only her students she hated leaving. He laid down his pencil. "What about James?"

She stared out the window, not meeting his eyes. "It's been quiet here. The police are watching our houses." He'd moved her and James, too, to a new home, two doors from his own. "It was probably a random attack like they said."

Shawn stared at the manuscript paper. He hadn't told her how personal the man seemed, calling him by name and asking about the Bruce. She would point out that all of Scotland knew his name, and there *were* approximately ten million hits to multiple YouTube videos of him announcing he'd been fighting with the Bruce. He sighed. She was right. And it *had* been quiet.

"Are you ever going to tell me what they say?" She was staring at him.

"What who says?" Shawn grabbed his pencil, jotting in vamping on the piano staff. "You want some thirteen chords here?" Maybe if he didn't make eye contact....

"You know what I mean. Your body language gives you away, Shawn. Every time. Why the big secret?"

With a sigh, he laid down the pencil, as rapier-sharp as the weapons in Glenmirril's armory. He stared out the window, with the sheer curtains pulled back to the frame. Children played outside. A dog barked.

Amy stood up, gathering her pencils. "I have rehearsal in an hour."

"Amy, wait!" He jumped to his feet, grabbing her arm. "It's not a secret. I just don't know...."

She waited, the pencils poised above her purse.

"I don't know how to talk about it. There's too much to say, and nothing that *needs* saying. You know I didn't talk about...feelings. What is there to say?"

"I got the impression you were really good at talking to Dana."

"Dana?"

"Yeah, I got another e-mail from her explaining how you two could *really talk.*"

"Yeah, we could."

"Okay, so talk to me. Or don't. I'm not trying to pry, but you know, we can't spin gold out of hay. What do we really have if we can't share our deepest thoughts and pain with each other?"

"You think it hurts?"

The pencils fell in a soft wooden shuffle on the table. "Of *course* it hurts. I only spent a week with Niall, and it hurts to know what kind of life he's stuck in. You spent two years with them. They meant something to you. They meant *everything* to you. You saw brutal warfare. I can't even imagine. *Talk* to me about it."

He said nothing.

"If you can talk to Dana," Amy said softly, "then that's who you should be with." She indicated his phone lying on the keyboard. "Call her." She gathered her purse.

He took a step forward. "Amy, that's not fair. What is this? A threat? You're leaving me if I don't tell you?"

Amy sighed. "Think whole score, Shawn, not single measure."

"But you're walking out because I'm not telling you."

"I'm walking out because we're done. If there are walls between us, we don't really have much. Why is this threats in your mind?" Her hair swung as she turned.

"I quit reading them," he said quickly, wanting her—needing her—to stop.

She paused at the front door, her hand on the knob. "Do you understand, Shawn, this isn't about forcing you to talk? Something very traumatic happened to you."

"Traumatic?" His brow furrowed. "No it was just...life."

"Warfare," Amy insisted. "Losing people you loved, seeing men die, seeing women widowed and children orphaned. You *killed* men, Shawn, in a time and place where you had to, and now you live in a world where nobody can possibly understand that."

"Can you?"

"I've had a year to reconcile the Niall I knew, someone kind and good, with someone who killed men. Yes, apart from Angus who you can't stand, I'm about your best hope of anyone ever *getting* that it was a different time and our standards don't apply."

He said nothing.

She turned the knob. "Shawn, you need someone, and if that's Dana, then that's what you need to do."

He shook his head. "You don't understand about Dana."

"So she told me." Amy spoke dryly. Cool air crept in, where she'd opened the door a crack.

Shawn snorted. "That's *not* what I meant. I could talk to her about *some* things. *Some* thoughts."

"I imagine." Amy's voice scraped out even more dryly than before.

"Would you stop that," Shawn snapped. "I mean like, did you ever have someone you could talk music with forever, but anything else, and you realize you have no connection?" He watched her, knowing she was fighting the urge to make another sarcastic crack. He figured he deserved it, and was profoundly glad she didn't make it.

Her shoulders relaxed.

Shawn took a step forward. "I can't talk to her about important things. *Real* things. She just wants to party and have fun."

"Sounds familiar." Amy's back was still to him.

"Even if she believed me about this, she wouldn't have anything profound to say. She'd tell me to have a beer, find a girl, and move on."

Amy stared out the door. "You know I have something better to offer. But I can't if you don't give me the chance."

"Please." He took another step forward and brushed her hair off her shoulder. "Shut the door."

She didn't move. But she didn't leave. "Why did you stop reading them?"

He reached around her, and pressed the door, till it clicked softly. She didn't stop him. "I didn't get an e-mail off to Ben because I was reading them. I didn't check out those musicians as carefully as I should have. I fudged the truth, pretending I had. Because I was reading them instead of doing what I need to do."

She turned, finally, studying him, her eyes searching his. "These were your closest friends. Life and death. Living together, your lives dependent on each other. Saving Niall from hanging. And you quit reading because you're too busy?"

Shawn swallowed and stared at the floor, arms akimbo, tense.

"What's happening to them?" When he didn't answer immediately, her hands flew to his chest. "Shawn, are they all right?"

He shrugged, his eyes glued to a smudge on the linoleum. "MacDougall—the one whose son I killed—he's locked in their tower, and seems to be a model prisoner, but Niall doesn't trust him."

"Can he get out? Do they have guards on him?"

"Yeah, they have guards, he's locked in. They're letting him send letters to his steward at Creagsmalan, and Niall says there's nothing amiss...." He stopped at his use of the archaic word. "Nothing *wrong* with the letters." His head shot up, his gaze met Amy's forcefully, and he exploded. "But I wish MacDonald would quit being so damned merciful and be *careful*! MacDougall is bad news. He's hateful and vindictive. He never forgets. He thrives on revenge."

"Then...." Amy stopped.

Shawn gave a harsh laugh. "Exactly. Then? Then *what*?" His voice rose. "See why I quit? It's like watching a train heading for a washed-out bridge, and there's nothing I can do. *Nothing!*"

"I'm sorry." Her hands inched up, around his neck, hugging him.

"Allene keeps asking for my prayers." His arms circled her. "I told her once—when I'd done my part with Christina, and we were riding to meet Niall, but it all depended on Bessie—I said I felt so helpless, there was nothing I could do. She told me I could pray."

"Did you?"

"A little. But now, it's all seven hundred years ago. Even praying can't help them. It's already happened, whatever *it* is." He held her close, feeling comfort in her touch. But his mind stayed in the fourteenth century. "It's more than that," he whispered. "I feel like I've been split in two. My mind is always half here and half there. I have a foot in each world, and I can't shake it off and get all the way into this one."

"Take it day by day." She touched his arm. "Set the parchments aside just for the tour."

"Are you coming with me?" He raised his eyes, burning with a need she'd never seen in them.

"I don't know," she whispered. "It's been perfectly quiet here."

It *had* been quiet.

She glanced at her watch. "Shawn, I have to go."

He nodded, numbly, wanting her to come home with him. But he'd promised Christina he was going to do better. He couldn't push this on her.

She laid wrapped her arms around his neck. "I'll see you tomorrow."

Inverness, Present

When Clive headed out on a morning call, Angus let himself into his office, locking the door behind him. He should have done it days ago, he chided himself. At the same time, he wasn't sure he should call even now. He didn't know who the man pulled off the field was. Tension creased his forehead. He wanted nothing to do with Shawn. But he was better than petty jealousy. He pulled up Shawn's file and, glancing from it to his phone, punched in the number. He swiveled his chair, gazing up at the thriving fern as the phone rang the first time. He cleared his throat as it rang the second time, trying to think how to start. He should have thought this part through. But then, he'd not call at all, if he kept thinking. Every fiber of his being rebelled at talking to this eejit. What had Amy ever seen in him? What did she see in him now? The phone rang a third time. *Voice mail,* Angus prayed. *Go to voice mail.*

"Shawn here!" The arrogant voice erupted like a bull through the phone line, snorting foul breath in his face.

Angus drew back; his lips puckered as surely as if said bull had been eating rotted lemons.

"Hello!" Shawn snapped. "Who is this?"

"Angus." Angus named himself tersely. He wanted nothing to do with this undeserving fool who had breezed back into the twenty-first century and ridden off into the sunrise with Amy.

Silence fell for just a moment over the line, before Shawn's voice came out, as icy as his home state. "What do you want?" It was a demand, accusation, curse, and slap in the face, rolled into four small words.

A dozen harsh retorts whipped through Angus's mind. He let his breath out slowly. This was for Amy and James. "I found something," he said.

There was a heartbeat of silence, before Shawn replied, his voice a shade less wintry than before. "What?"

"I sent a link," Angus replied. "Are you near a computer?" He swiveled to his own, pulling up the video.

"Hold on," Shawn said.

In the silence that followed, punctuated by the faint click of computer keys, far away in Bannockburn, Angus stared at the fern, drawing in long, slow breaths. This was for Amy. This was for James. He slid his desk drawer open, removing their picture. He studied her high cheekbones, cobalt eyes, and long, thick hair. After a moment, he pinned it back to his cork board.

"Okay, I got it," Shawn said. "What is this?"

Glenmirril, 1317

Conal appeared at Niall's side an hour later. "The Laird wishes to see you."

Niall limped after him to the tower, up the stairs to the laird's rooms.

"Sit," MacDonald commanded, before the door closed.

"Thank you, my Lord." Niall tried to lower himself with dignity, but collapsed gracelessly into the chair at the table. He leg throbbed. Noon sun poured through MacDonald's windows. Green hills showed in the eastern casement. He resisted the urge to lean back on the chair.

"Eat. Drink." MacDonald indicated bread and cheese on the table.

Niall waited for the Laird to say grace, before reaching for it. MacDonald pulled up a chair, joining him. "Read the letters." He smoothed them out on the table.

Niall wiped the crumbs off his hands and leaned in, studying MacDougall's lengthy letter to Roger. The steward in turn informed MacDougall of feral pigs in the forest, hunts, orchards, a woman caught in adultery, that he had not found a Franciscan monk for Creagsmalan. "Routine castle business," Niall said.

MacDonald nodded. "They appear innocent."

"Yet your gut says summat is amiss." Niall lifted the wine to his lips for a long draft, hoping it would quench the fire in his leg soon.

"Aye." MacDonald scowled into his ale before downing half the tankard. He slammed it down on the table. "A wild boar does not behave like a house cat. He cannot possibly be so accepting of his fate."

"No," Niall agreed. "He'll forever hold Duncan's death against us."

"He will exact his revenge." MacDonald rose, pacing to the window to stare out over the loch.

"At least, he will try." Niall finished his wine and poured more.

"Now," said the Laird, "perhaps you're ready to see the physician."

"Perhaps." Niall blinked. Black closed in on the sides of his vision.

"I think," said the Laird, "the physician will come to you. Lie down."

Bannockburn, Present

"Start at 30:25." Angus's voice came over the line as Shawn settled himself on his forest green bedspread, the laptop propped on his knees.

From downstairs came a knock on the door. Amy. His mother would let her in. Shawn shut his door, and went back to his laptop. "Just a sec," he told Angus.

"Blow the screen up as large as you can and watch the upper right."

Shawn was surprised to find his hand shake as he slid the bar across the bottom of the video. As he settled at 30:25, warriors appeared in mosses, russets and browns, momentarily frozen in battle tableau. He hit play.

"Give it ten seconds," Angus said.

Shawn watched, unblinking, the phone stuck to his ear as warriors burst into action, stalking in *schiltrons* toward charging cavalry. Prickles rose on Shawn's neck. He felt his chest constricting, remembering Adam falling to his knees that day; remembering the carnage there, and at Skaithmuir, the moans of the dying; fleeing on his galloping pony with Hugh at his side; on his hands and knees, vomiting. His stomach turned, as if the moment had never ended.

"Watch the upper right," came Angus's voice.

Shawn drew a deep breath, pulling himself from the flashback. In the corner, an English knight bent over his destrier's neck, his helmet half obscured by its flying mane. His right arm rose behind his back, sword high. Shawn's stomach knotted. It could be one of the men of Glenmirril, one of Niall's friends, he was about to fell. But before the blow came, a Highlander on a garron burst from off camera, slamming into him. The knight tumbled to the ground, an unheard clatter amidst the shouts of actors at the forefront of the scene. His helmet rolled off, revealing thick black hair, a curling, black beard. Shawn drew in a sharp breath. It could—maybe—be the man who had attacked Carol. Downstairs, Amy laughed. James answered with a sharp squeal of glee.

"You see him?" came Angus's voice over the line.

"Lots of men had black beards," Shawn said. He knew what Angus was suggesting. He didn't want to believe it.

"*Could* it be the man who attacked Carol?" Angus asked.

"Hold on." Shawn hit *pause,* squinting at the tiny figure. He replayed it three times. A foot soldier came from off camera, swinging his sword down. As the felled knight rolled, the weapon glanced off the side of his head. The English knight slumped, as if dead.

"I can't tell," Shawn finally said. "It's impossible to see his face."

"Aye, 'tis," Angus agreed. "But *could* it be the perp?"

"Well, yeah, it's *possible.*" Shawn watched as the victor in the skirmish spun, fighting off his own attacker. "But it's a stab in the dark." His attention was distracted by fighting at the forefront, and the Bruce shouting to the English, "Your king has fled!"

"Watch what happens now," Angus advised.

Amy's voice floated up the stairs. "Where's Shawn?"

Shawn looked to the corner of the video. A man in a russet jerkin shouted, pointed at the felled knight, and lifted him under the arms, pulling him from the field. Blood streamed from his temple. The rescuer raised his head, shouting, his words drowned by the sound of re-enactors near the cameraman. Two more actors raced up. Together, they pulled the injured man off the field.

"Is there more?" Shawn stared at the corner of the screen where the knight had disappeared. Downstairs, Carol's voice sounded, soft words unintelligible.

"That's all," Angus said.

Shawn hit pause. "You think the guy who attacked my mom crossed at the battle?"

"Not only that," said Angus, "I think he's the man who came to Monadhliath with me and Amy. Something wasn't right about him."

"How do we find out for sure?" Shawn asked.

"His coat of arms," Angus said. "Did you see the front of his tabard?"

"A rearing animal." Shawn squinted, trying to make it out. "Of some sort."

"I've called a few friends," Angus said. "My guess is he was injured severely enough to warrant hospital. I'll let you know what I find."

"Yeah. Do that." Shawn nodded, feeling numb. If a medieval madman had crossed into their time with some vendetta against him, modern police were no help.

Downstairs, Amy laughed again. Shawn's stomach lurched. It was one of the first things he'd noticed about her—her laugh, as she walked down the hall backstage with another man, before he even knew her name. Fear lurched up his throat, to think of that madman after her.

"I don't like the way he found Amy at Melrose," Angus was saying. "Or the way he looked at James on our hike. He lied to her about the translation. And now Carol. I think he was looking for Amy at Melrose."

"But why?" Shawn asked. "If he crossed over at the re-enactment, how could he know who I am, much less who Amy is? What could he want with either of us?" He frowned. There was Amy's wall, but why? Even if this guy *was* from Niall's time—why?

"I don't know," Angus said. "But keep Amy and James away from him."

"Yeah." Footsteps sounded on the stairs. Shawn glanced at the door.

"Shawn?" his mother called.

"Look." Shawn turned his back to the door, lowering his voice. "Don't mention this to her, okay? I don't want to scare her. I'll make sure he can't get at them. I'll take care of it." A knock sounded on the door. "Thanks for calling." He hung up as he jumped off the bed and flung the door open to Carol, holding James.

"Where's Amy?" he demanded, his heart pounding.

"She's gone to rehearsal. Shawn, what's wrong?"

Inverness, Present

"I'm sorry," the woman said, when Simon returned to the church. "but he's ill. He'll ring in a few days. Do you not have a phone where he could reach you direct?" She blinked at him.

"My *phone*...." he pronounced the word carefully, "has broken. I'm close by. It's no trouble to drop in. He'll be well soon, do they think?"

"Oh, aye," she agreed. "They seemed sure of it."

"I'd like to *meet* him," Simon stressed. "He has something he promised me."

"I told him," she replied. "He said he's misplaced it."

Simon's lips tightened. "Has he now? How very convenient."

The woman cocked her head, frowning. "Sure an' he's a sick, old man. These things happen."

"Can you not tell me where he lives?" Simon asked. "Surely it would be easier for *him*. I could help him look for the misplaced item."

"I'll ask. It does seem 'twould be easier." She shrugged. "Old people get set in their ideas, do they not?"

He smiled tightly, and took his leave.

Glasgow, Present

Doubt flickered as Shawn made his way down the hall, following the swell of music. *Till Eulenspiegel.* One of his favorites. *Because you relate to him,* Amy had teased him. He had no proof that Carol's attacker was a medieval madman. But as he'd wrestled through the morning with the decision, the two incidents—the attack and the hole in Amy's wall—convinced him this was the right one. If only he could convince her without scaring her and his mother.

Shawn slid into the wings, watching the Royal Scottish Orchestra rehearse, Amy far across the stage, in the middle of the first violins, her face rapt in concentration, her eyes locked on the page before her. He smiled, remembering the years of playing with her in their own orchestra.

The trombones, with their backs to him, lifted their instruments as one, and with the trumpets, came crashing in on the final measures. The conductor leaned in, his eyebrows knit in fierce concentration, his baton slicing the air, stabbing, one hand beckoning for more from the violins. Their sound swelled. Amy leaned into her stand, drawing her bow across her strings. Tympani rolled, like chargers across a battlefield, powerful and dangerous, with a final *thump*!

And it all stopped.

Shawn smiled. It was good to be back. He never would have experienced this again, in Niall's time. A peace came over him that he'd only ever felt in Christina's presence, or in the midst of performing, himself, when he lost himself in the music, became one with the sound flowing from his instrument.

Amy lowered her violin and raised her head. Her eyes met his. She smiled, a small, tentative smile. Shawn's own smile grew. He had all his arguments in place. She would agree—he was sure. She *had* to!

Around the orchestra, instruments lowered, musicians slapped black folders closed, rose. Some chatted in groups of two or three, some left the stage, calling back over their shoulders, or laughing as they went. Several greeted Shawn with nods. One man held out his hand, shaking, and saying, "Welcome home!"

Shawn smiled, thanking him, and his eyes cut back to Amy. She spoke to her stand partner, then turned to meet his eyes, and came toward him, skirting the front of the stage. In the wings, Shawn took her hand, and gave her a swift kiss on the cheek. She'd hated it when he'd made a production of it. "Lunch?" he asked. He'd pressed his mother to stay with Ina while he was gone.

Twenty minutes saw them seated at a pub, their orders placed. He cleared his throat, the multiple notes of persuasion running one last rehearsal through his head before he launched the performance. "I leave in three days. You're done with your concert tomorrow, no more rehearsals, no more subbing scheduled?" At her nod, he reached across the small table, clasping her hands. "I *have* to go back. It's my job, my work. But it would mean everything to me if...."

"If I'd go back with you." All hint of smiles fled. "For James's sake, of course, not yours." She pulled her hands from his, taking a napkin and twisting it. Her hands became still. Her eyes settled on the Bruce's ring, glinting on her finger.

He saw, as if he watched himself across the years, cajoling, pleading, pushing her—for her sake, for the orchestra's sake, for Dana's sake. *Always* for someone else, never admitting that every single thing he'd ever pushed for, had been what he himself wanted, with no regard for anyone—except as it helped him cajole her into giving him his way. He hesitated, a battle raging. He didn't *know* she was in danger. But Angus believed she was. He drew breath. "I bullied you." He touched her fingers. "I manipulated. I used other people to pressure you. I'm sorry."

She lifted her gaze from the ring. "I don't *want* to leave Scotland."

Shawn felt the breath still in his lungs. Angus hovered, a palpable presence between them. Yes, he acknowledged to himself, he wanted her away from Angus. His lips tightened; he stared at their hands, asking himself, how much did he *really* fear for James's safety? He'd left his mother and son almost alone, after all. But he was only twenty minutes away—not across an ocean.

He *did* fear for them, but he feared for himself, too—feared losing her to Angus if he had to keep leaving her here, close to him. He closed his eyes, reminding himself he'd come back to do it right, to be the man she'd believed in. He could tell her what Angus had told him. He didn't want to scare her. And they didn't *know* who the man really was.

"I can hire...." His words came out scratchy, as weak as a flute with worn pads. He lifted his eyes, and lifted his voice. "I'll hire a guard, someone to be there with you. If you want to stay." He stared at his hands, knowing there was still another step he could take for her safety. He didn't want to. But she would be only a job to a hired guard. He drew breath, not looking at her, and said, "If you stay, I want you to consider...." He stopped, hating the words, hating the thought.

"Consider what?" she prompted.

"Moving near Angus. Even moving in with him. I want you and James safe."

Inverness, Present

As Angus finished a meeting with the chief, the call to Shawn burned on his mind. It hadn't been as bad as he'd feared. He and Shawn were on the same side. They both wanted to protect Amy and James. He resisted a snort. Who was he kidding. Amy was still with Shawn. He still couldn't stand the eejit.

A hand fell on his shoulder. He turned to see Pete. "Checked your equipment?" Pete asked.

"Done."

"The forms? Mick's after me."

Angus shook his head in irritation. "Haven't we been checking our equipment for years without filing a report telling him we did so?"

Pete grinned. "I'm with you, Angus. But the lad's breathing down my neck. Ten minutes to fill out his silly forms and get him off all our backs."

"Ten minutes I could be doing something useful," Angus grumbled. "I'll get it done." He hurried to his office to open his e-mail, warning himself not to expect much so soon. He wasn't disappointed.

His cousin, Professor Jamieson, was the only answer. *Tabard and arms,* he wrote. *I used university equipment to zoom in on them. Take a look at the tail. What happened with that translation I sent you? Is it coincidence that within hours her boyfriend showed up—in a place Columba slept—claiming to have been in medieval Scotland? What's up, Cuz? PJ*

Angus studied Paul's words, deciding how to answer. He had believed the evidence Amy presented, yet he found it hard to admit to anyone that he had, *and did,* believe that two men had hurtled across centuries—and now believed a third man had done so. Struggling to ease the frown creasing his forehead, he opened the picture of the rearing beast. He squinted at the tail. Blown up, it became blurry. He leaned closer. It appeared to be forked, but it was hard to tell.

He contemplated a moment before picking up his phone and scanning his contacts. His eyes settled on Brian. He hadn't answered. With his enthusiasm for history, Angus would have expected his to be the first and longest reply, including not only whose arms were on the tabard, but a twenty page history of the family in question. It was unlike him to resist such a tantalizing historical puzzle.

Angus hit *call,* waiting through several rings until he was taken to voice mail. He cleared his throat. "Brian, how's things? Haven't heard from you in awhile. Did you get my e-mail? Listen, another question, about a coat of arms with a rearing...animal of some sort. I'll send you a picture. It seems to have a forked tail. I'm hoping you can tell me whose it is. Let's meet up for a pint."

He ended the call, and returned to the e-mail. It was a quick matter to forward Paul's picture to Brian, his mate Charlie at Glenmirril, and several others. He clicked back to the picture of the tabard and zoomed in on the rearing animal. It filled his computer monitor.

"Mail!" Sticking her head in the door, Claire tossed a pile of envelopes on Angus's desk. Her smile disappeared. "What is it, Inspector? You look as if you've just lost your last can of Who hash!"

Angus looked at her in surprise.

She laughed. "I've been reading to my nephew. Perhaps you're not fond of Who hash and don't mind losing your last can?"

Angus smiled. "I can't say I've ever tried it, though Hamish did often ask me what it tastes like."

"I tell my niece it tastes like the best haggis in the world." She glanced at his computer. "You're studying tabards now?"

Angus hesitated only a second. It could hurt nothing. And maybe she'd have an idea. "I need to know whose coat of arms that is."

Claire tilted her head. "Why?"

Again, he hesitated. But she was easy to talk to. "The man who was asking after Amy, the one who went to Monadhliath with us. I think he was at the re-enactment."

"You think he wore that?" she asked.

Angus nodded.

"Why does it matter whose arms he wore?" she asked.

Angus frowned, seeking an explanation more believable than *I think he's a medieval madman.* And, as Shawn had asked—even if he *was* a medieval madman, why would he be interested in Amy? Or was it Shawn he was after? It was Shawn's home he'd attacked. Angus stared at the image, and gave the only answer he could summon. "I've reason to think he wore his own family's arms that day."

"Do you not know his surname?" she asked. "I mean, the man who went to Monadhliath with you. Look up that family's arms and see if it might be a match."

Angus shook his head. "If he told me his surname, I don't remember."

"How did you meet him?" Claire asked. "Maybe...."

The shrill of a bell cut off her words. Feet pounded in the hall. "Angus!" Clive, breathless, skidded to a stop in the doorway. "Hiker with a broken leg. Let's go." Angus jabbed a button on his computer, shutting it down. Simon would have to wait.

Bannockburn, Present

I lie awake late into the night, staring at the ceiling. From the crib beside my bed comes the smooth, even rise and fall of James's breathing. Shawn is smart. He reads people like he reads notes on a page. He manipulates people as easily as he lays notes on a page, too, placing each trill and emotion exactly where he wants it. He knows that backing off, playing the self-effacing repentant, the self-sacrificing hero is exactly how to get what he wants right now.

But the truth is, I'm worried about James, too. I haven't forgotten the damaged wall in the professor's home. I don't like leaving him and Carol alone for rehearsals. I already promised myself I would accept no jobs while Shawn is gone. But who am I fooling? Do I really think I'm going to stop an attacker? Shawn is equipped to fight. What am I going to do? Subdue him with a Telemann Sonata? It's what I'm really good at. And it's absolutely useless at protecting my own son.

And Angus—he can't quit work to be with me all the time. Besides, it's not fair to him to ask that, when I can't give him my whole heart.

I sigh, staring at the black tree swaying outside my window. I know the police said it was random. I know 'strong, swarthy, medium height' is a vague description, and no proof it was Simon. What did Simon really do? Pound on my window, wanting a ride? I'm spinning entire oratorios from fragments of melody, the way Dvorak spun symphonies from folk songs. And yet...

...those symphonies were right, in every way.

Outside, a dog barks. The moon floats, a silver beacon on the dark ship of clouds that carries it across the black sky. James sighs, then gives one of his short chuckles. I smile, wondering what dreams sail through his sleep. I think of Angus holding him, looking down and smiling, too, at James laughing in his sleep.

Angus knows about the attack. I don't even doubt that. A police report was filed. It was all over the internet. He may have walked away from me, but he cares about James. If he were worried—if he thought it was Simon—he'd have called. He didn't.

I sigh, as heavily as James. It's been months. Angus is seeing someone else, while I remain torn, and missing him. It's October. Thanksgiving and Christmas are coming. I can go for awhile—no commitment. It's just taking James to meet my parents; supporting Shawn as he rebuilds his life. It's just temporary.

And the attack has left me nervous. My mind will be more at peace, in the States, regardless of Shawn's intentions. I make my decision, and as James lets out another soft chuckle, I slip into my own dreams—restless, disturbed dreams of Simon; of calling Angus, telling him I don't want to leave. The phone cord twists around his neck, his legs, his arms, pulling him into a deep, dark sea. I let go of the phone, let go of Angus, trying to stop hurting him. I have to give him peace.

FOURTH MOVEMENT

CHAPTER THIRTY-TWO

Inverness, Present

Simon tamped his impatience as he arrived yet again at the church. Each time he'd come, there had been some reason why Eamonn couldn't meet him yet. His irritation mounted when he saw the reception area empty, papers scattered on the desk, and one of those black boxes blaring.

It showed a man talking earnestly. "The rescuers were out all night, a really rough time up there, but they got the boys down." The picture changed to show men moving slowly down the mountain, bearing a litter, and then switched again. Simon stared. It was Angus, wearing heavy leggings and jacket, with the straps he'd been working on in his yard across his chest.

"Team members credit Angus MacLean with getting the young men out at some grave risk to himself."

"Oh, you're here!" The woman appeared from a hall and snapped off the box. "Your timing couldn't be better. Brother Eamonn is just after calling."

Simon rose, trying not to appear too eager. "He has what he promised me?"

She sifted through the papers on her desk, chose one, and read. "He says he'll bring you the key to...to get you home?" She stared at him, puzzled.

"When?" Simon did not answer her unspoken question.

"A few days." Her voice took on a more professional tone, though she looked disappointed not to have an answer to the mystery. "He's still on the mend."

"Aye, I'm sure." Simon gave a curt nod, fuming at the old man's games. He turned to leave.

"Oh, Sir!" the woman called.

Simon looked over his shoulder.

"He says it's at Glenmirril."

"*What* is at Glenmirril?" Simon demanded.

"The key," she answered. "He said the key is at Glenmirril, and he'll bring it to you when he's well, but sure you're welcome to get it yourself."

"*Where* in Glenmirril?"

The woman looked momentarily confused, but then said, "He mentioned the chapel, though I'm not sure what he meant. He talked quite a bit, you see." She tapped her head. "I'm not sure he knows what he's about."

"Of course," Simon said tersely. He turned to leave.

"And Sir?"

Simon stopped, heaving a sigh.

The woman leaned over her desk, her brows knit. "He says Christmas is but weeks now. He says you know what he means. Do you know what he means?"

Simon turned and left.

Midwest America, Present

Lights flashed in Shawn's eyes as he climbed from his Jaguar. He blinked, shook the spots from his vision, and grinned at the reporters. "Just like old times," he said. He rounded the car, pushing through the crowd, to open the door for Amy.

"Welcome back!" A woman flashed her camera. "Still wearing Ren-faire?"

Shawn glanced at his trews and *leine.* "They're comfortable."

"Where were you for a year?" A man thrust a microphone forward.

"Visiting the Sultan." Shawn opened the back door, lifting James from his car seat. He rose, his son on his shoulder, and added, "He swore me to secrecy. I can't say more." He handed James to Amy, and hefted out his trombone.

"Seriously, Mr. Kleiner! Where were you?"

"Seriously, I like my body parts where they are." He edged through the group, his case hoisted before him, his free arm around Amy. Cameras flashed. "I have to get in and warm up. Thanks."

"Your son is beautiful," a woman called.

Amy looked up, smiling at the words. A light flashed in her eyes.

The stage door opened. Shawn ushered her in, and slid through behind her.

"You made it through the gauntlet," Aaron said. "Welcome back." He gave Amy a hug and welcome, too.

She kissed Shawn on the cheek. "I'm going to go say hi, and head home." She disappeared down the hall.

Aaron slid his arm around a gangly boy who shared his olive complexion and black hair. "This is Jon. He's excited to meet you. He just started trombone."

Shawn smiled, offering his hand. "Great choice. How do you like the Midwest?"

The boy stared, then thrust out his hand, shaking hard. "I got to go canoeing! I never did that in L.A."

"Canoeing's great. I could take you and your dad out on a sailboat, too, if you want."

The boy's eyes shone. "Really? Could you show me how to play trombone like you do?"

"Lots of air," Shawn said. "Blow hard. You want some lessons?"

Jon nodded vigorously.

"You'd do that for him?" Aaron asked.

"Sure." He owed Aaron at least that much. Before he could say more, Rob burst around a corner, at the head of a group shouting his name. They surrounded him, a sea sweeping him to the green room, greeting, chatting. Amy wasn't there. He raised his hand high, hailing Zach. Zach's trumpet swung from his right hand,

and Sophie rode on his left hip, thrilled at the excitement around her. Kristin held Emma by the hand, talking with Celine. Celine saw Shawn, flushed, and turned away.

The glory of his return dimmed.

Across the room, Caroline looked him up and down, curled her lip, and turned her back. The glory withered.

Feeling a fraud, Shawn heaved the fawn-colored case to a table and soon long, golden tones flowed from his instrument. He played through a few scales, scanning the musicians as he did so. No women flirted with him. Caroline scowled at him as she flashed up and down her own scales, and through a passage from *The Firebird.* Dana looked in the door, gave him a small, sad smile, and left. Celine never looked at him at all. Nobody asked if he had a party planned after the concert. Not that he wanted one, he reminded himself. He'd come back to make things right with Amy.

He laid the trombone on a table, to don his tuxedo jacket. By twos and threes, the musicians left the green room, heading out to the stage. Shawn glanced around. Amy wasn't there to tie his tie or hook his cummerbund for him.

"Need help?" Kristin appeared at his side.

"Yeah," he said. "Amy told me I need to figure this out for myself."

"She's right." Kristin knotted the tie deftly, gave it a sharp yank, and melted away to Zach's side. They stood with their girls, listening over the loudspeaker to the orchestra warming up. A woman whom Shawn guessed to be Celine's mother chatted with Aaron's son. The boy looked at Shawn, awe on his face. The woman touched his arm, stopping him, when he made a move to approach Shawn. Shawn's heart fell.

Peter lifted his hand in farewell. "Break a leg," he said, and left. A minute later, applause erupted over the loudspeaker, followed by the A of Peter's violin. Shawn closed his eyes, listening as the A hummed down the strings, moved into the winds, starting at the flutes—he could pick out Caroline's—and down to the dark sounds of French horns, trombones, and tuba. More clapping signified Conrad's entrance.

They played Amy's arrangement of Tommy Dorsey's *Boogie Woogie.* Shawn smiled, appreciating it more fully than he had on paper. She had a gift. He hoped she was watching the performance.

He grinned at Zach, anticipating the next piece. "You ready?"

Zach returned his broad smile. "I was born ready. Let's go. Kristin, the girls should be able to see from backstage."

Shawn turned to Jon and the woman. "Go with them—you'll get a great view."

The woman tightened her lips and turned away. Shawn was sure now it was Celine's mother. He gave a quick smile, trying to ignore the snub, snatched up his red and white plunger mute, and headed out with Zach. They parted ways, heading to balconies on opposite sides of the concert hall. The snub faded as his anticipation rose. He climbed to the second floor of the concert hall, as familiar to him as his own home. His feet made no sound on the thick carpeting in the empty hallway. He nodded at the usher, and slipped through the door, into the dark hall, a story above the orchestra. Across the concert hall, he saw a bar of gray as Zach opened his own door and slid into position. He gave a thumbs up, grinning, and Zach flashed one in return. *Take that, ye auld cow,* he thought to Celine's mother. It wasn't entirely fair, he chided himself. But he didn't care. It was time to have fun!

Below, Conrad talked about the great jazz trombonists around whom the concert revolved. Dorsey, Miller, Teagarden. He paused, looked around, peering into the wings, cleared his throat, and added some more information. He peered into the wings again, and glanced at his watch, and finally groused, in a parody of his own cranky ways, "Where are Shawn and Zach? Anybody seen them?"

Shawn lifted his trombone and let out a single, long B flat. Conrad, he knew, would be shielding his eyes, peering up into the balcony. Across the hall, Zach added a matching pitch, an octave higher.

"What are you two doing up there?" Conrad demanded.

Shawn grinned, lowered his trombone, and as the spotlight swept across him, his eyes met Zach's. He bobbed his head in time with his trombone, one, two, three, swung it to his lips, and they came in on the upbeat, singing out *Tuxedo Junction.* One measure, and the pianist onstage hit his chords. Another measure, and Aaron was on the trap set, his brushes circling and slapping in time.

Life surged through Shawn! They'd been right, he and Zach, back in the conference room in Inverness. The audience loved it, cheering and whooping! They did another piece from the balconies, to more applause, and descended to the stage while a vocalist sang *Sunny Side of the Street.*

The concert passed away quickly to intermission, with Shawn's double tall latte waiting for him. He sipped it, thinking of Niall. *A twice as tall would taste good right now,* he'd joked the morning after escaping MacDougall's noose. And in the Bat Cave, Christina's eyes had shone in the torchlight, watching him play. His stomach turned, missing it. He finished the second half, playing Tommy Dorsey's and Glenn Miller's great solos, regaining his enthusiasm, forgetting where he was, and feeling himself back in the cave with the Laird and Allene and Christina.

He lowered the trombone to the sound of applause washing over him; to Zach lifting his hand high in the air, and swinging down into a joint bow. He drew in a breath, smiled, remembering where he was, and wanting to call Amy.

Inverness, Present

"Come in!" The chief looked up as Angus entered, beetling heavy eyebrows at him. "Good work, MacLean. Sit down."

"Thank you." Angus seated himself.

"I'm surprised to see you. I thought you'd need another day to recover."

Angus shrugged, his mind on his request. "Getting them out took a wee bit longer than we expected," he admitted. "But I slept all of yesterday. I'm good."

"Twenty-four hours in the hills, MacLean. Don't know how you do it." The chief shook his head. "There've been some very nice interviews on the telly— grateful families and all. Have you seen them?"

Angus shook his head. "I've been sleeping."

"Well, what can I do for you?" The chief grinned. "Take advantage. I'm inclined to say yes to almost anything after what you did out there!"

There was no point beating around the bush. Taking a seat, Angus explained what he wanted, what had spun through his mind, waiting up there in the mountains with the injured hiker, later as he sank into exhausted sleep in his own home, and as he woke again hours later. He laid his list of Bannockburn area hospitals on his superior's desk. "It's a short list," he said. "It'll not take much time away from my work. But I'd like to be able to call in an official capacity."

The chief sat back, furrowing his eyebrows at the ceiling a moment, before leaning his forearms on his heavy desk and asking, "What makes you think he has anything to do with the attack in Bannockburn? And what's it to do with us?"

Angus cleared his throat. Throughout his restless night, he hadn't thought of an answer to that. He edged toward the truth. "'Twas Amy's son yer man attacked. I think he may be the same man who came to Monadhliath with myself and Amy. He found her at Melrose shortly before we went. And I suspect this man in the video is him, so if...."

"I understand your concern for *Amy,*" the chief interrupted, his bushy eyebrows bristling, "but how does that make it the interest of the *Inverness* police?"

"It doesn't." Angus forced himself to sit still, trying to look sure of himself.

His superior harrumphed.

"Could I not take the matter in hand, call hospitals officially and find out if such a man was brought in? As a professional courtesy to Bannockburn PD?" Angus leaned forward, his voice lifting in excitement. "Because if I'm right, and he's the man who went to Monadhliath with us, I already know something of him, and can help them."

The chief settled back in his chair, hand on his chin. "What I want to know is...." He paused, studying Angus with sharp eyes that showed the intelligence that had brought him to the head of the department. "I understand how you saw the link between this attacker and the man who went to Monadhliath. But how do you connect either of them to the re-enactment?"

Angus shifted uneasily. "I...well...things he said on our hike. I don't remember specifics. It just popped into my head."

"Your unerring gut instinct," the chief mused. "Like knowing Kleiner would turn up at Glenmirril."

"Yes!" Angus agreed. "Yes, Sir, a gut feeling. So I looked. And there it was...." His voice trailed off. Niall flashed through his mind; and he sent up a silent *Ave,* asking God to pave the way for him.

"I see no harm in it," the chief finally said, nodding. "A half hour, an hour, maybe, making calls? Yes, do it. But I'll say nothing to Bannockburn unless you've something to tell them."

"Thank you." Angus rose, taking his list. His mind still on Niall, he resisted the urge to bow. He smiled. The chief would insist he take another day to rest, if he started bowing. He headed down the hall to his office.

Glenmirril, Present

The anger did not leave Simon as he rode in one of their large wagons, filled with irritating women and elderly men, down to Glenmirril. The old monk delighted in games, did he? It was anyone's guess if the crucifix was really at Glenmirril. But if it was, if he found it before meeting Eamonn, he could kill the old monk. If not, Christmastide was only weeks away. No! He *would* find the crucifix! He would *not* be forced to dance to the old scoundrel's pipes!

The *bus* pulled into the paved lot above Glenmirril, disgorging Simon into crowds swarming toward the castle in October's gray chill. Simon glanced at the visitor's center—in his own time, a forested hill rose above the castle—and joined the flow of parents and children through the gatehouse. It took only a question or two, and climbing the tower stairs, to find the chapel.

It was empty, but for two pews, a small altar under a rose window, and a life-sized crucifix in gleaming satiny wood, the shade of honey. *She dropped it,* Eamonn had said long ago. *It got caught in a crack.* With a glance around to ascertain he was alone, Simon dropped to his knees, searching the wooden floor. There were no cracks large enough to catch Amy's crucifix. He went over the floor a second time, in a widening arc, into the circle of sunlight falling through the rose window.

Voices floated in from the hall. Simon rose to his feet, seating himself in a pew. A family came in, a boy and girl bouncing around, looking up at the window, and running to the man on the cross. "It's gorgeous now, is it not?" the woman asked, turning to her husband.

Simon's lips pursed. He studied the chapel while they looked around, trying to think where else a crucifix might be—if, indeed the wily monk had told the truth and not just another story.

The boy bounded up to Simon, black curls dropping over his brow. "Do you live here?" he demanded.

Simon stared back, malice in his eyes.

"Joseph." The woman took the boy's arm. "Of course he doesn't live here. He doesn't want to be bothered. Ian, Grace, let's go see the gatehouse."

The family disappeared out the door, the boy glancing back. Simon scowled at him as his mother dragged him away. The moment they left, he shot to his feet, going straight for the altar. He ran his hands over its smooth top, of the same satin honey as the large cross, along the sides, down the legs. He wedged his fingers in where legs and top joined, and dropped to his knees, peering up from underneath, searching for springs, panels, hidden places.

Once more, voices sounded in the hall. He rose, wandering to the crucifix, as a man and girl entered. Simon stood close, inspecting the cross for any possible hiding place, while the girl complained about spending a sunny day in an old heap of stones.

"Imagine the people who lived here," her father replied. "Can you imagine knights praying at this altar the night before battle? Can you imagine the man who carved that crucifix, working on it day and night, pushing his tools over it, sanding it, polishing it?"

Simon glanced over his shoulder at them.

The girl plopped herself on a pew, legs kicked out, arms thumped across her chest. "That was like a million years ago."

"Seven hundred," Simon corrected.

The girl sniffed. Her father smiled.

"So what," said the girl. "It's hardly like they're real."

"They're more real than you can possibly imagine," Simon said.

She glared at him.

"Aren't you an insolent child." Simon lifted a lip in a sneer at her.

The man's smile slipped. His arm around the girl, he hurried her out.

Simon returned to his study of the crucifix, running his hands over it, searching for any secrets it might hold. He stooped to search the bottom, and felt along each side. There was nothing.

He went to the pews, giving them the same thorough examination. Once again, he found nothing. He closed his eyes, seething. He'd failed to get information from Amy, Angus, or Eamonn. He'd learned nothing of de Soulis, Michael Scot, Thomas of Erceldoune, or Einstein.

He *needed* the crucifix. He would search all of Glenmirril, he vowed. He opened his eyes, scanning the chapel one more time. He returned to the altar. And there, far back around a curve in the wall, was a doorway, almost completely hidden behind the life size crucifix. He slipped into it, finding a dark, narrow passage that twisted into the depths of the castle.

Inverness, Present

Excited to start calling hospitals, Angus headed back to his office.

"Hiya, Inspector." Claire glanced up, and lowered her eyes quickly.

"How's things?" he replied.

She gave a fleeting smile that didn't touch her eyes. "All right." She leaned into her monitor, typing quickly.

Strange, he thought, as he continued down the hall. Pete approached, scanning a report in his hands. He mumbled a greeting, lowered his head, and hurried by. Angus frowned. Maybe Pete and Claire had had a falling out? He wasn't sure they'd seen enough of each other to have a falling out. He smelled the mocha hazelnut as he approached his office. In the doorway, he saw Clive studying his monitor. Clive looked up guiltily, and stabbed at the keyboard. "Never mind about it!" he said.

Angus saw a news site blink away into Clive's desktop photograph of Ben Nevis. "Never mind about *what?*" he demanded. At the same time, he saw the coffee sitting on his desk beside two of his favorite donuts. He turned back to Clive. "Claire?"

Clive nodded, looking miserable. "She hoped to cheer you up."

Angus cast a suspicious eye on the computer that now told him nothing. "And why would I need cheering?"

"She didn't tell you?" Clive sounded surprised.

"Claire? What would Claire be telling me?"

"Amy," Clive corrected.

Alarm shot through Angus. "Is she or James hurt?"

"They're fine." Clive lowered his eyes. "They've gone back to America."

Angus dropped into his chair, sure he didn't want coffee or donuts. She hadn't even *told* him! "What site were you on?" He guessed there was more Clive wasn't saying.

"Is it worth seeing?" Clive protested.

"What site?" Angus repeated. Clive mumbled the name and left the office. Angus brought it up. On the front page, Shawn grinned out at him, wearing his *leine*, open at the throat, and his medieval trews. His auburn hair blew in a breeze. In his left hand, he held his trombone case. His right arm wrapped around Amy, with James on her shoulder. She leaned close to him, beaming.

Beaming! She was quite happy without him. Had probably never looked back.

As harshly as the picture stabbed at his heart, Angus stabbed the X in the corner, shutting the page. He turned his eyes to the picture of her and a much younger James, on his board. *She hadn't even said good-bye!* He shot to his feet, hands on hips, turned, staring at the wall, at the fern. He sat down again, taking her picture from his cork board, staring at it. His heart pounded. How could she walk away without even *telling* him? Had everything they had together been so meaningless to her?

He stood again, anger and pain snapping like an angry beast. There was nowhere to go. He could barely move in the small office. He couldn't walk out there, with all of them acting like he'd just been dealt a blow, watching as if at an accident.

But he *had* been dealt a blow.

He sat down, drawing a ragged breath, trying to reason with himself. She just went for a recording. Or to visit her parents. Maybe.... He took a slow breath. No. It was the way they acted. He suspected the accompanying article might clue him in. He didn't want to know.

He picked up her picture, from where he'd dropped it next to the donut, staring at it. What did he expect? He'd *told* her not to call him. She'd done exactly as he asked. But he'd hoped she'd find him worth coming back for. He'd told her to call if she decided that. And she hadn't.

Sorrow crept in. He'd spent months putting his life on hold, hoping, waiting, and she'd flown away without even saying good-bye. The smile on her face told him she was quite happy.

Clive stuck his head in. "You all right, Mate?"

Angus nodded numbly, but made no more answer.

Clive entered, dropping into his own chair. "I know it's not what you want to hear right now," he said, "but you never believed that attack was random. I know it's not what you want, but if your unerring gut is right once again, aren't she and James safer in America?"

"She's gone for good, then?" Angus heard the dullness in his own voice.

Clive touched his shoulder. "For his tour, anyway. Angus, you were worried. If you're right, she's safer there, aye?"

Angus looked up, hoping his eyes didn't look as hollow as he felt inside. But he nodded. *Love is patient, love is kind,* he'd told Amy. *Love is not self-seeking...it always protects.* "You're right, Mate," he said.

Clive patted his shoulder. "I've...uh...work." He left, closing the door softly.

Angus propped his elbows on his desk, dropping his forehead onto clasped hands. Yes, she was safer. His heart sank into prayer. *Help me remember it's better for her. Now what?*

He lifted his eyes, studying her picture. She was gone for some months. It *did* take the pressure off learning who the attacker was—which was good, because it was the busy season for rescuing. On top of police work, it wasn't leaving him much time. He glanced at his list of hospitals. It didn't matter much anymore. She was safe in America, and he had work to do. He stuck the list to his cork board, and opened his reports.

Midwest America, Present

"Got a party, Shawn?" Rob asked in the green room. He asked without hope.

"We're taking the girls for ice cream," Zach volunteered, when Shawn didn't answer immediately. "Want to join us? Maybe Celine and Aaron would like to come with Jonathan." He raised his voice to be heard by Aaron, standing nearby. He and Celine glanced at one another. Jonathan's eyebrows shot up, his eyes full of hope. Celine shook her head. It didn't surprise Shawn. Still—something wilted inside him. It would have been fun, if that shadow hadn't hung between them. Jonathan looked from her to his father. Celine murmured to Aaron. His raised eyebrows that asked, *Are you sure?* She nodded. Her lips moved.

Aaron cleared his throat. "Jon would love to. Can we ride with you, Shawn?"

"In the Jaguar?" Awe filled Jonathan's voice.

Shawn smiled at his enthusiasm. It was a long time since he'd remembered the joy of owning such a car. "In the Jag." He tugged at the tie and cummerbund, and dropped them into his case. "Let me change." He was already working at his cuff links. He tossed his keys to Aaron. "Show him the Jag." He took the garment bag to a bathroom, emerging shortly in trews, *leine,* and leather boots laced to the knees.

Out in the cool evening, Jonathan stared. "Mr. Kleiner?" He touched the bell sleeve. "Why do you dress like that?"

"Jonathan." Aaron's eyebrows dipped warningly.

"I'm sorry," the boy said. "I didn't mean anything. I was just curious. I mean, they're cool, you know."

"It's okay," Shawn said to Aaron. And to Jonathan, "They're comfortable."

"Where did you find them?"

Shawn winked. "In my closet. There were all these women who sewed all day, and every day when I woke up, I had a fresh, clean shirt."

Jonathan smiled. "It sounds like a fairy tale."

The smog and cynicism of his youth seemed to lift off the boy in that moment, and Shawn saw, suddenly, the child he really was. *Nothing we do here matters.* His words mattered. Something he had said, even so little and unintended, had given a little piece of childhood back to a boy who badly needed it. He thought of Red, the same age as Jonathan. His own smile grew, and he added. "Castles and princesses and villains and all." He thought of Christina and MacDougall, with a sense of foreboding. "Even a magic tower. But you don't want to hear about that."

"Yes, I do!"

Shawn grinned. "Let's get ice cream before Emma and Sophie eat it all, aye?"

Glenmirril, Present

Searing pain jolted Niall from deep slumber. Allene sat in a chair between the bed and William's cradle, spinning thread. She lowered the spindle. "Are you feeling better?"

"Better than MacDougall's arrow." Even to himself, he sounded groggy.

"I imagine. 'Tis fortunate you are. He barely grazed you. Though you ran a fever for several hours."

Niall fumbled with the covers, his muscles sluggish and uncooperative. Allene rose, helping him. He pushed himself up against the pillows, murmuring, "That explains the dreams."

"You were restless." Allene placed her hand to his forehead. After a moment, she nodded approval.

"Though the dreams rose from the letters between MacDougall and his steward."

Allene seated herself at his side on the bed, twining her hand with his. "Was summat amiss?"

"Naught," Niall replied. "Have you read them?"

She nodded. "As you say, all seems well. It bothers me, too."

The cradle swayed. Allene rose, as William made his first mewling sounds. She lifted him out, wrapped head to toe in swaddling clothes. "Will you hold him?"

Niall accepted him into his arms, as he leaned against the pillows. William blinked in surprise at the new face. "You don't remember me, either?" Niall asked. "Well, we've a wee bit of time." He spoke heartily, pretending to himself that it was enough. William would no more remember him from a couple of weeks, than if he'd stayed away all together.

Allene touched his hand. "You'll remember, even if he won't."

He turned to her, studying her dark blue eyes. "Can you see my thoughts?"

She smiled. "We've known one another since we were bairns."

"Aye, we've known one another long," he said. "And something has changed in you in the last years."

"Life," she said. "It's changed you, too. You're far more sober."

Niall laughed softly. "A few injuries." His leg throbbed. "A few battles, a few weeks in a different century, a secret other self who opened worlds to me I never dreamed of."

"And left," Allene said softly.

"Yes, left the world a wee bit more ordinary than it was." He watched William, watching him. Shawn had hated swaddling clothes. Niall slid the end of the band from the cloths, twisting them away. The boy lay still. Niall moved his son's hand up and down, then windmilled his small feet. "See, you can move," he said.

"The swaddling clothes comfort them." Allene's voice held gentle reproach.

A smile broke across William's face. He flung his hand out on his own.

"So I heard." Niall laughed suddenly. "Yes, I've changed. I hope 'tis not a bad thing."

"No. I love you more each day."

He kissed her, his hand in her hair. "I'm barely home."

"One day, you will be. And Scotland will be better for our sons, for your sacrifice."

William's smile turned to a frown, and he began to whimper. Allene gathered him up. "He needs to be fed. I'll fetch the nurse." She left the room. Niall climbed stiffly from bed, inspecting his aching leg, though there was little to see apart from the fresh bandage. He pulled on a fresh shirt and trews, and limped to the solar, where he took parchment and a quill from the desk, and began a letter to Shawn.

When Allene returned, he set the quill in its holder. "Is Christina reassured?"

"Mostly." She rested her hands on his shoulders. "Though now, she worries how my father will give James Angus back to her."

"Is your father still angry?"

"He's not happy." She leaned down, studying his words. "But he's a good heart. He finally understands it may not be Shawn's doing." Her face became grim. "Or hers." She touched a finger to the parchment. "D' ye think he'll ever find these?"

"I don't know." He touched his leg, wishing for a large jug of wine to kill the pain. "But I feel better for writing. And we promised we would."

"He seems very close," Allene said. "As if he only went to a different place."

"Because 'tis too incomprehensible to think the other," Niall replied. "Even now, I sometimes think we must have all been deceived, even having seen it myself."

"Do you still think about his world?"

"Our world," Niall corrected. "Only a different time. Yes, I think a great deal on it. I think he is home with Amy and his son, eating well, expecting many a year with them. I never know when death will separate us from one another, or our bairns."

"We are blessed," Allene said. "We will look with gratitude on what years God grants us. I hear discontent in your voice. Thinking Shawn's life is far better."

"Shawn's life *is* far better." Niall laughed harshly, realizing his gratitude of only yesterday had once again slipped. Still, he asked, "Do you think Shawn was gored by a boar today?"

"Considering he's not yet been born, no." Allene raised an eyebrow at him.

"You mock me," Niall accused.

"Aye. Someone must." Allene ran her hand through his hair, and kissed the top of his head. "In truth, Niall, did you not tell me, when you first came back, that they all seemed discontent there? Angry over one thing or another?"

"I did say that." Niall studied his own words on the parchment. "Perhaps I misunderstood. How could they be, when they are so abundantly blessed?"

"I dinna ken, Niall. But I believe you'd not be as happy there as you imagine."

"If you were there, and William, and James, I would be."

"What would your life be, there? What would you do?"

"Play music all day like he does."

Allene's hands slid from his shoulders. He turned, to see her wrapping her arms about herself. "I can't but feel," she said, "that summat would be missing."

"Death, pain, separation." Niall sanded the letter and rolled it. "I'd not mind their loss."

Allene smiled, but sadly. "No, Niall, summat else."

He cleared his throat as he stood, painfully, shifting the weight off the injured leg. "I've not told you everything."

Her clear eyes clouded. She raised a slender, questioning eyebrow, that still managed to be as threatening as her father's lowered bushy brows. "Have you not?"

"I've barely been home," he reminded her. He backed up a step, gripping the table for support. "I'd no wish to spoil the first night. And since then, I've been dealing with Christina's baby...."

"Which you mustn't call him."

"And MacDougall...and your father."

Allene sniffed. "'Twould not have taken so long, had you done as you were told."

"You were equally concerned with his stays in the Bat Cave," Niall snapped.

"I obeyed him, nonetheless!"

Niall sighed. "Allene, the Bruce wants me back in Scone for his council."

Her annoyance fled like mist in hot sun. Her fingers wrapped in his shirt. "When, Niall?"

"I leave in a week."

Allene shook her head in agitation. "A week? I thought you were home to bide a wee bit."

"D' you see why I might feel discontent," Niall said angrily. "Why I might envy Shawn's life?"

She took a deep breath, hugging herself.

"He goes home to her every night! He has no wars!" Niall gestured at his leg. "No vicious animals!"

"A week?" Her voice came out as soft as the coral pink of a seashell.

Niall wrapped his arms around her. "Let us not spend that time angry with one another. I but wanted not to spoil our first night together."

"I see that." In his arms, she relaxed, her head on his chest. "I'd have been upset had you told me then, as well. When will you be back?"

"I don't know. There is much more to do for Scotland. Berwick is still in English hands."

"Sir James has tried thee times to take it." Worry filled Allene's voice. "He was injured in the last attempt."

"And he'll continue to try until it is ours. Which is why we *will* win this war, Allene. Because of Douglas and Bruce."

"And you. Bruce knows this of you." She spoke as certainly as if she'd seen the future. "They'll lay siege to Berwick again, and he'll want you there."

"'Tis likely." Niall agreed, though he hadn't thought that far ahead.

"I wish...."

"We both do," he said. "I wish our lives were different. I wish we could go into the tower and walk out into Shawn's world where there is no war." He shifted unsteadily, his leg throbbing in pain.

Midwest America, Present

Emma and Sophie were carrying banana splits to the table when Shawn and Aaron arrived with Jon. Emma dropped her bowl on the table and ran to Shawn, hugging his leg and chanting, "Mr. Finer! Mr. Finer!" Shawn laughed, though his heart did a funny flop at her innocent acceptance and love—healing balm after the snubs in the green room. He ruffled her hair, and she dashed back to her table.

Jon joined them, while the two little girls whispered and giggled, looking at him. He seemed to take it as a compliment, and launched into a story, while they listened in rapt attention. Aaron grinned. "It's fun, having kids." They joined Zach and Kristin at the nearby table, and Shawn fell into the rhythm of this milder after-concert event, enjoying an Oreo blizzard instead of bourbon. He relished Jon's thrill at the Jaguar, and the joy shining on his face. He liked knowing he'd done that for him. He'd do more of it, and the Tessas and Celine's mothers of the world would fade away.

Zach leaned toward Sophie. "Knock, knock," he said.

She giggled. "Who's there?"

"Emma."

She glanced at her sister. "Emma who?"

"Emma 'bout to eat your ice cream if you don't eat it yourself!"

Kristin shook her head. "Corny!"

They left shortly after, carrying their daughters out. Jon brought his sundae to the table. He looked from his father to Shawn. "Emma said you can turn invisible. She said her parents said so."

Shawn bowed his head, hiding a laugh.

"Jonathan, that's ridiculous," Aaron said.

Jonathan shook his head. "Sophie said he can make dimes disappear."

"I can," Shawn confirmed. "But trombones are more interesting." He looked to Aaron. "Can you bring him over Sunday? I film the talk show Monday and fly out Tuesday for Texas."

"Right after church," Aaron confirmed. And to Jonathan, "Finish up. I'm using the restroom, and then you need to get to bed." He gathered his empty dish and spoon and left.

Shawn and Jonathan stared at one another. "What kind of a horn do you have?" Shawn asked.

Jonathan leaned forward, dropping his plastic spoon. "Celine's nice. You're nice. Why does she hate you?"

Shawn's face fell. "She hates me?"

"She wouldn't come with us. I wish she would. I like her."

Shawn swallowed. He'd apologized to so many people already. And here was one more, a boy he'd only just met, impacted by the things he'd done. "I hurt her." Pain stabbed at his heart, hating the thought that Jonathan would one day refuse to look at him, as Celine did. He swallowed. "I didn't mean to. I didn't think."

"She seems okay to me," Jonathan said. "You don't seem like you'd hurt anyone."

Shawn stared at the table, then lifted his eyes to Jonathan's. "Sometimes, people hurt inside. Where we can't see." He took a breath, looking back to his hands on the table. "I lied to her. All you need to know about it is, be kind, don't lie, and you'll have fewer regrets."

"I wish she would have come, though."

"If you wish something," Shawn said, "wish that I hadn't caused this. Don't blame her." He saw with relief that Aaron had emerged from the bathroom. He stood up, digging for his keys. "Come on, another ride in the Jag, and I'll see you Sunday."

CHAPTER THIRTY-THREE

Inverness, Present

As twilight fell, Simon pressed through the cold alley behind his house. The opening of the time slip was fast approaching. After more than a week of searching Glenmirril fruitlessly—plagued by ill-mannered urchins who asked questions and stared—Simon decided to search Angus's home for information on Amy. He might have to simply face her and forcibly find what she knew of the crucifix.

He had time. From listening through walls, Simon knew Angus spent a great many an evening, of late, in the pub with Clive. Anticipating a leisurely search, he crossed the wall into Angus's back garden, a sad jumble of dead plants and fallow earth under chilly autumn rains. Simon jiggled the doorknob—locked—and tested the window. He smiled as it gave. The fool had left a window open. So much for the great hero these people thought him! He didn't even have sense enough to guard his own home. Simon smiled at the irony as he eased the glass up and hoisted himself over the ledge.

He landed inside with a soft thump of leather boots, and looked around. It was a small kitchen, like his own, lit by moonlight pouring through the square of window. Though everything was tidy and clean, the table in one corner was covered by a frayed cloth. Simon's lip curled. He'd never allow his servants to treat his home so shabbily!

There would be little in the kitchen worth finding. Simon moved down the narrow hall, where a cross hung with two palm fronds fanning out behind it. Simon stopped, studying them. If God were on this man's side, He certainly wouldn't allow his home to be so easily invaded. God would have given him more sense, or perhaps a neighbor to notice or care.

Simon turned into the front room. Ashes lay cold and gray in the ridiculously small hearth. But then, they didn't use these to cook. In the street light pouring through the front window, he studied the pictures on the walls—an older man and woman. The man was the image of Angus. It must be his father. Another showed the same couple, this time with Angus, a man who looked very like him, and a short, round woman with a curl flopping almost over one eye. Angus's brother and sister, Simon mused. They could come in handy, if he desired to pressure Angus. He moved around the room, finding a smaller picture standing upright on a table. He picked it up. Street light flashed off the glass covering it. He angled it till he could see. A man and woman posed with two young boys. Simon glanced back to the picture on the wall. Yes, it was the same woman. So this must be Angus's sister, with her husband and two small boys. Simon's smile grew. Children were particularly useful in convincing a man to do as he was told.

A movement outside caught his eye. Picture in hand, he crossed to the window, standing back against the wall. Angus walked down the street. Simon watched. Not what he'd planned on, but it didn't matter. He could wait here, press Angus to lead him to Amy and James, when he came in unawares, and, then dispense of him before dealing with the child. His problem would be solved and he could get back to his own time. He smiled. Yes, it was a good plan. He slid his knife from his belt.

♫

As Angus trudged through soft drizzle dancing in the blue-gray sky, the door across the street from his own flew open, spilling a cheerful rectangle of light across the cold steps. Mrs. MacGonagle, in a gray house dress, sturdy hose, and practical shoes, beckoned. "I've dinner on the stove, Angus! Far too much to eat by myself!"

He glanced at the bags in his hands. He dearly wished to be in his own front room with a Guinness.

"Never you mind that," she said. "Sure an' you can eat it tomorrow. Come in!"

With a sigh, he obeyed, crossing under the rain-swirled street lamp and up her steps. "I do appreciate it, Mrs. MacGonagle." He patted his stomach. "It was going to take a wee bit of time to make my own." Stamping his feet, he set his bags of vegetables in her front hall.

"You're losing weight, Angus," she said sternly, when she had him cornered at her kitchen table. "Are you taking care of yourself?"

"I am, Mrs. MacGonagle," he reassured her with a smile. "Do you not see the groceries?"

She sniffed as she set a roast, rich vegetables swimming in a dark sauce, on the table. "It's *that girl*. The one who was...." She lowered her voice. "*Pregnant*. She took off with that American musician, did she not?"

"She's in America for Christmas." Angus sidestepped the issue of Shawn. The truth was, he realized, it *had* been since June he'd lost his taste for cooking, for eating, for much of anything, really.

"You're a far better man," Mrs. MacGonagle snipped, her nose in the air. "She's a fool, going with him."

"It smells grand, Mrs. MacGonagle," Angus said. "Shall we say grace?"

She removed her apron before settling herself, hands folded, and murmuring words of thanks.

She looked up expectantly. He rose, dipping the serving fork and knife in, and carving off a rich piece of meat for her. He spooned up a ladle full of carrots and potatoes onto her plate, and served himself.

"The neighbor girl is on about ghosts again," Mrs. MacGonagle said, as he sat.

"Is that so?" he asked. "Kathleen does have a grand imagination."

"Doesn't she." Mrs. MacGonagle rarely achieved a full smile, but she made a fine attempt to lift a little of the sour pucker from her lips. "She has all the neighbor-hood children in an uproar."

"Which house is it this time?" Angus asked.

"The one that's been empty for months now—next door to yours."

♫

Simon's fingers twitched on the knife as he watched the house into which Angus had disappeared. It didn't matter. He would return. But the old woman annoyed him. He'd seen her studying his house, with narrowed eyes. Ah, well, she was no threat. Easily dispatched, if she made trouble. He set the picture down, careful to leave it at a different angle than he'd found it—playing with a man's mind was half the fun—and scanned the rest of the room. The shelves on the far wall caught his eye. Wary of the lace curtain that might allow a glimpse of his shadow, he moved to the shelf, studying the titles in the falling evening light. Angus had a number of books on what these people called history—specifically, Simon's own time.

But there was nothing here to lead him to Amy. Glancing out the window, he saw no sign of Angus. He climbed the dark stairs, daring turn on a light in the back room, where a heavy curtain covered the window. He ran a finger along the books on the shelf, and dug through clothes in the wardrobe. None of it would lead him to Amy.

In the front rooms, lit by moonlight, he rifled drawers, finding socks and undergarments, and a picture of Amy holding her violin. A desk held piles of papers. Holding them up to the light coming in the window, he made out enough to guess they were household accounts. He went through a number of them, glancing constantly out the window at the old woman's house, before deciding he'd find nothing helpful here. He may as well wait for Angus.

Back in the downstairs room, he squinted in the dim light to scan book titles. Half a shelf was devoted to medieval warfare. Simon pulled out a book on the art of swordplay to take to the kitchen at the back of the house. There, he dared turn on a light. Browsing Angus's cupboards for food, he found a bag of carrots in the small cold-box under the counter, and settled at the table to read as he ate. It was a good book, he decided. They'd gotten some things wrong, but he found a few thoughts—in the section on the Far East—that might help his own skills.

♫

Mrs. MacGonagle sawed at her roast vigorously. "I told her ghosts are not interested in empty houses. Where's the fun of that? If I were a ghost, I told her...." She stopped to pop the meat into her mouth, chewing and swallowing before resuming. "If I were a ghost, I said, sure an' I'd find it more fun to be haunting a house where I can *see* people jump in fear!"

Angus, his knife halfway through his own roast, looked up and laughed. "But Mrs. MacGonagle, you are aware, are you not, that the neighborhood children don't *know* you've a sense of humor,."

Her mouth puckered primly. "And whose fault is that? They're not making them like they used to, Angus! All these children sitting in front of their tellys, and i-this and i-that and i-everything. How could they possibly know what a sense of humor is, when they never *talk* to one another?"

Angus smiled. "There may be some truth to that."

She sniffed, and poked a potato into her mouth. "There is a *great* deal of truth to it. I did, however, take pity on young Kathleen when I saw I'd but scared her the more, and assured her these houses are far too new for ghosts. At least a hundred years old, they've got to be, I told her. The silly ninny insisted she's seen a shadow behind the curtains. Are you aware, by the way, that the Frasers down the road are having another child?"

"When did you find that out?" Angus asked.

"Oh, weeks ago. They're all after talking about it down at the market."

She updated him on more of the neighborhood's doings as they ate, in between lecturing him that he must keep up his strength if he was to continue his rescue work. "We can't have you going over a cliff and breaking your leg, too," she warned. "And all because you aren't feeding yourself. She's gone, now, you know. You've so much to offer. Look around and you'll find plenty of young ladies interested in you."

Angus smiled politely, removing his napkin from his lap and setting it beside his empty plate. "I'll keep that in mind." He rose. "Mrs. MacGonagle, will I help with the washing up?"

She waved him off. "No, no, you're my guest. You go on home now, and get a good night's sleep."

Gathering his groceries, he headed out into the cold night, torn between relief at escaping and thankfulness for the company and good food. She could be sour, but she cared for people in her own way. He only wished, he thought as he crossed the small street, under eddies of mist trembling in the street light's halo, that she wouldn't keep mentioning Amy. It hurt enough, even without her not-so-helpful reminders. As he reached for his house key, deep in a coat pocket, his phone rang. He juggled it, and the grocery bag, as he stood on his stoop, trying to open his door.

♫

Simon was finishing the chapter on Eastern sword technique, when a sound at the front door alerted him. He jumped, hitting the switch on the wall. Darkness swallowed him. A heartbeat later, the door opened. Angus's voice, full of cheer, filled the hallway. "Aye, Clive, too much on my mind. I'll see you in the morning. I have to put away my groceries."

Simon melted into the kitchen wall, drawing his knife from his belt.

"Thanks for checking in. But really, I'm fine. Bye, now."

The light came on in the hallway, turning the black night of the kitchen to charcoal shadows. Simon raised the knife. Angus's footsteps came down the hall. Simon dropped into a half crouch, ready to spring.

A melody sang out. The footsteps stopped. "How are you, Mairi?" Angus was so close, Simon could have reached around the door and slit his throat. He waited, listening to the treble sounds of a voice coming over the instrument. He wondered if Mairi was the woman in the picture.

"I have it somewhere," Angus said. "I'll grab it."

The voice trilled on at length. There was a soft thump on the floor, as if something had been set down, and Angus's footsteps headed back to the front door. The stairs creaked. "Of course you can bring them over, but wouldn't it be easier...."

The voice faded away up the stairs. Simon waited, listening, in the dark kitchen. He could search at leisure, with all the lights on, once he slit Angus's throat. On second thought, though, an obvious murder would garner attention. Besides, he couldn't get information from a dead man. And, Simon thought, he had time, still, until Christmastide. There were ways that could be more fun.

He glanced at the table and chairs. It took him only minutes to carve a deep gouge at the top of one chair leg, listening the while to Angus moving about in the hall and rooms above. When the stairs creaked, Simon snatched the book off the table. He slipped out the back door into the misty night, and hoisted himself over the wall, back to his own home.

♫

"Aye, I've plenty on medieval warfare," Angus told Mairi over the phone, as he flipped on the light in his front room. "I've one more down here—maybe a wee bit advanced, but it might help with his report." He scanned the book shelf, frowning, before saying, "It seems I've misplaced that one. But I've others. I can drop them by on my way to work tomorrow."

"That would do nicely," Mairi agreed. She hesitated a moment, and then asked in a rush, "You're doing all right?"

Angus sighed. "I'm fine, Mairi. Clive is just after calling, too. I'm playing with the pipe band again in January. I've gone out a few times with a lovely girl at work." The picture of Mairi and the boys caught his eye. He frowned. Had he really left it at that peculiar angle?

"Oh, now, Angus," she began.

"Really, Mairi." He straightened the picture. "I'm fine. I'll see you tomorrow, aye? Give my love to Hamish and Gavin." He hung up, picked up his laptop, and headed down the dark hall to the kitchen. The vegetables waited beside the door in their canvas bag. He hit a switch, flooding the kitchen with bright light against the black night peering through the fragile lace curtain. He put the vegetables in the crisper and grabbed a Guinness. He'd resisted the urge for two weeks, but now, he was going to have a Guinness and look at pictures from the eejit's Christmas tour, and make himself sick to his stomach—all so he could see where Amy was, if she took James to his concerts...if maybe he could see her in a picture, see how she looked.

He pulled out the chair and sat down.

With a crack and sharp report, it buckled under him, dropping him with a thud that jarred his tailbone, onto the kitchen floor.

CHAPTER THIRTY-FOUR

Midwest America, December, Present

Jonathan proved to be a quick learner with natural talent. Shawn enjoyed teaching him, in between concerts. "Can I go to the taping for your next interview?" the boy asked after his fifth lesson, as he snapped his case shut.

"Let me talk to your dad about it," Shawn said. "There's a waterfall out there. It's pretty cool when it's frozen. Why don't you see if you can find it?"

He and Aaron followed Jonathan out the front door, shrugging into warm coats, and watched him dash across the wide snow-covered lawn, toward the wooded copse, before Aaron spoke. "Your comeback is incredible. The interviews are going great."

Shawn smiled. "Yeah. This next one has a huge audience."

"Next week?"

Shawn nodded. "Yeah, I have a bit of a break. I needed it."

"It's been intense," Aaron agreed. "Don't know how you do it." They watched Jonathan for a moment, their hands deep in their jacket pockets, before Aaron added, "I really appreciate what you're doing for him. He can't stop talking about you."

Something unpleasant stirred in Shawn, remembering Jonathan's questions at the ice cream parlor. "Listen," he said, as they trailed fifty yards behind the excited boy, "I'm not sure about him coming to the interview."

Aaron stopped in surprise.

"Not because of him," Shawn said hastily. "Celine—you know...." Aaron started to speak, but Shawn stopped him. "It's my fault. I know that. But how does she feel about him going on about me?"

"She smiles and says you're very good at trombone."

"And leaves the room?" Shawn guessed.

Aaron nodded, staring at his feet. Jonathan darted into the woods, disappearing into snow-covered pines.

"It's hard on her," Shawn confirmed.

Aaron nodded. "But she wants him to have this."

Shawn hated the words he was about to say. But he had to. "Then it's better I don't spend time with him. I'll pay for him to take lessons with anyone you pick. But I laid awake last night thinking, what if my kid came home telling me how great Clarence is?"

"Clarence?"

Shawn hesitated. He rarely discussed it, even with Amy. "He killed my father."

"Oh." Aaron spoke on a quick intake of breath. And again, "*Oh.* You never told me his name."

"I was sixteen," Shawn said, not knowing why. That he'd been sixteen didn't matter. "Yeah, I wouldn't like to hear my kid going on about Clarence."

Aaron started to speak, but Shawn cut him off. "I'm leaving, anyway. I have no idea when I'll be back. So it's a non-issue. Find someone really good. I'll pay for a few lessons. I'll pay for a whole year. But let Celine have peace."

Inverness, Present

"No more accidents?" Clive asked as he returned to their office after lunch. "You've had a bad run this past month."

Angus shrugged. "I tripped a wee bit on the back stair to the garden. Cracked my knee badly. I've not seen it becoming worn and chipped under the snow."

"The mantle falling—strange business, that."

"The place is old." Angus dismissed it. "My real worry is how often I'm misplacing things these days."

Clive dropped into his desk, not meeting Angus's eyes. "You need to get out more. Get your mind off things. It's stress, that's what it is."

Angus said nothing.

Clive wiggled the mouse, bringing his monitor to life. "Have you stayed away from his tour photos like I told you to?"

"I only looked the once," Angus answered tersely.

"She and James are safer. On a different matter—or maybe not—I'm just after chatting with the chief." Clive sipped his coffee as he studied his monitor. "He wants us to look into this report from your friend—peculiar goings-on at Glenmirril."

Angus glanced at him. "Are there now?" Clive had said little of the strange events surrounding Shawn's return. Angus didn't particularly want to think about anything to do with Glenmirril. It left a sour taste in his mouth. But it was his job. "What's happened?"

Clive adjusted his monitor so Angus could see. He tapped the words. "Visitors are complaining about a man there."

"What's he done?" Angus's senses sharpened.

"Nothing."

"So what's their complaint?"

Clive scanned the words. "There daily, a month now. Scowls at children."

"Scowling's not a crime," Angus said. But he understood. On a gut level, something was bothering people. "Has anyone asked him why he's there so often?"

Clive nodded. "He says he enjoys history, imagining those who lived there."

"As do I," said Angus.

"Do you scowl at children while you enjoy history?" Clive asked.

"No." Angus smiled. "Nor do I kick dogs. Have you a description?"

"No," said Clive. "But the chief wants us to drop by."

With a sigh, Angus set aside his reports and gathered his heavy coat and gloves.

Half an hour later, they stood in the director's office. "Good to see you again, Angus," the man said. He held up his hand. "Yer man's about so tall. Thick black hair, swarthy, dark eyes, muscular. I'd not want to tangle with him."

Simon. The attacker. The description hit Angus like a wash of cold water. And here he was haunting Glenmirril where the switches had happened. He kept his voice flat, asking, "What's he doing?"

"Searching." The director ushered them out of his office, explaining as they crossed the drizzling parking lot. "He seems to be making a methodical round of the castle. The staff says he spent a great deal of the first days searching the chapel, asking questions of the staff about it. He spent the next several where the kirk stood. Then he went to the wing on the loch, working his way down floor by floor."

Clive looked up from jotting in his notebook. "So we should be able to predict where he'll go next."

"He's here today?" Angus asked.

"Aye, he's here." They passed through the gatehouse, the heavy arch briefly blocking the soft patter of rain, and dropping a cool pall around them. They emerged into the renewed spattering. The director looked worried. "He's done nothing illegal now, you know. But he's worrying people. I do appreciate you coming out as a personal favor."

Angus nodded absently, his mind churning. "Given the pattern, we'd expect him on the lowest level of the loch wing or in the southern bailey."

"I think so," the director agreed.

"I'll take the southern bailey," Clive volunteered.

Angus nodded. "John and I will watch the loch wing." He didn't add that if Simon showed up, he hoped not to be seen.

They split apart, Clive splashing through puddles to the south. Angus patted his pocket, feeling his phone there, as he and John entered the wing in which Niall had lived, centuries ago. John headed to the north end, while Angus wandered the large, barren ante chamber at the southern end, trying to appear interested in placards he knew by heart. He gazed out the window at the rain-spattered loch, wandered into the adjoining chamber, and returned to the first room as the rain retreated to sporadic drops. He checked the time on his phone, and looked out into the chilly courtyard. His mind strayed to the inhabitants of Glenmirril, to Niall, MacDonald...Shawn.

He had lived here during some of those two years. He might have attended Niall's marriage to Allene. Angus gazed at the spot where the chapel had stood, centuries ago. Medieval weddings had been brief exchanges of promises, often on the church stairs. Had Shawn watched? Had he scoffed at the beautiful ideals of marriage and commitment? Had he stayed away altogether? Angus's heart hurt.

He should be married to Amy. She'd accepted. Yet she was back in America with Shawn, without so much as a good-bye.

Angus turned back into the antechamber. Weak sunshine shot through the thinning clouds, splashing a puddle of sunshine on the cold stone floor. The thoughts he barred from Amy jumped back to Shawn, wondering how often he'd come through this chamber. What had he and Niall talked about? How had a man like Niall been able to stand the eejit's ostentatious, self-centered arrogance? Angus wandered to a plaque, tracing its raised letters.

They'd both been involved in Niall's escape from MacDougall's dungeon. Or Shawn's escape. There was no telling who had been there, and who had been with Douglas. Shawn had been in the dungeon, he decided—because it would have been Niall who behaved honorably and nobly, to be knighted by the Bruce. So Niall had saved Shawn. Again—honorable and noble. Angus wanted to hear the story. But that would require talking to Shawn. He wasn't sure he wanted to hear it that badly. Maybe.

He trailed his fingers off the plaque, and wandered back to the other chamber, watching for Glenmirril's visitor. Why had Niall rescued Shawn? Because Niall would do that, Angus decided. Because Niall wouldn't leave a man to die an awful death. Yes, Niall had been the hero in all events.

But you don't know, his conscience reminded him. And his own words came back to him. *I've never stopped to ask if they're good or bad before I rescue them.* Wasn't he engaging in all sorts of judgments against Shawn now? Claire said rumor was he'd come back changed—two years in medieval times just might do that to a man. And Shawn had saved James.

It's his son, Angus argued with himself. *Even an ogre loves his own son.*

But he *had* protected James, and for that, Angus felt gratitude, drop-to-the-knees, tears-streaming, the-horror-of-what-could-have-been gratitude. And it angered him to feel gratitude for Shawn. It angered him to be indebted to someone like Shawn.

The soft bleating of Clive's ring tone drew Angus back to the present. He answered softly, "Is he there?" Adrenaline rose in his body, wondering what he'd face in the next moments. You couldn't arrest a man for scowling, but if it was, indeed Simon, there was something very wrong, and the man was violent.

"I believe 'tis him," Clive answered. "One Seamus P. Martin."

"He gave you his name?" Angus frowned, wondering if Simon would make up a name. "You checked ID?"

"No need." Clive's voice sounded behind him. Angus spun. Face to face, Clive chuckled as he stowed his phone. "He was in our jail this summer past. I checked him out myself when he left."

Angus pushed his phone into his pocket. "What was he in for?"

"Unruly behavior is all. Lost his temper a wee bit."

Angus frowned, still trying to adjust his thinking. It wasn't Simon. "What does he say he's doing here?"

"Said he's a professor, doing some work on the history of Glenmirril."

It didn't sit right. "A professor?" Simon had claimed to be a professor. "Is he still there?"

Clive shook his head. "He was leaving when I called you."

Angus bolted to the door, scanning the northern bailey. It was empty. He raced across the lawn, green and damp with rain, and through the gate house. Seamus P. Martin was nowhere to be seen.

Scone, 1317

The meeting at Scone dragged on as meetings always had. Niall had to admire the way Bruce sat, hour after hour, in his heavy royal tabard with threads of gold depicting the rearing lion, the circle of gold on his head, in the straight-backed throne. The gathered lords and knights discussed and argued endlessly over the Irish war and the raids into northern England, while Niall reminded himself that Bruce, too, was far from his wife and child, and made no complaint.

They broke for meals and for a hunt in the forests around Scone, dragging in a great stag and a boar—Hugh grinned at Niall, while Niall threw a sour look back— and returned to vehement discussions about their future course.

"We must press farther into England," one lord insisted.

"We must secure all of Scotland first," objected James Douglas. "'Tis not safe for me to push my men farther."

"As far as you've gone has not won peace," roared the first. "We *must* go further."

"We take Berwick first," insisted Douglas, refusing in his gentle way, to yield.

"We've tried to take Berwick many times," another lord reminded the gathering. "'Tis time to change tactics."

The deliberations raged, voices rising, and fists thumping on tables.

Niall offered his opinion when asked, sweating in the heat of Scone's great hall in June, his leg itching under the bandages, and pondered Allene's certainty that they would once again besiege Berwick. In last January's attempt, James Douglas had scaled a wall with his own invention of a hanging ladder. Halfway up, he'd been pierced by an arrow and the attempt had been called off.

A nighttime attack from the sea, by Bruce and Douglas, had been thwarted when the moon came out and a dog barked. Despite their many David and Goliath victories, Berwick seemed destined to remain in English hands. Niall hoped Allene was wrong. Berwick was bound to be disaster. It always had been.

Don't do it, Niall!

Niall jolted upright in his chair. No one spoke. Beside him, Hugh leaned in, listening to Douglas outline his plan for Berwick. No one paid him mind. There was no servant boy nearby who could have spoken. He sank back against his chair, feeling sweat prickle his forehead. It was the injury...fever...stress. That was all. It had to be, because if it were a premonition, he could hardly tell his king to change battle plans because he, Niall, was hearing voices.

Inverness, Present

Angus sat at his desk, his chin planted atop his fist, his elbow resting on top of a manila folder. He stared at the picture of Amy and James, pinned on top of receipts and the schedule for pipe band rehearsals, and a drawing from Gavin. It was good she'd gone back to America. She *was* safer there. He'd been unable to shake the feeling all week. Something was very wrong. Everything pointed toward it being Simon haunting Glenmirril. It *fit.*

Simon and Seamus P. Martin mixed in his head. Could Seamus have been a re-enactor—*merely* a re-enactor? Could the blow to his head have made him believe he was the medieval warrior he portrayed? It was odd for a professor to be picked up for disorderly conduct, but a head wound could cause erratic behavior.

It couldn't, however, explain his meeting with Amy at Melrose, or his desire to go to Monadhliath.

Angus stared blankly at his screen saver—a photograph of Glenmirril. Say it *was* Simon at Glenmirril, he thought, and Simon *was* a medieval knight pulled from a battle into modern Scotland. How would he know of Shawn's return, or its tie to Glenmirril? He'd hardly be watching the telly—would he? But it had been big news. People talked. And if Niall could learn quickly here, so could Simon.

He turned abruptly, yanking Kleiner's file from the cabinet. He took a sheet of blank paper and headed it. *How it might have happened.*

Pulled from field, nursed to health. His pen stilled. It wasn't much. How had he found Amy at Melrose? Angus lifted his eyes to her picture. He frowned, thinking about Simon approaching her that day at Melrose. What had he known?

The door swung open, abruptly, and Clive burst in, setting a steaming mug on Angus's desk. "Claire asked me to bring it for you," he said. "Chief doesn't like it."

"The coffee?" Angus closed Kleiner's file.

"Yer man at Glenmirril." Clive tossed himself into his chair, taking a gulp of his own coffee. He set it down, wiping his mouth. "It's been eating you. You thought 'twould be the attacker. Why?"

Angus stared at the folder. He couldn't tell Clive it was too coincidental, a professor matching Simon's description at Glenmirril—exactly where a medieval knight trapped in this time would go, if he knew about Shawn. But the question was whether it *was* Simon. "You're sure it's the same man we booked?" he asked, instead of answering Clive's question.

"Course I'm sure. I processed him and sent him out of here myself."

Angus was already tapping at his keyboard, pulling up records. Moments later, Seamus P. Martin's driver's license appeared on screen. He fit Clive's description. Thick black hair, stocky, a square face like Simon's. He smiled broadly. Simon rarely smiled, making it hard to compare. Angus turned to Clive. "You checked his license?"

"Aye, course I did."

"How carefully did you look?"

Clive put down his pen with a sharp *harrumph.* "Given 'twas nothing but disorderly conduct, and the chaos—Kleiner showing up in his ridiculous get-up...."

"He was there *that* morning?" Angus stared at Clive. Another coincidence clicked into place.

"Aye, does that make a difference?"

Angus turned his monitor toward Clive. "Is this the man you released?"

Clive scooted his chair across the small divide, studying the driver's license on the screen. "He looks very like him," he said.

Angus heard the hesitation in his voice. "But?"

"I can see how I'd glance at it and think 'twas the same man."

"But you're not so sure."

Clive tilted his head, studying it. "Well, now, the picture's a few years old, and people moving and talking always look different than their pictures."

"You're not sure," Angus repeated. He pulled up Seamus P. Martin's booking picture. It was Simon. Angus smiled. He'd been right. He turned to Clive. "Is that who you saw at Glenmirril?"

"That's him." Clive frowned. "Put it with the driver's license."

Angus clicked the mouse and the two pictures appeared side by side.

"It's not the same man," Clive said.

Angus rose, his eyebrows carving a deep furrow over his nose. "What *exactly* was Seamus Martin brought in for?"

"Hold on." Clive tapped his keyboard, and a moment later gave a grunt. "Well, now, isn't that interesting. I'd have made the connection if I'd booked him."

"What?" Angus leaned in.

"Disturbance of the peace." Clive tapped the screen. "He went off on yer man, the old monk from Monadhliath we brought down from the mountains." Clive lifted his eyes. "Angus, there are far too many coincidences here. Amy, Monadhliath, Glenmirril, this man in the thick of it all. What's going on?"

"I don't know. Exactly." Angus sighed. Even if he knew, he doubted he could tell Clive. Amy and James were in danger if they came back. Yet Simon hadn't actually done anything arrest-worthy—that they *knew* of. And why *would* he be after Amy? Or was it Shawn he was after? And why would he attack James? He glanced at her picture again. The short list of hospitals stuck out from underneath. It was time to make those calls. Amy *might* be back. And, Angus chided himself, if Simon was the Bannockburn attacker, he was violent and might be hurting others.

♫

Simon brushed white flakes from his coat as he entered the church office in the late afternoon dusk. His anger had grown through a restless week. Unable to return to Glenmirril, he was stuck waiting on the monk. He stomped snow from his boots, cursing the Scottish weather, and looking forward to the day he could wipe the God-forsaken country off the face of the earth. The new one across the ocean would be much more suitable for such as himself.

The woman behind the desk, her face lit by the glow from her *computer,* was deeply engrossed in her work. On her last visits, she had looked no more happy to see him than he was to see her, asking twice now, "Your phone is still broken?"

"I dislike phones," he'd said. "I don't mind at all stopping by." He'd smiled. The promise he would return encouraged her to press Eamonn for answers.

He cleared his throat.

She almost jumped from her seat, starting at the sight of him, and saying in a rush, "He's left a message! He'll meet you on the twentieth." She named the church, and glanced down at the note in her hand, her brow furrowing. "At *Vespers?*"

Simon smiled, not indulging her curiosity. "Vespers will do quite nicely," he said. "Thank you."

He took himself back out to the chilly streets of Inverness, to women leaning into white swirls, and babies in prams reaching for the fat flakes dancing around their heads. The twentieth was a week away, pushing right into Christmastide. Anger chilled his stomach, to be left once more at the old monk's mercy. He made his way to an alley, dark with shadows, behind one of the expensive taverns. He slid his knife from his belt, ready to vent his anger and replenish his money. Yes, he would meet the old monk on the twentieth at Vespers, and then he would vent his rage again—as soon as he had what he wanted.

Inverness, Present

Angus waited until Clive left before taking down the list and dialing the first hospital. It was awkward with no name or specific injury. "He'd have been brought in after the re-enactment," Angus repeated to various people. "It appears to have been a rather serious head wound." But computers were not equipped to look up whether a patient's stay had anything to do with the re-enactment of a 700 year old battle. He reached the last hospital on his list before a woman said, "Aye, there *was* such a man brought in. *Terrible* head wound!"

Excitement quivered in Angus, like a retriever after a kill.

"I remember it well," the woman continued. "My daughter telling me of strange doings at the re-enactment. I couldn't be there, you see, being at work...."

"But he *was* brought in?" Angus asked, re-directing her.

"Aye, no sooner had I hung up, than there was a wee stir, and yelling at the door, and them racing in with him on a gurney. One of the medics was after telling me about the blood, couldn't understand how such a thing happened at a re-enactment."

"A head injury?" Angus clarified.

"Aye, and a terrible one. It *did* look as if a sword had struck him. I mean, 'tis not the first injury at these events. But this one was vicious."

Angus was about to re-direct her again, when he decided he'd do better to listen.

"Blood everywhere," she added. "I thought he'd not live."

"He did?" Angus realized he'd never even considered that the man on the video might have died, so sure was he that he'd watched Simon emerge into the present as Niall disappeared into the past.

"Oh, aye!"

"Did he not have ID?" Angus asked.

"No. They never found a name."

Angus smiled. Another piece *fit*. "How long was he in hospital?" he asked.

"Hold on, now, a wee minute."

Angus listened over the phone to the tapping of keys.

"Here we are," she announced. "He was in a coma for some time. No identification. Bannockburn PD interviewed the re-enactors, and no one had any notion who he was. They were all accounted for. There were no missing persons reports to tell us who he might be."

Angus's gut tingled. His instincts had not failed. He jotted as he asked questions. "No family ever came looking for him?" But he knew.

"None," she confirmed.

"He eventually woke up?"

"Aye, that he did, and the commotion! Himself shouting, yelling, lunging at the staff. It took ten of them to hold him down. *Ten!* Like a raging bull. Stronger than any man they'd ever encountered, they said."

As Shawn had described the attacker, Angus thought. Medieval knights, with years of hard training, carrying heavy weapons and armor, would be far stronger than most men today. He listened as she talked about the day, about going in to see him herself, after he'd been restrained, and his angry demands, barked out in an unintelligible language.

It didn't surprise Angus. "When did he leave and where did he go?" he asked.

There came another tapping of keys. "He was sent to the psychiatric ward," she said. "I know nothing of what became of him then. I can give you their number."

Jotting it down and thanking her, Angus hung up. He sat, chin on hand, staring at the picture of Amy and James a moment before he dialed the psych ward. It took fifteen minutes, but a secretary made him an appointment, a frustrating two weeks out. "Christmas and Hogmanay and all," she apologized. "It gets difficult to add anything to the schedule this time of year."

Hanging up, Angus glanced at the clock. His shift was nearly over. He still had to stop at the market for dinner. He didn't fancy the walk home through the snow. What he'd once found beautiful, now reminded him of last winter with Amy. He shut off his computer and left for a quiet night at home, missing her, wanting her safe in America, and wishing she were here. Maybe he'd find he'd over-reacted. Maybe someone had been injured in the chaos on the battlefield, and the incident in Bannockburn was just a random attack. He hoped, for once, that his unerring gut instinct had finally erred. But in the meantime, he thought, he had to think what more he could learn of Simon, until he could get in to see the director of the psych ward.

CHAPTER THIRTY-FIVE

America, Present

"Tell me about your new style." Ella Erin dimpled at Shawn.

Shawn rose from the couch, turning with outspread arms to show off his trews and bell-sleeved shirt. He grinned at the hostess. "Like them?"

She smiled, waiting for his usual raunchy conclusion.

"They're comfortable." He sat down, to audience applause, grinning at her.

She looked confused for a second, behind the painted-on smile, and then said, "But...why? Why did you *start* dressing like that?"

Shawn shrugged. "Just something I found I liked. You should try it." He smiled, using the trick of unnerving her with silence to get her to move on.

"They do look medieval," she said, "and one of your stories is that you spent a year in medieval Scotland."

"Two years," he corrected, beaming at the audience.

They laughed.

She leaned close, half-lowering her lids, and said, "Tell me where you really were." Glancing coyly at the audience, she added, "Just whisper in my ear. I won't tell," and leaned closer.

Irritation mounting at her refusal to talk about music, Shawn leaned close. His lips brushed her ear. "I was in a monastery with the Monks of Monadhliath in the mountain fastnesses of Scotland. Showing cleavage is not impressing me." He sat back, grinning at the audience.

Ella's face turned red. She sat up abruptly, yanking at her gaping blouse.

"You'll keep your word not to tell them?" he said into his microphone.

She nodded, quickly recovering, with a little laugh. "Oh, I won't tell. But be assured, I'm going to look them up and ask them if it's the truth."

"Check their archives." The smile fell from Shawn's face. "I left music. Let's talk about music."

"Oh, of course." She laughed again, looking uncertain, flashed a bright expanse of white teeth at the audience, and said, "It beats the Easter Island story." She turned back to Shawn, with more professional decorum, and continued with questions about his music, the tour, the musicians.

He relaxed, enjoying the interview, before picking up his trombone and welcoming Elinore on stage to accompany him. "*Trombonology*," he said. "One of

Tommy Dorsey's pieces," and began. The audience chanted for *Blue Bells* when he finished, and he indulged them, closing his eyes and feeling himself back in the Bat Cave, but for the tinkling of piano keys. He sailed up an arpeggio to the high C, and back down, remembering Christina's eyes bright with excitement in the torchlight; he hung onto a note, and launched into triplets, swaying with the music, lost in the flash of the slide and deep, relaxing breaths pouring back out into the instrument in pedal tones that quivered in the soles of his feet, and flew back up to the highest registers. He slid into the last low note like Babe Ruth into a home run, with elation and a final lift of the trombone, beaming at the audience. They cheered, for the music—and for him. They loved him!

He swept a hand out to Elinore, who bowed, glowing, and disappeared offstage. Returning his trombone to its stand, he resumed his seat opposite Ella. He could live this new life! Be this new man!

"Wow!" she said. "Wow! O-*kay*! Let's take questions."

He answered the typical ones. *How long did it take you to learn that?* from a boy. *How long do you practice each day?* Shawn answered them, relishing his return, his triumph. Every concert had sold out. Pre-orders were rolling in for albums not even recorded yet.

The phone rang on the table beside him. Ella picked it up. "Hi, Caller. What's your name?"

"Cassie."

"What's your question?"

"Shawn, do you remember me? Cassie. Ron's wife."

"Ron?"

"He played clarinet in the orchestra."

"Oh, yeah, yeah, yeah!" Shawn leaned forward. "We had a lot of fun together. How is he?"

"I know he made his own choices, Shawn," came the soft feminine voice over the phone. "But I wish you hadn't pushed him to gamble with you all the time. He kept thinking he'd get as lucky as you." In the background, a child spoke unintelligibly. "He lost the house instead."

Shawn shifted uncomfortably in the couch, smiling a tight, embarrassed smile at Ella, grateful Jonathan was not in the audience—and wishing no one was.

Inverness, Present

Simon entered the dim church, seething over the monk's games, and his own repeated failures. Great arches reached to a high vaulted roof, lost in shadow above. Outside, thunder rumbled. Rain pelted the windows.

Simon lowered his eyes, searching the dim interior. Eamonn stood in a side chapel, in his brown robe, hands clasped behind his back, looking up at a statue of a monk. Candles in chips of colored glass flickered, row upon row, at the statue's feet, casting shadows over the pair of faces that gazed at one another. Simon considered plunging his knife into the man's back. It would be easy enough to find the crucifix in the folds of the robe. He inched forward, silent as an owl on the hunt.

Eamonn turned. The shadows made valleys of his gaunt cheeks. His eyes sank under hooded brows. His mouth twisted in a ghoulish smile. His voice came out a soft rasp. "You'd not be thinking I'd be so foolish as to carry the crucifix with me?"

Simon stopped. A cold splash of fear washed over him. The monk looked like the wizened healer who had stirred potions at Claverock, years ago when Simon had been a boy—though that man had been even older than this monk.

Simon remembered as if it had just happened. He had crept around a corner in the deep kitchens, where he was forbidden to go. The old man had turned, slowly, crooking his finger, beckoning. "You'd like to see, would you?" he croaked. "Come closer. I can heal you of many things. I'll tell you secrets you may not wish to know...but perhaps should."

Simon had backed away. The old man let his huge, wooden ladle slide down in the cauldron, to step forward. Simon turned, running for the stairs, biting his tongue not to scream like one of the girls when he dropped spiders on their embroidery. His anger grew, at himself, at his fear, at the old man. He swore vengeance! But on asking, no one had ever seen such a man. "I've seen him often!" Simon shouted at his nurse. "Tell my father! Command him to bring this wretch to me!"

His father gazed at him sadly, sending heat up Simon's cheeks, flaming his anger. "The healer is a woman," he said. "She lives in the forest, not in our kitchens."

"Come closer," Eamonn said. "You wished to know my secrets. It is time to tell. Promise you won't run."

Simon drew breath, his face devoid of expression. "I've never run," he whispered harshly. But fear inched up his spine. He hadn't felt fear in years.

Eamonn chuckled, a wisp of breathy sound. The few white hairs on his head stirred in a draft. "There was the once."

"Who are you?" Simon demanded, forcing his voice out in anger.

Eamonn stepped forward. Behind him, the marble monk, stony, cold, glared down at Simon over Eamonn's shoulder. The jeweled glasses flickered with candle light. "The question is, who is *Angus*?"

Simon's lips tightened, waiting. Thunder rumbled outside.

"'Tis Angus will teach the boy to fight," Eamonn whispered.

Angus. Lightning flashed through the stained glass high above, illuminating the old man for just a moment before darkness once again drenched the church.

Simon smiled. "You are a fool after all. If I don't find James, I shall merely kill Angus. James will show up as weak and soft as all men here."

Eamonn's eyebrows rose. "Ah, then you shall do what you shall do. But you still need a way *to* your own time. I believe I promised you something." He reached in his robes, and withdrew his hand.

The smell of wax grew thick in the air. Simon's head swam. He took a step back, bumping into a pew.

"You don't wish to have it?" Eamonn extended his hand. Something silver glinted in it.

Simon shook his head, shook off the light-headedness.

"No?" Eamonn asked in surprise.

"Yes!" Simon snapped. He snatched it from Eamonn's hand, holding it up as another bolt of lightning lit the place. A large silver key glinted in his hand. His head shot up. Anger flashed from his eyes. "You promised me the crucifix!"

"So I did," Eamonn agreed. "This is, one might say, the *key* to retrieving the crucifix." He chuckled inanely.

Simon's mouth tightened. "What does it unlock?" he asked.

"The secrets you desire." Eamonn cackled again.

The marble monk stared down over his shoulder. Simon's eyes flickered across it's pensive face and back to Eamonn. "Quit your games," he hissed. Outside, thunder rumbled. "What does it unlock?"

Eamonn sighed. "Ah, your lack of humor is not good for your health. Anger has a way of eating one's heart."

Simon stepped forward, chest to chest with Eamonn. "*What* does the key un*lock*?" he bit out.

"The altar."

"*Which* altar? You may have noticed an *abundance* of altars in Scotland."

"And in England." Eamonn turned his back, looking up once more to the statue. "He was a fine man, our St. Fillan."

"You're mad!" Simon hissed. "Which altar?"

"Ah, that!" Eamonn looked back, resting a gaze of childish delight on Simon. "Aye, altars. Alter thy clothes, alter thy ways, alter thy time."

Simon's lip curled in anger. "I could kill you, Monk."

"But you'd be no happier, for you'd not have altered your relationship with God." Eamonn tucked his hands in his sleeves, and strolled down the aisle between pews and shrines. "How He looks down, wishing you'd heed His voice. He longs so for your soul. 'Tis not too late."

"God smiles on me!" Simon strode after the monk, wanting to crush his neck. But he needed information. "Has He not done wonders, bringing me to a time filled with knowledge, which will give me power?"

"Except the knowledge you need." Eamonn stopped at the next shrine. A woman looked down over her own garden of flickering candles. Thunder crashed, shaking the church. Lightning flashed, illuminating a mischievous smile playing on her lips. "Margaret Morrison," Eamonn said. "Of Glenmirril. She played tricks on Niall when she was young. He likely deserved them." He smiled to himself, as if watching children at play.

"The altar," Simon reminded him.

Eamonn turned. His head tilted. He looked quizzically at Simon. "Why would we be speaking of altars?"

"The key!" Impatience reared in Simon.

"Ah, yes!" Eamonn's face brightened. "Well, you see, if I tell you which altar, you shall surely kill me, and decrepit though I am, I believe God is not quite through with me." He smiled, beatifically. His few strands of white hair floated about his head like a weak halo. "Surely you understand my dilemma. But I'm thinking there's a solution."

"Is there?" Simon asked sardonically. His fingers twitched on his knife.

"Oh, aye!" Eamonn spoke as if discussing an anticipated party. "I'm thinking I can leave a note at the church desk telling you which altar. That way, you've all I promised you, and I've my life. A fair trade, is it not?" He beamed as thunder rolled.

Simon glanced up at Margaret Morrison of Glenmirril. She seemed to laugh at him. He snarled at her, and looked back to Eamonn. The monk had pulled his hood up over his head, shielding his face. "You made me a promise, Monk."

"And I've kept it. I've given you the key to your return home, as I promised. I shall even give you more. The door opens on December 26. Perhaps because that's Margaret's feast day? I imagine she might still like to have fun with Niall. Imagine the tricks she has up her sleeve."

Simon's mind spun. "Six days from now?"

"Aye." Eamonn's head bobbed arthritically. "But you shall need the crucifix. I'll leave that note, will I? Perhaps on the very day." He smiled. "But only if James is alive."

Simon's lip curled in anger.

Eamonn looked up at the statue. "Now, Margaret, you promised me a bit of help, aye?"

Simon spun, looking at the statue. She laughed down at him. "What game is this!" Lightning flashed, revealing the empty spot where the monk had stood. Simon spun again, scanning the aisle. It was empty. He searched the small shrine, stretched up to look behind the statue. Anger lashed through his stomach, launched into his chest, and trembled in his arms. He wanted to smash, hurt, kill, destroy! But the monk was gone.

Simon drew in a slow, tight breath. His lips hurt, so tightly did they press together. He would go to the church tomorrow and see if Eamonn had left the information. If he had, Simon promised God, he would leave alms. If not, he would tear the place down. If not in this time, then in his own.

He reminded himself he was another step ahead. He had a date. He had but days to outwit the monk—to find the crucifix, and kill James—or Angus. He didn't care which. Still, he'd been played for a fool. He stormed out of the church. It had happened at Glenmirril. The key *must* fit something there! He would tear it apart! Room by room, stone by stone! He would find whatever was there!

He stopped suddenly in the dark, rainy street. No. First, he would make sure Angus would not be teaching James anything.

America, Present

Shawn sat at the back of his local church, staring at the crucifix over the altar, far down the aisle. Amy and his mother would be waiting for him at home. They would say nothing. But he couldn't face them just yet. He needed to be here— here where he felt Niall. And Christina. He felt sick, his stomach in knots.

Humiliation. He'd never felt humiliated in his life. Worse, he felt remorse, a deep, profound regret and desire to turn back the clock, to fix what he'd brought on Cassie and the child in the background. But how was he supposed to fix this?

He lifted his eyes to the crucifix. *What do you want from me?* he asked. It was a hopeless asking, with no expectation of a response.

Silence hummed around him. He closed his eyes, slipping back into his many mornings in Glenmirril's chapel. A thought entered his head. He opened his eyes. "That's too much," he murmured. "I didn't make him." His brow furrowed as he stared at the crucifix. He felt Christina at his side, her hand on his shoulder. No reprimand, no condemnation—she only stood, a silent, invisible presence.

Shawn pulled out his phone even as he rose and moved to the foyer. Ben picked up on the first ring, listening to Shawn's command. "You have the last gig to worry about," Ben objected.

"You know I'm good for it," Shawn said. "Just find out, okay?"

He returned to the pew, staring the length of the church. Memories flooded him, of raiding churches, gold, women screaming, children fleeing—sometimes alone—in terror through dark cobbled streets. He didn't know why he thought of it now.

His phone *ka-chinged.* He moved once again to the foyer, listening to Ben's answer. "Yeah, thanks," he said, and returned to the pew, hunched with his elbows on knees, hands clasped together. High above, the light faded behind the stained glass. He'd come back to make things right with Amy, to give her the world. But Cassie and her child were living in a dump. No matter how much he told himself Ron had made his own choices, the guilt would not leave.

Christina's presence stirred. He felt her watching him. *You know Amy doesn't care about money.* He swore he heard her soft brogue. *It's why you're so scared of Angus.*

Angus was being lauded in the wake of his most recent rescue, Shawn thought bitterly, not shown for a fool to the whole world.

Christina's presence squeezed his shoulder. *What you're thinking would be far more valuable to Amy than the horse you want for her.*

Who was he kidding, he thought. He could still get Amy a horse. Maybe it was the things *he* thought of owning someday that would be affected. But Christina was right. His character mattered to Amy. His thoughts drifted to Jimmy. *Big feckin' star, ye think ye can jest throw mooney at it all?*

He hung his head. He *did* want the world to know he'd made amends. He'd thrown six hundred pounds down in that pub, for everyone to see. It wasn't like that, he protested. Jimmy had been in a pub. How else was he supposed to give it to him?

In an envelope? suggested the snide Shawn Kleiner of two years ago. *Without announcing to the whole crowd how much it was?* Shawn's head dropped further, staring at his clasped hands. It was true: a fantasy had filled his mind of his arm around Cassie, her gratitude, articles telling the world how wonderful he was—like Ebeneezer Scrooge, hailed with open arms, the hero of his story! The Grinch sailing into town with the sleigh full of toys, greeted with love by all of Whoville!

Toys he stole in the first place, Shawn thought. The comparison did not flatter him. People would accuse him of grandstanding. But what was the other choice? Do nothing?

You know what to do. Christina's lyric voice filled his mind. He did know. He wanted things for Amy? He would just sell more albums, write more music, play more concerts. She wouldn't pay for his misdeeds. He snatched his phone from his pocket in the dimming church, scrolled through his contacts and hit call, his eyes locked on the crucifix.

"Matt," he said, when his agent answered. "I want you to contact a woman named Cassie."

"Right *now*?" Matt asked. "I can get to it maybe next..."

"Not now. In four months."

"Four months? Why are you calling me now?" Matt asked.

"Because I don't want her to associate this with me. Take her to find a house. Anything she wants, up to half a million, understand?" He listened to Matt, and replied, "It's going to be in her name. *Hers*, not her husband's." He listened another moment and said, "I'm setting up a fund. My name will not be associated with this in any way. Is that clear? You don't tell your friends, you don't tell your wife. You don't tell your therapist or priest, understand? No one is to *ever* know who bought that house, or it's the last time you and I do business."

He thanked Matt, hung up, and returned to staring at the crucifix, lit only by candles, now that night pressed up against the stained glass. The humiliation of the phone call stung—having to admit to Matt that he'd harmed someone. It stung, too, that the world would never know he'd made amends. But he felt Christina's warm smile, her hand on his shoulder. *I know*, he felt her say. *And* you *know*. Yes, *he* knew he'd done the right thing.

Berwick, July 1317

The pounding of hammers and scraping of saws and crashing of trees in the forest echoed in Niall's head even in his dreams, so many hours did he listen to it each day. June's council passed directly into action. Bruce and his men swarmed the forests around Berwick, constructing siege engines. Niall's days in the Bat Cave with the Laird helped him build mining cats for burrowing under the walls, belfries to push against them, and giant trebuchets to launch stones and Greek fire over them.

He worked in his shirt, sweat flowing freely, in the warm July days, chopping, pounding, building, drilling men for war. He couldn't remove the shirt, lest any notice he lacked Shawn's scar from Bannockburn. Some days, he rode with the hunt in search of meat for the great army. Some days, he scouted Berwick, studying the soldiers on the walls, from the safety of the forest, and reporting back to Bruce and Douglas as they pored over maps of the vicinity and town, in Bruce's tent.

"They've not let up on their defenses," Douglas murmured. "They *must* show a weakness sooner or later."

"Berwick is their last jewel," Bruce countered. "They'll guard it well."

After another evening of playing his harp around campfires, singing of victories past and victories to come, Niall wrapped himself once more into his tartan under the trees, missing Allene and his sons who would no longer recognize him when he got home. As he lay listening to the steady *drip drip* of rain pattering down from the leaves above, he pondered MacDougall's letters. He had gone over the Laird's copies repeatedly, in the evenings around campfires. Naught was amiss. *Nothing!* They spoke of castle affairs, of servants. But each time he read them, he felt something was wrong, something just out of sight, that he should be seeing.

He sat up, staring at the embers, and suddenly, it came to him. *The orchards in the northern glen.* He'd ridden hard through that glen, Bessie clinging to his back, November wind cold on his bare head. There were no orchards. He frowned, trying to fathom what it meant.

Don't do it!

Niall shot to his feet, his hand on his knife. The words were faint and far away. He moved softly, prowling the dark edges of the camp, his ears straining.

All was silent, but for men snoring and fires crackling. Stress was getting to him, he decided. He returned to his place, tugging his tartan close. But he lay awake long into the night, listening, and trying to guess why MacDougall had written about orchards that didn't exist.

Inverness, Present

"Busy season," Clive muttered as they unpacked rescue gear at the cavernous station house. "Seems worse than usual this year."

"Aye," Angus agreed. "It's the awful weather. The hills are more treacherous." Between more rescues, more paper work, talks to school and scout groups on mountain safety, and a smattering of requisite Christmas parties, he'd had no time to look further into who the man on the battlefield might be.

Before he could say more, the door flew open, admitting young Mick O'Shaughnessy. "Lads!" He beamed. "Did you not get the memo?"

Angus and Clive glanced at one another. "What memo?" Clive asked.

"The station equipment is being gathered for a thorough check." He indicated the plastic bins into which he wanted it loaded. "You're to bring in your own equipment. Did you not read the e-mail I sent round yesterday?"

Angus shook his head. "Sorry, I was on holiday in the mountains."

Clive snickered.

Mick frowned. "Aye, well. Get it in straight away, aye?"

"I will," Angus said, and Mick left.

"I've a meeting with Pete," Clive said. "Can you finish up here?"

Angus nodded, grateful for time alone after the whirlwind of the last days. As he coiled ropes, his mind turned to the man pulled off the battlefield. He could go back to the internet, or talking to historians, to learn whose coat of arms the fallen warrior in the video had worn. But so far, they'd found nothing.

He dropped the ropes into a bin, wanting to call Amy—but he'd taken himself out of her life. It only made sense to call her if he had anything to pass on. He had to find out more about Simon. Although, he reminded himself, he didn't *know* it was Simon who had attacked Carol. There were plenty of strong, stocky, swarthy men, and Shawn had been sure his accent was nothing unusual.

His thoughts turned back to starting from a surname, rather than the coat of arms. What had Claire suggested? Their conversation had been cut short by an alarm. *I don't know his surname,* he'd said. *How did you meet him?* she'd asked.

How *had* he met him? Angus dropped down on a canvas bundle, staring at the bins, trying to remember. Simon had called out of the blue, talking about research, archives. Angus pulled his phone from his jacket pocket. He frowned, trying to remember when Simon had called—it had been just before he and Amy left for Monadhliath in early April. He hit *call log,* scrolling back, back, back. He slowed on April 1, March 31, March 30. Every call had come from someone on his contact list. He weaved up and down the few days again, backed up to March 28, and moved forward again—Amy, Amy, Mairi, Clive, the station....

"Inspector?" Claire opened the door, scanning the cavernous garage.

Angus glanced up at her and back at the names—his brother, his father, Amy. Helen O'Malley. Angus stared at the name—the professor to whom Rob had sent Amy's crucifix and ring. Why had she called in March, three months after giving them the story of the crucifix? Why didn't he remember talking to her?

"Inspector? It's just, the Chief says you're to be in your meeting."

Angus glanced up. "What?"

"The new software."

Angus nodded, his eyes returning to Helen's name. And he remembered. It hadn't been Helen. It had been Simon, calling from Helen's phone.

"Be right there," he said, punching in a text to Helen.

Inverness, Present

Simon had watched from a window until Angus disappeared through the morning mist, before heading downstairs, out his back door, and over the wall, to enter Angus's home through the kitchen window. He'd delighted in seeing Angus tumble on his step. But the fun was over. This time, he'd make sure Angus wouldn't be teaching James anything. He climbed the stairs, to the first bedroom.

It held a bed, a table at its side, and more books. A few *photographs* hung on the walls. He studied them. One showed Angus with several men, all of them wearing straps across their chests, smiling broadly. In another, a man hung off a cliff, dangling as if from a spider's thread. Simon peered closer. It was Angus. The same harness crossed his chest, attached to the rope that supported him. There were two more of Angus with other men, one by a loch, and one up in the mountains.

A bookshelf filled the wall under the window. Simon squatted down to read titles, and picked several to flip through. They all involved *rescue work*—going into mountains, wilderness, lochs, to bring out the wounded or lost—and *first aid*—healing injuries, he gathered. He dropped down on the bed, turning page after page, studying pictures of the equipment they used. *They go up there with all their gear,* the boy had said as Angus and other men poured from the station, long ago. *One of them may be hanging off a cliff in midair.* This was what Angus did. Simon turned pages, fascinated by their methods of healing injuries. He decided to take this book with him, too, to heal his own soldiers.

He glanced out the window. Though heavy clouds covered the sky, the filtered glare of the sun behind them shone higher than it had. The mist hovering over the frosty gardens below had thinned. Fat flakes of snow fell from the clouds. He couldn't forget himself, or his purpose.

Tucking the *first aid* book into his shirt, he opened the closet to the web of wide, heavy straps, with multiple clips attached to them that Angus had been laying out in the back yard—the harness Angus wore in the painting, and shown in the books. Simon touched it. It would hold Angus securely to ropes as he dropped over steep mountainsides—or not. Studying it, Simon thought of his own gear. He checked it carefully before battle, running his hands over each piece, inspecting by sight as well as feel. Angus would do the same.

Smiling, Simon slipped his knife from his belt and made numerous small cuts, invisible to the eye, in the threads where each part of the harness joined another. He glanced out the window to snow swirling in big, fat flakes. Angus would not be teaching James anything. And there would be no alarm over murder—only laments over a tragic accident.

CHAPTER THIRTY-SIX

Inverness, Present

Angus stamped snow off his feet as he entered the station two days later, his equipment left in the garage. "Cold day, Inspector," said Claire.

"The wind is something else," he agreed, as she handed him a pile of mail.

"I'm just after putting on coffee. It'll be ready any minute."

"Thanks." Angus hurried past, pulling off his gloves and hat, and feeling, as always, like a great galoot for keeping it strictly professional with her. Deleting the Glenmirril Lady from his phone had hardly deleted Amy from his mind. The familiar argument waged as he sifted through the envelopes while heading down the hall. Maybe he'd forget Amy if he went out with Claire again. No, that would be using Claire. But, the argument continued, she knew where he stood and was still offering. She hadn't gone out with Pete again.

"You made it!" Clive greeted him as he entered the cramped office. "Got your equipment here?"

"Aye, in the garage."

The smell of coffee filled the small room, as the machine burbled cheerfully on top of the filing cabinet. "Claire's been in," Clive said.

"Aye, she has." Angus hung his jacket on the coat tree and tossed his gloves and hat on his desk where they spread a puddle of melting snow.

"Keeps the plants looking chipper."

Angus glanced at the fern, thriving on the cabinet. Maybe he would, too, if he gave her a chance. It had been months since the fiasco at Glenmirril. Amy had left. He had to move on. "Snow's hitting hard," he said, ignoring Clive's hint.

"Aye!" Clive rubbed his hands together. "I'm hoping for a day of paperwork."

"'Tis one day I'd welcome it." Angus's chair squeaked as he dropped into it, already pulling letters and forms from the pile of paperwork, sliding them like cards in a poker game to piles—those needing immediate attention, those that could wait till afternoon. "Got your Christmas turkey?"

"Aye, and a good thing, too, what with the weather. You?"

"Mairi's having us all again." Angus scooted his chair to the file cabinet, yanked a folder to check information, and jotted a note for the coroner. Clive pecked at the keyboard with his index fingers, leaning close, and muttering.

"It's not so hard to learn to type," Angus said.

"It's not so hard to let a pretty girl fawn all over you," Clive returned.

"Did I say I want to talk about this?"

"Coffee's ready." Clive grunted in victory as he stabbed at another letter.

As Angus pushed his chair back, and rose to fill a mug with the coffee steaming in the glass pot, his phone beeped. He picked it up. Helen O'Malley had texted. *Simon Beaumont.* Angus stared at the name. It sounded familiar.

Send it on to Shawn, he told himself. *Let him deal with it.*

As soon as I have more information, he argued. He should call Bannockburn P.D. He would, he told himself—as soon as he ran a search on police records. He might have more to tell them. Because he still had no proof that the man who went to Monadhliath was the same man who attacked Carol.

He ran the search, but no Simon Beaumont had been brought into the station this decade. There had been no rescues involving anyone by that name. So why was it so familiar? He searched wider, but found only a twenty-year-old shoplifter down in Carlisle. So why was his gut ringing?

He typed the name into an internet search. It yielded Facebook pages, linked in profiles, men prominent in their fields, and historical figures. He studied the list, wondering if there was a quicker way than sifting through all of this.

Suddenly, he knew. And he knew why he'd avoided it. But it did no good to avoid. He entered a new search—*Simon Beaumont coat of arms*—and hit *images.* He opened Paul's photo beside the search results.

Those in the first five rows didn't match the blurred enlargement at all. He began to hope, scrolling down, his eyes flickering between the results and Paul's magnification. Life would be easier, if he'd made a mistake, a foolish embarrassing mistake, and Amy was in no danger.

He hit *next.* The screen blinked, refreshed, and he found himself staring at a match to the coat of arms of the man pulled from the field. *Simon Beaumont,* read the text beneath it. *The Butcher of Berwick.*

Midwest America, Present

Shawn stopped suddenly, just inside the vast, flashing glitz of the Mall of America, patting his trews' pockets.

"What?" Amy, pushing James in his stroller, stopped, looking back.

"My phone."

Amy's mouth quirked up.

"What?" Shawn demanded. "It's my *phone!*"

"Um, yeah," she said. "We'll be okay. We won't be trapped in this wilderness."

"This is serious," he protested. "Tonight's the last concert. I have to be in touch with Ben."

"Call Ben and have him call me if there's any emergency."

Under his *leine,* Shawn's shoulders relaxed. "Okay, yeah." He took her phone, calling as they walked through the crowd, past displays draped in holly garlands, and decked with bright red berries.

"Good?" she asked, as he handed it back. "You'll be okay now?"

A girl stopped suddenly, her eyes widening. "Shawn *Kleiner*?"

Shawn stared. Fear gripped his heart. Was she going to chastise him for harming Cassie, chew him out in public, humiliate him? Was she condemning him?

Amy stared at him. "Shawn?"

"Can I...get a picture with you?" the girl asked at the same time, making a grab for her purse. A hopeful smile lit her face. She thrust out her cell phone.

Shawn let his public relations smile break out. "Of course." He leaned in, mugging with her. To the accompaniment of Victorian-clad carolers, she gushed thanks, cast a fleeting glance at his hair, and, clutching the phone, raced past the carolers toward another girl.

"If Ben needs something, he can tweet," Amy said. "The fan girls will find you and let you know."

"You're making fun of me," Shawn retorted.

She laughed. "*Somebody* has to! Keep your head just small enough to squeeze back into your car so you can *get* to the concert tonight."

"Seriously," he said. "I have to go from here straight to the school to set up. I won't have time to get my phone."

"By then," Amy said, "you'll be with Ben anyway, and he can call the musicians, if someone doesn't show up. Which never happens. Okay?"

"Yeah." Shawn relaxed, realizing she was right. "Okay."

"So let's enjoy the day." She took his hand, pushing the stroller with the other. "It's James's first Christmas! You're home, your mother is on cloud nine. Your career is skyrocketing. It's good to have a day with just us, no phone, no internet."

"Yeah." He laughed. "Yeah, that could be good." His thoughts drifted as they walked past window displays. Neither Amy nor his mother had mentioned Cassie. Nor had Ben or any of his musicians given any sign they knew. It left him humbled, quick to thank people and offer help, and hoping maybe—*maybe*—they could see good in him *now*, despite his past mistakes. And *he* knew he was making amends.

He relaxed in the excitement of Christmas, of carolers, glittering balls in whites, greens, reds, and blues, excited children, people wearing antler headbands and Santa caps. They joined his mother for lunch at the Jungle Room, where James ogled the wild animals. At Glenmirril, there would be only holly, garlands, candles, and Mass.

"See," Amy said, as they filled his mother's car with their new purchases. "Ben didn't call. I told you it would be fine. On to set up, you you could live without your phone. Break a leg!" She kissed him and he headed to his Jaguar and last concert.

Inverness, Present

The moniker *Butcher of Berwick*, Angus read, *arose from the Sack of Berwick. Legend says Edward called off the slaughter only when he saw one of his men hacking a woman to death in the very act of giving birth. Local tradition names that man as Simon Beaumont, Lord of Claverock.*

The picture that accompanied the article showed a stocky, swarthy man. It proved nothing. There'd been no photographer to capture his likeness. But there had been artists, and the similarity to Simon was disturbing. Angus stared at the picture, tapping his pen on the edge of his desk. He knew what he believed. But did he have any real proof? He spun suddenly, yanking a sheet of paper from the printer and jotted a list in short, sharp strokes, of what he knew.

Glenmirril searcher, Simon, and Seamus P. Martin are the same man.

Seamus/Simon attacked Eamonn. Why?

Simon's accent is somewhat like medieval accents on YouTube.

He stopped. YouTube? Had he come down so far as to make critical decisions based on YouTube videos? On the guesses of modern men as to how a medieval accent *might* have sounded? They were educated guesses—but still *guesses*. Besides, accents varied greatly, town to town and century to century. To say a man had a medieval accent was as meaningless as to say he had a modern accent. Leave that a moment, he told himself, and continued his list.

A man was dragged off the battlefield in medieval gear—not a re-enactor.

Again, Angus stopped. Eyewitness accounts could conflict greatly. Maybe the police had missed the one actor who knew the man dragged off the field. Maybe someone had been at the field—like Niall had been—who was not on any list. Angus frowned. Of course, Niall *had*, in fact, been in the wrong century. Still, someone *could* have joined the actors. Lack of identification hardly proved time travel. But it brought him to his next points.

Man dragged off field spoke gibberish. Medieval English? Didn't understand modern English. It proved nothing. But it hinted at yet another connection. Angus put the pen back to paper: *Overly interested in Amy. Knew about translation linking Glenmirril to strange events. Could read medieval English!*

Angus frowned. The man *claimed* to read medieval English. Had he lied about the translation because he *couldn't*? But then why claim to in the first palace? He knew one more thing, Angus thought. Simon, *whoever* he was, took far too great an interest in Amy, Monadhliath, and Glenmirril.

He made a separate column labeled *What I don't know:*

That Simon is the man dragged off the field. That Simon attacked Carol.

But the descriptions fit in all cases. They were only descriptions, he reminded himself. He scanned his lists and knew he couldn't avoid it. Copying then into an e-mail, he added Shawn's address, and hit *send*.

He stared at the screen as the e-mail blinked away. Simon had killed a woman and helpless child in the very act of birth. An e-mail wasn't enough. He should call Amy. But Shawn had asked him not to alarm her. She would be gone at least through Hogmanay anyway. As long as she was safe, it was best to avoid contact with her. He picked up his phone, stabbing Shawn's name. It rang repeatedly, before taking him to voicemail. "It's Angus," he said tersely. "The attacker is from Niall's time, I'm sure of it. Don't let Amy or James come back here." He stopped, his voice threatening to break, cleared his throat and said, "He'll kill them both.

Don't let them back here." He hung up, wishing he could have spoken directly to Shawn. But a man like Shawn would check his phone frequently.

Outside, the wind whistled, loud enough to be heard through the brick walls. Angus rose to pour coffee, glad he didn't have to be out there today, and dropped back into his chair, staring at the picture of Amy and James. Much as he disliked the eejit, Angus trusted that Shawn, more than anyone in the modern world, was equipped to protect her from Simon...and would.

Midwest America, Present

"Maple Grove?" Ben groused. They stood behind velvet curtains, on a high school stage, waiting with the eighteen member big band while the audience filled up a room full of tables set for dinner. Fifty dollars a head, half of it to the education department. "Who ever heard of Maple Grove? Why are we playing here?"

Shawn swung the trombone in his left hand, eager to start. Amy had been right. He hadn't needed his phone. Ben had everything under control as always, and he'd arrived to find things moving without a hitch. Ben's grousing was par for the course. Just as well he hadn't had his phone, or he'd have had to listen to it all day at the Mall. "I went to school here," he said. "It's called giving back."

"It's called *not cost efficient*," Ben retorted. "Who the hell *lives* in Maple Grove? Or *Billings*? They don't have big enough audiences to justify the expense of hauling a big band here."

In their seats, the musicians glanced over, and returned to their chatter.

"Making an effort for people is always cost efficient," Shawn replied. "The Laird said so."

"Who the hell is the laird? *What* the hell is a laird?" Ben asked.

Shawn sighed. "Just a saying." He really had to watch what came out of his mouth, he thought.

"But what's a laird?"

"You never heard of a laird? They're Scottish clan chiefs."

Ben's sarcasm burned like a torch in the dim backstage. "And you know a lot of Scottish clan chiefs dishing out pearls of wisdom, do you?" He glanced up and down Shawn's medieval clothing.

"Only the one, really." He moved his slide up and down, testing it. Smooth as Trombone Shorty. From beyond the heavy curtain came the rising chatter of the audience. Another sold out performance, despite the incident with Cassie.

"Where *were* you for a year?" Ben exploded. The drummer looked over at them, scratched his ear and turned away, trying not to listen. "Sultans! Easter Island! Medieval Scotland! Why are you so *difficult?*"

"I'm not trying to be," Shawn said mildly. "I just don't have a story that makes sense to anyone. What does that leave me to say?"

"The truth! How hard is it to tell the *truth!*"

"Does it matter?" Shawn asked wearily. "As long as I'm cranking out money and paying you well?"

"Do you know how many people hound *me* for an answer?" Ben demanded. "Reporters, family, friends, anyone connected to me professionally. They all think *I* know something. Why can't you just tell me and tell them and maybe they'll all shut up? What is it, something you're embarrassed about? Although nothing would have embarrassed the man I knew." He snapped his fingers suddenly. "Alcohol rehab! Sex addicts rehab. That would explain the change in you, right?"

Shawn sighed. "So would two years in medieval Scotland."

"You were only gone a year." Ben eyed Shawn's tawny breeks and leather boots laced to the knee. "You forgot the vest," he said dryly. The high school band director stuck his head backstage, beckoning, and Ben grunted, "Showtime." He stepped through the curtains to a smattering of applause.

Behind the curtains, Shawn gave a thumb's up to the drummer, and grinned at the trombones. He danced on the balls of his feet, wanting to be moving, playing. He listened as Ben gave a blessedly short introduction, then bounded through the curtains, into waves of cheering, that filled him and breathed life into him. They packed the high school's lunch room at table after table in crisp white linen, while band students in black delivered salads to old women, couples, young men who looked like they played football, housewives with children.

Every one of them smiled; their hands pounded together, thundering applause —for him. Someone whistled. Shawn beamed, he and the audience feeding off each other, energy rising exponentially, till the stage vibrated beneath the leather soles of his boots. Shawn raised his hand for silence. They kept clapping.

"So we came here...." He leaned into the microphone, waited for the shush to fall, and tried again. "We came here today to talk about why we put so much time and energy and money into music education." It was a departure from his usual talk. They quieted, straining to hear.

"Why does music matter?" he said softly into the microphone. "It doesn't save lives." He made eye contact with several in the audience, holding their gaze. "We don't fight wars. We don't face hardship." He looked from one to another, letting silence give weight to his words. "But music makes our lives better." He walked the width of the stage, letting the words sink in. "Music was important enough that Glenn Miller died taking music to our troops in World War II."

His heart turned to the night before Bannockburn, and he wondered, as he often had, if his music had aided their victory. Bruce had chosen and prepared the land with military genius, but he liked to think he'd played his part for men facing an army four times their size. He thought of Niall playing his harp in famine-ridden, war-torn Ireland.

A tentative pair of hands clapped, questioningly. Shawn came back to the present, realizing with a shock that he'd been standing silent at the microphone, lost in a different world. When he looked at the crowd staring back at him, now with chicken and potatoes, they burst into assured applause. He grinned at them as if he'd intended a dramatic pause, stepped back with a snap of his fingers and, "A one, a two, a one, two, three, four," as the curtains swung open, and the waiting jazz band burst into the rapid-fire opening of *Opus One*. He lifted his trombone and joined in, strutting before the band. He stepped back for Elinore to take her solo at the piano, and for Al on the trumpet to screech out higher and higher notes, till the audience laughed at the effect.

"Nothing like starting the night on a high note," Shawn wisecracked, and it delighted the audience as much his antics ever had.

They finished the night with excitement, audience and musicians alike. Shawn's spirits soared. They still loved him. After an hour of signing autographs, of meeting and greeting, he helped pack the tour bus, loading drums, mics, and stands as snow shimmered down in the parking lot lights, laughing with the other musicians, until one by one they climbed on the bus.

"You did it!" In the bus's stairwell, Ben beamed. "I'm proud of you, Shawn!"

Shawn grinned. "Here's to the next one!" He shook Ben's hand, waved as the bus rolled out, and headed around the school for his car, eager to get back to Amy and James, at his mother's house. Despite his mistakes, they'd cheered him, feted him. He stopped, looking up into great flakes of white floating in the parking lot lights, against a pink winter sky. He was fixing the harm he'd done Cassie. He would fix any other damage he'd caused. *Thank you,* he thought.

The moment was shattered by the sound of smashing glass, and heavy crunch of metal. He burst into headlong flight, skidding around the school, to see a large man with a sledgehammer attacking his Jaguar. "Hey!" Shawn shouted. "That's my car!"

The man swung the hammer down, panting. It came to rest by his feet. As white flakes swirled into his hair, he shouted, "Be glad it's your car and not your face!"

Inverness, Present

As the coffee swirled, rich and black, to the rim of Angus's mug, his phone rang. He reached for it, as he sipped the invigorating brew. Hazelnut, he thought. Claire must have bought it. The station stocked basic black. "Inspector MacLean." He spoke into the phone.

"MacLean," came the chief's voice. "How'd you like to do a little hill-walking?"

Angus set the mug down beside the damp hat. Everything in him revolted at the thought of going out. "It's a particularly poor day for bagging munros."

"Well, now, you've more sense in your one head than the four boys between them who decided to do just that. We've got one frantic mother on the phone saying they went out yesterday and aren't back. How fast can you get the team out there?"

Berwick, 1317

With a message sent home to Glenmirril regarding the absent orchards, Niall devoted himself to his work. He could do no more, from such distance. He almost forgot MacDougall as his weeks wore away in the dull business of siege warfare, and the eternal drizzle that continued to destroy crops. With engines, cats, and belfries built, and tens of thousands of arrows honed, Bruce's men closed in on Berwick. The siege ground on with dull predictability, a few skirmishes, and scattered exchanges of rocks flung between trebuchets inside the town and out. The belfries sank in the mud, never coming near enough the walls of Berwick to help Bruce's army. Lachlan led the men in piling straw and wood and anything they could find, into the moat to fill it in and give them a crossing. Everything sank.

As Niall stood beside the muddy moat that swallowed all their hard work, two men of the cloth, lifting their fine hems out of the mud with distaste, approached Lachlan. Niall paused, a bundle of hay on his shoulder, watching. After a brief interchange, Lachlan led them to Niall. "Sir Niall." He bowed, handing Niall a letter. "From home," he said, then nodded toward the two men. "They come from cardinals Jocelin and Luke. They've a message for our king."

With a glance at the Laird's strong script on the outside of the letter, Niall pushed it into his belt and turned to the messengers. One was tall and thin with a rich cap of brown curls, only a bit older than Niall himself. The other stood several inches shorter, and appeared to have eaten well during these years of famine. Wisps of gray hair clung to his nearly-bald pate. Jocelin and Luke were friends of the Pope—who had been no friend of the Bruce, despite Bruce's love for the Church. Even now, Niall knew, the relics of a Saint or two resided in Bruce's tent with him. Niall glanced to the walls, assuring himself no archers had appeared, and, conscious of his filthy state beside their finery, asked, "Your names?"

"Master Aumery," the younger introduced himself, "and the Bishop of Corbeil."

"Come with me." Niall led them through the maze of men, catapults, and bales of hay; through tents, and men cooking on griddles over open fires. The bishop lifted a kerchief to his nose. Master Aumery stepped carefully through the mud, lifting his hem higher. "I trust you had a good journey?" Niall said.

The bishop coughed delicately.

"We traveled with the bishop-elect," Master Aumery said. "We were accosted by bandits and our money stolen." His tone left little to guess as to his feelings toward the Scots. "They are holding the bishop—the *bishop!*—for ransom!"

"My condolences." Niall kept his face impassive. A bishop's ransom would fund the war effort for a long time. "I trust you are unhurt."

The bishop snorted derisively. "If one calls being accosted *unhurt.*"

"You are not injured?"

"We are not," Master Aumery said. "And they left our papers to us."

"'Tis glad I am to hear it." Niall smiled. It had Bruce's mark all over it. Whoever had accosted the clerics wanted only money and had had no intention of harming their persons.

Niall found Bruce hauling on the arm of a catapult, shouting to the men on the other side. He turned, wiping his hands. "Sir Niall." He looked at the two men.

"Clergy sent by Cardinals Jocelin and Luke," Niall said. "The Bishop of Corbeil and Master Aumery."

Bruce waited.

The two men looked at one another. Finally, Aumery bowed.

"Join me for refreshment," Bruce said. "Sir Niall, send for Douglas, Moray, and my lords and barons."

Niall bowed. "Aye, Your Grace." As the king and clergymen left, he searched the wide swath of army for the nobles. The scowls on the barons' faces bore proof of the Scots' mistrust of the church in England, as they flowed by twos and threes to meet with the clerics.

At Bruce's headquarters, Niall found Bruce, in his tabard and crown, chatting over mead with Douglas and Moray. Bruce waited until the barons settled, before turning to the clerics, who stood in the middle of the three heavy wooden tables full of heavily bearded Scots, scanning their surroundings anxiously.

"Tell us," Bruce said, "why our good cardinals have sent you to my humble home."

Niall noted the twinkle in his eye. The cardinals, and these clergymen, were used to far better than a war camp.

The bishop stepped forward, pulling himself as tall as he could from his plump shape. Taking a parchment from his cloak, he read a lengthy call for peace, while the lords exchanged looks of growing irritation. Bruce lounged in his makeshift throne, with amused patience, till the priest concluded, "The Pope pleads for peace among his children." He lifted his eyes expectantly to Bruce.

Bruce sat, with furrowed brows for a time, before saying, "Give us a moment."

Guards escorted the clerics out. Barely had the door closed, when the barons' voices erupted. "Peace!" bellowed Moray. "They ask for *peace*, as if we ourselves have not requested it over and over!"

"Edward had but to say the word!" Douglas's heavy black brows drew down.

"'Twill do but little to remind them of this," said Moray. "Throw them out, Your Grace."

Nods went around the assembly.

"Summon them." Bruce smoothed his tabard with the prancing lion. His crown shone in the afternoon sun piercing through the hall's tall arched windows.

The clerics returned, guards behind them. They cast anxious glances at the weapons in the room, before their eyes fell on Bruce's benign countenance.

"We are in accord with our Holy Father." Bruce leaned toward the two trembling men. "'Tis what I have offered England many a time, on the easiest of terms. Has the Pope sent an emissary to Edward to tell him he must stay out of our country?"

De Soulis laid his dirk on his knee, smoothing a hand over its blade.

The priests exchanged nervous glances. "We've only the message given us."

Master Aumery reached into his robes. "Cardinals Jocelin and Luke have sent you a personal message from the Pope." He stretched a creamy parchment, sealed with wax, out to Bruce.

Bruce gave a nod to Niall, who left his seat, took it from the priest's hand, and, on one knee, offered it to his king. Bruce accepted it, studied the elegant script on the back, and looked up with a genial smile. "My apologies for your troubles, my good fathers. But I cannot accept this. It is not addressed to me."

Confusion flitted across the Bishop's face. "It is addressed to Robert Bruce.

Surely that is you?"

Bruce's smile grew. "I am. However, it is addressed to *Robert Bruce governing in Scotland.* Among my barons, there are many of the name of Robert Bruce, who share in the government of Scotland. These letters may possibly be addressed to some one of them, but they are not addressed to me, for *I* am King of Scots. I can receive no letters not addressed to me under that title, unless with the advice of my parliament. I shall assemble my parliament, and with their advice return my answer."

"My Lord." The bishop stepped forward. A shuffle of steel accompanied him. He looked frantically from the restless Scottish lords to Bruce's pleasant smile. "I do apologize for the address. Please understand, Holy Mother Church is eager not to say or write aught which might be interpreted as prejudicial to the claims of either of the contending parties."

Bruce's smile slipped only a little, as he said, "Since my spiritual father and holy mother would not prejudice the cause of my adversary by bestowing on me the appellation of King during the controversy, they ought not to have prejudiced *my* cause by *withdrawing* the appellation." He leaned forward, his eyes stern. "For I am in possession of the Kingdom of Scotland. My people call me King. Foreign princes address me under that title. But it seems my parents are partial to their English son." He looked from one to the other. "Had you presumed to present letters with such an address to any other sovereign Prince, you might perhaps have been answered in harsher style. But I reverence you as the messengers of the Holy See."

The bishop took a step back. Master Aumery cleared his throat. "We but brought the message, Your Grace. Will you not consent, at least, to temporary cessation of hostilities?"

"I can by no means consent without the advice of my parliament." Bruce raised an eyebrow. "Especially while the English are in the daily practice of spoiling the property of my subjects and invading all parts of my realm."

Douglas rose, tapping his dirk in his palm, and approached the priests, who pressed close together like a pair of frightened sheep. Douglas circled them once, twice, and stopped before them. He waited until they raised their eyes, before saying, "Had these letters been properly addressed to the king of Scots, negotiations would immediately have been re-opened."

"I believe," said de Soulis, rising from his seat, "there is *intrigue* between the English court and the Pope."

"Oh, no, my Lord," the bishop said hastily.

"None!" Master Aumery protested.

"And yet," said Douglas, stepping closer to the priests, so that they took another step backward, "it seems we are ordered to make peace while England— who invaded our land, butchered our people at Berwick, killed our priests and nuns, pillaged and massacred and burned—is not."

"I think it best you depart now." De Soulis picked idly at his nails with his knife blade, a smile tilting one corner of his mouth.

The priests looked once more to Bruce. "My Lord?"

"I am not your lord," Bruce said evenly. No hint of humor remained. "I am *Your Grace*." He rose to his feet, and all his court with him, and spoke more forcefully, still. "*King of Scots*." Around the room, blades slid from sheaths before Robert spoke again, softly. "When you bring a letter addressed to the King of Scots, I shall be happy to read it. I suggest you go before my men find their tempers short."

The unfortunate clerics bowed and hurried out.

CHAPTER THIRTY-SEVEN

Scottish Highlands, Present

"We were told there were four." Angus addressed the tallest of the three boys they'd found holed up in a shelter they'd built of snow against the mountainside. They were sorely under-dressed, even considering they'd expected to be back before the snow hit. The boy shivered in the Mylar blanket Clive had thrown over his shoulders. Wind howled across the mountainside. Clive hunched into it, yanking his scarf up and pounding his hands together. Angus wished they'd gotten the call even ten minutes earlier. The weather was turning fast. "Where's the fourth?"

"He s-slipped over the s-side," the boy managed to say through chattering teeth.

Angus groaned, already summoning his crew together to follow the boy's directions. "Why didn't you bring jackets?" he asked another boy.

"W-we did," he said. "But we p-passed two of ours to him so he wouldn't freeze. We figured we could stay warm together inside." He gestured to their snow fort.

"Aw' right, you may have saved his life," Angus conceded, and to one of his team, "Get something hot in them, and get back out here to see what we can do." He pulled his collar up against the gusting wind, an eye to the gray sky. The sooner they got this boy out, the better.

His team brought his rappelling equipment. "Can you see him?" he asked, as they laid out ropes and clips, ready to help him descend.

Clive, on his knees at the edge, looked up. "'Tis not far a' tall. He's waving. Looks pale, but I think he's all right, considering."

Angus wiggled into his harness that would see him down safely down the cliff, and in minutes, was eight feet down the mountainside, squeezed on a narrow ledge with a teenage boy bundled in two jackets and sitting on a third.

"I'm good," he called up to Clive. "Though he's fortunate. Past this ledge, 'tis a much sharper drop." He turned to the boy. "I take it you've spent more comfortable nights." He dug in a pocket for a flask of hot cocoa, and with bulky gloved fingers, unscrewed the lid. "What's your name?"

"Ewan. It's me leg." His chalk-white face showed relief at sight of the bottle.

"Careful, now, it's hot," Angus warned. He thought of Amy, so many months

ago at the monastery, reeling from the brandy he'd given her after she'd seen
Shawn in the church. He smiled, remembering how she'd thrown herself at him,
wondering what path their lives would have followed had he accepted. Maybe
she'd be waiting at home for him, even now. Then again, he thought, feeling the
boy's leg gently, maybe his heart would only be cut that much more deeply to know
she could share that with him and go back to Shawn anyway. His fingers settled on
the break, feeling through the boy's jeans how the leg bent where it ought not.
Ewan let out a groan.

Angus dug in his gear for an analgesic lozenge. "It'll dull the pain," he said, as
the boy took it. "You're going to want that when we lift you out of here." He
probed again, hating the pain he knew he was inflicting.

"How are you getting on?" Clive called down.

"We can't lift him like this," Angus called back. "The leg's broken too badly."

"Can you splint it?"

"I've no choice," Angus shouted up the face of the cliff. He glanced over his
shoulder to the long drop behind, and up again to Clive, holding the rope above.
He swung the pack off his back, edging over to make room for it, and touched
Ewan's leg again. Ewan jolted in pain, flinging out an arm.

Angus, squatting at the edge, lost his balance. He gave a shout as he tumbled
backwards into open space. The rope jarred him, snapping his head and bringing
him up short. As he struggled to steady himself against the cliff wall, he heard a
slow hiss. He grappled for the rope above him, as he realized with horror—his
harness was slowly tearing apart at the seams! He looked frantically below to the
long drop, and tried to wrap his hands around the rope. Suddenly the harness tore
apart, leaving him tumbling head over heels into the chasm, shouting for help.

Midwest America, Present

Shawn stared in shock, in the dim light shining down from the light posts.
"Mr. Olsen? *Brian's dad?*" He gestured at his car. "*Why?*"

"You can't figure it out?" The man glared, breathing heavily like a bull about
to charge.

"Brian was my best friend all through school!" Rage raised its head, a roaring
monster, Nessie bursting in fury from the loch. "Why would you do this to me?"

"I guess you got too big to bother about Brian anymore."

"So we drifted apart the last few years," Shawn shouted, goaded. "So you
destroy my car? What the hell is wrong with you?"

"Drifted apart so far you didn't even notice he was gone." He spoke bitterly,
lifting the hammer for another swing.

Shawn threw himself at Mr. Olsen, wrestling for the weapon. It was far easier
than fighting the Gascons. The older man fought viciously, swinging the hammer
at Shawn's face. Shawn grabbed it behind its head, wrenched it, and flung it across
the parking lot, resisting the urge to bash the man's head with it. Mr. Olsen panted,
his hands on his knees. "Now what!" he demanded, glaring up at Shawn. "I've
heard about that temper of yours. You want to finish it off, just like you did my

son?"

"What the hell are you talking about?" Shawn demanded. "Brian was my best friend. Didn't he just get married and have a kid? We used to have a great time."

"A great time *drinking*!"

His words, his tone, stilled the anger in Shawn—diminished chords humming in the background. Mr. Olsen had warned them sternly, the one time he'd caught them. They'd learned to be more careful—careful not to get caught.

"I knew what you were going through, Shawn." Snow fell in the man's hair, turning it white, flake by flake. His shoulders stooped as his anger drained. "I felt for you. I tried to help. You wouldn't listen."

The warning chord crescendoed. "What does this have to do with Brian?"

"He kept going, just like you did. Loved every one of your stories on Facebook. Your parties you talked about on those interviews. He looked up to you."

"What happened?" Shawn demanded.

"You always came out on top. He thought he would, too. He was drunk." The man's voice cracked. "Swerved in front of a semi."

Shawn closed his eyes. The cold night air froze in his lungs. "When?" The word came out in a frosty puff that hovered before his face.

"Seven months ago."

Shawn stayed in the darkness behind his eyelids, calculating—it had been while he was in 1316. Brian had driven a Cooper Mini. His own voice floated somewhere above him. "Is he okay?"

"Oh, yeah, he's *fine*." The man's voice was flat. "If you consider dead *fine*."

Berwick, 1317

In the cool evening, with the fire snapping cheerfully, Niall set aside his harp. His music had soothed the worst of the anger over the legates' visit, as the men sang of battles and love. As they drifted away for the night, he pulled the letter from his tunic, studying the Laird's strong hand that addressed it. Letters might bring good news. Or bad. He thought of his last night with Allene, his trips to the wee bit of shore with James, and holding William in his arms in the window sill where Shawn had loved to sit. He played them in his mind, tasting the sweetness of each moment, lest the Laird's letter shatter the joy, and cast those memories down into the grave.

His pondered the dichotomy of the miracle on the battlefield and the woman and child dead in the Irish town. He stared at the Laird's script, wondering which this letter brought—battlefield miracles, or famine deaths—and struggling to understand why the God who granted the one allowed the other.

Across the small clearing, two of the men from Glenmirril talked softly. Niall felt, before he saw, someone loom over him, and turned.

Hugh sank down on the log beside him. "A letter from home?"

Niall nodded. "He sent you one, too?" He swatted at buzzing midges.

Hugh grinned, nodding.

The tension in Niall's heart loosened. "'Tis good news, then?"

"Not bad." Hugh clapped Niall on the shoulder. "Quit your fashing, and read it."

Niall broke the wax seal and unfolded the paper carefully. Another letter, from Allene, nestled inside. He tucked it in his shirt, saving it for last. Evening fell earlier now, and the rich velvet sky and dancing shadows of the firelight made it hard to read even the Laird's firm hand. Niall liked it that way. It let him enjoy the taste of home that much longer, savoring each word.

Christina reveled in her son, and had played to perfection the surprise at being asked to take on a foundling. Lachlan's sister had wed. Ronan had requested the hand of the widow Muirne. Niall smiled. They would make one another happy. His care for her had long been evident. The rain had eased, finally, and the crops, though not plentiful, were better than they'd been in two years.

Niall barely noticed Hugh rise and wander away. Every curling letter wrapped Glenmirril warmly around his heart, taking him away from the pounding and yelling and flying arrows of the siege. MacDougall remained peaceable. Roger made no further attempt to communicate. That, too, sat wrong with the Laird, and he had no notion, either, why MacDougall might speak of orchards his glen did not have, but all seemed quiet. *I pray daily in the Bat Cave for the good of all,* he finished. *Blessings on you, my son.*

There was nothing to explain Hugh's grin.

The men had rolled into their tartans. The chirping of insects filled the night. Niall gazed up past the dark shapes of trees, swaying in the breeze, to the pinpricks of light in the velvet sky. He smiled at Shawn's explanation of stars as masses of fire and gas. He preferred his own view of them as lights shining from heaven.

Finally, he opened Allene's letter and read, even more slowly than the dying firelight forced him to. He wanted it to last forever, hearing her voice in the written words, seeing her pale, slender hand on the same parchment his hands now touched. James learned ever more words, in both Gaelic and English. William pulled himself to his feet, and delighted, like James, in going to the shore. Niall smiled, thinking maybe, just maybe, when he got home, he'd stand in the water with them, up to his knees even, show them, as Shawn had shown Hugh, how to put their faces in, to be unafraid, to float.

He closed his eyes, lost in the happy memory of Shawn and Hugh in the water of an evening, while MacDonald on the walls above, kept the guards from witnessing the swimming lessons. *Breathe out, sing,* he'd said. Niall wondered if he'd married Amy as he'd sworn he would, if they had a second child, perhaps, too.

He swatted at the midges stirring around his face, and poked a stick in the fire to raise more light. There was only a page left. He didn't want it to end. He shifted the top page to the back, tasting each word about Christina, Margaret, Muirne, because each was written by Allene's hand. *And my dear,* she wrote, at the end, *God has blessed your brief stay. I am with child. In February, we shall have a third.*

That was the cause of Hugh's grin! He'd known. Niall felt the smile spread across his face, even as the worry set in. Childbirth could kill a woman. Worry, pride, and joy danced a trio in his stomach. He wanted to shout out to the sleeping men, *I'm going to be a father! Again!* He merely stared at the words, grinning.

May God watch over you, and bring you home safe, Allene's fine script whispered. He almost felt her fingers touch his face, his ear, her breath flutter against his cheek, as it had when she'd whispered the same words to him, leaning up as he sat astride his horse, ready to cross the drawbridge at dawn. He folded the letter, tucked it inside his shirt against his heart, and curled into his tartan, next to the dying fire.

War killed men. And the clerics' insult to the Bruce today guaranteed war would continue. He prayed he, too, would be alive when their child was born. He sank, finally, into dreams of a restless shadow, prowling Bruce's camp, calling his name, over and over, warning him—warning him.

Inverness, Present

Claire returned to her desk from watering the fern in Inspector MacLean's office. She tipped the can over the plant on her own desk, and smiled at Judy. "Got your prezzies all bought, then?"

Judy rolled her eyes. "Five nephews, now, that's a lot of trucks and rugby gear!" She laughed. "I'd not miss it for the world. Yourself?"

"I've two nieces, all into make-up and nail polish. Easy to shop for, at least." She laughed, adding, "Their mum despairs, and wishes they'd like a nice engineering set, which is why they like gifts from me." She cast an eye at the snow swirling heavily outside the station's glass doors.

"It's getting worse," Judy commented, noting her look. "I'd hoped to hear from Inspector MacLean by now. The mother has called back twice, absolutely frantic."

"He'll be fine," Claire said. But her voice came out weak. She cleared her throat and spoke more forcefully. "He's the best at what he does." She rounded her desk, and tapped at her keyboard. She had e-mail reminders to send out to all the staff about the Christmas party this evening. Angus would be there. Surely, with Christmas nearly here, and Amy in America with her boyfriend, he'd relent. She'd bought a new dress, black and sparkly and cut to show off her legs.

"He'll need to be, and have a couple angels good at what they do, too."

"He'll be *fine*," Claire said more forcefully, but she glanced out the doors, where snow blew in straight lines. A passerby bent into the wind, clutching a hat to his head, and gripping his scarf to his chest.

The phone jangled suddenly on her desk. She jumped, then gave a little laugh at her own nerves, and lifted it. Her hand trembled. It was just Judy's warnings getting to her, she told herself. "Precinct office, this is Claire," she said.

"Claire." It took her a second to realize she was hearing Clive's voice. It shook. "Get the rest of the team and the heavy equipment out here as fast as you can. Call the team from Fort William, too."

"Who is it?" Her voice came out a dry whisper.

"Angus." His voice broke. "As fast as you can, Claire. He needs help."

She nodded and dropped the phone in the receiver. Her hands shook as she pulled up the numbers on the computer and lifted the phone again.

Midwest America, Present

Shawn knelt by the stone, snow soaking his trews. Mr. Olsen stood over him. Shawn brushed the dusting of flakes off the grave marker, revealing the name *Brian Michael Olsen* and the two dates with barely twenty-five years between them. *Beloved Husband, Father, Son.* He'd last seen Brian the Christmas before the orchestra went to Scotland. Three years ago in his life, two by the world's reckoning. He'd called Brian two days before Christmas, saying, "Let's go out."

Brian had laughed. "Come on, Shawn, I've got a wife, and a baby due any day."

"Getting old," Shawn chided. "She's fine for one night. She'll call if it's born."

"She asked me to quit, Shawn. Come over for eggnog and a movie. She'd love to meet you."

"I'm not sitting around like an old man," Shawn complained. "Life is about having fun!"

"I really want to quit, Shawn."

"Come on," Shawn wheedled. "One drink for old time's sake. I thought you got yourself a wife, not a ball and chain."

Brian gave in, laughing. "Just one, though."

One drink became two, two became four. A trip to a bar became a stop at Déjà Vu downtown, and another couple of drinks. He'd trundled Brian into his Jaguar somewhere between hysterical laughter and passing out, and weaved his way to Brian's apartment, to deliver a happy and wobbly Brian to his wife, laughing at her annoyance. Brian vomited in his entryway.

"Are you going to clean that up?" his wife snapped.

"You'll be happier if I get home before I vomit, too," he told her cheerfully, and walked away, leaving Brian snoring on the floor, while his heavily pregnant wife tried to pull him far enough in to shut the door.

Heat flamed up Shawn's face, as he knelt by Brian's grave. He tried to imagine the face he'd known, the nutmeg brown curls and square jaw and laughing eyes, still and somber beneath the snow. He didn't want to think what a collision with a semi had done.

"How old is his son?" he whispered.

"Two tomorrow. Christmas Eve. He won't even remember his father."

Shawn traced the indents that spelled *Brian* with a finger numb in the December cold. The collision had happened nearly a year and a half after that last drunken get-together. He'd had nothing to do with it.

Mr. Olsen laid his hand on Shawn's shoulder. "I know it wasn't you directly." His voice cracked. Shawn looked up. Tears rolled silently down Mr. Olsen's face.

Shawn shook his head, numb all over, not knowing what to say. If he wasn't responsible, in any way, for Brian's choices—then Clarence wasn't responsible, in any way, for his. But Clarence *was* responsible. For him, for this. He closed his eyes, the indents in the stone cold under his fingers, trying to believe it.

"I tried to help you, Shawn." Brian's father spoke in short gasps. "After your father died. For your sake. For Brian's." His voice broke. "I shouldn't have done that to your car. I'm sorry."

The hand slid off his shoulder, and some time later, Shawn realized he knelt alone in the dark cemetery, snow coating his shoulders in white, wishing he'd watched a movie with Brian and his wife that night. Wishing Brian were here to watch a movie with tonight. He could fix the house for Cassie. He couldn't fix this, ever, no matter how many albums he sold.

Inverness, Present

Claire backed against the wall, watching in horror as orderlies lowered a gurney from the ambulance, and raced it through the hospital's glass doors. She caught only a glimpse of Angus, in his heavy rescue jacket, an oxygen mask clamped over his face, as the medics ran. A doctor appeared in scrubs, shouting and running after them. If they were running, she thought, he was still alive. It had been hours since Clive had called. None of the updates had been good.

The doors slid open again with a soft swish. Clive and the rest of the team burst through in their heavy snow gear. Clive saw her. She pointed after the running medical team, not trusting herself to speak, and they hurtled down the hall after him.

"Claire?"

She turned to see Judy coming down the hall with a Styrofoam cup in each hand.

"Come on," Judy soothed. "Have a cuppa, and we'll go to the chapel and pray."

Claire nodded numbly, accepting the hot cup into her hands. Then she shook her head. "Clive won't know where to find me."

"We'll pray," Judy repeated. "Then I'll find Clive. All right? Now, it's the best we can do for him. You come with me."

Claire nodded again, her brain thrashing in the nettles of shock in which it had been caught for hours. This couldn't happen. *Not to Angus.* She let herself be led through a maze of halls, past somber visitors and chatting nurses, sipping now and again at the coffee. She'd started drinking hazelnut, Angus's favorite, and missed it.

"Here we are." Judy pushed open a wooden door the color of soft honey, and ushered her to a bench covered in a red velvet cushion. A silver cross hung at the front of the room above a small altar. A single candle flickered under it, and from somewhere came the soft burble of running water, as calming as harp music.

Slowly, the shock subsiding, Claire's focus settled on the cross. "He made it this far," she said.

"Aye, he did," Judy agreed. "Our Angus is tough. A little fall won't stop him."

"He was out in this weather all night. Might he have frostbite?"

"He might," Judy said. "Frostbite won't kill a man." She patted Claire's arm. "He's here, he's breathing, Claire. They're taking good care of him."

They fell to sipping their coffee, while Claire's thoughts churned out two words in a steady rhythm like the clack of a train on a track. *Please, God. Please, God.*

Judy squeezed Claire's shoulders. "I'll go find Clive."

Claire nodded, her eyes locked on the cross. She barely registered the soft click of the door behind her, as the words *Please, God* circled through her mind. The world wouldn't be the same without Angus.

It seemed a long time later she heard the door open again. Clive settled his bulk on the bench beside her. He looped his arm around her shoulder.

"Is he alive?" she whispered, terrified of the answer.

"Just barely," Clive said, and she'd never heard him sound so sad.

She looked up at him. His face was red with wind burn, his eyes red with grief. "Is there anything I can do?" she asked.

He handed her a small bag. "Find his parents and tell them."

She glanced in the bag. It contained Angus's cell phone, keys, and change. "What can I do to help *Angus*?"

"I think what will decide his fate," Clive said slowly, "is the will to live. He needs the people he loves at his side." He pushed himself heavily from the bench. "I've calls and paperwork to deal with. Thanks for coming, Claire."

She nodded, wondering what else he could possibly have expected from her. She lifted her eyes to the cross again. New words took up the place of the old ones. *He needs people he loves.* She stared at the few things in the bag. *He needs people he loves.* She pulled out his cell phone.

Midwest America, Present

"You're late," Amy said softly, as Shawn stumbled in. She sat in the rocker in his mother's living room. The flames from the fire crackled, casting a sheen on her satin peach robe. A thick braid hung over her shoulder. James slept in her arms, one hand protruding from the blanket and thrown across his brow. "Your mother went to bed."

Shawn slumped into the wing chair, still in his jacket, staring at James, at her, beautiful and waiting for him—for *him*. He didn't deserve her, not the way he'd lived. He didn't deserve James. Pain crushed his heart, piercing it, till he felt he could hardly breathe. He didn't deserve it. Somewhere, Brian's wife rocked her son alone. Brian would never walk in.

"Shawn?"

He didn't answer.

"Have you been drinking?" Amy's eyes narrowed.

He shook his head, squeezed his eyes, and dropped his head into his palms. Brian and Clarence circled one another in his head.

Amy rose. "We expected you five hours ago."

He lifted his head, tried to ask, *Where are you going,* but his tongue was thick in his mouth, his mind in shock. *He couldn't fix this!* No words came out. She started past him with James. He pushed himself out of the chair, trying to speak. He couldn't admit to her where he'd been.

She stopped, a hand to her nose. "You *have* been drinking."

"Amy...." He managed to croak the word out. "Please, this time...."

Her robe swirled around her feet, taking James down the hall. He followed her, his head spinning, sick to his stomach over Brian. She laid James in a bassinet, and yanked her suitcase from under her bed. "Some woman?"

"Amy, please."

She flipped the suitcase open, and jerked her head up. Color flushed her cheeks. "You know, I don't even care who it was this time."

"Brian."

Her eyebrows drew down fiercely. *"What?* Brian who?"

"My best friend—high school—college. Brian Olsen." He slumped into the wicker chair beside the dresser, swallowing the stale aftertaste of liquor. "We were at the cemetery."

Amy's arms became rigid. She whispered fiercely, "Let me get this straight. You and Brian spent five hours getting drunk in the snow in a cemetery two nights before Christmas? It's pretty sad, Shawn, when *I disappeared into medieval Scotland* is more believable than the garbage you come up with."

He shook his head, fighting the headache, fighting the nausea that rose every time he thought of Brian in the cold ground. "No," he whispered. "Brian is dead." His voice crumpled as his head dropped into his hands.

"Dead?" The pitch of her voice rose. "Tonight?"

"Every night. He died seven months ago. I was at his grave."

"Oh." Her voice fell; the peach robe and her feet swished into his view. She dropped to her knees in front of him. Her hands came to his face, lifting his bleary eyes to hers. "You've been out in the cold all this time?"

He nodded.

She pressed her hands around his, a brief moment of warmth, confirming it, and spun for a blanket from the closet. She seemed to notice, then, the dusting of snow on his shoulders, and brushed at it as she swung the blanket around him. "You just found out?"

He nodded again. "His dad was at my car." He couldn't say the rest. She might blame him, too. She'd already forgiven enough.

"What happened? Did he get murdered or something?"

He pushed at the blanket, pushed away her comforting hands, felt blindly for the door. He stopped in the hall, unsure momentarily where to go, and turned for his own room. He peeled off the wet jacket, dropping it on a chair, and sank, sitting on the bed, lost in memories. He had been the one to bring the alcohol, the first time he and Brian drank, out by the lake. His mother never suspected. He'd never done it before. He'd been the one to bring it the second time, and the third, convincing Brian each time it was no big deal, no harm done. He'd invited Brian to parties—drinking parties—throughout college.

"Shawn?" She was back.

He stared at her blankly.

Her hands fell on his shoulders. Her breath brushed his ear. "Tell me about it."

"You're going to hate me," he said.

"Why? You weren't even *there* seven months ago."

"You'll hate me."

"Going back to drinking isn't the answer. Trusting someone in this world is." She squeezed onto the bed beside him. Her arm crept around his back. She laid her head on his shoulder. "I saw your car. Is that how his dad told you?"

"Yeah."

"His dad blames you and you're afraid he's right."

Shawn nodded, grateful to be spared saying the words himself.

"You two drank a lot. Was it something to do with alcohol?"

Shawn nodded, whispering, "A semi."

She said nothing, but embraced him, cradled his head.

He rested there, trying to see through the alcohol. Niall, Allene, Christina— they'd all be unhappy with him taking this route. Amy offered comfort. Just this once, it was understandable. A trill came from somewhere beyond the gin-stained haze. *Pachelbel's Canon.*

Amy started. "Shawn, I have to get that. I'm sorry. I'll be right back."

CHAPTER THIRTY-EIGHT

Glenmirril, December 1318

"Join me for a game of chess, Taran." MacDougall peered through the bars of his door. "I've not seen you for some time."

The boy shook his head. "The Laird said no more chess."

MacDougall exaggerated a shrug. "I've shown myself to be a trustworthy and good-natured prisoner, have I not? But as you wish. We may as well both be bored as pass the time." He crossed to the window, looking down into the courtyard. As she did every morning, Christina emerged from the north tower in her blue cloak. Today, she carried linens to the kirk. The altar cloths she sewed, he guessed. She would certainly stay for Mass. He pictured her, kneeling, with her hair flowing down her back, her face at peace, and wished she would just once look up. He'd heard the guards whisper of the foundling discovered under a tree, and turned over to Christina to raise. A boy.

He watched the bailey. He could be ready when she returned from the kirk—if only Taran would enter the cell. Patience, he told himself. Taran, despite his youth, was no fool. And there was work to be done. His meal would come when the people of Glenmirril broke their fast—which guaranteed the passageways would be largely empty. Except, if he was lucky, for Christina. Allene would serve equally well, but he preferred Christina. Glancing to assure the bars in his cell door were covered, he pulled the makeshift knife and rope from under his bed. Eyes on the door, he loosened the leg from the table.

Soon, footsteps hurried down the hall, a soft brush of leather against stone, a swish of skirts, and a breathless voice. "Taran!"

"Marsailli," Taran said, and MacDougall heard his voice drop in pitch, the name stretched out. It meant one thing. MacDougall smiled. Taran would be cheerful, relaxed, when he brought the ale in. Off guard. The spindle came free. Clutching it in one hand, he seated himself on the bed with a book, staring at the page while straining for any piece of information they might drop outside.

They lowered their voices. The other guard spoke and laughed. Marsailli's giggle burst out, like a pigeon from a dovecote, and Taran shushed her. MacDougall swung the spindle at his side, testing its weight. Against an armed soldier, it was useless. Against a lovesick boy, it would do. It would do admirably. He hoped it was the lovesick boy, and not the soldier, who walked in. Niall and

MacDonald trained their men well. He would not get a second chance.

"I must go," the girl said in a breathless rush. "My Lady has warned me once not to tarry. She'll not abide it a second time."

There was a smile in Taran's voice as he said, "I'd not want you removed from ale duty. Hurry along!"

"It seems you've won our Marsailli's favor." Gregor chuckled.

"Aye," Taran said, in the husky voice of a lovesick boy.

MacDougall smiled. The unseen Marsailli had done him a great service. The key clicked in the lock. Taran drifted in, bearing the trencher and jug, grinning like a fool, his mind caught up in Marsailli.

MacDougall's hand swung up, his club catching Taran's temple, crumpling him. The jug smashed to the floor, ale exploding across the stones. MacDougall wrenched the knife from the boy's belt, storming the door as the older man burst in, sword drawn. MacDougall veered, grabbing his arm and spinning him, one hand clapping over his mouth as he drove his knife into his back. The man sagged to the floor.

MacDougall hauled Taran onto the bed, covering his prone form with a blanket. He took the keys off the other guard, pushed him under the bed, and left, locking the door behind him, his thoughts skipping ahead to Christina. He descended swiftly to the second floor and down the empty hall to the chambers where he'd found her so many months ago. Her room was empty. He opened the wardrobe, his hands lingering on each of the fine gowns, smiling as he thought of the days he'd watched her at Creagsmalan in her beautiful dresses.

But it wasn't what he'd come for.

At the far end, he found what he'd guessed he would: the gray robe worn by the monk who traveled with Niall, the monk who had not been seen since the battle, followed by lights in the sky and words called from the clouds. He slipped it from its peg and pulled it on. Lifting the cowl over his face, he slipped into the solar, just as the door flew open, and a woman entered cradling a baby.

Midwest America, Present

Shawn woke to winter sunshine flooding his room. Out of tune trumpets scraped his brain, making him sit up and grip his head. Worse, Brian's death scraped his mind raw. He threw himself back onto the pillow, palms to eyes, wanting it all to go away, trying to shut out the gravestone with Brian's name on it.

"Shawn?"

He lowered his hands carefully, squinting to control the sunlight flooding in and re-igniting the headache. Amy had held him last night, taken the edge off the grief. She'd be here, taking care of him as she always had. He rolled his head, peering through narrowed eyes at the door. His mother stood there.

He pushed himself up, fighting grogginess.

She studied him with pursed lips. "You know this wasn't the answer."

"The answer?" He swung his legs to the floor, trying to shake the kaleidoscope of unpleasant feelings.

"Amy told me what happened. I can't believe you went and got drunk again."

Shawn closed his eyes, breathing in deeply enough to pick a double-high E out of the blue. It was as bad as being back with the Laird and Niall. *Dry yer eyes,* he could almost hear Allene saying. *Quit yer greeting.* He risked opening his eyes. With the sun behind him, it wasn't so bad. "Where's Amy?" he asked.

"Get up and have coffee. Then we go for a drive."

Shawn raked his hand through his hair. His mother's stance, and the expression on her face, called to mind Douglas riding into battle. "What time is it?" It was mostly a ploy to stall the disagreeable act of standing up. He hadn't had a hangover in two and a half years, and didn't like it.

Her voice came out with the sting of a whip. "It's time to get up and shake this hangover. It was stupid! It hasn't helped Brian or you."

Harsh words sprang to his mind. But of all the people he'd never bullied—well, on second thought, *all the people he'd never bullied* amounted to only one: His mother. He gave his head a sharp shake and pushed himself off the bed, grumbling about lattes.

"You get black coffee and toast," she said. "Then you're going to shower and put on clean clothes and we're going out."

A steaming mug and buttered toast waited for him on the bedside table. She disappeared while he ate. He glanced at the clock. Eight. The house was strangely silent. His mother had been dressed in jeans, a sweater, and hiking boots.

"Are you ready?"

He spun at the sound of her voice. Coffee sloshed over his hand. He jumped, muttering, "Damn!"

"Not in my home," she snapped. "No drunkenness, no swearing."

Shawn's jaw tightened. "Where's Amy?" he asked. "Where's James?"

"We leave in fifteen minutes. Your teeth better be brushed."

"I'm not going anywhere! Where is she? What's come over you?"

Carol took a step closer, pushing a finger into Shawn's chest. "What's come over me is we've all put up with your antics long enough—me, Amy, everyone in that orchestra. I hoped and prayed you'd come to terms with what happened, and I think you're a step closer, but if you decide to backslide now, you do it on your own time, not mine, not Amy's, not in my house."

"I *gave* you this house!"

"*Gave.* It's *mine.* And you're not going to blackmail me into allowing what I never would have allowed in my home before. You think I'm going to sit back and watch you self-destruct again? You get showered and dressed and out to the car in the next fifteen minutes, or you're leaving my home. Forever."

Shawn considered pointing out he was quite capable of driving his Jaguar, battered as it was, straight back to his own, much larger, much nicer home. He closed his eyes, furious at her, but unwilling to break the tie they'd always had.

"You're about to spill the coffee," she said.

Shawn's eyes flashed open. He righted the mug, his jaw tense, and set it on the dresser.

Carol lifted it back off.

"I'll be out," he said.

"Darn right you will." She turned on her heel, taking the mug from the bedroom.

Glenmirril, December 1317

Christina's heart almost stopped at the sight of the gray robed figure of Brother Andrew entering the solar from her room. "Sh—!" She stopped. Shawn had not come back. She spun for the door, clutching William to her body.

He was on her in a flash, grabbing her arm. "Finish the name," he whispered harshly. "Is it the one that was called from the sky? Who did you expect in a gray robe?"

She knew MacDougall's voice. His fingers bit through the long sleeve of her underdress. Her arms tightened around William, her heart racing.

He threw back his hood, revealing the course black beard and yellow teeth. "Niall's child?" He drew his knife. "Give him to me."

"My Lord." She forced her voice to the melodious calm that had served so well with Duncan. "Whatever would you do with a bairn?"

"Same as he did to my son."

She let a slow smile curve her lips, and lied as smoothly as Shawn on his best day. "Then, my Lord, you would kill your own son."

William's eyes opened. He looked up at MacDougall, and whimpered.

MacDougall's eyes narrowed. "So it's true."

"Aye," she said, and repeated words Shawn had long ago thrown at her. "Surely you know how these things happen."

MacDougall glared at her, but dropped his eyes to the child. He touched the boy's cheek gently, his hard face softening into a smile. "Then he comes with us."

"Us?" She arched an eyebrow. Her heart hammered.

"We're leaving. You're coming with me."

"You will need to flee quickly and far," Christina said. "Surely, Alexander, you don't think to take a wean on such a journey, with MacDonald pursuing you."

"Us."

"Us," she acceded. The first thing was to get him away from Niall's son. "The child will lead them to us with his greeting."

MacDougall hesitated. In the brief moment, Christina pulled from him, gliding across the solar to lay the boy briskly in his cradle. His mouth puckered. "Come now." She swept back across the room, her cloak billowing behind her. "An infant will but slow us. We'll come back for him."

Midwest America, Present

Shawn let out a deep sigh, staring at the snow-shrouded tombstones outside the car. They sat for long moments in the warmth of his mother's Ford. Finally, Shawn removed his seat belt, opened his door, and swung his feet out.

Snow crunched under his leather boots. He went, half-blind, to a large cross with a carved angel kneeling beside it. He'd had it erected as soon as the albums started selling, before he bought the house or the Jaguar. His throat closed up, hot on the December day. His breath hung in the air in frosty puffs. He stared at the name etched in the silver-gray marble. *James Kleiner.* Forty years old. Not nearly old enough to die. He stared for a long time. The chill bit through his jacket.

"Where does it end, Shawn?"

He turned to his mother.

She hunched against the cold, her hands buried in her pockets, her knit hat low and her scarf high over her chin. "You have to finally let go of hatred and blame."

"I'm blaming myself this time. Brian's dead."

"You played your role and Brian made his choices. Just like Clarence played his role and you made your choices. Including getting drunk again last night."

"Is that why Amy's gone?"

"No."

They fell silent before James's grave. Amy, Brian, Niall, and a dozen others hovered, as formless and unsettled as Scotland's morning mist, in his mind. He had to tug them together, yank the misty threads into something solid and weave them, as the women of Glenmirril did with the threads of their tapestries, into a life better than he'd lived.

"Do you see how everything you've done has stemmed from your hatred of Clarence?"

"What *should* I feel about someone who killed my father?" Shawn demanded.

"Pity."

The word was a punch in the heart.

"He was trying to cope with the trauma in his own life, just like you've tried to cope with yours."

"So who's to blame for Dad's death? His mother? Her boyfriends?"

"Who turned his mother into a woman so desperate and weak she'd let men abuse her child? Who turned those men into what they were?"

"*Somebody* has to take responsibility!" Shawn stared at the granite angel. "It can't just end like this, everyone passing the buck. It has to be *someone's* fault."

Carol slipped her hand through his arm, laying her head on his shoulder. "It's the fault of every person, through generations, who chose to pass on the misery. You know, at least for Clarence, he was so young. His mother and the boyfriends, they were adults. They should have helped themselves by their ages."

"What about me?" Shawn asked. "I'm twenty-six."

Carol peered up at him quizzically. "You're twenty-five."

"Yeah. That's what I meant. I guess you could say the same about me."

"I guess I could. That's why we're here." She stretched out a hand, tracing the J of *James*. "He wouldn't want this for you, Shawn. He tried to be the brick wall where it all stopped, and put out something good on the other side."

"Look where it got him." Bitterness erupted in the air beside their frosty breaths.

"I see something different about where it got him. I see where it got all the people whose lives he touched."

"Clarence is a murderer in prison." A lone flake fluttered down on James Kleiner's tombstone.

"I understand how hard it is for you to hear," Carol said, "but in time, he learned from your father. He's doing good there. He's turning lives around. Because of your father's influence."

Shawn stared, his jaw hard, at his father's tombstone.

She touched his arm. "It's time you went to see Clarence."

"I tried," he said at last.

"You didn't tell me."

"No." He stared at the angel. "It didn't go so well."

"Why not?"

Shawn snorted. "I guess because he murdered my father and it makes me sick to look at his smirking, smarmy face playing *Look at me, I'm reformed and now I'm a big hero.* Other than that, no real reason."

"I always see Clarence at Christmas. Let's go."

Shawn snorted.

Glenmirril, December 1318

MacDougall lifted his hood, and grabbed Christina's arm, pressing his knife to her side, as she stepped into the hall. She yanked back, fighting panic. In the room, William whimpered. "You're quite safe," he whispered, holding tightly.

Her mind flew from one thought to another, swift as pigeons fluttering in the dovecot. She was still inside Glenmirril's walls. She might escape if she only kept her head about her. "You've a knife to my back," she said calmly. "Is this how you propose to show me I'm safe?"

"You're quite safe so long as you don't scream and alert the guards." He turned her to the stairs.

"You said you loved me. Yet you'd kill me?"

"Never. Unless you force my hand. I'd rather have you with me, Christina. *Much* rather." He led her down the hall, past arched windows looking down into the rain-smeared courtyard. "I suspect your affection for me is not so genuine as you led me to believe." As he looked down at her, the ugliness in his face softened for a moment. "I wish you'd been honest. It makes me little more than an animal, what happened between us."

She bit back her angry rejoinder, saying smoothly, "My Lord, certainly you *knew* a knife in hand would not get you an honest answer."

"Tell me now," he said. "What was the truth in the stable? What was the truth in Niall's chamber?" As a servant approached, he lowered his head, shielding his face under the gray hood.

Christina murmured, as the steps hurried away behind them, "My Lord, a knife to the back is but little different. How will you believe me this time?" He wouldn't kill her here in the hall where anyone could see. She hoped.

"I'll put the knife down when I'm safely beyond Glenmirril's walls," he said. "Then you'll tell me the truth. About many things."

Her chest tightened. "My Lord." She strove to keep her voice even. "I'm no use to you. I'll but hinder you on the road." She regretted the words instantly, lest he think the same and kill her, leaving her body in a deep ravine for wild boar to feast upon.

"You shall be *quite* useful," he said softly, turning her down the tower stairs.

Her blood went cold, wondering at his meaning.

"Tell the guards Brother Andrew wishes to escort you to feed the poor."

Her heart thundered. She might never see her son again. But she glided beside him, head high. Staying calm was her only hope with the father, as it had been with the son.

"If the guards attack me," he said, "the knife goes through your back first."

She smiled. "Ah, my Lord, and you doubt I could love you sincerely? How could I not, with such words of endearment?"

"Were I not in need of safe passage from *your* lord's hospitality, you'd never hear such words from me. I do love you, Christina. I think of little else!"

"And yet," said Christina, "you would throw me under a bus."

He stopped, startled, at the bottom of the stairs. "What is a *bus*?"

"A large wagon."

He furrowed his eyebrows. "I've thrown you under nothing." He glanced around the courtyard. "There's no wagon. Go quietly, now." He ushered her into the gray courtyard, staying close to her side.

"'Tis a saying, my Lord. It means you'll sacrifice me for your own wants." She didn't know whether to pray for or against help arriving. It could end badly either way, with his knife at her back. But the courtyard was quiet, everyone in the great hall.

In the gatehouse, Gil stepped forward. "My Lady? I wasn't told you were going out." He looked at the monk beside her. "When did Brother Andrew return?"

Christina hesitated. She felt the knife at her side. "Aye, he's back." The knife pressed harder. "We're going to feed the poor, Gil. Brother Andrew is concerned for my safety. Is he not good?"

"How kind," Gil said. But he frowned at Christina, questioningly.

"Please, Gil." The increasing pressure of the knife against her side threatened to shake her calm demeanor. Her voice shook.

"Are you not well, Milady?" Gil asked.

"I'm as well as can be." A line of sweat erupted across her forehead, prickling like ice. "Gil, we must be away."

"Why is he holding your arm?"

Christina fumbled for an answer. Why, indeed, would a monk clutch a lady's arm so? "He's not well, himself. But, honorable man that he is," she turned to the gray-robed MacDougall, "*so very honorable*, he insists on seeing me safe all the same."

"I can send for another who is in better form," Gil offered. "The Laird would not care to see the good brother out and about if he's ill."

"Gil." Christina spoke sternly to keep fear from shaking her voice. " The widow Muirne awaits us. Her wean is poorly."

Gil stepped back, though he looked doubtful. Christina sailed through the gatehouse, torn with relief and terror; death now or death in the wilderness; gratitude Gil had tried and frustration he hadn't seen through her lies; fear she'd pay in MacDougall's rage that he'd doubted her at all and relief MacDougall had not yet plunged his knife into her back.

"Well done," MacDougall said sardonically. Their leather boots brushed the wood of the drawbridge. She considered wrenching away and throwing herself into the murky waters below. Shawn swore staying afloat was easy. Then again, he'd not tried it in a gown and cloak.

"If only I could spice my head and stick an apple in my mouth for you." Shawn's sarcasm flowed freely from Christina's mouth. "To serve you even at cost of my own life gives me such joy." Her feet touched the frosty grass on the far side of the drawbridge, her hope sinking as surely as if her heavy gowns pulled her down through murky waters.

CHAPTER THIRTY-NINE

Midwest America, Present

The same warden who had talked with Shawn before greeted him again. Carol, her purse slung over one arm and juggling a Christmas package, hugged the man.

"It's great to see you again, Carol!" His bushy handlebar mustache lifted with his big smile for her. His arm stayed around her shoulder longer than necessary. Something inside Shawn turned over unpleasantly. He suspected there was more he hadn't been told. The warden glanced at Shawn's *leine* and trews and knee-high leather boots, and stuck his hand out. "You, too. Merry Christmas!"

"Or not." Shawn's impulse was to ignore the hand. He forced himself to go through the motions, giving a smile that was anything but sincere, and they shook.

The man seemed fully aware of, and unconcerned by, Shawn's antagonism. With a hand on Carol's back, he led them down the hall, through a clanging metal door that rattled shut behind them, leaving Shawn to follow, ignored. In the visitor's room, Clarence waited behind the glass partition. Carol handed the box to the warden to take through a security door.

Clarence's eyes, even as he accepted the package on the other side of the glass, darted from Carol to Shawn.

"He knows," Carol assured him. "How are you?"

Again, Clarence's eyes went to Shawn, sprawled on a chair, legs out, arms across his chest. Clarence licked his lips. "Fine. Good. You?" He spoke with a voice lower, clearer, and more self-assured than he had so many years ago. He sat with a quiet demeanor he'd never had in the days he'd lived with the Kleiners. Then, he had seemed ready to jump at the slightest sound, always perched on the edge of his chair, listening, assessing, preparing to fight or flee. He'd had a nervous energy then that he no longer had. His eyes darted once more to Shawn, and then he seemed to forget him, to relax in talking with Carol. He smiled and chatted as if they were old friends. Shawn supposed they were.

He wondered what Christina would say if she were here, expected to sit and play nice with someone who had done something so heinous. In her time, of course, Clarence would have been promptly hanged, maybe with a little disemboweling before he died, just to drive the point home. Christina, Niall, none of them, would ever be in this situation. Even Duncan, who had, technically speaking, done less, would never bother her again. They talked a fine talk, but none of them had any need to actually *deal with* this forgiveness garbage.

Carol laughed, her fingertips touching the bottom of the glass; Clarence's rested on the other side, meeting hers. Shawn's mind turned to Duncan and Christina—to his own knife driving through flesh and hard, resisting muscle, up in the tower of Glenmirril. Duncan had died angry, vengeful, and unrepentant, sure of his right to abuse and hate.

Shawn watched them talk, feeling the hunch of his own shoulders, the scowl of his own face—so like Duncan's in his dying moments. The disturbing thought came to him that he wasn't so different from Duncan, in his own hatred eating him, driving him. Clarence smiled, and laughed. Shawn wondered what Duncan's life might have been, had he let go of his anger. The thought burned deeply, as he recognized his own guilt, in his judgment of Duncan.

And then, Carol was standing. "Shawn, you and Clarence need to talk."

Shawn sat motionless, studying Clarence, as Carol walked away. He wanted to jump up, grab her skirts, cry not to leave him here to face this alone. He tensed his jaw against the weakness, and stared at Clarence's forehead, pretending to meet his eyes. Behind him, a door clicked.

He was alone with his father's killer.

Clarence bowed his head for a moment, and when Shawn said nothing, looked up. "I would do anything, I would give my own life, to undo it," he said softly.

Except, Shawn thought, feeling disoriented, he wasn't alone. He felt Christina at his side, and Brian. He felt his father's presence. They encouraged him to let his eyes drift up and really see Clarence. He was no longer the scrawny, unkempt, scowling boy Shawn remembered from so long ago, but a good-looking man, with a scar running from the corner of one eye up across his temple. He'd gained height and muscle. He'd need that in prison, Shawn thought. But what tried to be a sardonic, even vengeful, thought turned quickly to distaste and pity. Clarence had had enough trouble growing up, and had managed to land himself into something even worse.

"What happened that day?" he asked. He hadn't intended to. But the stories his mother had told suggested Clarence had left their house, that last time, for more misery. "I drank to get away from it," he added. "You did drugs." Without meaning to, his hatred slipped a little. They weren't so different.

"Not the smartest way to deal with it," Clarence said.

"I guess drinking wasn't, either," Shawn answered. He felt Brian's hand on his shoulder so strongly that he almost reached up to touch it. "I guess if I was trapped in a situation as a kid, and couldn't get out, maybe I'd have gone that route, too. So I'm thinking something in particular happened that day." The idea had only just sprung to mind. Intuition, Amy would have called it. He didn't think he'd previously been much given to great insights about others.

"Yeah." Clarence stared at his hands on the table. "Something happened that day. I was desperate to kill the feelings."

Shawn cleared his throat.

"I'm sorry." Clarence hung his head. "Worst possible choice of words."

"What happened?" Shawn asked.

Clarence shook his head. "There are evil people in the world." He gave a harsh croak. "Technically, I'm one of them."

Possibilities sifted through Shawn's mind. He suspected he didn't want to know what had happened that day. But he asked, "What kind of people?"

"Men who don't belong around children. Men who had been in jail and were less than honest with my mother about their past." Shawn noticed Clarence's knuckles turning white where his hands gripped one another behind the glass. "Not that it would have mattered. She believed what she wanted to."

"I'm sorry." Shawn dropped his gaze to his hands, clenched between his knees.

"It was all I could think of, that day, stopping the thoughts. The images."

Shawn nodded. He knew the feeling.

"And when your dad stood between me and relief, I snapped. I didn't know what I was doing. When I saw, when I came out of it, I thought about killing myself, but I couldn't do it. So I blamed your dad. I blamed the boyfriend. Eventually, I knew I played my own role in it. I was stupid. I was already out of my mom's house. If I'd just taken a few deep breaths, I would have realized I was away, and never had to go back. Your dad would have helped me. And in a day, I could have thought straight. In a week, I would have seen some hope. In a month, I would have started healing. And someday I would have been like Lazarus. Remember him? A surgeon now. Doing lots of good for people."

"The warden and my mother seem to think you are, too." It was a statement, not intended as an accolade.

Clarence let out a sigh, frowning. "I hope so."

They regarded each other through the glass. "We used to drive my mother nuts, staying up at night telling ghost stories," Shawn said. The words surprised him. He didn't want to reminisce. He felt Christina squeezing his shoulder.

Clarence chuckled. His face lightened. He looked younger, like any man Shawn might see on the street, at a bar, in an office; relaxed and happy, as good as anyone else. "Remember the one you told me about the island in the middle of Fish Lake? You nearly had me convinced."

"It *could* have been true." A little more of Shawn's anger drained. "But you got me back good for that."

"The face in the window?"

"You never told me who that was." Shawn's shoulders relaxed.

"Dan Wilson."

Shawn laughed. "No way! You roped Dan Wilson into that!"

Clarence blew on his fingernails and rubbed them on his shirt, smirking. "I had connections!"

The surprise of it hit Shawn. He was laughing with his father's murderer! A frown crossed his face. He wanted to feel sick inside. It was wrong. But he didn't feel sick. He felt lighter than he had in years. He felt ready to hear more, to listen. "So what happened?" he asked. "You came in here angry, hating everyone, blaming everyone. And now you're clean-cut and running ministries and—we're talking."

"Your mother."

When Clarence didn't elaborate, Shawn pressed. "Yeah?"

"She started coming about six months after. I was terrible. Acted like she was guilty of something."

He stopped, and Shawn tried again. "Then what?"

"She kept coming, every month. Talked a little. Sometimes left me something."

"Didn't she blame you?"

Clarence nodded. "She and I both knew—and still know—I made my choices as much everyone else. But she had compassion, and I'd never had that from anyone. She showed me love." His voice broke. He swallowed, blinked, and stared at his feet. His next words came out softly. "She finally got to me. She convinced me there was hope. Even here. Your mother is an incredible woman, Shawn. I used to envy you that, your parents, your house in the 'burbs. She gave me an incredible gift, they both did, including me in that, and it took me a long time to realize not every kid in my situation gets someone like that in their lives." He laughed, a harsh sound. "Ironic I learned gratitude here, isn't it?"

"Not so ironic." Shawn heaved a sigh. "You'd think I'd have appreciated all I had without having it ripped away."

Clarence frowned, his brows knit together. "This has something to do with where you disappeared to?"

Shawn shifted in his chair. "Yeah. You knew about that in here?"

"Of course I knew. Carol was distraught. Beside herself. Have you told her where you were?"

Shawn cleared his throat. The feeling he was being reprimanded, however gently or inadvertently, by a convict, was strong. Worse, he deserved it. "I can't tell her."

"Why not?" Clarence's brows furrowed deeper still. "If you can tell anyone, it's her."

"No." Shawn shook his head in irritation. "No, she'd think I was making light of it. She wouldn't believe me."

"Well it's got to be more believable than the stories you're telling. The pyramids! Medieval Scotland!" His eyes flickered up and down Shawn's outfit, and came back to his face.

Shawn coughed. He studied the toes of his leather boots.

"Why do you *say* those things?" Behind the glass, Clarence leaned forward, his nose almost touching the partition. "Is life really just one big joke to you? Did you just need some time off, or what? Why didn't you just say so instead of scaring people half to death and coming back and acting like it's a joke?"

Shawn shook his head, counting the specks on the gray floor. Tension flooded back into his shoulders. He forced himself to look back up, to meet Clarence's eyes. "You tell me. What am I supposed to say when the truth is not going to be believed by anybody?"

"Try me."

Shawn lifted his hands in resignation. "I was in medieval Scotland."

"Seriously."

"Seriously," Shawn repeated.

Clarence shook his head, irritation clear on his face.

"You asked," Shawn snapped. "One thing I've come to believe is God has a wicked sense of humor. I spent years lying to Amy and anyone else it suited me to lie to and now when I'm finally telling the truth, no one in their right mind would believe it. Does that meet the definition of ironic, or what?"

"It would if I believed you for half a second."

Shawn stood up so abruptly he nearly knocked over the chair behind him. He spread his arms, turning to show the breeks and woven shirt. It was the one he'd worn the night he returned, sewn by Christina. "People keep asking why I wear this stuff. It's because I got used to it." He lifted a foot, stomping it onto the small ledge in front of the partition. "Made in November 1314 by the cordwainer at Glenmirril Castle. Do you have internet here? Look up James Douglas—raiding northern England in 1314, 1315, and the first half of 1316. You might find some minor mention of a man named Niall Campbell with him. That was me. Niall was in a dungeon in Creagsmalan Castle in the west of Scotland. MacDougalls. Look it up. He called himself Fionn of Bergen. There was a woman named Christina...."

Clarence stood, his hand pressed to the glass. "Your mother's worried sick about you," he said. "Where *were* you? What *happened* to you?"

Everything crumpled inside Shawn. He pressed one hand to his face, bowed, trying to hold in the sick feeling. An entire two years of his life had disappeared and he could never talk about it to anyone except Aaron, Celine who wouldn't speak to him, Amy who had left him, and Angus whom he couldn't stand.

His lungs felt tight. He struggled to get breath. With all the force of will that had ruled an orchestra, he pulled himself together, pushed himself upright. "Nothing. You're right. I just needed a break from the pressure. Did a little soul-searching. There's this nice old couple who let me stay with them, kept it real quiet. I don't want to bring the press down on them." His hands went to his hips. "So I make up stories."

"You could at least tell your mother and your girlfriend the truth."

"Yeah, I think I'll tell her that." With the tendons taut on his neck, Shawn stared up at the ceiling.

Clarence dropped into his chair. "I'm sorry, Shawn. I, of all people, have no business calling you out on anything. It's just—she was devastated. Thought you were dead."

The word hung between them.

Shawn hung with it, over an abyss between two cliffs—one of a past and present with a Clarence he liked, the other of the safety of hatred. If he absolved Clarence, there was no one left to blame for his father's murder. He couldn't strike out with hatred at a faceless woman, or her nameless boyfriends. He couldn't imagine life without the hatred to bolster him, strengthen him, and drive him. He closed his eyes, breathing the stale, cold smell of the prison, of antiseptics, and somewhere beyond it, he smelled the pines around Glenmirril, and felt Christina and Brian beside him, each touching one of his arms. She'd had peace. He wanted it. He wanted his life to be the peace he'd had these few minutes with Clarence. He didn't want to die like Duncan, with hatred in his heart and shooting from his eyes.

His father stood behind him, a silent presence with the other two, his hands on Shawn's shoulders. *Forgive him,* he whispered. *He didn't know what he was doing.*

Shawn opened his eyes. Tears rolled down his cheeks. He swallowed over the hot pain in his throat; his mouth moved, trying to breathe. And his father's death let go of him, leaving him weak—and free.

"Shawn?" Beyond the glass, confusion crossed Clarence's face. He rose slowly to his feet. Both hands pressed the glass as if he wanted to melt through.

Looking at him, feeling Christina and Brian and his father all around, as real and present as Clarence himself, ten years of hatred melted away. He didn't know where it went. He didn't know why. He wanted to grab it back, for strength, but Christina whispered softly, *Let it go. You'll be aw' right without it, now.*

Shawn pressed his own hands, palm to palm through the clear surface. "It's okay, Clarence. You can say the word dead. You can tell me how it hurt my mother. It's true. I'm sorry for all that happened, for you, for me, for my father, my mother. For everyone I've hurt. I'm sorry for all of it. We're brothers again."

Glenmirril, December 1317

"The cover of trees will protect me soon enough if I tire of your tongue and drive a knife through your heart after all," MacDougall snapped, as he dragged her up the hill beyond Glenmirril.

"My screams will carry far," Christina replied. "Will you outrun their horses?" Hope rose in her that Gil would send MacDonald's men after her. "What have I done to you," she asked, as they passed into the wood, "that you should wish to hurt me?"

"I've no wish to hurt you." His eyes traveled over her body. He smiled. "Quite the opposite."

A rustle came from the firs towering over them. Christina yanked against MacDougall's arm, her heart hammering a sharp staccato.

He gripped her more tightly, saying, "'Tis only Roger."

His steward emerged from the trees, gripping the reins of three ponies. A tight hood covered his head, leaving his eyes, sharp nose, and bristling black beard showing. He grunted a greeting that only increased her fear. MacDougall pulled his knife from his belt. Christina let out a yelp and spun, slamming into Roger who gripped her arms.

"I gave you my word," MacDougall snapped. "No knife." He turned the hilt toward Roger and handed it over. "Are they ready to ride?" Roger grunted again, and to Christina, MacDougall said, "Up." He cupped his hands, boosting her onto the pony. Leaves rustled ahead, and a group of men appeared. MacDougall hailed them and called, "Ride ahead. I've business with Duncan's wife."

"I'm not his wife," Christina whispered fiercely.

He ignored her, but kicked his pony into a quick trot, taking her reins and keeping her close. "The knife is gone," he said. "Were you honest in the stables? In Niall's room?"

Christina's eyes darted over the party of armed men ahead. She had no idea where MacDougall was taking her or why. Either answer might lead to pain. "I spoke truly. I wanted a kind touch."

"But not mine."

"My Lord, I wasn't particular about whose. Duncan was hurting me."

"When was the child born?"

She stared straight ahead, saying nothing.

"What is he called?

"James Angus."

He reached a hand to her. "I won't hurt you, Christina."

She met his eyes angrily. "You *are* hurting me, taking me from my home and my son."

"I've no choice."

"You're free now. Let me go back." She glanced at her pony's reins in his hand.

"You'd sound the alarm. And I need your help."

"I've no wish to help you."

He didn't answer. Ahead, his men laughed at something. Christina's thoughts churned. When Gil told them she'd gone with Brother Andrew, MacDonald would know something was amiss. She scanned the men ahead, guessing their number at thirty. It wasn't many, but Gil would say she'd left with one monk, not thirty knights. The beauty of the narrowing glen was lost on her, as she worried that MacDonald would endanger himself, pursuing her with only a dozen men. She thought of Shawn, wondering what his life had been, these two years with Amy, with his own son, and fought a wave of self pity.

"Tell me who he is, Christina."

She looked up, drawn from her thoughts. "Who, my Lord?"

"The man who looks like Niall."

She jolted, startling her pony. "I know of no such man."

MacDougall held its reins tight. "*Who is he*, Christina?"

It hardly mattered, now Shawn was gone, if MacDougall knew. Still, she would keep MacDonald's confidence. She stared at him with the bland half-smile she'd perfected with Duncan. "There is no such man, my Lord."

MacDougall sighed. "I've had plenty of time to think, these many months. Clearly, a man does not walk through walls, neither at Stirling nor Creagsmalan. There is one man with a scar across his middle and one without. There are men who look like Niall who play harp, recorder, and sackbut."

Christina laughed. "My Lord, you imagine an entire army looking like Niall. Surely you can't believe such a thing."

"Two men, three instruments, perhaps? There is a man who loves Allene, and another, coming out of the kirk from marrying Allene who thought only of you. That seems odd for a man who had just escaped hanging and barely finished speaking vows to his new wife, for whom he'd waited so long. The man in my dungeon had no scar. The man at Allene's side on her wedding day has the scar and thought first of you. He is not Niall. Therefore 'twas Niall in my dungeon."

Christina laughed again, as light a sound as she could manage. "My Lord, you speak of fairy tales. Allene would never marry anyone but Niall. The Laird would not break his promise to Niall. I assure you Allene is married to Niall, not a ghost who looks like him."

"Niall hates water. Won't go near it, even at risk of disobeying the Laird he loves so well. Yet this same Niall supposedly fought gallantly on a boat in Jura, as if born to water. Who is he, Christina?"

"Such a man does not exist." *Stick as close to the truth as you can,* Shawn had said. She smiled, letting the birdsong of the glen brighten her. He did not exist. He wouldn't be born for seven centuries.

"It means it wasn't Niall who was knighted at Tynedale, for Niall was in my dungeon at the time. What would the Bruce think to hear he had an imposter with him?"

Christina turned to him in astonishment. "Surely, my Lord, you've no plans to tell the Bruce such a thing. For your own sake. He already knows you'd a traveling minstrel in your dungeon who bore some likeness to Niall. My Lord, you'll make your own life the more difficult, throwing such stories about."

"You know who he is, Christina. I want him."

"This man you believe looks like Niall?" A little of her fear slipped. Her self-pity vanished in relief. Shawn was safe in the future, safe with Amy and his wean, safe from MacDougall.

"Him, Niall. Like you, I'm not particular."

Her relief faded. Shawn was safe. Niall was not.

MacDougall watched her. "You love him, do you not, this man who looks like Niall? It's why you kept his robe."

She stared at him, not answering.

"I believe he loves you, too." MacDougall smiled, the yellow teeth showing. "He'll come for you, he or Niall—but I'm thinking they both will. I *want* them both, and with your help, I *will* have them."

CHAPTER FORTY

Glenmirril, December 1317

The pounding on Margaret's door jarred Allene, making her miss a stitch. She and Margaret looked up. "Enter," she called.

Gil burst in. "Milady! Christina left with Brother Andrew to care for the widow Muirne's wee one."

Allene stared blankly at him. "Brother Andrew cannot be back."

"And the widow Muirne is here with her bairn, who is quite well." She turned to Allene, frowning. "But Christina was caring for William."

Uneasiness settled on Allene. "Gil, who is guarding MacDougall?"

"Taran and Gregor."

"Margaret, go find William immediately." She dropped the altar cloth on the settee. "Gil, find my father, and pray I am wrong." She pushed herself up off the settee, awkward in advanced pregnancy.

Margaret rose. "Milady, you canna leave in your condition."

"I must see Taran." She hurried down the stone halls, hitching her surcoat up around her ankles, one hand pressed to her swollen stomach. At the end of the hall, she saw MacDougall's door, firmly shut. Ronan lounged in a chair in front of it. When he saw her, he jumped to his feet, smoothing his tunic. "Milady. You shouldn't be about in your condition! What will your father say?"

"Where's Taran?" she demanded.

"It's been quiet in the lord's cell." He looked at his shoes.

Her alarm heightened. "I did not ask that. I asked where Taran is. I was told he was on duty."

"I came on just now." He paused, looking as if he'd been about to say more.

"What is it?" Fear fluttered in her stomach.

"He's young, Milady," the man said. "You'll not be hard on him?"

"For what?"

"He left his post early. 'Tis unlike him. He must have had reason."

Alarm shot up and down her arms. "Did you not find out why?"

"There was no one to send." He stood stiffly; had he been less well-trained, he'd have been shifting from foot to foot, she thought.

"Gregor was supposed to be here, too." Allene stepped to the door, peering through the bars. MacDougall lay on the narrow cot, the blanket pulled up over his shoulders and head. "Ronan," she said. "Open the door."

"There's no reason to...."

"Open the door now."

He grabbed the keys at his belt.

"MacDougall!" she shouted through the grate. "Get up!"

The man didn't move. Ronan touched her shoulder. "Step back," he said. "Milady, stay out of this cell. He's up to something." He pulled his knife, edging in carefully. "MacDougall!" he snapped.

The man didn't move. Allene saw the foot protruding from under the bed. "It's not MacDougall," she whispered. "Pull the blanket off him."

Ronan reached for the rough-spun blanket and yanked it off.

Taran lay on the mattress, a gash oozing blood across his temple.

Midwest America, Present

"You're scowling." Back home, Carol tucked her legs under herself, sipping hot chocolate. "You seemed good when we left. What changed?"

"Not scowling," Shawn said. "Thinking." His mind jumped among Clarence, Amy, Brian, and all the faces of his life. He rose, restless, and tossed twigs into the fireplace. He reached for his sporran, feeling once, twice.

"What are you looking for?" his mother asked.

"Flint." He turned, blinking to see his own mother instead of Niall's, her hair a soft halo of brown around her shoulders, instead of bound up in a headdress. He frowned, trying to remember how to start a fire without flint.

"Flint?" She kicked her feet to the floor, leaning forward. *"Flint?"*

"I'm joking." He rose to his feet irritably. *"Matches*! Do we have matches? In the kitchen?" He felt her gaze follow him as he left the room.

"Top drawer next to the stove," she called.

He returned with the matches and cupped a small flame in his hands, nursing it to life. He thought of Adam, so long ago around Hugh's camp, and his widow, left with seven daughters and a son. He pushed them from his mind. He had to live in the present. The flame caught the first twig. A tiny burst of red and yellow curled up and caught the second. Shawn blew gently, till it grabbed a third.

He watched the flames lick at the kindling and swirl up around the log. They crackled with a pleasant sound that called up years of cozy winter nights, with his parents in modern Minnesota, and in Glenmirril's lively medieval hall, playing harp before the Laird with the great brazier warming him. He turned to the tree, with James and Amy's presents under it, wrapped in green and blue and red foil. The silence of the house settled on him. "When's she coming back?" he asked.

His mother stared at the fire. "I don't know."

The unease of the moments before battle filled Shawn's gut. He rose, heading down the hall to Amy's room. But he knew. Her closet was empty. He tore out her dresser drawers one by one. They were empty. James's clothes were gone. Her suitcases were gone! After she'd cradled his head and comforted him last night!

He stormed back to the great room. "Because I got drunk?"

Carol lifted her eyes to him. "No."

"Something else I said or did?" He thought of Cassie's call, shame flooding him, and of Brian, under a granite tomb.

"No." Her gaze dropped to her hands.

"Just tell me!" Shawn burst out. "Did she go to her parents? Did she leave me?"

"Angus was injured."

"Angus?"

"He's hurt quite badly," Carol said softly.

"Yeah, but...what are you saying?" Uneasiness crept over him. "Where *is* she?"

"On her way to Scotland."

"Scotland?" Images of the nameless attacker, strong enough to defeat three modern men, flared up in his mind. "No." He shook his head, searching for his phone, even as he reminded himself he didn't *know* the attack was anything other than random. "No, she can't go back."

Carol rose angrily. "Can you set your ego aside for once?"

Shawn stared at her blankly. Angus didn't *know* the man on the video was the attacker. Still, he jabbed Amy's name on his phone. She had to know.

"Can't you have any compassion for a man who's been very badly hurt?"

Amy's phone rang....rang...rang. He stabbed it off, and turned for the computer, searching, dialing an airline, interrupting before the woman could finish her spiel. "I need a ticket to Glasgow."

"What are you *doing,* Shawn?" Carol hissed.

He pulled out his credit card, reeling off numbers. He didn't *know,* he told himself, as he jotted down flight information. She might be fine.

"How can you do this to Angus?" Carol demanded as he hung up the phone. "He needs her!"

"Please, Mom." He rose, his flight information in hand. "I have to be at the airport in an hour."

"I am not helping you...."

"Please!" His eyes begged her. "There are things I didn't tell you. *Can't* tell you. Take me or I'll get a taxi, but I need to go."

Glenmirril, December 1317

"What happened?" MacDonald asked again.

Taran stood, dazed, before MacDonald's chair in the great hall. Morrison and Darnley sat at the table on either hand, Darnley in a fury, Morrison looking on with concern as Taran rubbed his head. "I dinna ken, my Lord. I only remember walking in with the ale, and next thing, Milady is shaking me."

"Father, he's hurt," Allene said. "He must go to the infirmary with Gregor."

"You, Allene, are meant to be in your chamber." He looked at her with heavy disapproval.

Allene lifted her chin. "*Amy* did not stay in her chambers."

"You are not Amy!" MacDonald snapped.

"Who is Amy?" Morrison peered quizzically at MacDonald.

"In the *future*," Allene said with a hard stare, "people will know 'tis quite safe for women to be about when their time is near."

MacDonald harrumphed. "He's *impertinent*! He admitted he knew nothing of medicine!"

"Yet women do not die in childbirth in his—country."

Darnley looked from one to the other, and back to Taran. "Of whom do we speak, my Lord? Taran has said naught of medicine."

Taran stared miserably at the floor, his face pale.

"Was it called a *concussion*, that..." Allene coughed and emphasized the name, "*Niall* said he had after the joust? Father, Taran can tell us no more. He needs rest."

"He was careless." MacDonald spoke sternly, though he didn't raise his voice.

Taran cringed as if from a blow. "My Lord, I beg your forgiveness. I *thought* I paid heed."

"Not enough," MacDonald barked. "He is gone, Gregor near dead, Christina abducted, and Sir Niall in danger. And you can't even tell us how or why."

Taran hung his head. "I'm sorry, my Lord."

"Pack your things," MacDonald said. "'Tis time you joined the men."

"Father!" Allene objected. "If he has a concussion...."

MacDonald rose, eyebrows drawing tight.

She lowered her head. "I'm sorry, Father."

"Guards," MacDonald called. "Escort him to his room."

"What of Christina?" Morrison asked, as they led Taran from the hall. "My brother entrusted her to my care, and this has happened!"

"I sent men to track him the moment I learned," MacDonald said. "They went north, around the loch, and down the south shore, presumably heading for England."

"Just MacDougall and Christina?" Morrison asked.

"There were more waiting in the hills. More than a score." He turned to Conal. "I want forty men ready to ride at dawn. We'll track MacDougall and deliver Taran to Niall at Berwick."

"What of Christina?" Allene clenched her skirt in nervous hands. "We'll leave her alone with him through the night? We must set out immediately to warn Niall! We know he'll go after him!"

"We can do naught in the dark." Her father sighed. "Yes, he'll no doubt head very quickly for Berwick."

Midwest America, Present

"Mr. Kleiner!" The perky reporter bounced in front of him as he approached the airport's glass doors. "Your tour was a huge success! Just a few questions!"

"I have a plane to catch." The fawn-colored trombone case hung from his hand.

"Where were you?" She hurried along beside him.

"It's really simple." Shawn glanced at one of the large clocks on the wall, as he raced for check-in, the reporter hurrying beside him. "The pressure got to me. I took some time off with a very nice older couple. You can understand I wanted to protect their privacy. So I made things up. I trust you'll leave them alone."

"Oh, yes!" She bobbed her head eagerly.

He could see her mind spinning as he stopped at a kiosk and jabbed his passport in. He didn't *know* the attack was targeted, he told himself for the hundredth time. She might be perfectly safe. But he wished she would answer her phone.

"Are they in the west of Scotland? The Hebrides?" She scanned his breeks and boots, and the backpack slung on his shoulder. "What did you do for that year?"

"I have a flight." Shawn snatched his boarding pass from the kiosk.

"Tell us about your son." The woman almost ran beside him in his charge for the security gate. "What's his name? Will you be staying in Scotland with his mother?"

"His name is Ewan." Shawn watched impatiently while the agent studied his passport. He didn't know the attack *wasn't* random. "He's actually a girl. His mother and I are moving to Peru." He accepted his documents back and started through the line.

"Mr. Kleiner!" She grabbed his sleeve. "Can't you tell the truth for once?"

He stopped, letting a slow smile cross his mouth. "Would you believe me if I told you you have really beautiful eyes?"

Her cheeks turned pink. "Really?"

He leaned close, whispering, "Really, especially beautiful. I wish I could stay." He patted her cheek, turned, and plowed through security, down the bustling concourse. The trombone swung, skimming past strollers and wheelchairs. He lifted it abruptly, up over the head of an escaped toddler. He pushed through the kaleidoscope of voices over loudspeakers, languages from all over the globe, businessmen chatting in earnest, college students laughing loudly, and mothers calling children, searching for his gate.

"Passenger Kleiner, please report to Gate D4."

He moved more quickly, the trombone thumping his leg. He raised his hand, signaling the attendant. "Here!" He gave his most charming smile, and her irritation melted. "I was helping this old lady," he said. "So sorry." He flashed his boarding pass and hurried down the long tunnel.

The flight attendants greeted him like a returning hero. "Mr. Kleiner! So glad you made it!"

Another laid her hand on his arm. "We were worried we'd have to leave without you! Can I take the trombone for you?"

He shook his head. "No, thanks." Nobody touched his trombone. He followed her, only half hearing her chatter, to his seat in first class, hoisted the instrument into the overhead bin, and swung his backpack to his feet before collapsing into the soft, wide seat. Twenty-four hours since his mother had insisted he get in her car and go to the prison. A lifetime ago. He closed his eyes.

"Fasten your seat belt, Mr. Kleiner." An attendant leaned close. He could smell her perfume. He opened his eyes, and buckled the belt. She flashed teeth as white as clouds, and went back to her duties. Shawn dug in the backpack. His mother had pushed something into it when she'd dropped him off. He found an oversized lime-green envelope, and removed a card. The Grinch stood on the front, with the words, *His heart grew three sizes that day.*

In a previous life, just twenty-four hours ago, he wouldn't have found that funny. Now, even in his fear for Amy, he smiled and opened it. *I'm proud of you,* she'd written. *Love, Mom.* He pushed it back in the backpack with a deep sigh. Amy would be fine. He was overreacting. The police said it was a random attack.

His pulled his phone from the backpack. It had been two days since he'd checked his voice mail. He pulled it up. A few requests for interviews, Christmas greetings from friends and colleagues. Conrad asking about an appearance next May. Then Angus's voice came over the line. *Butcher of Berwick...killed a woman giving birth. Don't Amy or James come back here! He* will *kill them both. Don't let them back here!*

CHAPTER FORTY-ONE

Inverness, Present

Amy hurried into the hospital room, clutching a sleeping James to her shoulder. Sitting beside Angus's bed, Claire looked up, Angus's hand in hers. She stood, laying his limp hand gently on the white sheet, and rounded the bed, to hug Amy. "I'm so glad you came. It'll mean the world to him, really it will."

Amy's heart nearly stopped, looking at the gray form on the bed. "Has he woken up at all?" she asked in horror. This wasn't the strong and vital Angus she knew, but a shell. He looked smaller, wasted.

"Oh, he's woken," Claire assured her. "Not for long, though, and he's in a great deal of pain."

Reassured, Amy turned to the girl. She seemed young. It was clear she was in love with Angus. Amy wondered if she had fought for her better nature, or if it had come easily to her to dial and ask Amy to come. Amy squeezed the girl's hand, and moved to the bed. James stirred in his sleep, and stretched an arm. Amy touched Angus's hand. "Angus?" she said softly. "It's Amy." He didn't respond.

Claire stood across the bed. She knit her fingers together, hands clasped. "He's only woken the once, and he seemed not to recognize much. But they say he may be aware, even when he appears unconscious. They said talk to him. They believe it helps."

"I've heard that, too." Amy gazed at the passive face. His hair had grown longer. She wrapped a curl around her finger, smiling. In her other arm, James sighed.

"Is this arm okay?" Amy asked Claire. When the girl nodded, Amy laid James in the crook of Angus's elbow. "James is here," she told his still form. She stood close, guarding against James falling, not knowing what to say. She ran her finger up and down his forearm, and pushed a curl off his forehead. Claire sat silently on the other side of the bed, her hands in her lap, her head down. "What happened?" Amy asked.

"Teenagers out hill walking." She gave a brief account, finishing with, "The second drop was much farther and full of sharp stones."

"Why didn't his harness catch him?" Amy asked.

Claire stared at Angus, blinking back tears. "It broke."

"Why?" Amy asked. "He takes good care of his equipment."

Claire shrugged. "Things can always go wrong." She brushed the back of her hand across eyes glistening with tears. "It took them hours to reach him and get him out. They didn't think he'd make it."

Guarding James, Amy reached across the bed. "Thank you for calling, Claire."

Claire took her hand. "Thank you for coming. He'll get better, hearing your voice and holding your hand."

Amy stared down at his still form, thinking back to the first time she'd met him, sitting beside Niall's hospital bed. She'd barely seen him that day, or the next two times he met with her about Shawn. She'd only really noticed him when he brought her coffee behind the Heritage Centre in Bannockburn. She traveled the halls of memory, polishing off each moment with him. There were no bad ones. She touched Angus's cheek. She knew her heart had settled. She hoped it wasn't too late.

♫

"He did indeed leave a note!" The woman at the church thrust it at Simon. She turned to her *computer,* typing, glancing up at him nervously as he scanned the note.

The hospital, it said. *I'll see you at the front door on the 26th and show you.*

"I'll be back if he's not there," Simon said softly. He liked the agitation on her face. Smiling, he headed out into the cold street, past trees sparkling with fairy lights, for the hospital.

Berwick, December 1317

"Another messenger from England." Lachlan spoke in Niall's ear.

Niall paused in drilling the men. He wanted to believe this messenger brought news that might lead to peace—that he might feel confident he'd be going home to Allene and their growing family. His breath frosted the air before him. "Owen, take over," he said, when they slowed to watch. Owen spun into the fray, shouting orders, and the men charged back to their drills, stamping in the snow. "Where?" Niall asked.

Owen pointed across the field to Bruce's makeshift hall, where Niall saw a young priest, tall even among the rangy Scots. He clutched a thick black cloak around his thin body. "He was here a few days ago," Niall murmured.

"Aye," Lachlan said. "He left his papers at Berwick. The Bruce gave him safe-conduct to go get them."

Barons and lords were heading toward the assembly hall.

"D' ye think he's brought a letter properly addressed this time?" Owen asked.

"We'll soon know," Niall returned. "Go back to your work." He stopped at the stream to splash icy water over his work-stained face, before heading for the hall.

"Adam Newton is back," de Soulis said, as they joined the stream of men.

James Douglas met them at the door of the hall, brushing dirt from his hands.

"Let us pray more sense has been shown this time. Bruce will not be peaceable forever in the face of these insults."

They entered the hall. Already, two dozen barons had seated themselves, all of them silent, all with swords and dirks, all staring hard at the unfortunate man chosen to deliver the message.

Adam Newton stood in the center of the hall, his black robes emphasizing his tall, slender frame, like a gladiator in the ring; his jaw set, though his eyes flitted from one lord to another as if any one of them might release the lions on him.

Bruce's throne alone remained empty. When all had assembled, Sir Alexander Seton strode forward to address the now-trembling Adam Newton. "Our king will not see you. However, he will look over the correspondence you have brought."

"I was promised...." Newton's voice came out in a squeak. He cleared his throat.

Before he could try again, Seton stopped him. "You were promised safe-conduct to *bring* the documents." He held out his hand. Newton wavered.

Beside Niall, Douglas shifted his hand to the hilt of his sword. A stir rippled throughout the room, of similar, muted motions. Newton's eyes flitted around the crowd. His Adam's apple bobbed. He dug in his robes and thrust the letters at Sir Alexander, his chin raised.

Sir Alexander raised an eyebrow. "Let us hope they are properly addressed this time." He turned and marched out the door at the far end of the hall.

Newton swallowed again and looked around the crowd of lords, his head high. They gazed back placidly, hands on swords. A few feet shuffled. The angle of the sunbeam sharpened. A servant entered to pile more kindling in the braziers. Adam Newton shifted from one foot to another.

Suddenly, the door burst open at the far end of the hall. Bruce himself, resplendent in his gold crown, sunlight flashing off the threads of gold on his tabard, stormed up to the priest, shaking the documents under his nose. "What did you think by bringing these here?" he demanded. "Did I not make myself clear to the last messengers that I *will not* accept improperly addressed communication?"

"My *Lord...*"

"I am *not* your lord, I am *Your Grace,* King of Scots. Would you *dare* to address Edward of Carnarvon in so slovenly a manner!" Bruce flung the documents, still sealed, on the floor.

Newton scrambled to retrieve them as if they were pearls. His hands shook, but as he uncoiled his lanky frame, he tried again. "Your Grace, I am but a messenger, doing as bidden by my superiors."

"Your superiors support the man who butchered my people at Berwick!" Bruce's eyes blazed. Never had Niall seen him in such rage. "Were you there that day?" Bruce pushed his face into Newton's.

The priest backed up, papers clutched to his chest, shaking his head vigorously.

"Did you walk the streets of Berwick when they were through?" Bruce demanded.

Again, the priest shook his head, his eyes wide.

"I did." Bruce swept a hand around the assembled lords. "Many of these men did. We were ordered to swear allegiance to Longshanks at Berwick. He left them there, rotting in the street, heads rolling in the gutters, limbs chopped from bodies, for us to walk among. *Children!* Men trying to protect their families." His face grew red with rage. "Women in the very act of giving birth!"

In a flash, Niall understood Bruce's decision to risk a whole army for Roysia.

"No, no!" Newton shook his head. "Edward stopped them when he saw that!"

Niall's fingers curled on the hilt of his sword in revulsion. The man was a fool.

Bruce's hand flashed out, gripping the cleric's robes. "Small good it did her, aye? She was fairly dead by then, and her child as well."

Newton trembled, on his toes in the king's grip.

"Did you see the streets running red with their blood?" Bruce asked. "Did you see the flies buzzing over headless bodies? Did you watch strong men on their knees retching at the stench in the town?"

"No, My-Lord-Your-Grace!" Newton quivered.

"I did." Bruce released him. Adam stumbled, grappling at his papers, his eyes wide, and scurried back two steps. "The Good Sir James lost his father there. Every man here lost loved ones to Longshanks' butchery that day, and many days afterward. My brothers' heads rotted on pikes on England's walls—for what? For protecting our people. For protecting my wife and daughter. If you persist in doing the bidding of *superiors* who slaughter our loved ones, you will find no friends here."

"My Lord, Your Grace, might I but have safe-conduct back to Berwick?"

Niall closed his eyes, willing the man out of his foolishness.

Bruce rounded on him. "*Safe conduct?* For bringing me insults?" He gestured in disgust at the documents crumpled to the cleric's chest. "Go! Leave before my men draw their swords!"

"I was ordered...."

"*Leave!*" Bruce roared in the man's face. "And let your masters know Berwick will soon be mine."

Newton scrambled from the hall, his feet slipping once, before he righted himself, and flew out the door. The barons rose from their seats and followed.

"Sir Niall."

Niall turned at Bruce's soft words. "Retrieve the papers when he's left camp."

"Aye, Your Grace." Niall bowed.

"And Niall."

"Your Grace?"

"As always, no real harm shall ever come to a man of God. I will not be Longshanks, nailing clerics to church doors. Come, let us see if he is wise enough to be on his way. But methinks his sense of duty outweighs his *common* sense."

Niall followed Bruce to the door. They stood in its shadow, watching. In the clearing of the snowy woods, Newton had jumped onto a stump in front of a large oak, as if in the center of a town square. "The Pope proclaims a truce!" he shouted.

The barons ringed him, in their heavy fur-lined cloaks and bushy beards. Foot soldiers emerged from the woods around, craning to see the spectacle. "A truce?" one lord jeered. "Such as we have been offering England for years?"

"Our Holy Father insists the fighting must stop!" Newton persisted.

"Then may England stop," shouted another baron. "Would they had stopped before Berwick!"

"They raped my sister," yelled a soldier. "Would they had honored the Holy Father's truce instead of being in my village!"

"Peace, we must have peace!" On the stump, Newton waved his arms.

"They killed my son!" shouted another. "Is that what you call peace?"

"The Holy Father says...."

"Does the Holy Father say they might lie with our women on our wedding nights?" demanded another.

"Or kill our people?"

"Burn our churches?" A pine cone flew threw the air, striking the tree.

The cleric cringed. The shouting of the crowd grew; a stone flew. Newton's pleading for peace died, his arms over his head, as he searched the crowd frantically for a way out.

In the doorway of the hall, Bruce spoke softly to Niall. "Get him out of here." He watched another rock sail through the air. "Though I think he's earned the right to have a little fear put into him. Perhaps he might lose his clothes on his way home, if he is uncooperative."

"No clothing in December, Your Grace. 'Twould be harmful indeed."

"Catch him near a village where he's bound to find more quickly. 'Tis better by far than the way our priests have been treated." He turned and spit, but before the moment of anger, Niall saw the flash of grief, of a king who loved his people. Then, in an instant, he straightened, and marched through the doors, erupting like a lion into the fray. His men froze. Adam Newton, on his stump, froze.

"Be gone!" Bruce roared. Sunlight dazzled off the lion on his tabard.

"Safe-conduct, Your Grace! Look how they ill treat me!"

"'Tis your own doing. Leave!"

The young priest jumped from his stump, gathered his robes, and ran, pine cones and rocks sailing after him.

CODA

Inverness, Present

Angus's eyes flutter open, move around looking glazed, and settle on me. Slowly, he focuses. I squeeze his hand. "You're here," he says. His voice scrapes out, rusty nails on old wood.

I smile. His hand is warm. "I'm here." Relief and hope flow around my heart, as warm as the smell of eggnog coming from the hall. "I came as soon as Claire called. How are you feeling?"

The vagueness returns to his eyes. He squeezes them shut, spreading small lines at the corners of his eyes, and opens them again, focusing on me with effort. "Like I fell off a cliff," he whispers. "Is there anything left of me?"

"Not much." I lean down to kiss his forehead, pushing aside a stray curl. "But I'm happy with what is."

It takes him a minute to answer, rasping in pain. "You spoke—to—doctors?"

I hesitate.

"I do this...for a living." When I don't speak, he whispers, "Will I walk again?"

"They're not sure," I say.

"Spinal cord?" His eyes lose their focus.

"They're worried about it," I admit. His eyes close. He sighs into sleep, while I hold his hand, watching him, praying.

Suddenly, his eyes fly open. "James?" He struggles vainly to rise.

"He's with your mom." I lay a hand on his arm, trying to calm him.

"Go home," he whispers angrily.

"I'm not leaving you," I say, surprised and hurt.

"You need—take James...." His words come out with difficulty. "Shawn."

"When Claire called, what I needed was to get on the first plane. That tells me all I need to know."

"I can't take care of you," he whispers.

Mairi appears in the doorway, holding James. He squeals, a short, staccato sound, when he sees me. I go to the door, taking him. Mairi glances from me to her brother, gives me a fleeting smile, and leaves. I bring James to Angus's bedside. He squeals and reaches for Angus, straining to get down to him. "There's a lot more to you than your legs, Angus," I say. Doesn't James reaching for him *prove it?*

He ignores James, asking, "Did Shawn come with you?"

"No."

A nurse appears in the doorway, a needle in hand. "Now then, Inspector, just a wee jag."

"He let you come?" he rasps, seeming not to notice her as she swabs his arm.

I shake my head, as she slides the needle under his skin. "He was asleep."

He looks at her suddenly, his eyes wide, saying, "No, I have to...."

"It's okay." I slip my hand back around his, reassuring myself he's really alive. James babbles, straining for him.

His eyes flutter to James. "Go back," he whispers harshly. He struggles, but the drugs take over. He sinks into sleep.

Inverness, Present

"Niall, is it?"

The words brought Shawn up short, in his rush through the hospital's antiseptic halls. He looked around, seeing no one, until his eyes fell on the open door of the hospital chapel. In the softly lit room, a gaunt, old monk perched on the edge of a small pew, his back bowed and gnarled hands resting on a cane.

"What do you know of Niall?" Shawn asked softly. He glanced down the hall, wanting to find Amy.

"Amy is quite safe at the moment. 'Tis James we ought speak of."

"James?" Shawn looked down the hall toward Angus's room. Amy *was* safe in a hospital. He entered the chapel. A silver cross hung on the wall over an altar. "What about James?"

"'Tis a fine thing, to see you in the flesh at last." The monk reached out a hand, grasping Shawn's.

"As opposed to?" Shawn thought the monk was hardly the sort to follow his tour.

The monk patted the red cushion covering the pew. "I've a story to tell."

"About my son?" Shawn studied him a moment, before sitting. "Who are you?"

The monk stared at the cross for a time, while water rippled softly from some unseen fountain. Then he cleared his throat. His voice rasping, he pulled Shawn into a different world.

I am Brother Eamonn, a monk of Monadhliath. I arrived there to take over the archives at the age of twenty-four. Brother Sebastian died soon after my arrival, leaving me to learn the records alone. They were in terrible disarray, as he had been ill a good long while. For months I read, sorted, organized.

I'd been working for a year when I came upon a document that seemed at odds with what I'd previously read. I sought quite some time, before finding Malcolm MacDonald of Glenmirril Castle, early fourteenth century. But when I reviewed those records, all agreed with that in my hand. I was mystified, as I had an excellent memory. It was why they'd assigned me to the archives. I took it to

Brother Win, the abbot. He questioned had I been drinking.

Here, Brother Eamonn gave a rusty laugh. *Thinking 'twas better to be thought drunk than mad, I apologized, and left. But before I filed the document, I copied it into my own notebook in my cell. I almost forgot the incident until two years later, when I found another inconsistency. Again, I searched the records for what I thought had been there. Again, I copied, word for word, what I had in my hand. I went back to the Glenmirril records and read again. What was there was indeed different from what I'd copied it into my book. I thought perhaps I was mad.*

"History changed," Shawn said. "What does this have to do with James?"

Brother Eamonn smiled. *Everything. 'Twas two years more, you see, when the days were at their longest, that I woke in the night, restless, and went out to the cloisters. There stood a man with long, golden hair, about my age. He moved stealthily, keeping to the shadows. He seemed to call over his shoulder to someone and there I saw another man, his twin.*

"Niall?" Shawn asked. "You saw Niall? He and I have been to Monadhliath. But that didn't happen."

It hasn't happened, Eamonn said.

"You're saying I go back?" Shawn became still inside. "What are you saying? I don't *want* to go back."

The candle on the altar flickered.

They were seeking, silent. Then Niall saw me. He looked to his twin and pointed at me. The twin saw me and smiled, as if at an old friend. I felt he knew me, though I'd never seen him. "You'll be fine," he told me.

Shawn stared at his hands, clasped between his knees. Life was good here. He'd come back to rebuild his life, not to give it up again.

Shouting rose outside the cloister. A door burst open; a young abbot stumbled in, followed by a knight in black, shouting, "Where is he, Brother William?"

"Brother William?" Shawn's head shot up. "Did they hurt him?"

No more so than anyone in that time.

"Was that meant to be reassuring?" he demanded.

Eamonn's liver-spotted hands gripped the cane. Water burbled softly. *I stood frozen, not thinking to hide myself, as the knight's men poured through the door. "Where is Campbell?" the black knight shouted. "Find him yourself, Beaumont," the abbot threw out defiantly.*

"*Simon* Beaumont?" Shawn's eyes narrowed. "Who attacked my mother?"

The same. I shook myself, thinking I must escape. I looked to Niall. He and his men melted back into the cemetery. I stood in plain sight, unable to move, though I knew I should. But the soldiers stormed past me, as if I didn't exist, into the kirkyard, the abbey, the church. Beaumont towered over Brother William, who had fallen to his knees. Brother William looked up, defiant, and shouted, "You'll not find Niall!"

Beaumont struck him. He fell again, his palms hitting the dirt, blood streaming from his temple, but he sprang to his feet, charging Beaumont. I stepped forward. What I thought I'd do, I've no idea, as I seemed to be invisible. But Beaumont saw me. He laughed, and I felt he, too, knew me. In that moment's distraction, Brother

William lunged, pulling a knife from his robes.

Beaumont spun, his sword raised, but Brother William scrambled under it, and as Beaumont turned on him, Niall charged from the tombs. They fought, my Lord of Claverock trying to call his men, but they were two upon him, though good Brother William had but the knife. Then Niall's twin burst from the graveyard, shouting, "Your men are dead, Beaumont!"

Simon ran. Niall stood before me, panting with the exertion of the fight. "Read the archives," he shouted. He was frantic, as he began to fade from sight. "Glenmirril. Read it now, when Simon has just escaped. You are in the time between times, and you must understand. It all depends on you understanding."

As dawn broke, I walked back through a monastery I barely recognized. 'Twas silent—no bells or sound of prayer. The place had an air of desolation. Vines crept in through empty casements. The archives was in ruins, the cabinets unlike those I knew. But they were full.

I stared at them, dozens of them, thousands of documents, spanning centuries. It would take weeks to search them all. And I'd no idea what I was looking for. I stood with my Rosary beads in one hand, praying, not knowing when or where I was, or if I'd ever see my fellow monks again. I didn't know who or what I'd seen, who this man Simon was who seemed to know me and laugh at me. I stood for some time, knowing I must have a better plan than searching randomly.

It came to me that their clothing narrowed the time in which they lived, at least a wee bit. So I searched our records for an abbot in those possible years—still far too many—named Brother William. There were several, as you may guess. I read in the days of one, then another, and a third, seeking any Beaumont or Niall Campbell. I read till the sun went down. I rose at dawn. I read as the sun grew bright, but found naught to say who they were. I grew hungry, but found no food in the refectory. I found root vegetables growing wild. I drank from the spring.

'Twas late evening I found Niall Campbell of the fourteenth century. I lost myself in the reading from there, following one trail after another to other parts of the archives. I spent three days in that abandoned ruin, keeping our offices alone in the chapel at the appointed hours, eating from the orchard and wild garden...reading in the archives as long as it was light, growing more horrified as I read.

I watched a history unfold, as horrible as anything your Hollywood has dreamed up. Eamonn turned his gaze to Shawn. *'Twas the tale of a man given great power."*

"Simon," Shawn said. And he knew. The attack had not been against his mother, but against his son.

Eamonn nodded. "I saw what might be, what *will* be."

Shawn's jaw tightened. "What does he do?"

Eamonn spoke softly. *On returning to his own time, he meets Edward, and prophesies. As his predictions come true, Edward grants him prestige and power. Simon, more competent than Edward, does what the king cannot. He decimates Scotland. Solidifies control of Wales and Ireland. He rewards those who swear fealty to him. His power grows. He turns on France and Spain.*

"What does this have to do with James?" Shawn asked.

I knew history well enough, Eamonn continued, as if Shawn had not spoken, *to see all that was missing. The Declaration of Arbroath is never written because Scotland is destroyed at the Battle of Dumfries in 1319.*

Niall would likely be fighting any Scottish battle in 1319. If Scotland was destroyed, so were Niall, Hugh, Allene, and so many more people he knew and loved. "The Declaration of Arbroath?" Shawn cleared his throat. "I don't even know what that is. What does it have to do with my son?"

"They say your own Declaration of Independence drew a great deal from the Declaration of Arbroath."

"Our founding fathers took their ideas from other places, too," Shawn said. "The Declaration of Independence will still exist."

"Not if America never exists."

"No." Shawn shook his head, denying, remembering the man he had wrestled on the stairs. "No. Simon Beaumont does *not* have the power to stop the United States from existing."

With what he knows of history, Eamonn rasped, *with what he has learned here of weapons, he has the power to control England. He wields that power well. He knows Isabelle and Mortimer's ambitions. They and the young prince Edward will be found dead in their beds. Which leaves Simon unopposed, to overrun Europe. Aragon.* He paused, meeting Shawn's eyes. *Castile.*

"Ferdinand and Isabella." Shawn's brows knit. "They funded Columbus."

They do not, Eamonn whispered, *for their families are wiped out more than a century before their births.*

"No." Shawn shook his head. "*No!* Someone else will give him money."

Columbus will not exist, Eamonn said placidly.

"Then someone else will cross the ocean. I mean, obviously someone *did* because here I am! I'm American, so America exists."

Eamonn's eyes were steady. *You remember music that no longer exists.*

"So what!" Shawn almost shouted. "*So what!* All I care about is James!"

Eamonn turned, staring at the candle flickering on the altar, till Shawn whispered harshly, "What does this have to do with *James*?"

His life is tied to Simon's. Eamonn paused a long moment, only the burbling water breaking the silence, before saying, *He must kill Simon, and Simon knows it. That is why Simon will not stop until he kills James first. He'll kill Amy just for fun.* He shook his head slowly. *No, Simon must be sent back to his own time before he can harm the bairn.*

"But you're telling me if Simon goes back, he destroys history, the very world, as we know it."

Eamonn fixed Shawn with a hard stare belying his age. "If he does not go back, he *will* kill James."

"And if he goes back, he kills us all."

Eamonn nodded, his eyes on the candle. "Unless James stops him."

"No, not James."

"Your son will be a man, then, not the bairn you're imagining."

Shawn shook his head angrily. "I'll put them on a plane and send them back to the States. Simon's medieval. He has no idea how to fly across an ocean."

"Did Niall not learn in our time? Did you not learn in his?"

"He has no money," Shawn objected.

"How do you think he feeds himself?" Eamonn countered. "'Tis simple enough to take money from the unwary by night."

"He has no identification," Shawn tried. "He can't get onto a plane without it."

Eamonn's eyes bored into Shawn's. "Would Niall have found a way to America, here in your time, had he needed to? To save Allene and his children?" Eamonn whispered. "Would he find a way?"

Shawn swallowed.

"Are there not those who create false identities?" Eamonn pressed. "Simon's type has existed throughout history. They find one another, he and his kind who will provide, for a price—which he will acquire in a dark alley—all he needs to get on a plane. Amy is not safe."

"He can't search the whole United States," Shawn argued. But his words came out weakly.

"He can hire those who can find her through your internet," Eamonn persisted. "A musician with a symphony is easy to find. Do you wish her to live in hiding her whole life? But," Eamonn added. "'Tis not the heart of the matter."

"Not the heart of the matter?" Shawn objected. "My wife and child being killed by a madman? I'd say it is!"

Eamonn smiled sadly. "Aye, to you, and so it should be. But Simon must be stopped, not for James and Amy, but for the whole world. Sending him to America will not change that." He leaned forward, his hands pressed to the gnarled wooden head of his cane. *These things will happen...unless James stops him.*

A pair of cold fingers pinched Shawn's neck, lifting the small hairs there. "But you said Simon has to be sent back." He rose in agitation, pacing to the altar and back. "My son is *not* going there. I won't let him."

Eamonn's blue eyes sharpened. "If you prevent him going back, he may never exist at all."

"He *does* exist!"

Aye, he exists, and he is called.

"His calling has nothing to do with a medieval madman. He'll be a musician, he'll be...."

There are men, Eamonn said, his eyes drifting back to cloudy memories, *who stand in the places between time, who see all that was, all that might be. Men destined to walk between times. Men shown where wrongs must be righted to keep history as it must be.*

"Not my son." Shawn shook his head. "No. I'll fight Simon."

"If you do so, who's to say you'll return?" Eamonn mused.

"Why wouldn't I?" Shawn asked. "I've crossed twice now."

Eamonn chuckled softly. "Do you not read fairy tales? 'Tis always three."

"Life isn't a fairy tale."

"Ah, but fairy tales draw their truths from life, do they not?" Eamonn smiled.

"If you go, you will not come back."

♫

I stand at Angus's bedside, watching him sleep, his breathing labored. My heart breaks. Just a year ago, we walked through Inverness's snow-globe world to Christmas Mass. I remind myself his world has turned upside down. My thoughts trail back to the summer months, sitting in the chapel at Glenmirril, his steady strength by my side—and now I have no way to help him. I think of his words there, amidst the ancient stone walls, before the magnificent life-sized crucifix.

It's what I like about these old places. I feel I'm soaking up the wisdom of all who have gone before me.

Niall would have gone to the chapel hundreds of times, perhaps gazed on the same crucifix.

"Amy?" It's Mairi's soft brogue.

I turn. Her brow wrinkles with concern. James squeals and grabs my hair.

"'Tis the drugs talking. He doesn't mean it." She reaches for James, who leans in, laughing, and goes to her. "A wee break would do you good," she says. "I was thinking I'd take the bairn a wee while, if you'd like to go for a cuppa. There are some lovely places by the river, now."

I cast a fleeting glance at Angus. He'll sleep for hours. I want to be near Niall. Tension melts from my mouth, and a smile eases the ache of sore muscles. I turn to Mairi, easing James's chubby fist from my hair. I kiss him. "I think I'll go to Glenmirril, if that's okay."

Mairi smiles, relief flooding her face. "Of course, Love. I'll bring James and meet you there." She glances at her watch. "Sunset's a bit over an hour. It's not much time." A brief wrinkle of concern returns to her forehead as she pushes away the curl there. "If you'd still like tea afterward, I can take James...."

"No, an hour's plenty. Meet me at Glenmirril. I'll be in the chapel." Already feeling better at the prospect of sitting where Niall sat, I thank Mairi, and head down the hall to a time of peace and contemplation, and the hope of feeling the wisdom of the ages.

Berwick, December 1317

Niall moved softly through the snowy wood with Hugh, Lachlan, and Owen. They traveled high on the tree-covered ridge, keeping Adam Newton, walking the easier path of the glen below, in sight. The words, *it's a trap* spun in a loop through his mind. It didn't matter. Even if it was, he had no choice but to obey his king. But it left him on edge, though he and four others followed one lone, scared priest.

"Let us be done with this and back to camp," Owen whispered. He glanced at the sun, sinking fast in the west.

Niall shook his head. "Near a village are our orders." He wanted, as badly as Owen, to be back to his warm fire and safety.

"He had the nerve...."

"He is a *cleric*," Niall replied. Under the dark pines, he tugged his cloak close.

"I see smoke," Hugh rumbled in the softest voice of which he was capable.

Below, the priest craned his neck, peering up the hill. The men shrank behind trees. Newton scanned the valley, its shadows long and dark. When he moved again, Niall dared a few words. "That will be a village. Give him another furlong or so."

Trailing the unfortunate man, they began their descent down the steep slope. Once, twice, Newton paused, searching the dark forest. Another step, and the village would be around the bend. Niall jerked his head, leading the three closer, edging ahead of the cleric.

"Now!" Niall whispered, and they burst onto the dusky path, shouting.

Newton yelped, shrinking back inside his cloak.

"The papers," Niall demanded. The wind rippled the edge of his cloak. He hoped the man would co-operate for his own sake.

"Be gone!" Newton waved at them as at recalcitrant pups. "What I carry is for the Pope and Bruce alone."

Niall sighed. "You're brave, but foolish. D' ye not see our swords?"

Newton cast frantic glances down the glen, as if help might come from the forest.

"Don't make this worse on yourself," Niall said. "Give us the papers." Lachlan and Owen circled him.

Newton's hand went to his chest, making it easy to guess where the documents hid, and suddenly bolted, aiming for the gap between Niall and Lachlan.

Hugh had him rolling on the ground in a heartbeat, while he kicked and thrashed, with ear-piercing shrieks. "Hold him!" Hugh roared. "Clamp a hand over his mouth! He'll bring the whole village on us!"

Owen and Lachlan lunged into the fray. The man put up a good fight for his slight build. Niall dove in, yanking at his cloak, fishing for the papers. The cloak tore from the cleric's neck. He sprang from the ground, pulled back instantly by Hugh, Lachlan, and Owen.

Owen grunted as an elbow connected with his eye. "We have our orders." Niall snapped. He fished through the cloak's lining till his fingers grazed soft vellum, the sounds of the tussle grinding in his ears. A black robe sailed threw the air, followed by a pair of trews. Niall snagged them from the air. He stuffed the documents in his own pocket even as he retrieved the black robe.

"I got his shirt!" Owen shouted, waving it triumphantly.

"It's cold!" the cleric wailed in a high-pitched voice. He danced up and down in his baggy breeks knotted around his waist, rubbing his hands up and down skinny arms. "You can't leave me like this! Heathens!" He raced at Hugh, but found himself in a headlock, squirming to get free.

"D' ye think the English would have treated us half as kindly had we insulted Edward so?" Hugh gave him a shake, and tossed him aside. He landed, sprawling in his underwear, in the powdery snow of the glen.

"Let's go." Niall waved an arm to the other three. He took one last look at the man scrambling off the cold ground, tossed the cloak back, and the four of them sprinted up the hill, into the trees.

"Niall!" The voice cracked like a whip through the fores.

Niall spun, his heart pounding, scanning the trees. It was empty but for the others running ahead.

"Don't go!" the voice hissed urgently. "It's a trap! Don't do it, Niall!"

Inverness, Present

"Amy."

The weak, rasping voice stops me in the lobby. I turn, surprised to see Brother Eamonn, bundled in a long, brown coat over his long woolen habit. A wool cap perches on his head. He rises, more steady than I've ever seen him. "I believe I'll go with you," he says.

I'm taken aback. I like Brother Eamonn. But I expected to be alone.

He smiles, as if reading my thoughts. "It all comes out right in the end. Shall we?" He takes my arm, glass doors slide open, and we're in cold, tiny flakes glittering in the air, not quite snow. I'm about to ask if he really wants to go to Glenmirril when another voice speaks my name.

I stop, tugging my blue coat close. On the cold sidewalk, Brother Eamonn stumbles suddenly, catching my arm, leaning heavily as he melts into weakness. I know the voice behind me—the smooth, velvet timbre, the vowels that are neither Scottish nor entirely English. Fear chills me. I think of the hole in my wall, of the door in Shawn's house half ripped out. Angus is helpless upstairs.

We're on a public sidewalk, I assure myself. He can't do anything, here with witnesses. On the street, a car roars by, a bright flash of red, a sharp honk of its horn, kicking up a spray of slush. I turn.

Simon Beaumont stands behind us. He is clean-shaven. His eyes, a rich golden-brown, wrinkle at the corners as he smiles. My stomach tumbles between the damage to our homes, and the innocent delight on his face. I'm imagining things. Shawn has taught me to be paranoid. Surely this is just a professor beaming at me, a poor, injured professor, who had nothing to do with the attack on Carol or my wall.

But he lied to me about the translation.

I set a smile on my face. "Simon! What a surprise!" I'll just move Eamonn along, get in my car and drive away.

"What a pleasure to see both you and the good Brother," he replies, with a bow.

Doubt wavers in my mind.

"An odd note," Simon says. "I'm thinking the key does not fit anything here."

"I left the wrong note?" Eamonn taps his head. "How foolish! But you're here now."

"But we're leaving," I say hastily. "It was nice to see you again, Simon."

"Certainly you could use help," Simon says. "Where are you away to?"

Eamonn's hand tightens on my arm.

I pull from his grip to slip my right arm around his back, supporting his frail weight. "I'm driving him to the nursing home."

Simon steps to the old monk's other side, cupping the man's elbow. "Surely this is not a job for a lady alone. Let me help."

"Said the spider to the fly," Eamonn murmurs.

I glance at him. Before I can respond, Simon leans across Eamonn, meeting my eyes. "And where is your bonny son this lovely day? Surely a mother doesn't like to be long from her child."

"In America." Eamonn speaks forcefully. His hand bites into mine through my glove. "Across an ocean, Simon." Eamonn sighs heavily. "A shame, but he's far, far away. She's quite sad."

"Oh, now!" Simon laughs easily. "Planes are wonderful, are they not? America is not so far away as it once was."

My mind jumps from the old monk, accused of drinking too much, to my own doubt. Simon seems unconcerned. He seems incapable of kicking holes in doors.

Eamonn laughs, a dry chuckle that ends in a wheeze. "Fortunately for the child, my Lord, you've no passport, and you'll not be getting on a plane without one."

My eyes narrow, moving between Eamonn and the cheerful Simon. If he's a medieval killer, surely he'll show some anger. But his smile remains pleasant, innocent. "A shame." Sunlight hits his eyes, lighting their depths. He could be any of my fellow musicians, any of the concert-going crowd who gather in foyers to meet us, any man offering help to the elderly. "Still..." He meets my eyes. "He'll be back soon?"

His words are too intense. His smile is gone. My gut knots, flips over, and settles. There's no reason for him to be so interested in my son. My doubts smooth as abruptly as wind dropping, leaving calm sea in its wake. I was right all along. He's from Niall's time. Peace comes in the knowledge, despite fear swelling softly beneath it. What if Mairi chooses now to walk out of the hospital with James?

"He'll be back soon?" Simon asks more forcefully.

"Next month." The lie flows easily. I have to get him away from James. "You'll be the first to know." I smile pleasantly. It can only help to play dumb, to keep Simon thinking he's ahead in the game I suddenly see myself caught in. "He certainly did take to you." I let my smile grow. The wind cuts down the street. In front of me, a small boy ducks his chin down into his jacket and buries himself in his mother's side.

"Delightful!" Simon replies. "As I to him! Such a bonny lad!"

"You'll be wanting to get home." Eamonn starts his slow shuffle down the sidewalk, pulling me and Simon along. "Not long before the unfortunate incident in the chapel, in which I so carelessly injured myself, I read a very interesting story of events in late December of 1314, concerning the mighty Lord of Claverock."

"Where's Claverock?" I rush Eamonn faster than he can go, disliking pushing him, but fearing Mairi will come out of the hospital.

"Northumberland." Simon's chin lifts. "The finest castle in England."

"No doubt," I murmur. I bet Claverock is—was—his home.

"How far is your car?" Simon asks.

"A block," I say. I wonder where Simon will go once I get Eamonn in the car

and leave. I'll call Mairi the second the doors close, and warn her not to leave Angus's room. My heart flutters a trill of agitation, a quick set of thirty-second notes that end in calm as I feel the crucifix against my chest, under my sweater. "Brother Eamonn," I ask, as I pull him along, "what happened to the Lord of Claverock?"

"King Edward made a surprise visit there," Eamonn wheezes, "in which the lord, a seer of sorts, warned him of future events. It was the day the Lord of Claverock came to glory and power. But as Edward will not return to Northumberland for some time, 'twould be a shame if that lord were not...had not been...is not there, when he calls...called." He chuckles, bringing on a dry cough that causes him to stop and double over. His weight pulls on my arm.

I rub his back, looking over my shoulder. Mairi doesn't appear at the hospital door. There's no reason she should, I tell myself. Still, fear is stronger than reason. Cold wind gusts down the street. The old monk coughs harder. I tug my white scarf tight, whispering. "Let's get you into the car, Brother Eamonn."

He inches himself upright, patting his chest as the cough dies. "Forgive a foolish old man...too much of Brother Jimmy's brew. Strong stuff." He smiles down at me.

I reach up to tug his wool cap down firmly. Tufts of white hair stick out from his ears. Liver spots stand out on his neck. I touch his cheek, scared for him and my son. "Simon, can you go down the street and find someone to help me get him to the car?" Maybe I can get away while he goes looking.

"We'll move faster by simply doing it, the two of us!" Simon sweeps into motion, hurrying the old man, nearly dragging him. I search for words to protest, but he's moving us along. "Brother Eamonn, I do need to get home." He leans again across Eamonn to speak to me. "I hoped you could show me the crucifix again. As a historian, it fascinates me."

My heart lurches. I hold my tongue. Fear boils up inside me that he can see the crucifix hidden under my layers of clothing.

"Now, now," Eamonn says, "I did tell you the crucifix is at Monadhliath."

"You did not say Monadhliath." Simon's smile grows with the intensity of his voice.

Eamonn laughs. "Ah, yes, I do mix things up. If only I had not so carelessly injured myself, I'd have shown it to you sooner."

I glance from one to the other, and over my shoulder again. No sign of Mairi. I breathe a sigh of relief, as we turn the corner. My car is half a block away. I'll get Eamonn in, slam the door, and drive away.

"Then we shall go to Monadhliath." Simon says, as if suggesting a lakeside walk on a spring day.

I stop. A woman with a pram edges around me. A car honks in the street. "He can't hike to Monadhliath!" I don't care what he does to me, I am not dragging this old man into the hills in winter. He'll do worse to us there, anyway, than here on a busy street.

Simon smiles pleasantly. "You and I will help him." He pulls Eamonn along.

I hurry to keep up, holding Eamonn around the waist. "No, you and I will not help him. It's winter. He's...."

"You don't need the crucifix," Eamonn interrupts. "What you need is much closer. Just at Glenmirril."

"Not Glenmirril!" Panic shoots up my arms, into my throat.

"Is it Glenmirril after all?" Simon studies the old man with interest.

"'Tis but a short walk." Eamonn chuckles. "Historians walk and ride many miles, do they not?"

"Your car?" Simon stops beside my Renault, faint red under a thin layer of snow. "Let us get him in."

I click the fob. Simon opens the door, and eases Eamonn in, patting his shoulder.

I scramble around the car. I'll drive away, call Mairi—all will be well. I slide into the driver's seat, reaching for my phone. A door slams. I spin. Simon sits in the back seat. My heart pounds. My hand freezes on the phone. "Get out!" I want my words to be strong, commanding, but they are breathless and weak.

Simon smiles. "Drive."

I'll go the other way, I decide, to Culloden. At least it's away from James, no matter what Simon does to me. I'll think of a better plan as I drive. I turn the key in the ignition, feeling strength in the power of the engine humming to life.

From the back seat comes Simon's smooth, easy voice. "I'm well acquainted with the road to Glenmirril. Even in your day."

I glance into the rear view mirror, through which his eyes meet mine. The smile doesn't leave his face. I understand his meaning. My hand goes to my chest. I can drive part way, get Simon away from the hospital, and give him the crucifix. It's what he wants. Then he'll go away. Or I can throw it out the window, into the wooded slopes. He'll have to go hunting for it. My heart flutters in panic.

"All is well, Amy." Brother Eamonn speaks firmly, the usual rustle of his voice replaced by a veneer of steel. He touches my hand, pulling it from the hidden crucifix. "Take us to Glenmirril."

I stare at him helplessly, shaking my head, unable to tell him, in front of Simon, why I can't do that.

His face wrinkles into a smile. He winks one watery blue eye at me. "Have faith." His eyes hold mine. Strength flows from his ageless eyes.

Still I hesitate. My hand slips into my pocket, feeling my phone, wondering if I can dial for help without Simon noticing. A motion from the back seat draws my attention. Sunlight flashes off metal. My heart trips once, becomes still a moment too long, and suddenly knocks hard against my sternum.

Simon smiles, at odds with the knife in his hand resting against Eamonn's wrinkled-parchment throat. "Yes, take us to Glenmirril, Amy."

"Do not be afraid, Amy," Eamonn whispers. He sighs and leans back against his seat, humming softly, undisturbed by the knife at his throat.

I glance from one to the other, at the insane smiles on both their faces, as if neither is aware of the deadly steel between them.

Simon's voice drops to its smoothest, most velvety tone. "Now, Amy." He holds out his free hand. "And the phone, please."

I swallow hard. With trembling hand, I pull the phone from my pocket, and give it to him. I shift into drive and ease into heavy traffic as thin flakes of snow slide down my windshield, leaving wet trails on the glass. There will be visitors at Glenmirril. He can't hurt us in front of witnesses. I'll think of something, before James gets there.

♬

"You'll go quietly," Simon murmured. The pleasant smile never left his face. "My knife can do him a great deal of harm. By the time anyone realizes it's not just an old man's heart, I'll be gone."

Amy stared up at Glenmirril's stone walls with snow dancing over them. Heavy gray clouds scooted across the sky, darkening the winter sun. Snow had slowed traffic all the way to Glenmirril, eating up precious minutes in which Mairi might follow them. Under her heavy coat, cold crawled up her arms. She bit her lip. He would kill them, anyway, as soon as he got them alone somewhere.

"We'll walk in quietly," Eamonn assured him. He squeezed Amy's hand, and lowered his voice. "Be not afraid, Love."

Amy nodded, only half-hearing him. She'd been too trapped in fear, through the drive, to think up any way to warn Mairi. A big, fluffy flake of snow caught in her eyelash. She blinked, wiping it away.

"She should be very afraid." With a smile, Simon inserted himself between them. Linking his arms firmly through theirs, he led them down the cement path winding across the snow-covered lawn outside the castle, and through the gatehouse. The arched tunnel blocked the snow and what little sunlight there had been, dropping a cold shadow over them as they passed through.

Shadows covered the courtyard, too. Wind whispered down over the high walls. The flags on the parapets gave a weak wave and dropped limply. Amy's hopes sank as she saw the empty courtyard.

"Where to, good Brother?" Simon's voice rang with cheer.

"The chapel," Eamonn said with assurance.

"I've searched it quite thoroughly," Simon said.

"Ah, but I know just where."

Amy wondered how much Eamonn was making up. He'd lied easily to Simon about James. Maybe he was leading him astray now, too. Simon was watching her.

"Is he telling the truth?" He asked with casual interest.

She nodded, swallowing hard over the fear jamming her throat. "Of course. Monks don't lie."

"Hm." Simon contemplated only a moment, before saying, "Let us go, then."

Eamonn shuffled, his arm caught in Simon's, through the snow, toward the tower. Amy shivered as another wave of wind rolled across the bailey. A heavy cloud slid over the sun. She wondered what Eamonn knew, or if he was merely stalling for time, hoping to think of something, himself. If he stalled too long, Mairi would show up with James.

Eamonn lifted the skirts of his woolen robe. He grunted as he climbed the small step into the bottom of the tower. Amy peered with concern around Simon's broad frame. She couldn't reach Eamonn to help him, if he should trip or fall. She tried to guess how long it had been since they'd left the hospital. More than half an hour. Maybe forty-five minutes. Simon tugged her into the tower. The round, close walls shut out the sunlight, leaving them in a dim cavern of stone.

Far out on the road, she heard a car. She tensed, unwittingly stopping on the bottom step as Eamonn, his gnarled hand gripping the rope rail, started up.

"Come along." Simon chirped, as if they were heading to a picnic.

She stumbled up another stair after him, listening to Eamonn wheeze in the dark above her, and straining to hear if the car kept going.

"What will happen when we get there, old man?" Simon inquired. "Is it like your chapel at Monadhliath?"

"Aye, 'tis a thin place indeed." Eamonn stumbled, yanking Simon, who in turn yanked Amy. Her foot hit a stair hard, stubbing her toe. Eamonn grunted, catching himself on the rope, and pulled himself up another two stairs.

Far away, beyond the castle walls, a horn beeped a musical high-pitched beep, like Mairi's horn. Amy bit her lip. "Eamonn, can we go faster? There's a time limit. It only happens at certain times of day."

"Aye!" He agreed cheerfully with her lie. He moved more quickly, making her wonder again how much of what he said or did was truth. She hoped Simon would disappear. She couldn't believe he would. But then, she argued with herself, she had the crucifix. The prophecy said it did something. *But only for those in Niall's line of descent!* her mind screamed frantically. If that was Mairi's horn, James was on his way in. She pushed forward, feeling the walls in the oncoming twilight.

"You're in a hurry," Simon remarked as he twisted up the curving stairs. "You do realize I'll likely kill you before I go. Are you so weary of life?"

Fear flashed into anger. "You can't kill us!" Amy searched for a reason, a lie, to convince him he couldn't. She could think of nothing. She glared at him.

He laughed. "Whyever not? I see no gallant knight rushing to your rescue. And when your son shows up in my time, I'll kill him too, now that I'm forewarned."

Amy yanked against Simon's grip, her heart pounding. "My son is not...."

"Yes, Amy, he will," Eamonn said calmly. "Now come along."

Simon laughed. "Surely you didn't think I had such interest in your urchin for his charming looks?" He tugged her onto the landing of the second floor. The last of the winter light spilled through the big windows looking out on the courtyard. The snow had grown heavier.

"You're sick and evil," Amy hissed.

Simon chuckled. "Better that than weak and powerless."

She glanced out the window. It would have been impossible to see over the high walls into the parking lot even without the veil of falling snow. Lots of horns had Mairi's high-pitched bleat.

"Looking for something?" Simon inquired.

"The chapel, Amy, come along." Eamonn picked up his pace, moving down the stone hallway, the windows lighting their way. From outside came a heavy rumble.

"Eamonn," she protested, as she hurried them through the halls. "Wouldn't it happen in Niall's rooms?"

"The crucifix," Eamonn said to Simon, not answering her, "is of great importance to Niall. I believe we'll find him in the chapel and you can join him and go from there to meet your king."

"I found no crucifix here," Simon argued.

Eamonn tutted as if explaining to a child. "This is *another* crucifix, made by the Laird of the time. Touch it, and I think you'll be surprised. One can only hope you don't interrupt evening prayers. 'Twould be most disrespectful."

"Evening prayers!" Amy gaped. Maybe he was crazy after all. "He's going to *kill* us and you're worried about interrupting prayers?" She glanced at the window. Large flakes of snow floated down past the arch, coating the window ledge in white.

Eamonn led the way to the chapel. As they entered, a clap of thunder exploded outside, jolting all of them, even Simon. He looked up sharply. The chapel's one window, high up over the altar, darkened abruptly, leaving them only the light of two dozen candles flickering under the life-sized crucifix.

"Thunder snow," Eamonn said calmly. "Highly unusual here, but then many things at Glenmirril are highly unusual." He shuffled to the crucifix, standing before it and gazing up at the man who gazed down, his head crowned with thorns. "My Lord, you'll want to place your hand on it. Niall often does, and then I believe our times shall meet. When James arrives, you'll be ready, with your foreknowledge. Rest easy, you've naught to fear."

Simon tore his gaze from the dark window, stepping toward Eamonn. His pleasant demeanor slipped away. "I've no fear," he snapped. "Do not insult me!"

Amy took an inadvertent step backward. Eamonn remained motionless, staring up at the carved face. Self-loathing rushed up inside her. He'd kill them both if he wanted. Was she really going to run and leave an old man to his fate? She forced herself forward, one step, two. "Leave him alone!"

Simon swung his head slowly, a bull sizing its target before charging. He laughed. "There's a fine line between courage and foolishness. You're on the wrong side, Lass."

He slid the knife from the sheath at his hip.

Amy bit her lip.

"Between the ribs, up into the heart," Simon whispered. "So fast you'll hardly feel a thing. See? I'm not half so evil as you think."

"Amy, do not fear." Eamonn didn't move. "Look around you. Look carefully."

His words distracted Simon. The knife lowered, as he squinted into the candle-lit gloom of the chapel.

Amy wondered if she dared throw herself forward and try to wrestle the knife from him. She tensed. He turned his back to her, searching the shadows of the chapel.

"Touch the crucifix, and you'll be home," Eamonn said softly.

Amy hesitated. Maybe he'd touch the crucifix and disappear without harming them, if she just left him alone. The window darkened even more. The air before the candles shimmered. It was a trick of the light, of dozens of tiny halos surrounding dozens of flames. But the breath caught in her throat.

Another clap of thunder boomed outside. She jumped.

"Amy, there you are, thank *goodness*!"

A short, sharp squeal sounded.

Amy spun. Simon's head snapped away from the window. They both stared at Mairi, standing in the doorway of the chapel, holding James.

♫

It all happens at once. Simon lunges. Eamonn jumps, yelling, "He's no threat to you! Go home!" I throw myself at him, with no thought but keeping him from my son, screaming, "Run, Mairi!" My fingers catch his coat; it slips through; I grab with my other hand. Something hits my head; my knee jars to stone floor, but I hold tight. I hear voices, shouting; see people, see Eamonn rushing Simon.

Mairi, in the doorway, bends over James, her arms around his head, screaming. I hear, Run, run, run, coming from my mouth, and someone shouts, "What's this, Niall?" and Simon's coat slips from my fingers. I scramble off the floor, throw myself at him. I slam into the brick wall that is Simon, and crumple to the floor, scooting backwards, trying to get up. He grunts and stumbles; yells, "What's happening?"

"Go home, Simon!" Eamonn shouts. "He's no threat to you! There they are! Go to your king, get your power, before the window closes!"

I see them—Niall rising to his feet from a pew, anger flooding his face, an old man at his side with silver and red hair bristling like a lion's mane, and a giant of a man who must be Hugh.

Simon's back is to them. His hand, with the knife, comes up. He glowers at Mairi, still huddled over James, and in that heartbeat, I bolt off the floor, surprising him, throwing him off balance; he stumbles back, toward the crucifix, and the three medieval men racing for it, for him. Mairi's screams bounce off the stone walls. The men in tunics shout. Simon's head spins, taking it in—Niall, the great bear Hugh, the leonine Malcolm rising fiercely.

Simon backs away, spins on his heel, racing toward the crucifix—past it. Eamonn flings his frail old body at Simon, trying to push him into it before he can bolt up onto the altar, trying to send him back. The air shimmers. Outside, thunder snow erupts in a loud clap, shaking the very stones of Glenmirril.

I'm on one knee on the floor, unsure how I got here, breathing hard. Someone is sobbing. My cheeks are wet. I press my hands to my temples, trying to shut out the awful sound. My breath jars in my chest, like someone being jolted back to life.

"Sh, Amy. They're gone."

I pull in another deep breath, realizing it's me making these awful sounds. I fight the gasping sobs, brush at tears cascading down my face. Two more deep breaths.

"Amy, what just happened?" Mairi's voice shakes.

I close my eyes. My breath slows. My knee burns. "James?" As I speak, I hear his happy gurgle. I open my eyes. The chapel is empty but for me on one knee on the stone floor, and Mairi, clutching James, leaning over me.

Simon is gone. Eamonn is gone.

Shawn explodes into the room, shouting, "Amy!" He's scooping me up off the flagstones, and immediately pushing me away, reaching to his back for a claymore that isn't there. "Stay there!" he orders. He storms to the crucifix, to the wall behind it.

I gather my son into my arms, burying my face in his thick, black hair, breathing thanks to Niall, to Eamonn, to God, wherever, whenever, they are. James is safe. Nothing else matters. Not Shawn, not Angus, not Niall or Eamonn. James is safe.

The End...
...Until Book Five, The Battle is O'er
♫

Made in the USA
Monee, IL
22 September 2021